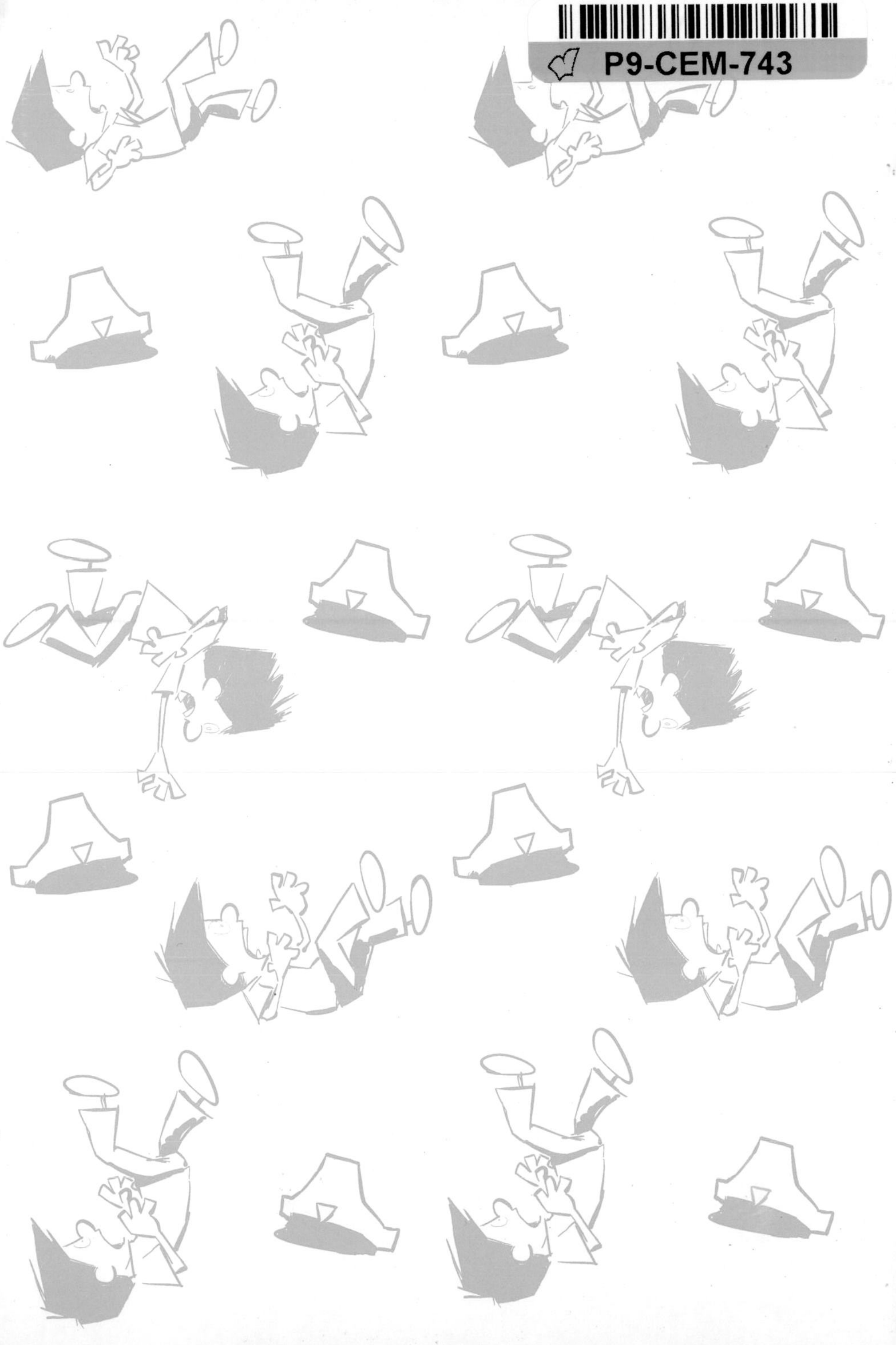

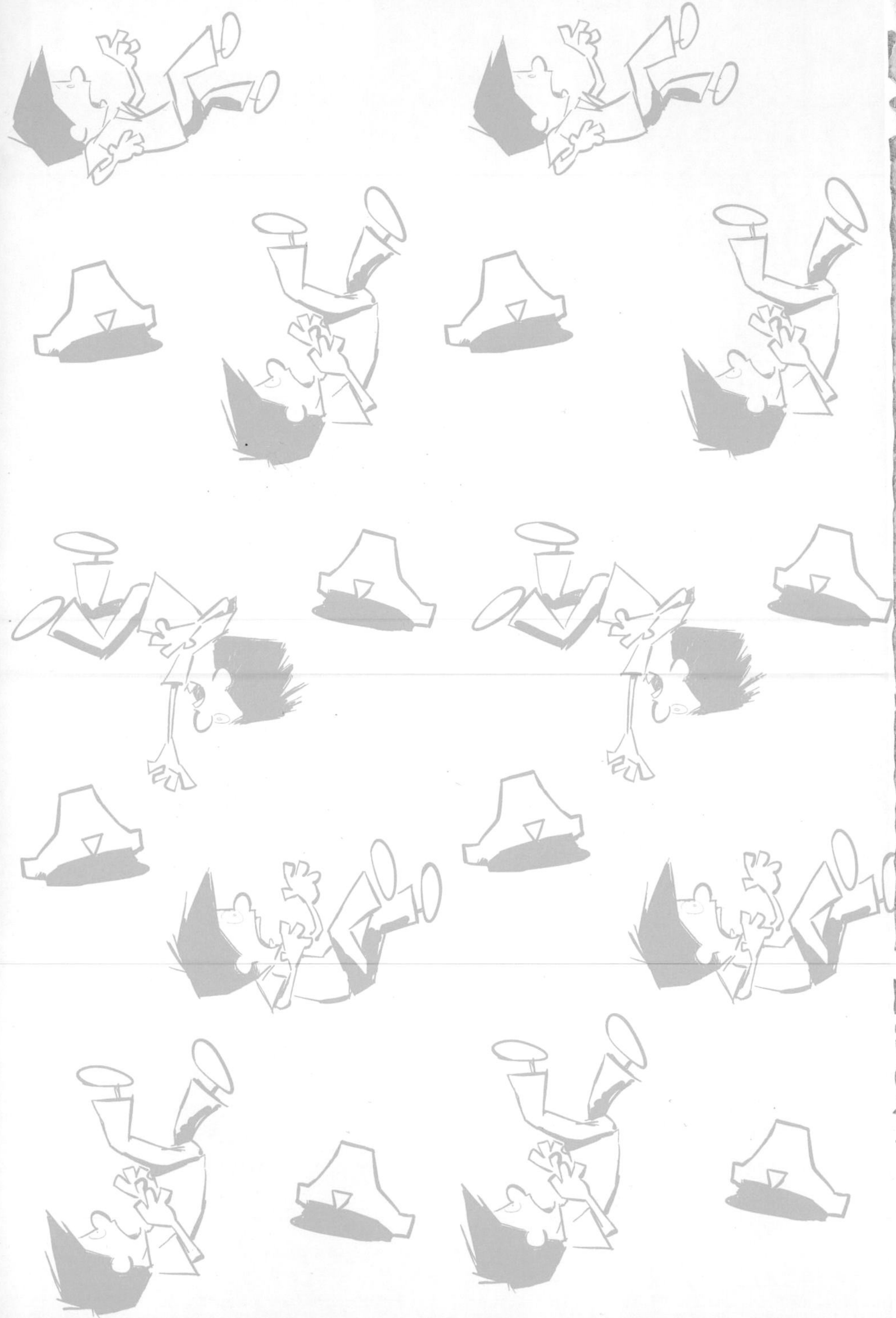

MIDDLE SCHOOL MISADVENTURES

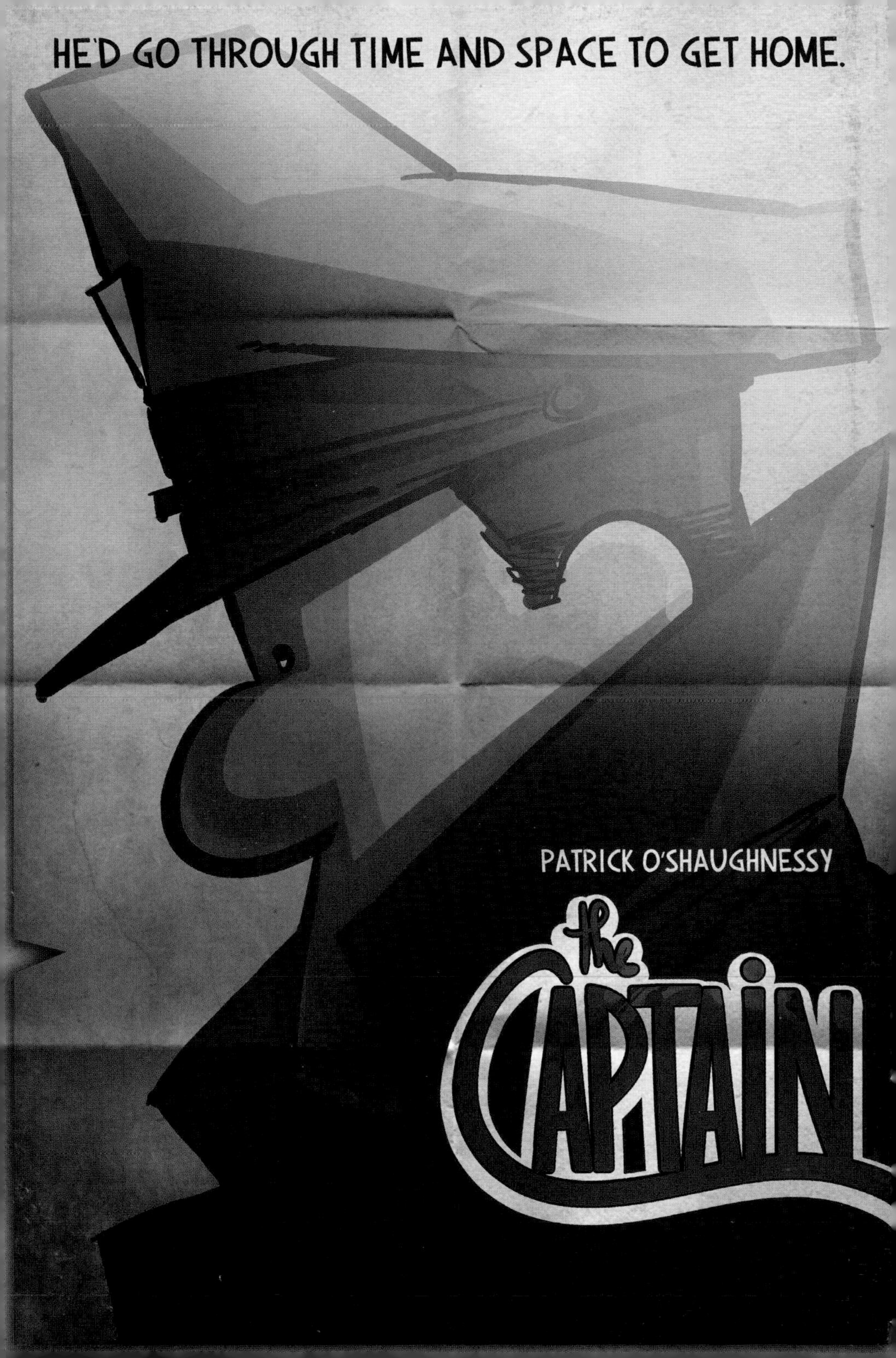
HE'D GO THROUGH TIME AND SPACE TO GET HOME.
PATRICK O'SHAUGHNESSY
the CAPTAIN

MIDDLE SCHOOL MISADVENTURES

OPERATION: HAT HEIST!

JASON PLATT

LB
LITTLE, BROWN AND COMPANY
NEW YORK BOSTON

ABOUT THIS BOOK

The illustrations of this book were done in Corel Painter on the Wacom Cintiq companion and colored in Adobe Photoshop. This book was edited by Rachel Poloski and designed by Christina Quintero. The production was supervised by Virginia Lawther, and the production editor was Lindsay Walter-Greaney. The text was set in MisterAndMeBook, and the display type is MisterAndMe.

Little, Brown and Company
Hachette Book Group
1290 Avenue of the Americas, New York, NY 10104
Visit us at LBYR.com

First Edition: April 2020

Little, Brown and Company is a division of Hachette Book Group, Inc.
The Little, Brown name and logo are trademarks of Hachette Book Group, Inc.

The publisher is not responsible for websites (or their content) that are not owned by the publisher.

Library of Congress Cataloging-in-Publication Data
Names: Platt, Jason, author, illustrator.
Title: Operation: hat heist! / Jason Platt.
Description: First edition. | New York ; Boston : Little Brown and Company, 2020. | Series: Middle school misadventures | Summary: When Newell's very special hat is taken away at school, he and his most talented friends concoct the perfect plan to get it back.
Identifiers: LCCN 2019022189 | ISBN 9780316416900 (hardcover) | ISBN 9780316416894 (pbk.) | ISBN 9780316416917 (ebk.) | ISBN 9780316537148 (library edition ebook)
Subjects: LCSH: Graphic novels. | CYAC: Graphic novels. | Stealing—Fiction. | Middle schools—Fiction. | Schools—Fiction. | Friendship—Fiction. | Fathers and sons—Fiction.
Classification: LCC PZ7.7.P55 Ope 2020 | DDC 741.5/973—dc23
LC record available at https://lccn.loc.gov/2019022189

ISBNs: 978-0-316-41690-0 (hardcover), 978-0-316-41689-4 (paperback), 978-0-316-41691-7 (ebook), 978-0-316-53717-9 (ebook), 978-0-316-53716-2 (ebook)

Printed in China

1010

Hardcover: 10 9 8 7 6 5 4 3 2 1
Paperback: 10 9 8 7 6 5 4 3 2 1

TO MY CHILDHOOD HEROES

* * *

REAL OR FICTITIOUS, YOU HAVE INSPIRED ME.
THANK YOU FOR ALL THE ADVENTURES.

CHAPTER ONE

I SWEAR THAT THIS IS A TRUE STORY

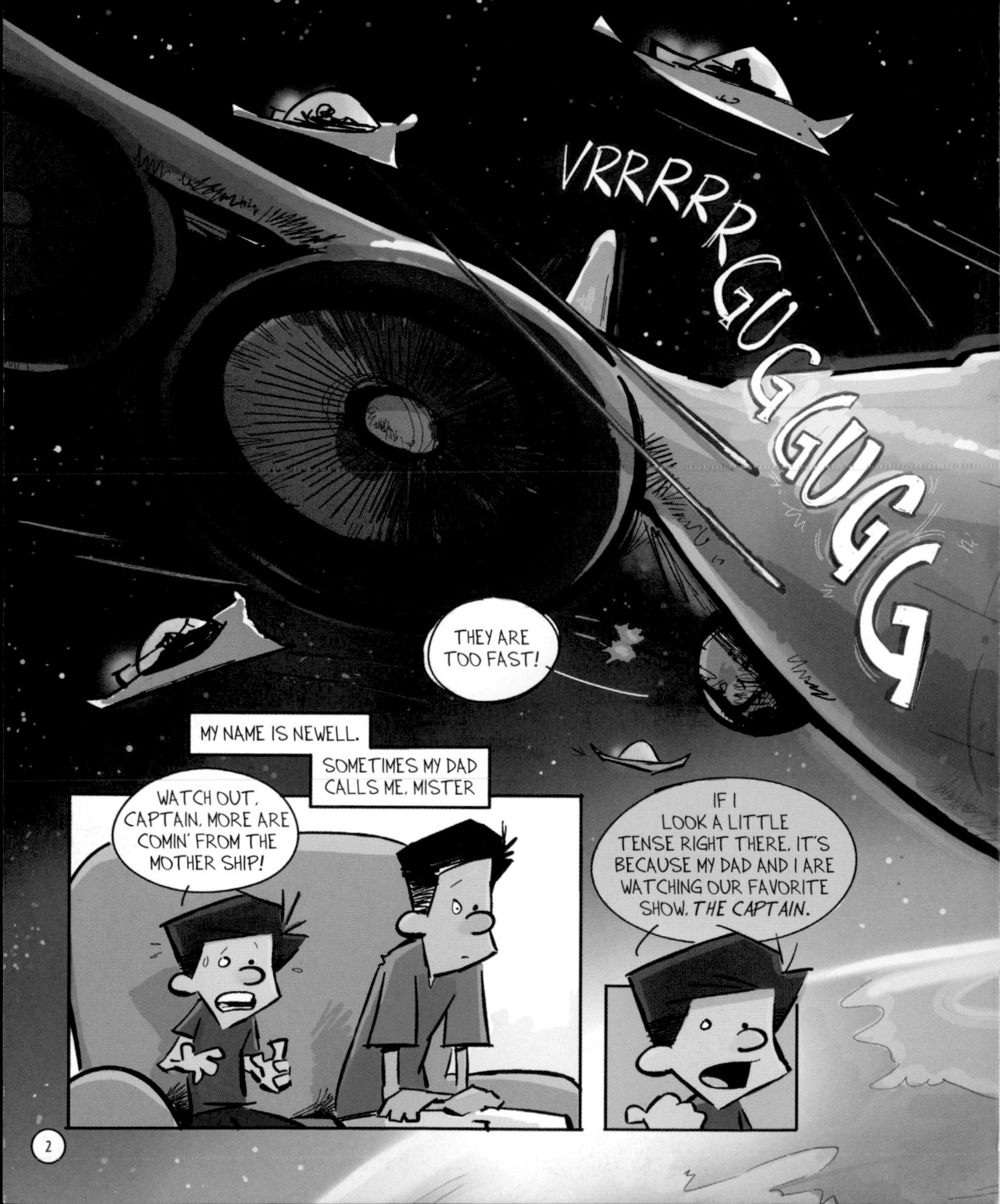

VRRRRRGUGGUGGG
THEY ARE TOO FAST!
MY NAME IS NEWELL.
SOMETIMES MY DAD CALLS ME, MISTER
WATCH OUT, CAPTAIN, MORE ARE COMIN' FROM THE MOTHER SHIP!
IF I LOOK A LITTLE TENSE RIGHT THERE, IT'S BECAUSE MY DAD AND I ARE WATCHING OUR FAVORITE SHOW, *THE CAPTAIN*.

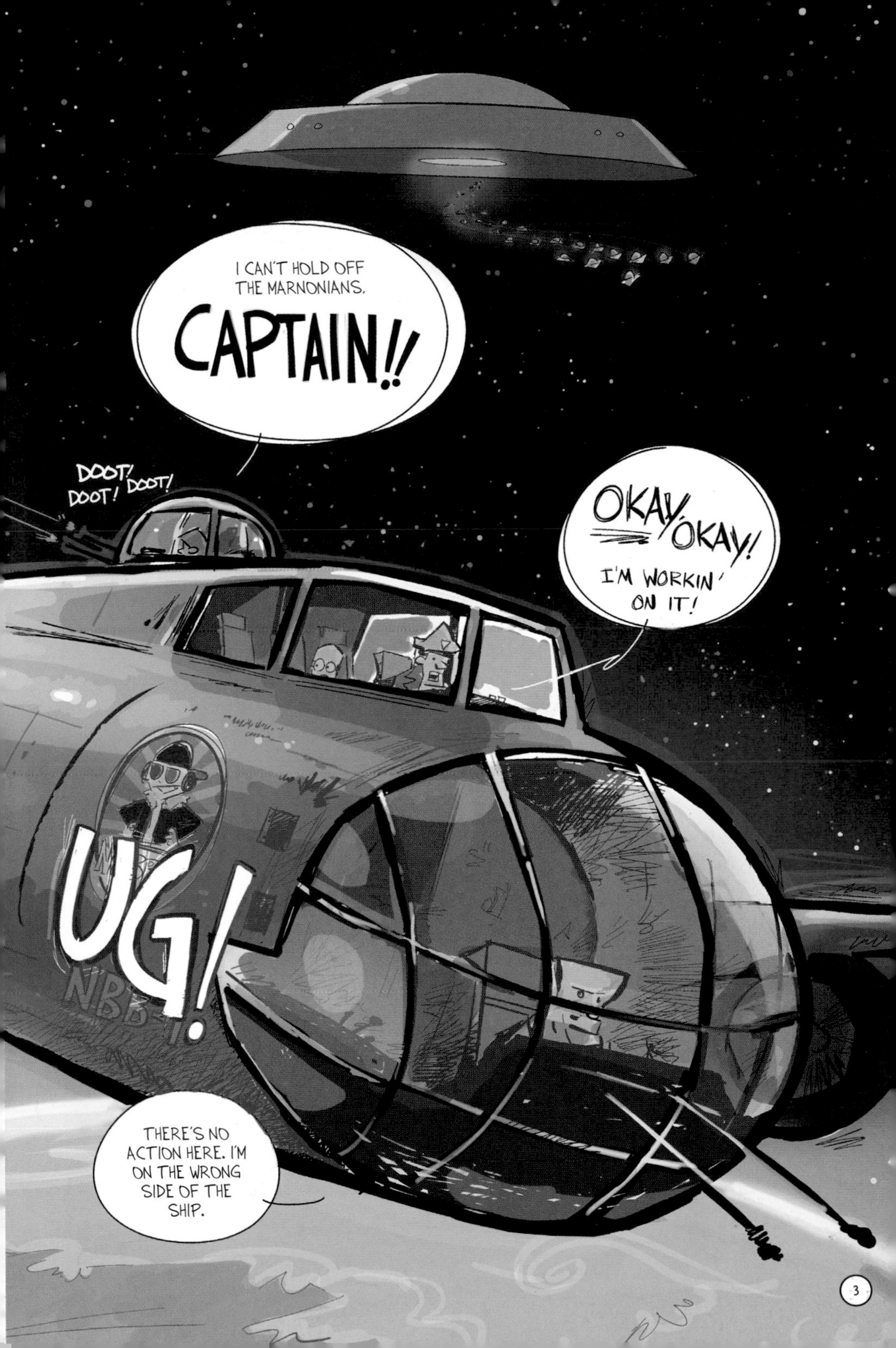
I CAN'T HOLD OFF THE MARNONIANS, CAPTAIN!!
DOOT! DOOT! DOOT!
OKAY, OKAY! I'M WORKIN' ON IT!
UG!
NBB-1
THERE'S NO ACTION HERE. I'M ON THE WRONG SIDE OF THE SHIP.

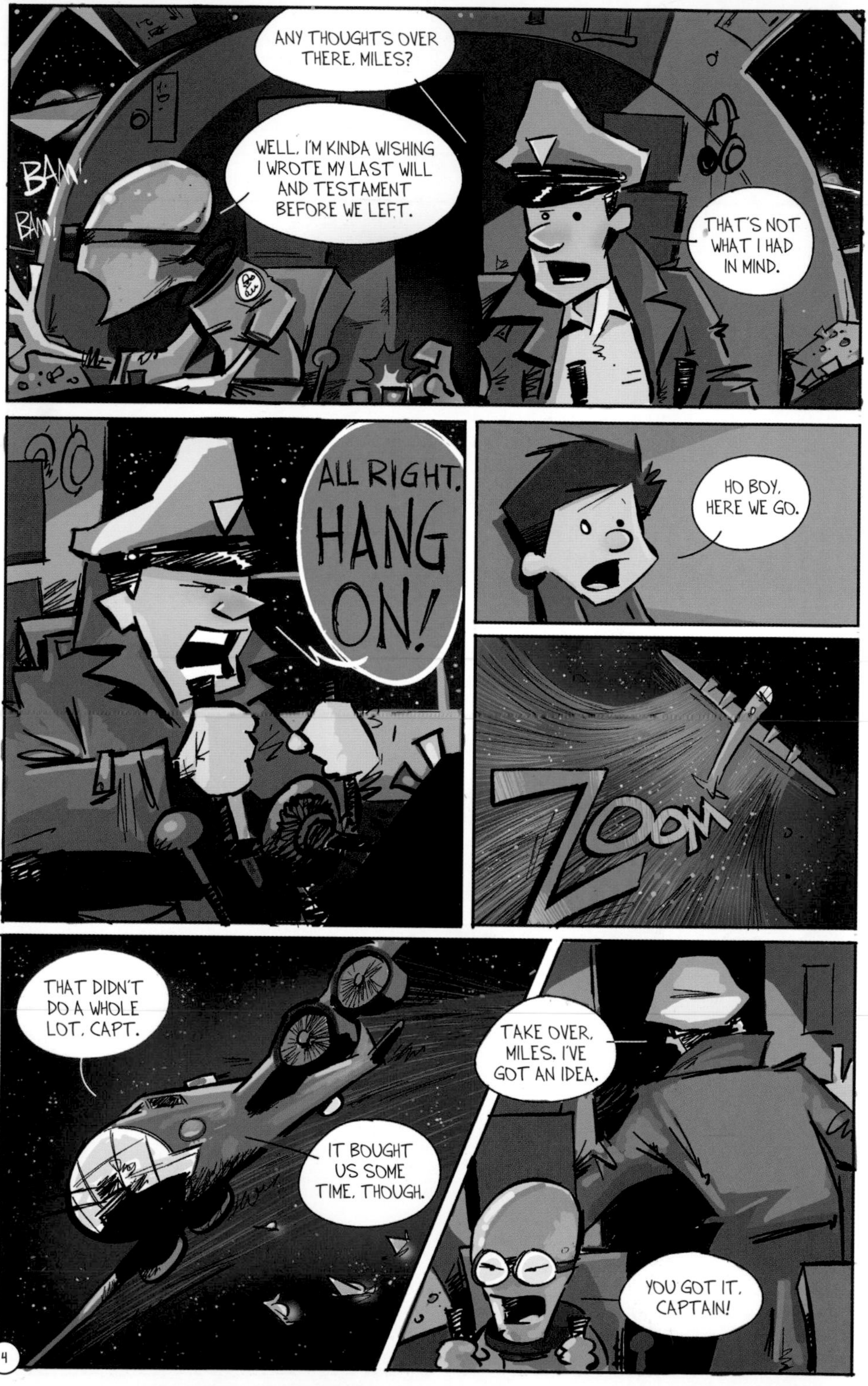
ANY THOUGHTS OVER THERE, MILES?
BAM! BAM!
WELL, I'M KINDA WISHING I WROTE MY LAST WILL AND TESTAMENT BEFORE WE LEFT.
THAT'S NOT WHAT I HAD IN MIND.
ALL RIGHT. HANG ON!
HO BOY, HERE WE GO.
ZOOM
THAT DIDN'T DO A WHOLE LOT, CAPT.
IT BOUGHT US SOME TIME, THOUGH.
TAKE OVER, MILES. I'VE GOT AN IDEA.
YOU GOT IT, CAPTAIN!

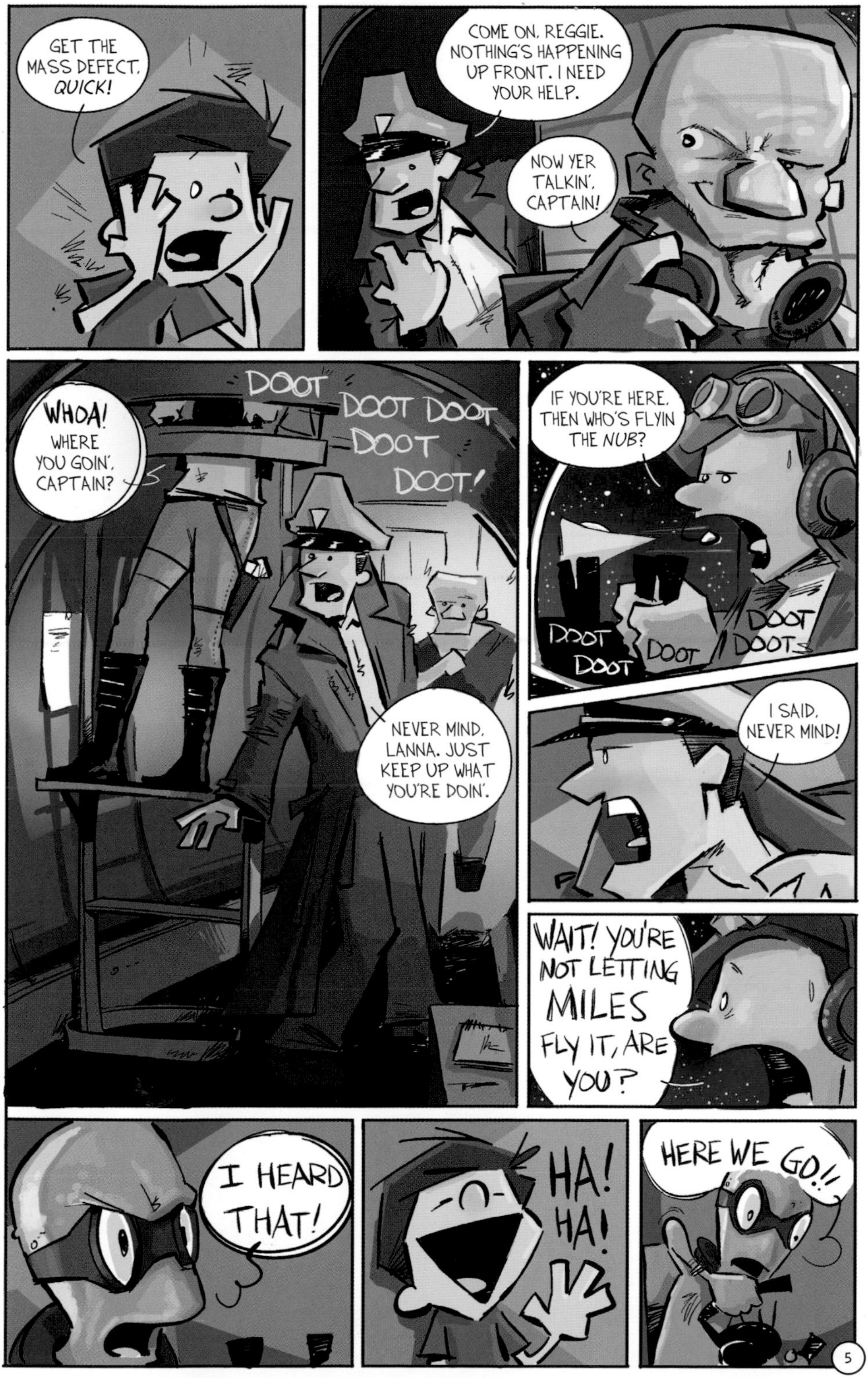
GET THE MASS DEFECT. QUICK!
COME ON, REGGIE. NOTHING'S HAPPENING UP FRONT. I NEED YOUR HELP.
NOW YER TALKIN', CAPTAIN!
DOOT DOOT DOOT DOOT DOOT!
WHOA! WHERE YOU GOIN', CAPTAIN?
NEVER MIND, LANNA. JUST KEEP UP WHAT YOU'RE DOIN'.
IF YOU'RE HERE, THEN WHO'S FLYIN THE NUB?
DOOT DOOT DOOT DOOT DOOTS
I SAID, NEVER MIND!
WAIT! YOU'RE NOT LETTING MILES FLY IT, ARE YOU?
I HEARD THAT!
HA! HA!
HERE WE GO!!

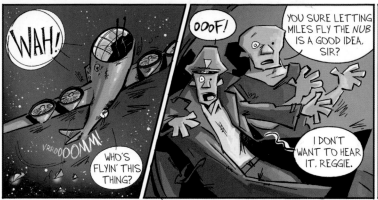

WAH!

VRROOOOMM!

WHO'S FLYIN' THIS THING?

OOOF!

YOU SURE LETTING MILES FLY THE *NUB* IS A GOOD IDEA, SIR?

I DON'T WANT TO HEAR IT, REGGIE.

UM...CAPTAIN? SHOULDN'T YOU BE UP FRONT PILOTING THE *NUBBY*?

I NEED YOU DOWN IN THAT BELLY TURRET, TARIS! AND BEFORE YOU ASK, YES, MILES IS FLYING THE NUB!

NO, SIR, I WASN'T GONNA SAY ANYTHING, CAPT!

SMART MOVE. HE'S TOUCHY ON THE SUBJECT.

GRUMBLE GRUMBLE! FINE.

BUT IT MIGHT BE GOOD IF MILES COULD PASS HIS FLYING TEST BEFORE HE GOT HIS MITTS ON THE NUBBY, THOUGH!!

PEW! PEW!

PEW! PEW! PEW!

THIS ISN'T GOOD.

CAPTAIN?! WHATEVER YOU'RE DOING, DO IT QUICK!

HURRY! THE MASS DEFECT IS IN THE BACK!

GAH!

UGH! I CAN'T WATCH.

CAPTAIN! ANYTIME NOW!

REGGIE, GIMME A HAND, QUICK!

OOOOF! HEAVY LITTLE SUCKER.

JUST PUT IT ON THE TABLE. HURRY!

POOM

FLUH- FLAP!

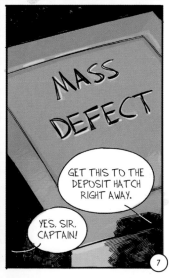

MASS DEFECT

GET THIS TO THE DEPOSIT HATCH RIGHT AWAY.

YES, SIR, CAPTAIN!

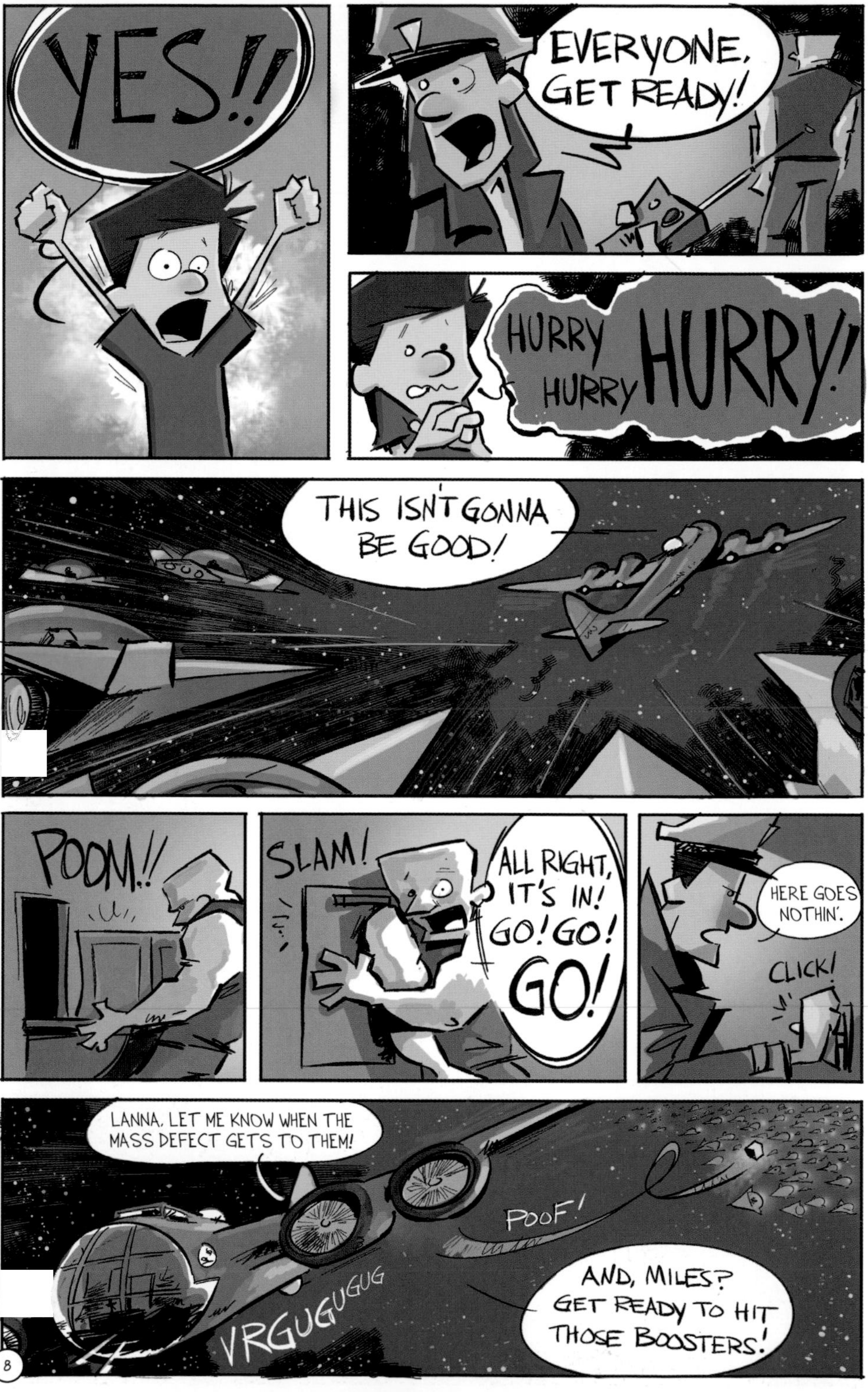
YES!!
EVERYONE, GET READY!
HURRY HURRY HURRY!
THIS ISN'T GONNA BE GOOD!
POOM!!
SLAM!
ALL RIGHT, IT'S IN! GO! GO! GO!
HERE GOES NOTHIN'.
CLICK!
LANNA, LET ME KNOW WHEN THE MASS DEFECT GETS TO THEM!
POOF!
VRGUGUGUG
AND, MILES? GET READY TO HIT THOSE BOOSTERS!

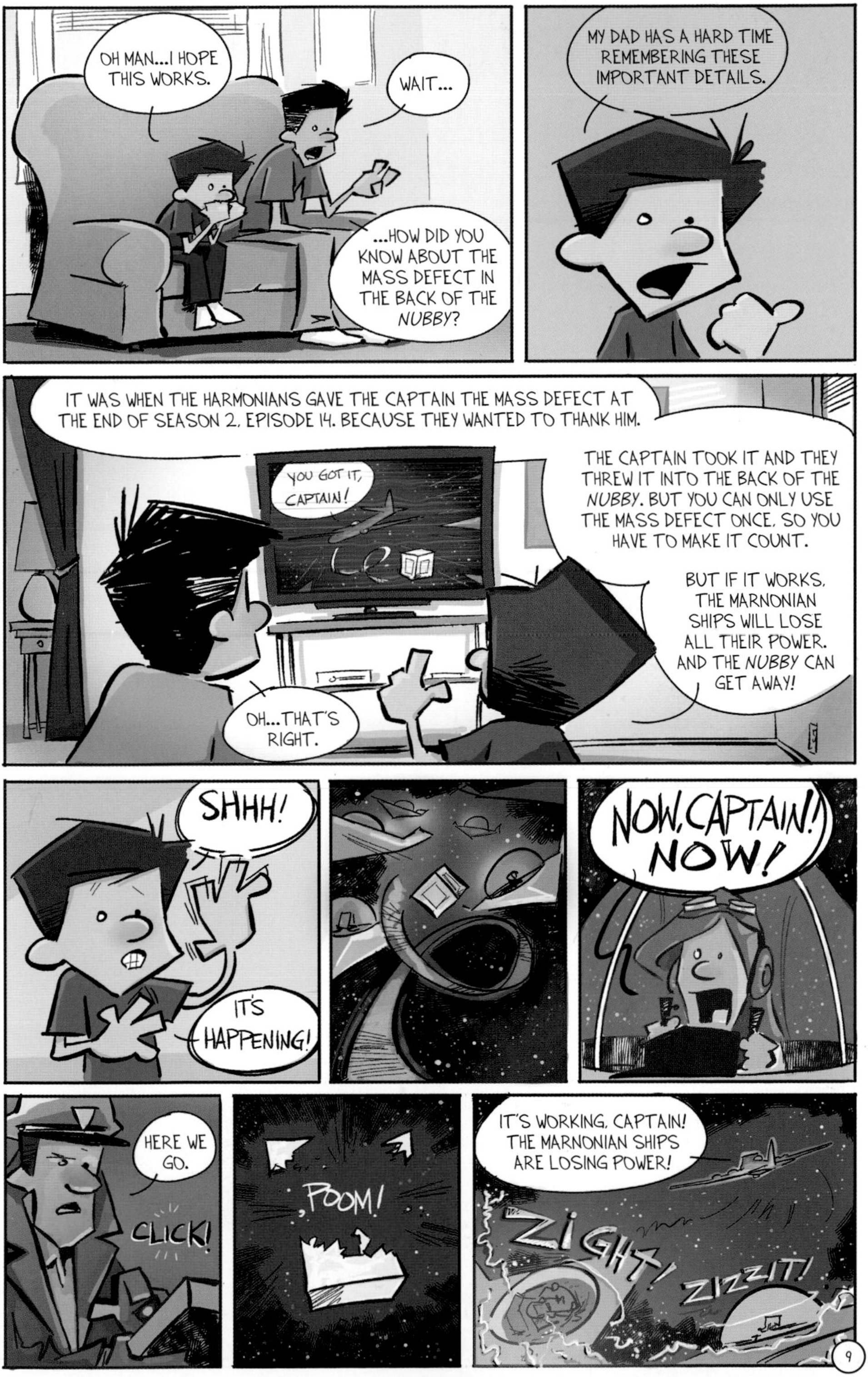
OH MAN...I HOPE THIS WORKS.
WAIT...
...HOW DID YOU KNOW ABOUT THE MASS DEFECT IN THE BACK OF THE *NUBBY*?
MY DAD HAS A HARD TIME REMEMBERING THESE IMPORTANT DETAILS.
IT WAS WHEN THE HARMONIANS GAVE THE CAPTAIN THE MASS DEFECT AT THE END OF SEASON 2, EPISODE 14. BECAUSE THEY WANTED TO THANK HIM.
YOU GOT IT, CAPTAIN!
THE CAPTAIN TOOK IT AND THEY THREW IT INTO THE BACK OF THE *NUBBY*. BUT YOU CAN ONLY USE THE MASS DEFECT ONCE, SO YOU HAVE TO MAKE IT COUNT.
BUT IF IT WORKS, THE MARNONIAN SHIPS WILL LOSE ALL THEIR POWER. AND THE *NUBBY* CAN GET AWAY!
OH...THAT'S RIGHT.
SHHH!
IT'S HAPPENING!
NOW, CAPTAIN! NOW!
HERE WE GO.
CLICK!
POOM!
IT'S WORKING, CAPTAIN! THE MARNONIAN SHIPS ARE LOSING POWER!
ZIGHT!
ZIZZIT!

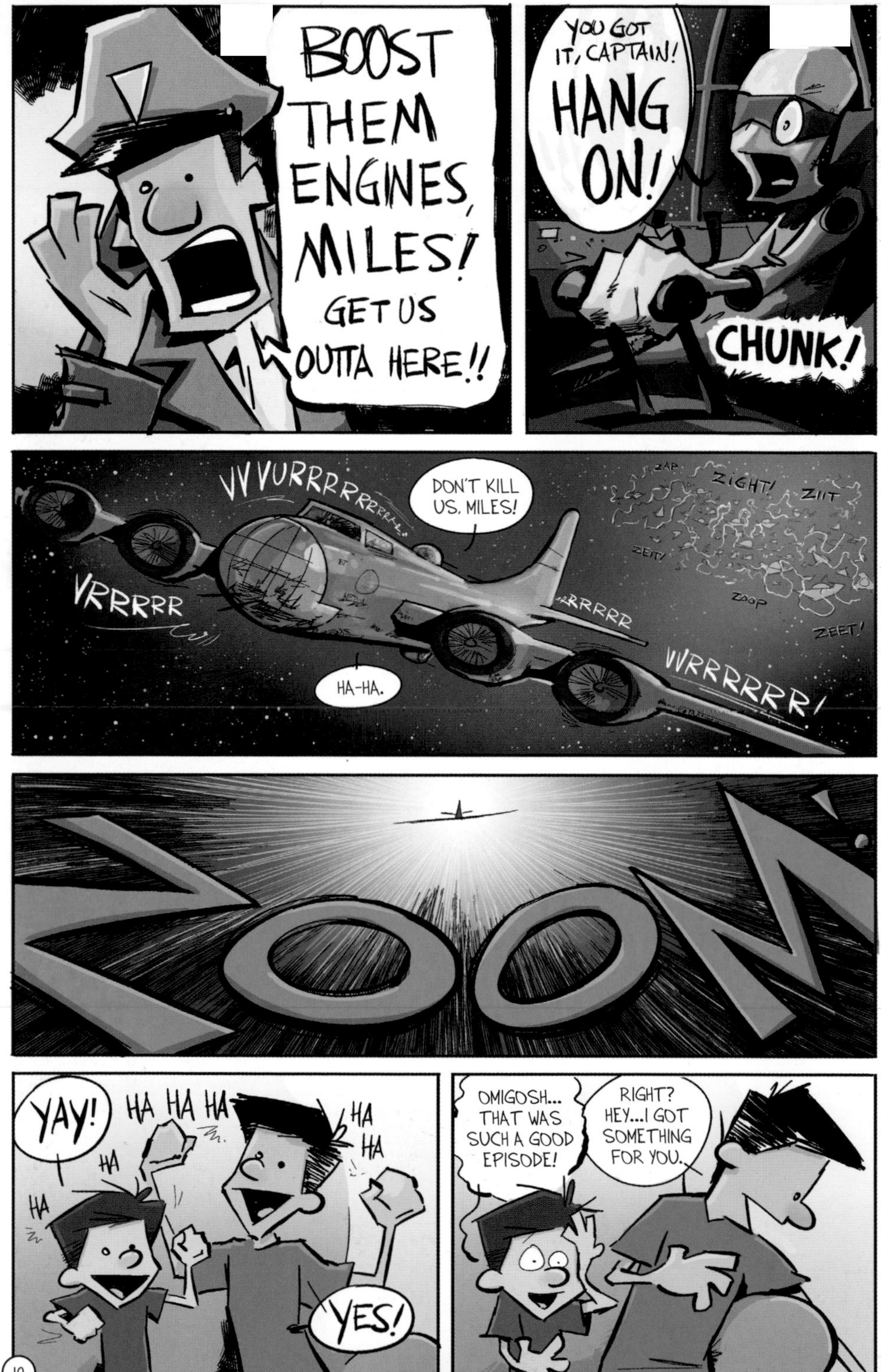

BOOST THEM ENGINES, MILES! GET US OUTTA HERE!!
YOU GOT IT, CAPTAIN! HANG ON!
CHUNK!
VVVURRRRRRRRRRR
DON'T KILL US, MILES!
ZAP
ZIGHT!
ZIIT
ZEIT!
ZOOP
ZEET!
VRRRRR
RRRRRR
HA-HA.
VVRRRRRRR!
ZOOM!
YAY!
HA HA HA
HA HA
HA
HA
YES!
OMIGOSH... THAT WAS SUCH A GOOD EPISODE!
RIGHT? HEY...I GOT SOMETHING FOR YOU.

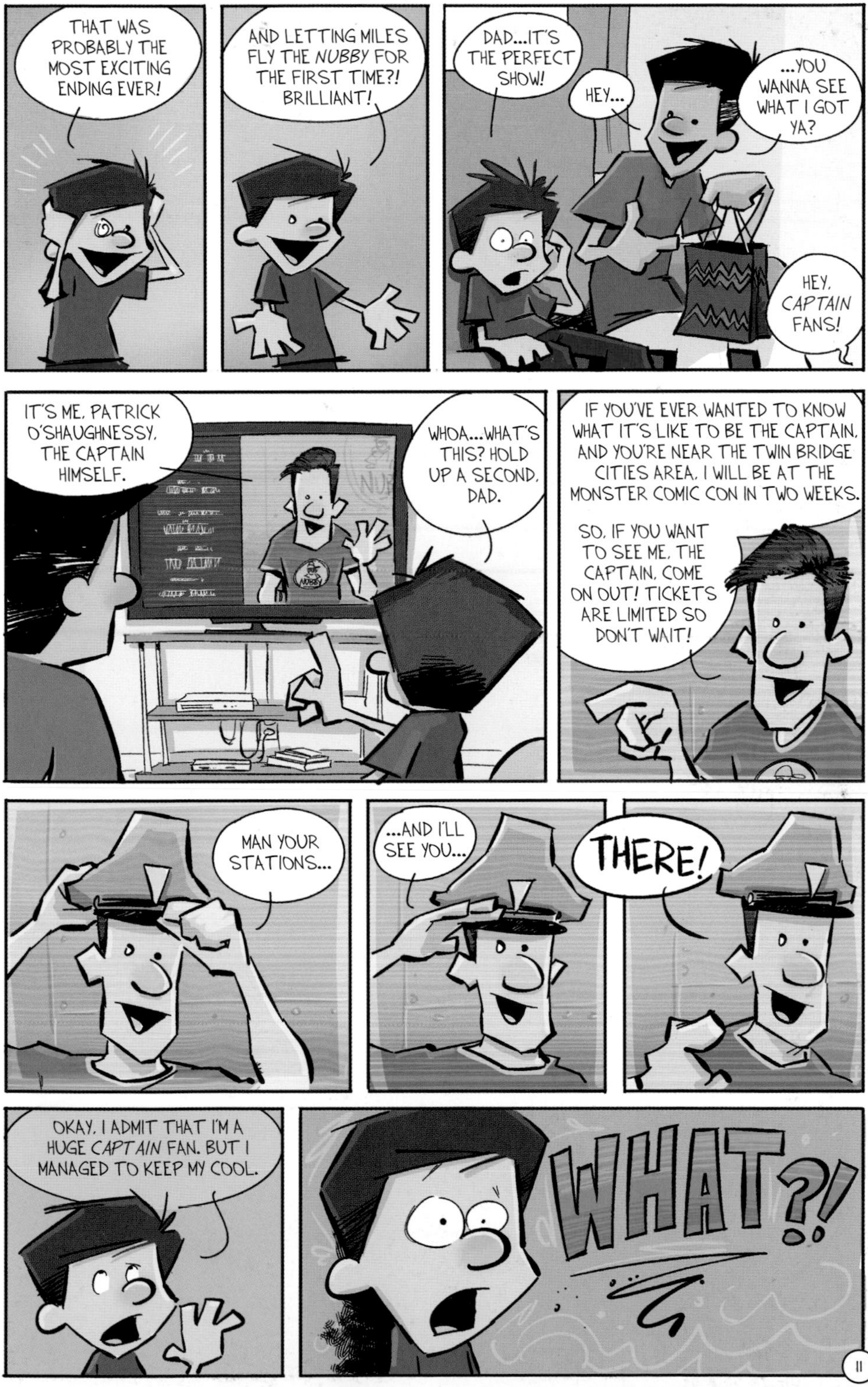
THAT WAS PROBABLY THE MOST EXCITING ENDING EVER!
AND LETTING MILES FLY THE *NUBBY* FOR THE FIRST TIME?! BRILLIANT!
DAD...IT'S THE PERFECT SHOW!
HEY...
...YOU WANNA SEE WHAT I GOT YA?
HEY, *CAPTAIN* FANS!
IT'S ME, PATRICK O'SHAUGHNESSY, THE CAPTAIN HIMSELF.
WHOA...WHAT'S THIS? HOLD UP A SECOND, DAD.
IF YOU'VE EVER WANTED TO KNOW WHAT IT'S LIKE TO BE THE CAPTAIN, AND YOU'RE NEAR THE TWIN BRIDGE CITIES AREA, I WILL BE AT THE MONSTER COMIC CON IN TWO WEEKS.
SO, IF YOU WANT TO SEE ME, THE CAPTAIN, COME ON OUT! TICKETS ARE LIMITED SO DON'T WAIT!
MAN YOUR STATIONS...
...AND I'LL SEE YOU...
THERE!
OKAY, I ADMIT THAT I'M A HUGE *CAPTAIN* FAN. BUT I MANAGED TO KEEP MY COOL.
WHAT?!

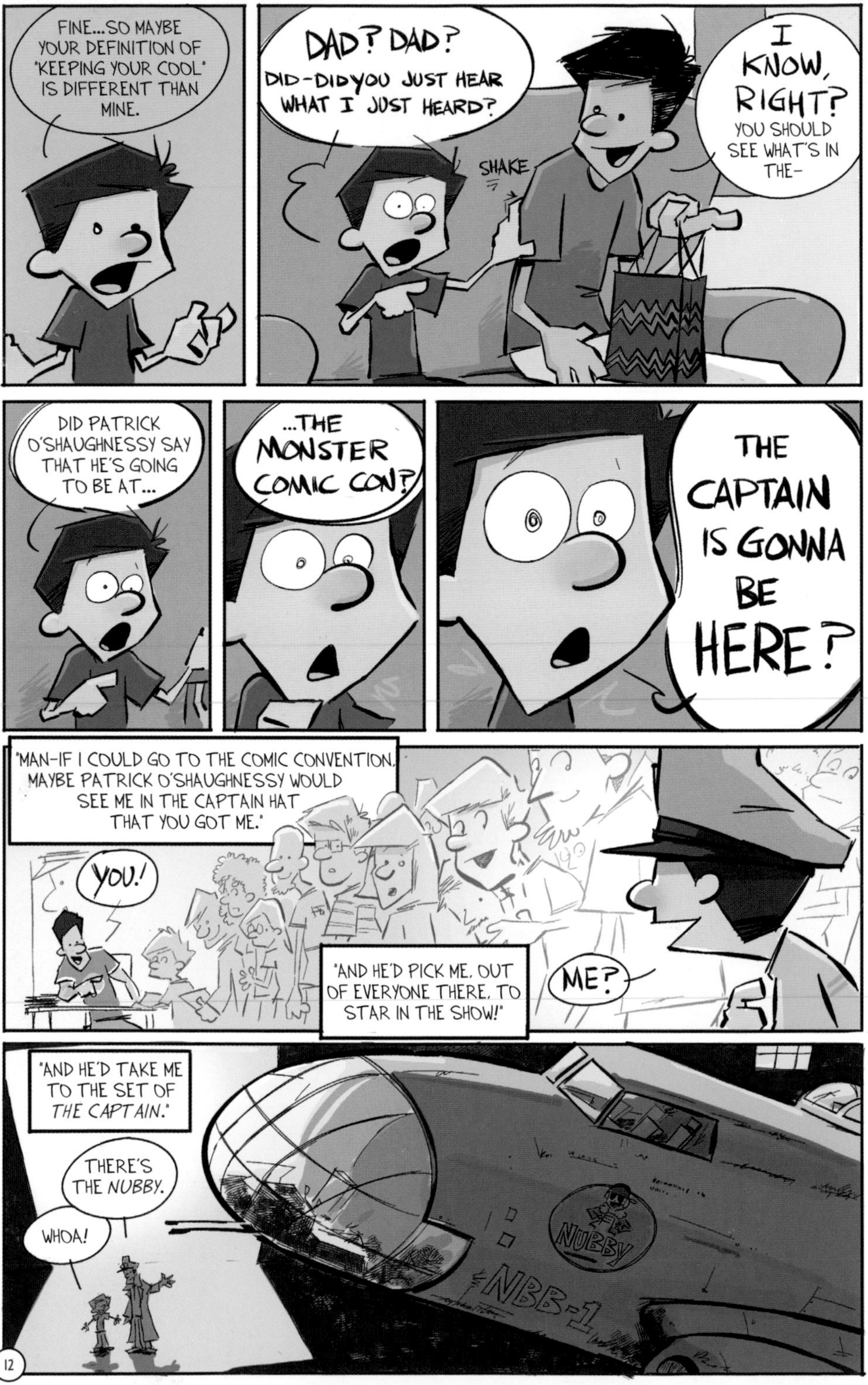

FINE...SO MAYBE YOUR DEFINITION OF "KEEPING YOUR COOL" IS DIFFERENT THAN MINE.
DAD? DAD?
DID-DID YOU JUST HEAR WHAT I JUST HEARD?
SHAKE
I KNOW, RIGHT?
YOU SHOULD SEE WHAT'S IN THE–
DID PATRICK O'SHAUGHNESSY SAY THAT HE'S GOING TO BE AT...
...THE MONSTER COMIC CON?
THE CAPTAIN IS GONNA BE HERE?
"MAN–IF I COULD GO TO THE COMIC CONVENTION, MAYBE PATRICK O'SHAUGHNESSY WOULD SEE ME IN THE CAPTAIN HAT THAT YOU GOT ME."
YOU!
"AND HE'D PICK ME, OUT OF EVERYONE THERE, TO STAR IN THE SHOW!"
ME?
"AND HE'D TAKE ME TO THE SET OF *THE CAPTAIN*."
THERE'S THE *NUBBY*.
WHOA!
NUBBY
NBB-1

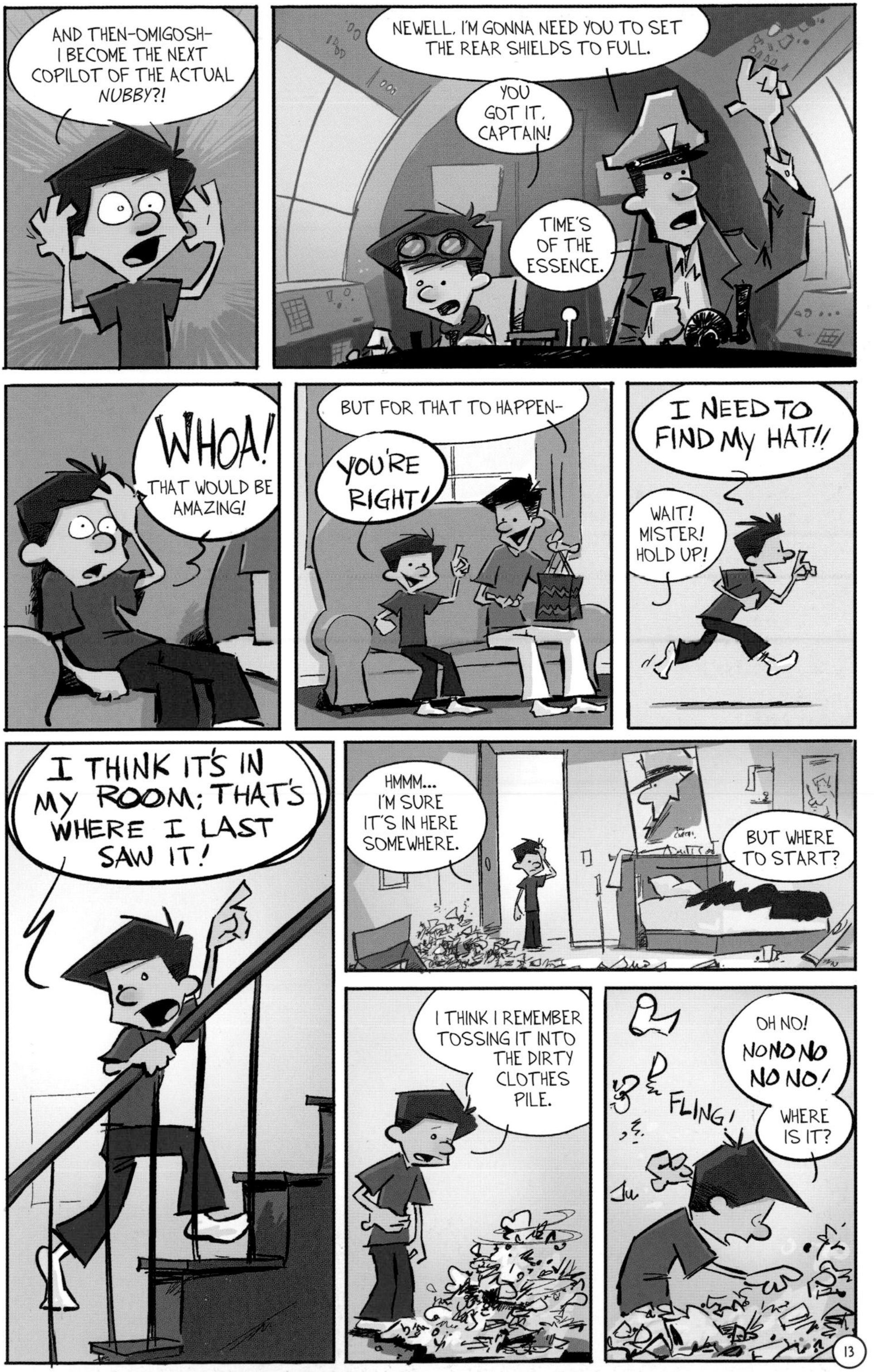

AND THEN-OMIGOSH-I BECOME THE NEXT COPILOT OF THE ACTUAL NUBBY?!
NEWELL, I'M GONNA NEED YOU TO SET THE REAR SHIELDS TO FULL.
YOU GOT IT, CAPTAIN!
TIME'S OF THE ESSENCE.
WHOA! THAT WOULD BE AMAZING!
BUT FOR THAT TO HAPPEN-
YOU'RE RIGHT!
I NEED TO FIND MY HAT!!
WAIT! MISTER! HOLD UP!
I THINK IT'S IN MY ROOM; THAT'S WHERE I LAST SAW IT!
HMMM... I'M SURE IT'S IN HERE SOMEWHERE.
BUT WHERE TO START?
I THINK I REMEMBER TOSSING IT INTO THE DIRTY CLOTHES PILE.
OH NO! NO NO NO NO NO!
FLING!
WHERE IS IT?

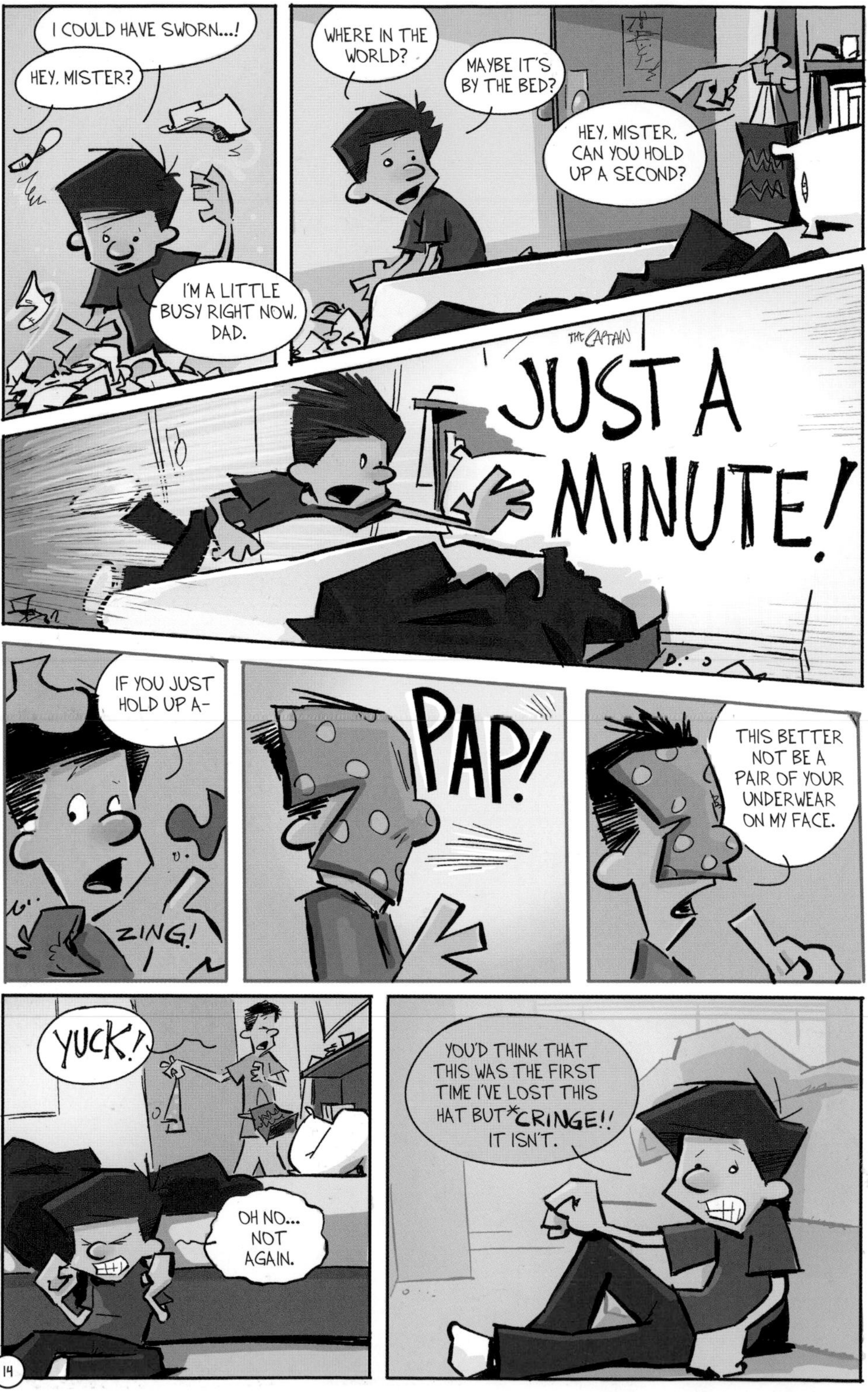

I COULD HAVE SWORN...!
HEY, MISTER?
I'M A LITTLE BUSY RIGHT NOW, DAD.
WHERE IN THE WORLD?
MAYBE IT'S BY THE BED?
HEY, MISTER, CAN YOU HOLD UP A SECOND?
THE CAPTAIN
JUST A MINUTE!
IF YOU JUST HOLD UP A-
ZING!
PAP!
THIS BETTER NOT BE A PAIR OF YOUR UNDERWEAR ON MY FACE.
YUCK!
OH NO... NOT AGAIN.
YOU'D THINK THAT THIS WAS THE FIRST TIME I'VE LOST THIS HAT BUT *CRINGE!!* IT ISN'T.

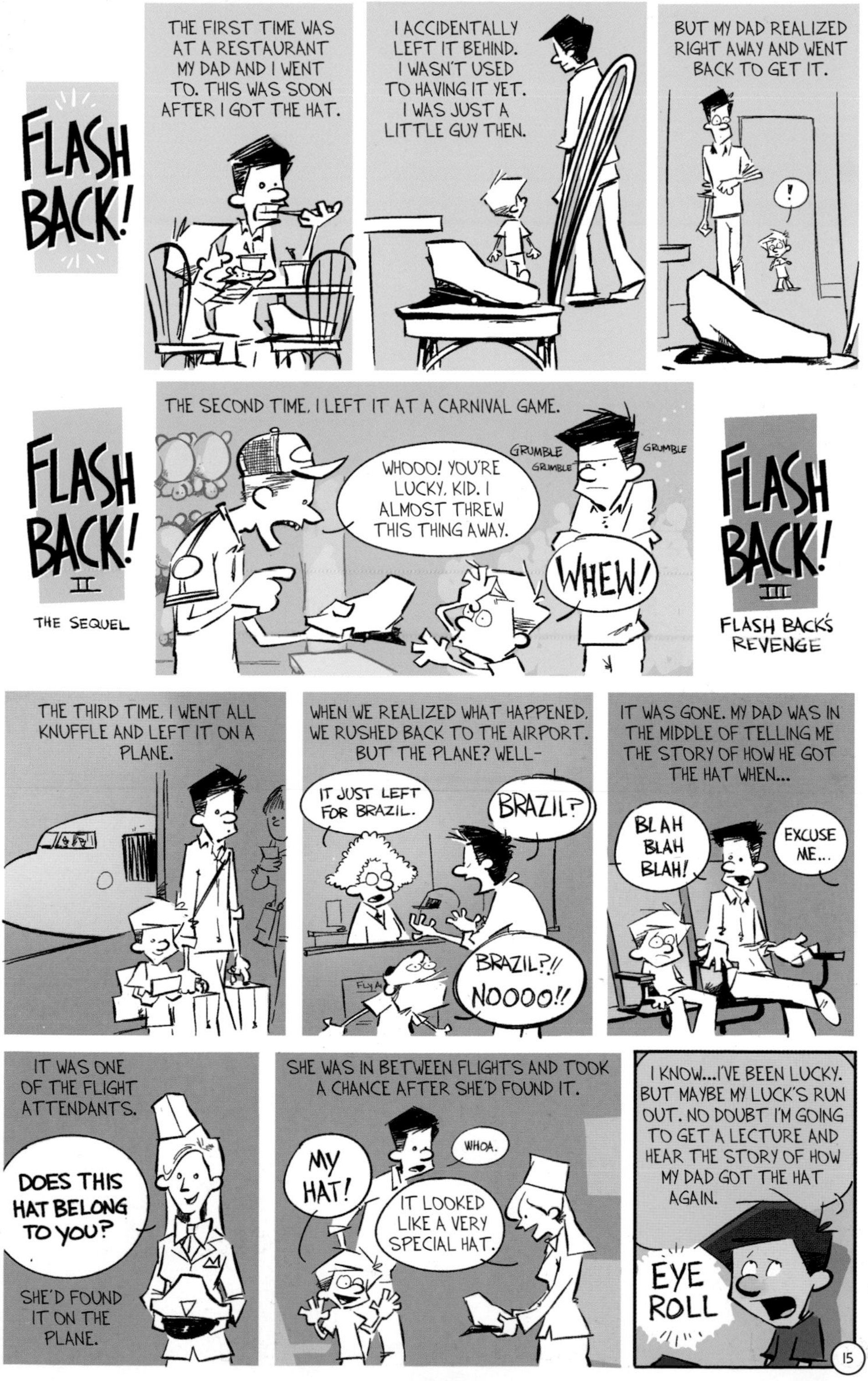
FLASH BACK!
THE FIRST TIME WAS AT A RESTAURANT MY DAD AND I WENT TO. THIS WAS SOON AFTER I GOT THE HAT.
I ACCIDENTALLY LEFT IT BEHIND. I WASN'T USED TO HAVING IT YET. I WAS JUST A LITTLE GUY THEN.
BUT MY DAD REALIZED RIGHT AWAY AND WENT BACK TO GET IT.
!
FLASH BACK! II
THE SEQUEL
THE SECOND TIME, I LEFT IT AT A CARNIVAL GAME.
GRUMBLE
GRUMBLE
GRUMBLE
WHOOO! YOU'RE LUCKY, KID. I ALMOST THREW THIS THING AWAY.
WHEW!
FLASH BACK! III
FLASH BACK'S REVENGE
THE THIRD TIME, I WENT ALL KNUFFLE AND LEFT IT ON A PLANE.
WHEN WE REALIZED WHAT HAPPENED, WE RUSHED BACK TO THE AIRPORT. BUT THE PLANE? WELL-
IT JUST LEFT FOR BRAZIL.
BRAZIL?
BRAZIL?!!
NOOOO!!
IT WAS GONE. MY DAD WAS IN THE MIDDLE OF TELLING ME THE STORY OF HOW HE GOT THE HAT WHEN...
BLAH BLAH BLAH!
EXCUSE ME...
IT WAS ONE OF THE FLIGHT ATTENDANTS.
DOES THIS HAT BELONG TO YOU?
SHE'D FOUND IT ON THE PLANE.
SHE WAS IN BETWEEN FLIGHTS AND TOOK A CHANCE AFTER SHE'D FOUND IT.
MY HAT!
WHOA.
IT LOOKED LIKE A VERY SPECIAL HAT.
I KNOW...I'VE BEEN LUCKY. BUT MAYBE MY LUCK'S RUN OUT. NO DOUBT I'M GOING TO GET A LECTURE AND HEAR THE STORY OF HOW MY DAD GOT THE HAT AGAIN.
EYE ROLL

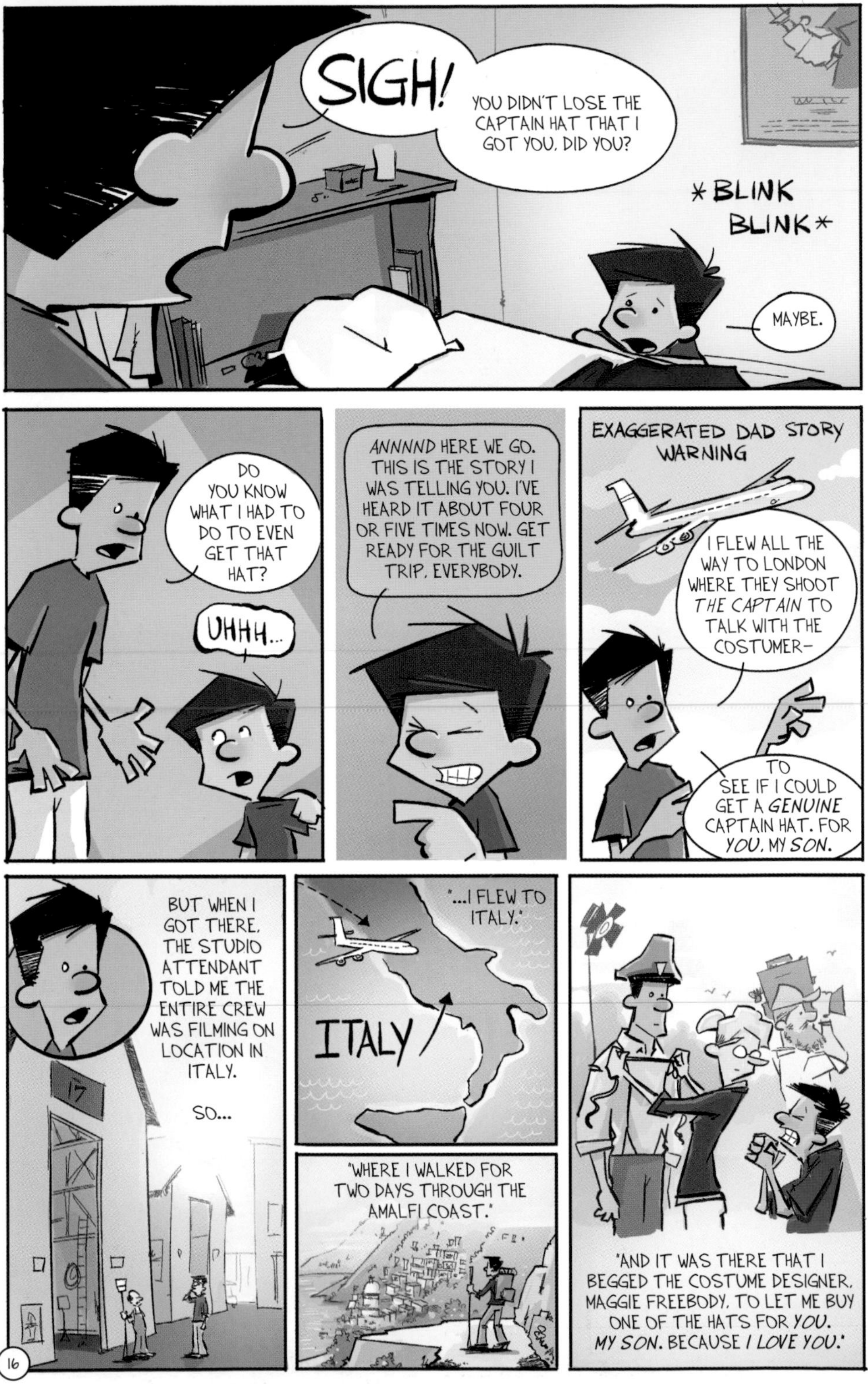
SIGH!
YOU DIDN'T LOSE THE CAPTAIN HAT THAT I GOT YOU, DID YOU?
BLINK BLINK
MAYBE.
DO YOU KNOW WHAT I HAD TO DO TO EVEN GET THAT HAT?
UHHH...
ANNNND HERE WE GO. THIS IS THE STORY I WAS TELLING YOU. I'VE HEARD IT ABOUT FOUR OR FIVE TIMES NOW. GET READY FOR THE GUILT TRIP, EVERYBODY.
EXAGGERATED DAD STORY WARNING
I FLEW ALL THE WAY TO LONDON WHERE THEY SHOOT THE CAPTAIN TO TALK WITH THE COSTUMER–
TO SEE IF I COULD GET A GENUINE CAPTAIN HAT. FOR YOU, MY SON.
BUT WHEN I GOT THERE, THE STUDIO ATTENDANT TOLD ME THE ENTIRE CREW WAS FILMING ON LOCATION IN ITALY.
SO...
17
"...I FLEW TO ITALY."
ITALY
"WHERE I WALKED FOR TWO DAYS THROUGH THE AMALFI COAST."
"AND IT WAS THERE THAT I BEGGED THE COSTUME DESIGNER, MAGGIE FREEBODY, TO LET ME BUY ONE OF THE HATS FOR YOU. MY SON. BECAUSE I LOVE YOU."

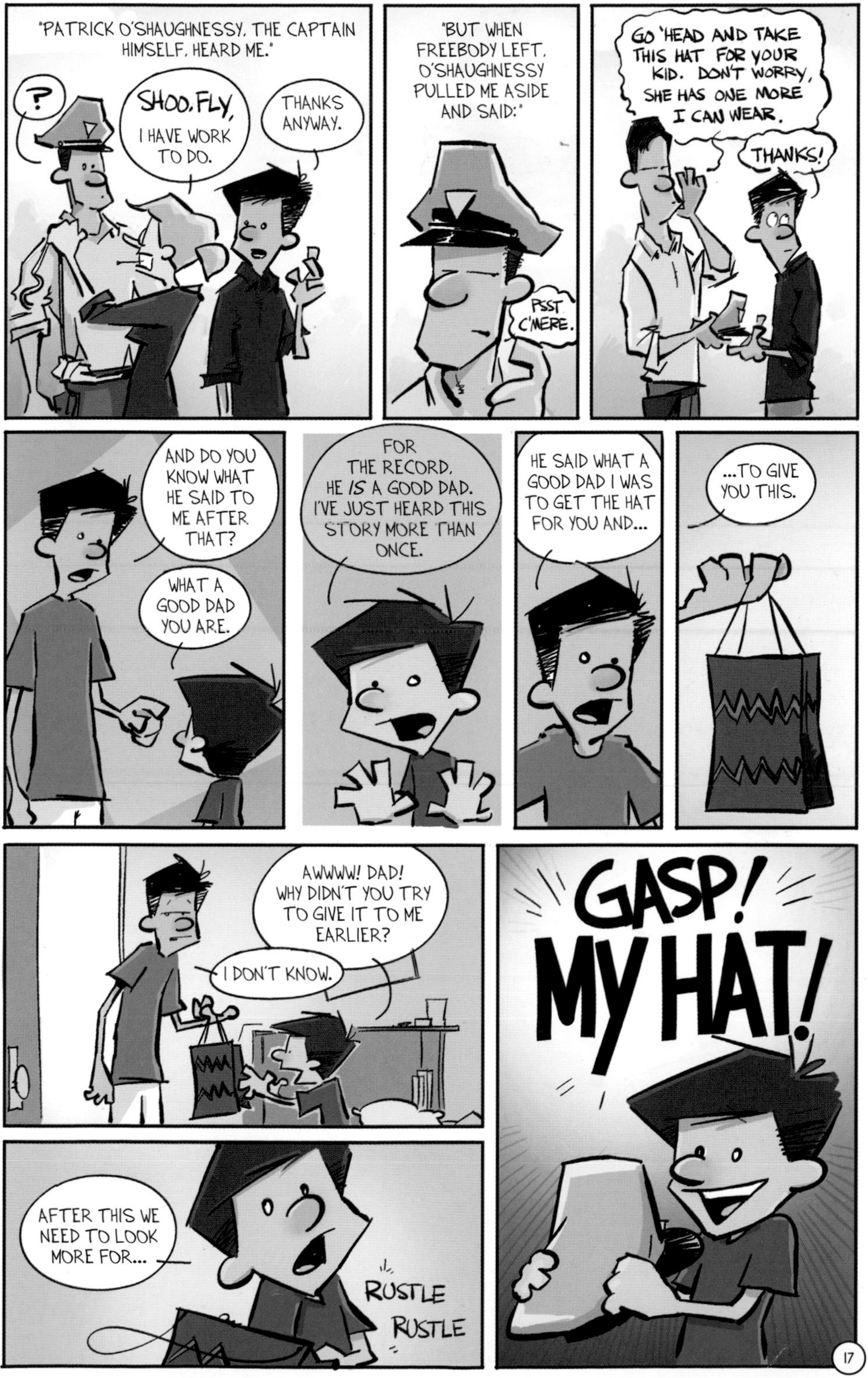
"PATRICK O'SHAUGHNESSY, THE CAPTAIN HIMSELF, HEARD ME."
?
SHOO, FLY, I HAVE WORK TO DO.
THANKS ANYWAY.
"BUT WHEN FREEBODY LEFT, O'SHAUGHNESSY PULLED ME ASIDE AND SAID:"
PSST C'MERE.
GO 'HEAD AND TAKE THIS HAT FOR YOUR KID. DON'T WORRY, SHE HAS ONE MORE I CAN WEAR.
THANKS!
AND DO YOU KNOW WHAT HE SAID TO ME AFTER THAT?
WHAT A GOOD DAD YOU ARE.
FOR THE RECORD, HE *IS* A GOOD DAD. I'VE JUST HEARD THIS STORY MORE THAN ONCE.
HE SAID WHAT A GOOD DAD I WAS TO GET THE HAT FOR YOU AND...
...TO GIVE YOU THIS.
AWWWW! DAD! WHY DIDN'T YOU TRY TO GIVE IT TO ME EARLIER?
I DON'T KNOW.
AFTER THIS WE NEED TO LOOK MORE FOR...
RUSTLE
RUSTLE
GASP! MY HAT!

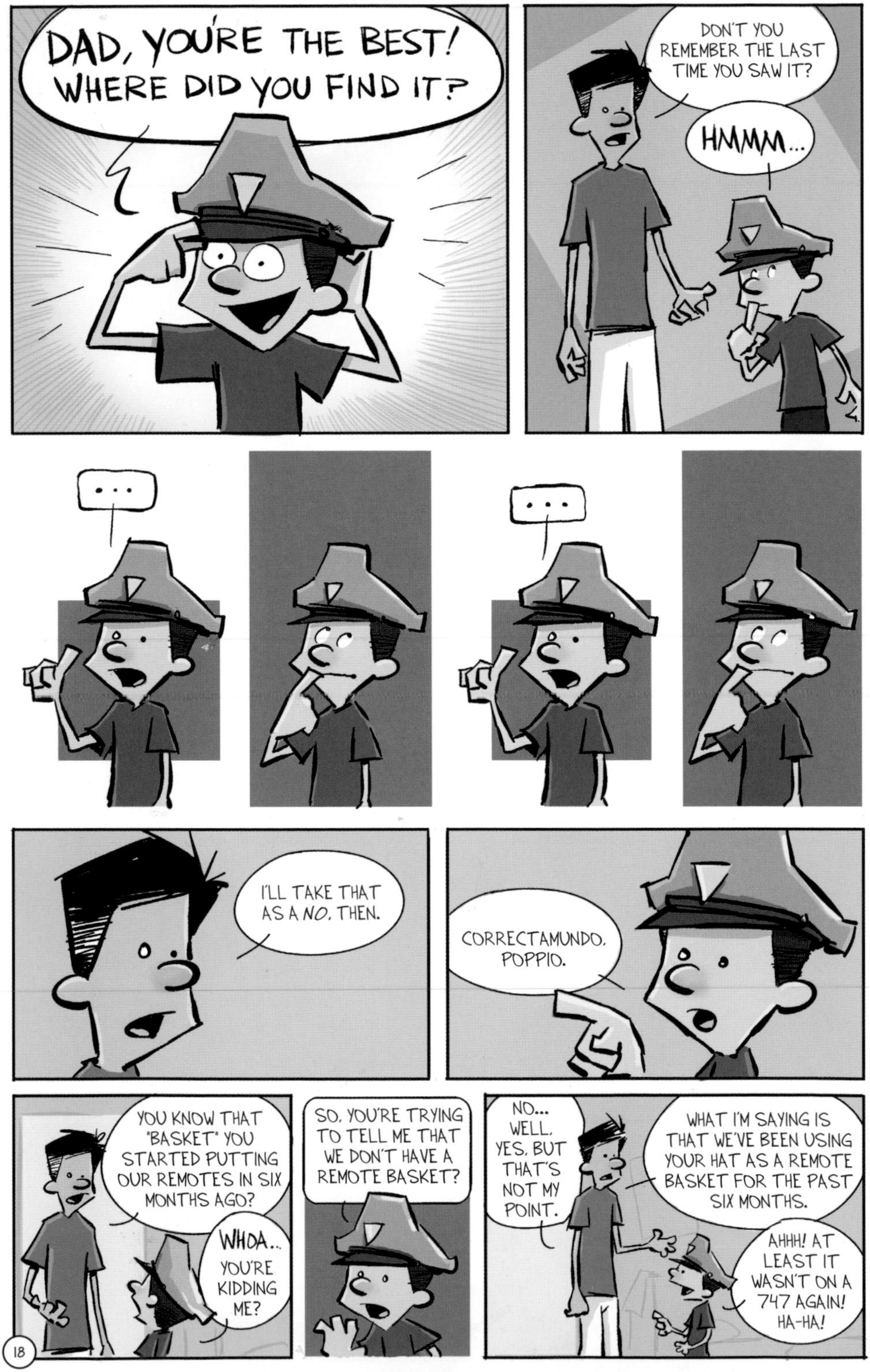
DAD, YOU'RE THE BEST! WHERE DID YOU FIND IT?
DON'T YOU REMEMBER THE LAST TIME YOU SAW IT?
HMMM...
...
...
I'LL TAKE THAT AS A *NO*, THEN.
CORRECTAMUNDO, POPPIO.
YOU KNOW THAT "BASKET" YOU STARTED PUTTING OUR REMOTES IN SIX MONTHS AGO?
WHOA...
YOU'RE KIDDING ME?
SO, YOU'RE TRYING TO TELL ME THAT WE DON'T HAVE A REMOTE BASKET?
NO... WELL, YES, BUT THAT'S NOT MY POINT.
WHAT I'M SAYING IS THAT WE'VE BEEN USING YOUR HAT AS A REMOTE BASKET FOR THE PAST SIX MONTHS.
AHHH! AT LEAST IT WASN'T ON A 747 AGAIN! HA-HA!

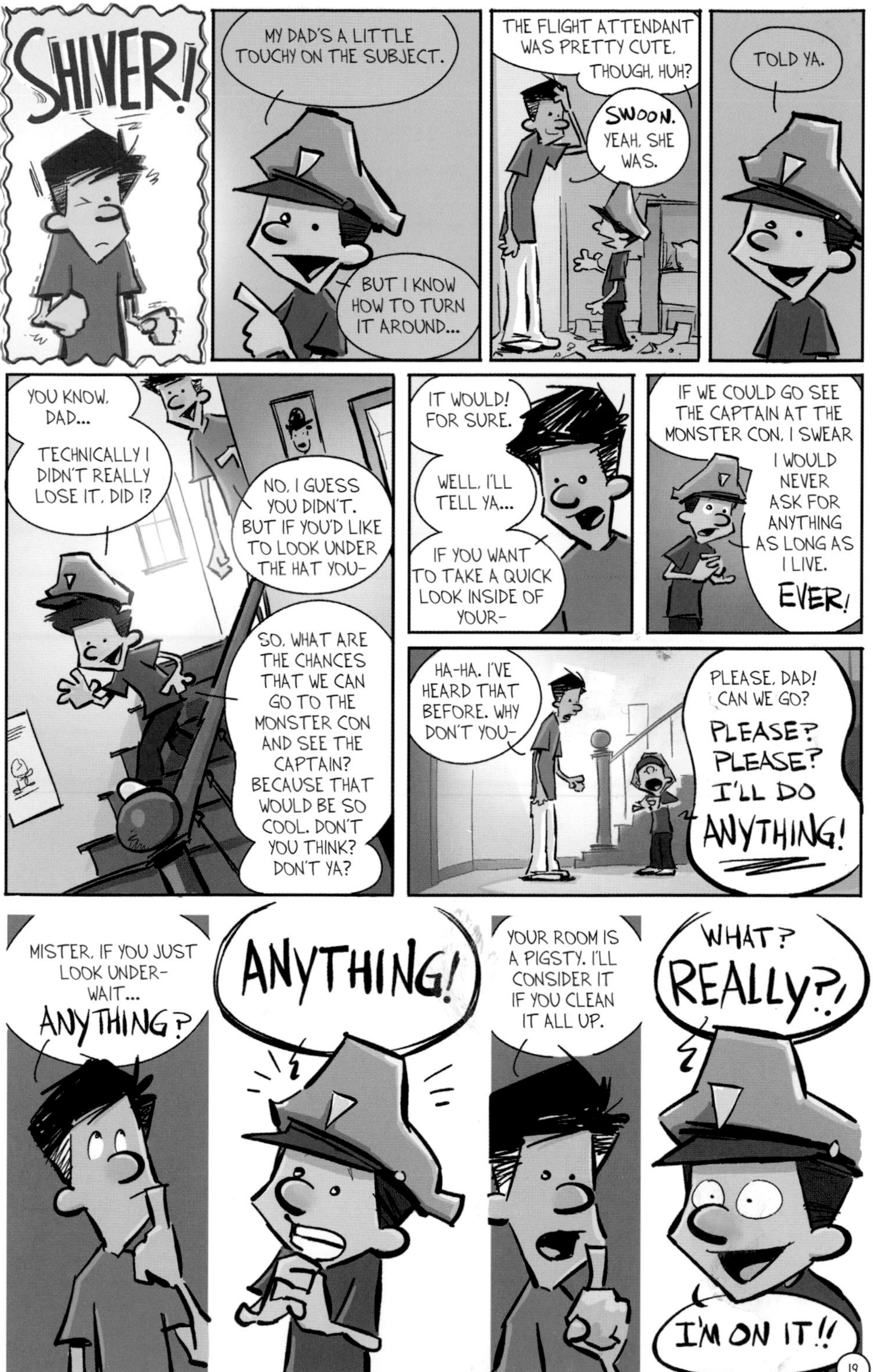
SHIVER!
MY DAD'S A LITTLE TOUCHY ON THE SUBJECT.
BUT I KNOW HOW TO TURN IT AROUND...
THE FLIGHT ATTENDANT WAS PRETTY CUTE,
THOUGH, HUH?
SWOON.
YEAH, SHE WAS.
TOLD YA.
YOU KNOW, DAD...
TECHNICALLY I DIDN'T REALLY LOSE IT, DID I?
NO, I GUESS YOU DIDN'T. BUT IF YOU'D LIKE TO LOOK UNDER THE HAT YOU-
SO, WHAT ARE THE CHANCES THAT WE CAN GO TO THE MONSTER CON AND SEE THE CAPTAIN? BECAUSE THAT WOULD BE SO COOL. DON'T YOU THINK? DON'T YA?
IT WOULD! FOR SURE.
WELL, I'LL TELL YA...
IF YOU WANT TO TAKE A QUICK LOOK INSIDE OF YOUR-
IF WE COULD GO SEE THE CAPTAIN AT THE MONSTER CON, I SWEAR
I WOULD NEVER ASK FOR ANYTHING AS LONG AS I LIVE.
EVER!
HA-HA. I'VE HEARD THAT BEFORE. WHY DON'T YOU-
PLEASE, DAD! CAN WE GO?
PLEASE? PLEASE? I'LL DO ANYTHING!
MISTER, IF YOU JUST LOOK UNDER-
WAIT... ANYTHING?
ANYTHING!
YOUR ROOM IS A PIGSTY. I'LL CONSIDER IT IF YOU CLEAN IT ALL UP.
WHAT? REALLY?!
I'M ON IT!!

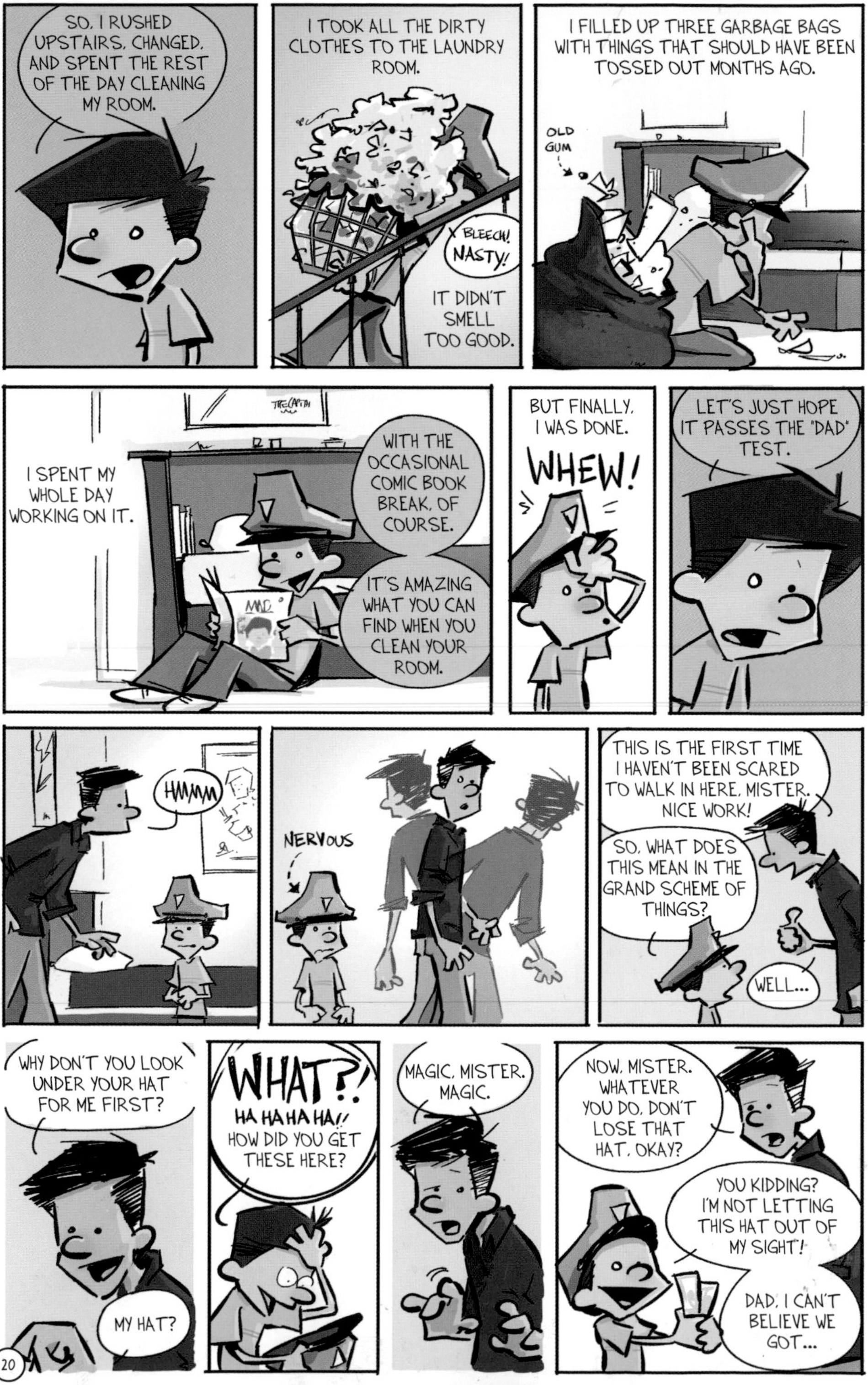
SO, I RUSHED UPSTAIRS, CHANGED, AND SPENT THE REST OF THE DAY CLEANING MY ROOM.
I TOOK ALL THE DIRTY CLOTHES TO THE LAUNDRY ROOM.
BLEECH! NASTY!
IT DIDN'T SMELL TOO GOOD.
I FILLED UP THREE GARBAGE BAGS WITH THINGS THAT SHOULD HAVE BEEN TOSSED OUT MONTHS AGO.
OLD GUM
I SPENT MY WHOLE DAY WORKING ON IT.
WITH THE OCCASIONAL COMIC BOOK BREAK, OF COURSE.
IT'S AMAZING WHAT YOU CAN FIND WHEN YOU CLEAN YOUR ROOM.
BUT FINALLY, I WAS DONE.
WHEW!
LET'S JUST HOPE IT PASSES THE "DAD" TEST.
HMMM
NERVOUS
THIS IS THE FIRST TIME I HAVEN'T BEEN SCARED TO WALK IN HERE, MISTER. NICE WORK!
SO, WHAT DOES THIS MEAN IN THE GRAND SCHEME OF THINGS?
WELL...
WHY DON'T YOU LOOK UNDER YOUR HAT FOR ME FIRST?
MY HAT?
WHAT?!
HA HA HA HA!!
HOW DID YOU GET THESE HERE?
MAGIC, MISTER. MAGIC.
NOW, MISTER. WHATEVER YOU DO, DON'T LOSE THAT HAT, OKAY?
YOU KIDDING? I'M NOT LETTING THIS HAT OUT OF MY SIGHT!
DAD, I CAN'T BELIEVE WE GOT...

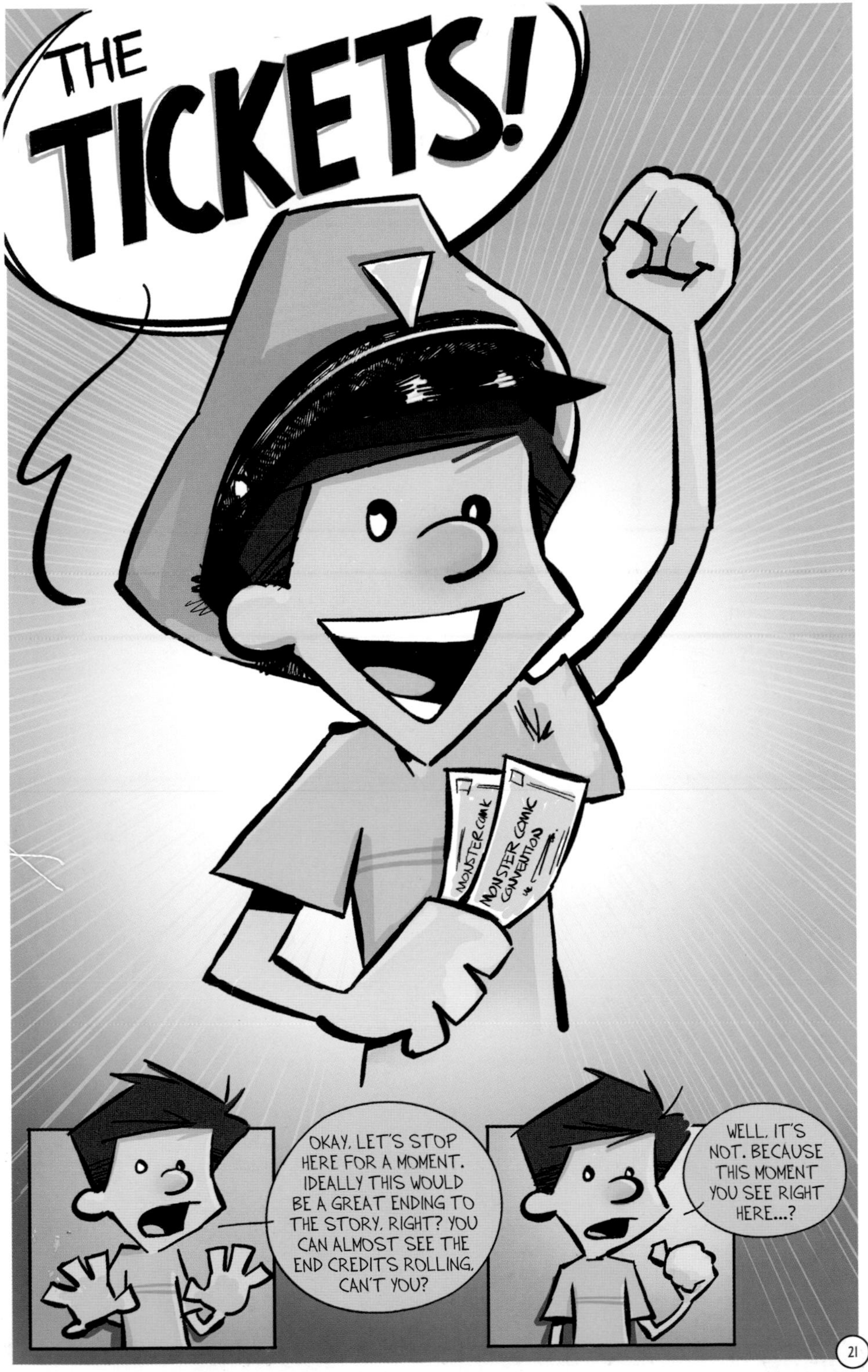
THE TICKETS!
MONSTER COMIC
MONSTER COMIC CONVENTION
OKAY, LET'S STOP HERE FOR A MOMENT. IDEALLY THIS WOULD BE A GREAT ENDING TO THE STORY, RIGHT? YOU CAN ALMOST SEE THE END CREDITS ROLLING, CAN'T YOU?
WELL, IT'S NOT. BECAUSE THIS MOMENT YOU SEE RIGHT HERE...?

CHAPTER TWO
THIS IS ONLY THE BEGINNING

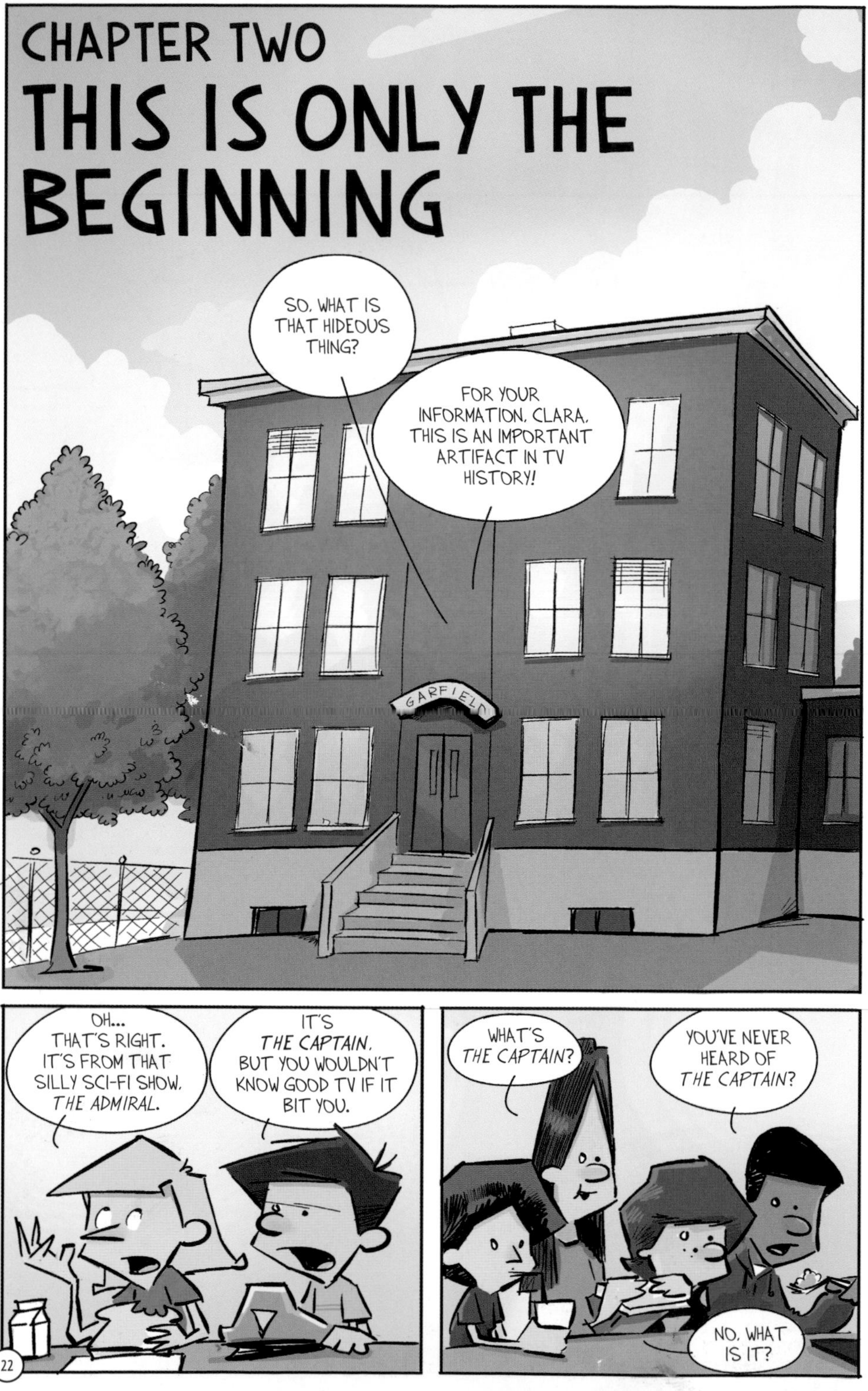
SO, WHAT IS THAT HIDEOUS THING?
FOR YOUR INFORMATION, CLARA, THIS IS AN IMPORTANT ARTIFACT IN TV HISTORY!
GARFIELD
OH... THAT'S RIGHT. IT'S FROM THAT SILLY SCI-FI SHOW, *THE ADMIRAL*.
IT'S *THE CAPTAIN*, BUT YOU WOULDN'T KNOW GOOD TV IF IT BIT YOU.
WHAT'S *THE CAPTAIN*?
YOU'VE NEVER HEARD OF *THE CAPTAIN*?
NO, WHAT IS IT?

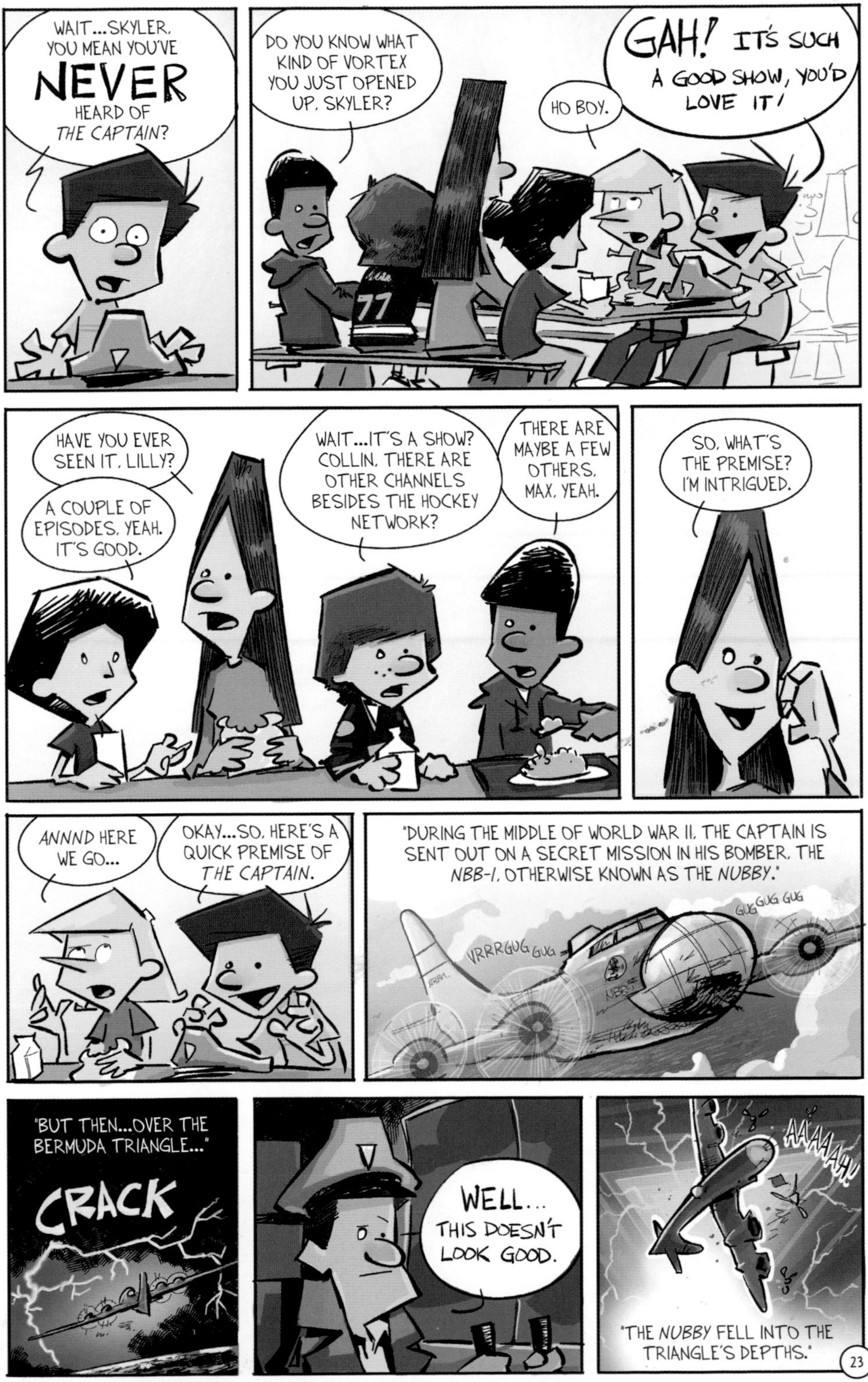
WAIT...SKYLER, YOU MEAN YOU'VE NEVER HEARD OF *THE CAPTAIN*?
DO YOU KNOW WHAT KIND OF VORTEX YOU JUST OPENED UP, SKYLER?
HO BOY.
GAH! IT'S SUCH A GOOD SHOW, YOU'D LOVE IT!
77
HAVE YOU EVER SEEN IT, LILLY?
A COUPLE OF EPISODES, YEAH. IT'S GOOD.
WAIT...IT'S A SHOW? COLLIN, THERE ARE OTHER CHANNELS BESIDES THE HOCKEY NETWORK?
THERE ARE MAYBE A FEW OTHERS, MAX, YEAH.
SO, WHAT'S THE PREMISE? I'M INTRIGUED.
ANNND HERE WE GO...
OKAY...SO, HERE'S A QUICK PREMISE OF *THE CAPTAIN*.
"DURING THE MIDDLE OF WORLD WAR II, THE CAPTAIN IS SENT OUT ON A SECRET MISSION IN HIS BOMBER, THE *NBB-1*, OTHERWISE KNOWN AS THE *NUBBY*."
VRRRGUG GUG
GUG GUG GUG
NBB
"BUT THEN...OVER THE BERMUDA TRIANGLE..."
CRACK
WELL... THIS DOESN'T LOOK GOOD.
AAAAAAH!
"THE *NUBBY* FELL INTO THE TRIANGLE'S DEPTHS."

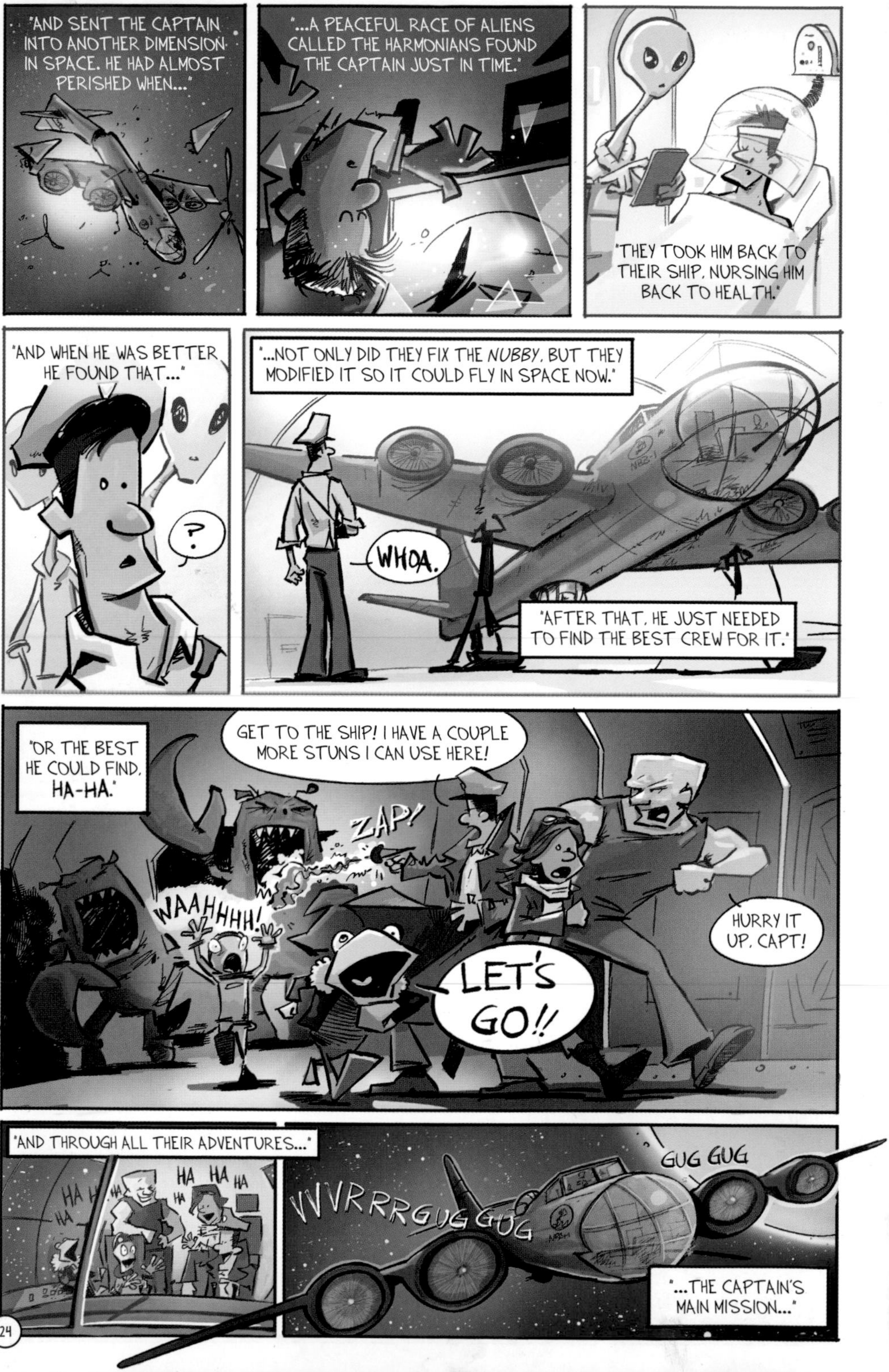
"AND SENT THE CAPTAIN INTO ANOTHER DIMENSION IN SPACE. HE HAD ALMOST PERISHED WHEN..."
"...A PEACEFUL RACE OF ALIENS CALLED THE HARMONIANS FOUND THE CAPTAIN JUST IN TIME."
"THEY TOOK HIM BACK TO THEIR SHIP, NURSING HIM BACK TO HEALTH."
"AND WHEN HE WAS BETTER HE FOUND THAT..."
?
"...NOT ONLY DID THEY FIX THE *NUBBY*, BUT THEY MODIFIED IT SO IT COULD FLY IN SPACE NOW."
WHOA.
"AFTER THAT, HE JUST NEEDED TO FIND THE BEST CREW FOR IT."
"OR THE BEST HE COULD FIND, **HA-HA.**"
GET TO THE SHIP! I HAVE A COUPLE MORE STUNS I CAN USE HERE!
ZAP!
WAAHHHH!
LET'S GO!!
HURRY IT UP, CAPT!
"AND THROUGH ALL THEIR ADVENTURES..."
HA HA HA HA HA HA HA
VVVRRRRGUG GUG
GUG GUG
"...THE CAPTAIN'S MAIN MISSION..."

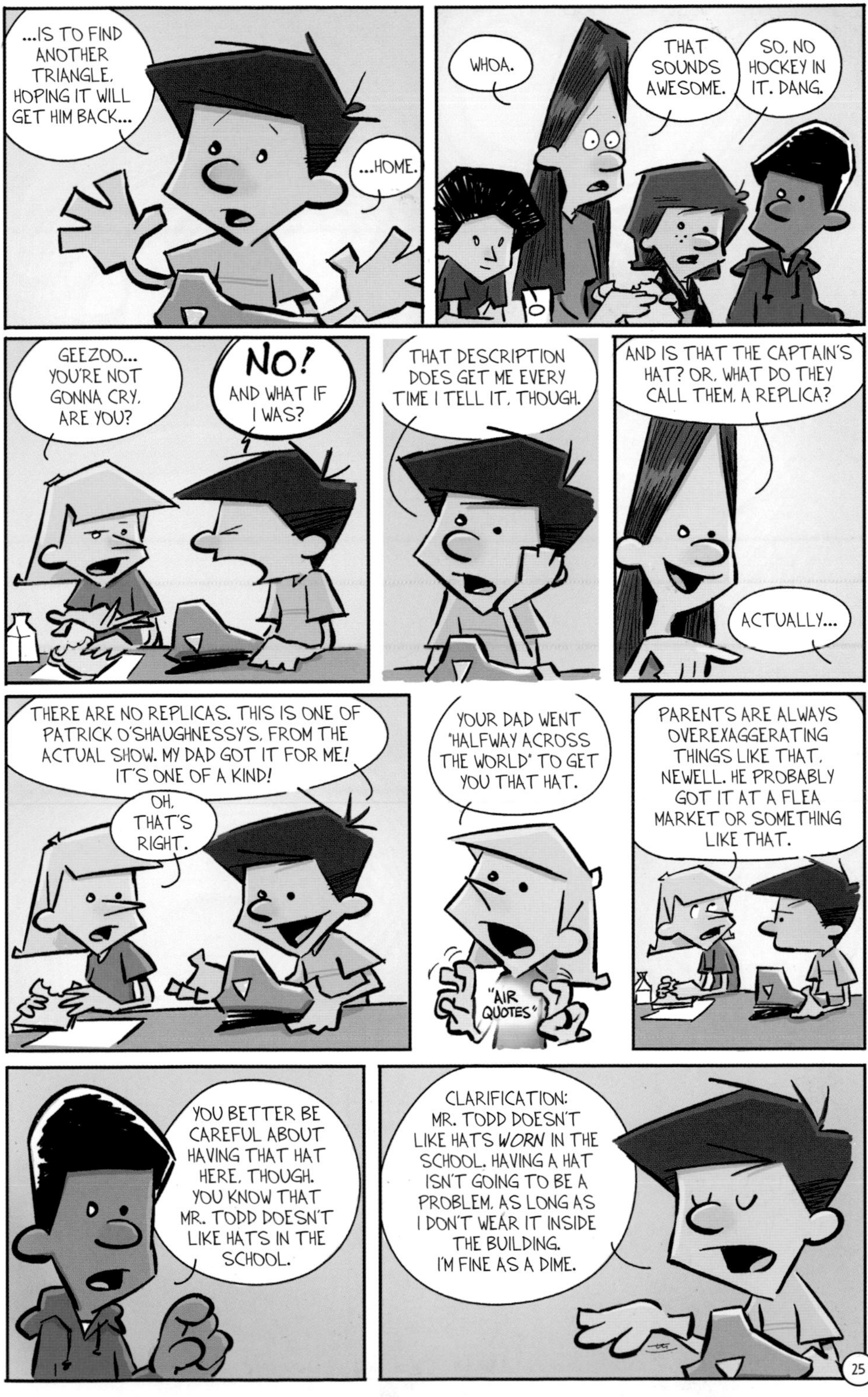
...IS TO FIND ANOTHER TRIANGLE, HOPING IT WILL GET HIM BACK...
...HOME.
WHOA.
THAT SOUNDS AWESOME.
SO, NO HOCKEY IN IT. DANG.
GEEZOO... YOU'RE NOT GONNA CRY, ARE YOU?
NO! AND WHAT IF I WAS?
THAT DESCRIPTION DOES GET ME EVERY TIME I TELL IT, THOUGH.
AND IS THAT THE CAPTAIN'S HAT? OR, WHAT DO THEY CALL THEM, A REPLICA?
ACTUALLY...
THERE ARE NO REPLICAS. THIS IS ONE OF PATRICK O'SHAUGHNESSY'S, FROM THE ACTUAL SHOW. MY DAD GOT IT FOR ME! IT'S ONE OF A KIND!
OH, THAT'S RIGHT.
YOUR DAD WENT "HALFWAY ACROSS THE WORLD" TO GET YOU THAT HAT.
"AIR QUOTES"
PARENTS ARE ALWAYS OVEREXAGGERATING THINGS LIKE THAT, NEWELL. HE PROBABLY GOT IT AT A FLEA MARKET OR SOMETHING LIKE THAT.
YOU BETTER BE CAREFUL ABOUT HAVING THAT HAT HERE, THOUGH. YOU KNOW THAT MR. TODD DOESN'T LIKE HATS IN THE SCHOOL.
CLARIFICATION: MR. TODD DOESN'T LIKE HATS *WORN* IN THE SCHOOL. HAVING A HAT ISN'T GOING TO BE A PROBLEM, AS LONG AS I DON'T WEAR IT INSIDE THE BUILDING. I'M FINE AS A DIME.

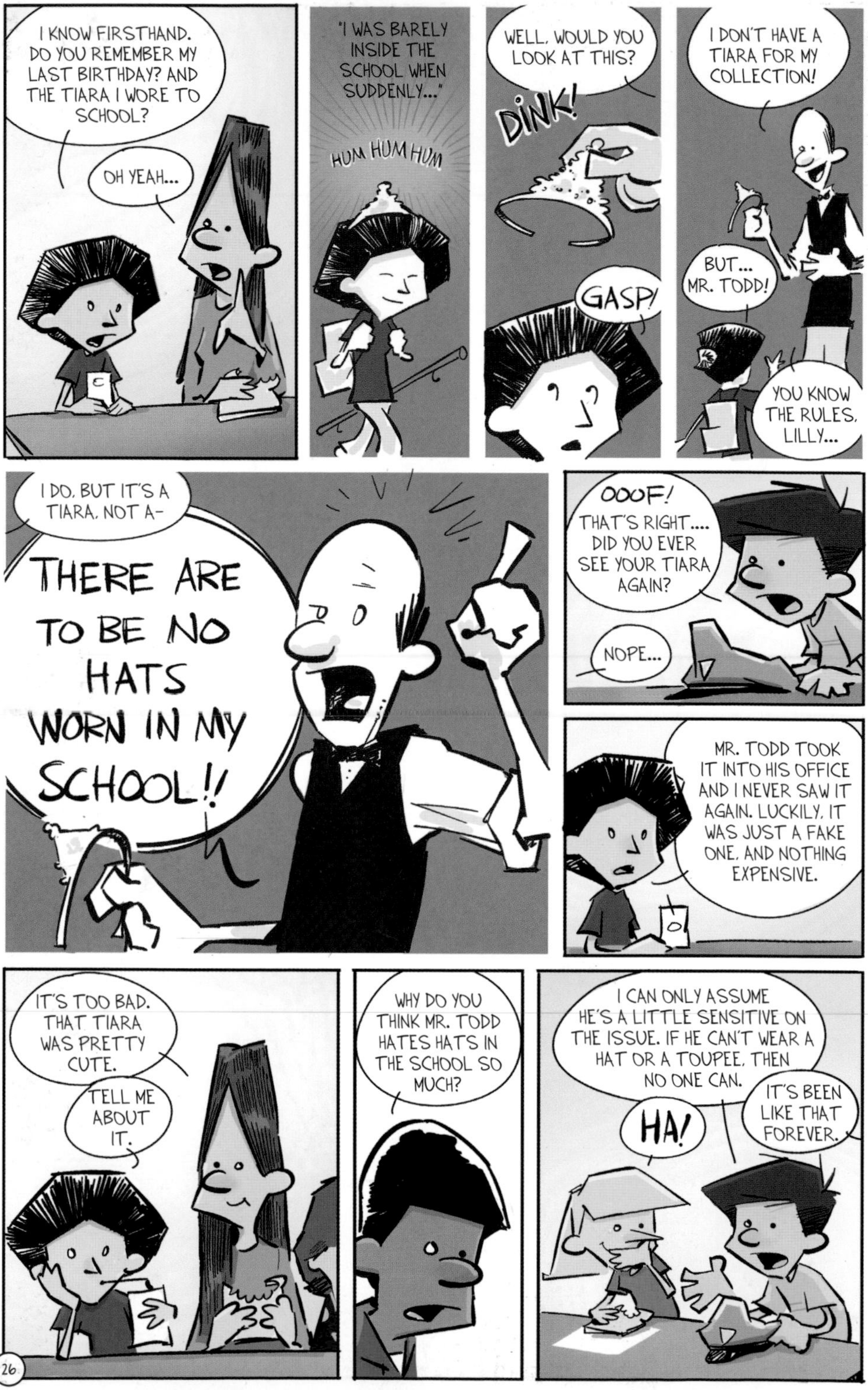
I KNOW FIRSTHAND. DO YOU REMEMBER MY LAST BIRTHDAY? AND THE TIARA I WORE TO SCHOOL?
OH YEAH...
"I WAS BARELY INSIDE THE SCHOOL WHEN SUDDENLY..."
HUM HUM HUM
WELL, WOULD YOU LOOK AT THIS?
DINK!
GASP!
I DON'T HAVE A TIARA FOR MY COLLECTION!
BUT... MR. TODD!
YOU KNOW THE RULES, LILLY...
I DO, BUT IT'S A TIARA, NOT A-
THERE ARE TO BE NO HATS WORN IN MY SCHOOL!!
OOOF!
THAT'S RIGHT.... DID YOU EVER SEE YOUR TIARA AGAIN?
NOPE...
MR. TODD TOOK IT INTO HIS OFFICE AND I NEVER SAW IT AGAIN. LUCKILY, IT WAS JUST A FAKE ONE, AND NOTHING EXPENSIVE.
IT'S TOO BAD. THAT TIARA WAS PRETTY CUTE.
TELL ME ABOUT IT.
WHY DO YOU THINK MR. TODD HATES HATS IN THE SCHOOL SO MUCH?
I CAN ONLY ASSUME HE'S A LITTLE SENSITIVE ON THE ISSUE. IF HE CAN'T WEAR A HAT OR A TOUPEE, THEN NO ONE CAN.
HA!
IT'S BEEN LIKE THAT FOREVER.

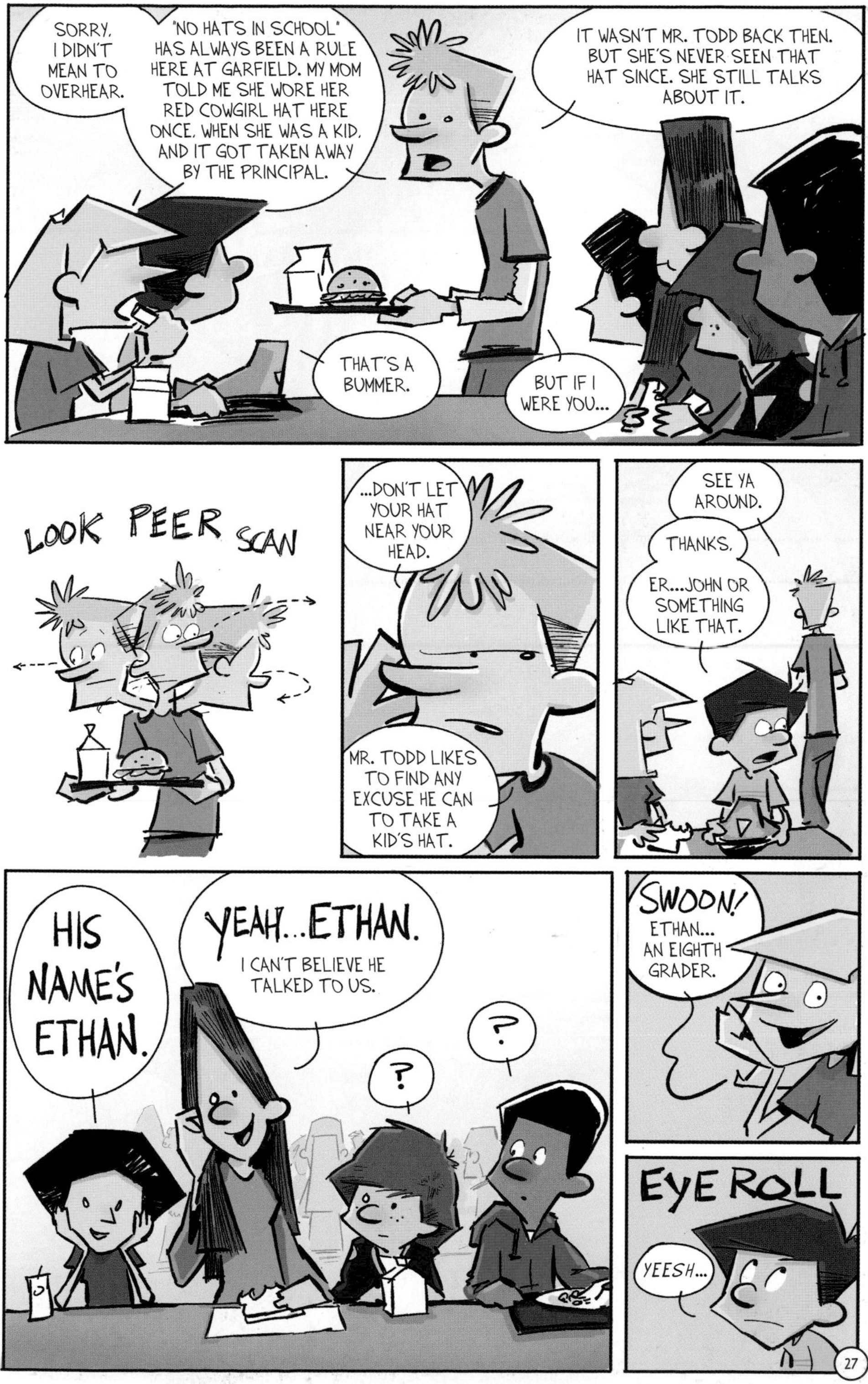
SORRY, I DIDN'T MEAN TO OVERHEAR.
"NO HATS IN SCHOOL" HAS ALWAYS BEEN A RULE HERE AT GARFIELD. MY MOM TOLD ME SHE WORE HER RED COWGIRL HAT HERE ONCE, WHEN SHE WAS A KID, AND IT GOT TAKEN AWAY BY THE PRINCIPAL.
IT WASN'T MR. TODD BACK THEN. BUT SHE'S NEVER SEEN THAT HAT SINCE. SHE STILL TALKS ABOUT IT.
THAT'S A BUMMER.
BUT IF I WERE YOU...
LOOK PEER SCAN
...DON'T LET YOUR HAT NEAR YOUR HEAD.
MR. TODD LIKES TO FIND ANY EXCUSE HE CAN TO TAKE A KID'S HAT.
SEE YA AROUND.
THANKS,
ER...JOHN OR SOMETHING LIKE THAT.
HIS NAME'S ETHAN.
YEAH...ETHAN.
I CAN'T BELIEVE HE TALKED TO US.
?
?
SWOON!
ETHAN... AN EIGHTH GRADER.
EYE ROLL
YEESH...

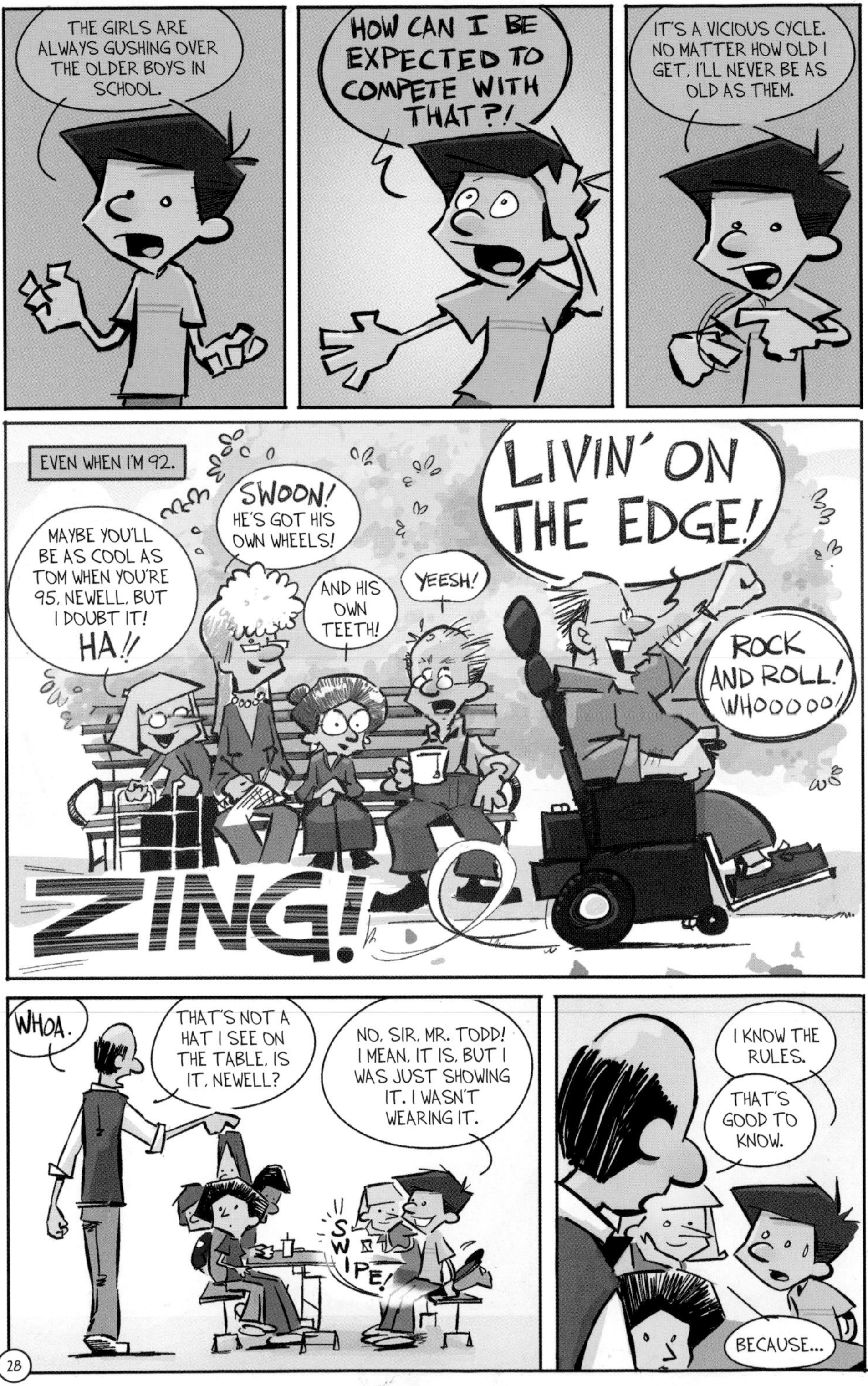
THE GIRLS ARE ALWAYS GUSHING OVER THE OLDER BOYS IN SCHOOL.
HOW CAN I BE EXPECTED TO COMPETE WITH THAT?!
IT'S A VICIOUS CYCLE. NO MATTER HOW OLD I GET, I'LL NEVER BE AS OLD AS THEM.
EVEN WHEN I'M 92.
MAYBE YOU'LL BE AS COOL AS TOM WHEN YOU'RE 95, NEWELL, BUT I DOUBT IT! HA!!
SWOON! HE'S GOT HIS OWN WHEELS!
AND HIS OWN TEETH!
YEESH!
LIVIN' ON THE EDGE!
ROCK AND ROLL! WHOOOOO!
ZING!
WHOA.
THAT'S NOT A HAT I SEE ON THE TABLE, IS IT, NEWELL?
NO, SIR, MR. TODD! I MEAN, IT IS, BUT I WAS JUST SHOWING IT. I WASN'T WEARING IT.
SWIPE!
I KNOW THE RULES.
THAT'S GOOD TO KNOW.
BECAUSE...

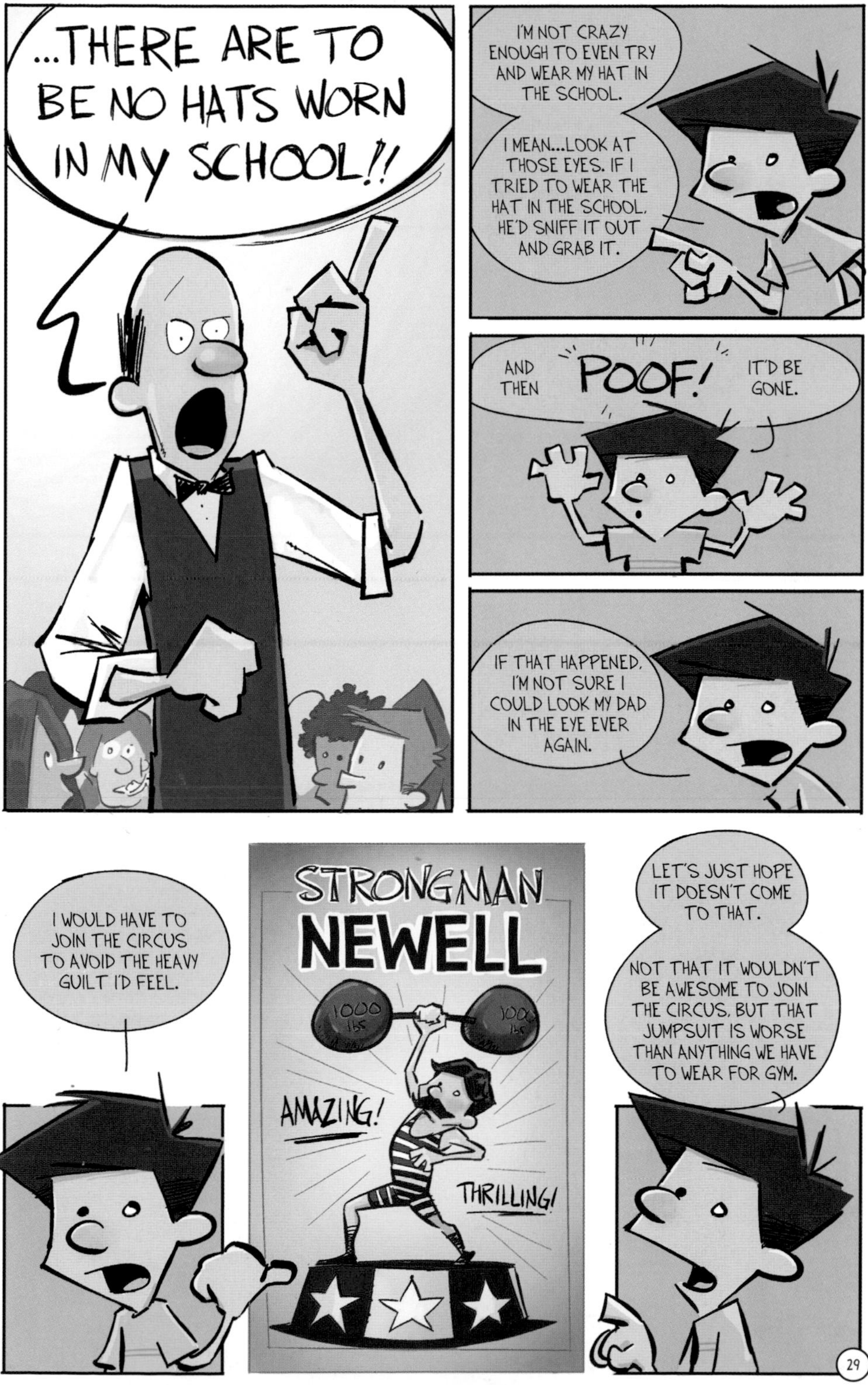
...THERE ARE TO BE NO HATS WORN IN MY SCHOOL!!
I'M NOT CRAZY ENOUGH TO EVEN TRY AND WEAR MY HAT IN THE SCHOOL.
I MEAN...LOOK AT THOSE EYES. IF I TRIED TO WEAR THE HAT IN THE SCHOOL, HE'D SNIFF IT OUT AND GRAB IT.
AND THEN
POOF!
IT'D BE GONE.
IF THAT HAPPENED, I'M NOT SURE I COULD LOOK MY DAD IN THE EYE EVER AGAIN.
I WOULD HAVE TO JOIN THE CIRCUS TO AVOID THE HEAVY GUILT I'D FEEL.
STRONGMAN
NEWELL
AMAZING!
THRILLING!
LET'S JUST HOPE IT DOESN'T COME TO THAT.
NOT THAT IT WOULDN'T BE AWESOME TO JOIN THE CIRCUS, BUT THAT JUMPSUIT IS WORSE THAN ANYTHING WE HAVE TO WEAR FOR GYM.

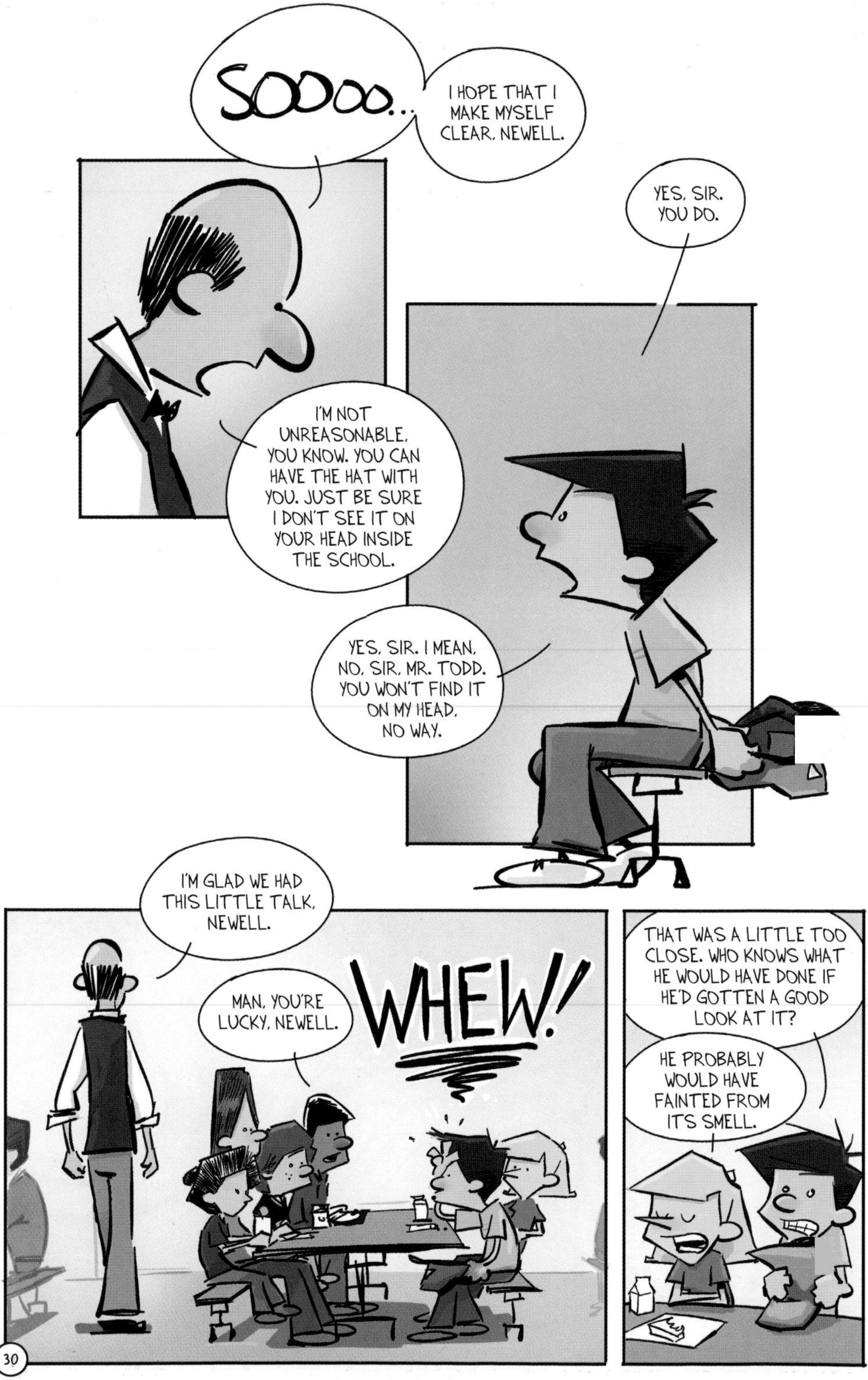
SOOOO...
I HOPE THAT I MAKE MYSELF CLEAR, NEWELL.
YES, SIR. YOU DO.
I'M NOT UNREASONABLE, YOU KNOW. YOU CAN HAVE THE HAT WITH YOU. JUST BE SURE I DON'T SEE IT ON YOUR HEAD INSIDE THE SCHOOL.
YES, SIR. I MEAN, NO, SIR, MR. TODD. YOU WON'T FIND IT ON MY HEAD, NO WAY.
I'M GLAD WE HAD THIS LITTLE TALK, NEWELL.
MAN, YOU'RE LUCKY, NEWELL.
WHEW!
THAT WAS A LITTLE TOO CLOSE. WHO KNOWS WHAT HE WOULD HAVE DONE IF HE'D GOTTEN A GOOD LOOK AT IT?
HE PROBABLY WOULD HAVE FAINTED FROM ITS SMELL.

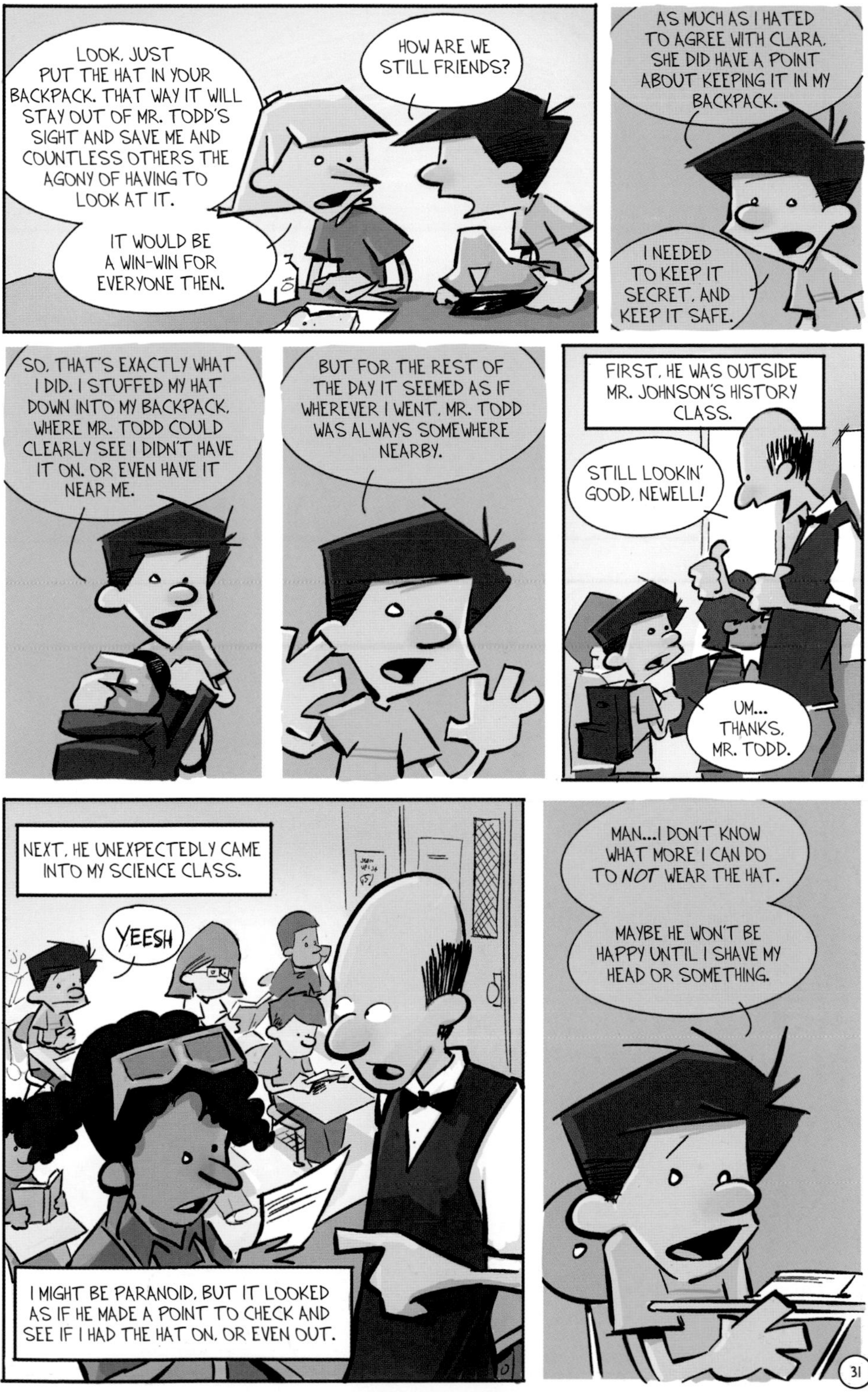

LOOK, JUST PUT THE HAT IN YOUR BACKPACK. THAT WAY IT WILL STAY OUT OF MR. TODD'S SIGHT AND SAVE ME AND COUNTLESS OTHERS THE AGONY OF HAVING TO LOOK AT IT.
HOW ARE WE STILL FRIENDS?
IT WOULD BE A WIN-WIN FOR EVERYONE THEN.
AS MUCH AS I HATED TO AGREE WITH CLARA, SHE DID HAVE A POINT ABOUT KEEPING IT IN MY BACKPACK.
I NEEDED TO KEEP IT SECRET, AND KEEP IT SAFE.
SO, THAT'S EXACTLY WHAT I DID. I STUFFED MY HAT DOWN INTO MY BACKPACK, WHERE MR. TODD COULD CLEARLY SEE I DIDN'T HAVE IT ON, OR EVEN HAVE IT NEAR ME.
BUT FOR THE REST OF THE DAY IT SEEMED AS IF WHEREVER I WENT, MR. TODD WAS ALWAYS SOMEWHERE NEARBY.
FIRST, HE WAS OUTSIDE MR. JOHNSON'S HISTORY CLASS.
STILL LOOKIN' GOOD, NEWELL!
UM... THANKS, MR. TODD.
NEXT, HE UNEXPECTEDLY CAME INTO MY SCIENCE CLASS.
YEESH
I MIGHT BE PARANOID, BUT IT LOOKED AS IF HE MADE A POINT TO CHECK AND SEE IF I HAD THE HAT ON, OR EVEN OUT.
MAN...I DON'T KNOW WHAT MORE I CAN DO TO *NOT* WEAR THE HAT.
MAYBE HE WON'T BE HAPPY UNTIL I SHAVE MY HEAD OR SOMETHING.

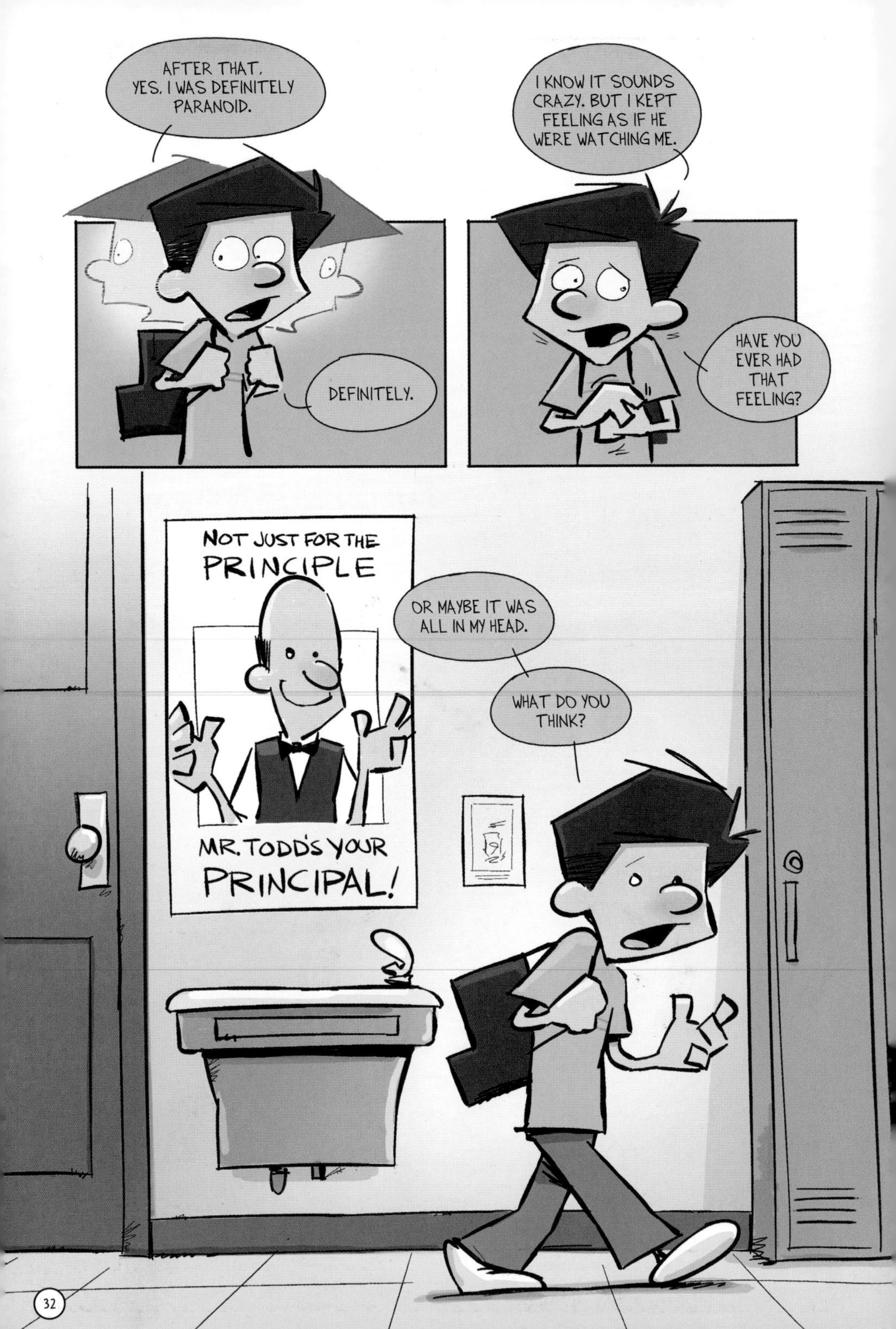
AFTER THAT, YES, I WAS DEFINITELY PARANOID.
DEFINITELY.
I KNOW IT SOUNDS CRAZY. BUT I KEPT FEELING AS IF HE WERE WATCHING ME.
HAVE YOU EVER HAD THAT FEELING?
NOT JUST FOR THE PRINCIPLE
MR. TODD'S YOUR PRINCIPAL!
OR MAYBE IT WAS ALL IN MY HEAD.
WHAT DO YOU THINK?

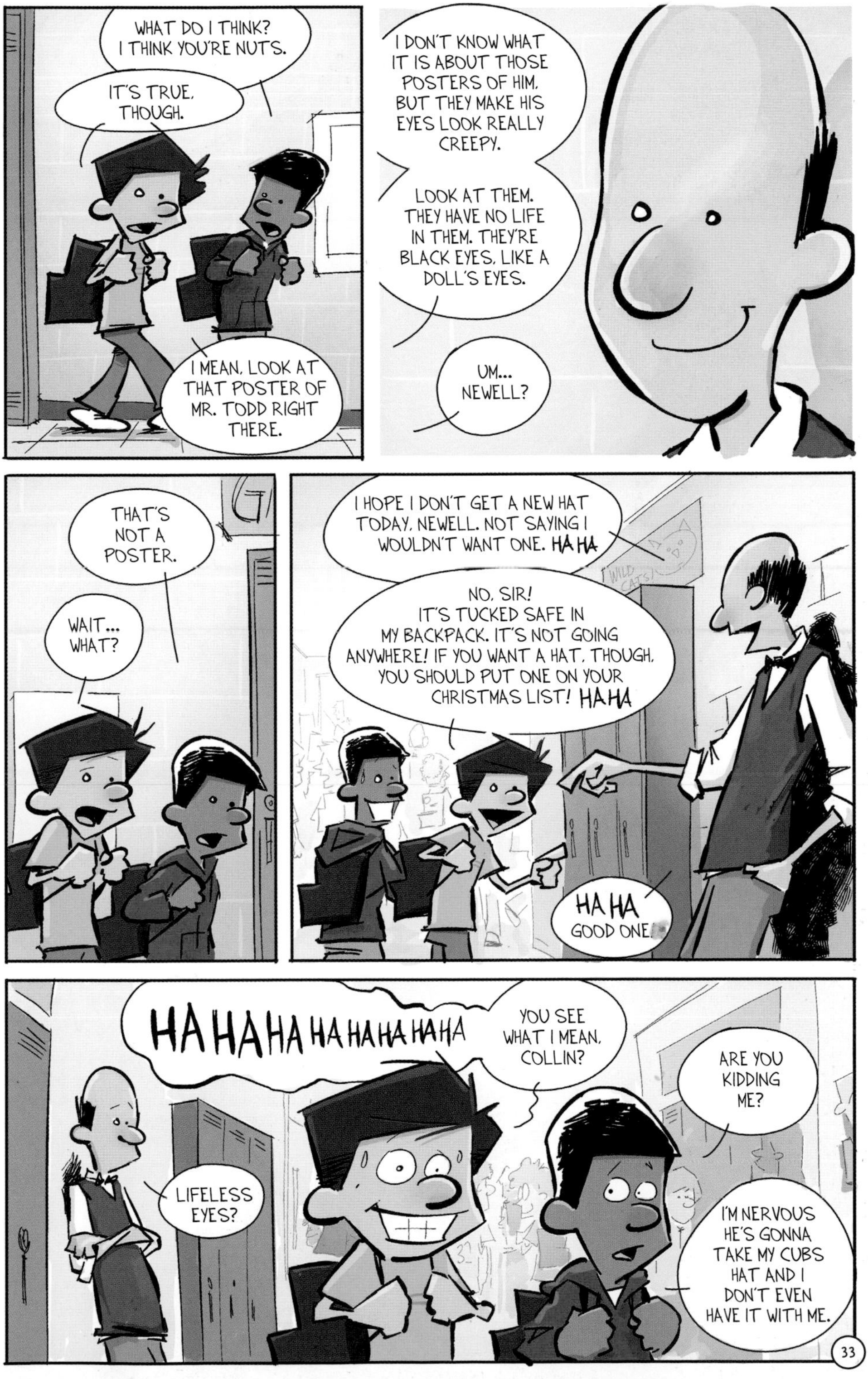
WHAT DO I THINK? I THINK YOU'RE NUTS.
IT'S TRUE, THOUGH.
I MEAN, LOOK AT THAT POSTER OF MR. TODD RIGHT THERE.
I DON'T KNOW WHAT IT IS ABOUT THOSE POSTERS OF HIM, BUT THEY MAKE HIS EYES LOOK REALLY CREEPY.
LOOK AT THEM. THEY HAVE NO LIFE IN THEM. THEY'RE BLACK EYES, LIKE A DOLL'S EYES.
UM... NEWELL?
THAT'S NOT A POSTER.
WAIT... WHAT?
I HOPE I DON'T GET A NEW HAT TODAY, NEWELL. NOT SAYING I WOULDN'T WANT ONE. HA HA
NO, SIR! IT'S TUCKED SAFE IN MY BACKPACK. IT'S NOT GOING ANYWHERE! IF YOU WANT A HAT, THOUGH, YOU SHOULD PUT ONE ON YOUR CHRISTMAS LIST! HA HA
HA HA GOOD ONE!
HA HA HA HA HA HA HA HA HA
YOU SEE WHAT I MEAN, COLLIN?
ARE YOU KIDDING ME?
LIFELESS EYES?
I'M NERVOUS HE'S GONNA TAKE MY CUBS HAT AND I DON'T EVEN HAVE IT WITH ME.

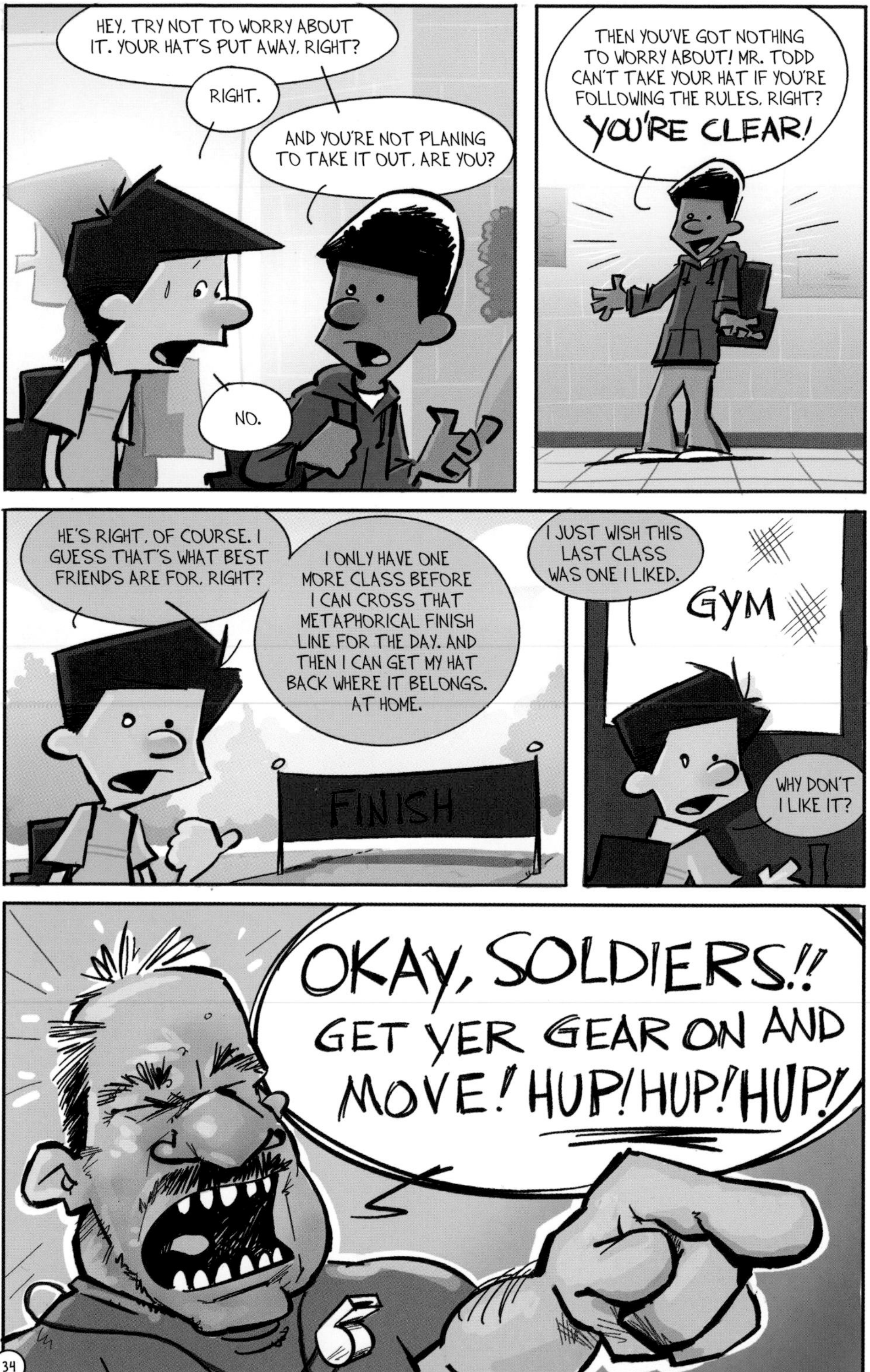
HEY. TRY NOT TO WORRY ABOUT IT. YOUR HAT'S PUT AWAY, RIGHT?
RIGHT.
AND YOU'RE NOT PLANING TO TAKE IT OUT, ARE YOU?
NO.
THEN YOU'VE GOT NOTHING TO WORRY ABOUT! MR. TODD CAN'T TAKE YOUR HAT IF YOU'RE FOLLOWING THE RULES, RIGHT? YOU'RE CLEAR!
HE'S RIGHT, OF COURSE. I GUESS THAT'S WHAT BEST FRIENDS ARE FOR, RIGHT?
I ONLY HAVE ONE MORE CLASS BEFORE I CAN CROSS THAT METAPHORICAL FINISH LINE FOR THE DAY. AND THEN I CAN GET MY HAT BACK WHERE IT BELONGS. AT HOME.
FINISH
I JUST WISH THIS LAST CLASS WAS ONE I LIKED.
GYM
WHY DON'T I LIKE IT?
OKAY, SOLDIERS!!
GET YER GEAR ON AND MOVE! HUP! HUP! HUP!

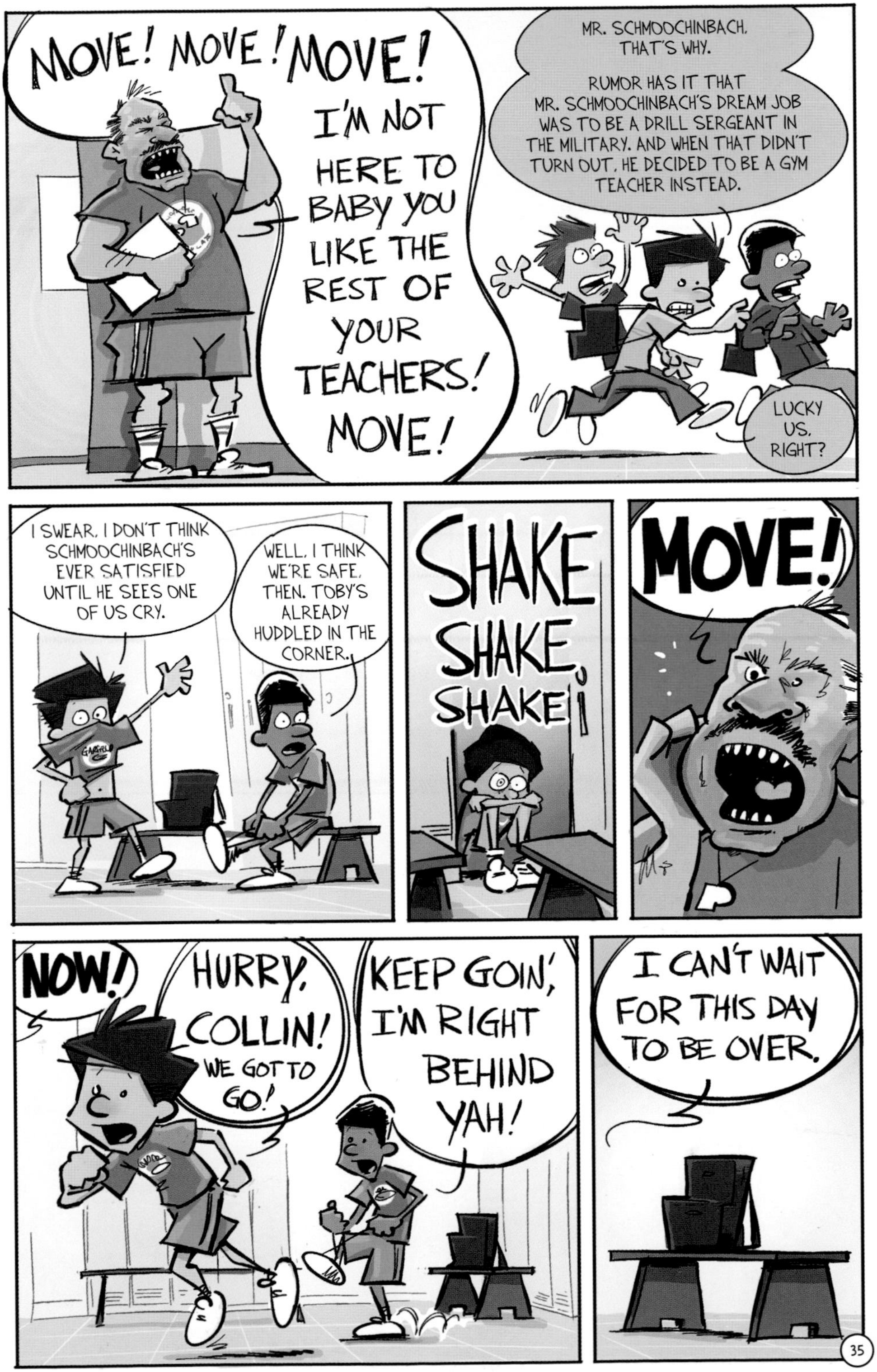
MOVE! MOVE! MOVE! I'M NOT HERE TO BABY YOU LIKE THE REST OF YOUR TEACHERS! MOVE!
MR. SCHMOOCHINBACH, THAT'S WHY.
RUMOR HAS IT THAT MR. SCHMOOCHINBACH'S DREAM JOB WAS TO BE A DRILL SERGEANT IN THE MILITARY. AND WHEN THAT DIDN'T TURN OUT, HE DECIDED TO BE A GYM TEACHER INSTEAD.
LUCKY US, RIGHT?
I SWEAR, I DON'T THINK SCHMOOCHINBACH'S EVER SATISFIED UNTIL HE SEES ONE OF US CRY.
WELL, I THINK WE'RE SAFE, THEN. TOBY'S ALREADY HUDDLED IN THE CORNER.
SHAKE
SHAKE,
SHAKE
MOVE!
NOW!
HURRY, COLLIN! WE GOT TO GO!
KEEP GOIN', I'M RIGHT BEHIND YAH!
I CAN'T WAIT FOR THIS DAY TO BE OVER.

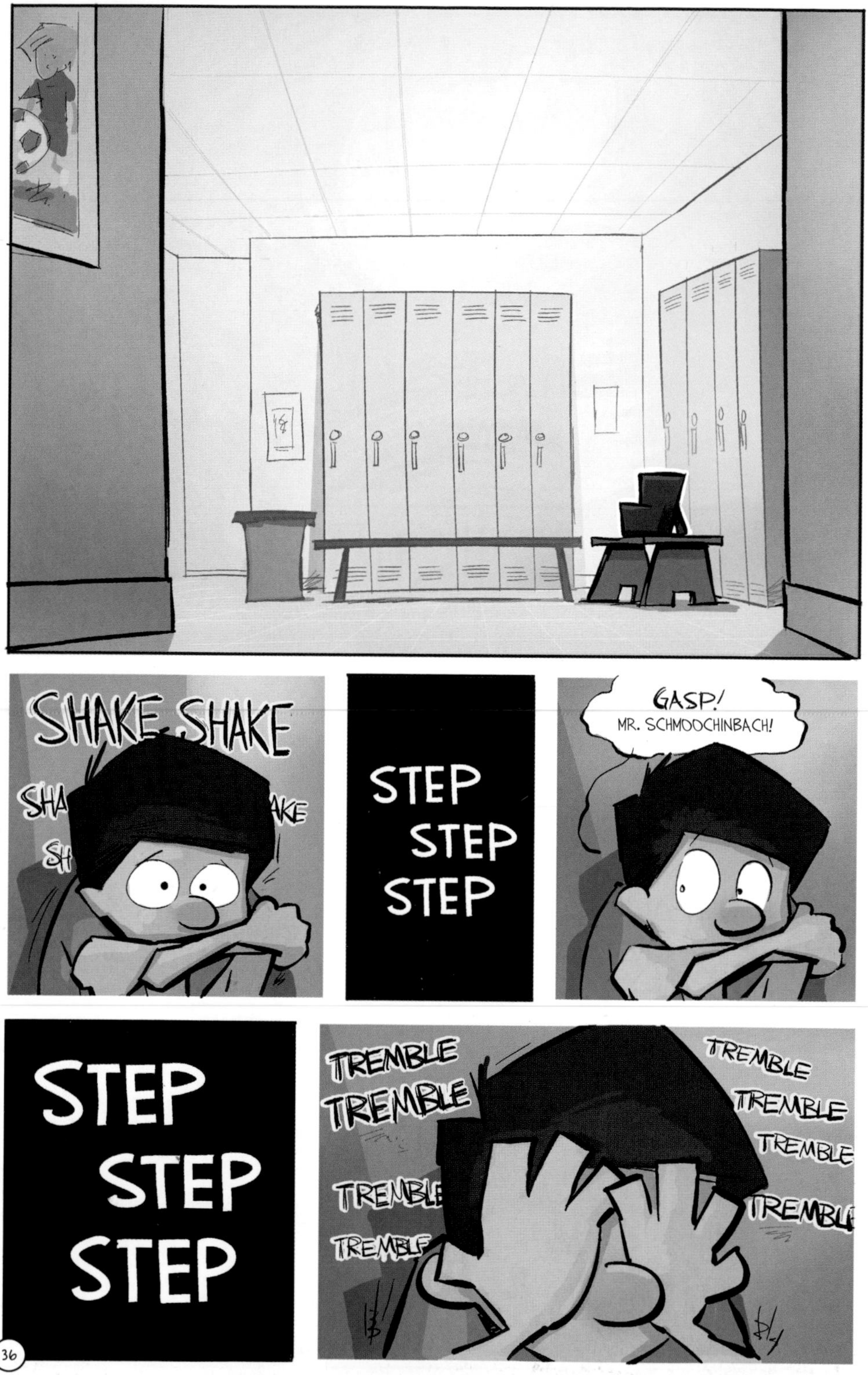
SHAKE SHAKE
STEP
STEP
STEP
GASP!
MR. SCHMOOCHINBACH!
STEP
STEP
STEP
TREMBLE
TREMBLE
TREMBLE
TREMBLE
TREMBLE
TREMBLE
TREMBLE
TREMBLE

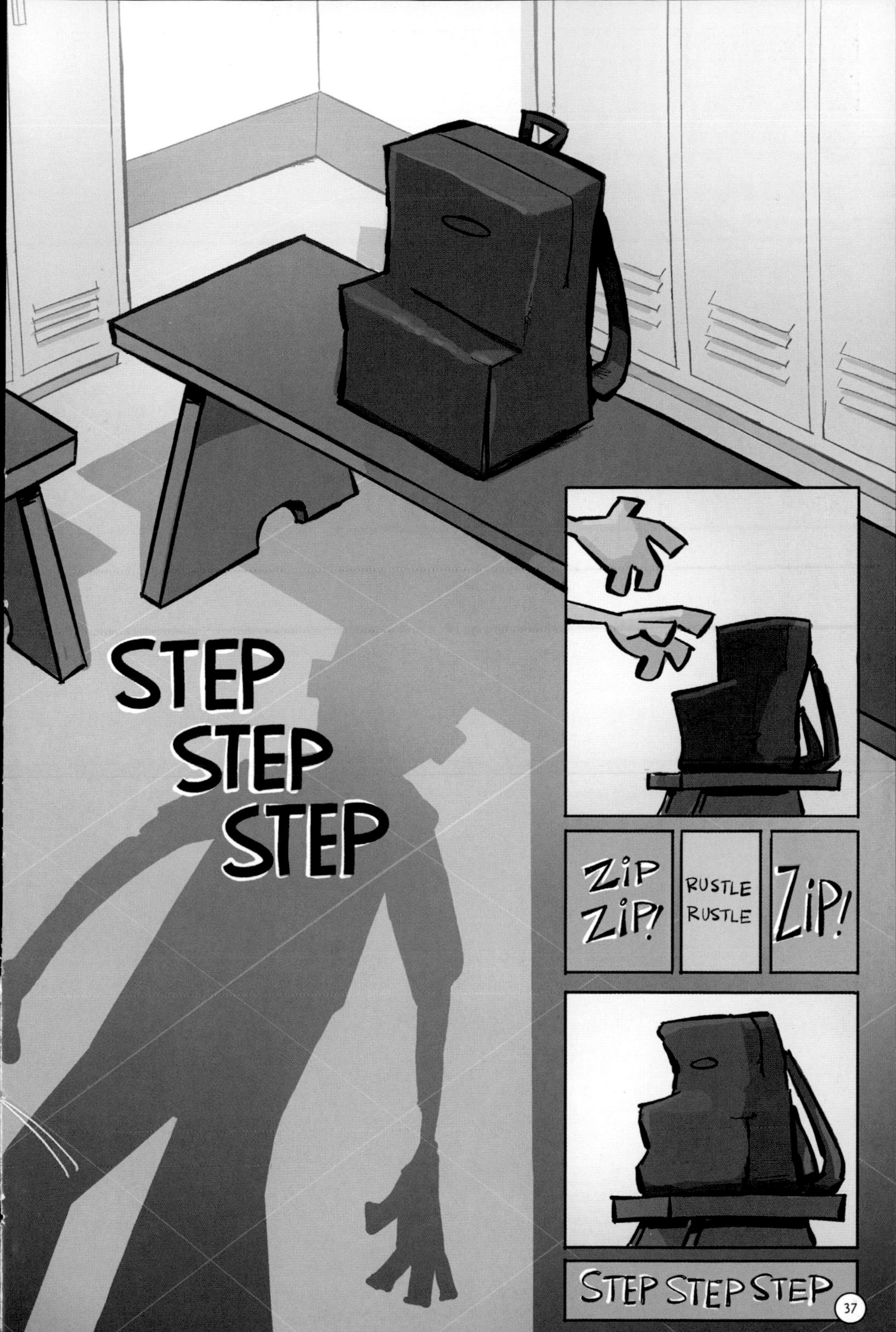
STEP
STEP
STEP
ZIP
ZIP!
RUSTLE
RUSTLE
ZIP!
STEP STEP STEP

CHAPTER THREE
SO CLOSE, AND YET SO FAR

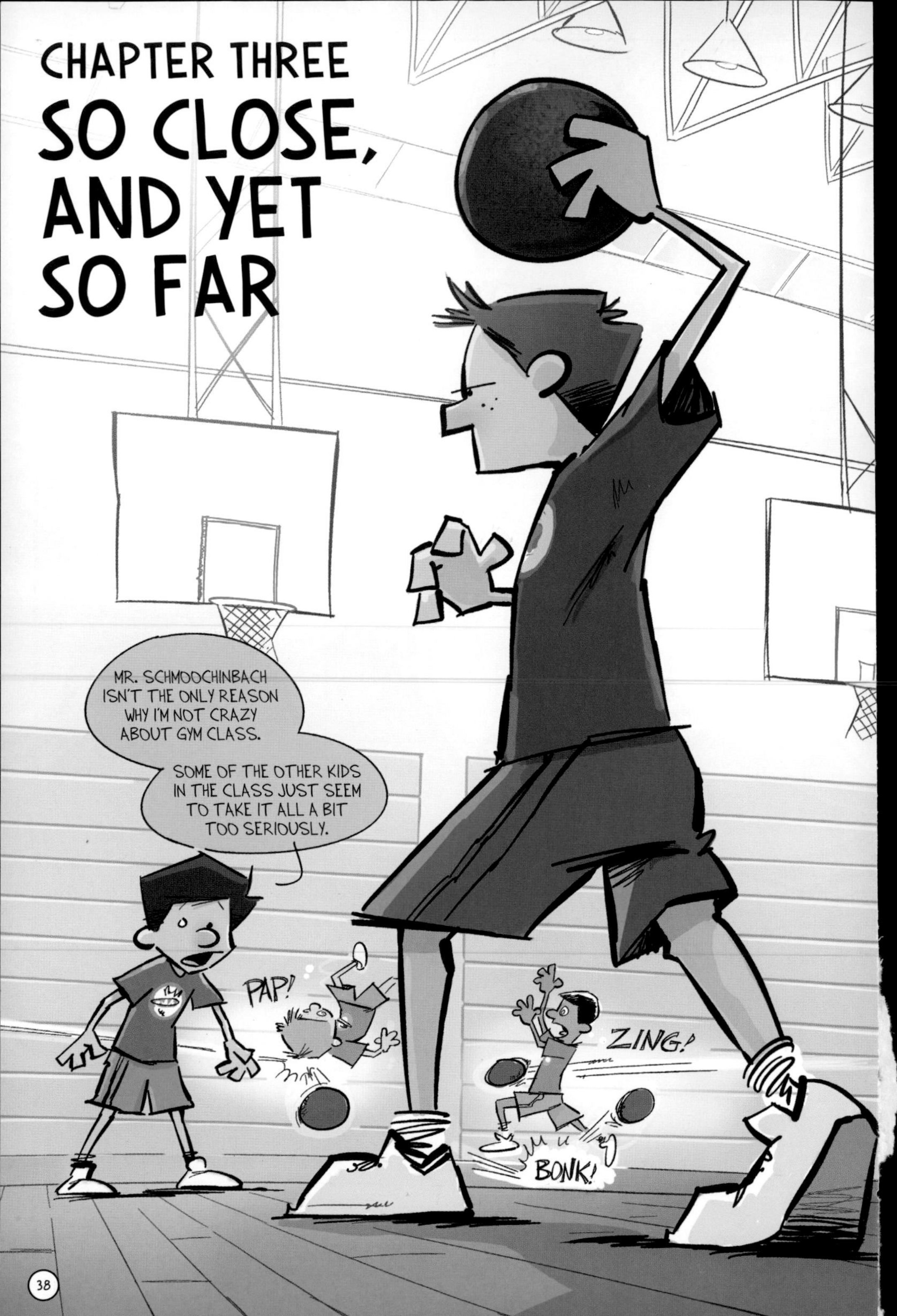
MR. SCHMOOCHINBACH ISN'T THE ONLY REASON WHY I'M NOT CRAZY ABOUT GYM CLASS.
SOME OF THE OTHER KIDS IN THE CLASS JUST SEEM TO TAKE IT ALL A BIT TOO SERIOUSLY.
PAP!
ZING!
BONK!

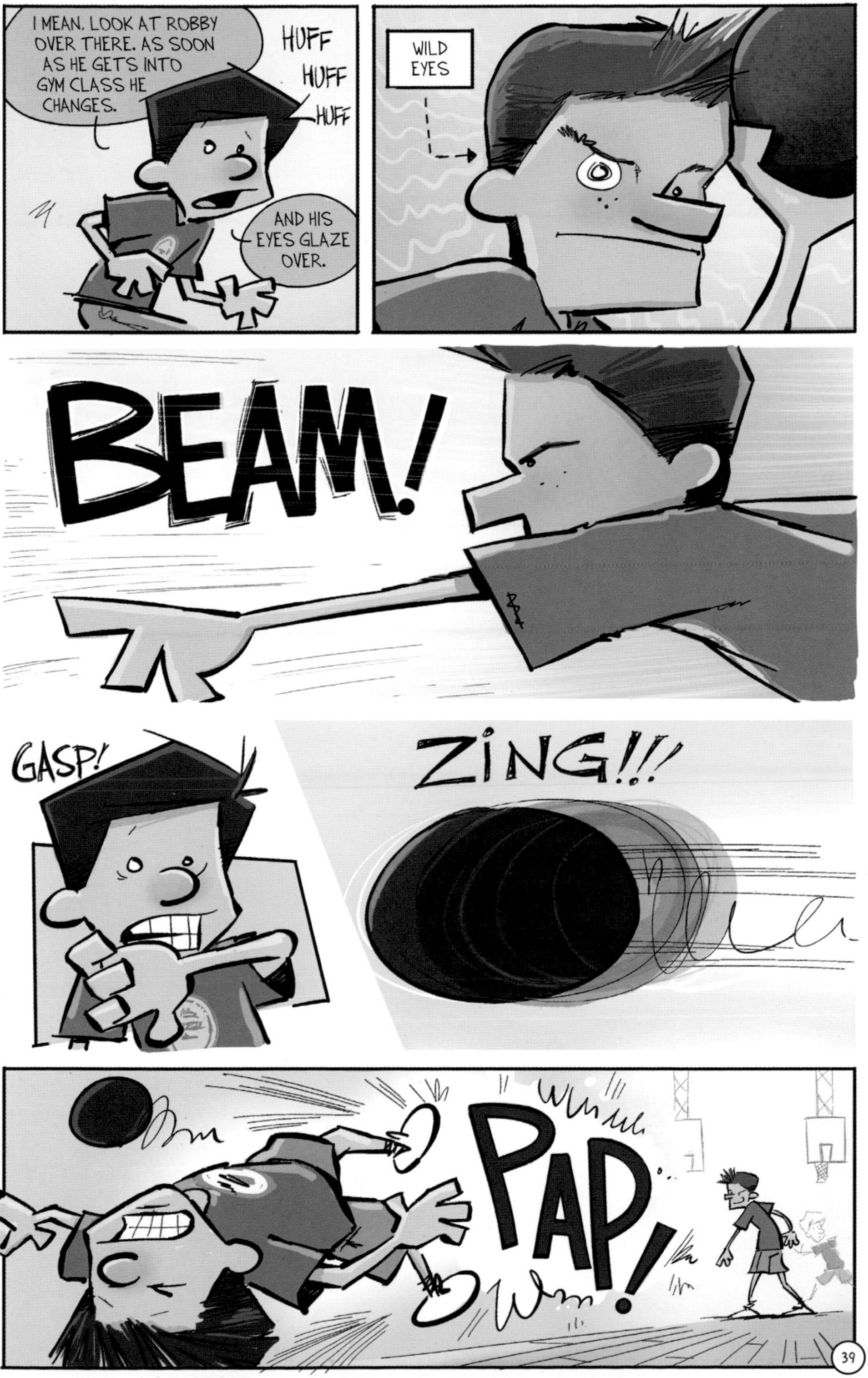
I MEAN, LOOK AT ROBBY OVER THERE. AS SOON AS HE GETS INTO GYM CLASS HE CHANGES.
HUFF HUFF HUFF
AND HIS EYES GLAZE OVER.
WILD EYES
BEAM!
GASP!
ZING!!!
PAP!

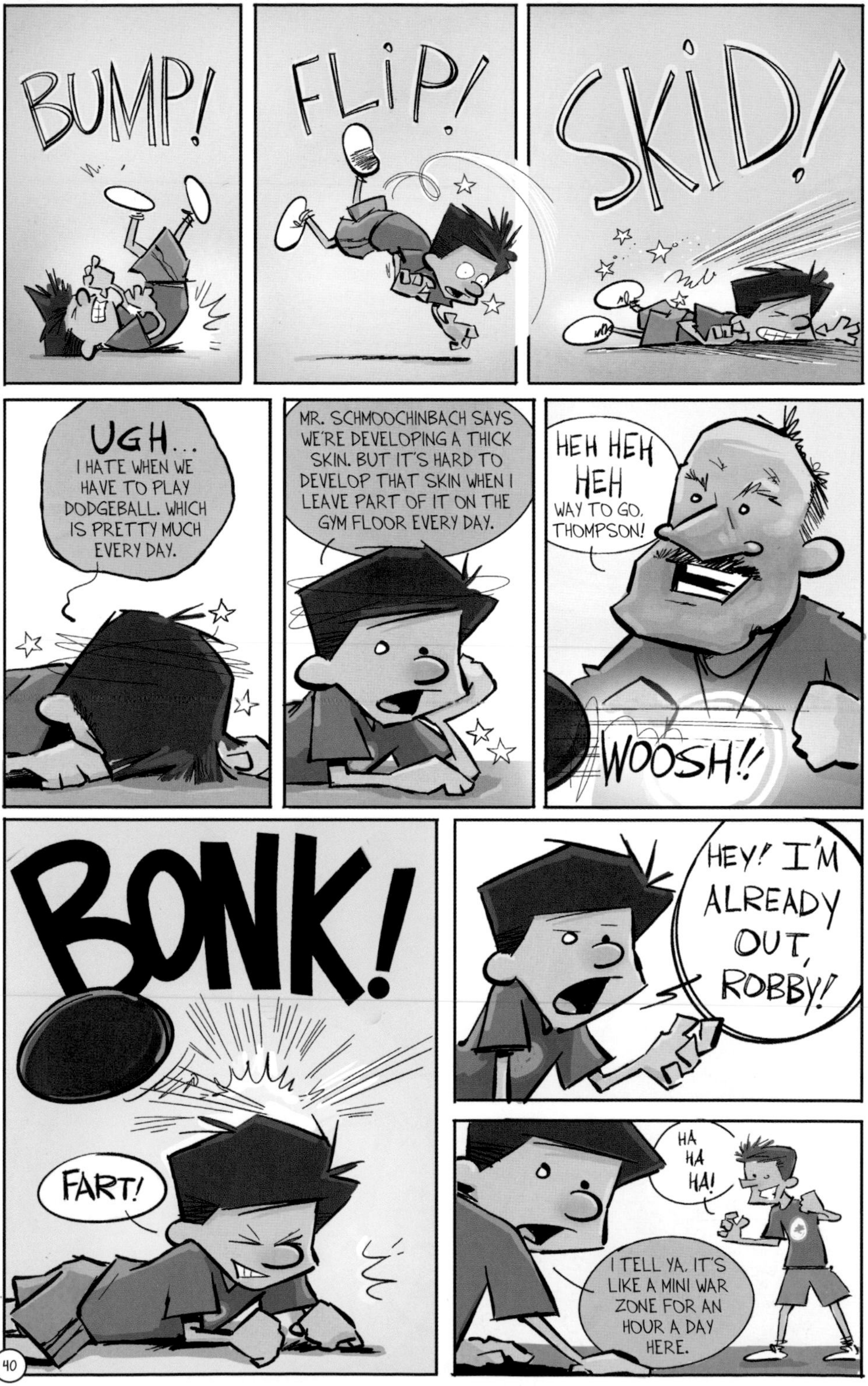
BUMP!
FLIP!
SKID!
UGH... I HATE WHEN WE HAVE TO PLAY DODGEBALL. WHICH IS PRETTY MUCH EVERY DAY.
MR. SCHMOOCHINBACH SAYS WE'RE DEVELOPING A THICK SKIN. BUT IT'S HARD TO DEVELOP THAT SKIN WHEN I LEAVE PART OF IT ON THE GYM FLOOR EVERY DAY.
HEH HEH HEH
WAY TO GO, THOMPSON!
WOOSH!!
BONK!
FART!
HEY! I'M ALREADY OUT, ROBBY!
HA HA HA!
I TELL YA, IT'S LIKE A MINI WAR ZONE FOR AN HOUR A DAY HERE.

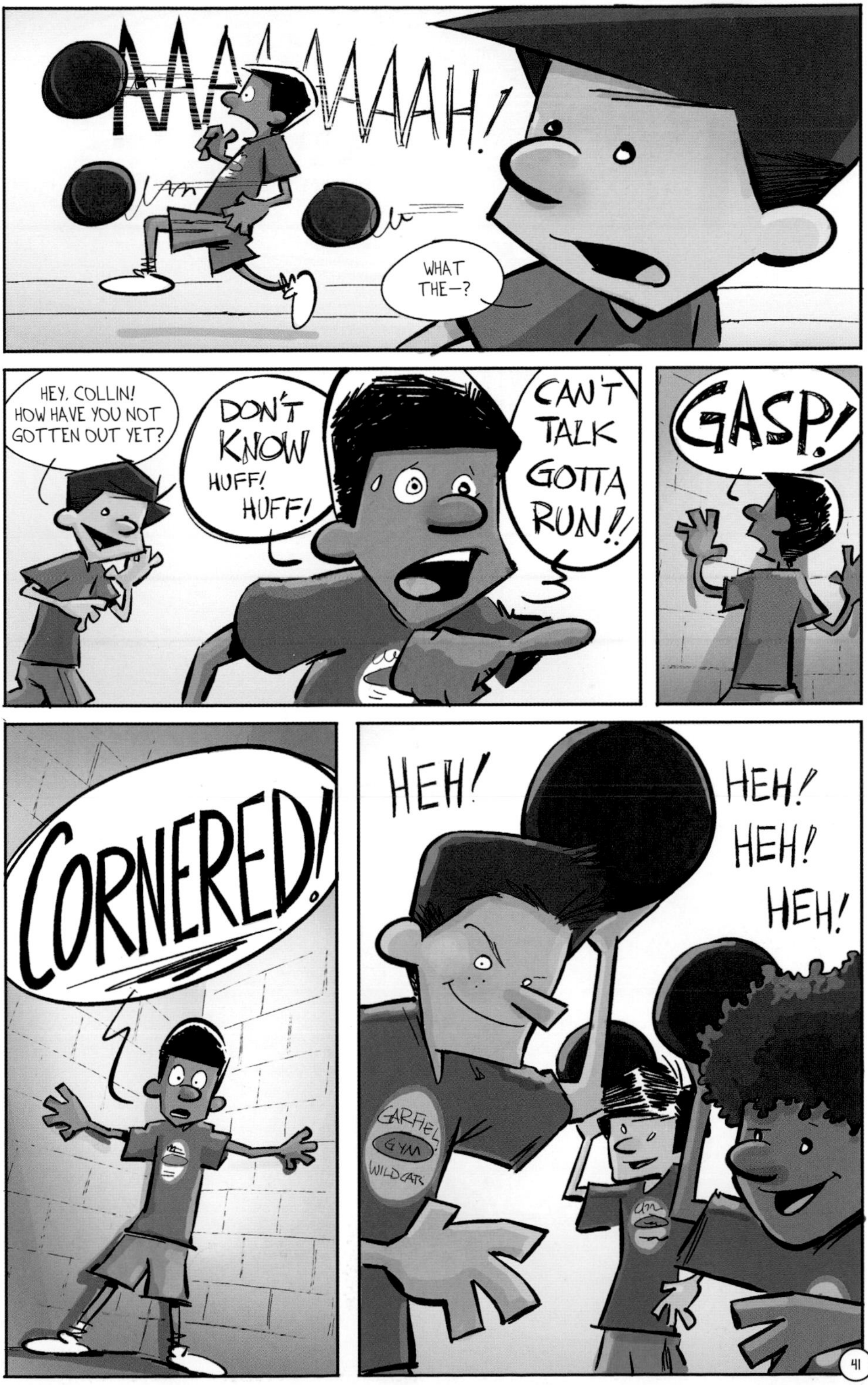

AAAAAAAAH!
WHAT THE—?
HEY, COLLIN! HOW HAVE YOU NOT GOTTEN OUT YET?
DON'T KNOW
HUFF! HUFF!
CAN'T TALK GOTTA RUN!!
GASP!
CORNERED!
HEH!
HEH! HEH! HEH!

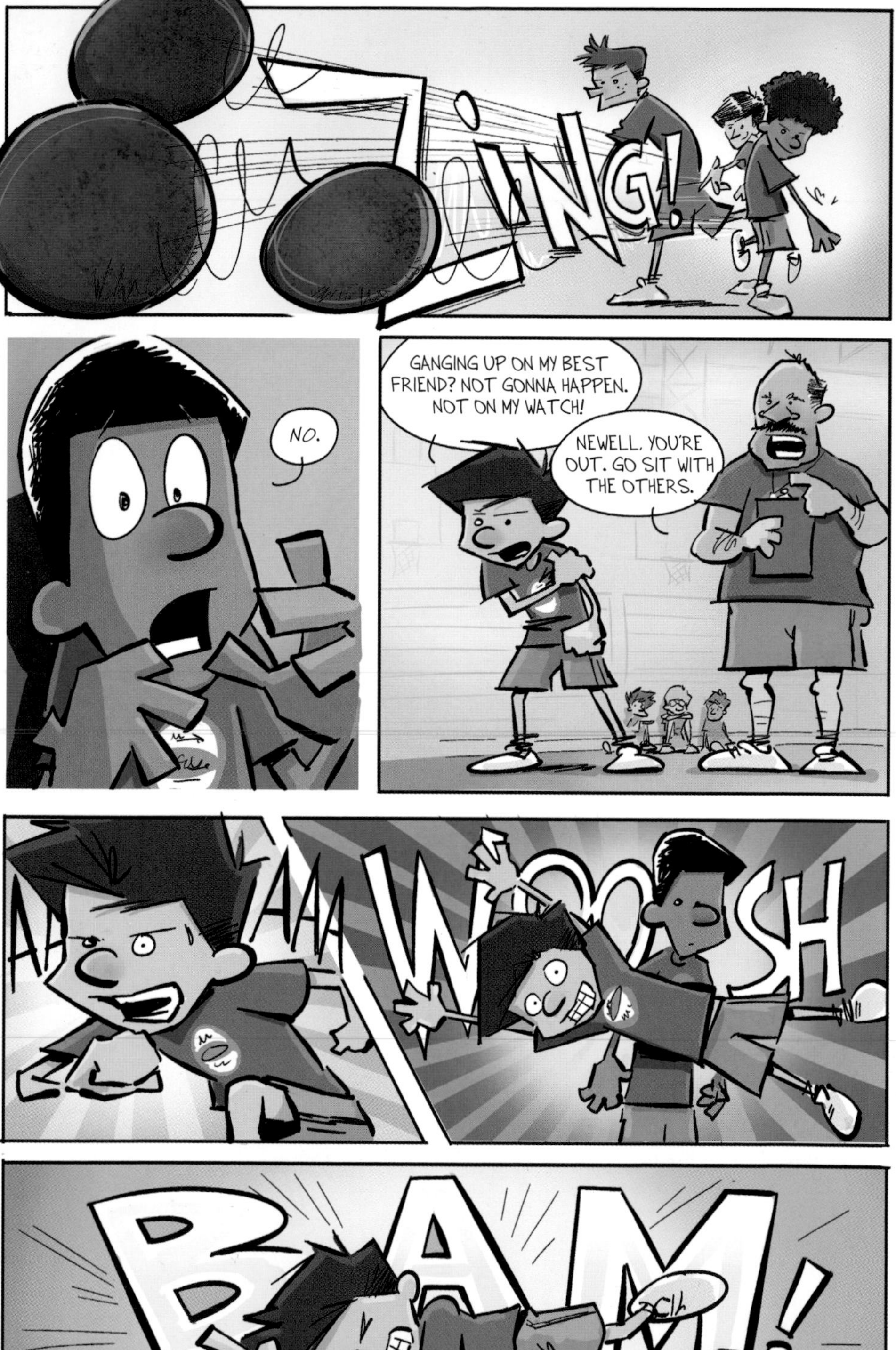
BOING!
NO.
GANGING UP ON MY BEST FRIEND? NOT GONNA HAPPEN. NOT ON MY WATCH!
NEWELL, YOU'RE OUT. GO SIT WITH THE OTHERS.
AAA AAA
WOOSH
BAM!

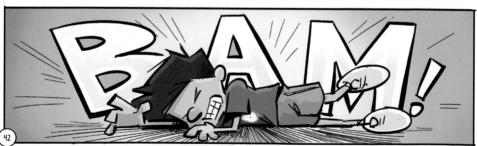

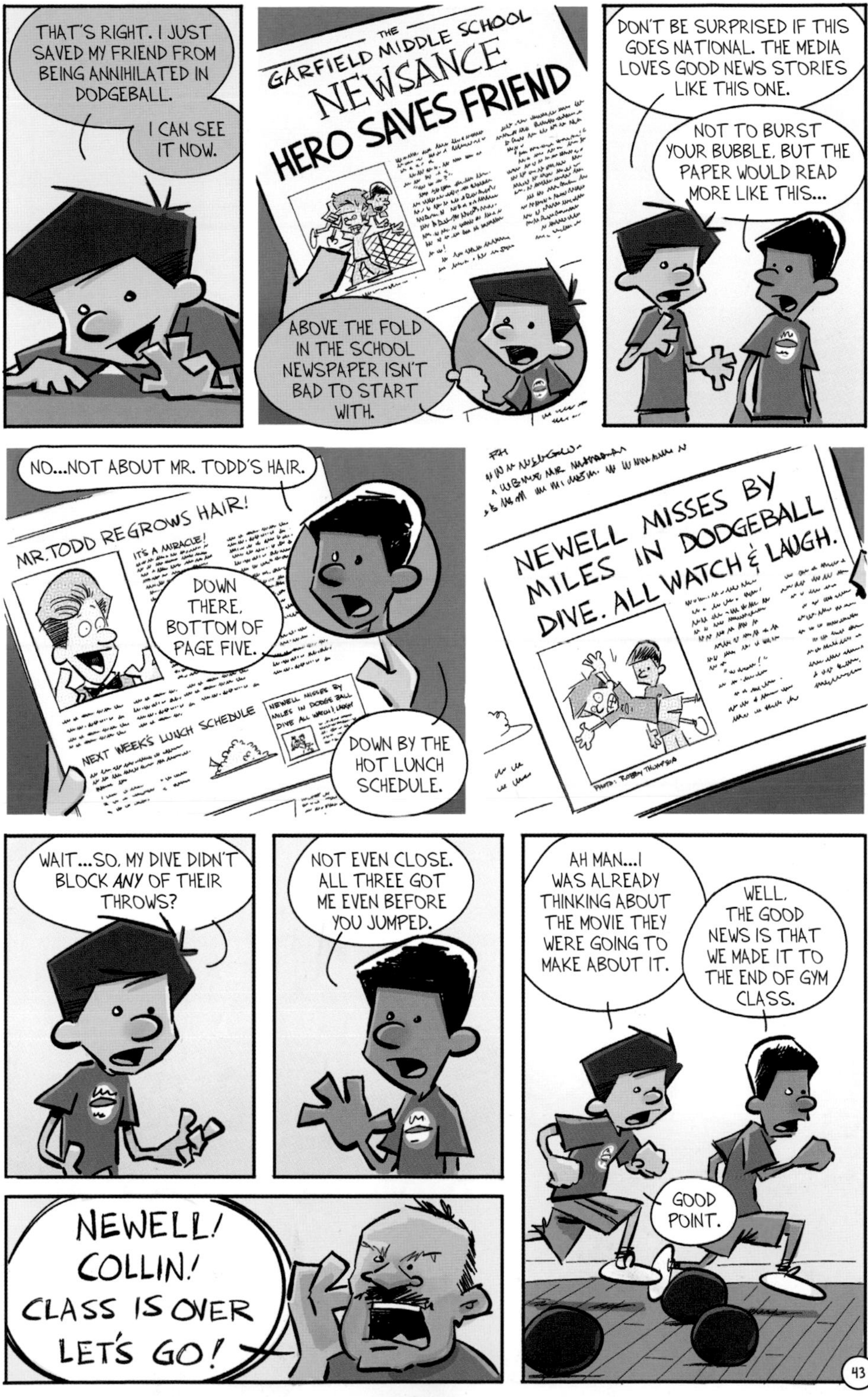
THAT'S RIGHT. I JUST SAVED MY FRIEND FROM BEING ANNIHILATED IN DODGEBALL.
I CAN SEE IT NOW.
THE GARFIELD MIDDLE SCHOOL NEWSANCE
HERO SAVES FRIEND
ABOVE THE FOLD IN THE SCHOOL NEWSPAPER ISN'T BAD TO START WITH.
DON'T BE SURPRISED IF THIS GOES NATIONAL. THE MEDIA LOVES GOOD NEWS STORIES LIKE THIS ONE.
NOT TO BURST YOUR BUBBLE, BUT THE PAPER WOULD READ MORE LIKE THIS...
NO...NOT ABOUT MR. TODD'S HAIR.
MR. TODD REGROWS HAIR!
IT'S A MIRACLE!
DOWN THERE, BOTTOM OF PAGE FIVE.
NEXT WEEK'S LUNCH SCHEDULE
NEWELL MISSES BY MILES IN DODGE BALL DIVE. ALL WATCH & LAUGH
DOWN BY THE HOT LUNCH SCHEDULE.
NEWELL MISSES BY MILES IN DODGEBALL DIVE. ALL WATCH & LAUGH.
WAIT...SO, MY DIVE DIDN'T BLOCK ANY OF THEIR THROWS?
NOT EVEN CLOSE. ALL THREE GOT ME EVEN BEFORE YOU JUMPED.
AH MAN...I WAS ALREADY THINKING ABOUT THE MOVIE THEY WERE GOING TO MAKE ABOUT IT.
WELL, THE GOOD NEWS IS THAT WE MADE IT TO THE END OF GYM CLASS.
GOOD POINT.
NEWELL! COLLIN! CLASS IS OVER LET'S GO!

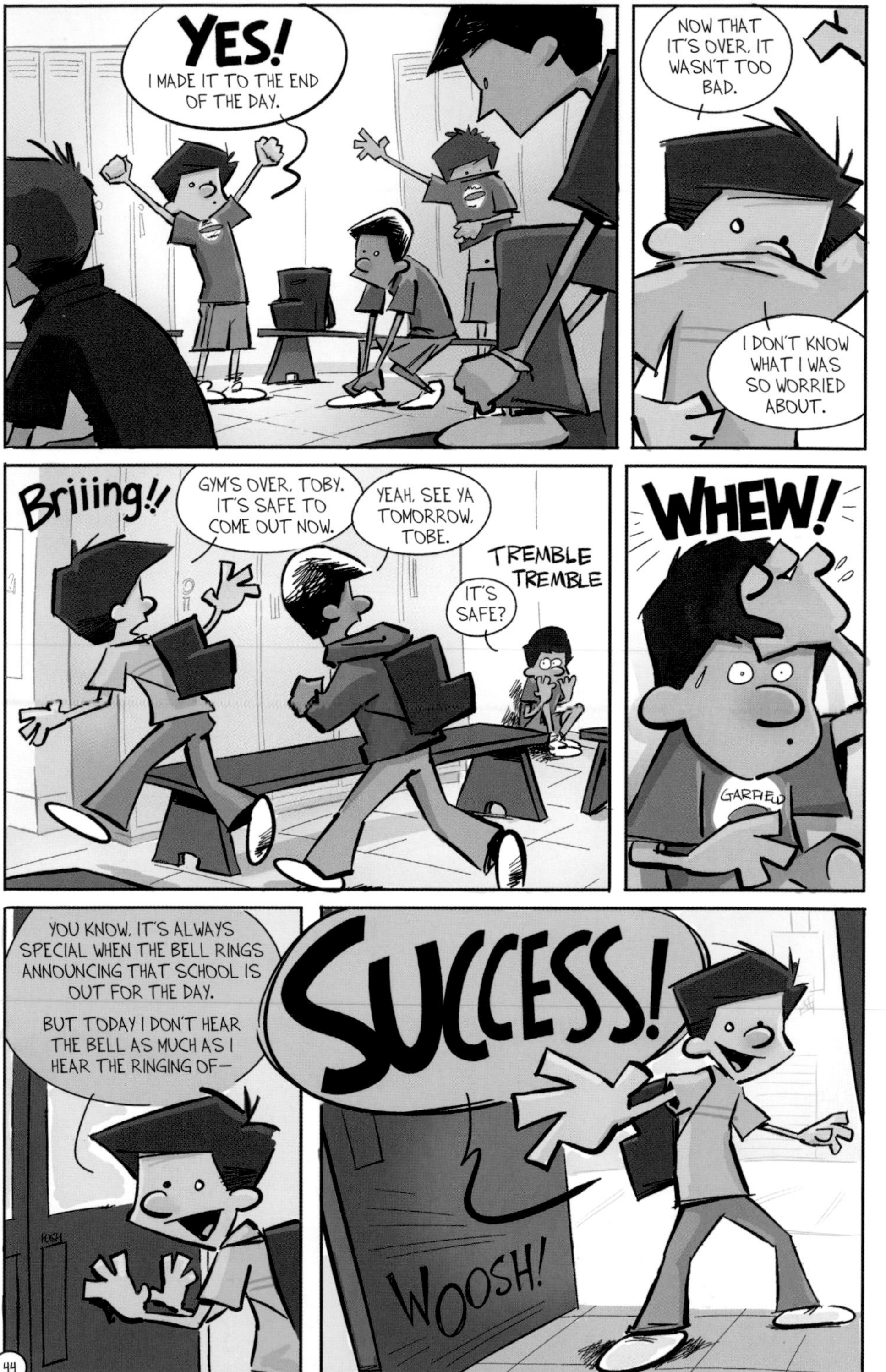
YES! I MADE IT TO THE END OF THE DAY.
NOW THAT IT'S OVER, IT WASN'T TOO BAD.
I DON'T KNOW WHAT I WAS SO WORRIED ABOUT.
Briiing!!
GYM'S OVER, TOBY. IT'S SAFE TO COME OUT NOW.
YEAH, SEE YA TOMORROW, TOBE.
TREMBLE TREMBLE
IT'S SAFE?
WHEW!
GARFIELD
YOU KNOW, IT'S ALWAYS SPECIAL WHEN THE BELL RINGS ANNOUNCING THAT SCHOOL IS OUT FOR THE DAY.
BUT TODAY I DON'T HEAR THE BELL AS MUCH AS I HEAR THE RINGING OF—
SUCCESS!
WOOSH!

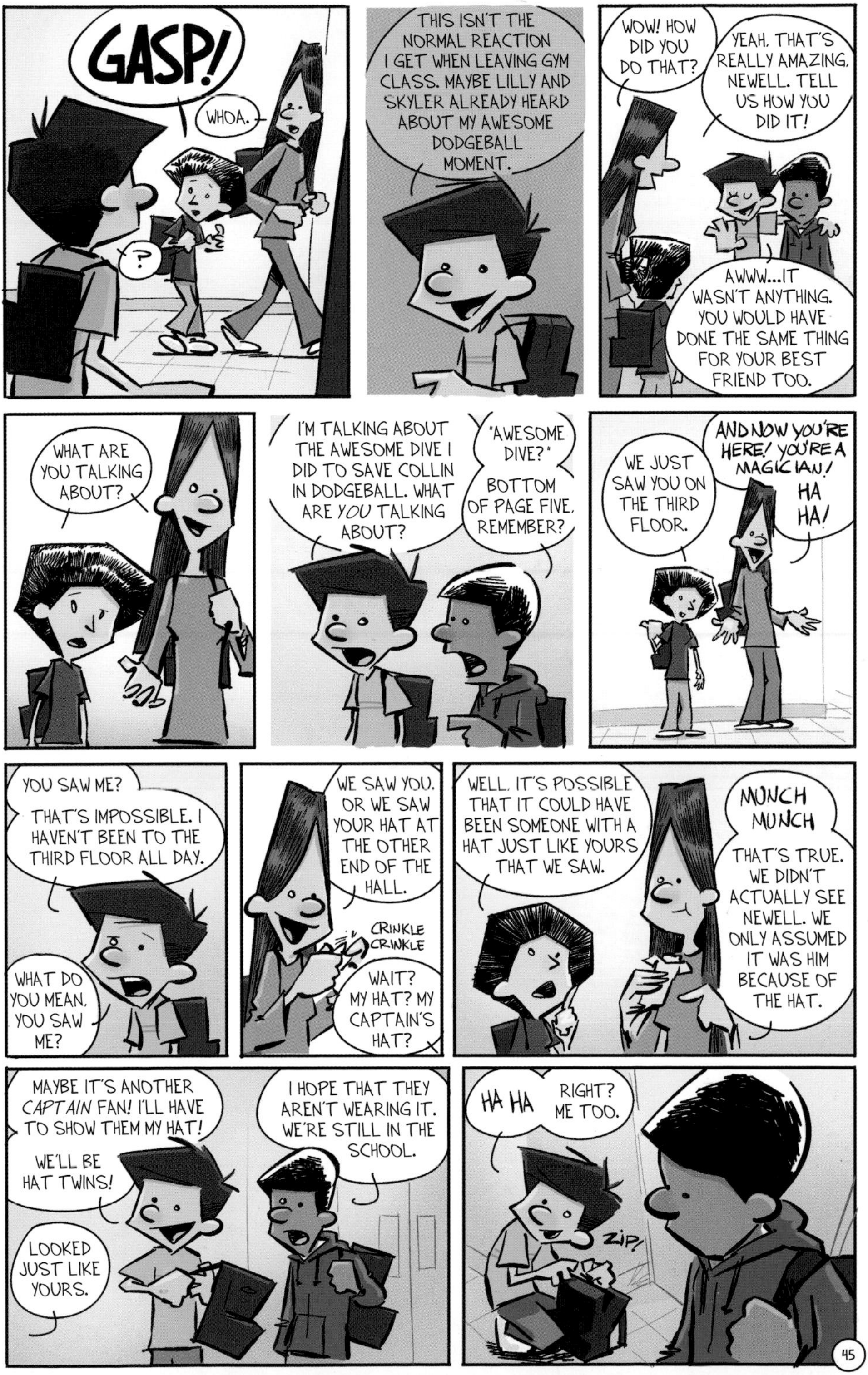
GASP!
WHOA.
?
THIS ISN'T THE NORMAL REACTION I GET WHEN LEAVING GYM CLASS. MAYBE LILLY AND SKYLER ALREADY HEARD ABOUT MY AWESOME DODGEBALL MOMENT.
WOW! HOW DID YOU DO THAT?
YEAH, THAT'S REALLY AMAZING, NEWELL. TELL US HOW YOU DID IT!
AWWW...IT WASN'T ANYTHING. YOU WOULD HAVE DONE THE SAME THING FOR YOUR BEST FRIEND TOO.
WHAT ARE YOU TALKING ABOUT?
I'M TALKING ABOUT THE AWESOME DIVE I DID TO SAVE COLLIN IN DODGEBALL. WHAT ARE *YOU* TALKING ABOUT?
"AWESOME DIVE?"
BOTTOM OF PAGE FIVE, REMEMBER?
WE JUST SAW YOU ON THE THIRD FLOOR.
AND NOW YOU'RE HERE! YOU'RE A MAGICIAN!
HA HA!
YOU SAW ME?
THAT'S IMPOSSIBLE. I HAVEN'T BEEN TO THE THIRD FLOOR ALL DAY.
WHAT DO YOU MEAN, YOU SAW ME?
WE SAW YOU, OR WE SAW YOUR HAT AT THE OTHER END OF THE HALL.
CRINKLE CRINKLE
WAIT? MY HAT? MY CAPTAIN'S HAT?
WELL, IT'S POSSIBLE THAT IT COULD HAVE BEEN SOMEONE WITH A HAT JUST LIKE YOURS THAT WE SAW.
MUNCH MUNCH
THAT'S TRUE. WE DIDN'T ACTUALLY SEE NEWELL. WE ONLY ASSUMED IT WAS HIM BECAUSE OF THE HAT.
MAYBE IT'S ANOTHER *CAPTAIN* FAN! I'LL HAVE TO SHOW THEM MY HAT!
WE'LL BE HAT TWINS!
LOOKED JUST LIKE YOURS.
I HOPE THAT THEY AREN'T WEARING IT. WE'RE STILL IN THE SCHOOL.
HA HA
RIGHT? ME TOO.
ZIP!

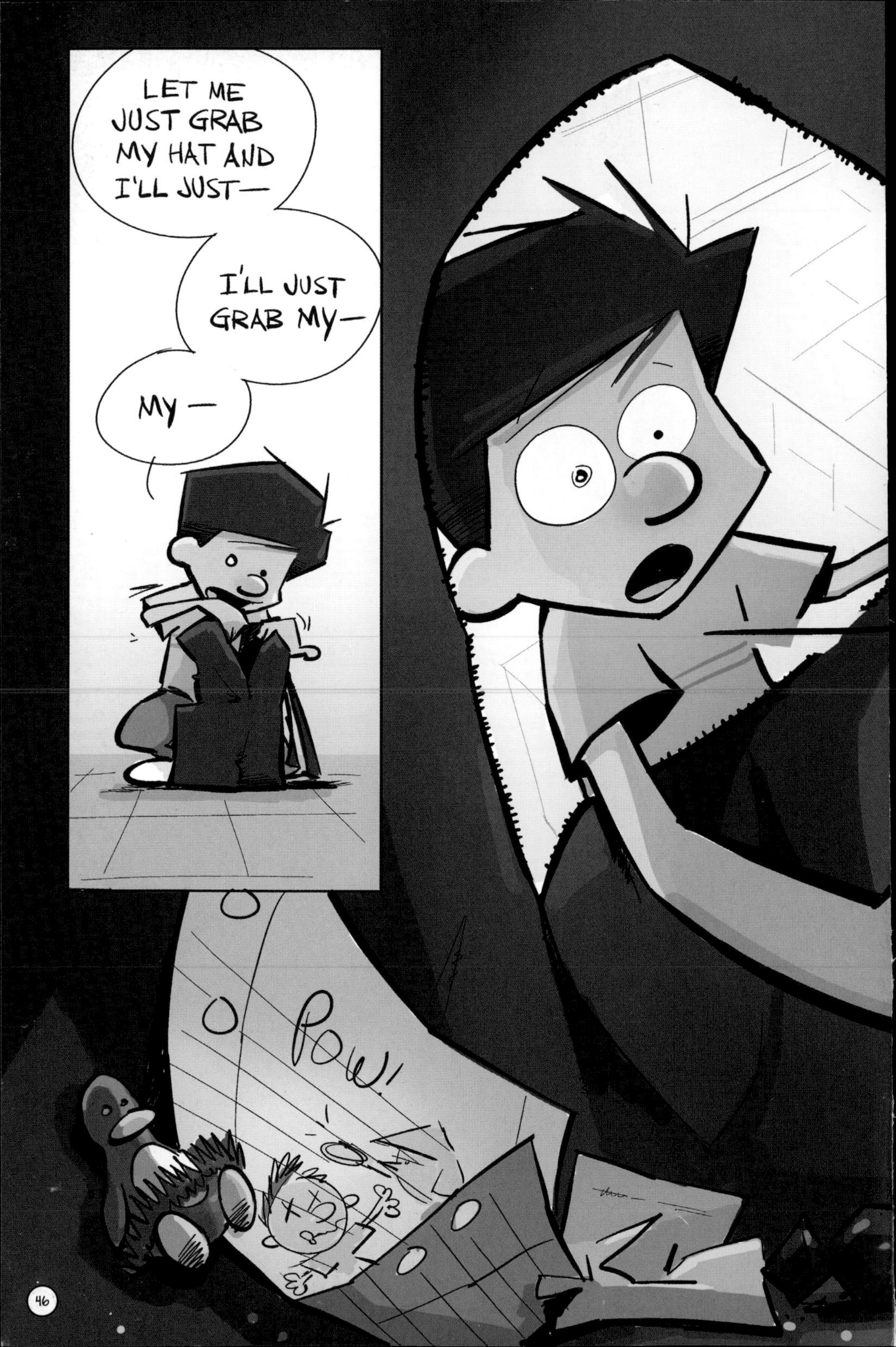
LET ME JUST GRAB MY HAT AND I'LL JUST—
I'LL JUST GRAB MY—
MY—
POW!

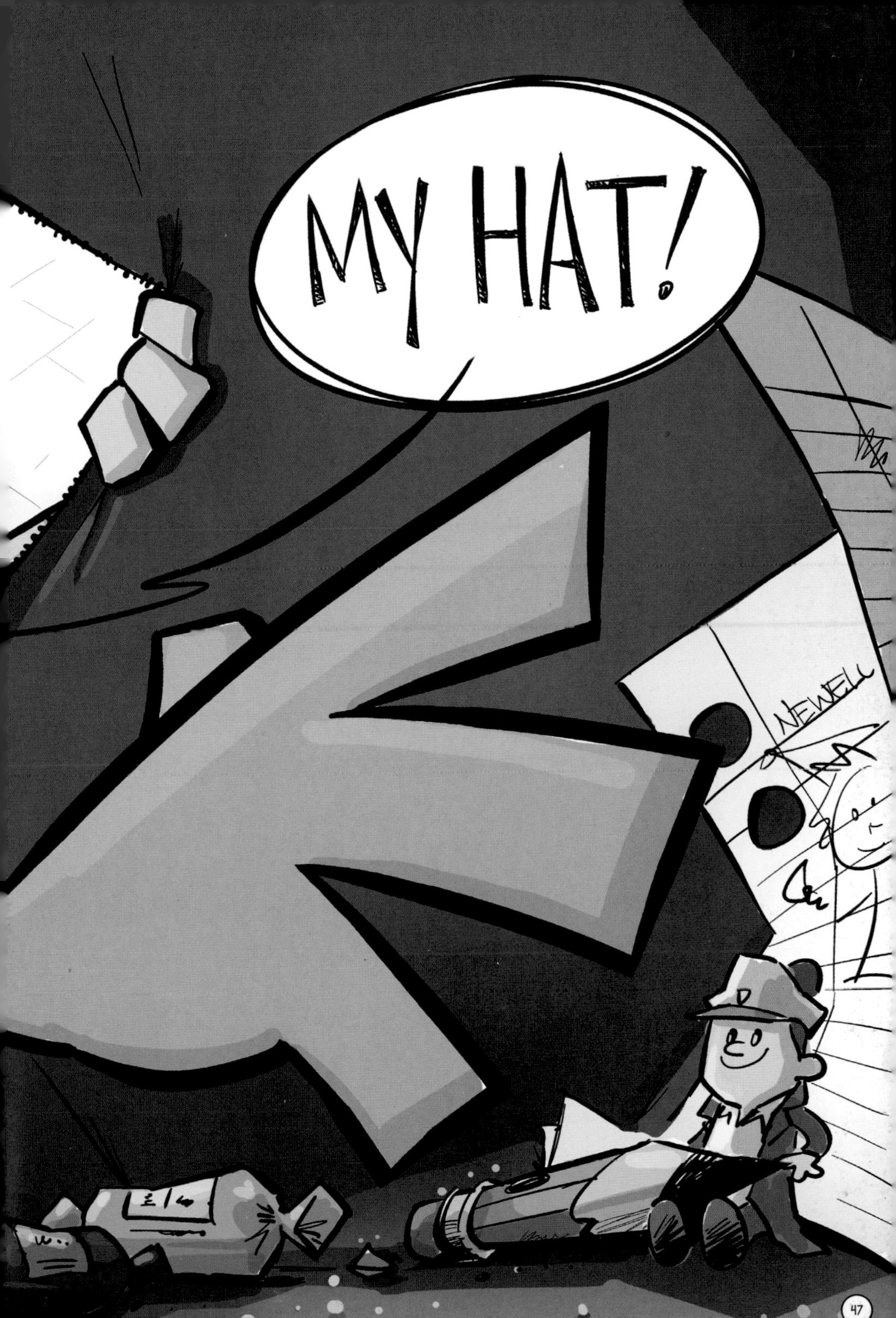
MY HAT!
NEWELL

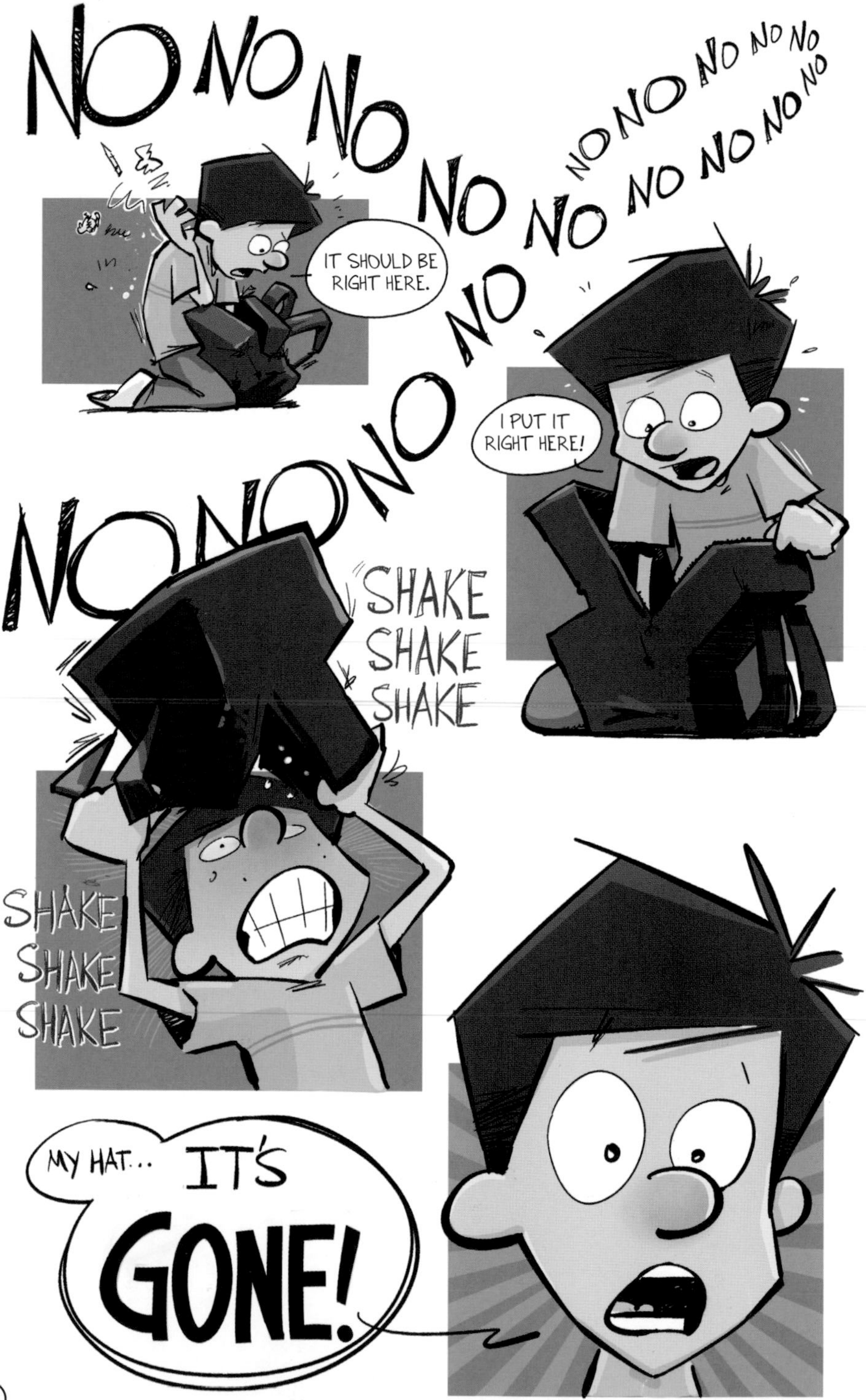
NO NO NO NO NO NO NO NO NO NO
NO NO NO NO NO NO
IT SHOULD BE RIGHT HERE.
NO NO NO NO NO
I PUT IT RIGHT HERE!
SHAKE SHAKE SHAKE
SHAKE SHAKE SHAKE
MY HAT... IT'S GONE!

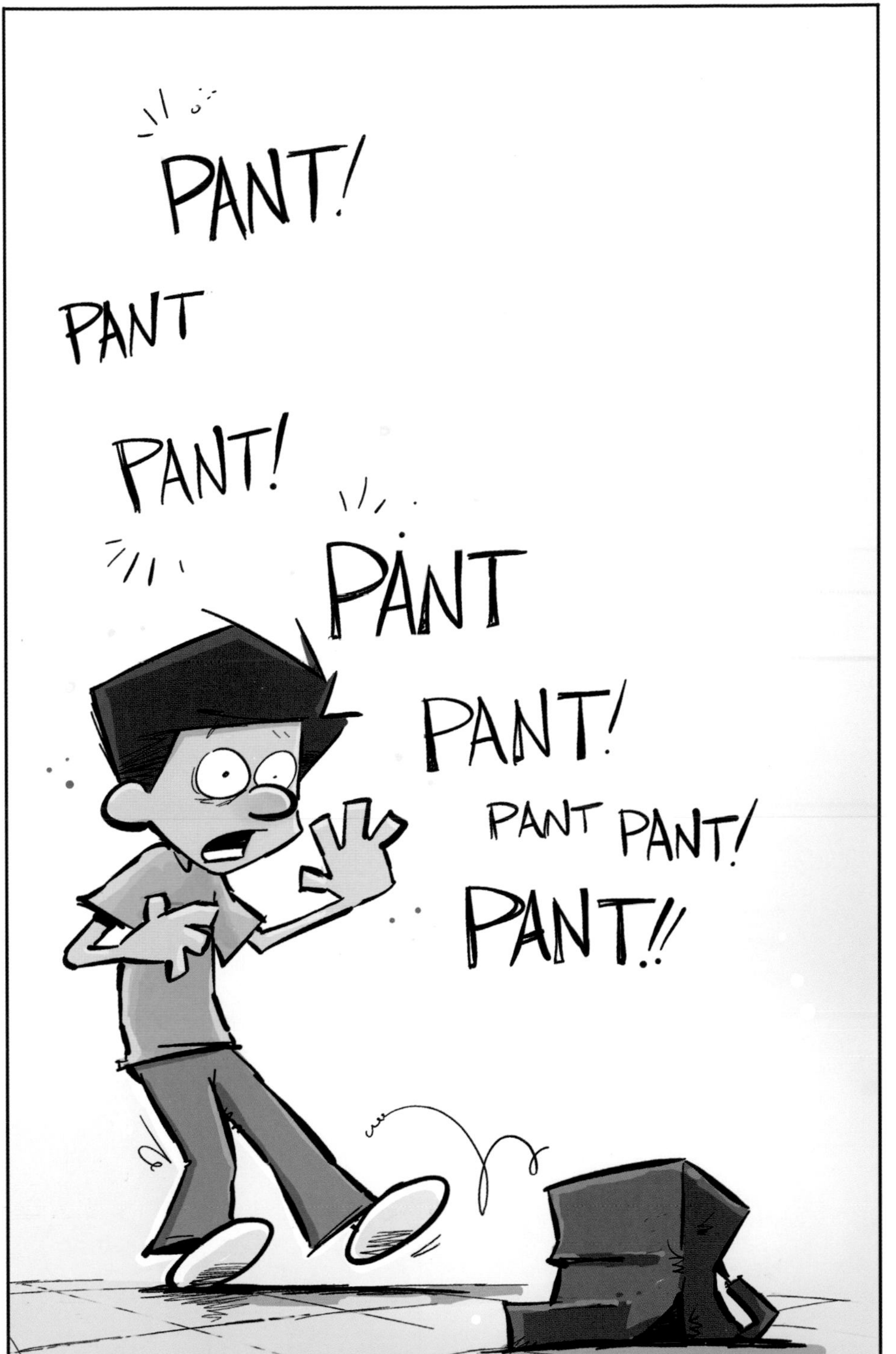
PANT!
PANT
PANT!
PANT
PANT!
PANT PANT!
PANT!!

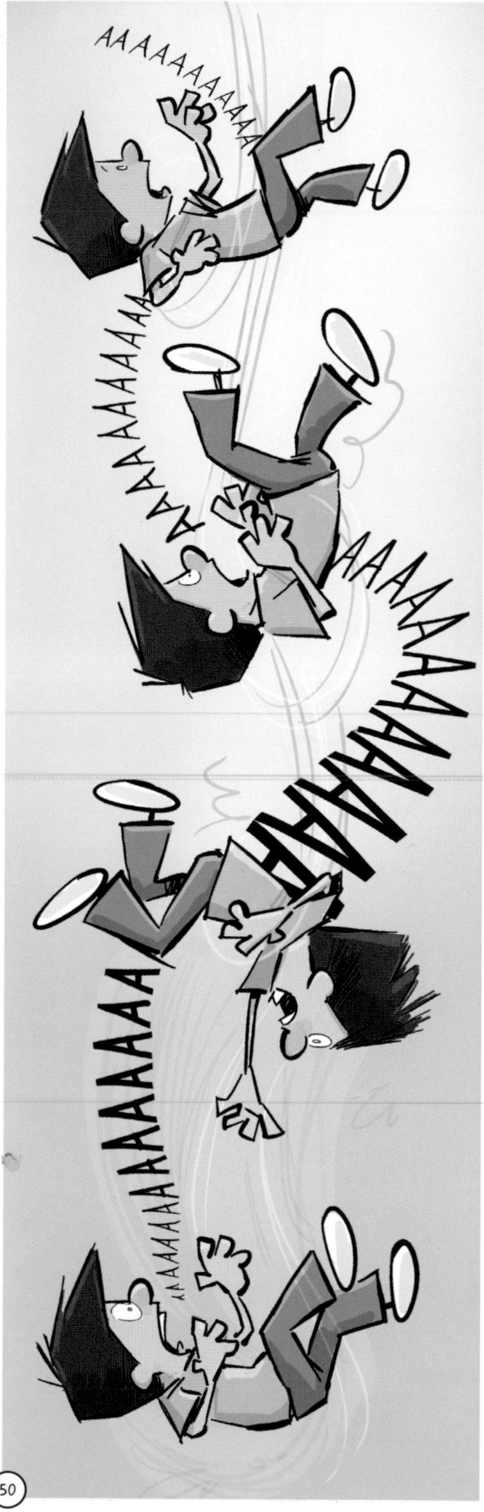
AAAAAAAAAAAAA
AAAAAAAAAAAAAAAAAAAAAAAAAAAAAAAAHHHHH
AAAAAAAAAAAAAAAAAAA

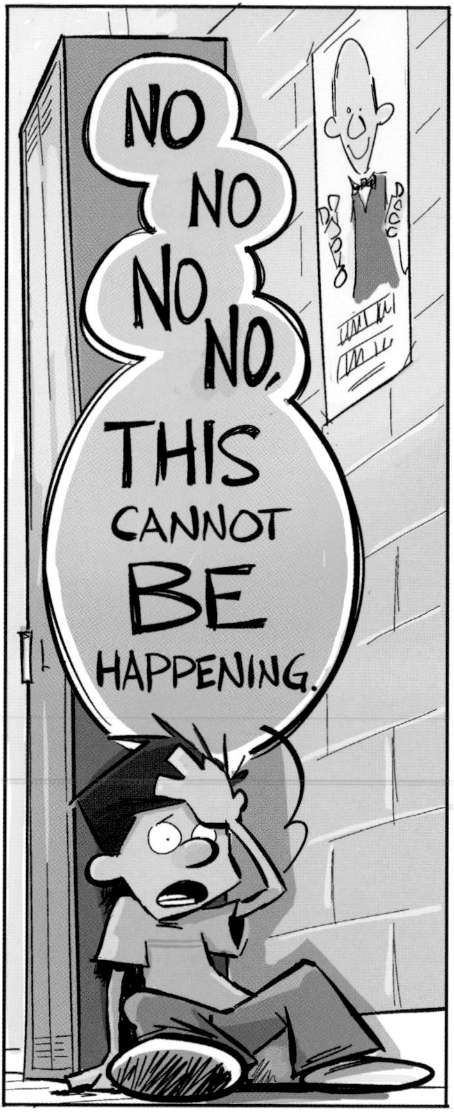
NO NO NO NO, THIS CANNOT BE HAPPENING.

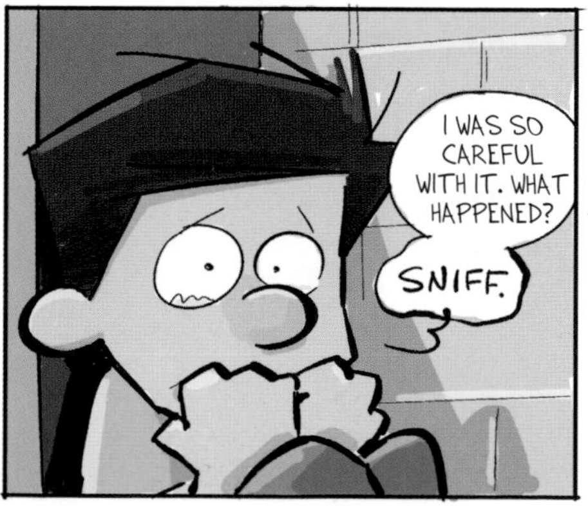
I WAS SO CAREFUL WITH IT. WHAT HAPPENED?
SNIFF.

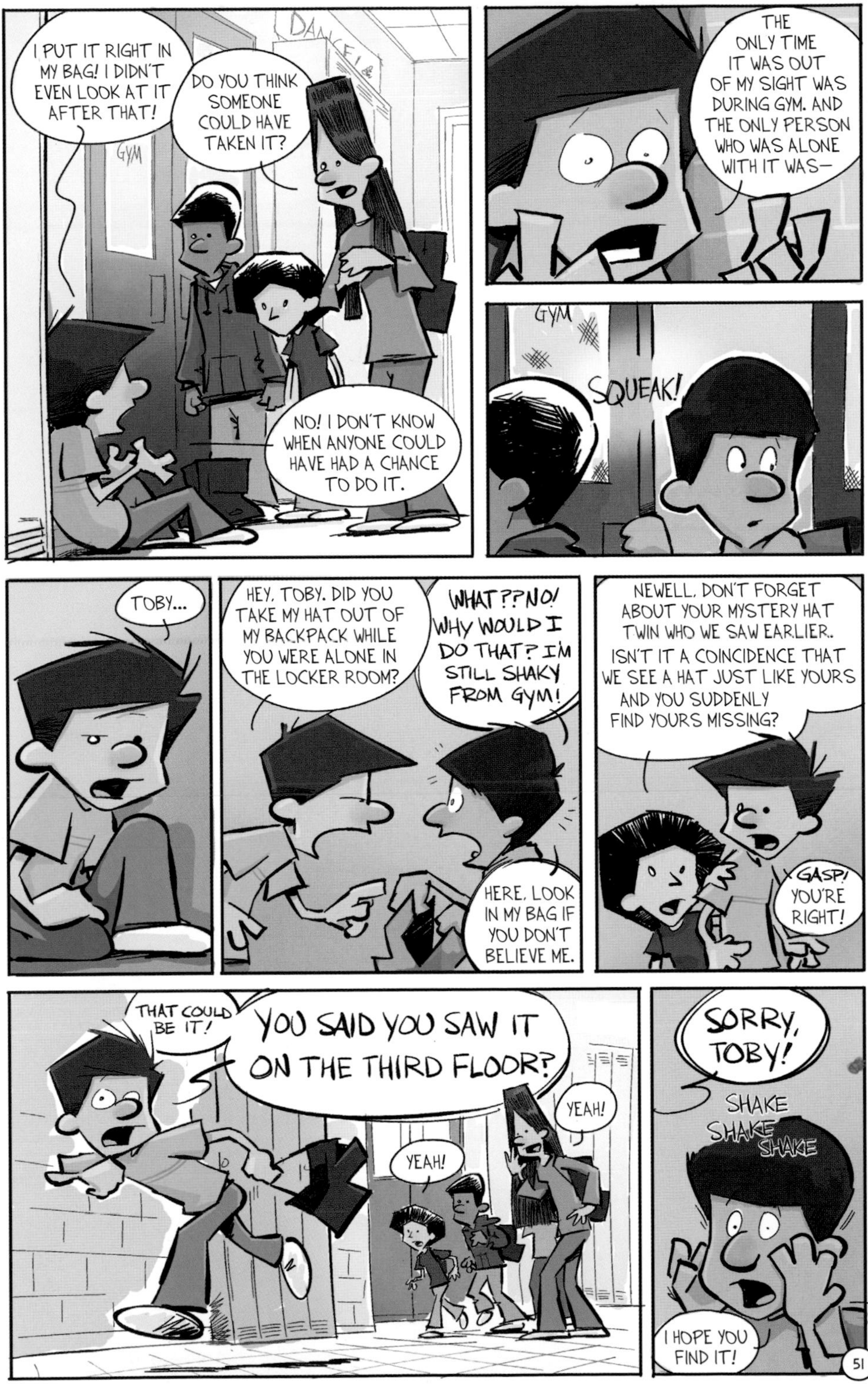

DANCE
GYM
I PUT IT RIGHT IN MY BAG! I DIDN'T EVEN LOOK AT IT AFTER THAT!
DO YOU THINK SOMEONE COULD HAVE TAKEN IT?
NO! I DON'T KNOW WHEN ANYONE COULD HAVE HAD A CHANCE TO DO IT.
THE ONLY TIME IT WAS OUT OF MY SIGHT WAS DURING GYM. AND THE ONLY PERSON WHO WAS ALONE WITH IT WAS—
GYM
SQUEAK!
TOBY...
HEY, TOBY. DID YOU TAKE MY HAT OUT OF MY BACKPACK WHILE YOU WERE ALONE IN THE LOCKER ROOM?
WHAT??NO! WHY WOULD I DO THAT? I'M STILL SHAKY FROM GYM!
HERE. LOOK IN MY BAG IF YOU DON'T BELIEVE ME.
NEWELL, DON'T FORGET ABOUT YOUR MYSTERY HAT TWIN WHO WE SAW EARLIER. ISN'T IT A COINCIDENCE THAT WE SEE A HAT JUST LIKE YOURS AND YOU SUDDENLY FIND YOURS MISSING?
GASP! YOU'RE RIGHT!
THAT COULD BE IT!
YOU SAID YOU SAW IT ON THE THIRD FLOOR?
YEAH!
YEAH!
SORRY, TOBY!
SHAKE
SHAKE
SHAKE
I HOPE YOU FIND IT!

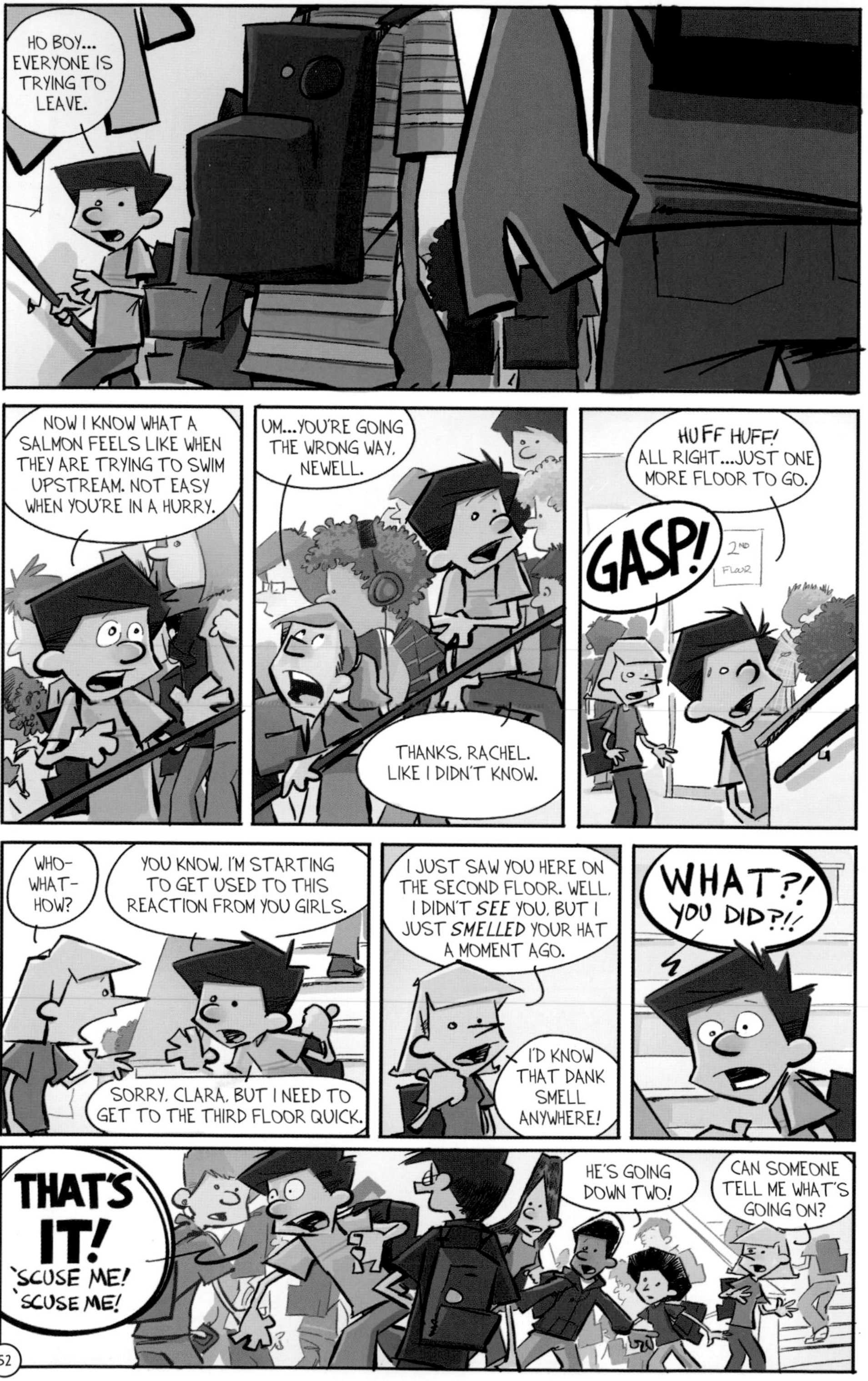
HO BOY... EVERYONE IS TRYING TO LEAVE.
NOW I KNOW WHAT A SALMON FEELS LIKE WHEN THEY ARE TRYING TO SWIM UPSTREAM. NOT EASY WHEN YOU'RE IN A HURRY.
UM...YOU'RE GOING THE WRONG WAY, NEWELL.
THANKS, RACHEL. LIKE I DIDN'T KNOW.
HUFF HUFF! ALL RIGHT...JUST ONE MORE FLOOR TO GO.
GASP!
2ND FLOOR
WHO- WHAT- HOW?
YOU KNOW, I'M STARTING TO GET USED TO THIS REACTION FROM YOU GIRLS.
SORRY, CLARA, BUT I NEED TO GET TO THE THIRD FLOOR QUICK.
I JUST SAW YOU HERE ON THE SECOND FLOOR. WELL, I DIDN'T *SEE* YOU, BUT I JUST *SMELLED* YOUR HAT A MOMENT AGO.
I'D KNOW THAT DANK SMELL ANYWHERE!
WHAT?! YOU DID?!!
THAT'S IT! 'SCUSE ME! 'SCUSE ME!
HE'S GOING DOWN TWO!
CAN SOMEONE TELL ME WHAT'S GOING ON?

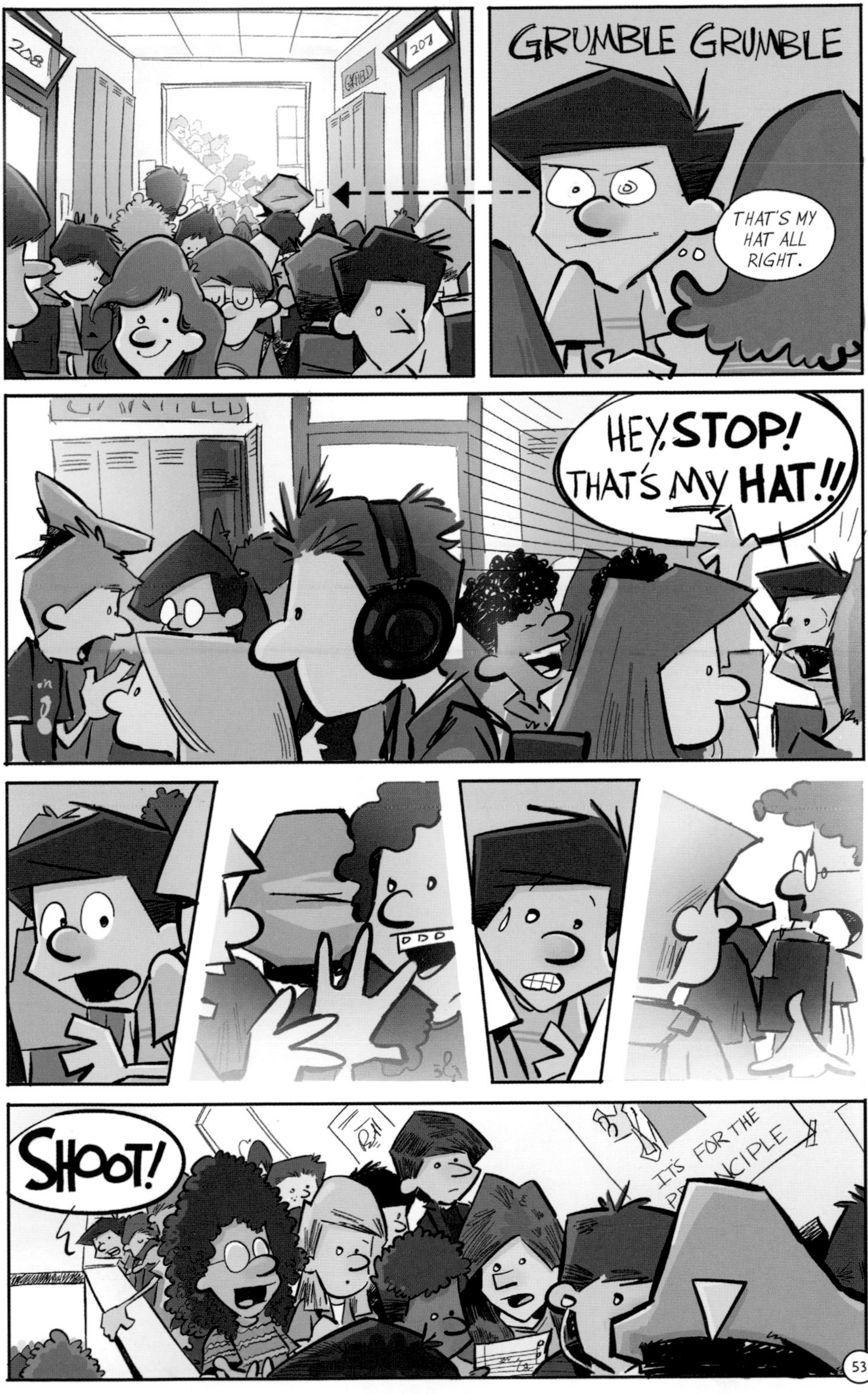
208
207
GARFIELD
GRUMBLE GRUMBLE
THAT'S MY HAT ALL RIGHT.
HEY, STOP! THAT'S MY HAT!!
SHOOT!
IT'S FOR THE PRINCIPLE

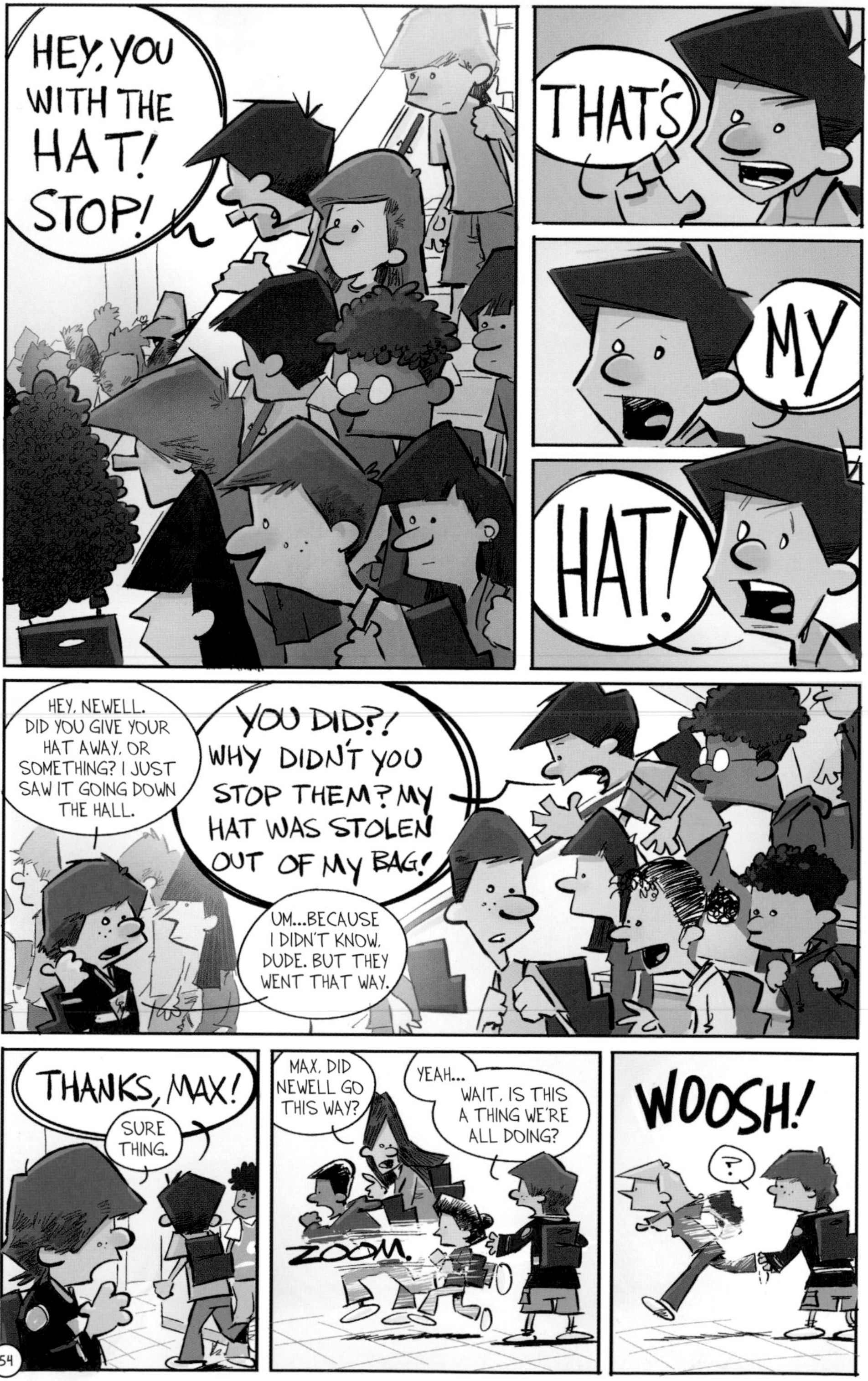
HEY, YOU WITH THE HAT! STOP!
THAT'S
MY
HAT!
HEY, NEWELL. DID YOU GIVE YOUR HAT AWAY, OR SOMETHING? I JUST SAW IT GOING DOWN THE HALL.
YOU DID?! WHY DIDN'T YOU STOP THEM? MY HAT WAS STOLEN OUT OF MY BAG!
UM...BECAUSE I DIDN'T KNOW, DUDE. BUT THEY WENT THAT WAY.
THANKS, MAX!
SURE THING.
MAX, DID NEWELL GO THIS WAY?
YEAH...
WAIT, IS THIS A THING WE'RE ALL DOING?
ZOOM.
WOOSH!
?

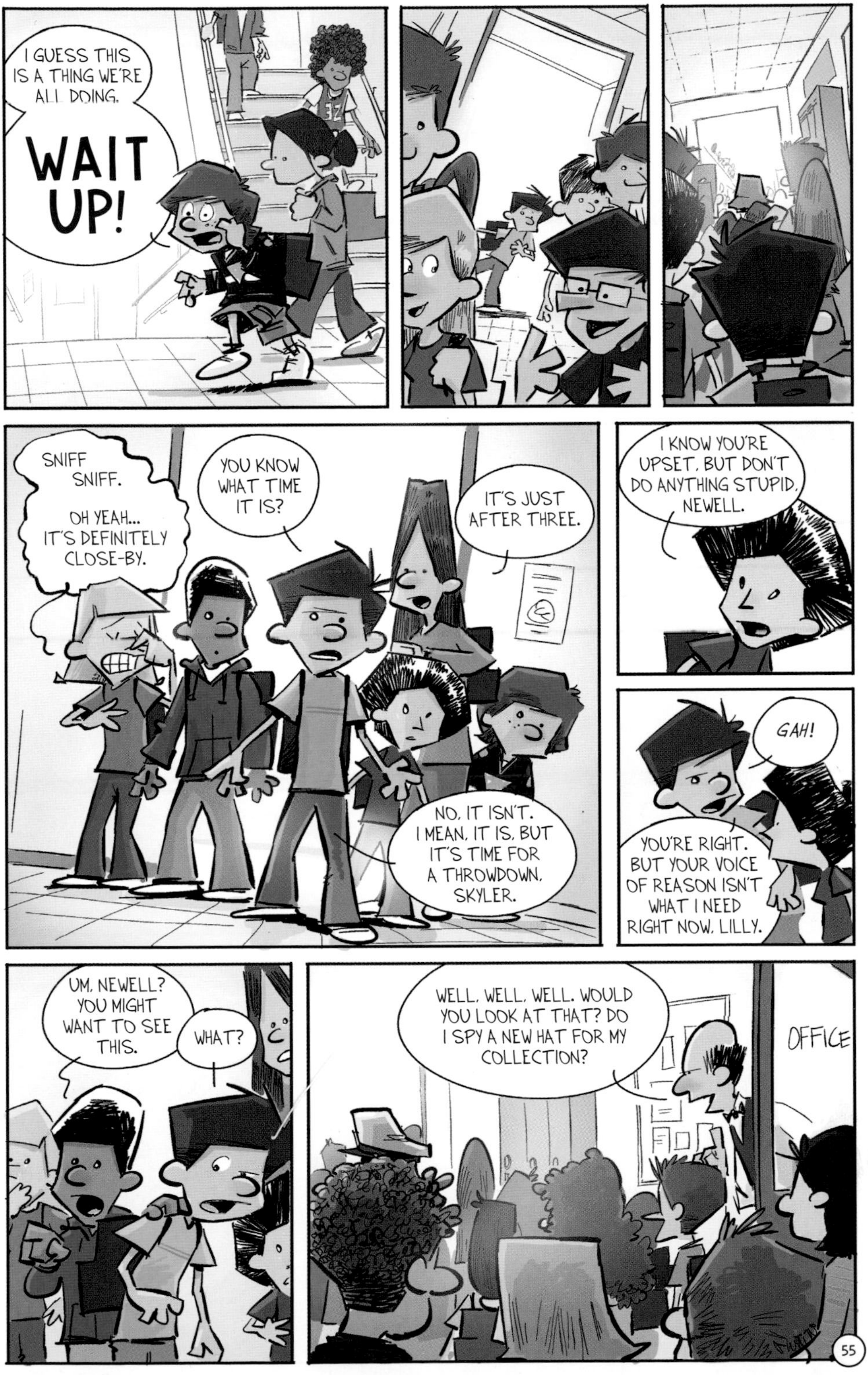
I GUESS THIS IS A THING WE'RE ALL DOING.
WAIT UP!
SNIFF SNIFF.
OH YEAH... IT'S DEFINITELY CLOSE-BY.
YOU KNOW WHAT TIME IT IS?
IT'S JUST AFTER THREE.
NO, IT ISN'T. I MEAN, IT IS, BUT IT'S TIME FOR A THROWDOWN, SKYLER.
I KNOW YOU'RE UPSET, BUT DON'T DO ANYTHING STUPID, NEWELL.
GAH!
YOU'RE RIGHT. BUT YOUR VOICE OF REASON ISN'T WHAT I NEED RIGHT NOW, LILLY.
UM, NEWELL? YOU MIGHT WANT TO SEE THIS.
WHAT?
WELL, WELL, WELL. WOULD YOU LOOK AT THAT? DO I SPY A NEW HAT FOR MY COLLECTION?
OFFICE

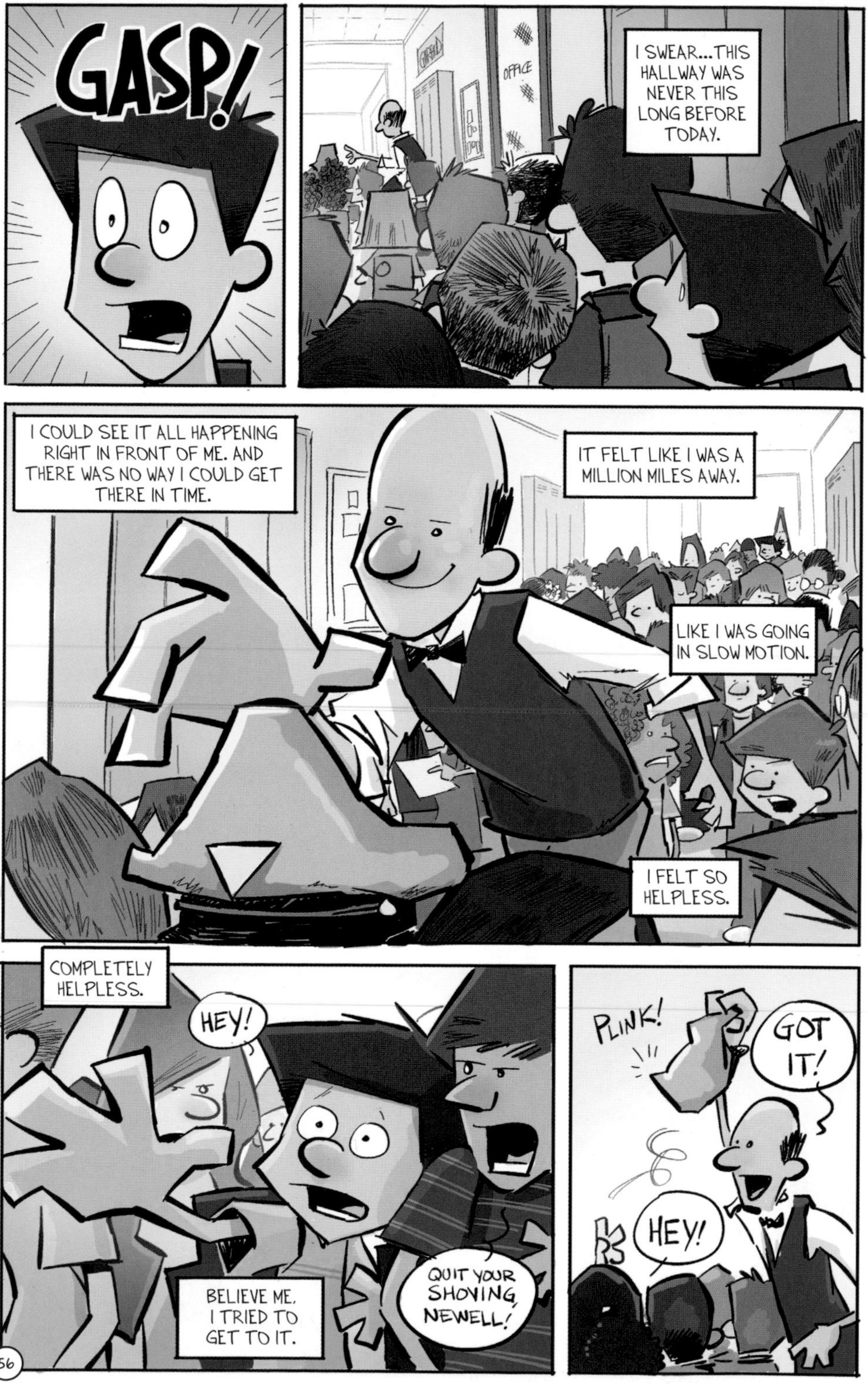
GASP!
OFFICE
I SWEAR...THIS HALLWAY WAS NEVER THIS LONG BEFORE TODAY.
I COULD SEE IT ALL HAPPENING RIGHT IN FRONT OF ME. AND THERE WAS NO WAY I COULD GET THERE IN TIME.
IT FELT LIKE I WAS A MILLION MILES AWAY.
LIKE I WAS GOING IN SLOW MOTION.
I FELT SO HELPLESS.
COMPLETELY HELPLESS.
HEY!
BELIEVE ME, I TRIED TO GET TO IT.
QUIT YOUR SHOVING, NEWELL!
PLINK!
GOT IT!
HEY!

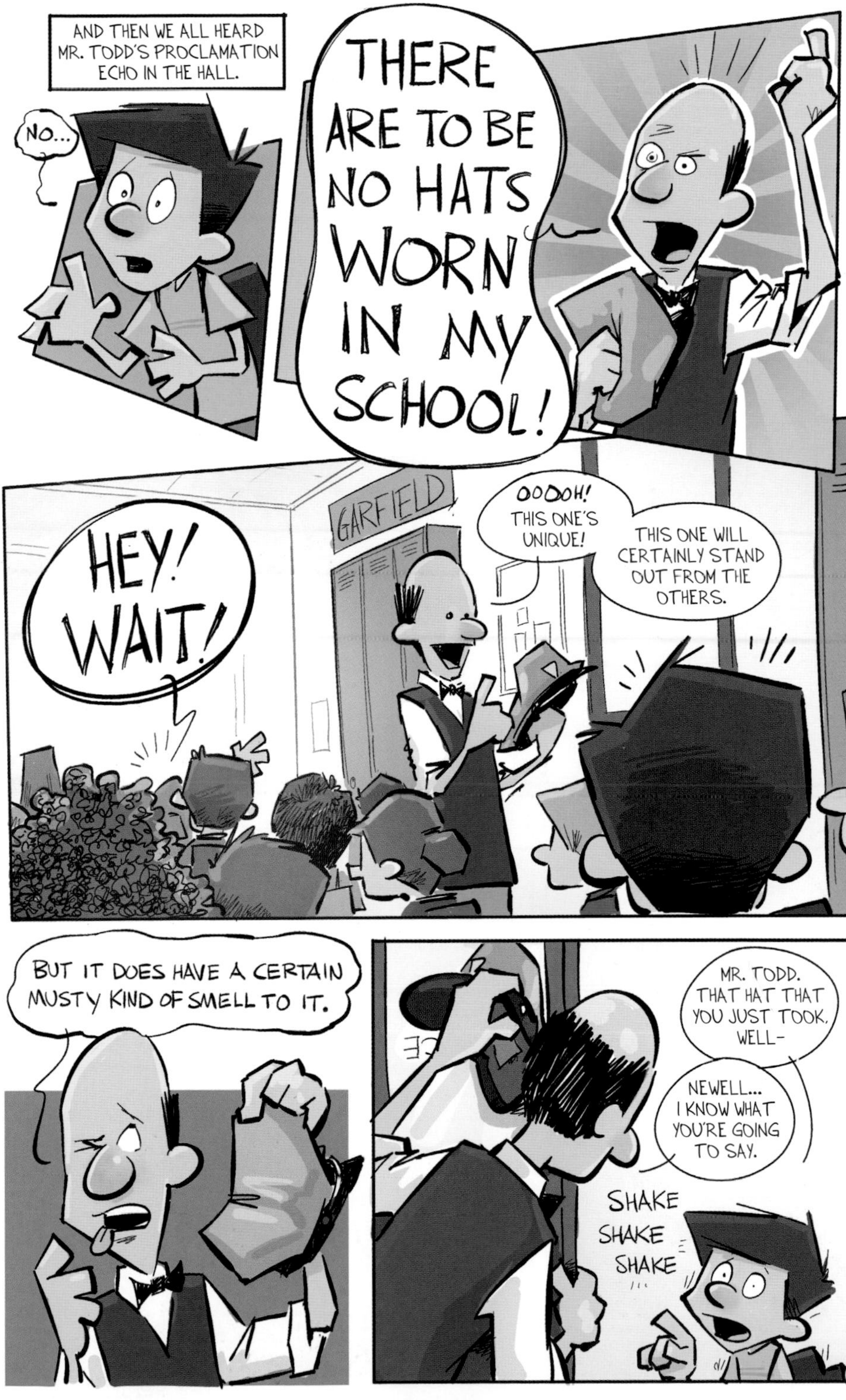
AND THEN WE ALL HEARD MR. TODD'S PROCLAMATION ECHO IN THE HALL.
NO...
THERE ARE TO BE NO HATS WORN IN MY SCHOOL!
GARFIELD
HEY! WAIT!
OOOOH! THIS ONE'S UNIQUE!
THIS ONE WILL CERTAINLY STAND OUT FROM THE OTHERS.
BUT IT DOES HAVE A CERTAIN MUSTY KIND OF SMELL TO IT.
MR. TODD. THAT HAT THAT YOU JUST TOOK, WELL-
NEWELL... I KNOW WHAT YOU'RE GOING TO SAY.
SHAKE
SHAKE
SHAKE

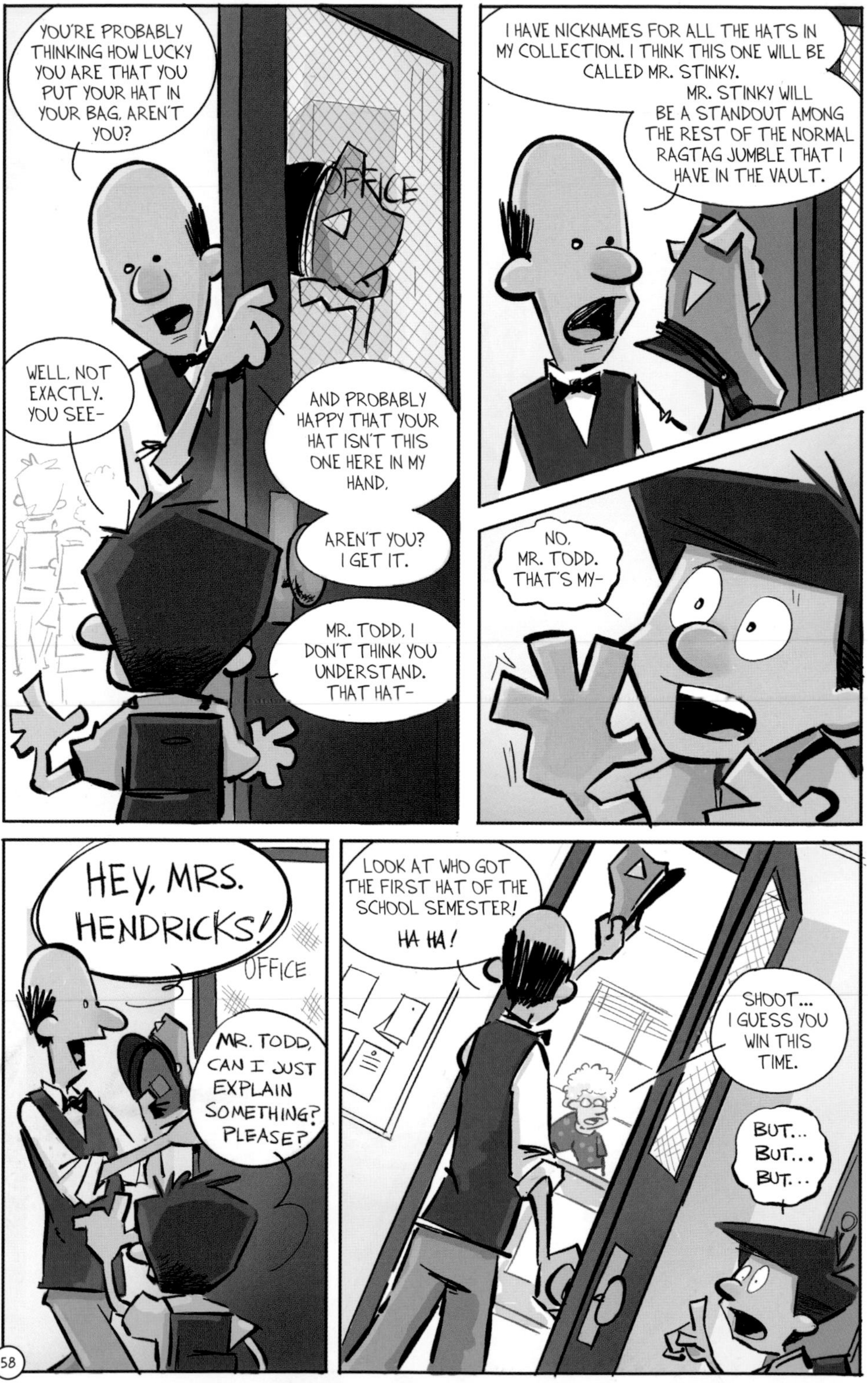
YOU'RE PROBABLY THINKING HOW LUCKY YOU ARE THAT YOU PUT YOUR HAT IN YOUR BAG, AREN'T YOU?
OFFICE
WELL, NOT EXACTLY. YOU SEE-
AND PROBABLY HAPPY THAT YOUR HAT ISN'T THIS ONE HERE IN MY HAND.
AREN'T YOU? I GET IT.
MR. TODD, I DON'T THINK YOU UNDERSTAND. THAT HAT-
I HAVE NICKNAMES FOR ALL THE HATS IN MY COLLECTION. I THINK THIS ONE WILL BE CALLED MR. STINKY.
MR. STINKY WILL BE A STANDOUT AMONG THE REST OF THE NORMAL RAGTAG JUMBLE THAT I HAVE IN THE VAULT.
NO, MR. TODD. THAT'S MY-
HEY, MRS. HENDRICKS!
OFFICE
MR. TODD, CAN I JUST EXPLAIN SOMETHING? PLEASE?
LOOK AT WHO GOT THE FIRST HAT OF THE SCHOOL SEMESTER!
HA HA!
SHOOT... I GUESS YOU WIN THIS TIME.
BUT... BUT... BUT...

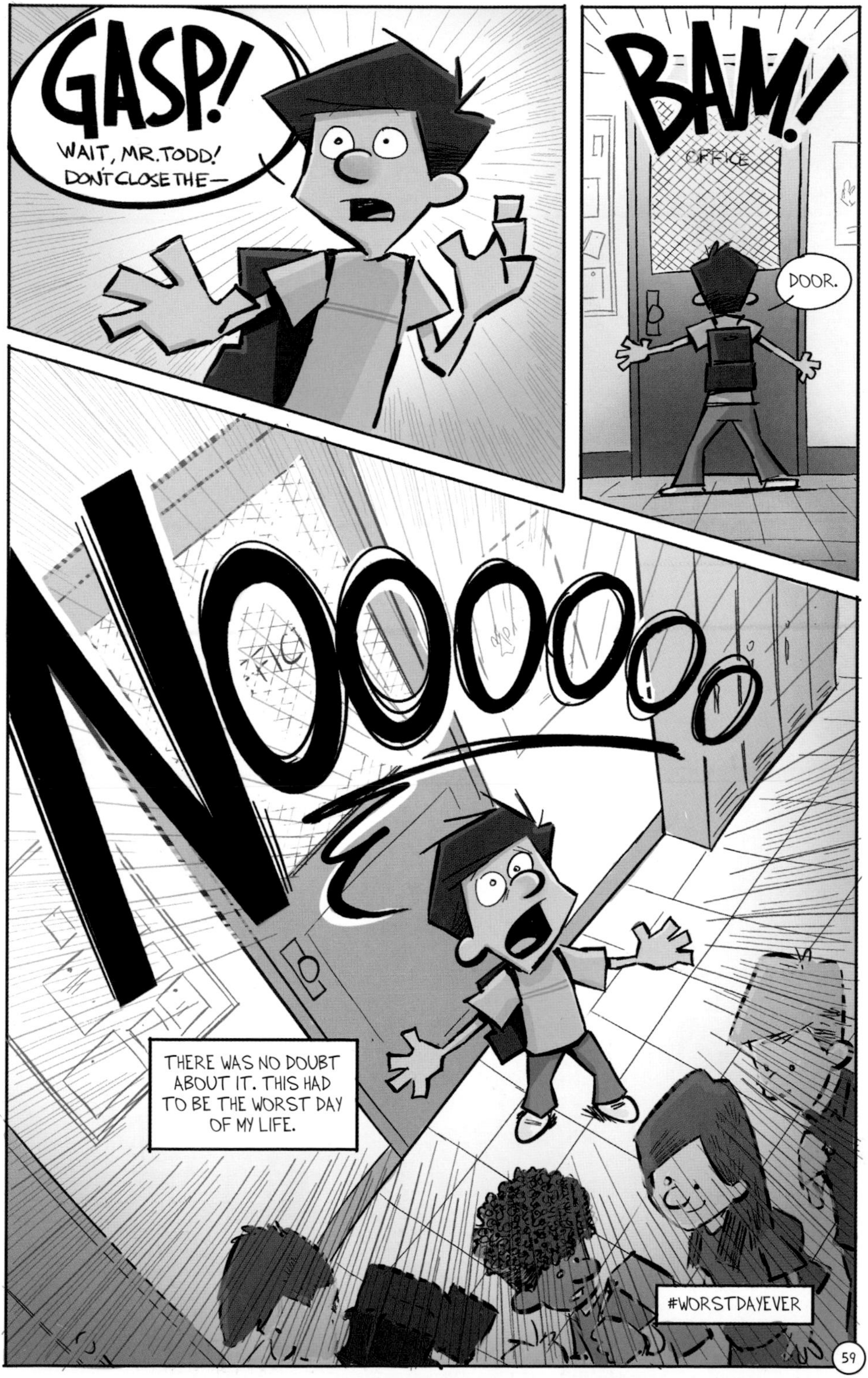
GASP!
WAIT, MR. TODD! DON'T CLOSE THE—
BAM!
OFFICE
DOOR.
NOOOOOOOO
THERE WAS NO DOUBT ABOUT IT. THIS HAD TO BE THE WORST DAY OF MY LIFE.
#WORSTDAYEVER

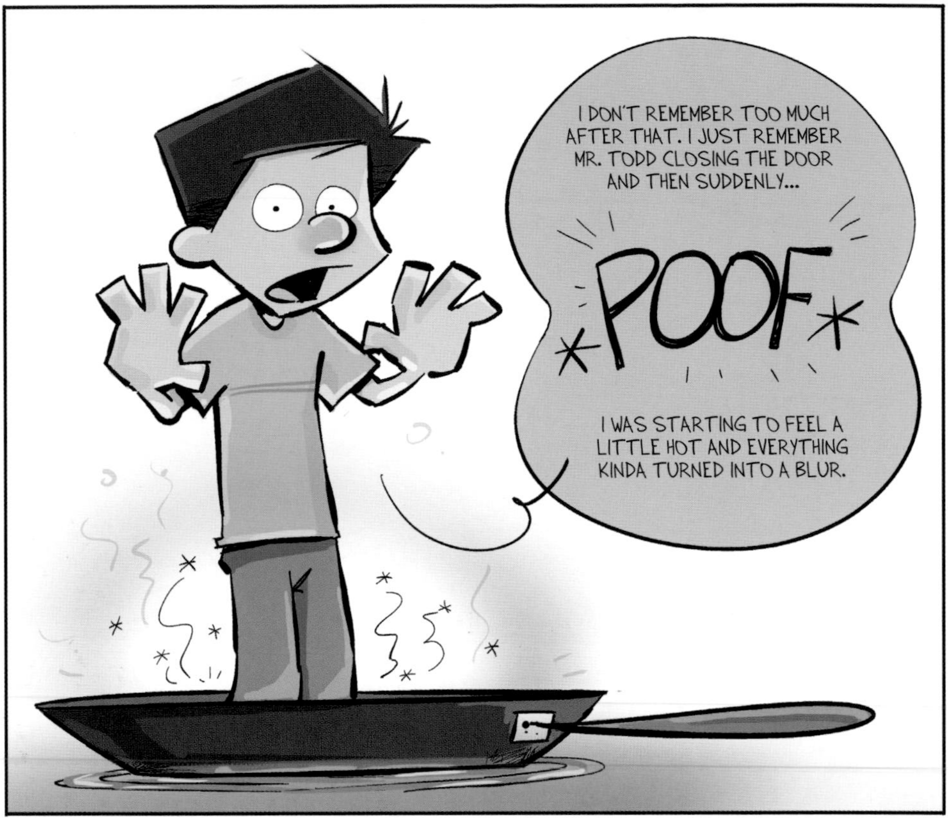
I DON'T REMEMBER TOO MUCH AFTER THAT. I JUST REMEMBER MR. TODD CLOSING THE DOOR AND THEN SUDDENLY...
POOF
I WAS STARTING TO FEEL A LITTLE HOT AND EVERYTHING KINDA TURNED INTO A BLUR.

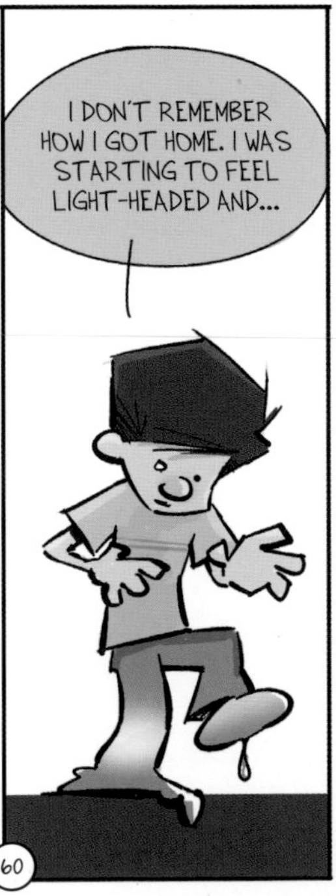
I DON'T REMEMBER HOW I GOT HOME. I WAS STARTING TO FEEL LIGHT-HEADED AND...

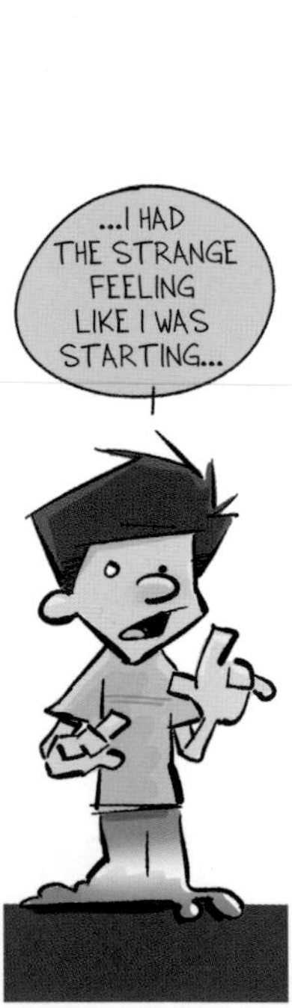
...I HAD THE STRANGE FEELING LIKE I WAS STARTING...

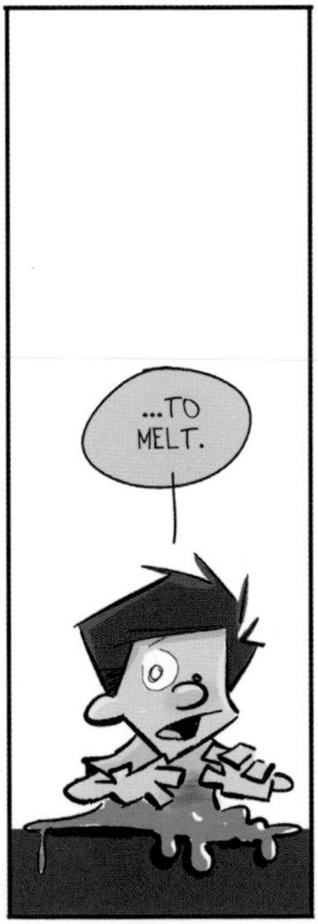
...TO MELT.

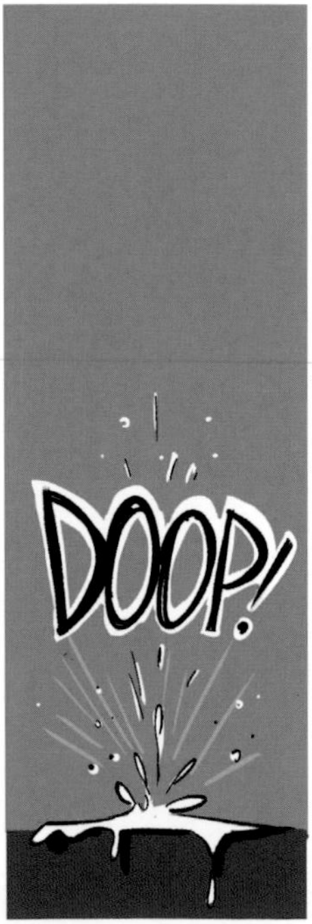
DOOP!

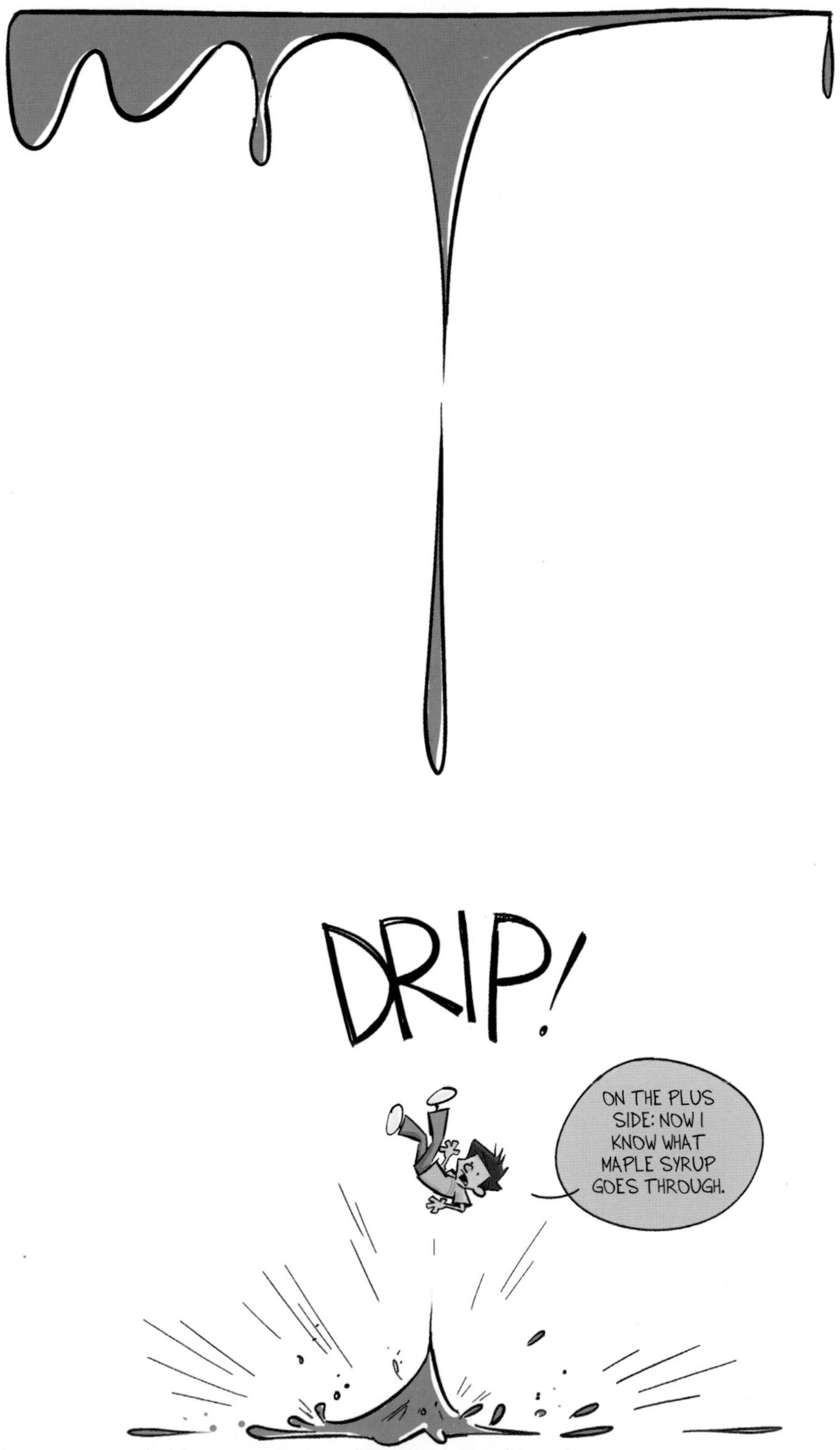
DRIP!
ON THE PLUS SIDE: NOW I KNOW WHAT MAPLE SYRUP GOES THROUGH.

CHAPTER FOUR
LIVING THE DREAM

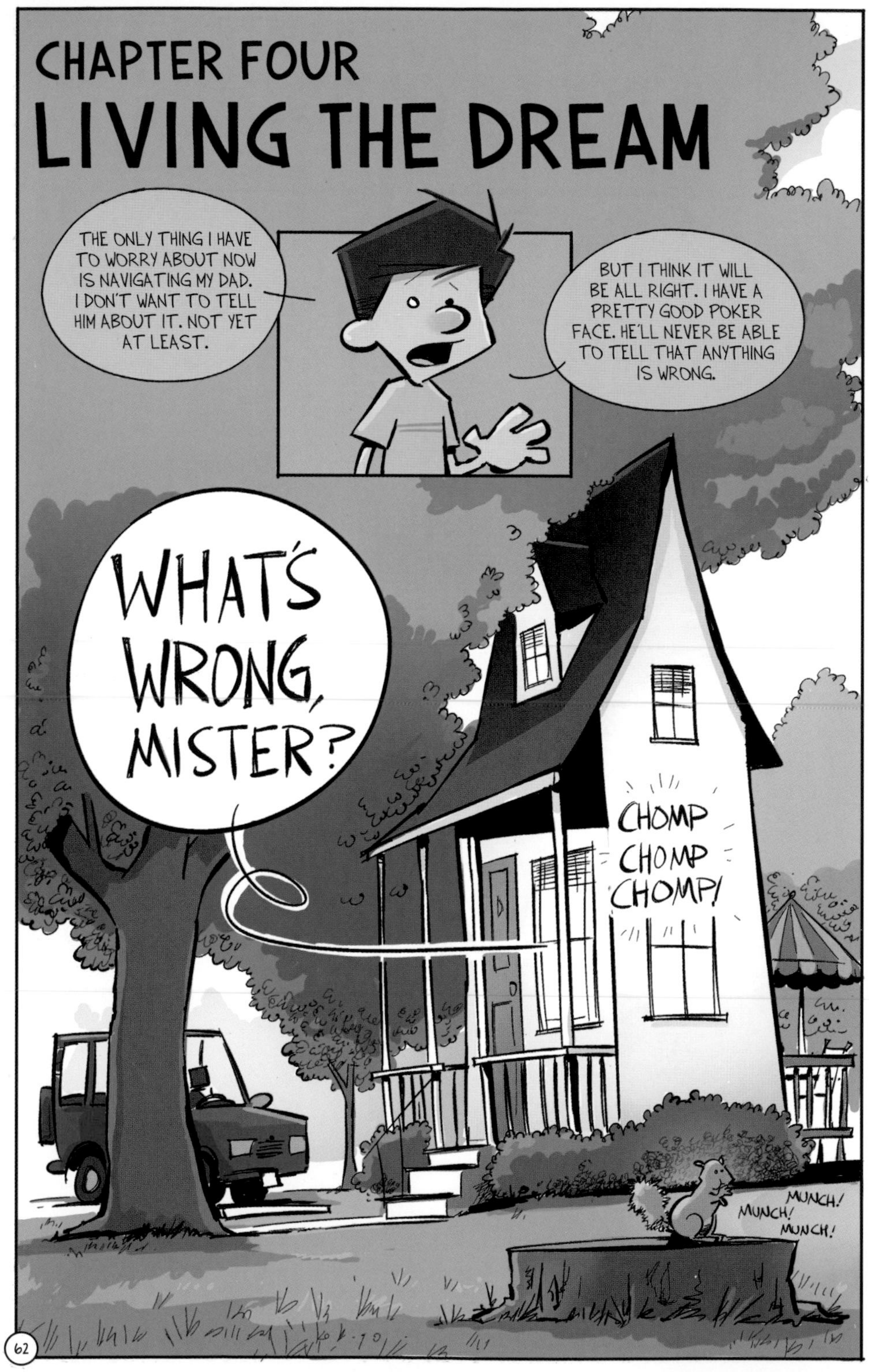

THE ONLY THING I HAVE TO WORRY ABOUT NOW IS NAVIGATING MY DAD. I DON'T WANT TO TELL HIM ABOUT IT. NOT YET AT LEAST.
BUT I THINK IT WILL BE ALL RIGHT. I HAVE A PRETTY GOOD POKER FACE. HE'LL NEVER BE ABLE TO TELL THAT ANYTHING IS WRONG.
WHAT'S WRONG, MISTER?
CHOMP CHOMP CHOMP!
MUNCH! MUNCH! MUNCH!

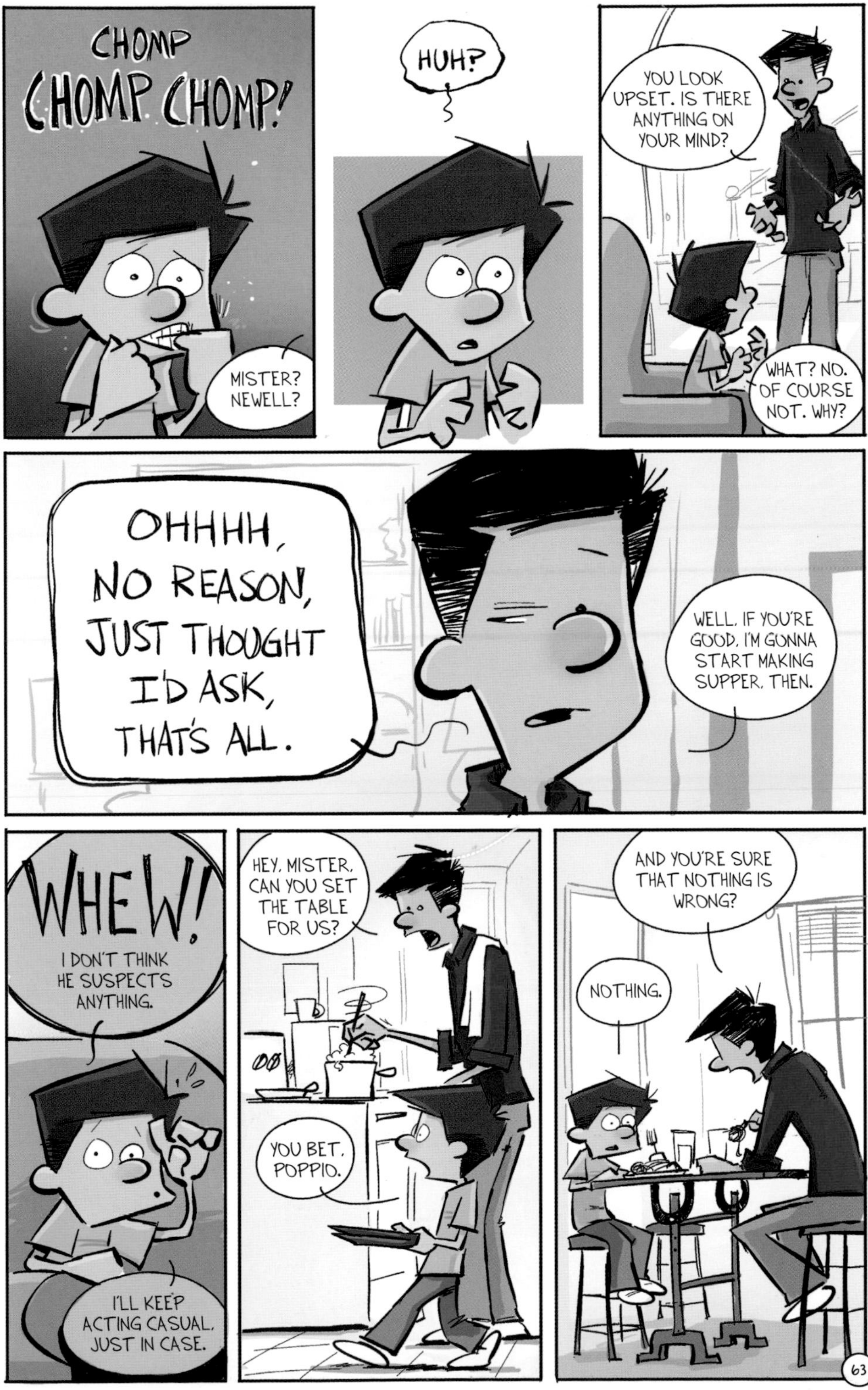
CHOMP
CHOMP CHOMP!
MISTER? NEWELL?
HUH?
YOU LOOK UPSET. IS THERE ANYTHING ON YOUR MIND?
WHAT? NO. OF COURSE NOT. WHY?
OHHHH, NO REASON, JUST THOUGHT I'D ASK, THAT'S ALL.
WELL, IF YOU'RE GOOD, I'M GONNA START MAKING SUPPER, THEN.
WHEW!
I DON'T THINK HE SUSPECTS ANYTHING.
I'LL KEEP ACTING CASUAL, JUST IN CASE.
HEY, MISTER, CAN YOU SET THE TABLE FOR US?
YOU BET, POPPIO.
AND YOU'RE SURE THAT NOTHING IS WRONG?
NOTHING.

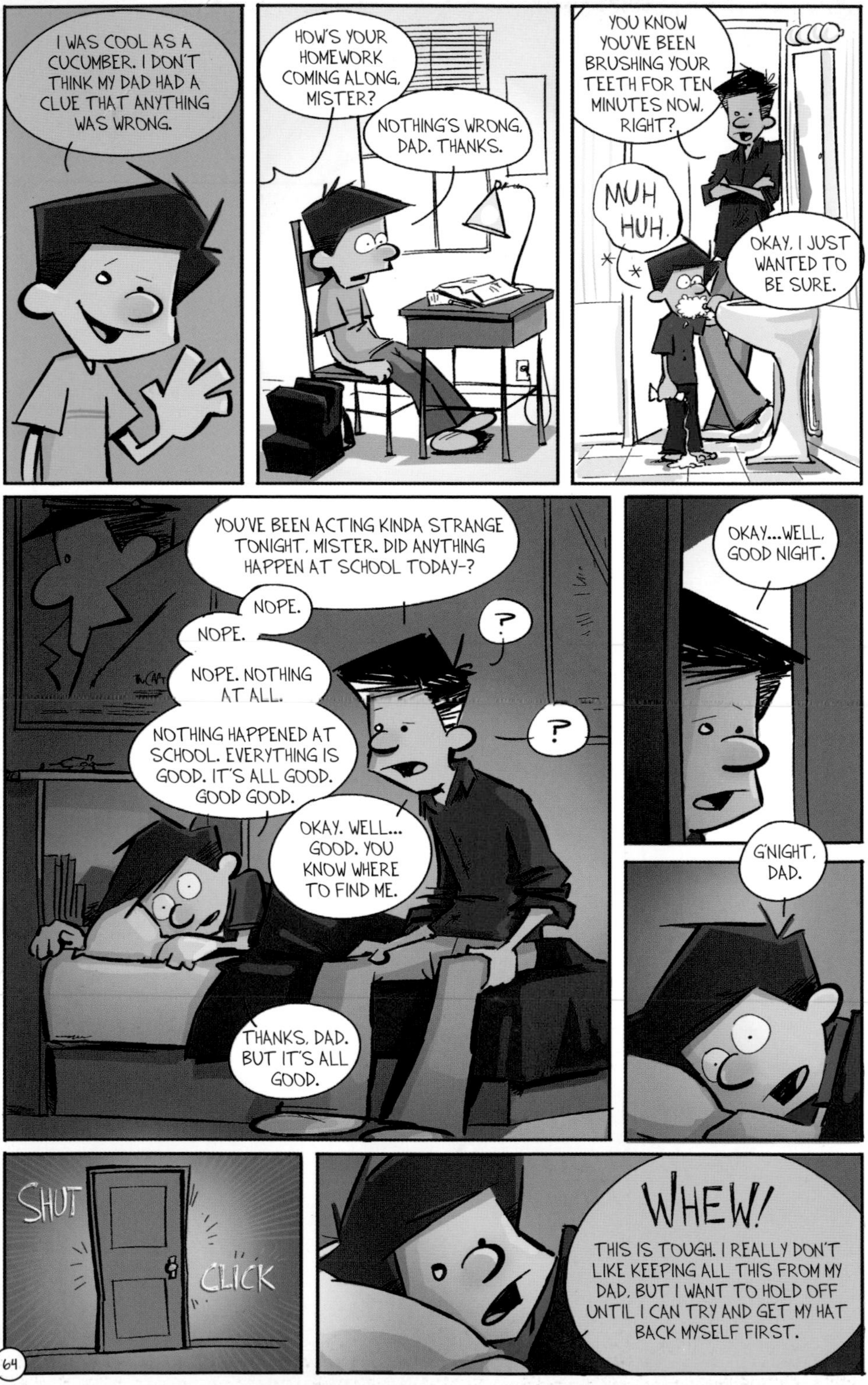
I WAS COOL AS A CUCUMBER. I DON'T THINK MY DAD HAD A CLUE THAT ANYTHING WAS WRONG.
HOW'S YOUR HOMEWORK COMING ALONG, MISTER?
NOTHING'S WRONG, DAD. THANKS.
YOU KNOW YOU'VE BEEN BRUSHING YOUR TEETH FOR TEN MINUTES NOW, RIGHT?
MUH HUH.
OKAY, I JUST WANTED TO BE SURE.
YOU'VE BEEN ACTING KINDA STRANGE TONIGHT, MISTER. DID ANYTHING HAPPEN AT SCHOOL TODAY-?
NOPE.
NOPE.
NOPE. NOTHING AT ALL.
?
NOTHING HAPPENED AT SCHOOL. EVERYTHING IS GOOD. IT'S ALL GOOD. GOOD GOOD.
?
OKAY. WELL... GOOD. YOU KNOW WHERE TO FIND ME.
THANKS, DAD. BUT IT'S ALL GOOD.
OKAY...WELL, GOOD NIGHT.
G'NIGHT, DAD.
SHUT
CLICK
WHEW!
THIS IS TOUGH. I REALLY DON'T LIKE KEEPING ALL THIS FROM MY DAD, BUT I WANT TO HOLD OFF UNTIL I CAN TRY AND GET MY HAT BACK MYSELF FIRST.

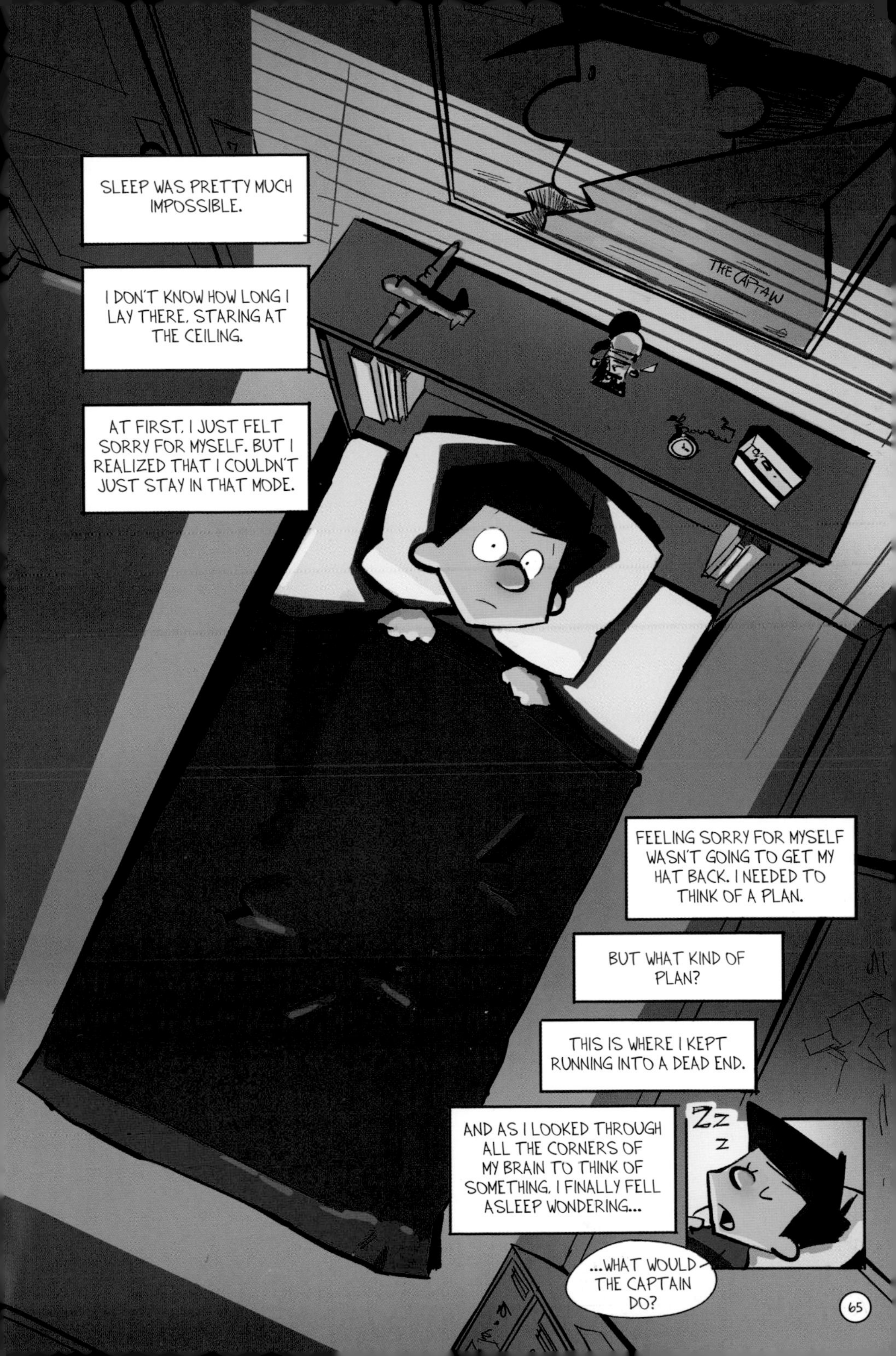
SLEEP WAS PRETTY MUCH IMPOSSIBLE.
I DON'T KNOW HOW LONG I LAY THERE, STARING AT THE CEILING.
AT FIRST, I JUST FELT SORRY FOR MYSELF. BUT I REALIZED THAT I COULDN'T JUST STAY IN THAT MODE.
FEELING SORRY FOR MYSELF WASN'T GOING TO GET MY HAT BACK. I NEEDED TO THINK OF A PLAN.
BUT WHAT KIND OF PLAN?
THIS IS WHERE I KEPT RUNNING INTO A DEAD END.
AND AS I LOOKED THROUGH ALL THE CORNERS OF MY BRAIN TO THINK OF SOMETHING, I FINALLY FELL ASLEEP WONDERING...
ZZ
Z
...WHAT WOULD THE CAPTAIN DO?

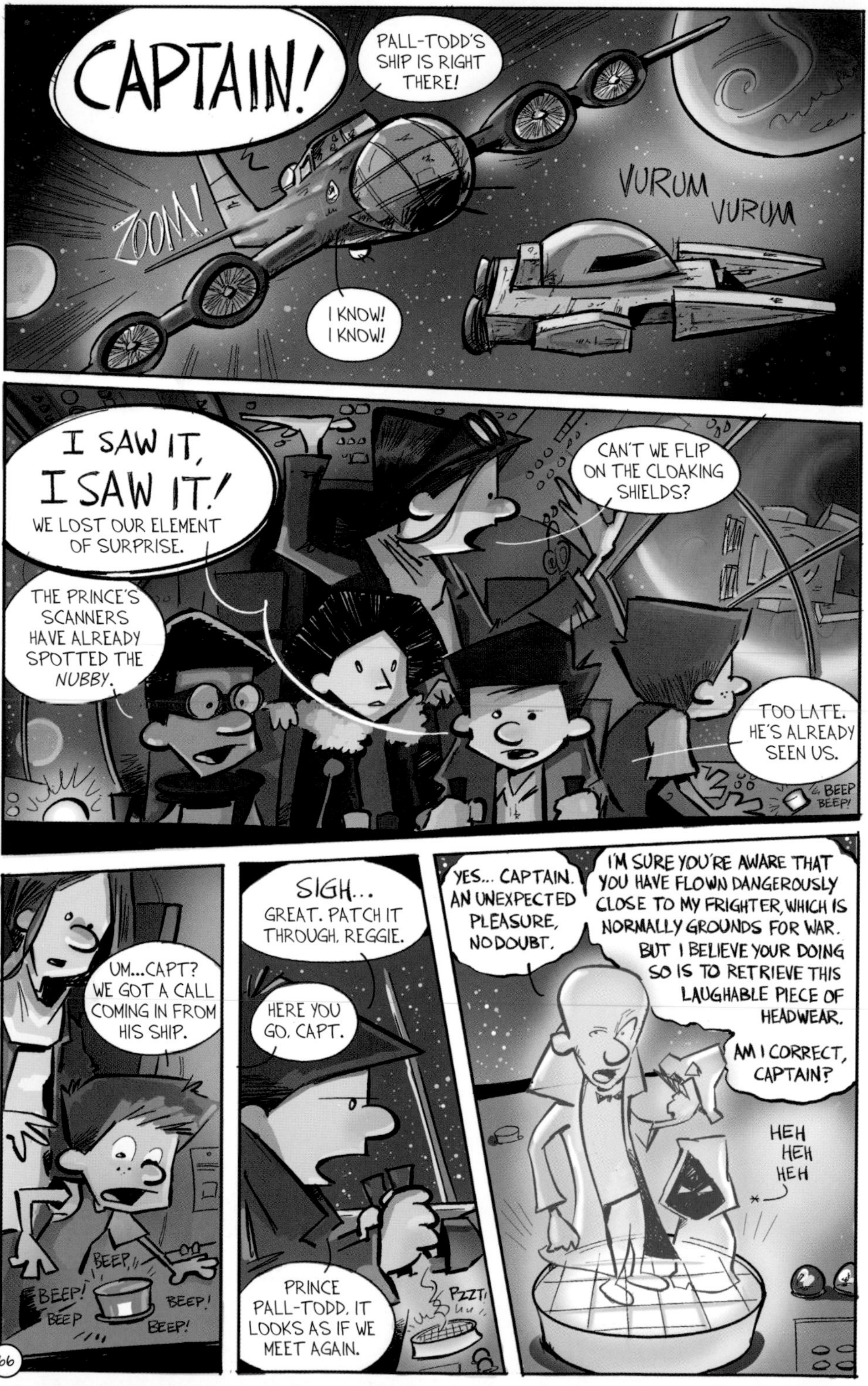
CAPTAIN!
PALL-TODD'S SHIP IS RIGHT THERE!
ZOOM!
VURUM VURUM
I KNOW! I KNOW!
I SAW IT, I SAW IT! WE LOST OUR ELEMENT OF SURPRISE.
CAN'T WE FLIP ON THE CLOAKING SHIELDS?
THE PRINCE'S SCANNERS HAVE ALREADY SPOTTED THE *NUBBY*.
TOO LATE. HE'S ALREADY SEEN US.
BEEP BEEP!
UM...CAPT? WE GOT A CALL COMING IN FROM HIS SHIP.
BEEP! BEEP BEEP! BEEP! BEEP!
SIGH... GREAT. PATCH IT THROUGH, REGGIE.
HERE YOU GO, CAPT.
PRINCE PALL-TODD, IT LOOKS AS IF WE MEET AGAIN.
PZZT!
YES... CAPTAIN. AN UNEXPECTED PLEASURE, NO DOUBT.
I'M SURE YOU'RE AWARE THAT YOU HAVE FLOWN DANGEROUSLY CLOSE TO MY FRIGHTER, WHICH IS NORMALLY GROUNDS FOR WAR.
BUT I BELIEVE YOUR DOING SO IS TO RETRIEVE THIS LAUGHABLE PIECE OF HEADWEAR.
AM I CORRECT, CAPTAIN?
HEH HEH HEH

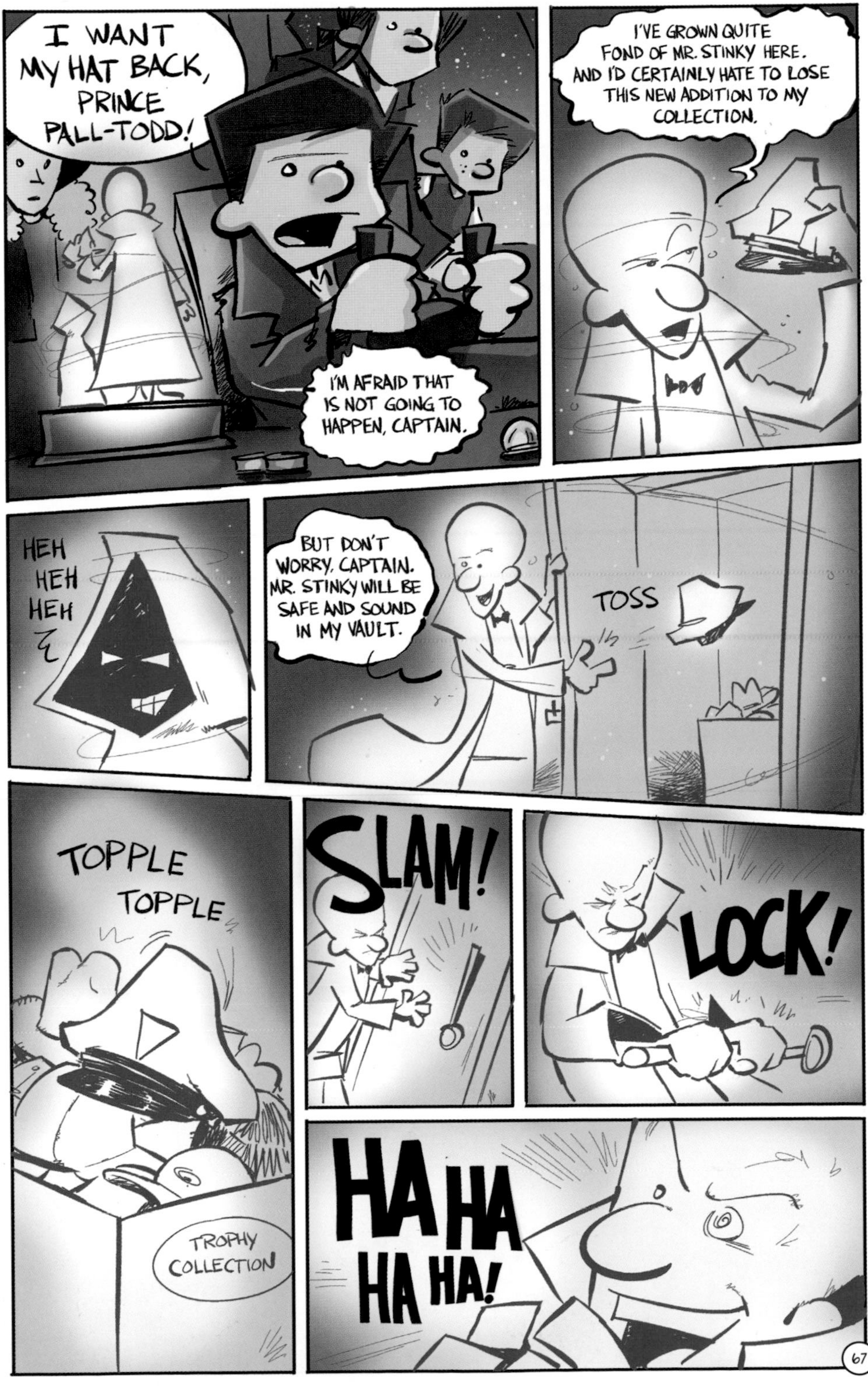
I WANT MY HAT BACK, PRINCE PALL-TODD!
I'M AFRAID THAT IS NOT GOING TO HAPPEN, CAPTAIN.
I'VE GROWN QUITE FOND OF MR. STINKY HERE. AND I'D CERTAINLY HATE TO LOSE THIS NEW ADDITION TO MY COLLECTION.
HEH HEH HEH
BUT DON'T WORRY, CAPTAIN. MR. STINKY WILL BE SAFE AND SOUND IN MY VAULT.
TOSS
TOPPLE TOPPLE
TROPHY COLLECTION
SLAM!
LOCK!
HA HA HA HA!

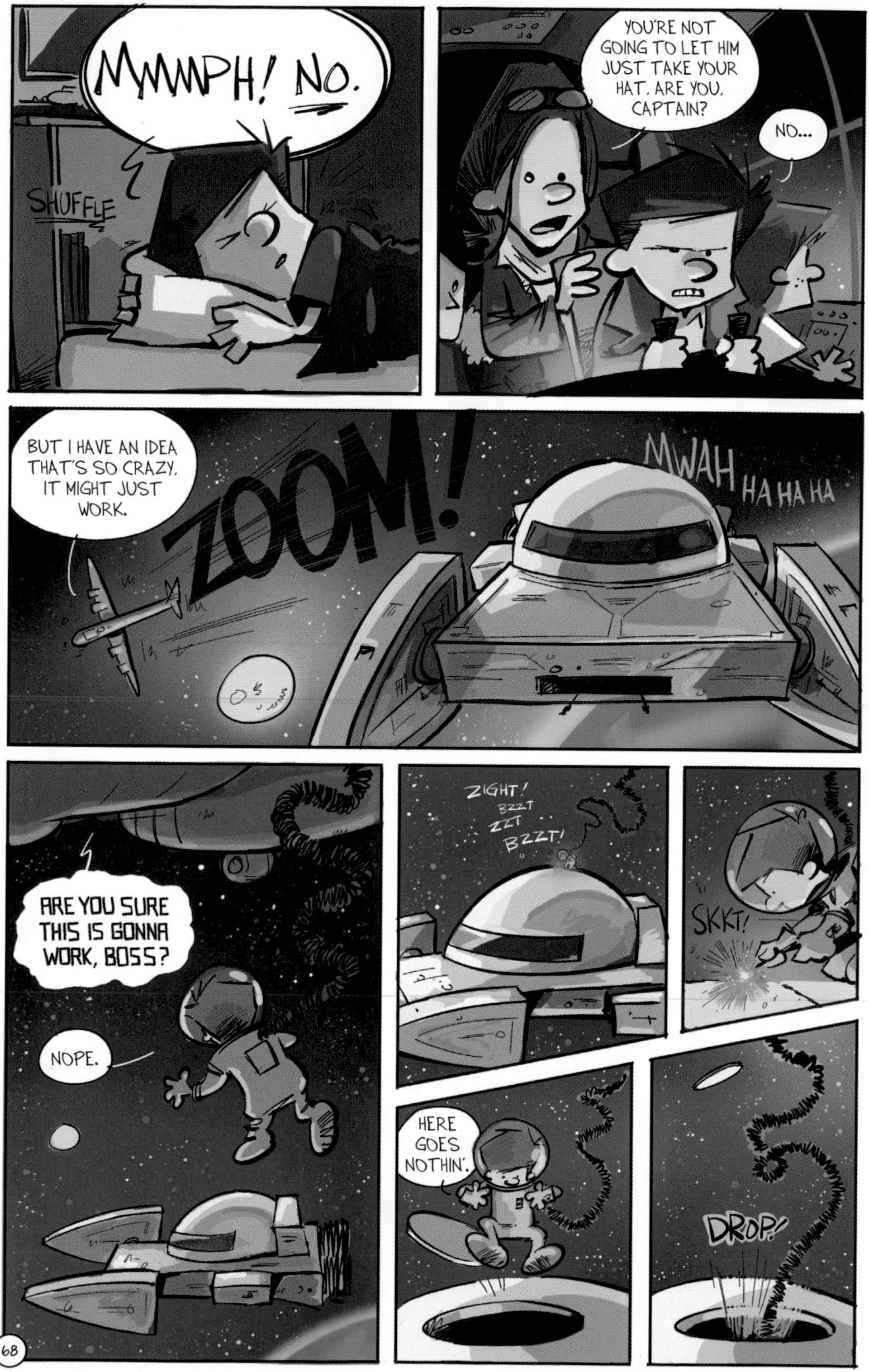

MMMPH! NO.
SHUFFLE
YOU'RE NOT GOING TO LET HIM JUST TAKE YOUR HAT, ARE YOU, CAPTAIN?
NO...
BUT I HAVE AN IDEA THAT'S SO CRAZY, IT MIGHT JUST WORK.
ZOOM!
MWAH HA HA HA
ARE YOU SURE THIS IS GONNA WORK, BOSS?
NOPE.
ZIGHT! BZZT ZZT BZZT!
SKKT!
HERE GOES NOTHIN'.
DROP!

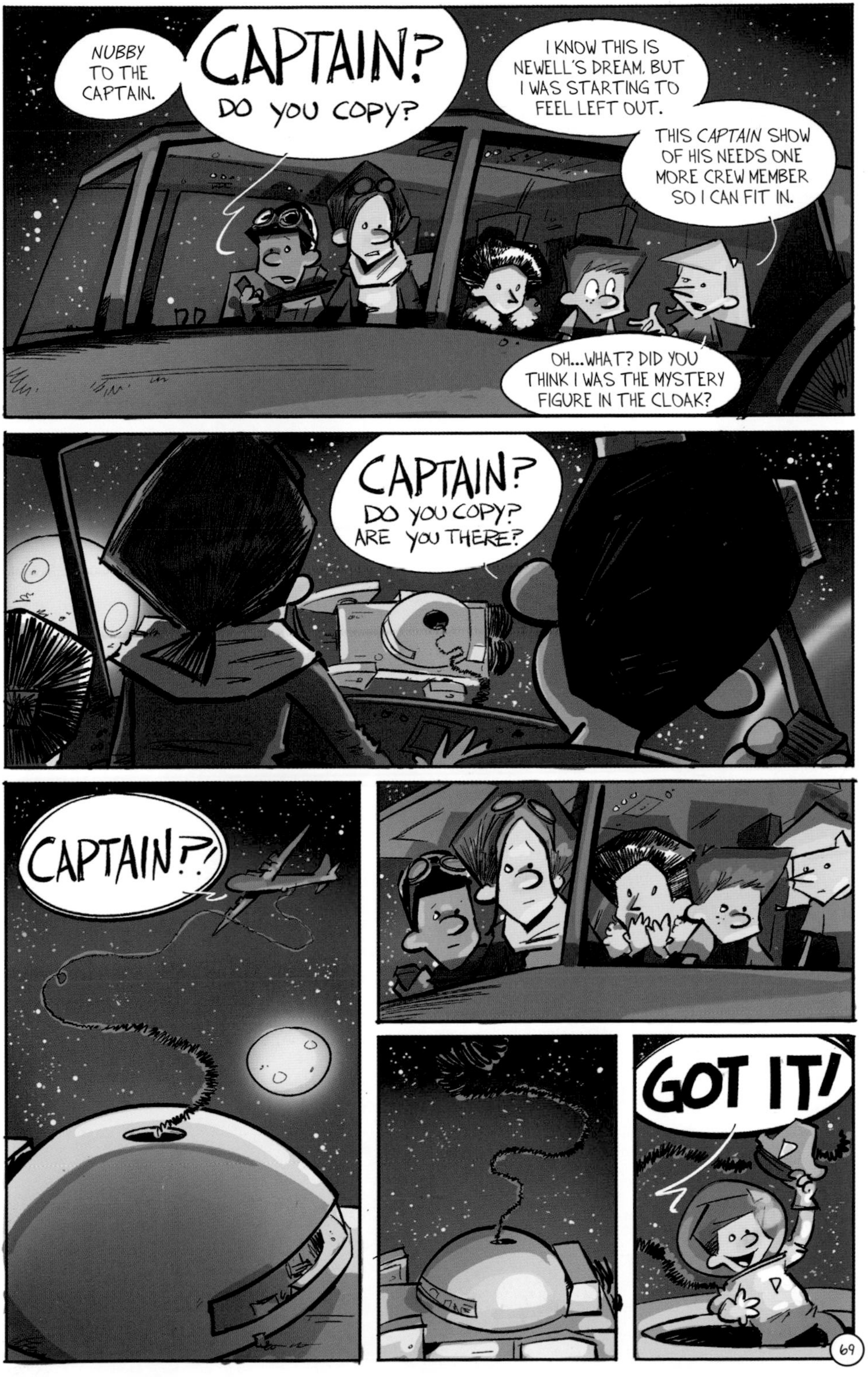
NUBBY TO THE CAPTAIN.
CAPTAIN? DO YOU COPY?
I KNOW THIS IS NEWELL'S DREAM, BUT I WAS STARTING TO FEEL LEFT OUT.
THIS CAPTAIN SHOW OF HIS NEEDS ONE MORE CREW MEMBER SO I CAN FIT IN.
OH...WHAT? DID YOU THINK I WAS THE MYSTERY FIGURE IN THE CLOAK?
CAPTAIN? DO YOU COPY? ARE YOU THERE?
CAPTAIN?!
GOT IT!

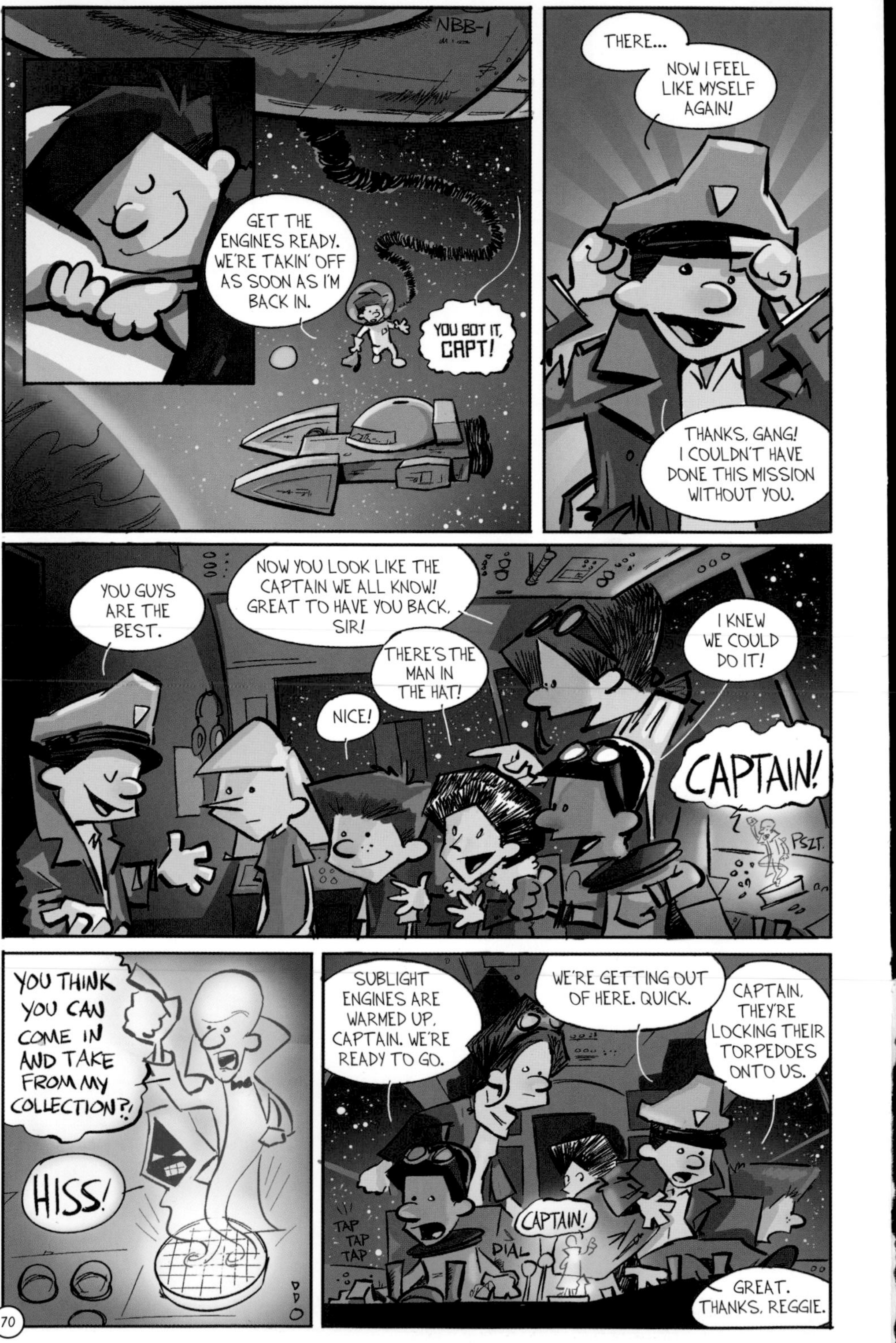
NBB-1
GET THE ENGINES READY. WE'RE TAKIN' OFF AS SOON AS I'M BACK IN.
YOU GOT IT, CAPT!
THERE...
NOW I FEEL LIKE MYSELF AGAIN!
THANKS, GANG! I COULDN'T HAVE DONE THIS MISSION WITHOUT YOU.
YOU GUYS ARE THE BEST.
NOW YOU LOOK LIKE THE CAPTAIN WE ALL KNOW! GREAT TO HAVE YOU BACK, SIR!
NICE!
THERE'S THE MAN IN THE HAT!
I KNEW WE COULD DO IT!
CAPTAIN!
PSZT.
YOU THINK YOU CAN COME IN AND TAKE FROM MY COLLECTION?!
HISS!
SUBLIGHT ENGINES ARE WARMED UP, CAPTAIN. WE'RE READY TO GO.
WE'RE GETTING OUT OF HERE. QUICK.
CAPTAIN, THEY'RE LOCKING THEIR TORPEDOES ONTO US.
TAP TAP TAP
CAPTAIN!
DIAL
GREAT. THANKS, REGGIE.

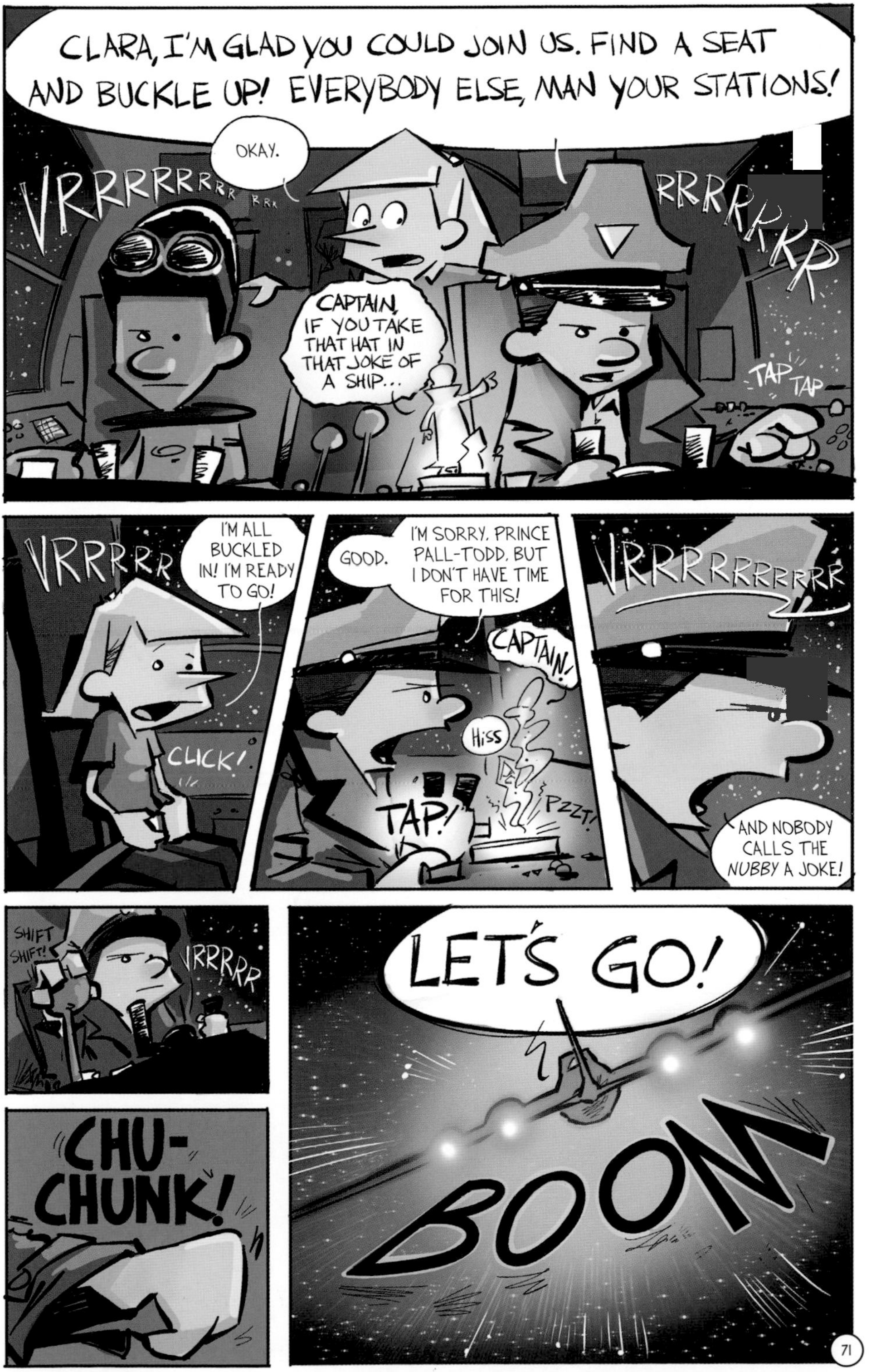

CLARA, I'M GLAD YOU COULD JOIN US. FIND A SEAT AND BUCKLE UP! EVERYBODY ELSE, MAN YOUR STATIONS!
OKAY.
VRRRRRRRR RRR
RRRRR[redacted]KRR
CAPTAIN, IF YOU TAKE THAT HAT IN THAT JOKE OF A SHIP...
TAP TAP
VRRRRRR
I'M ALL BUCKLED IN! I'M READY TO GO!
CLICK!
GOOD.
I'M SORRY, PRINCE PALL-TODD, BUT I DON'T HAVE TIME FOR THIS!
CAPTAIN!
HISS
TAP!
PZZT!
VRRRRRRRRRRR
AND NOBODY CALLS THE NUBBY A JOKE!
SHIFT SHIFT!
VRRRRR
CHU-CHUNK!
LET'S GO!
BOOM

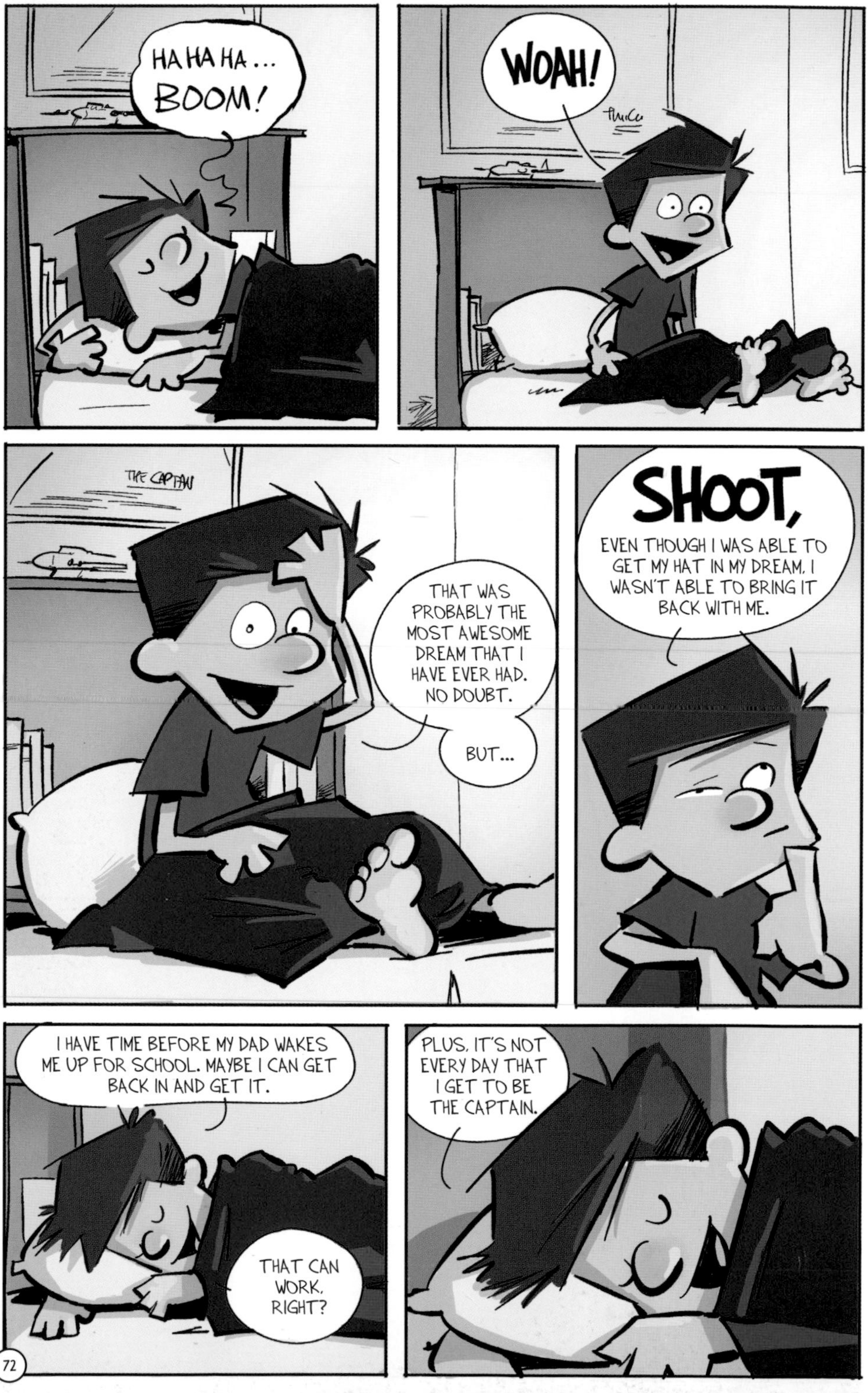
HA HA HA ... BOOM!
WOAH!
THAT WAS PROBABLY THE MOST AWESOME DREAM THAT I HAVE EVER HAD. NO DOUBT.
BUT...
SHOOT,
EVEN THOUGH I WAS ABLE TO GET MY HAT IN MY DREAM, I WASN'T ABLE TO BRING IT BACK WITH ME.
I HAVE TIME BEFORE MY DAD WAKES ME UP FOR SCHOOL. MAYBE I CAN GET BACK IN AND GET IT.
THAT CAN WORK, RIGHT?
PLUS, IT'S NOT EVERY DAY THAT I GET TO BE THE CAPTAIN.

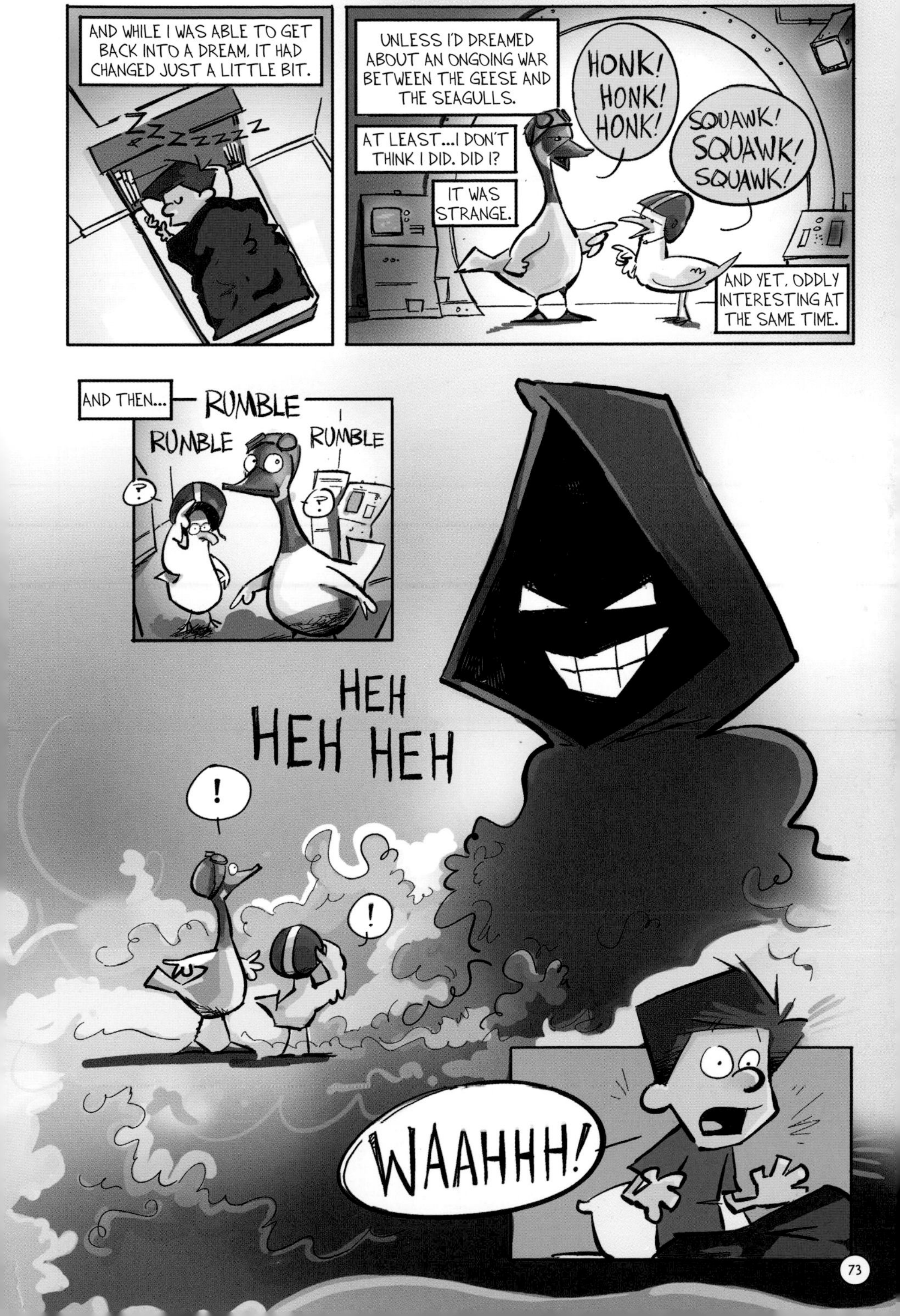
AND WHILE I WAS ABLE TO GET BACK INTO A DREAM, IT HAD CHANGED JUST A LITTLE BIT.
ZZZZZZZZ
UNLESS I'D DREAMED ABOUT AN ONGOING WAR BETWEEN THE GEESE AND THE SEAGULLS.
AT LEAST...I DON'T THINK I DID. DID I?
IT WAS STRANGE.
HONK! HONK! HONK!
SQUAWK! SQUAWK! SQUAWK!
AND YET, ODDLY INTERESTING AT THE SAME TIME.
AND THEN...
RUMBLE
RUMBLE
RUMBLE
?
?
HEH
HEH HEH
!
!
WAAHHH!

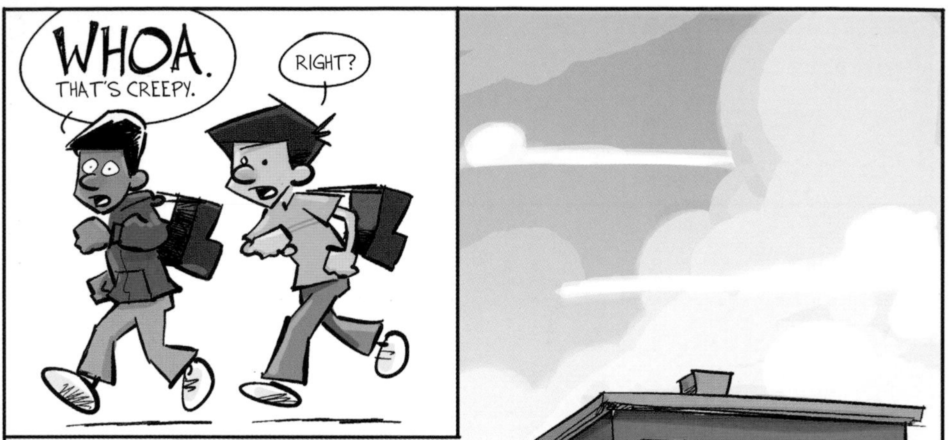
WHOA. THAT'S CREEPY.
RIGHT?
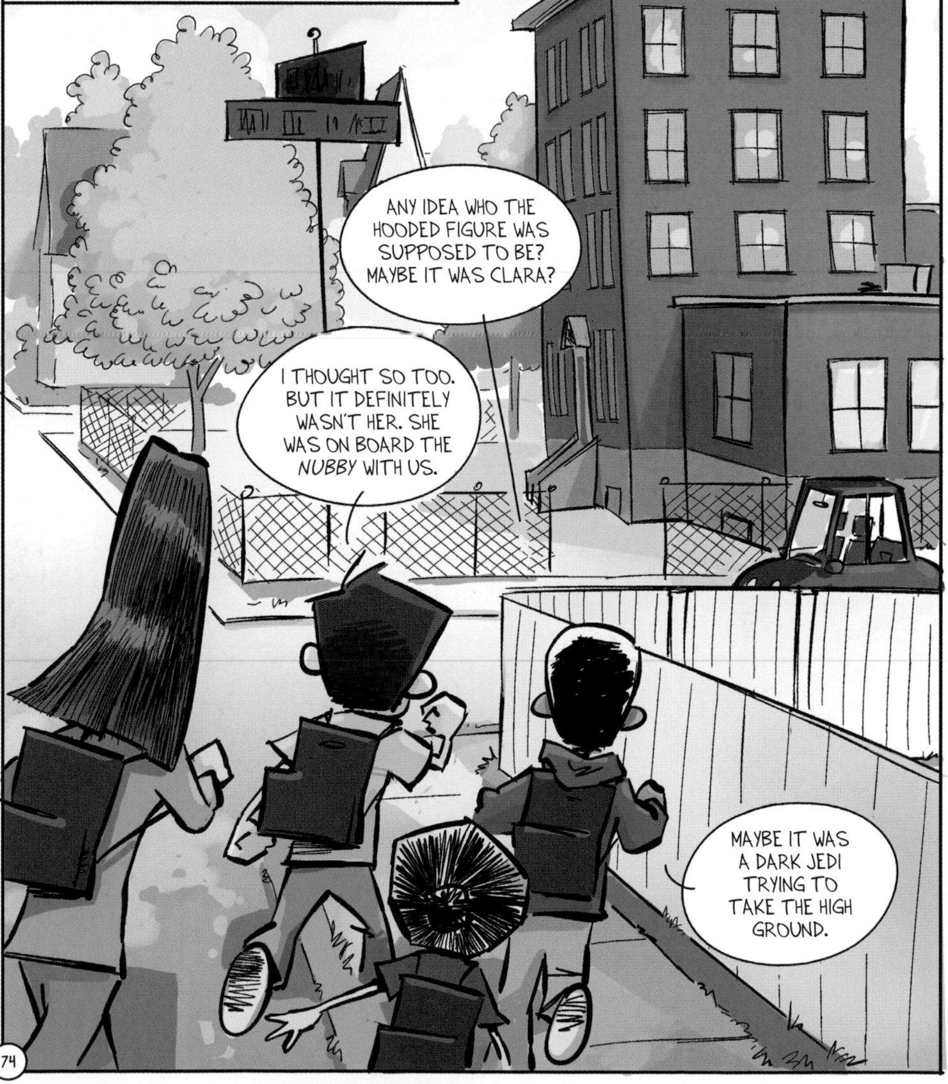
ANY IDEA WHO THE HOODED FIGURE WAS SUPPOSED TO BE? MAYBE IT WAS CLARA?
I THOUGHT SO TOO. BUT IT DEFINITELY WASN'T HER. SHE WAS ON BOARD THE *NUBBY* WITH US.
MAYBE IT WAS A DARK JEDI TRYING TO TAKE THE HIGH GROUND.

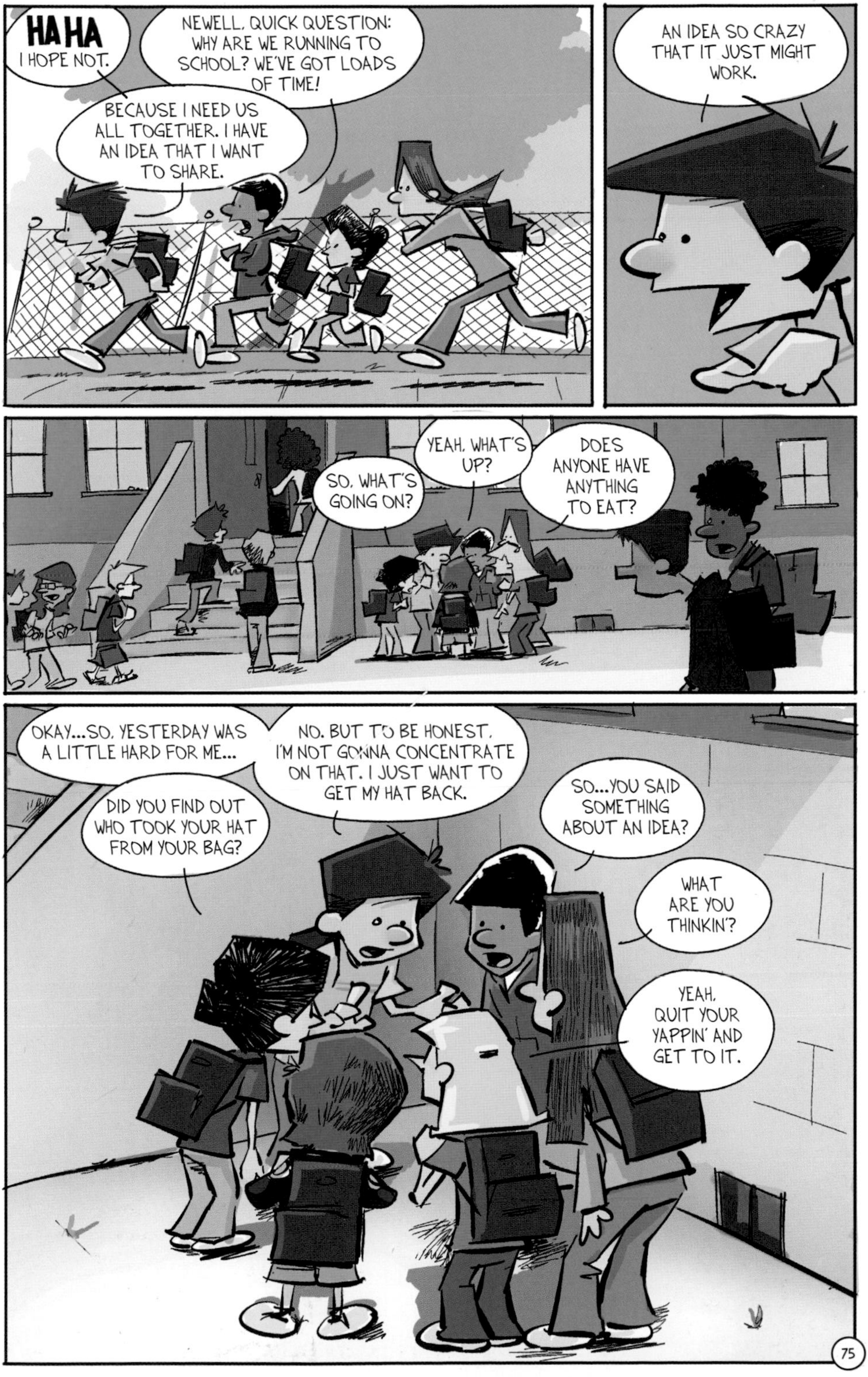

HAHA I HOPE NOT.
NEWELL, QUICK QUESTION: WHY ARE WE RUNNING TO SCHOOL? WE'VE GOT LOADS OF TIME!
BECAUSE I NEED US ALL TOGETHER. I HAVE AN IDEA THAT I WANT TO SHARE.
AN IDEA SO CRAZY THAT IT JUST MIGHT WORK.
SO, WHAT'S GOING ON?
YEAH, WHAT'S UP?
DOES ANYONE HAVE ANYTHING TO EAT?
OKAY...SO, YESTERDAY WAS A LITTLE HARD FOR ME...
DID YOU FIND OUT WHO TOOK YOUR HAT FROM YOUR BAG?
NO. BUT TO BE HONEST, I'M NOT GONNA CONCENTRATE ON THAT. I JUST WANT TO GET MY HAT BACK.
SO...YOU SAID SOMETHING ABOUT AN IDEA?
WHAT ARE YOU THINKIN'?
YEAH, QUIT YOUR YAPPIN' AND GET TO IT.

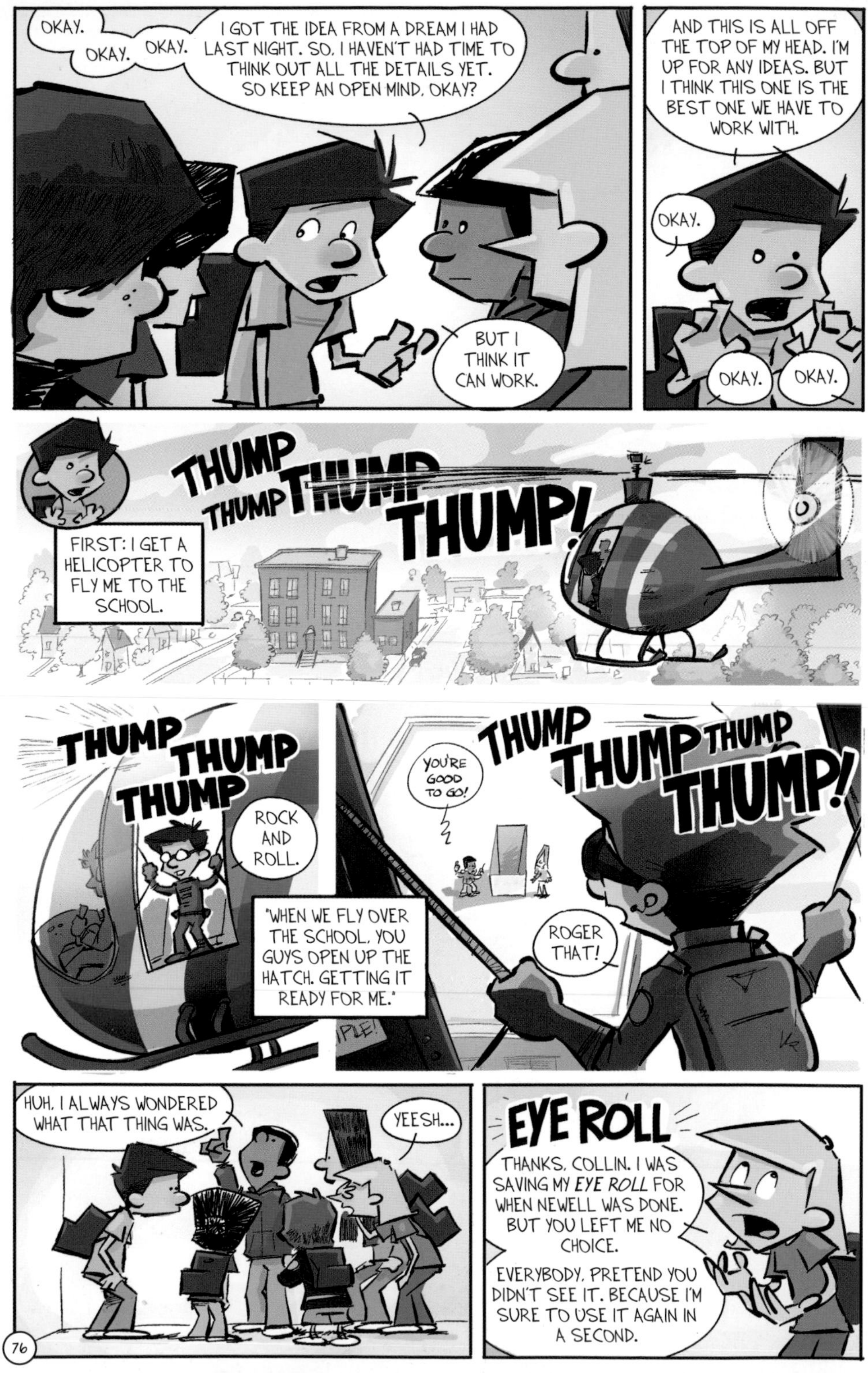
OKAY.
OKAY.
OKAY.
I GOT THE IDEA FROM A DREAM I HAD LAST NIGHT. SO, I HAVEN'T HAD TIME TO THINK OUT ALL THE DETAILS YET. SO KEEP AN OPEN MIND, OKAY?
BUT I THINK IT CAN WORK.
AND THIS IS ALL OFF THE TOP OF MY HEAD. I'M UP FOR ANY IDEAS. BUT I THINK THIS ONE IS THE BEST ONE WE HAVE TO WORK WITH.
OKAY.
OKAY.
OKAY.
THUMP THUMP THUMP THUMP!
FIRST: I GET A HELICOPTER TO FLY ME TO THE SCHOOL.
THUMP THUMP THUMP
ROCK AND ROLL.
"WHEN WE FLY OVER THE SCHOOL, YOU GUYS OPEN UP THE HATCH. GETTING IT READY FOR ME."
THUMP THUMP THUMP THUMP!
YOU'RE GOOD TO GO!
ROGER THAT!
HUH, I ALWAYS WONDERED WHAT THAT THING WAS.
YEESH...
EYE ROLL
THANKS, COLLIN. I WAS SAVING MY *EYE ROLL* FOR WHEN NEWELL WAS DONE. BUT YOU LEFT ME NO CHOICE.
EVERYBODY, PRETEND YOU DIDN'T SEE IT. BECAUSE I'M SURE TO USE IT AGAIN IN A SECOND.

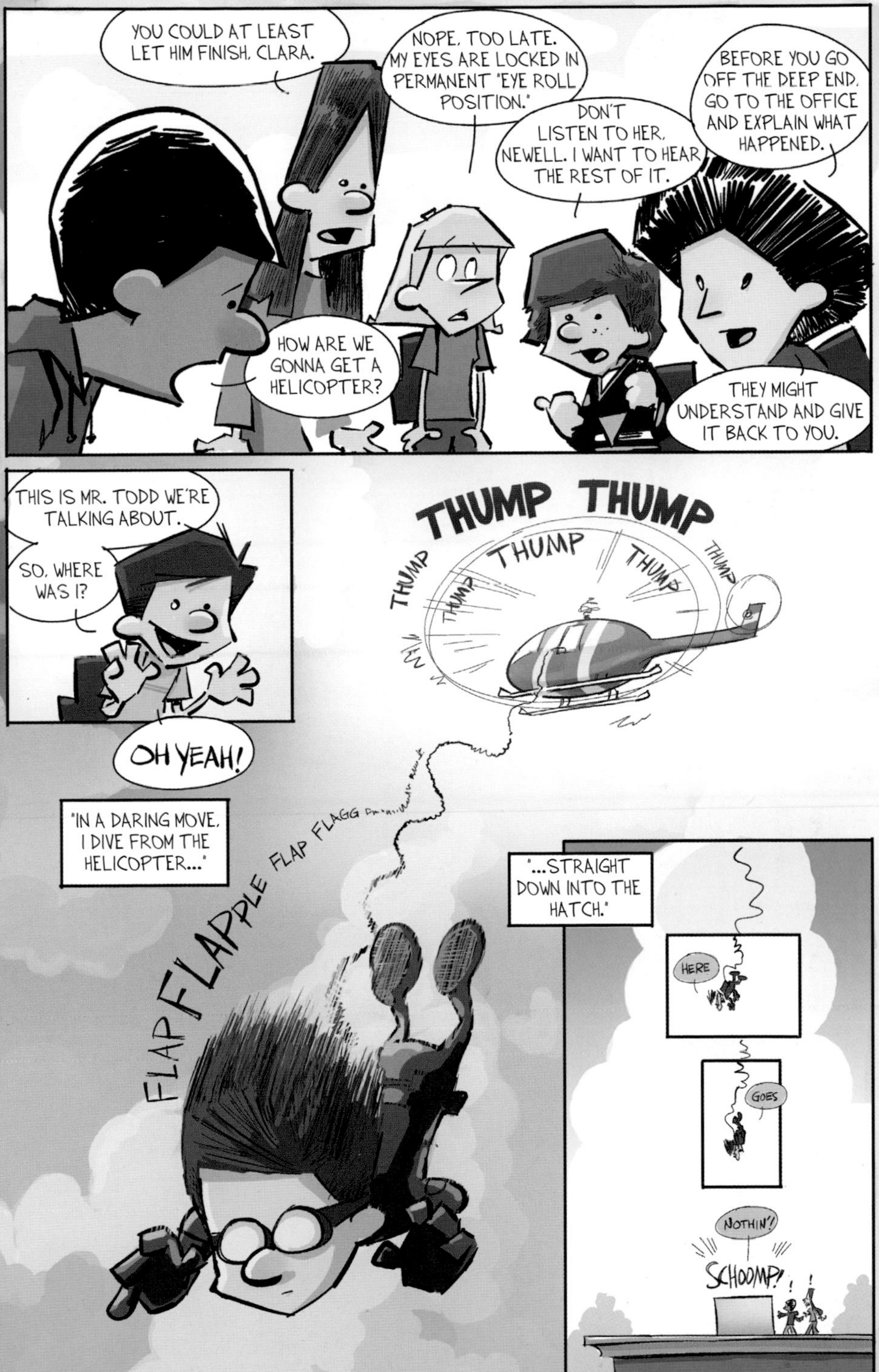
YOU COULD AT LEAST LET HIM FINISH, CLARA.
NOPE, TOO LATE. MY EYES ARE LOCKED IN PERMANENT "EYE ROLL POSITION."
DON'T LISTEN TO HER, NEWELL. I WANT TO HEAR THE REST OF IT.
BEFORE YOU GO OFF THE DEEP END, GO TO THE OFFICE AND EXPLAIN WHAT HAPPENED.
HOW ARE WE GONNA GET A HELICOPTER?
THEY MIGHT UNDERSTAND AND GIVE IT BACK TO YOU.
THIS IS MR. TODD WE'RE TALKING ABOUT.
SO, WHERE WAS I?
OH YEAH!
THUMP THUMP
THUMP THUMP THUMP THUMP THUMP THUMP
"IN A DARING MOVE, I DIVE FROM THE HELICOPTER..."
FLAP FLAPPLE FLAP FLAGG
"...STRAIGHT DOWN INTO THE HATCH."
HERE
GOES
NOTHIN'!
SCHOOMP!

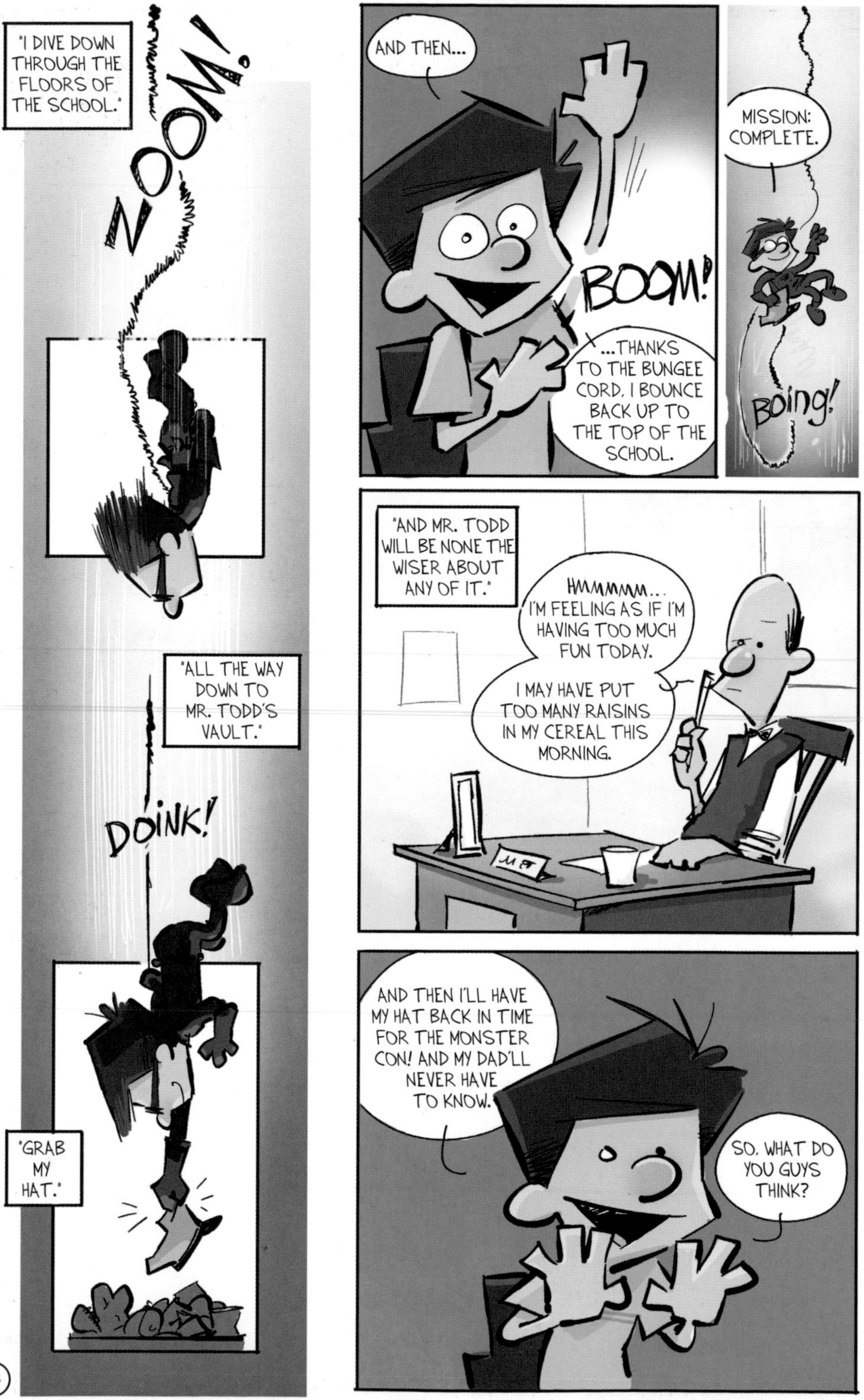
"I DIVE DOWN THROUGH THE FLOORS OF THE SCHOOL."
ZOOM!
"ALL THE WAY DOWN TO MR. TODD'S VAULT."
DOINK!
"GRAB MY HAT."
AND THEN...
BOOM!
...THANKS TO THE BUNGEE CORD, I BOUNCE BACK UP TO THE TOP OF THE SCHOOL.
MISSION: COMPLETE.
BOING!
"AND MR. TODD WILL BE NONE THE WISER ABOUT ANY OF IT."
HMMMMM... I'M FEELING AS IF I'M HAVING TOO MUCH FUN TODAY.
I MAY HAVE PUT TOO MANY RAISINS IN MY CEREAL THIS MORNING.
AND THEN I'LL HAVE MY HAT BACK IN TIME FOR THE MONSTER CON! AND MY DAD'LL NEVER HAVE TO KNOW.
SO, WHAT DO YOU GUYS THINK?

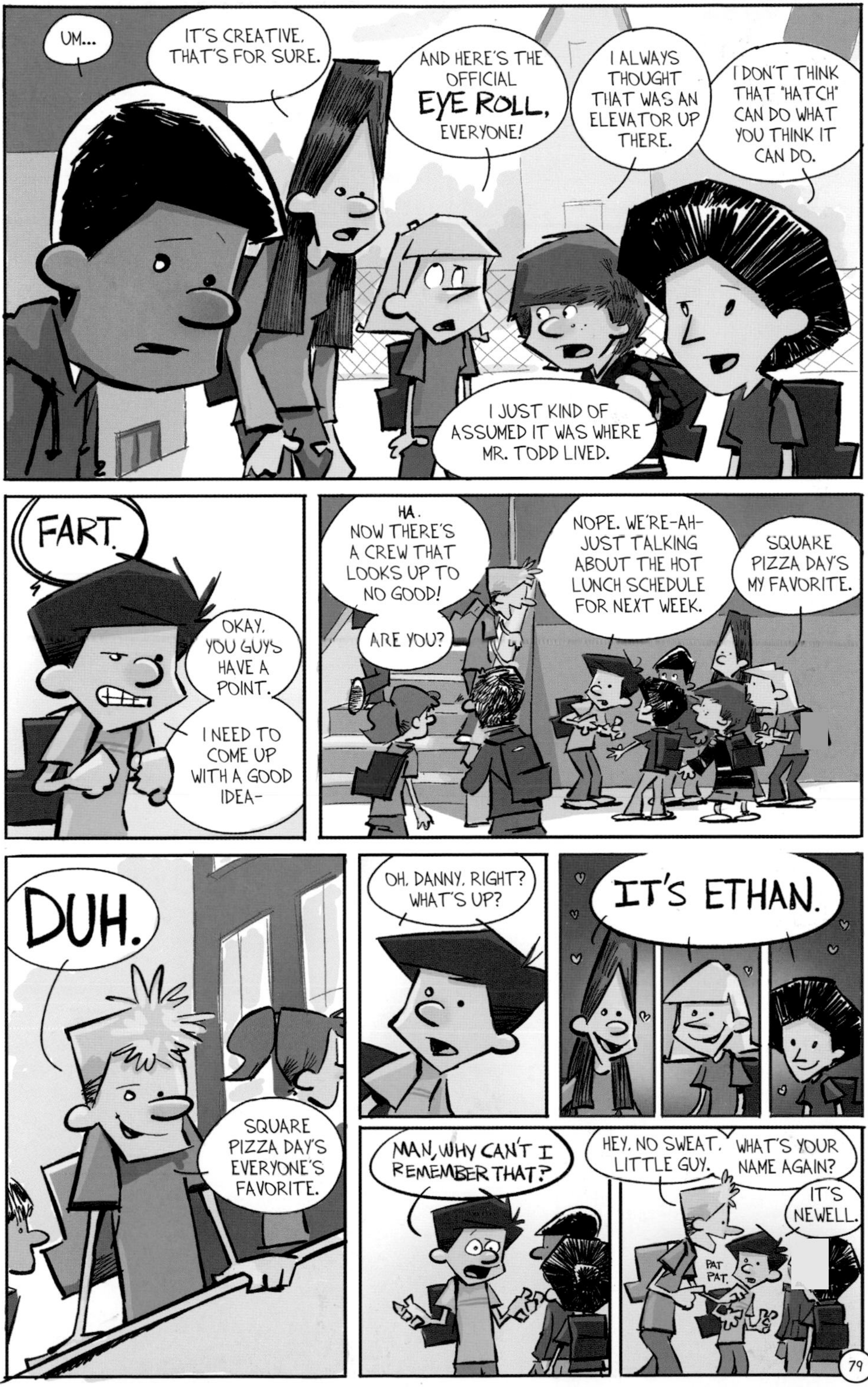
UM...
IT'S CREATIVE, THAT'S FOR SURE.
AND HERE'S THE OFFICIAL EYE ROLL, EVERYONE!
I ALWAYS THOUGHT THAT WAS AN ELEVATOR UP THERE.
I DON'T THINK THAT "HATCH" CAN DO WHAT YOU THINK IT CAN DO.
I JUST KIND OF ASSUMED IT WAS WHERE MR. TODD LIVED.
FART.
OKAY, YOU GUYS HAVE A POINT.
I NEED TO COME UP WITH A GOOD IDEA-
HA. NOW THERE'S A CREW THAT LOOKS UP TO NO GOOD!
ARE YOU?
NOPE. WE'RE-AH- JUST TALKING ABOUT THE HOT LUNCH SCHEDULE FOR NEXT WEEK.
SQUARE PIZZA DAY'S MY FAVORITE.
DUH.
SQUARE PIZZA DAY'S EVERYONE'S FAVORITE.
OH, DANNY, RIGHT? WHAT'S UP?
IT'S ETHAN.
MAN, WHY CAN'T I REMEMBER THAT?
HEY, NO SWEAT, LITTLE GUY.
WHAT'S YOUR NAME AGAIN?
PAT PAT.
IT'S NEWELL.

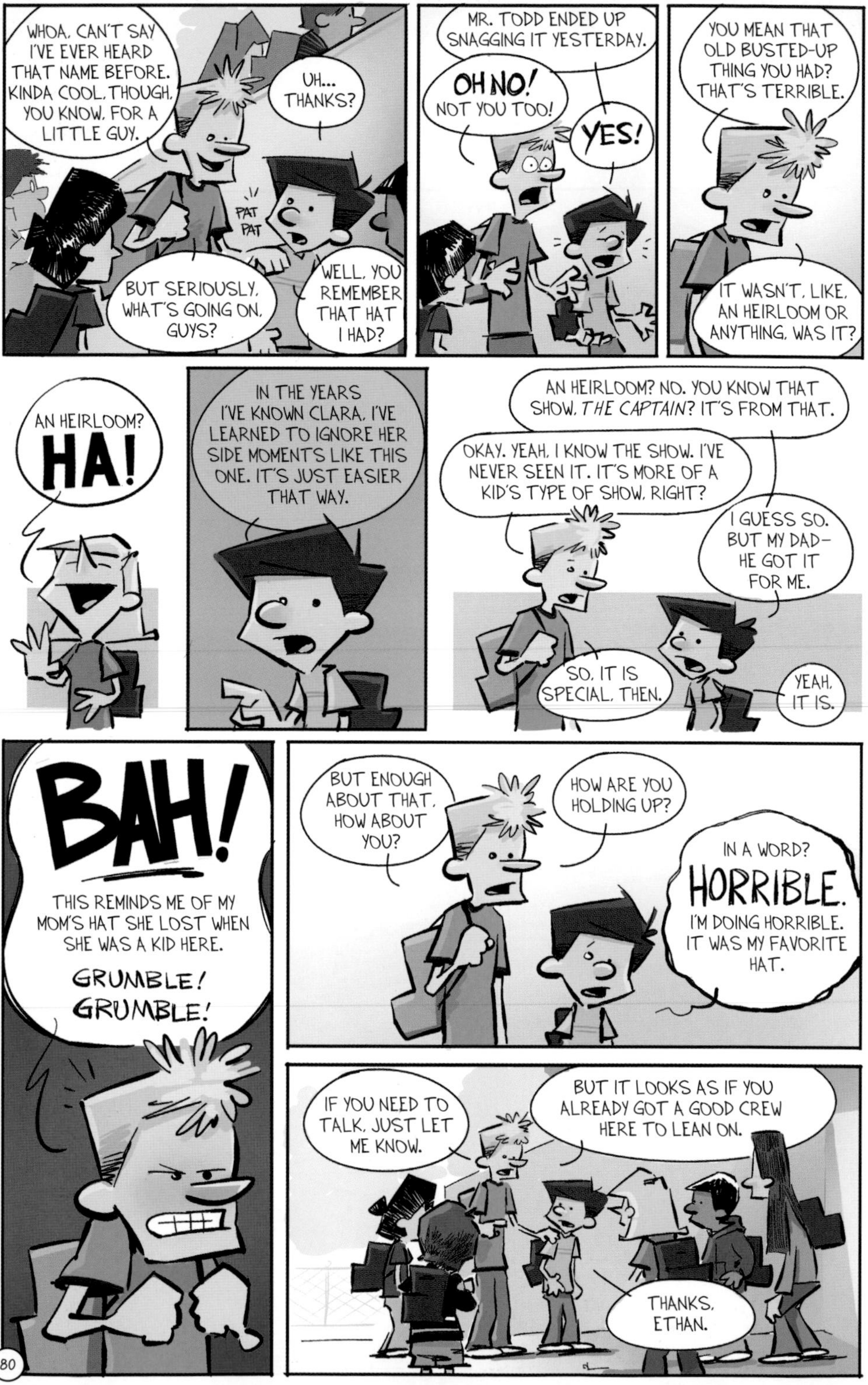
WHOA, CAN'T SAY I'VE EVER HEARD THAT NAME BEFORE. KINDA COOL, THOUGH, YOU KNOW, FOR A LITTLE GUY.
UH... THANKS?
PAT PAT
BUT SERIOUSLY, WHAT'S GOING ON, GUYS?
WELL, YOU REMEMBER THAT HAT I HAD?
MR. TODD ENDED UP SNAGGING IT YESTERDAY.
OH NO! NOT YOU TOO!
YES!
YOU MEAN THAT OLD BUSTED-UP THING YOU HAD? THAT'S TERRIBLE.
IT WASN'T, LIKE, AN HEIRLOOM OR ANYTHING, WAS IT?
AN HEIRLOOM? HA!
IN THE YEARS I'VE KNOWN CLARA, I'VE LEARNED TO IGNORE HER SIDE MOMENTS LIKE THIS ONE. IT'S JUST EASIER THAT WAY.
AN HEIRLOOM? NO. YOU KNOW THAT SHOW, *THE CAPTAIN*? IT'S FROM THAT.
OKAY. YEAH, I KNOW THE SHOW. I'VE NEVER SEEN IT. IT'S MORE OF A KID'S TYPE OF SHOW, RIGHT?
I GUESS SO. BUT MY DAD— HE GOT IT FOR ME.
SO, IT IS SPECIAL, THEN.
YEAH, IT IS.
BAH!
THIS REMINDS ME OF MY MOM'S HAT SHE LOST WHEN SHE WAS A KID HERE.
GRUMBLE! GRUMBLE!
BUT ENOUGH ABOUT THAT, HOW ABOUT YOU?
HOW ARE YOU HOLDING UP?
IN A WORD? HORRIBLE. I'M DOING HORRIBLE. IT WAS MY FAVORITE HAT.
IF YOU NEED TO TALK, JUST LET ME KNOW.
BUT IT LOOKS AS IF YOU ALREADY GOT A GOOD CREW HERE TO LEAN ON.
THANKS, ETHAN.

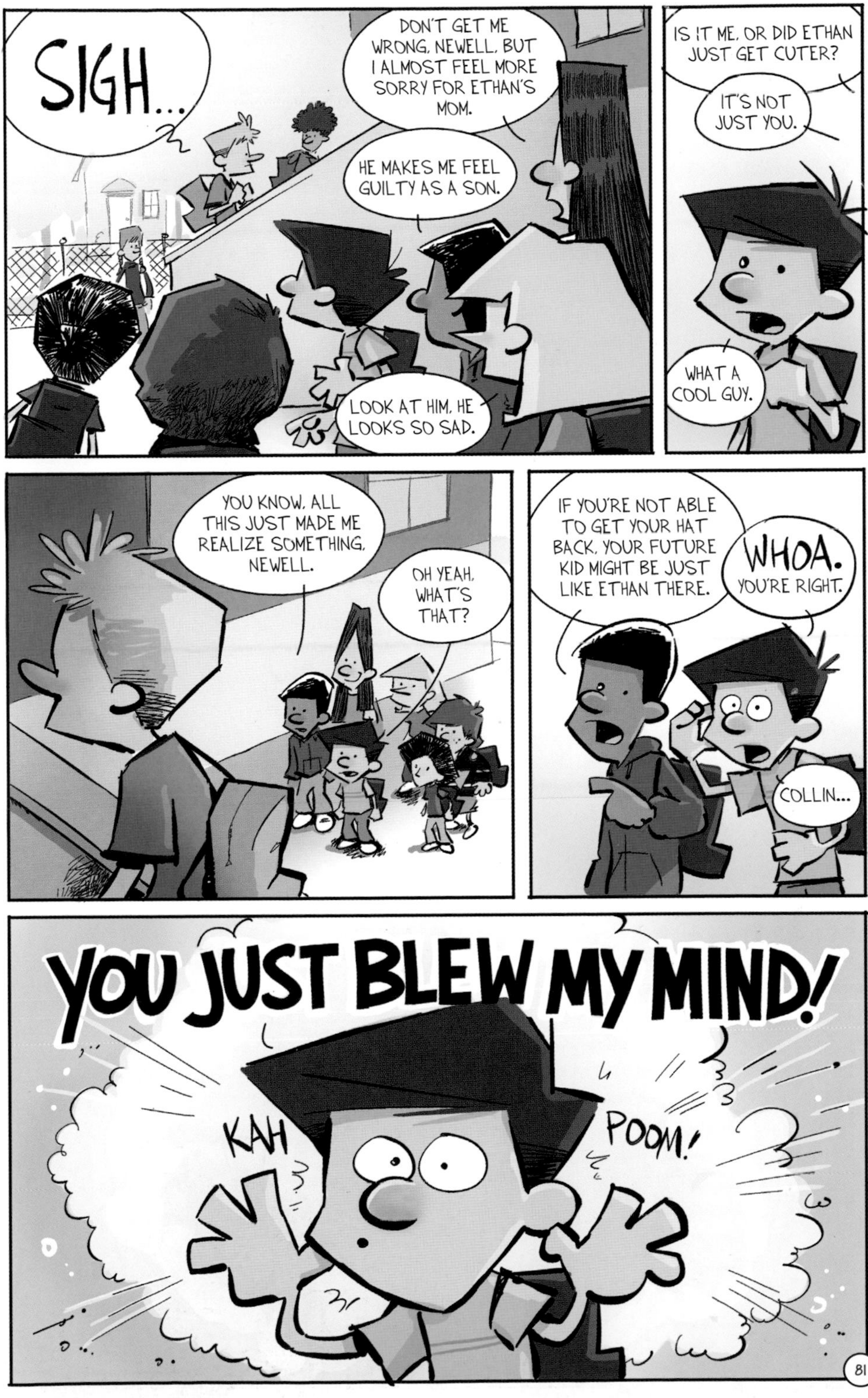
SIGH...
DON'T GET ME WRONG, NEWELL, BUT I ALMOST FEEL MORE SORRY FOR ETHAN'S MOM.
HE MAKES ME FEEL GUILTY AS A SON.
LOOK AT HIM, HE LOOKS SO SAD.
IS IT ME, OR DID ETHAN JUST GET CUTER?
IT'S NOT JUST YOU.
WHAT A COOL GUY.
YOU KNOW, ALL THIS JUST MADE ME REALIZE SOMETHING, NEWELL.
OH YEAH, WHAT'S THAT?
IF YOU'RE NOT ABLE TO GET YOUR HAT BACK, YOUR FUTURE KID MIGHT BE JUST LIKE ETHAN THERE.
WHOA.
YOU'RE RIGHT.
COLLIN...
YOU JUST BLEW MY MIND!
KAH
POOM!

CHAPTER FIVE
THE SETUP

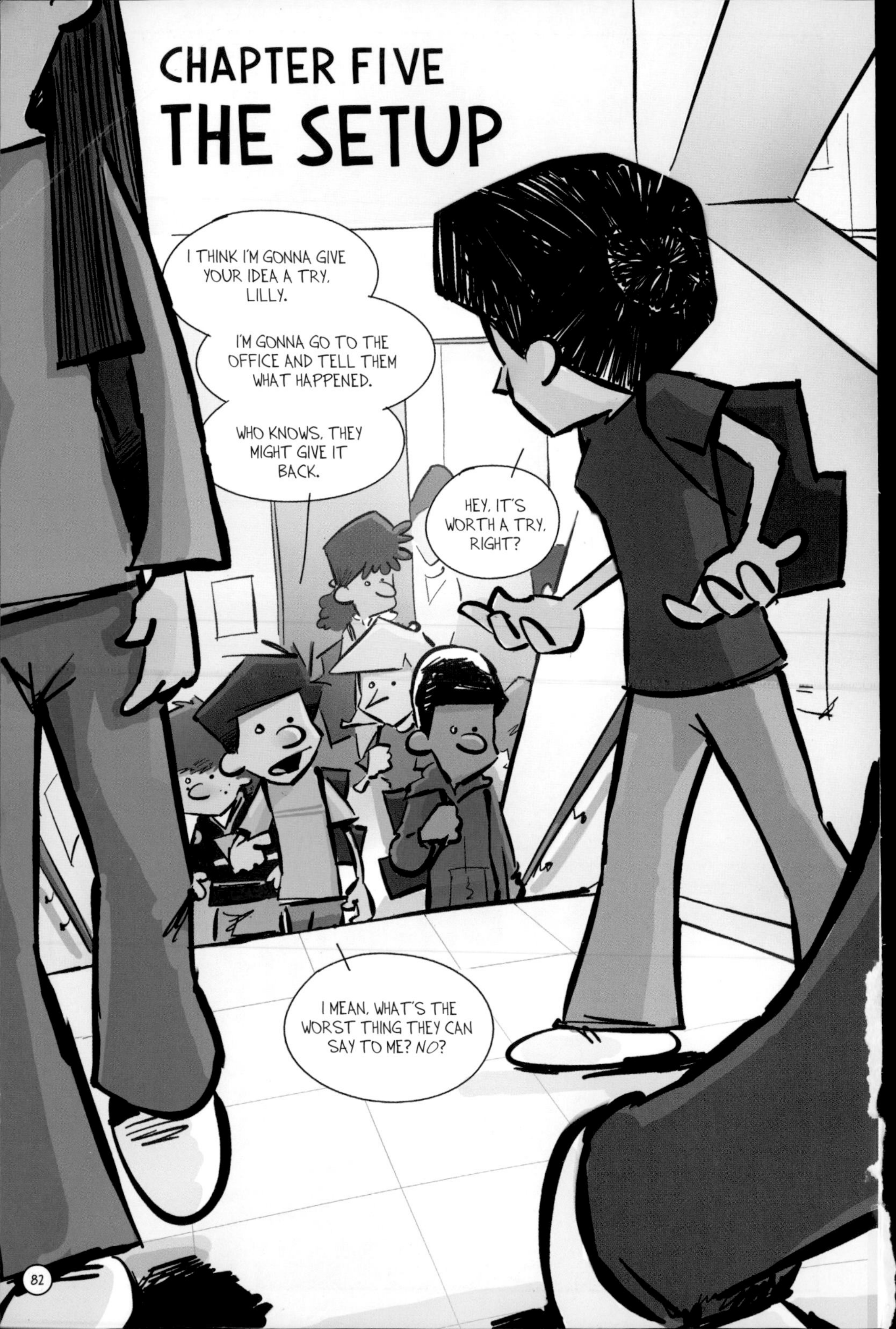
I THINK I'M GONNA GIVE YOUR IDEA A TRY, LILLY.
I'M GONNA GO TO THE OFFICE AND TELL THEM WHAT HAPPENED.
WHO KNOWS, THEY MIGHT GIVE IT BACK.
HEY, IT'S WORTH A TRY, RIGHT?
I MEAN, WHAT'S THE WORST THING THEY CAN SAY TO ME? *NO*?

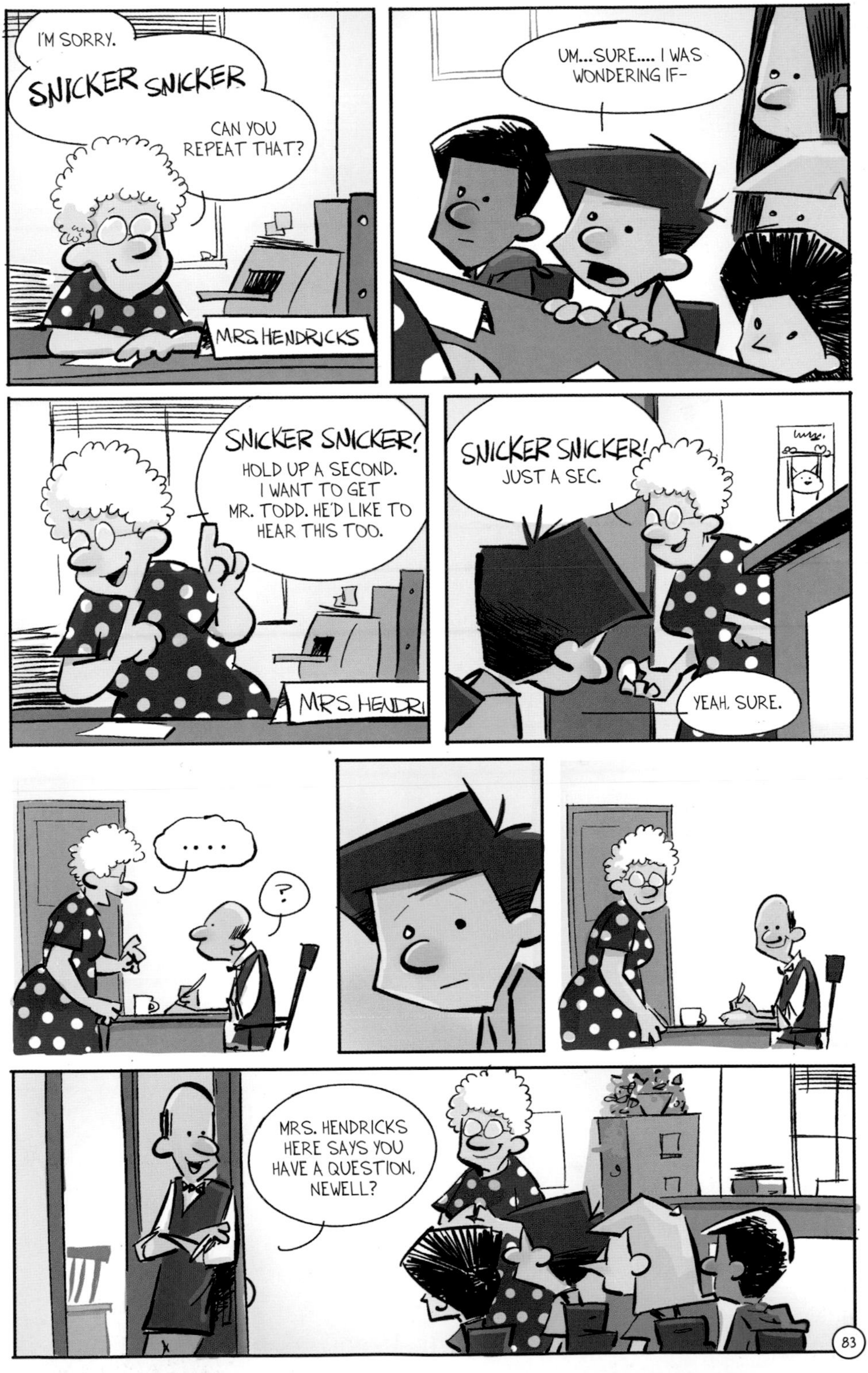
I'M SORRY.
SNICKER SNICKER
CAN YOU REPEAT THAT?
MRS. HENDRICKS
UM... SURE.... I WAS WONDERING IF-
SNICKER SNICKER!
HOLD UP A SECOND. I WANT TO GET MR. TODD. HE'D LIKE TO HEAR THIS TOO.
MRS. HENDRI
SNICKER SNICKER!
JUST A SEC.
YEAH, SURE.
....
?
MRS. HENDRICKS HERE SAYS YOU HAVE A QUESTION, NEWELL?

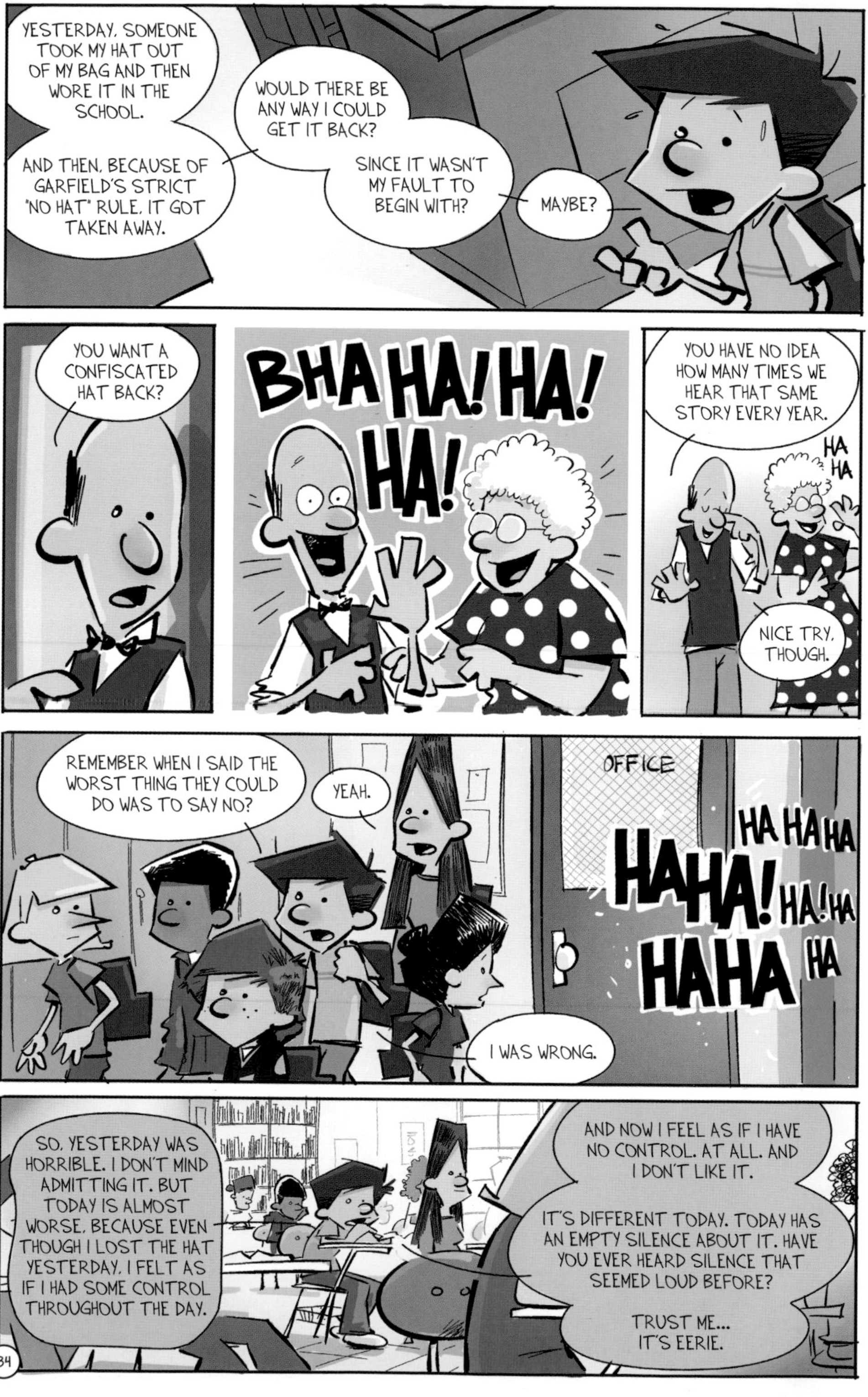
YESTERDAY, SOMEONE TOOK MY HAT OUT OF MY BAG AND THEN WORE IT IN THE SCHOOL.
AND THEN, BECAUSE OF GARFIELD'S STRICT "NO HAT" RULE, IT GOT TAKEN AWAY.
WOULD THERE BE ANY WAY I COULD GET IT BACK?
SINCE IT WASN'T MY FAULT TO BEGIN WITH?
MAYBE?
YOU WANT A CONFISCATED HAT BACK?
BHA HA! HA! HA!
YOU HAVE NO IDEA HOW MANY TIMES WE HEAR THAT SAME STORY EVERY YEAR.
HA HA
NICE TRY, THOUGH.
REMEMBER WHEN I SAID THE WORST THING THEY COULD DO WAS TO SAY NO?
YEAH.
OFFICE
HA HA HA HAHA! HA! HA HAHA HA
I WAS WRONG.
SO, YESTERDAY WAS HORRIBLE. I DON'T MIND ADMITTING IT. BUT TODAY IS ALMOST WORSE, BECAUSE EVEN THOUGH I LOST THE HAT YESTERDAY, I FELT AS IF I HAD SOME CONTROL THROUGHOUT THE DAY.
AND NOW I FEEL AS IF I HAVE NO CONTROL. AT ALL. AND I DON'T LIKE IT.
IT'S DIFFERENT TODAY. TODAY HAS AN EMPTY SILENCE ABOUT IT. HAVE YOU EVER HEARD SILENCE THAT SEEMED LOUD BEFORE?
TRUST ME... IT'S EERIE.

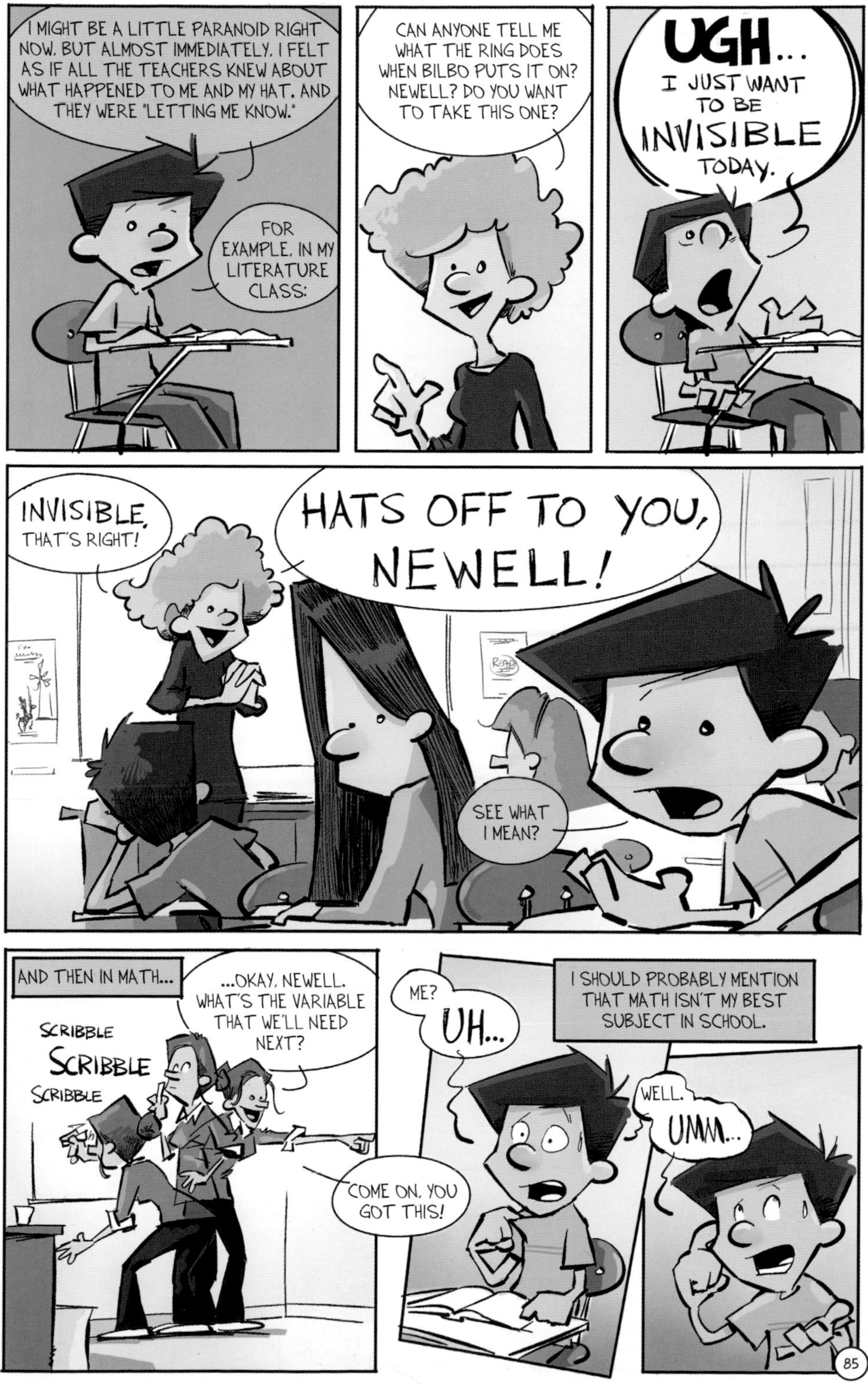
I MIGHT BE A LITTLE PARANOID RIGHT NOW, BUT ALMOST IMMEDIATELY, I FELT AS IF ALL THE TEACHERS KNEW ABOUT WHAT HAPPENED TO ME AND MY HAT. AND THEY WERE "LETTING ME KNOW."
FOR EXAMPLE, IN MY LITERATURE CLASS:
CAN ANYONE TELL ME WHAT THE RING DOES WHEN BILBO PUTS IT ON? NEWELL? DO YOU WANT TO TAKE THIS ONE?
UGH... I JUST WANT TO BE INVISIBLE TODAY.
INVISIBLE, THAT'S RIGHT!
HATS OFF TO YOU, NEWELL!
SEE WHAT I MEAN?
AND THEN IN MATH...
...OKAY, NEWELL. WHAT'S THE VARIABLE THAT WE'LL NEED NEXT?
SCRIBBLE
SCRIBBLE
SCRIBBLE
COME ON, YOU GOT THIS!
ME? UH...
I SHOULD PROBABLY MENTION THAT MATH ISN'T MY BEST SUBJECT IN SCHOOL.
WELL. UMM...

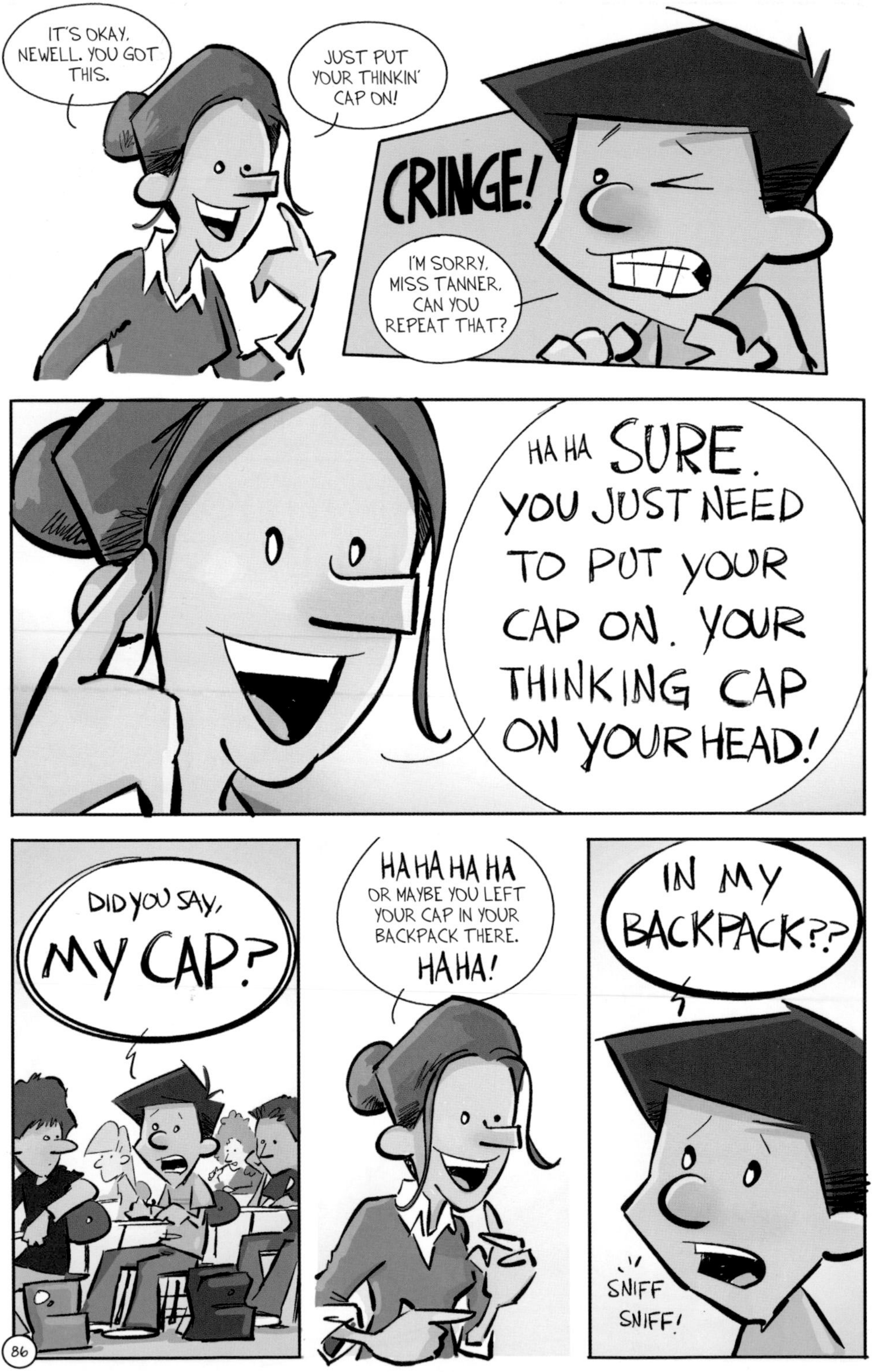
IT'S OKAY, NEWELL. YOU GOT THIS.
JUST PUT YOUR THINKIN' CAP ON!
CRINGE!
I'M SORRY, MISS TANNER, CAN YOU REPEAT THAT?
HA HA SURE. YOU JUST NEED TO PUT YOUR CAP ON. YOUR THINKING CAP ON YOUR HEAD!
DID YOU SAY, MY CAP?
HA HA HA HA OR MAYBE YOU LEFT YOUR CAP IN YOUR BACKPACK THERE. HA HA!
IN MY BACKPACK??
SNIFF SNIFF!

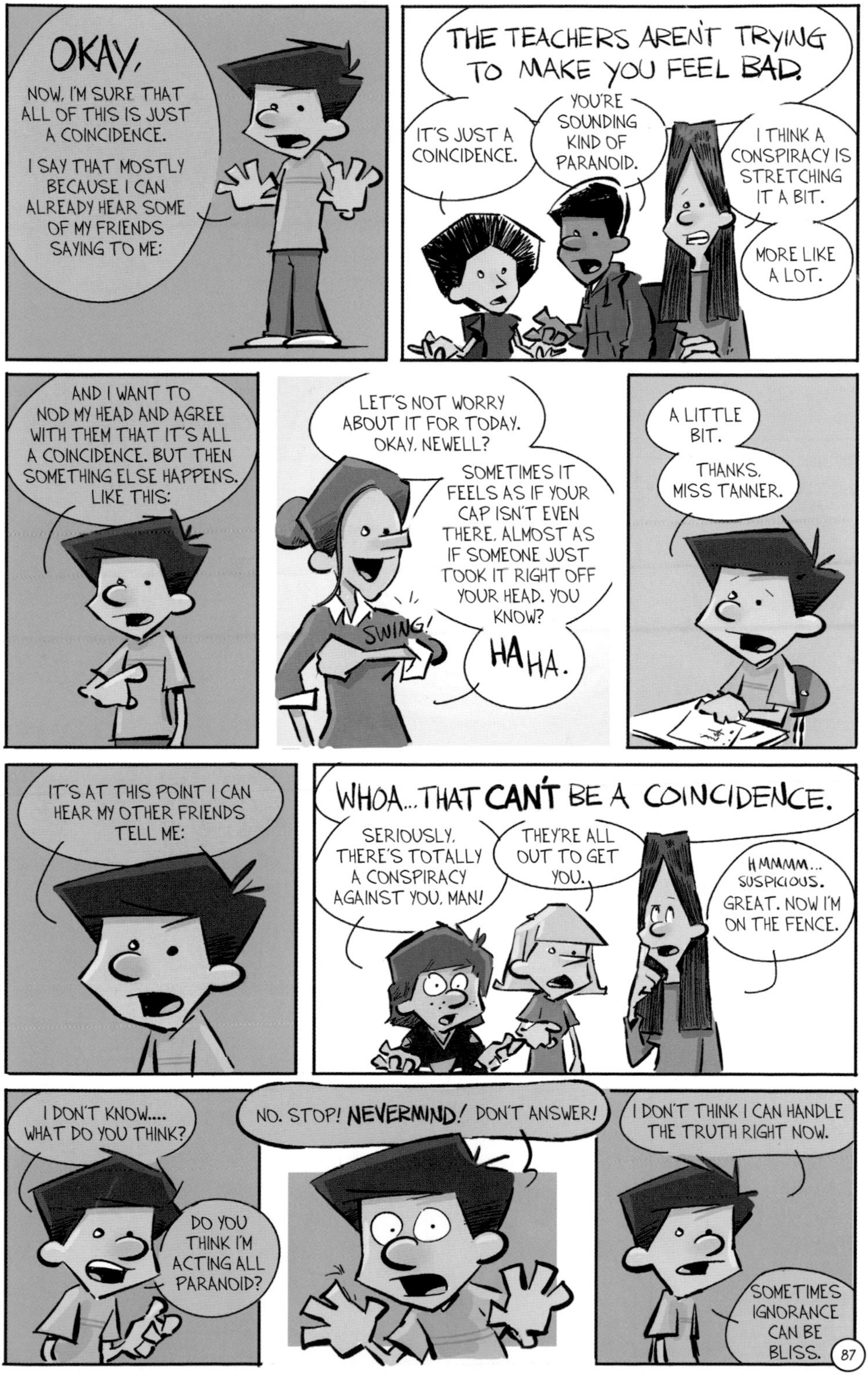
OKAY,
NOW, I'M SURE THAT ALL OF THIS IS JUST A COINCIDENCE.
I SAY THAT MOSTLY BECAUSE I CAN ALREADY HEAR SOME OF MY FRIENDS SAYING TO ME:
THE TEACHERS AREN'T TRYING TO MAKE YOU FEEL BAD.
IT'S JUST A COINCIDENCE.
YOU'RE SOUNDING KIND OF PARANOID.
I THINK A CONSPIRACY IS STRETCHING IT A BIT.
MORE LIKE A LOT.
AND I WANT TO NOD MY HEAD AND AGREE WITH THEM THAT IT'S ALL A COINCIDENCE. BUT THEN SOMETHING ELSE HAPPENS. LIKE THIS:
LET'S NOT WORRY ABOUT IT FOR TODAY. OKAY, NEWELL?
SOMETIMES IT FEELS AS IF YOUR CAP ISN'T EVEN THERE, ALMOST AS IF SOMEONE JUST TOOK IT RIGHT OFF YOUR HEAD. YOU KNOW?
SWING!
HA HA.
A LITTLE BIT.
THANKS, MISS TANNER.
IT'S AT THIS POINT I CAN HEAR MY OTHER FRIENDS TELL ME:
WHOA... THAT CAN'T BE A COINCIDENCE.
SERIOUSLY, THERE'S TOTALLY A CONSPIRACY AGAINST YOU, MAN!
THEY'RE ALL OUT TO GET YOU.
HMMMM... SUSPICIOUS. GREAT. NOW I'M ON THE FENCE.
I DON'T KNOW.... WHAT DO YOU THINK?
DO YOU THINK I'M ACTING ALL PARANOID?
NO. STOP! NEVERMIND! DON'T ANSWER!
I DON'T THINK I CAN HANDLE THE TRUTH RIGHT NOW.
SOMETIMES IGNORANCE CAN BE BLISS.

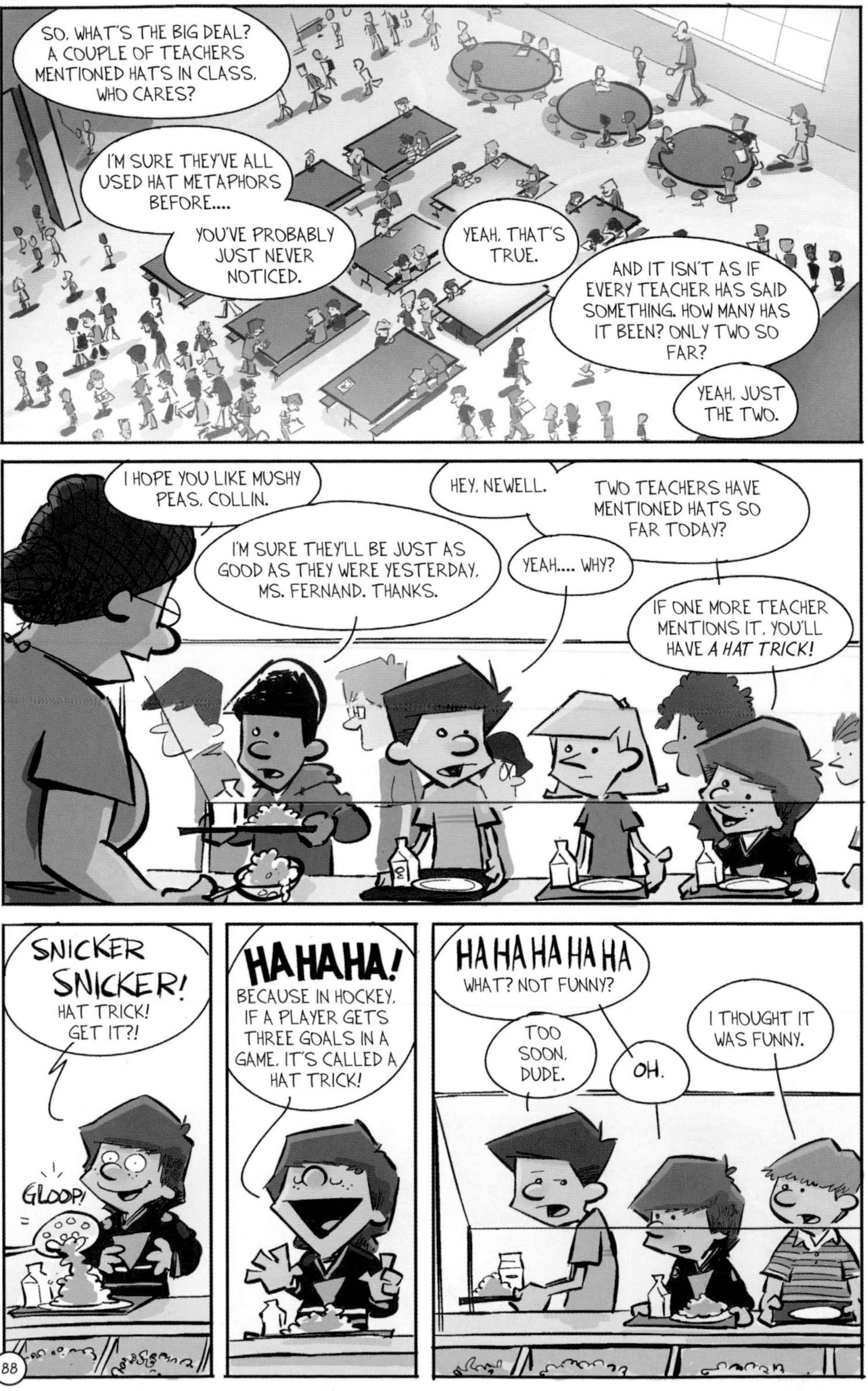
SO, WHAT'S THE BIG DEAL? A COUPLE OF TEACHERS MENTIONED HATS IN CLASS. WHO CARES?
I'M SURE THEY'VE ALL USED HAT METAPHORS BEFORE....
YOU'VE PROBABLY JUST NEVER NOTICED.
YEAH, THAT'S TRUE.
AND IT ISN'T AS IF EVERY TEACHER HAS SAID SOMETHING. HOW MANY HAS IT BEEN? ONLY TWO SO FAR?
YEAH, JUST THE TWO.
I HOPE YOU LIKE MUSHY PEAS, COLLIN.
I'M SURE THEY'LL BE JUST AS GOOD AS THEY WERE YESTERDAY, MS. FERNAND. THANKS.
HEY, NEWELL.
TWO TEACHERS HAVE MENTIONED HATS SO FAR TODAY?
YEAH.... WHY?
IF ONE MORE TEACHER MENTIONS IT, YOU'LL HAVE *A HAT TRICK!*
SNICKER SNICKER! HAT TRICK! GET IT?!
GLOOP!
HAHAHA! BECAUSE IN HOCKEY, IF A PLAYER GETS THREE GOALS IN A GAME, IT'S CALLED A HAT TRICK!
HA HA HA HA HA HA WHAT? NOT FUNNY?
TOO SOON, DUDE.
OH.
I THOUGHT IT WAS FUNNY.

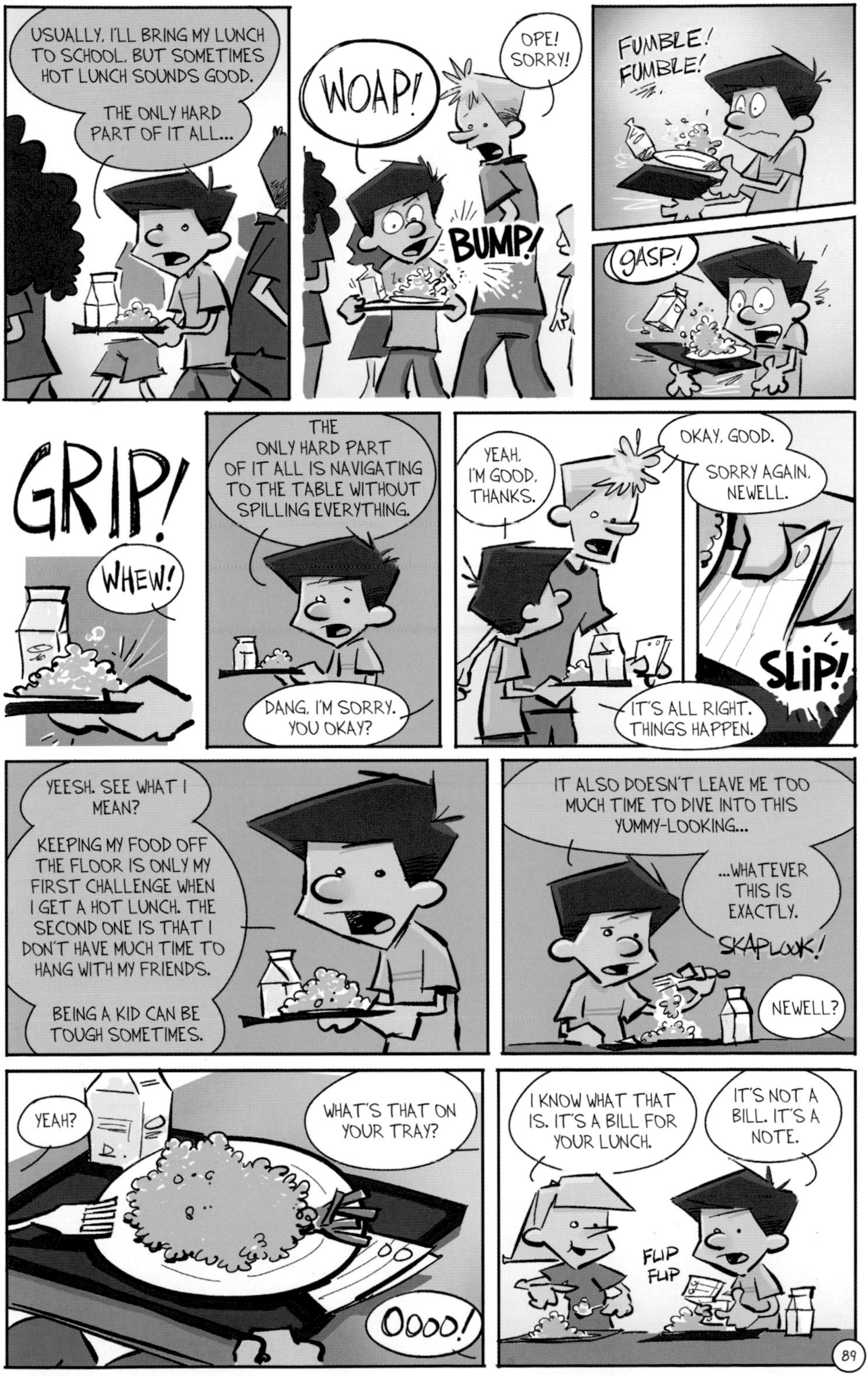
USUALLY, I'LL BRING MY LUNCH TO SCHOOL, BUT SOMETIMES HOT LUNCH SOUNDS GOOD.
THE ONLY HARD PART OF IT ALL...
WOAP!
OPE! SORRY!
BUMP!
FUMBLE! FUMBLE!
GASP!
GRIP!
WHEW!
THE ONLY HARD PART OF IT ALL IS NAVIGATING TO THE TABLE WITHOUT SPILLING EVERYTHING.
DANG, I'M SORRY. YOU OKAY?
YEAH, I'M GOOD, THANKS.
OKAY, GOOD.
SORRY AGAIN, NEWELL.
IT'S ALL RIGHT. THINGS HAPPEN.
SLIP!
YEESH. SEE WHAT I MEAN?
KEEPING MY FOOD OFF THE FLOOR IS ONLY MY FIRST CHALLENGE WHEN I GET A HOT LUNCH. THE SECOND ONE IS THAT I DON'T HAVE MUCH TIME TO HANG WITH MY FRIENDS.
BEING A KID CAN BE TOUGH SOMETIMES.
IT ALSO DOESN'T LEAVE ME TOO MUCH TIME TO DIVE INTO THIS YUMMY-LOOKING...
...WHATEVER THIS IS EXACTLY.
SKAPLOOK!
NEWELL?
YEAH?
WHAT'S THAT ON YOUR TRAY?
OOOO!
I KNOW WHAT THAT IS. IT'S A BILL FOR YOUR LUNCH.
IT'S NOT A BILL. IT'S A NOTE.
FLIP FLIP

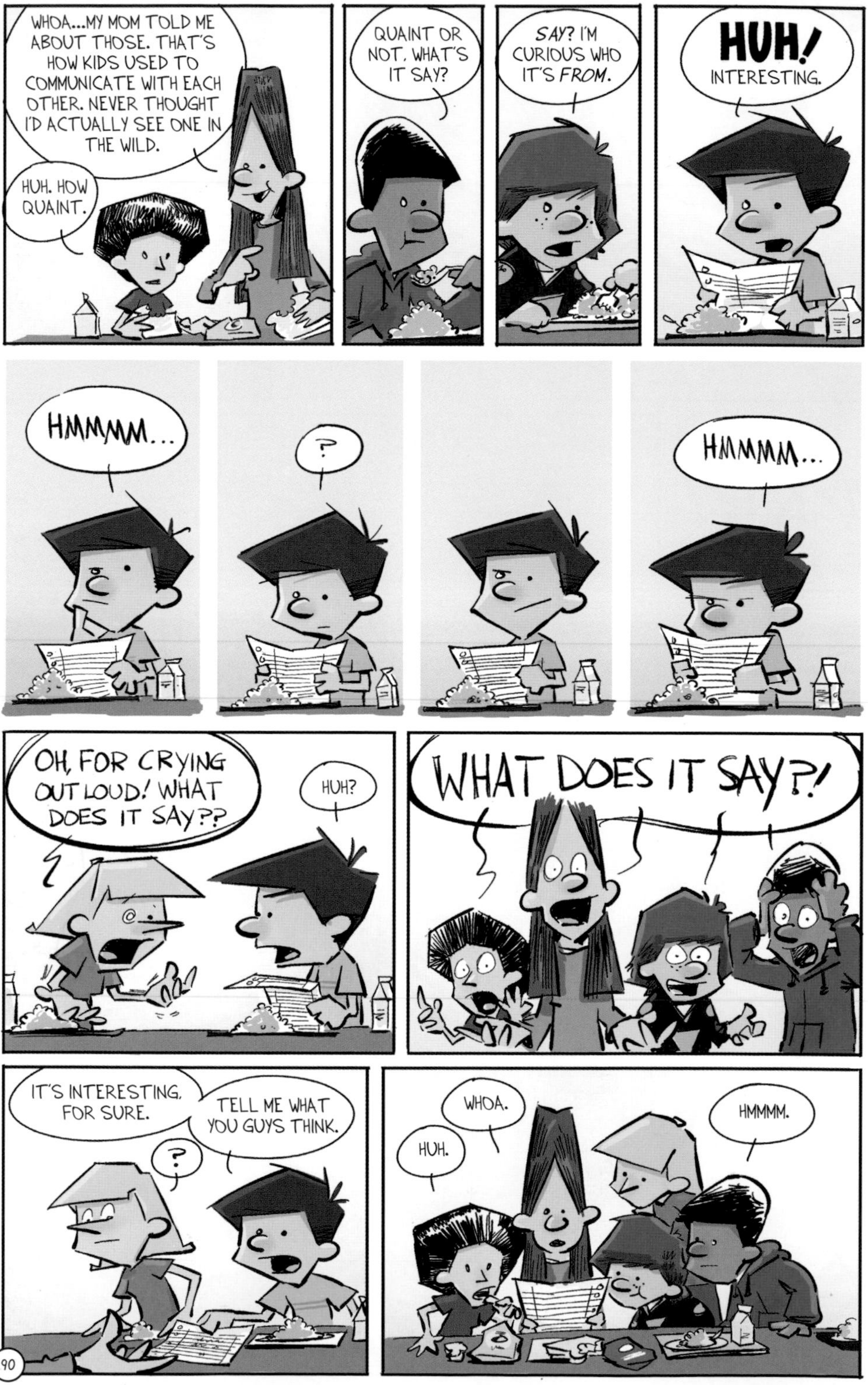
WHOA...MY MOM TOLD ME ABOUT THOSE. THAT'S HOW KIDS USED TO COMMUNICATE WITH EACH OTHER. NEVER THOUGHT I'D ACTUALLY SEE ONE IN THE WILD.
HUH. HOW QUAINT.
QUAINT OR NOT, WHAT'S IT SAY?
SAY? I'M CURIOUS WHO IT'S FROM.
HUH!
INTERESTING.
HMMMM...
?
HMMMM...
OH, FOR CRYING OUT LOUD! WHAT DOES IT SAY??
HUH?
WHAT DOES IT SAY?!
IT'S INTERESTING, FOR SURE.
?
TELL ME WHAT YOU GUYS THINK.
HUH.
WHOA.
HMMMM.

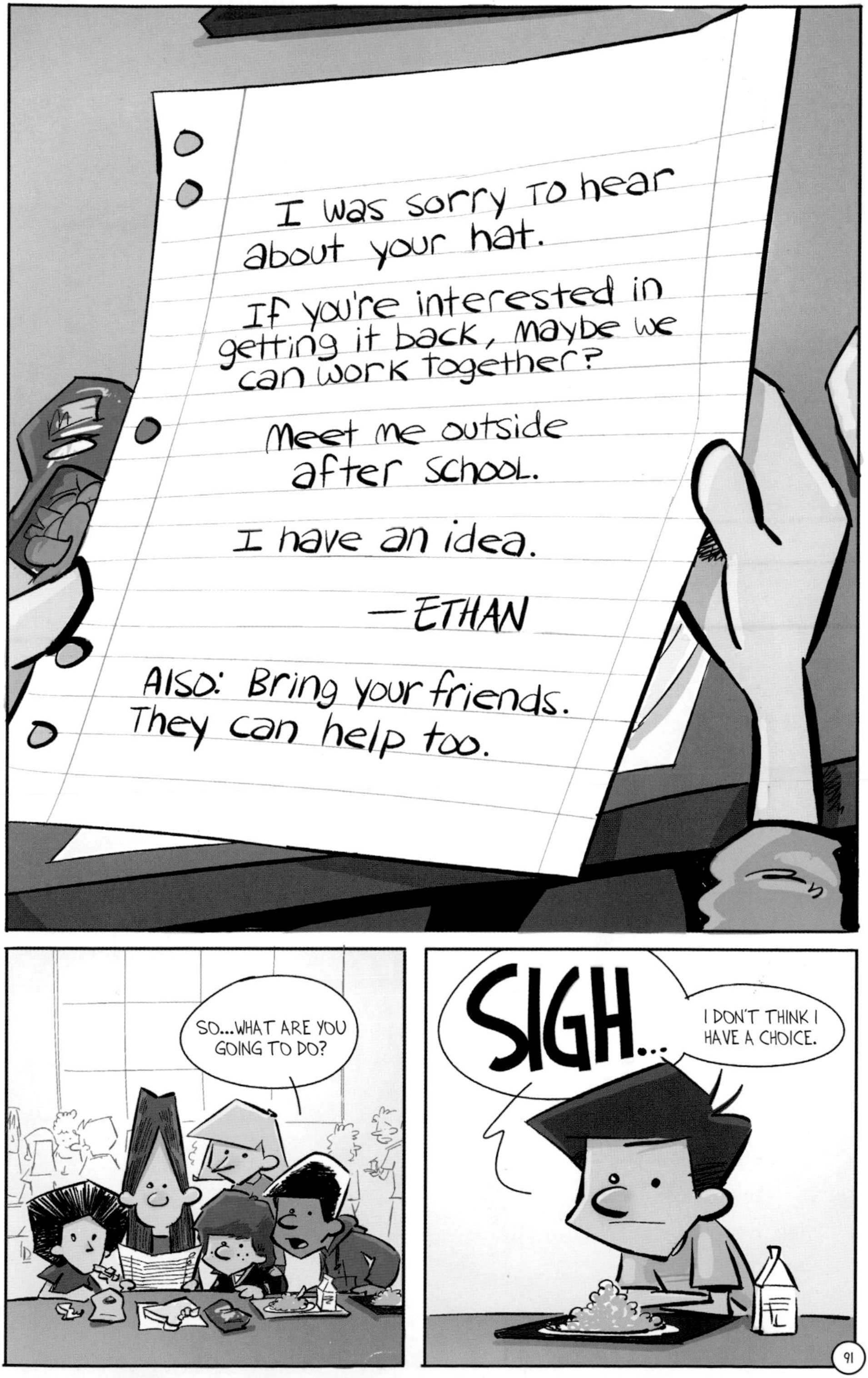
I was sorry to hear about your hat.
If you're interested in getting it back, maybe we can work together?
Meet me outside after school.
I have an idea.
—ETHAN
Also: Bring your friends. They can help too.
SO...WHAT ARE YOU GOING TO DO?
SIGH...
I DON'T THINK I HAVE A CHOICE.

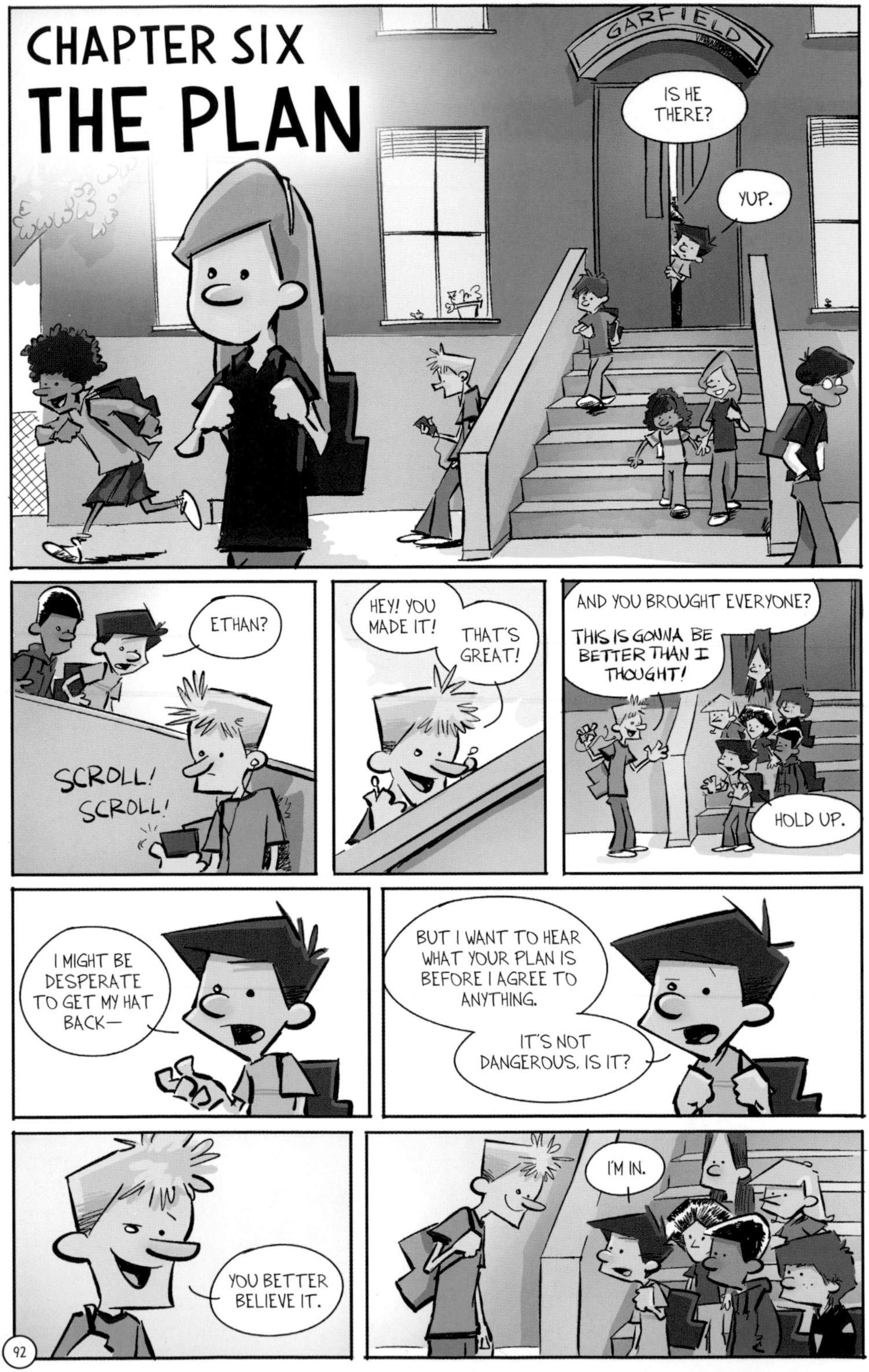
CHAPTER SIX
THE PLAN
GARFIELD
IS HE THERE?
YUP.
ETHAN?
SCROLL! SCROLL!
HEY! YOU MADE IT!
THAT'S GREAT!
AND YOU BROUGHT EVERYONE?
THIS IS GONNA BE BETTER THAN I THOUGHT!
HOLD UP.
I MIGHT BE DESPERATE TO GET MY HAT BACK—
BUT I WANT TO HEAR WHAT YOUR PLAN IS BEFORE I AGREE TO ANYTHING.
IT'S NOT DANGEROUS, IS IT?
YOU BETTER BELIEVE IT.
I'M IN.

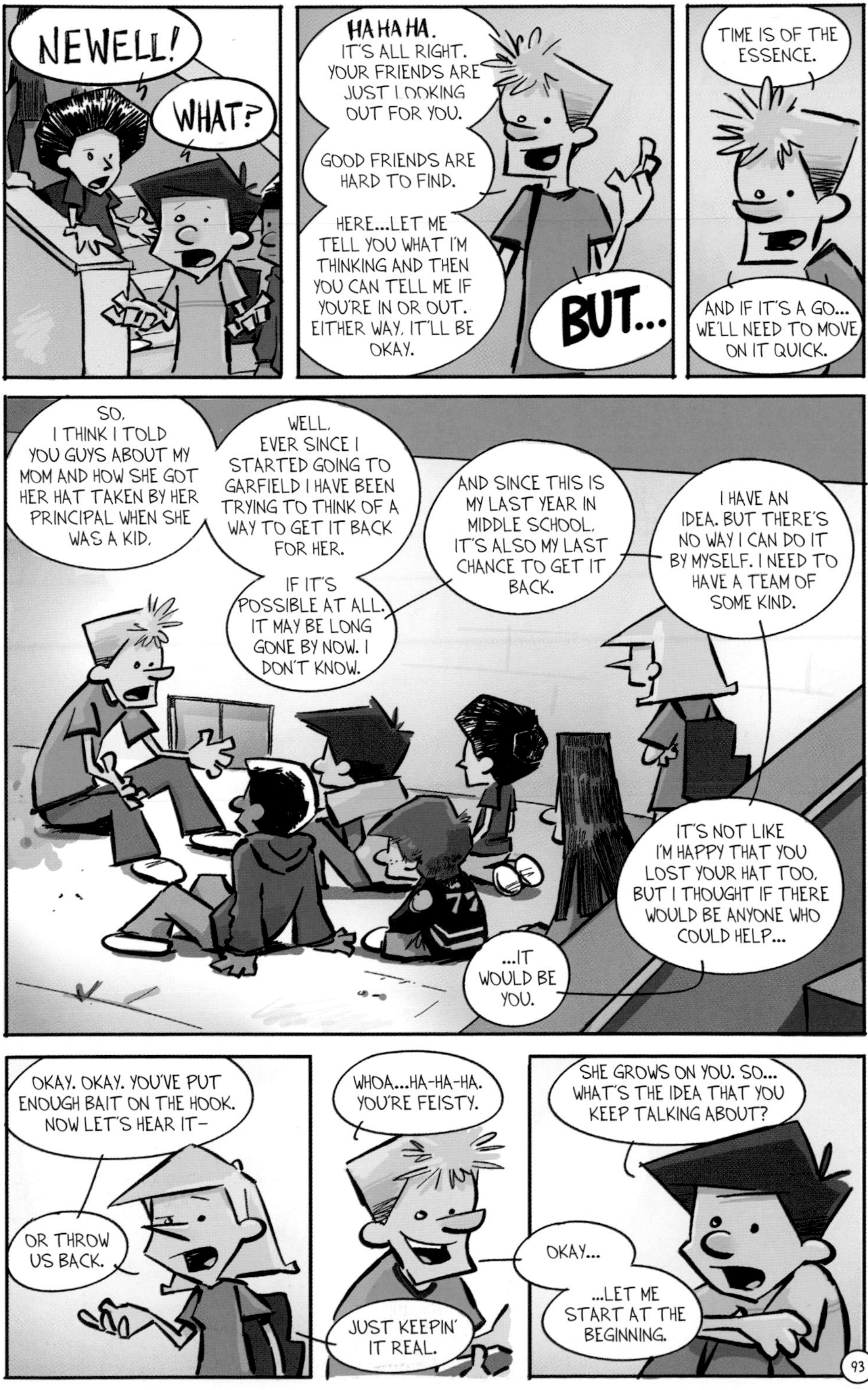
NEWELL!
WHAT?
HA HA HA. IT'S ALL RIGHT. YOUR FRIENDS ARE JUST LOOKING OUT FOR YOU.
GOOD FRIENDS ARE HARD TO FIND.
HERE...LET ME TELL YOU WHAT I'M THINKING AND THEN YOU CAN TELL ME IF YOU'RE IN OR OUT. EITHER WAY, IT'LL BE OKAY.
BUT...
TIME IS OF THE ESSENCE.
AND IF IT'S A GO... WE'LL NEED TO MOVE ON IT QUICK.
SO, I THINK I TOLD YOU GUYS ABOUT MY MOM AND HOW SHE GOT HER HAT TAKEN BY HER PRINCIPAL WHEN SHE WAS A KID.
WELL, EVER SINCE I STARTED GOING TO GARFIELD I HAVE BEEN TRYING TO THINK OF A WAY TO GET IT BACK FOR HER.
IF IT'S POSSIBLE AT ALL. IT MAY BE LONG GONE BY NOW. I DON'T KNOW.
AND SINCE THIS IS MY LAST YEAR IN MIDDLE SCHOOL, IT'S ALSO MY LAST CHANCE TO GET IT BACK.
I HAVE AN IDEA. BUT THERE'S NO WAY I CAN DO IT BY MYSELF. I NEED TO HAVE A TEAM OF SOME KIND.
IT'S NOT LIKE I'M HAPPY THAT YOU LOST YOUR HAT TOO, BUT I THOUGHT IF THERE WOULD BE ANYONE WHO COULD HELP...
...IT WOULD BE YOU.
OKAY. OKAY. YOU'VE PUT ENOUGH BAIT ON THE HOOK. NOW LET'S HEAR IT—
OR THROW US BACK.
WHOA...HA-HA-HA. YOU'RE FEISTY.
JUST KEEPIN' IT REAL.
SHE GROWS ON YOU. SO... WHAT'S THE IDEA THAT YOU KEEP TALKING ABOUT?
OKAY...
...LET ME START AT THE BEGINNING.

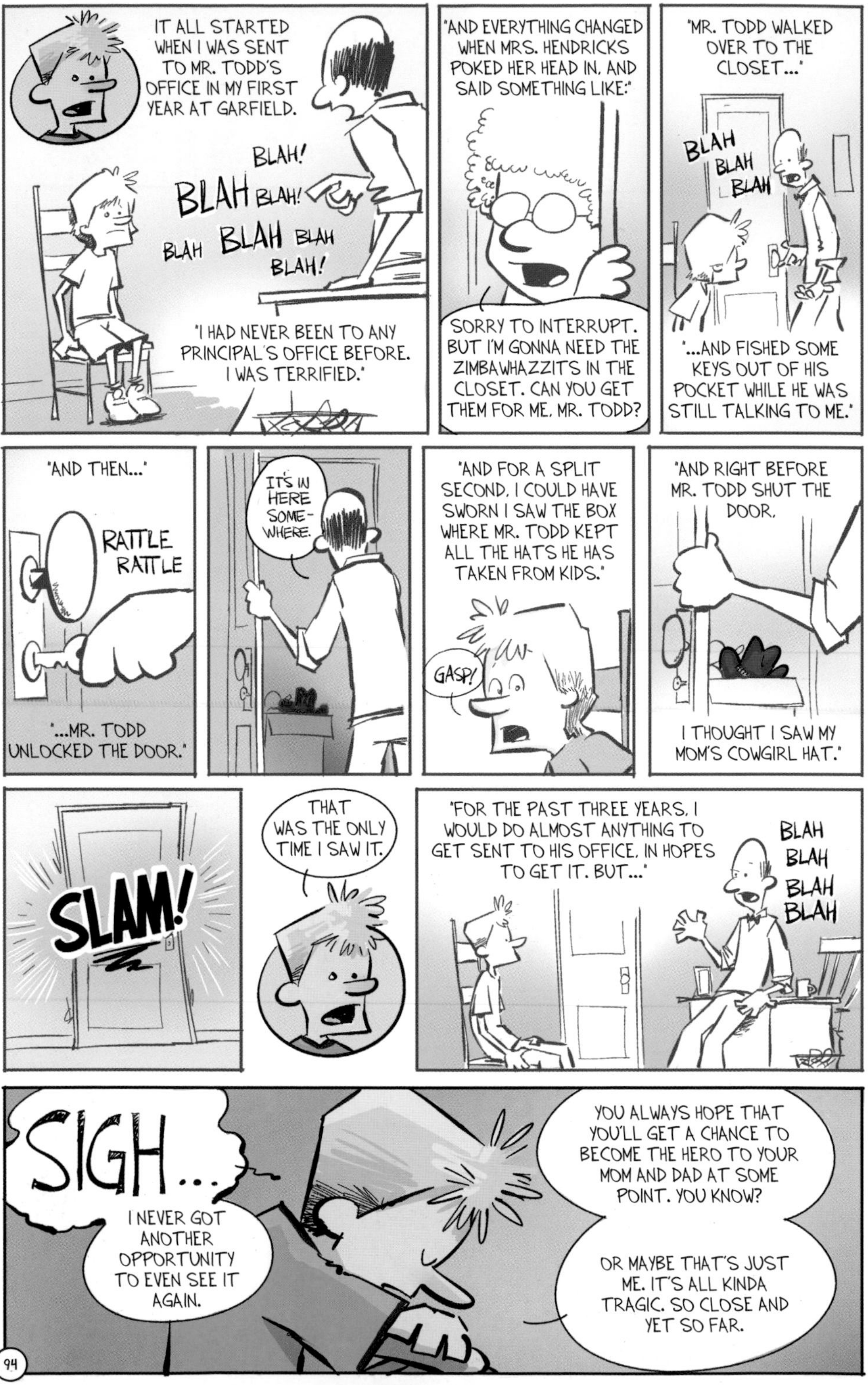

IT ALL STARTED WHEN I WAS SENT TO MR. TODD'S OFFICE IN MY FIRST YEAR AT GARFIELD.
BLAH!
BLAH BLAH!
BLAH BLAH BLAH
BLAH!
"I HAD NEVER BEEN TO ANY PRINCIPAL'S OFFICE BEFORE. I WAS TERRIFIED."
"AND EVERYTHING CHANGED WHEN MRS. HENDRICKS POKED HER HEAD IN, AND SAID SOMETHING LIKE:"
SORRY TO INTERRUPT, BUT I'M GONNA NEED THE ZIMBAWHAZZITS IN THE CLOSET. CAN YOU GET THEM FOR ME, MR. TODD?
"MR. TODD WALKED OVER TO THE CLOSET..."
BLAH BLAH BLAH
"...AND FISHED SOME KEYS OUT OF HIS POCKET WHILE HE WAS STILL TALKING TO ME."
"AND THEN..."
RATTLE RATTLE
"...MR. TODD UNLOCKED THE DOOR."
IT'S IN HERE SOME-WHERE.
"AND FOR A SPLIT SECOND, I COULD HAVE SWORN I SAW THE BOX WHERE MR. TODD KEPT ALL THE HATS HE HAS TAKEN FROM KIDS."
GASP!
"AND RIGHT BEFORE MR. TODD SHUT THE DOOR,
I THOUGHT I SAW MY MOM'S COWGIRL HAT."
SLAM!
THAT WAS THE ONLY TIME I SAW IT.
"FOR THE PAST THREE YEARS, I WOULD DO ALMOST ANYTHING TO GET SENT TO HIS OFFICE, IN HOPES TO GET IT. BUT..."
BLAH BLAH BLAH BLAH
SIGH...
I NEVER GOT ANOTHER OPPORTUNITY TO EVEN SEE IT AGAIN.
YOU ALWAYS HOPE THAT YOU'LL GET A CHANCE TO BECOME THE HERO TO YOUR MOM AND DAD AT SOME POINT, YOU KNOW?
OR MAYBE THAT'S JUST ME. IT'S ALL KINDA TRAGIC. SO CLOSE AND YET SO FAR.

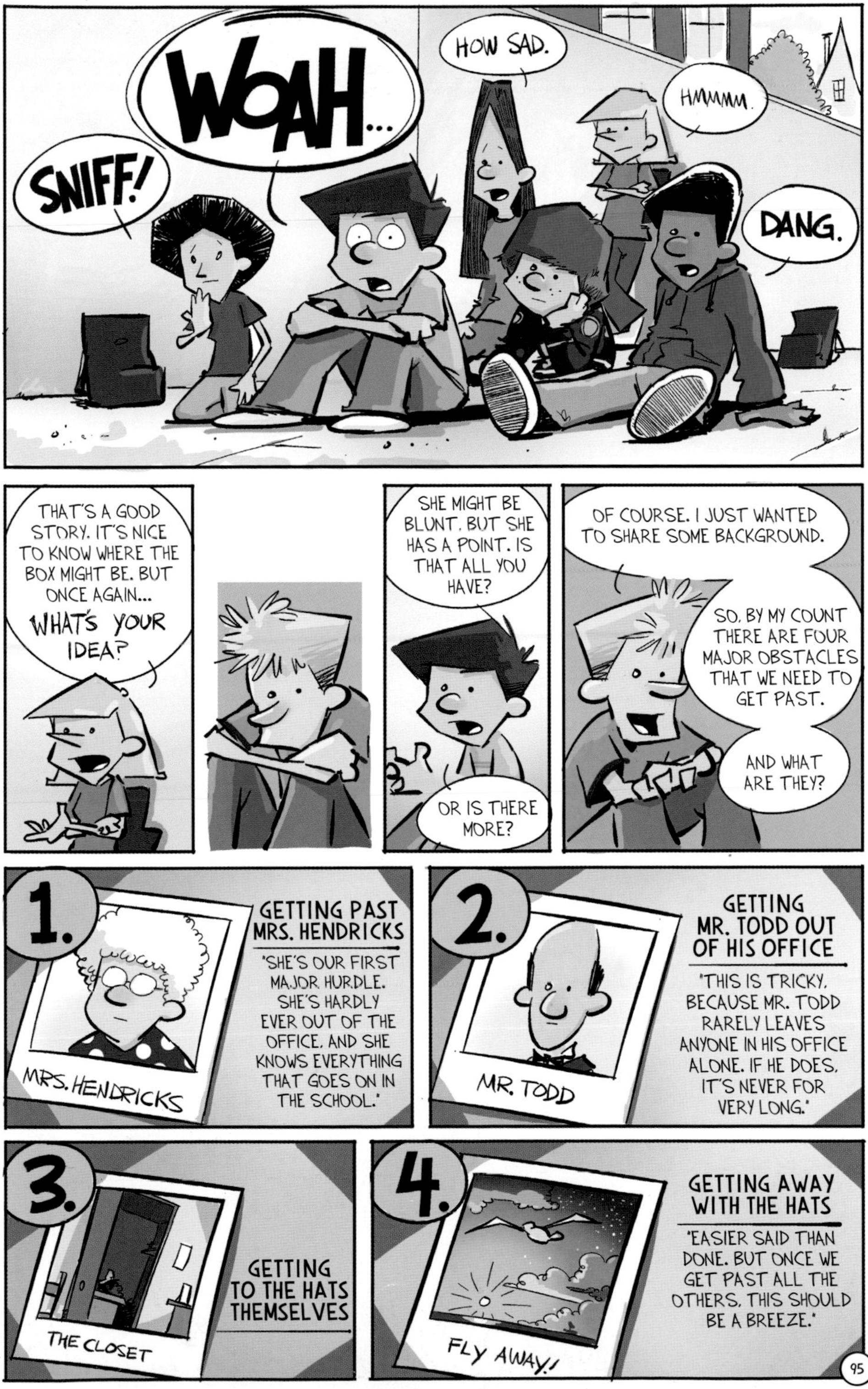
SNIFF!
WOAH...
HOW SAD.
HMMMM.
DANG.
THAT'S A GOOD STORY. IT'S NICE TO KNOW WHERE THE BOX MIGHT BE. BUT ONCE AGAIN... WHAT'S YOUR IDEA?
SHE MIGHT BE BLUNT, BUT SHE HAS A POINT. IS THAT ALL YOU HAVE?
OR IS THERE MORE?
OF COURSE. I JUST WANTED TO SHARE SOME BACKGROUND.
SO, BY MY COUNT THERE ARE FOUR MAJOR OBSTACLES THAT WE NEED TO GET PAST.
AND WHAT ARE THEY?
1.
MRS. HENDRICKS
GETTING PAST MRS. HENDRICKS
"SHE'S OUR FIRST MAJOR HURDLE. SHE'S HARDLY EVER OUT OF THE OFFICE, AND SHE KNOWS EVERYTHING THAT GOES ON IN THE SCHOOL."
2.
MR. TODD
GETTING MR. TODD OUT OF HIS OFFICE
"THIS IS TRICKY, BECAUSE MR. TODD RARELY LEAVES ANYONE IN HIS OFFICE ALONE. IF HE DOES, IT'S NEVER FOR VERY LONG."
3.
THE CLOSET
GETTING TO THE HATS THEMSELVES
4.
FLY AWAY!
GETTING AWAY WITH THE HATS
"EASIER SAID THAN DONE. BUT ONCE WE GET PAST ALL THE OTHERS, THIS SHOULD BE A BREEZE."

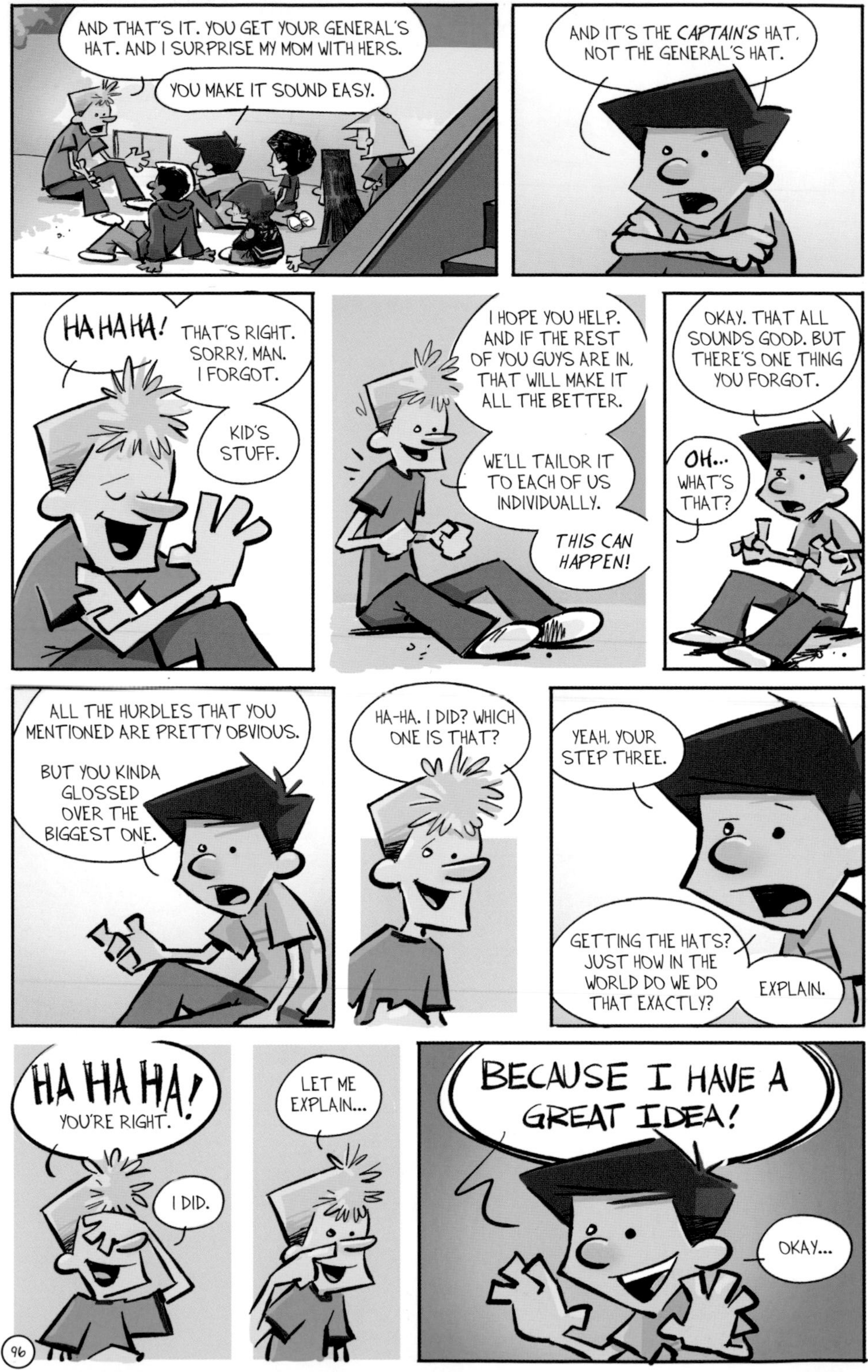
AND THAT'S IT. YOU GET YOUR GENERAL'S HAT. AND I SURPRISE MY MOM WITH HERS.
YOU MAKE IT SOUND EASY.
AND IT'S THE *CAPTAIN'S* HAT, NOT THE GENERAL'S HAT.
HA HA HA! THAT'S RIGHT. SORRY, MAN. I FORGOT.
KID'S STUFF.
I HOPE YOU HELP. AND IF THE REST OF YOU GUYS ARE IN, THAT WILL MAKE IT ALL THE BETTER.
WE'LL TAILOR IT TO EACH OF US INDIVIDUALLY.
THIS CAN HAPPEN!
OKAY. THAT ALL SOUNDS GOOD. BUT THERE'S ONE THING YOU FORGOT.
OH... WHAT'S THAT?
ALL THE HURDLES THAT YOU MENTIONED ARE PRETTY OBVIOUS.
BUT YOU KINDA GLOSSED OVER THE BIGGEST ONE.
HA-HA. I DID? WHICH ONE IS THAT?
YEAH, YOUR STEP THREE.
GETTING THE HATS? JUST HOW IN THE WORLD DO WE DO THAT EXACTLY?
EXPLAIN.
HA HA HA! YOU'RE RIGHT.
I DID.
LET ME EXPLAIN...
BECAUSE I HAVE A GREAT IDEA!
OKAY...

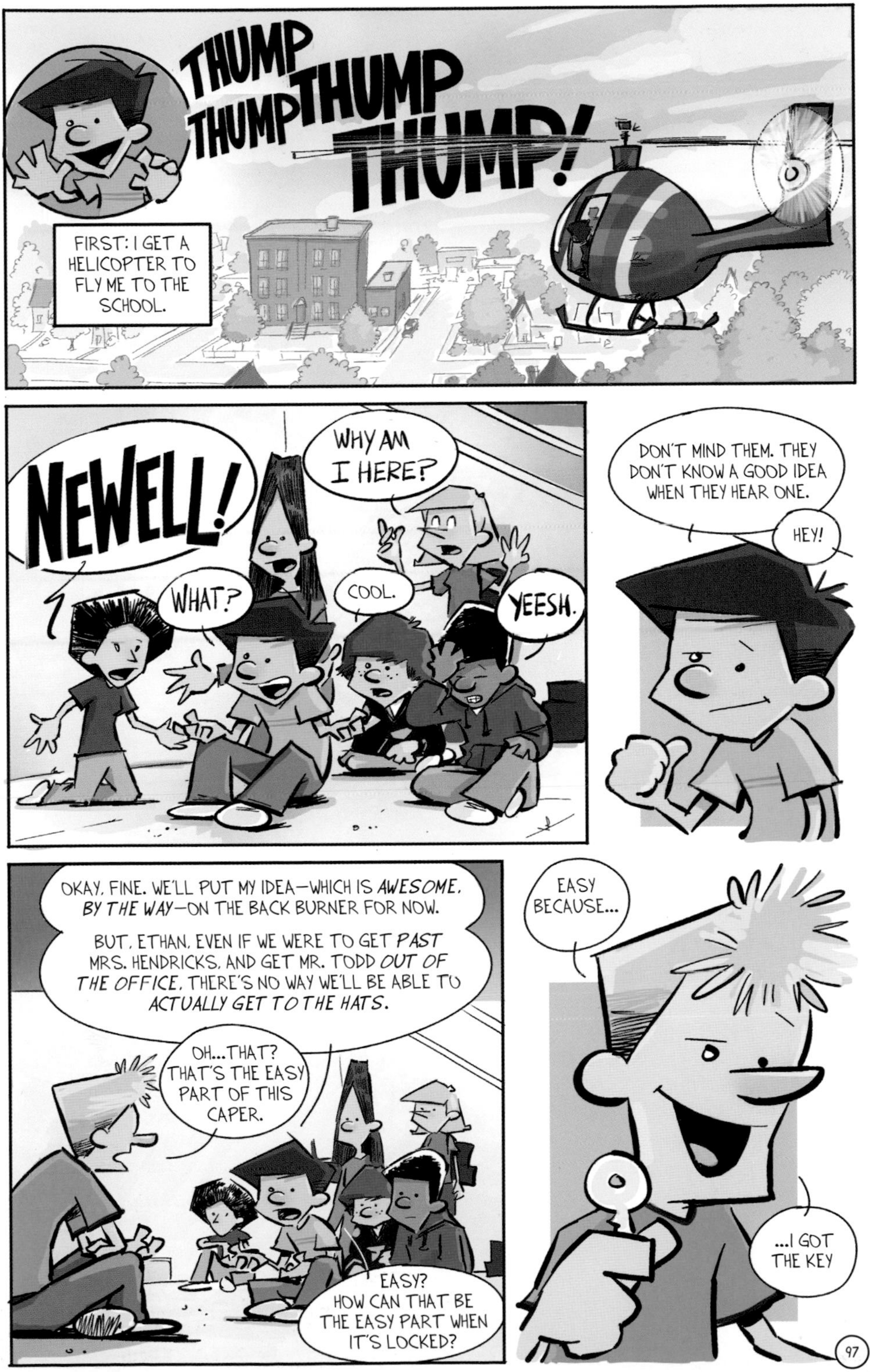
THUMP THUMP THUMP THUMP!
FIRST: I GET A HELICOPTER TO FLY ME TO THE SCHOOL.
NEWELL!
WHY AM I HERE?
WHAT?
COOL.
YEESH.
DON'T MIND THEM. THEY DON'T KNOW A GOOD IDEA WHEN THEY HEAR ONE.
HEY!
OKAY, FINE. WE'LL PUT MY IDEA—WHICH IS *AWESOME, BY THE WAY*—ON THE BACK BURNER FOR NOW.
BUT, ETHAN, EVEN IF WE WERE TO GET *PAST* MRS. HENDRICKS, AND GET MR. TODD *OUT OF THE OFFICE*, THERE'S NO WAY WE'LL BE ABLE TO *ACTUALLY GET TO THE HATS*.
OH...THAT? THAT'S THE EASY PART OF THIS CAPER.
EASY? HOW CAN THAT BE THE EASY PART WHEN IT'S LOCKED?
EASY BECAUSE...
...I GOT THE KEY

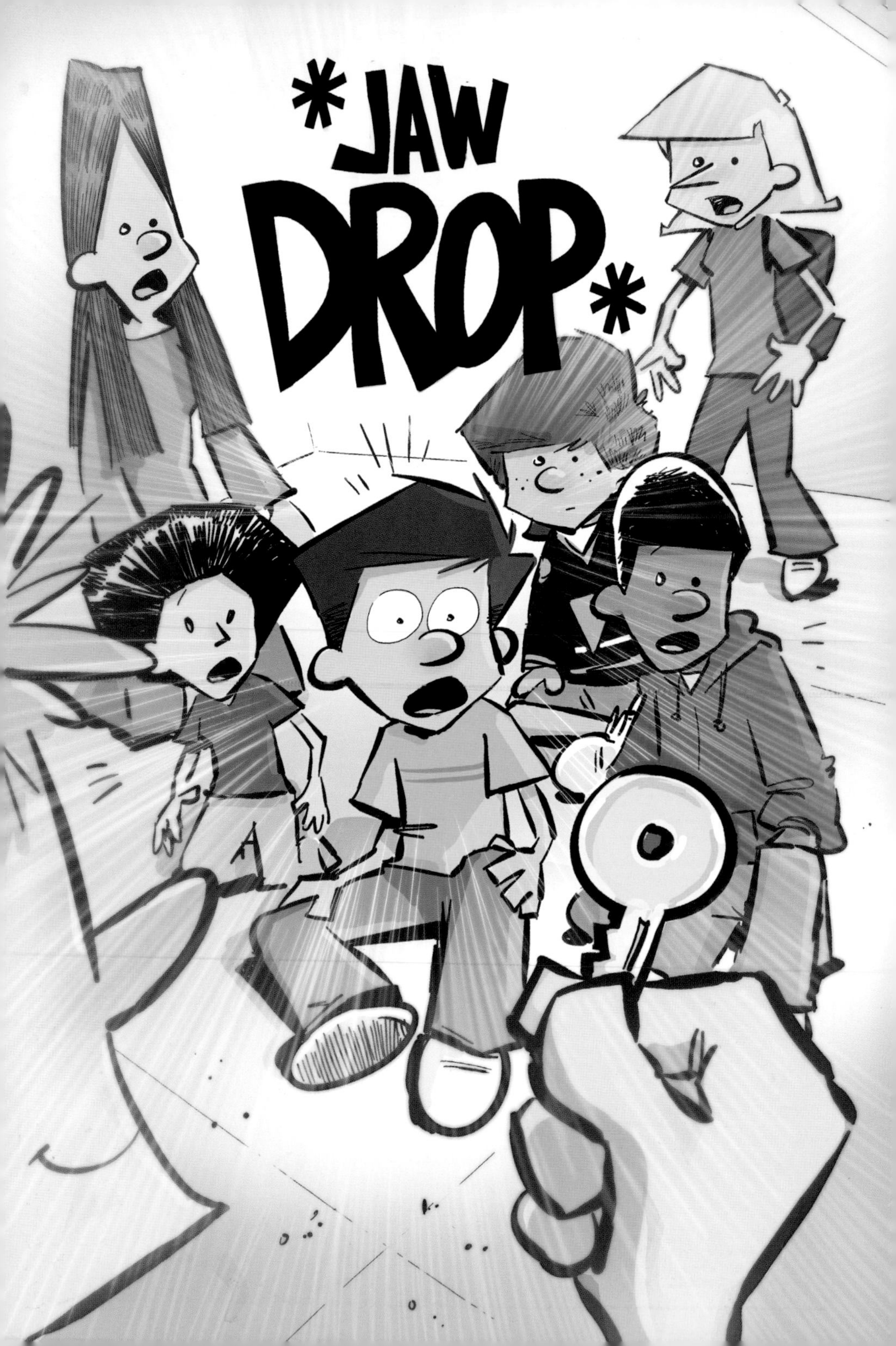
JAW DROP

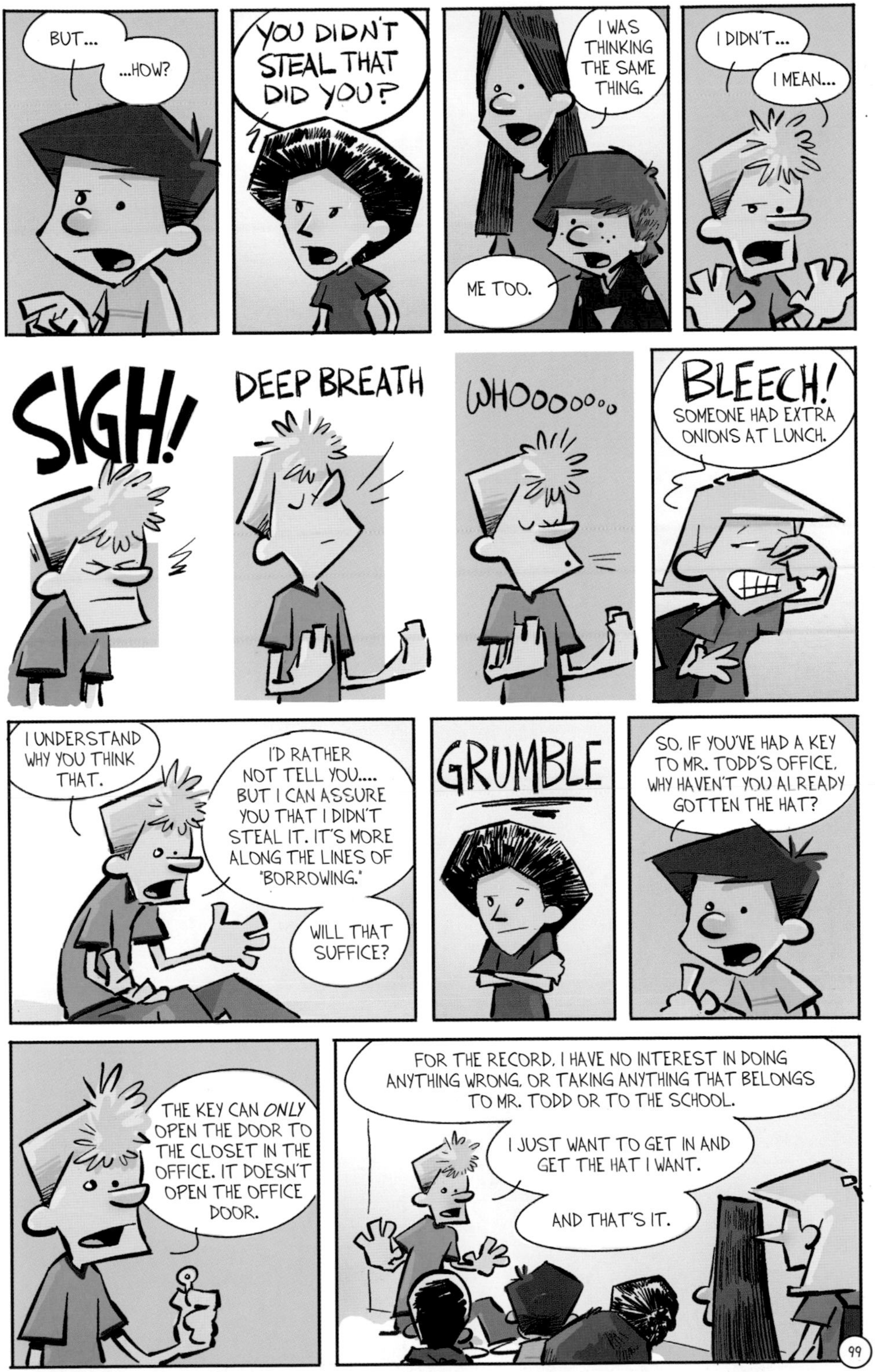
BUT...
...HOW?
YOU DIDN'T STEAL THAT DID YOU?
I WAS THINKING THE SAME THING.
ME TOO.
I DIDN'T...
I MEAN...
SIGH!
DEEP BREATH
WHOOOOooo
BLEECH!
SOMEONE HAD EXTRA ONIONS AT LUNCH.
I UNDERSTAND WHY YOU THINK THAT.
I'D RATHER NOT TELL YOU.... BUT I CAN ASSURE YOU THAT I DIDN'T STEAL IT. IT'S MORE ALONG THE LINES OF "BORROWING."
WILL THAT SUFFICE?
GRUMBLE
SO, IF YOU'VE HAD A KEY TO MR. TODD'S OFFICE, WHY HAVEN'T YOU ALREADY GOTTEN THE HAT?
THE KEY CAN *ONLY* OPEN THE DOOR TO THE CLOSET IN THE OFFICE. IT DOESN'T OPEN THE OFFICE DOOR.
FOR THE RECORD, I HAVE NO INTEREST IN DOING ANYTHING WRONG, OR TAKING ANYTHING THAT BELONGS TO MR. TODD OR TO THE SCHOOL.
I JUST WANT TO GET IN AND GET THE HAT I WANT.
AND THAT'S IT.

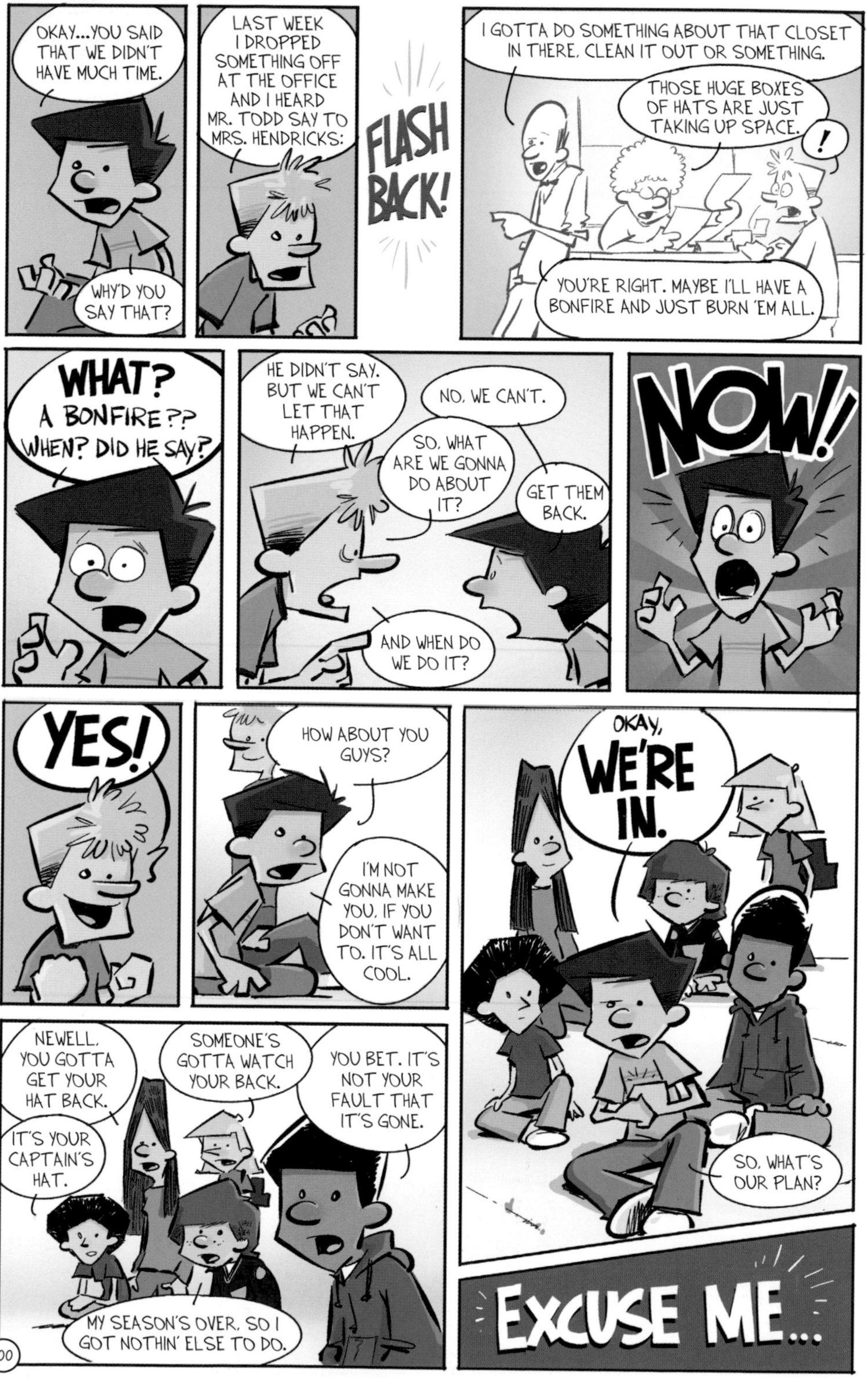
OKAY...YOU SAID THAT WE DIDN'T HAVE MUCH TIME.
WHY'D YOU SAY THAT?
LAST WEEK I DROPPED SOMETHING OFF AT THE OFFICE AND I HEARD MR. TODD SAY TO MRS. HENDRICKS:
FLASH BACK!
I GOTTA DO SOMETHING ABOUT THAT CLOSET IN THERE, CLEAN IT OUT OR SOMETHING.
THOSE HUGE BOXES OF HATS ARE JUST TAKING UP SPACE.
!
YOU'RE RIGHT. MAYBE I'LL HAVE A BONFIRE AND JUST BURN 'EM ALL.
WHAT? A BONFIRE?? WHEN? DID HE SAY?
HE DIDN'T SAY. BUT WE CAN'T LET THAT HAPPEN.
NO, WE CAN'T.
SO, WHAT ARE WE GONNA DO ABOUT IT?
GET THEM BACK.
AND WHEN DO WE DO IT?
NOW!
YES!
HOW ABOUT YOU GUYS?
I'M NOT GONNA MAKE YOU, IF YOU DON'T WANT TO. IT'S ALL COOL.
OKAY, WE'RE IN.
SO, WHAT'S OUR PLAN?
NEWELL, YOU GOTTA GET YOUR HAT BACK.
IT'S YOUR CAPTAIN'S HAT.
SOMEONE'S GOTTA WATCH YOUR BACK.
YOU BET. IT'S NOT YOUR FAULT THAT IT'S GONE.
MY SEASON'S OVER, SO I GOT NOTHIN' ELSE TO DO.
EXCUSE ME...

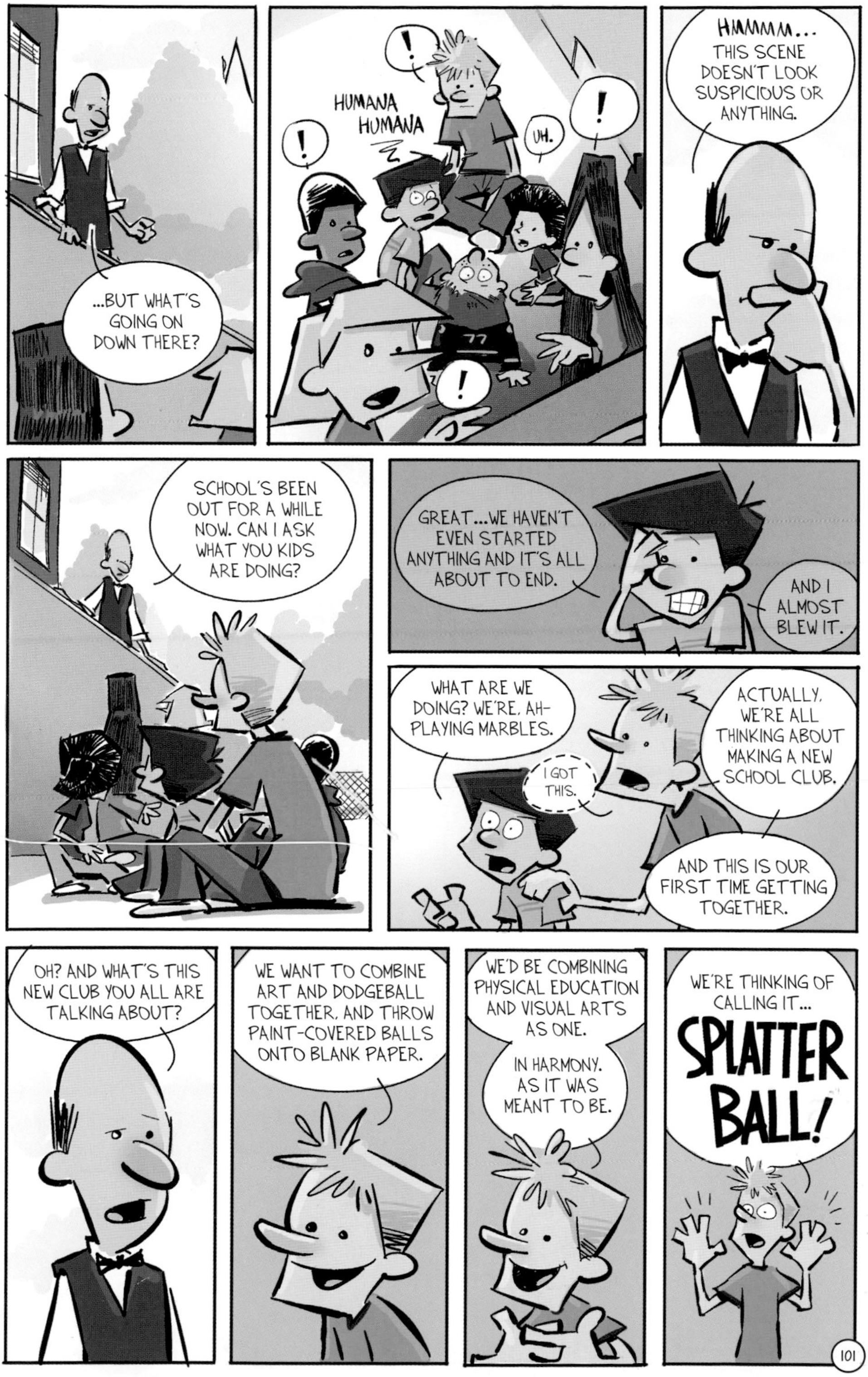

...BUT WHAT'S GOING ON DOWN THERE?
!
HUMANA HUMANA
!
UH.
!
!
77
HMMMM...
THIS SCENE DOESN'T LOOK SUSPICIOUS OR ANYTHING.
SCHOOL'S BEEN OUT FOR A WHILE NOW. CAN I ASK WHAT YOU KIDS ARE DOING?
GREAT...WE HAVEN'T EVEN STARTED ANYTHING AND IT'S ALL ABOUT TO END.
AND I ALMOST BLEW IT.
WHAT ARE WE DOING? WE'RE, AH- PLAYING MARBLES.
I GOT THIS.
ACTUALLY, WE'RE ALL THINKING ABOUT MAKING A NEW SCHOOL CLUB.
AND THIS IS OUR FIRST TIME GETTING TOGETHER.
OH? AND WHAT'S THIS NEW CLUB YOU ALL ARE TALKING ABOUT?
WE WANT TO COMBINE ART AND DODGEBALL TOGETHER, AND THROW PAINT-COVERED BALLS ONTO BLANK PAPER.
WE'D BE COMBINING PHYSICAL EDUCATION AND VISUAL ARTS AS ONE.
IN HARMONY. AS IT WAS MEANT TO BE.
WE'RE THINKING OF CALLING IT...
SPLATTER BALL!

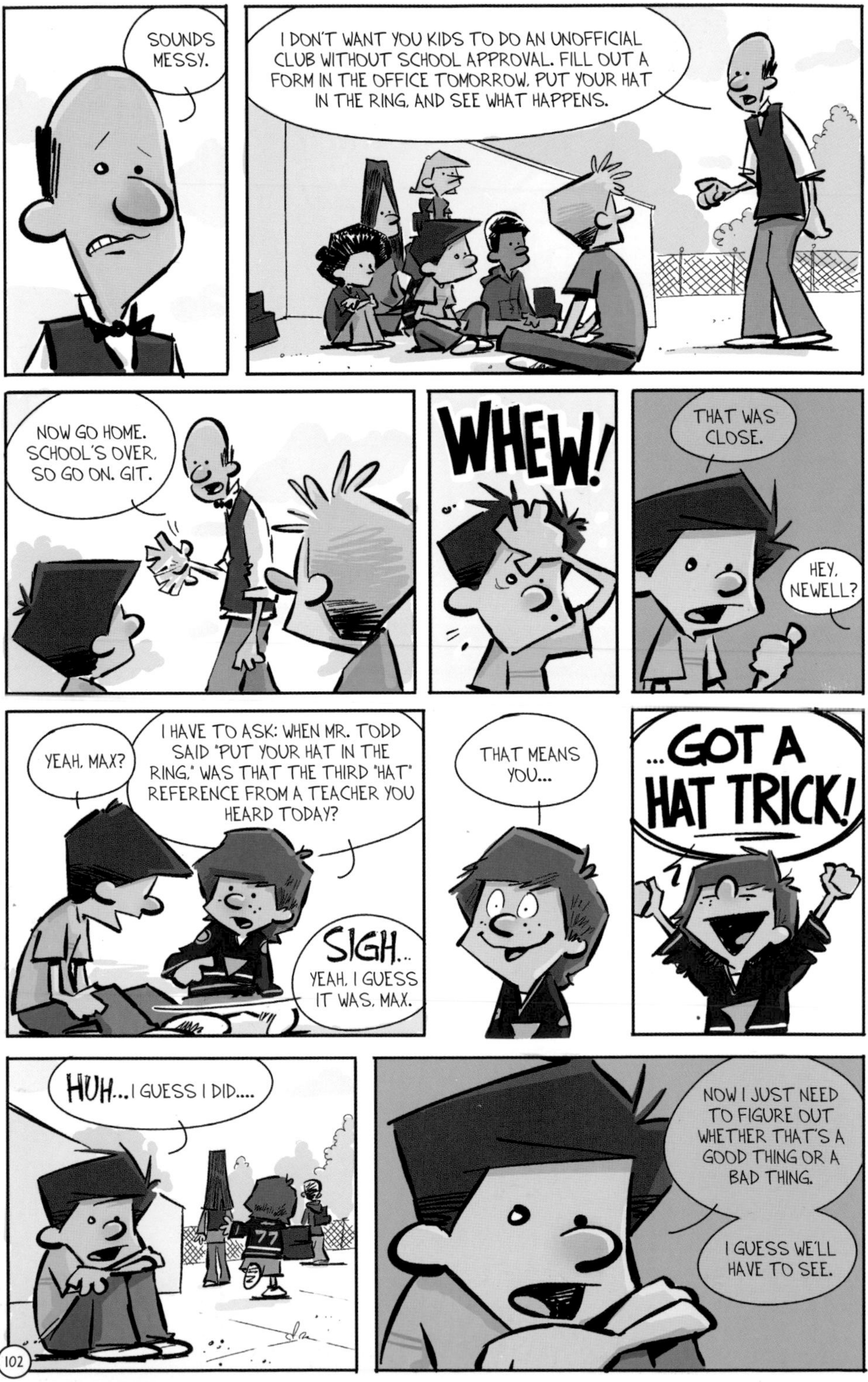
SOUNDS MESSY.
I DON'T WANT YOU KIDS TO DO AN UNOFFICIAL CLUB WITHOUT SCHOOL APPROVAL. FILL OUT A FORM IN THE OFFICE TOMORROW. PUT YOUR HAT IN THE RING, AND SEE WHAT HAPPENS.
NOW GO HOME. SCHOOL'S OVER, SO GO ON. GIT.
WHEW!
THAT WAS CLOSE.
HEY, NEWELL?
YEAH, MAX?
I HAVE TO ASK: WHEN MR. TODD SAID "PUT YOUR HAT IN THE RING," WAS THAT THE THIRD "HAT" REFERENCE FROM A TEACHER YOU HEARD TODAY?
SIGH...
YEAH, I GUESS IT WAS, MAX.
THAT MEANS YOU...
...GOT A HAT TRICK!
HUH...I GUESS I DID....
77
NOW I JUST NEED TO FIGURE OUT WHETHER THAT'S A GOOD THING OR A BAD THING.
I GUESS WE'LL HAVE TO SEE.

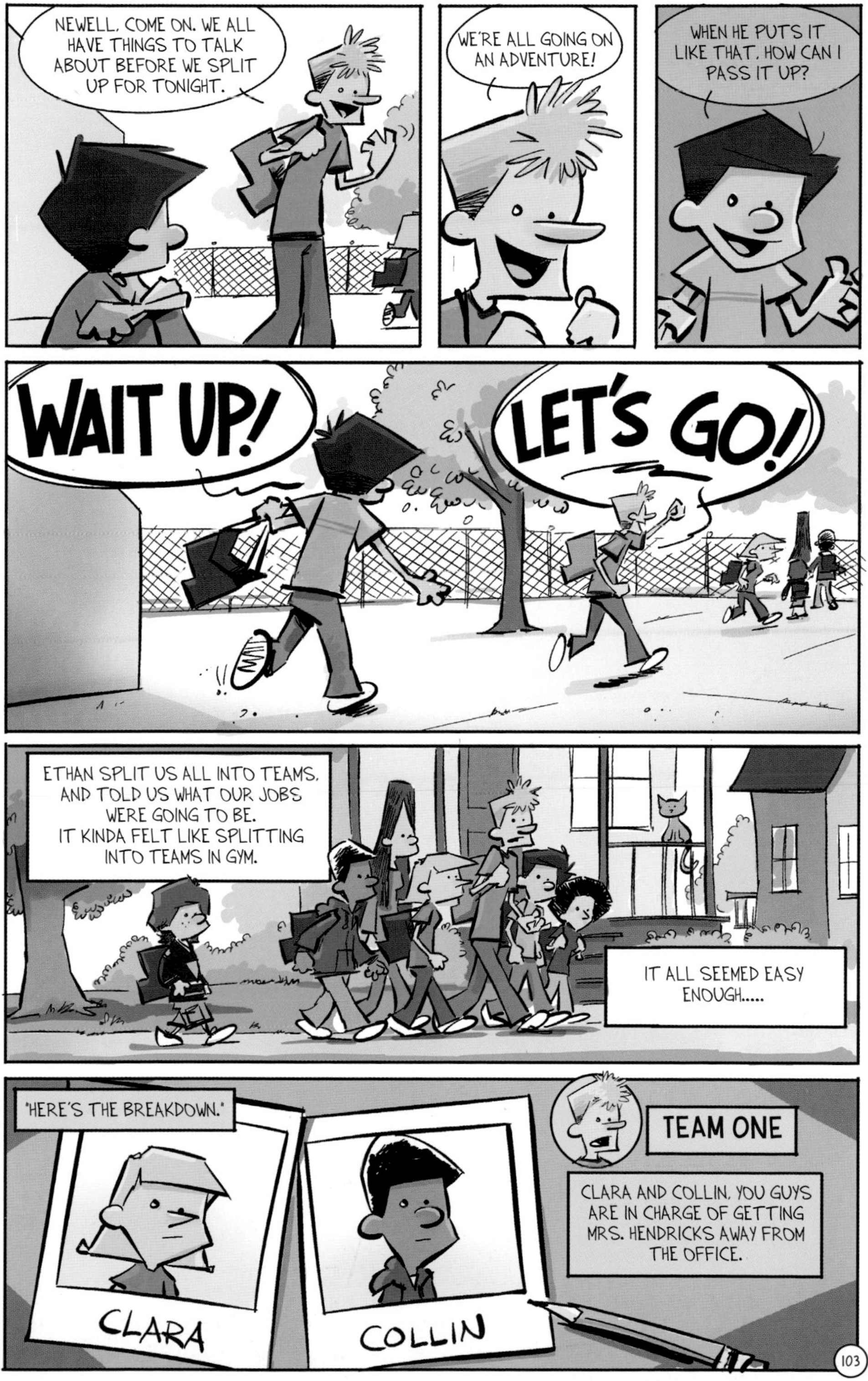

NEWELL, COME ON. WE ALL HAVE THINGS TO TALK ABOUT BEFORE WE SPLIT UP FOR TONIGHT.
WE'RE ALL GOING ON AN ADVENTURE!
WHEN HE PUTS IT LIKE THAT, HOW CAN I PASS IT UP?
WAIT UP!
LET'S GO!
ETHAN SPLIT US ALL INTO TEAMS, AND TOLD US WHAT OUR JOBS WERE GOING TO BE. IT KINDA FELT LIKE SPLITTING INTO TEAMS IN GYM.
IT ALL SEEMED EASY ENOUGH.....
"HERE'S THE BREAKDOWN."
TEAM ONE
CLARA AND COLLIN, YOU GUYS ARE IN CHARGE OF GETTING MRS. HENDRICKS AWAY FROM THE OFFICE.
CLARA
COLLIN

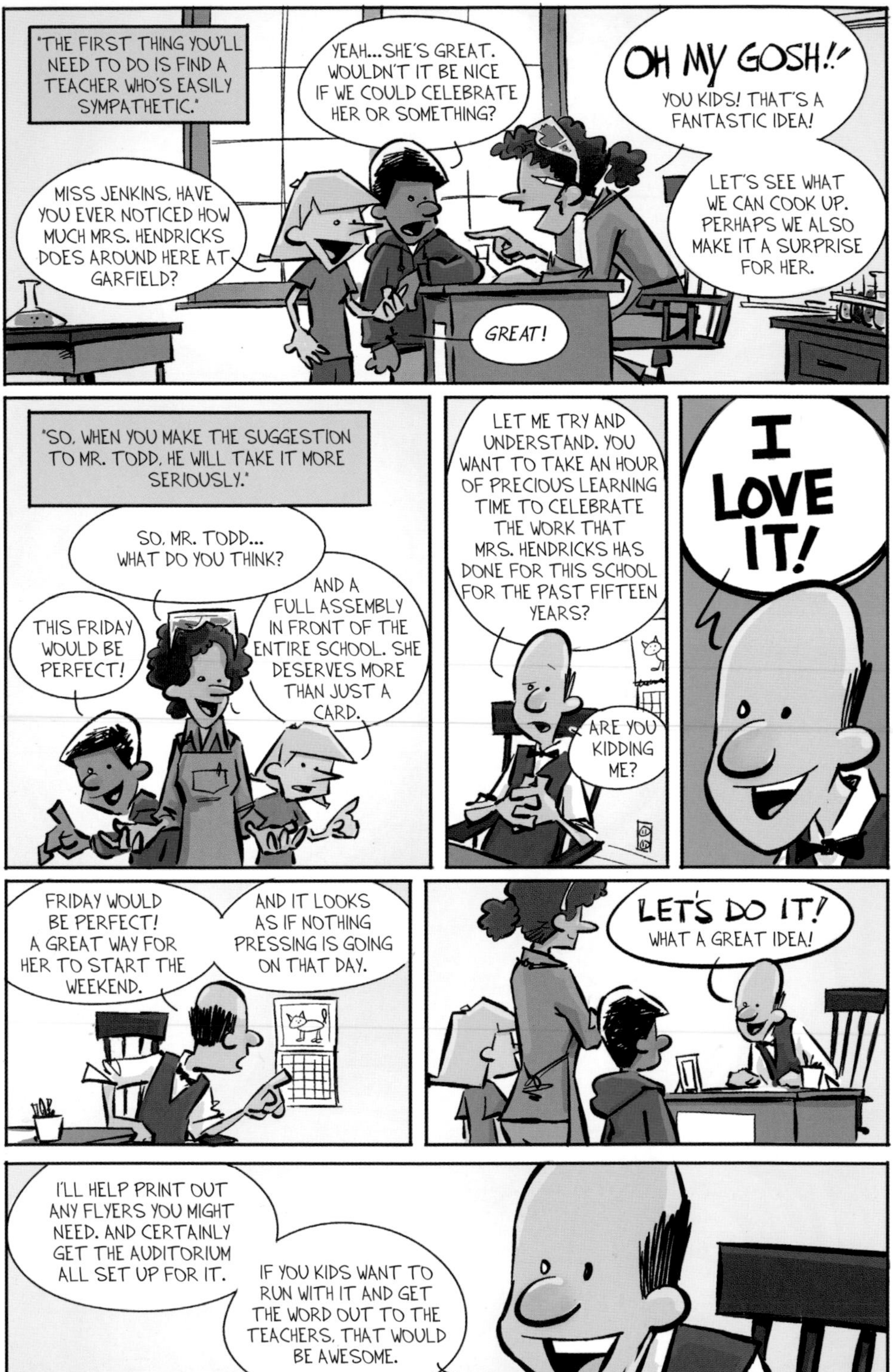
"THE FIRST THING YOU'LL NEED TO DO IS FIND A TEACHER WHO'S EASILY SYMPATHETIC."
MISS JENKINS, HAVE YOU EVER NOTICED HOW MUCH MRS. HENDRICKS DOES AROUND HERE AT GARFIELD?
YEAH...SHE'S GREAT. WOULDN'T IT BE NICE IF WE COULD CELEBRATE HER OR SOMETHING?
OH MY GOSH!! YOU KIDS! THAT'S A FANTASTIC IDEA!
LET'S SEE WHAT WE CAN COOK UP. PERHAPS WE ALSO MAKE IT A SURPRISE FOR HER.
GREAT!
"SO, WHEN YOU MAKE THE SUGGESTION TO MR. TODD, HE WILL TAKE IT MORE SERIOUSLY."
SO, MR. TODD... WHAT DO YOU THINK?
THIS FRIDAY WOULD BE PERFECT!
AND A FULL ASSEMBLY IN FRONT OF THE ENTIRE SCHOOL. SHE DESERVES MORE THAN JUST A CARD.
LET ME TRY AND UNDERSTAND. YOU WANT TO TAKE AN HOUR OF PRECIOUS LEARNING TIME TO CELEBRATE THE WORK THAT MRS. HENDRICKS HAS DONE FOR THIS SCHOOL FOR THE PAST FIFTEEN YEARS?
ARE YOU KIDDING ME?
I LOVE IT!
FRIDAY WOULD BE PERFECT! A GREAT WAY FOR HER TO START THE WEEKEND.
AND IT LOOKS AS IF NOTHING PRESSING IS GOING ON THAT DAY.
LET'S DO IT! WHAT A GREAT IDEA!
I'LL HELP PRINT OUT ANY FLYERS YOU MIGHT NEED. AND CERTAINLY GET THE AUDITORIUM ALL SET UP FOR IT.
IF YOU KIDS WANT TO RUN WITH IT AND GET THE WORD OUT TO THE TEACHERS, THAT WOULD BE AWESOME.

TOTALLY, NOT A PROBLEM, MR. T!

'SUCCESS!'

DOOP!

TEAM TWO

LILLY AND SKYLER? YOU TWO ARE GOING TO BE IN CHARGE OF THE GETAWAY.

LILLY

SKYLER

"YOU TWO ARE IN MR. JOHNSON'S HISTORY CLASS, RIGHT? SO ABOUT NOW YOU SHOULD BE DOING THE U.S. MONUMENT PROJECT. ASK IF YOU GUYS CAN WORK TOGETHER."

INSTEAD OF DOING TWO SMALL INDEPENDENT PROJECTS...

...CAN LILLY AND I WORK TOGETHER TO DO ONE BIG PROJECT?

WE'RE THINKING OF MAKING MOUNT RUSHMORE.

I'M SORRY, YOU WANT TO WHAT?

"AND YOUR PROJECT? IT NEEDS TO BE BIG. LIKE, REALLY BIG."

SIGH.

AS LONG AS YOU BOTH KNOW THAT I'LL BE GRADING YOU HARDER THAN THE OTHERS.

SURE, WHY NOT?

"THIS'LL BE THE BIGGEST PROJECT THAT WE'LL HAVE WITH ONLY A COUPLE OF DAYS TO MAKE IT. WE ALL SHOULD PITCH IN AND HELP. SKYLER AND LILLY SHOULDN'T HAVE TO DO IT ALL."

IT'S LOOKIN' GOOD!

HECK YEAH, IT IS!

WE NEED TO MAKE SURE THERE'S A DOOR ON THIS END OF IT.

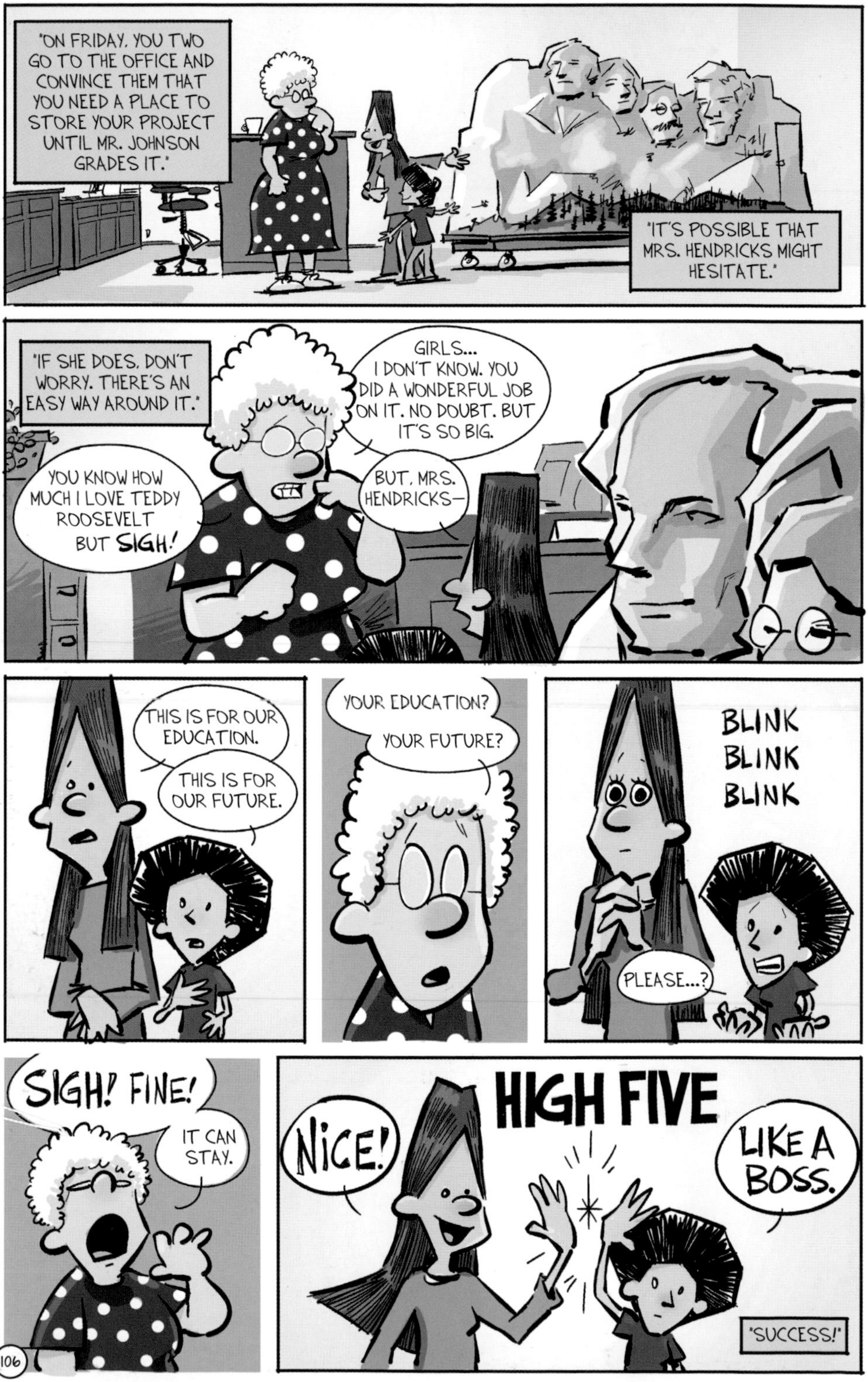
"ON FRIDAY, YOU TWO GO TO THE OFFICE AND CONVINCE THEM THAT YOU NEED A PLACE TO STORE YOUR PROJECT UNTIL MR. JOHNSON GRADES IT."
"IT'S POSSIBLE THAT MRS. HENDRICKS MIGHT HESITATE."
"IF SHE DOES, DON'T WORRY. THERE'S AN EASY WAY AROUND IT."
YOU KNOW HOW MUCH I LOVE TEDDY ROOSEVELT BUT SIGH!
GIRLS... I DON'T KNOW. YOU DID A WONDERFUL JOB ON IT, NO DOUBT. BUT IT'S SO BIG.
BUT, MRS. HENDRICKS—
THIS IS FOR OUR EDUCATION.
THIS IS FOR OUR FUTURE.
YOUR EDUCATION?
YOUR FUTURE?
BLINK
BLINK
BLINK
PLEASE...?
SIGH! FINE!
IT CAN STAY.
HIGH FIVE
NICE!
LIKE A BOSS.
"SUCCESS!"

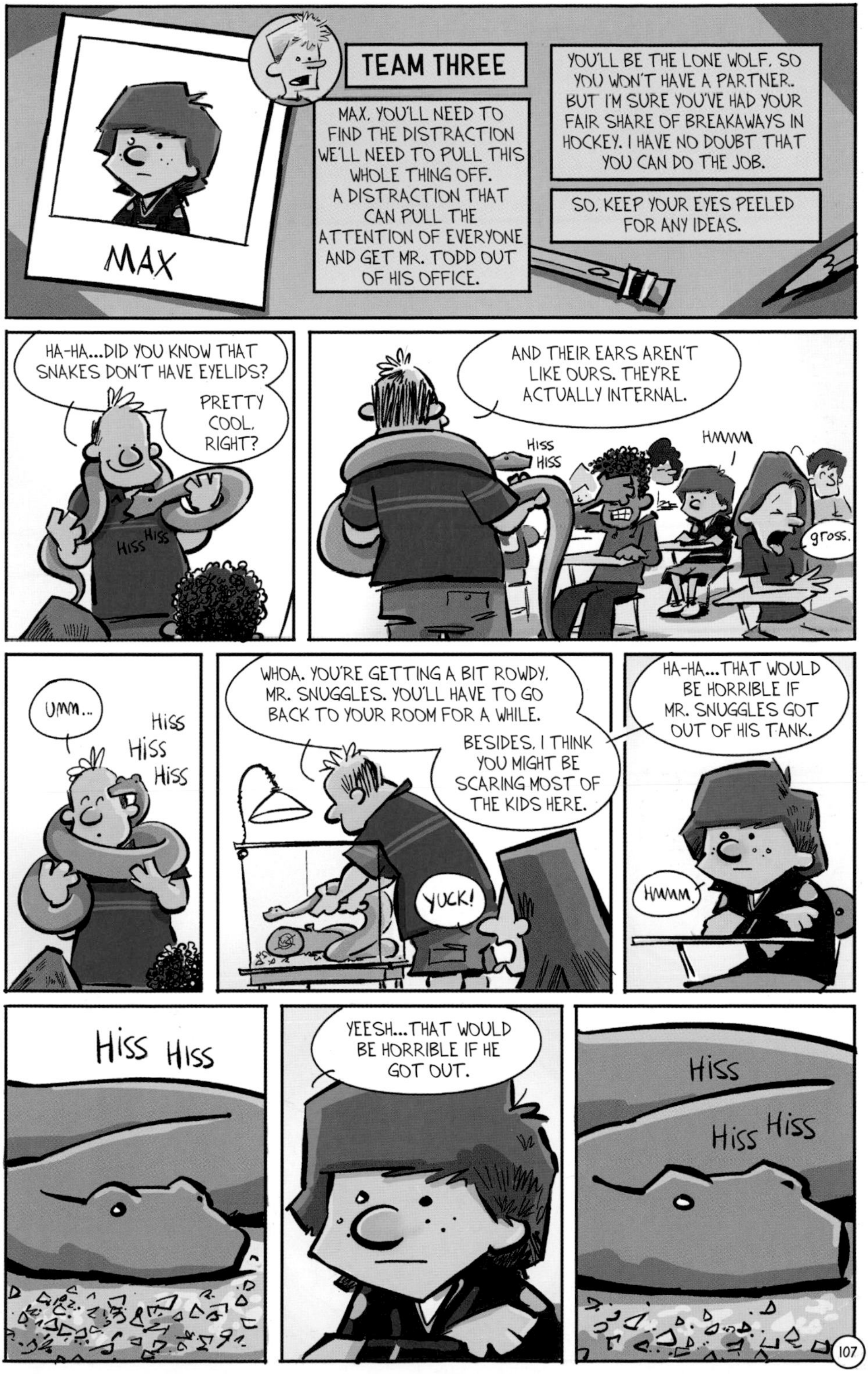
TEAM THREE
MAX
MAX, YOU'LL NEED TO FIND THE DISTRACTION WE'LL NEED TO PULL THIS WHOLE THING OFF. A DISTRACTION THAT CAN PULL THE ATTENTION OF EVERYONE AND GET MR. TODD OUT OF HIS OFFICE.
YOU'LL BE THE LONE WOLF, SO YOU WON'T HAVE A PARTNER. BUT I'M SURE YOU'VE HAD YOUR FAIR SHARE OF BREAKAWAYS IN HOCKEY. I HAVE NO DOUBT THAT YOU CAN DO THE JOB.
SO, KEEP YOUR EYES PEELED FOR ANY IDEAS.
HA-HA...DID YOU KNOW THAT SNAKES DON'T HAVE EYELIDS?
PRETTY COOL, RIGHT?
HISS HISS
AND THEIR EARS AREN'T LIKE OURS. THEY'RE ACTUALLY INTERNAL.
HISS HISS
HMMM
gross.
UMM...
HISS HISS HISS
WHOA. YOU'RE GETTING A BIT ROWDY, MR. SNUGGLES. YOU'LL HAVE TO GO BACK TO YOUR ROOM FOR A WHILE.
BESIDES, I THINK YOU MIGHT BE SCARING MOST OF THE KIDS HERE.
YUCK!
HA-HA...THAT WOULD BE HORRIBLE IF MR. SNUGGLES GOT OUT OF HIS TANK.
HMMM.
HISS HISS
YEESH...THAT WOULD BE HORRIBLE IF HE GOT OUT.
HISS
HISS HISS

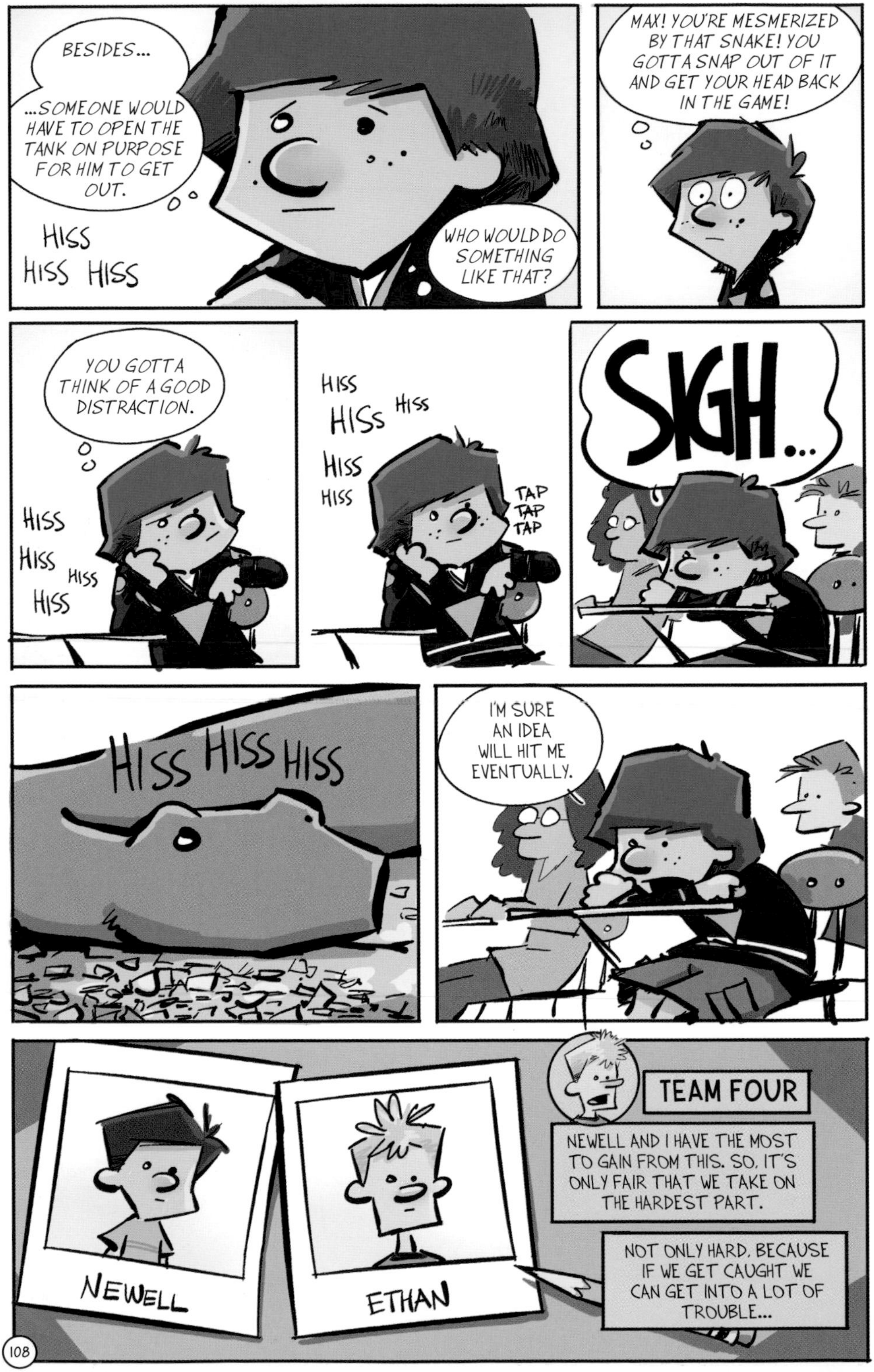
BESIDES...
...SOMEONE WOULD HAVE TO OPEN THE TANK ON PURPOSE FOR HIM TO GET OUT.
HISS HISS HISS
WHO WOULD DO SOMETHING LIKE THAT?
MAX! YOU'RE MESMERIZED BY THAT SNAKE! YOU GOTTA SNAP OUT OF IT AND GET YOUR HEAD BACK IN THE GAME!
YOU GOTTA THINK OF A GOOD DISTRACTION.
HISS HISS HISS HISS
HISS HISS HISS HISS HISS
TAP TAP TAP
SIGH...
HISS HISS HISS
I'M SURE AN IDEA WILL HIT ME EVENTUALLY.
NEWELL
ETHAN
TEAM FOUR
NEWELL AND I HAVE THE MOST TO GAIN FROM THIS. SO, IT'S ONLY FAIR THAT WE TAKE ON THE HARDEST PART.
NOT ONLY HARD, BECAUSE IF WE GET CAUGHT WE CAN GET INTO A LOT OF TROUBLE...

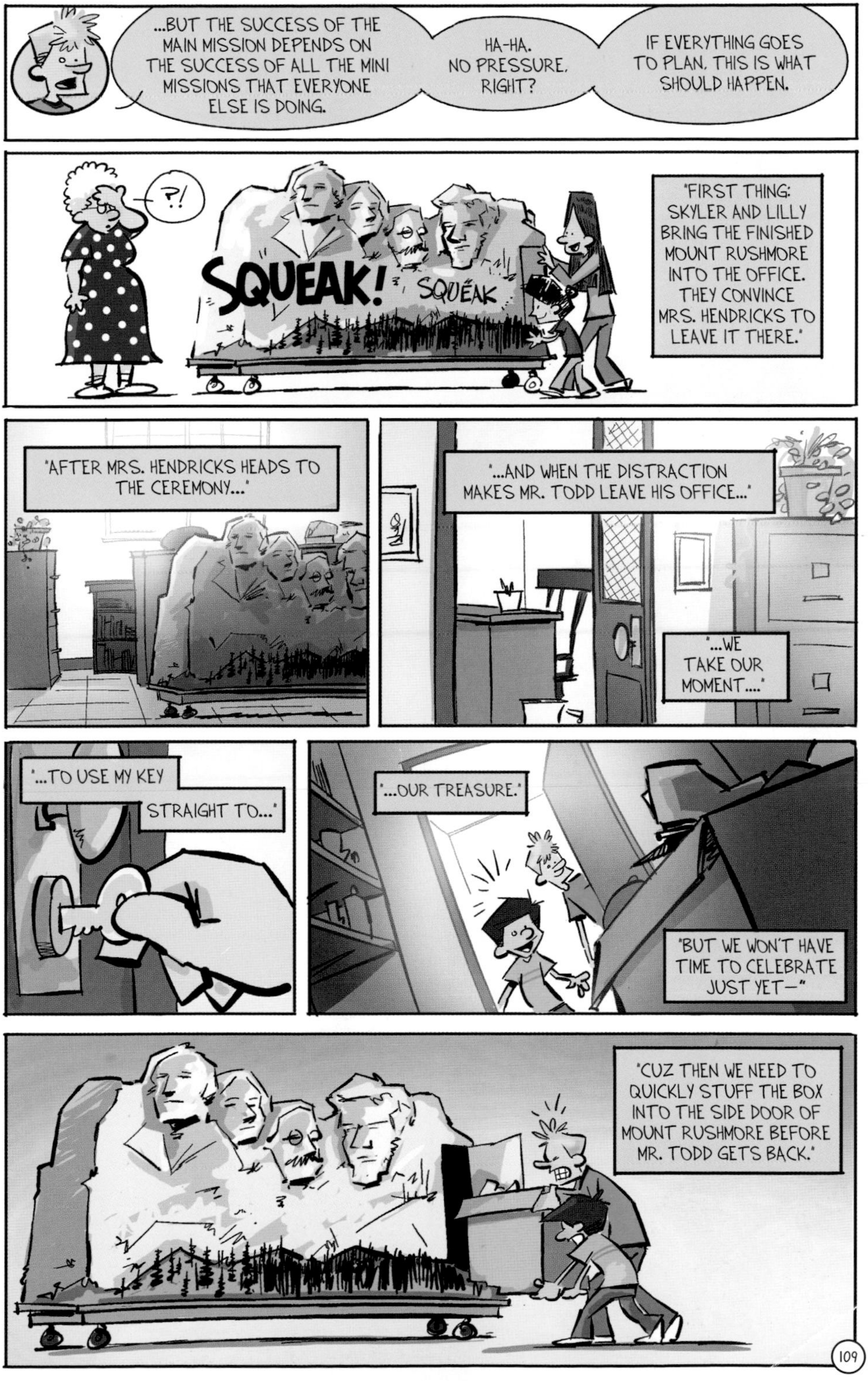
...BUT THE SUCCESS OF THE MAIN MISSION DEPENDS ON THE SUCCESS OF ALL THE MINI MISSIONS THAT EVERYONE ELSE IS DOING.
HA-HA. NO PRESSURE, RIGHT?
IF EVERYTHING GOES TO PLAN, THIS IS WHAT SHOULD HAPPEN.
?!
SQUEAK!
SQUEAK
"FIRST THING: SKYLER AND LILLY BRING THE FINISHED MOUNT RUSHMORE INTO THE OFFICE. THEY CONVINCE MRS. HENDRICKS TO LEAVE IT THERE."
"AFTER MRS. HENDRICKS HEADS TO THE CEREMONY..."
"...AND WHEN THE DISTRACTION MAKES MR. TODD LEAVE HIS OFFICE..."
"...WE TAKE OUR MOMENT...."
"...TO USE MY KEY
STRAIGHT TO..."
"...OUR TREASURE."
"BUT WE WON'T HAVE TIME TO CELEBRATE JUST YET—"
"CUZ THEN WE NEED TO QUICKLY STUFF THE BOX INTO THE SIDE DOOR OF MOUNT RUSHMORE BEFORE MR. TODD GETS BACK."

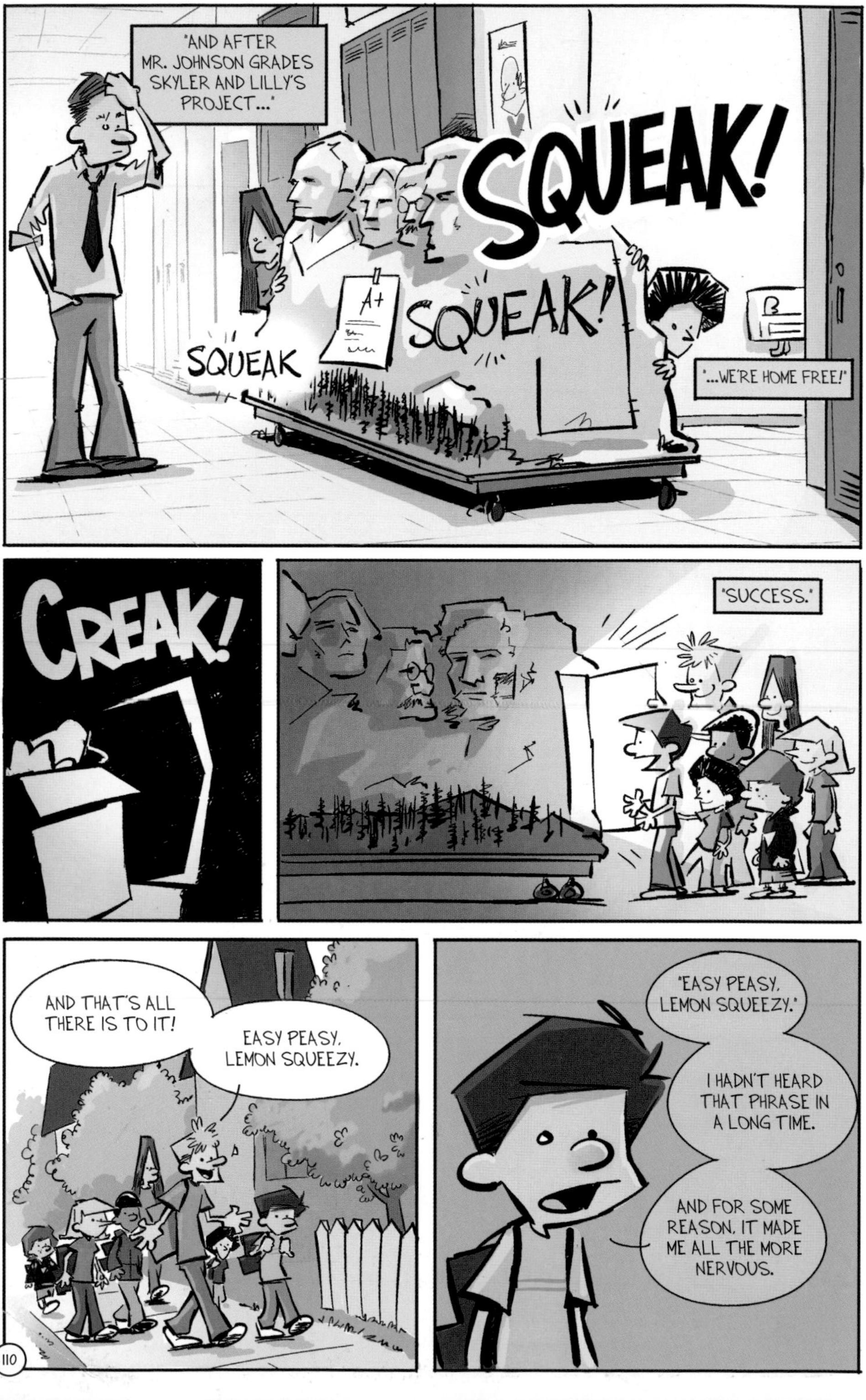
"AND AFTER MR. JOHNSON GRADES SKYLER AND LILLY'S PROJECT..."
SQUEAK!
A+
SQUEAK!
SQUEAK
"...WE'RE HOME FREE!"
CREAK!
"SUCCESS."
AND THAT'S ALL THERE IS TO IT!
EASY PEASY, LEMON SQUEEZY.
"EASY PEASY, LEMON SQUEEZY."
I HADN'T HEARD THAT PHRASE IN A LONG TIME.
AND FOR SOME REASON, IT MADE ME ALL THE MORE NERVOUS.

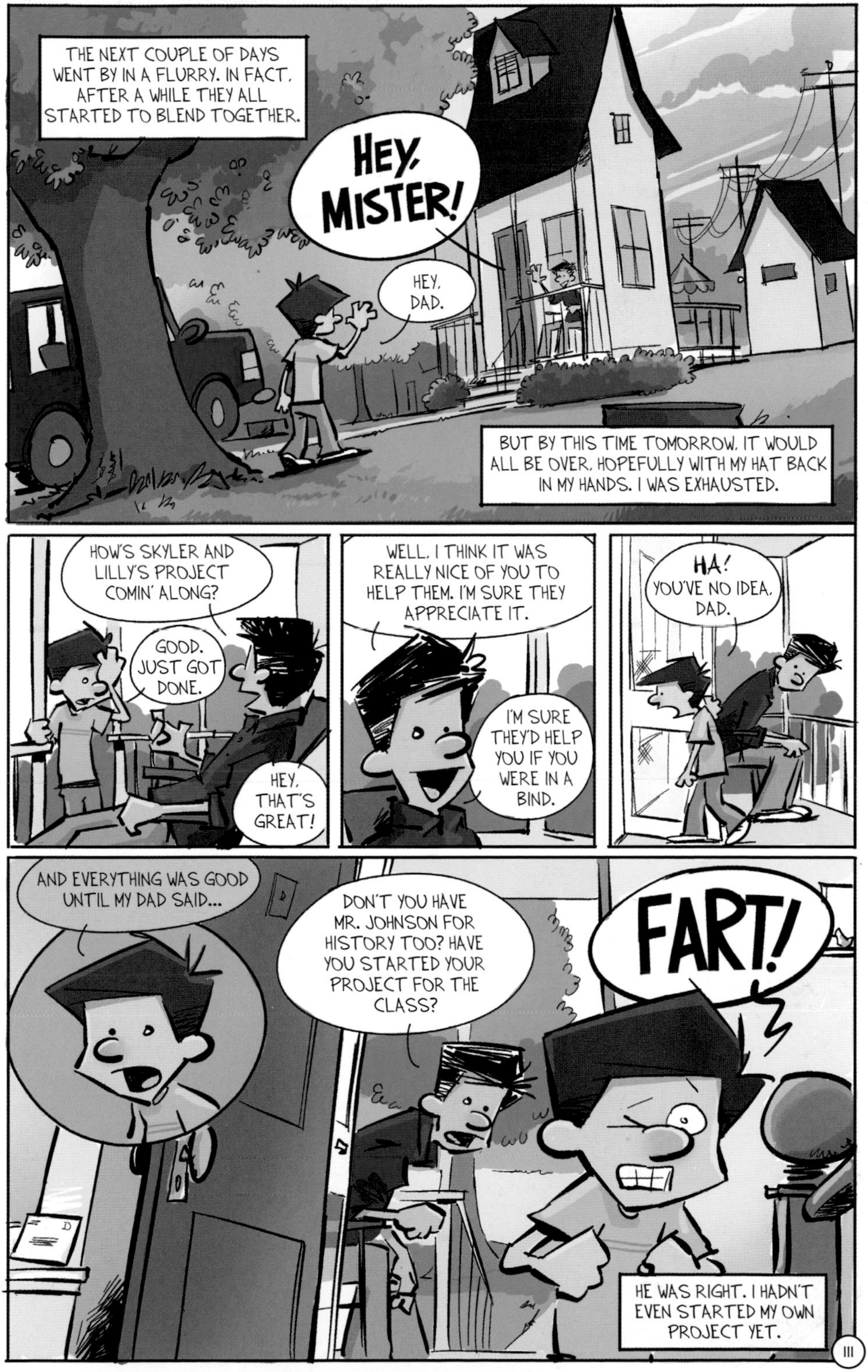

THE NEXT COUPLE OF DAYS WENT BY IN A FLURRY. IN FACT, AFTER A WHILE THEY ALL STARTED TO BLEND TOGETHER.
HEY, MISTER!
HEY, DAD.
BUT BY THIS TIME TOMORROW, IT WOULD ALL BE OVER, HOPEFULLY WITH MY HAT BACK IN MY HANDS. I WAS EXHAUSTED.
HOW'S SKYLER AND LILLY'S PROJECT COMIN' ALONG?
GOOD. JUST GOT DONE.
HEY, THAT'S GREAT!
WELL, I THINK IT WAS REALLY NICE OF YOU TO HELP THEM. I'M SURE THEY APPRECIATE IT.
I'M SURE THEY'D HELP YOU IF YOU WERE IN A BIND.
HA! YOU'VE NO IDEA, DAD.
AND EVERYTHING WAS GOOD UNTIL MY DAD SAID...
DON'T YOU HAVE MR. JOHNSON FOR HISTORY TOO? HAVE YOU STARTED YOUR PROJECT FOR THE CLASS?
FART!
HE WAS RIGHT. I HADN'T EVEN STARTED MY OWN PROJECT YET.

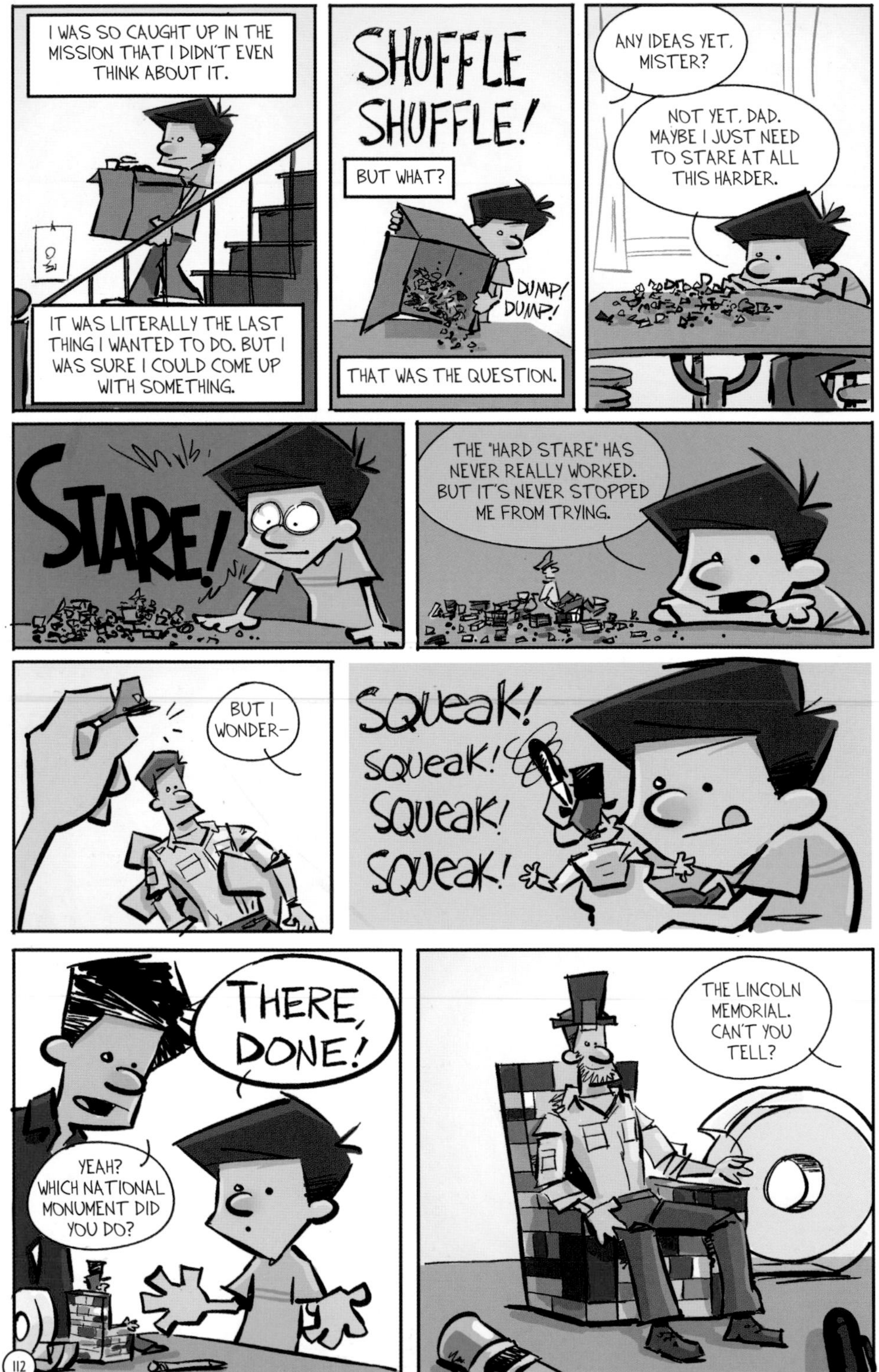

I WAS SO CAUGHT UP IN THE MISSION THAT I DIDN'T EVEN THINK ABOUT IT.
IT WAS LITERALLY THE LAST THING I WANTED TO DO. BUT I WAS SURE I COULD COME UP WITH SOMETHING.
SHUFFLE SHUFFLE!
BUT WHAT?
DUMP! DUMP!
THAT WAS THE QUESTION.
ANY IDEAS YET, MISTER?
NOT YET, DAD. MAYBE I JUST NEED TO STARE AT ALL THIS HARDER.
STARE!
THE "HARD STARE" HAS NEVER REALLY WORKED. BUT IT'S NEVER STOPPED ME FROM TRYING.
BUT I WONDER—
SQUEAK! SQUEAK! SQUEAK! SQUEAK!
THERE, DONE!
YEAH? WHICH NATIONAL MONUMENT DID YOU DO?
THE LINCOLN MEMORIAL. CAN'T YOU TELL?

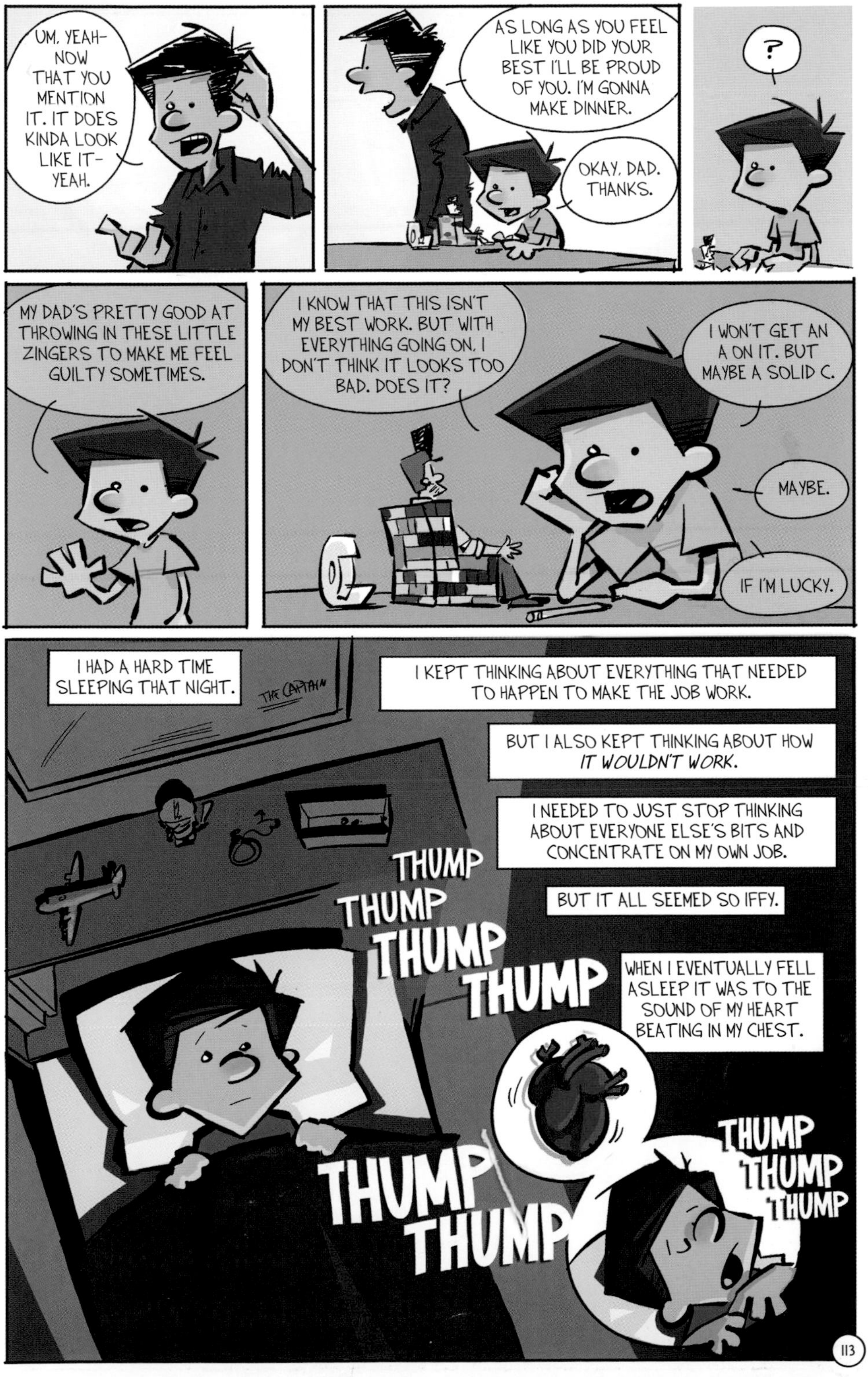
UM, YEAH- NOW THAT YOU MENTION IT. IT DOES KINDA LOOK LIKE IT- YEAH.
AS LONG AS YOU FEEL LIKE YOU DID YOUR BEST I'LL BE PROUD OF YOU. I'M GONNA MAKE DINNER.
OKAY, DAD. THANKS.
?
MY DAD'S PRETTY GOOD AT THROWING IN THESE LITTLE ZINGERS TO MAKE ME FEEL GUILTY SOMETIMES.
I KNOW THAT THIS ISN'T MY BEST WORK. BUT WITH EVERYTHING GOING ON, I DON'T THINK IT LOOKS TOO BAD. DOES IT?
I WON'T GET AN A ON IT. BUT MAYBE A SOLID C.
MAYBE.
IF I'M LUCKY.
I HAD A HARD TIME SLEEPING THAT NIGHT.
THE CAPTAIN
I KEPT THINKING ABOUT EVERYTHING THAT NEEDED TO HAPPEN TO MAKE THE JOB WORK.
BUT I ALSO KEPT THINKING ABOUT HOW *IT WOULDN'T WORK*.
I NEEDED TO JUST STOP THINKING ABOUT EVERYONE ELSE'S BITS AND CONCENTRATE ON MY OWN JOB.
BUT IT ALL SEEMED SO IFFY.
THUMP THUMP THUMP THUMP
WHEN I EVENTUALLY FELL ASLEEP IT WAS TO THE SOUND OF MY HEART BEATING IN MY CHEST.
THUMP THUMP
THUMP THUMP THUMP

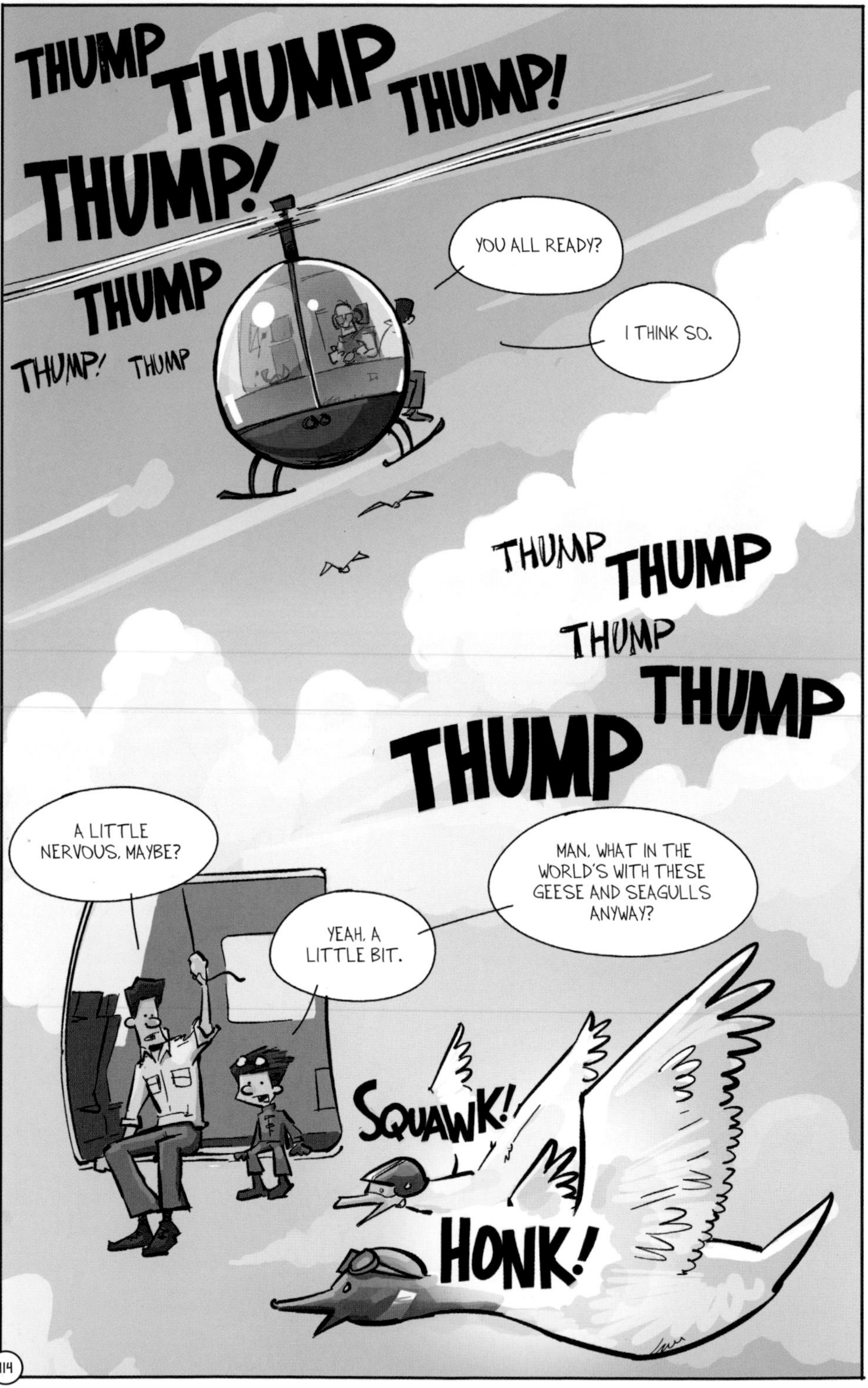
THUMP THUMP THUMP!
THUMP!
THUMP
THUMP! THUMP
YOU ALL READY?
I THINK SO.
THUMP THUMP
THUMP
THUMP
THUMP
A LITTLE NERVOUS, MAYBE?
YEAH, A LITTLE BIT.
MAN, WHAT IN THE WORLD'S WITH THESE GEESE AND SEAGULLS ANYWAY?
SQUAWK!
HONK!

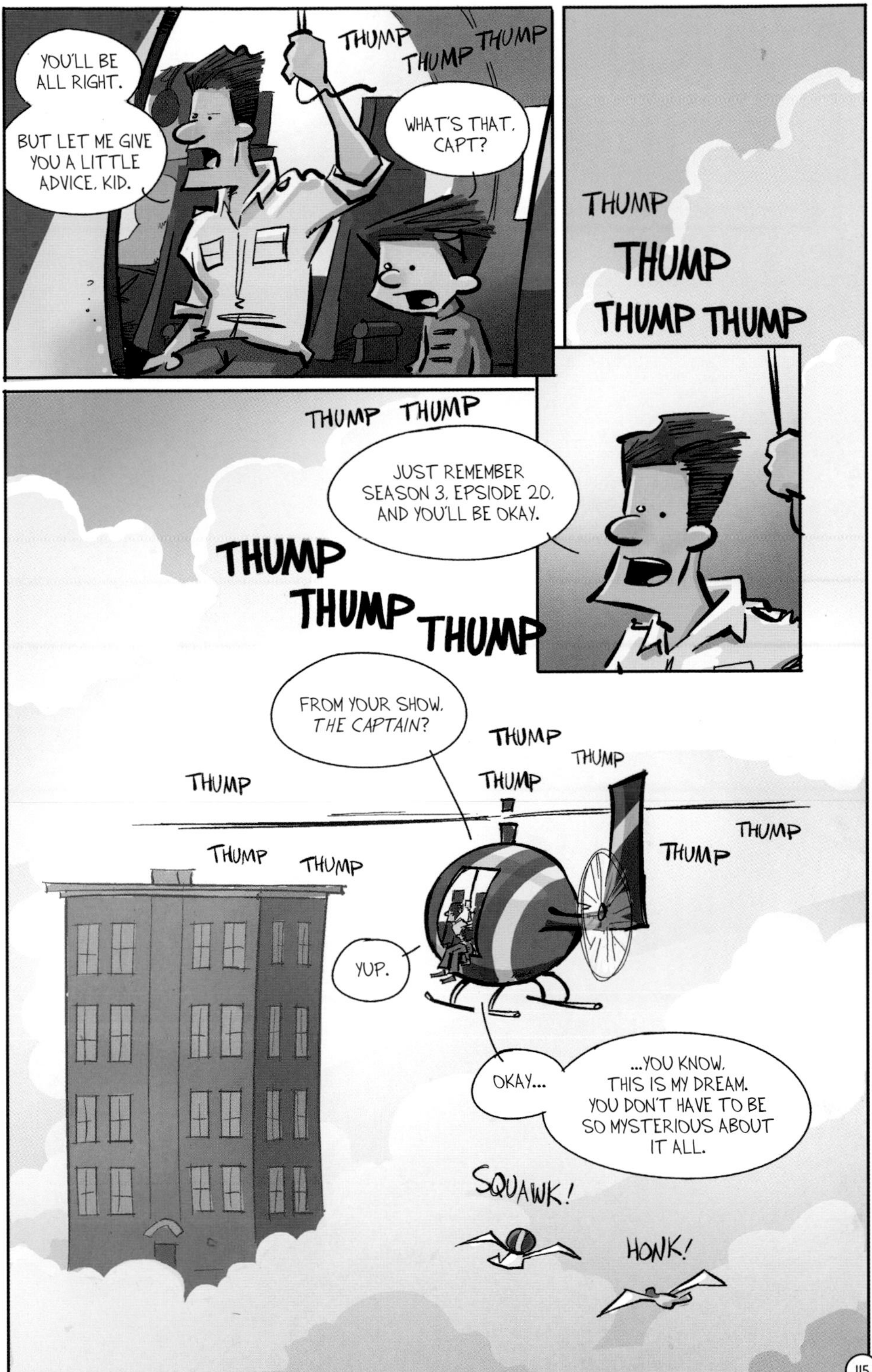
YOU'LL BE ALL RIGHT.
BUT LET ME GIVE YOU A LITTLE ADVICE, KID.
THUMP THUMP THUMP
WHAT'S THAT, CAPT?
THUMP THUMP THUMP THUMP
THUMP THUMP
JUST REMEMBER SEASON 3, EPSIDODE 20, AND YOU'LL BE OKAY.
THUMP THUMP THUMP
FROM YOUR SHOW, *THE CAPTAIN*?
THUMP THUMP THUMP
THUMP
THUMP THUMP
THUMP THUMP
YUP.
OKAY...
...YOU KNOW, THIS IS MY DREAM. YOU DON'T HAVE TO BE SO MYSTERIOUS ABOUT IT ALL.
SQUAWK!
HONK!

CHAPTER SEVEN
THE HEIST

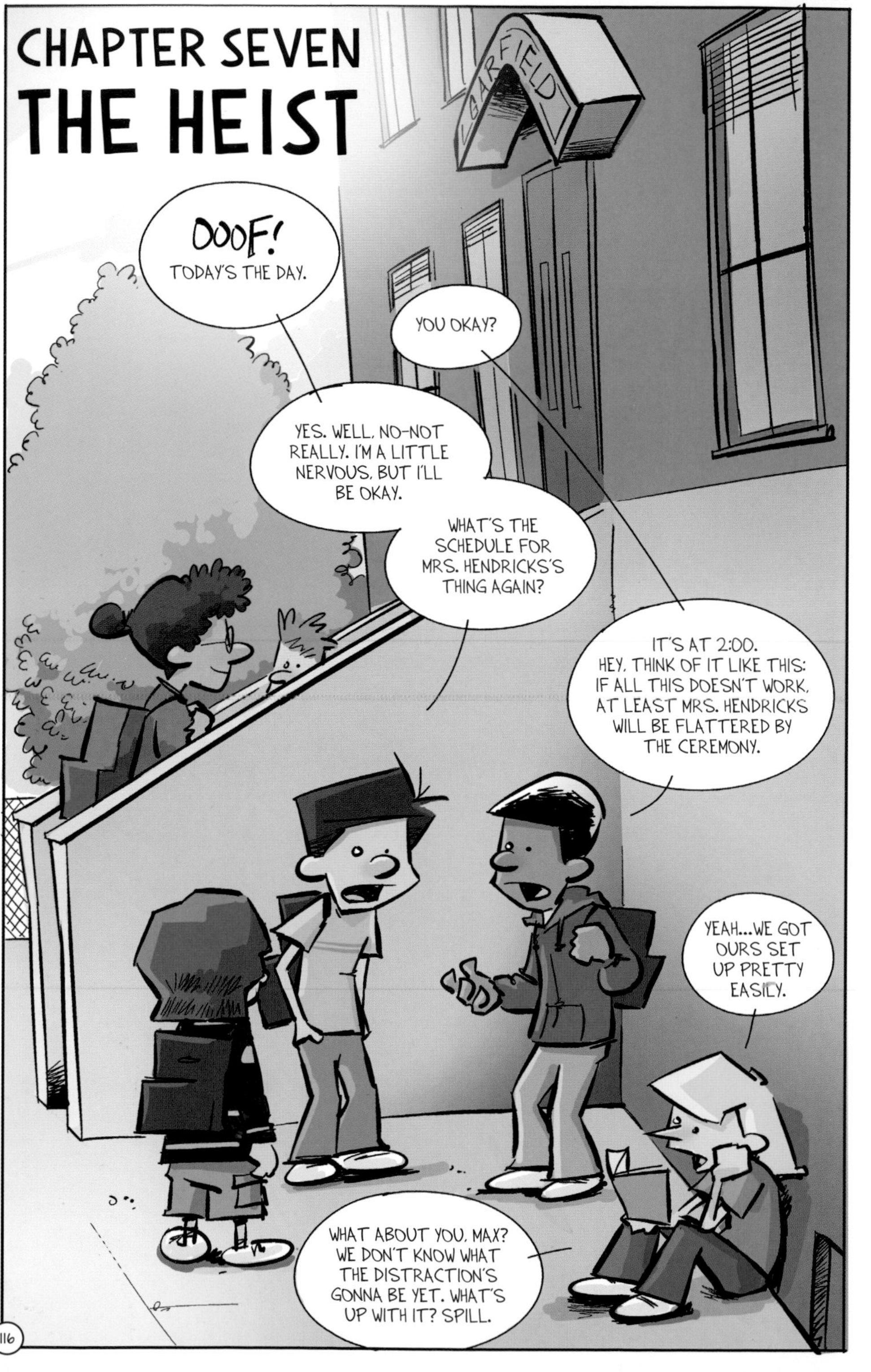

OOOF! TODAY'S THE DAY.
YOU OKAY?
YES. WELL, NO–NOT REALLY. I'M A LITTLE NERVOUS, BUT I'LL BE OKAY.
WHAT'S THE SCHEDULE FOR MRS. HENDRICKS'S THING AGAIN?
IT'S AT 2:00. HEY, THINK OF IT LIKE THIS: IF ALL THIS DOESN'T WORK, AT LEAST MRS. HENDRICKS WILL BE FLATTERED BY THE CEREMONY.
YEAH...WE GOT OURS SET UP PRETTY EASILY.
WHAT ABOUT YOU, MAX? WE DON'T KNOW WHAT THE DISTRACTION'S GONNA BE YET. WHAT'S UP WITH IT? SPILL.

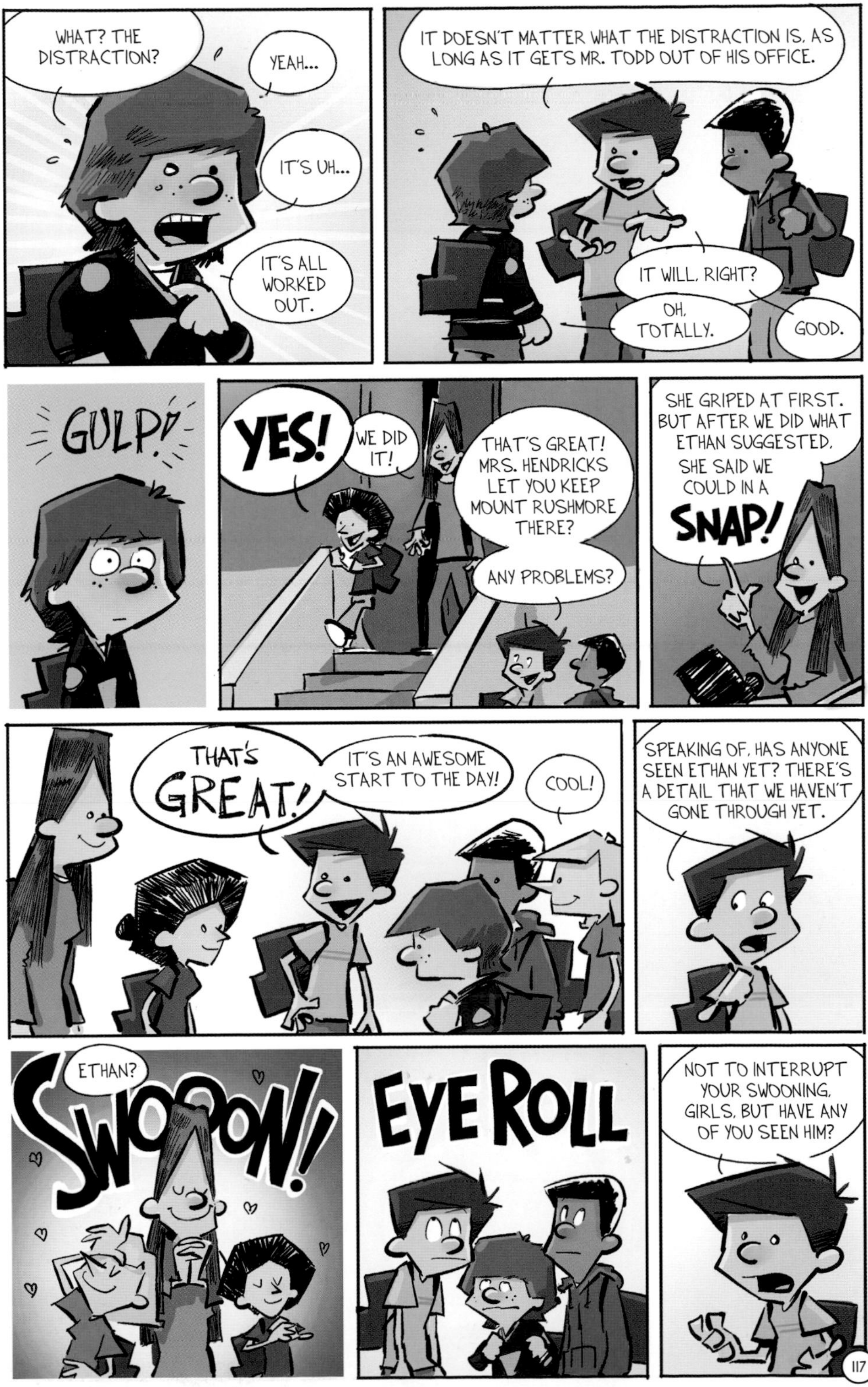
WHAT? THE DISTRACTION?
YEAH...
IT'S UH...
IT'S ALL WORKED OUT.
IT DOESN'T MATTER WHAT THE DISTRACTION IS, AS LONG AS IT GETS MR. TODD OUT OF HIS OFFICE.
IT WILL, RIGHT?
OH, TOTALLY.
GOOD.
GULP!
YES!
WE DID IT!
THAT'S GREAT! MRS. HENDRICKS LET YOU KEEP MOUNT RUSHMORE THERE?
ANY PROBLEMS?
SHE GRIPED AT FIRST. BUT AFTER WE DID WHAT ETHAN SUGGESTED, SHE SAID WE COULD IN A SNAP!
THAT'S GREAT!
IT'S AN AWESOME START TO THE DAY!
COOL!
SPEAKING OF, HAS ANYONE SEEN ETHAN YET? THERE'S A DETAIL THAT WE HAVEN'T GONE THROUGH YET.
ETHAN?
SWOOON!
EYE ROLL
NOT TO INTERRUPT YOUR SWOONING, GIRLS, BUT HAVE ANY OF YOU SEEN HIM?

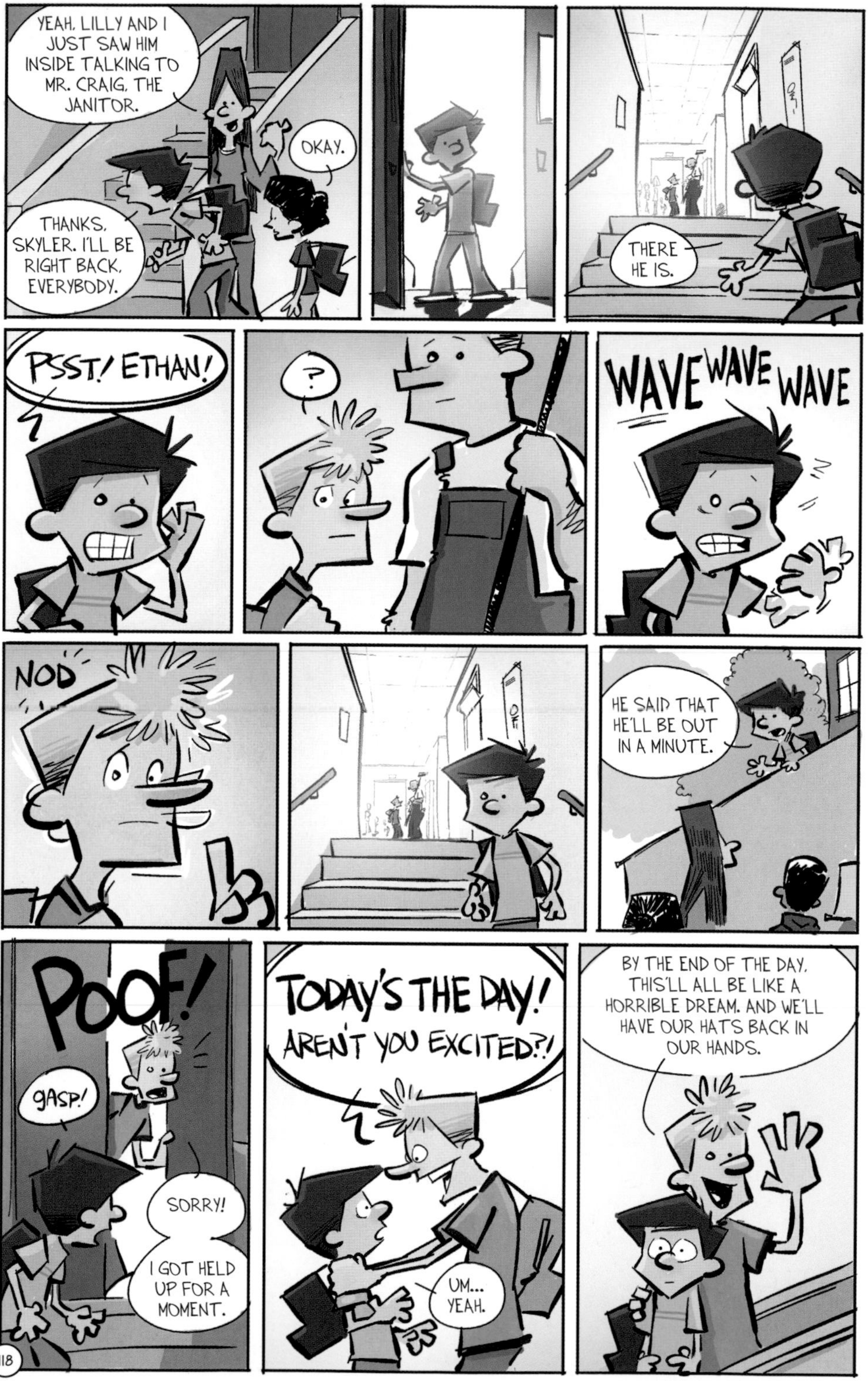
YEAH, LILLY AND I JUST SAW HIM INSIDE TALKING TO MR. CRAIG, THE JANITOR.
OKAY.
THANKS, SKYLER. I'LL BE RIGHT BACK, EVERYBODY.
THERE HE IS.
PSST! ETHAN!
?
WAVE WAVE WAVE
NOD
HE SAID THAT HE'LL BE OUT IN A MINUTE.
POOF!
GASP!
SORRY!
I GOT HELD UP FOR A MOMENT.
TODAY'S THE DAY! AREN'T YOU EXCITED?!
UM... YEAH.
BY THE END OF THE DAY, THIS'LL ALL BE LIKE A HORRIBLE DREAM. AND WE'LL HAVE OUR HATS BACK IN OUR HANDS.

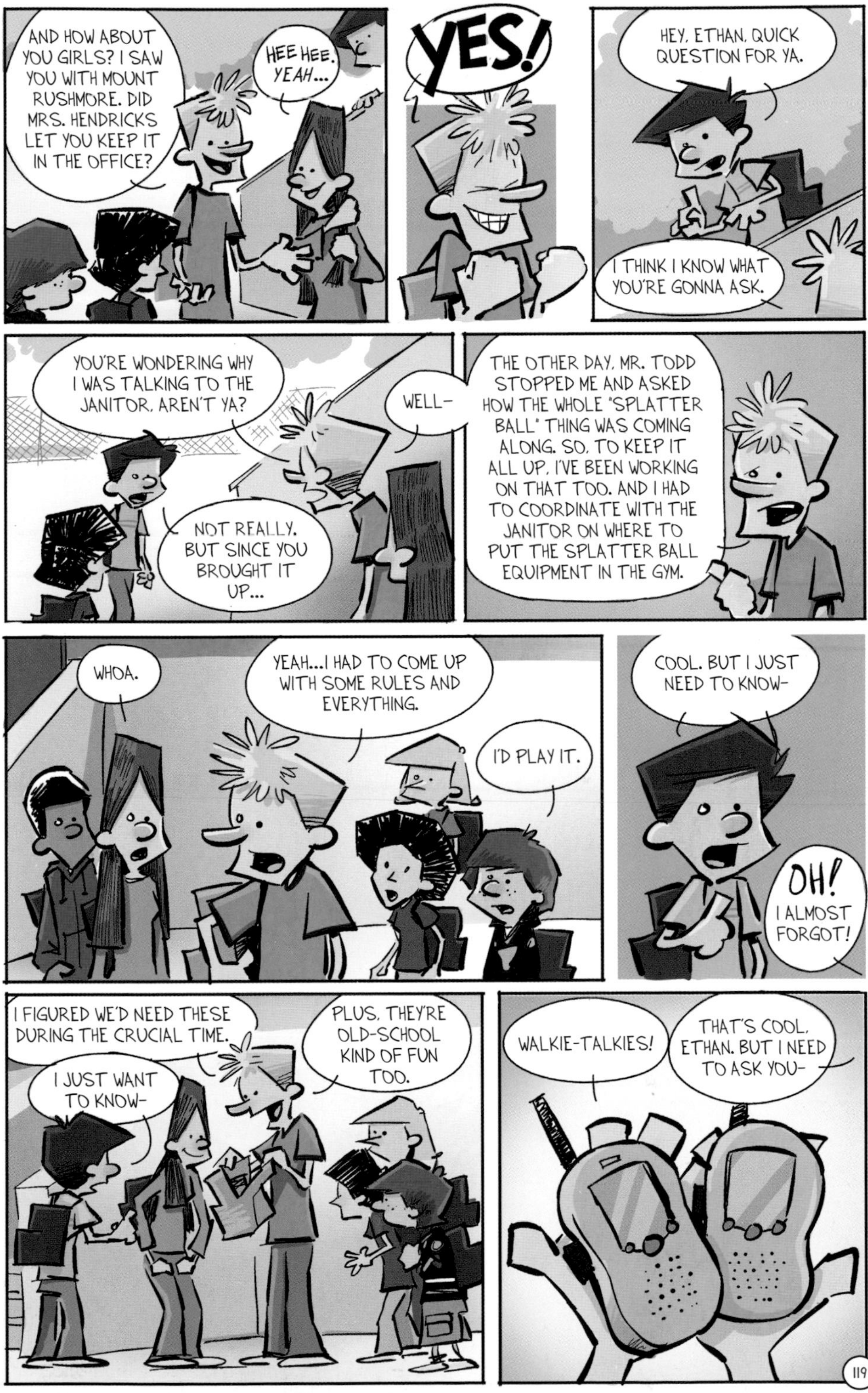
AND HOW ABOUT YOU GIRLS? I SAW YOU WITH MOUNT RUSHMORE. DID MRS. HENDRICKS LET YOU KEEP IT IN THE OFFICE?
HEE HEE. YEAH...
YES!
HEY, ETHAN, QUICK QUESTION FOR YA.
I THINK I KNOW WHAT YOU'RE GONNA ASK.
YOU'RE WONDERING WHY I WAS TALKING TO THE JANITOR, AREN'T YA?
WELL-
NOT REALLY. BUT SINCE YOU BROUGHT IT UP...
THE OTHER DAY, MR. TODD STOPPED ME AND ASKED HOW THE WHOLE "SPLATTER BALL" THING WAS COMING ALONG. SO, TO KEEP IT ALL UP, I'VE BEEN WORKING ON THAT TOO. AND I HAD TO COORDINATE WITH THE JANITOR ON WHERE TO PUT THE SPLATTER BALL EQUIPMENT IN THE GYM.
WHOA.
YEAH...I HAD TO COME UP WITH SOME RULES AND EVERYTHING.
I'D PLAY IT.
COOL. BUT I JUST NEED TO KNOW-
OH! I ALMOST FORGOT!
I FIGURED WE'D NEED THESE DURING THE CRUCIAL TIME.
I JUST WANT TO KNOW-
PLUS, THEY'RE OLD-SCHOOL KIND OF FUN TOO.
WALKIE-TALKIES!
THAT'S COOL, ETHAN. BUT I NEED TO ASK YOU-

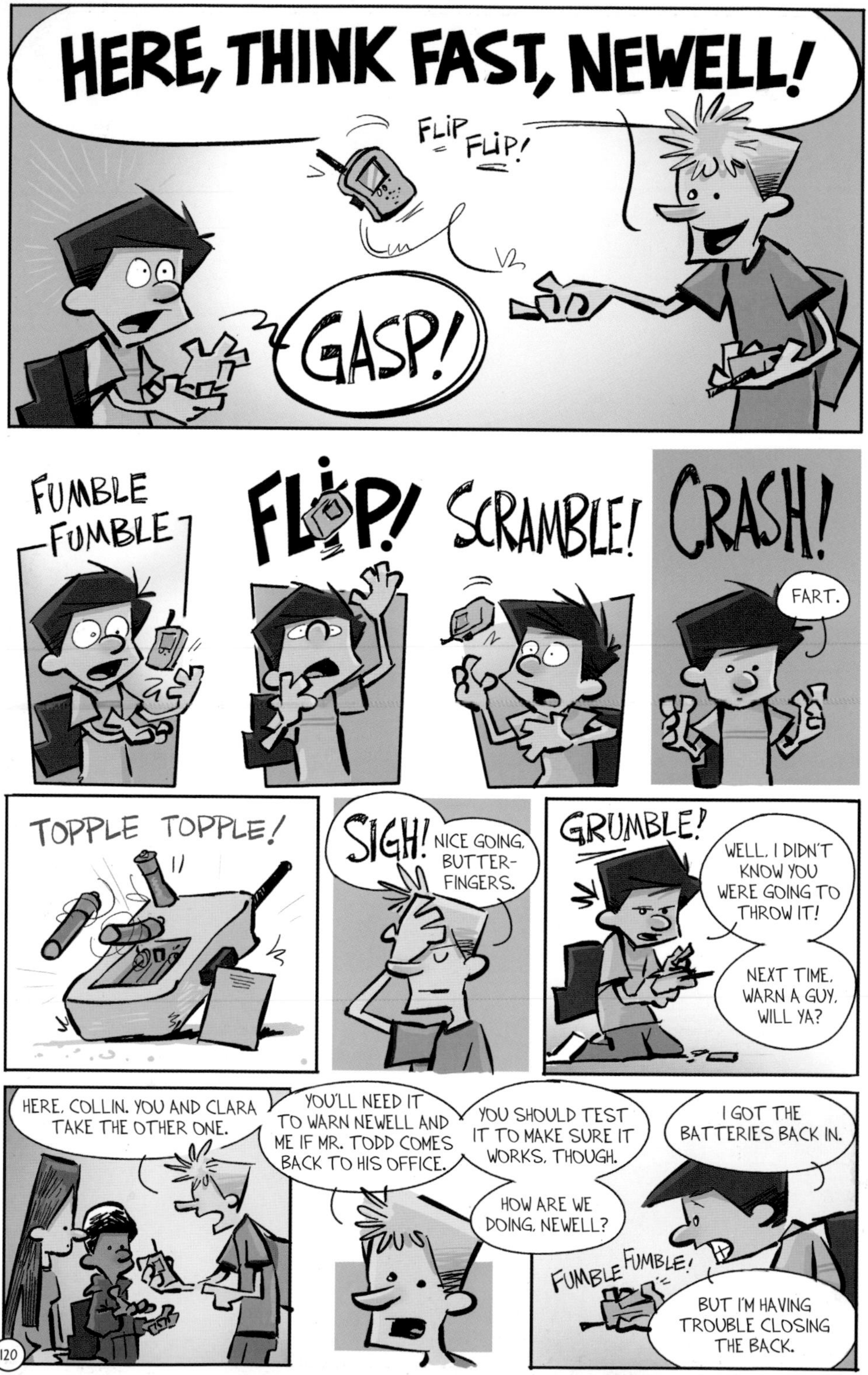
HERE, THINK FAST, NEWELL!
FLIP FLIP!
GASP!
FUMBLE FUMBLE
FLIP!
SCRAMBLE!
CRASH!
FART.
TOPPLE TOPPLE!
SIGH!
NICE GOING, BUTTER-FINGERS.
GRUMBLE!
WELL, I DIDN'T KNOW YOU WERE GOING TO THROW IT!
NEXT TIME, WARN A GUY, WILL YA?
HERE, COLLIN. YOU AND CLARA TAKE THE OTHER ONE.
YOU'LL NEED IT TO WARN NEWELL AND ME IF MR. TODD COMES BACK TO HIS OFFICE.
YOU SHOULD TEST IT TO MAKE SURE IT WORKS, THOUGH.
HOW ARE WE DOING, NEWELL?
I GOT THE BATTERIES BACK IN.
FUMBLE FUMBLE!
BUT I'M HAVING TROUBLE CLOSING THE BACK.

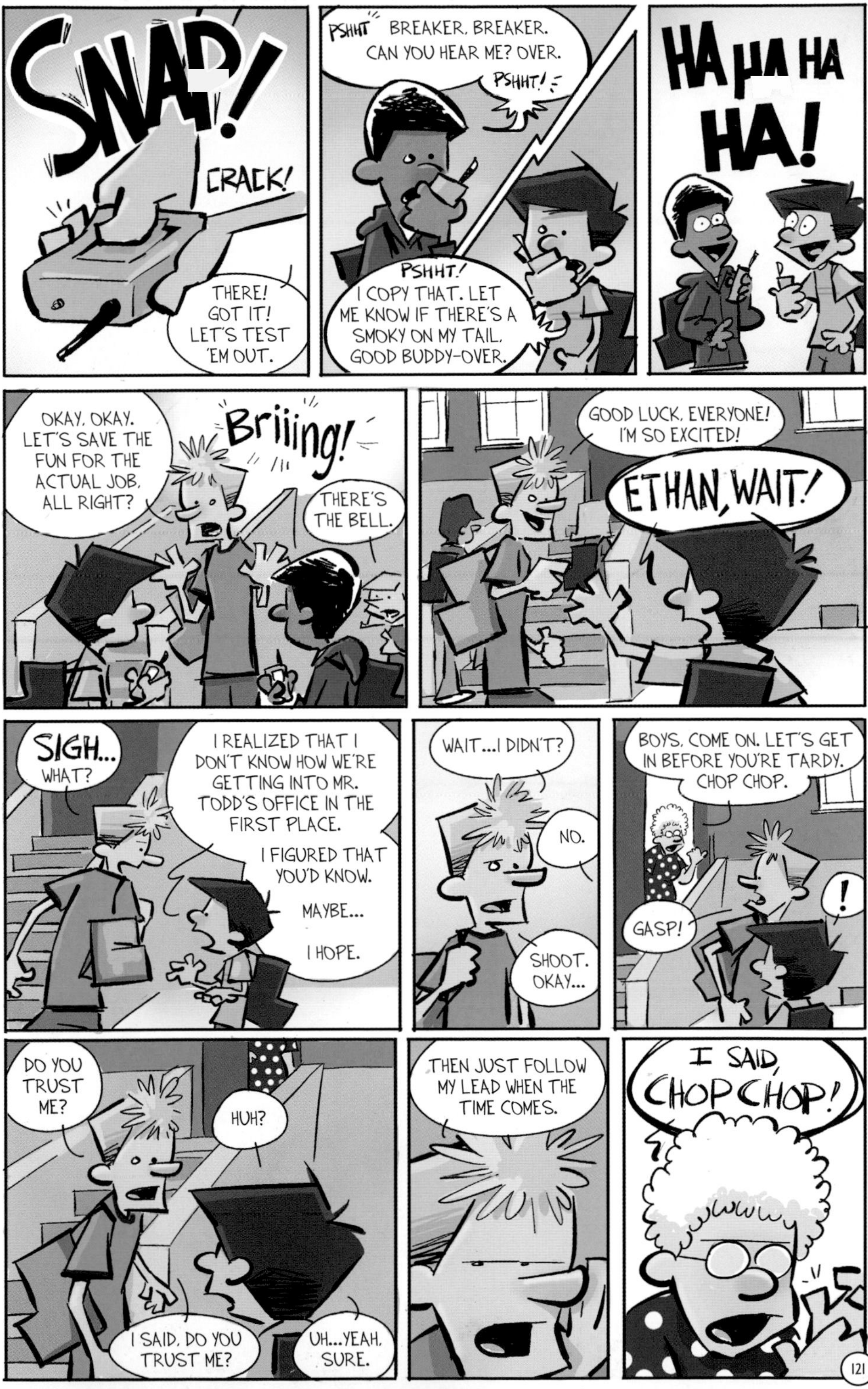
SNAP!
CRACK!
THERE! GOT IT! LET'S TEST 'EM OUT.
PSHHT BREAKER, BREAKER. CAN YOU HEAR ME? OVER. PSHHT!
PSHHT! I COPY THAT. LET ME KNOW IF THERE'S A SMOKY ON MY TAIL, GOOD BUDDY–OVER.
HA HA HA HA!
OKAY, OKAY. LET'S SAVE THE FUN FOR THE ACTUAL JOB, ALL RIGHT?
Briiing!
THERE'S THE BELL.
GOOD LUCK, EVERYONE! I'M SO EXCITED!
ETHAN, WAIT!
SIGH... WHAT?
I REALIZED THAT I DON'T KNOW HOW WE'RE GETTING INTO MR. TODD'S OFFICE IN THE FIRST PLACE.
I FIGURED THAT YOU'D KNOW.
MAYBE...
I HOPE.
WAIT...I DIDN'T?
NO.
SHOOT. OKAY...
BOYS, COME ON. LET'S GET IN BEFORE YOU'RE TARDY. CHOP CHOP.
GASP!
!
DO YOU TRUST ME?
HUH?
I SAID, DO YOU TRUST ME?
UH...YEAH, SURE.
THEN JUST FOLLOW MY LEAD WHEN THE TIME COMES.
I SAID, CHOP CHOP!

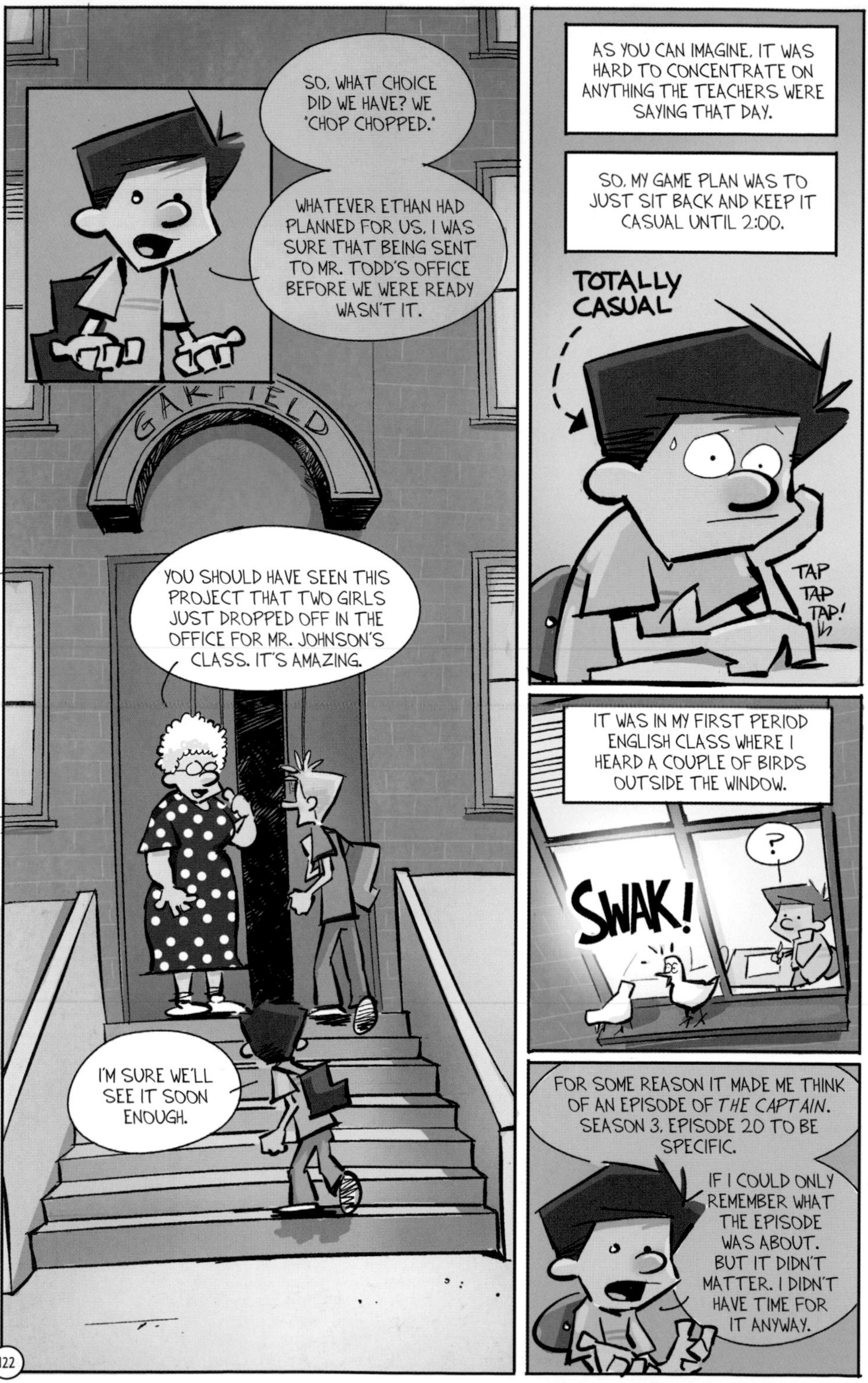
SO, WHAT CHOICE DID WE HAVE? WE "CHOP CHOPPED."
WHATEVER ETHAN HAD PLANNED FOR US, I WAS SURE THAT BEING SENT TO MR. TODD'S OFFICE BEFORE WE WERE READY WASN'T IT.
GARFIELD
YOU SHOULD HAVE SEEN THIS PROJECT THAT TWO GIRLS JUST DROPPED OFF IN THE OFFICE FOR MR. JOHNSON'S CLASS. IT'S AMAZING.
I'M SURE WE'LL SEE IT SOON ENOUGH.
AS YOU CAN IMAGINE, IT WAS HARD TO CONCENTRATE ON ANYTHING THE TEACHERS WERE SAYING THAT DAY.
SO, MY GAME PLAN WAS TO JUST SIT BACK AND KEEP IT CASUAL UNTIL 2:00.
TOTALLY CASUAL
TAP TAP TAP!
IT WAS IN MY FIRST PERIOD ENGLISH CLASS WHERE I HEARD A COUPLE OF BIRDS OUTSIDE THE WINDOW.
?
SWAK!
FOR SOME REASON IT MADE ME THINK OF AN EPISODE OF *THE CAPTAIN*. SEASON 3, EPISODE 20 TO BE SPECIFIC.
IF I COULD ONLY REMEMBER WHAT THE EPISODE WAS ABOUT. BUT IT DIDN'T MATTER. I DIDN'T HAVE TIME FOR IT ANYWAY.

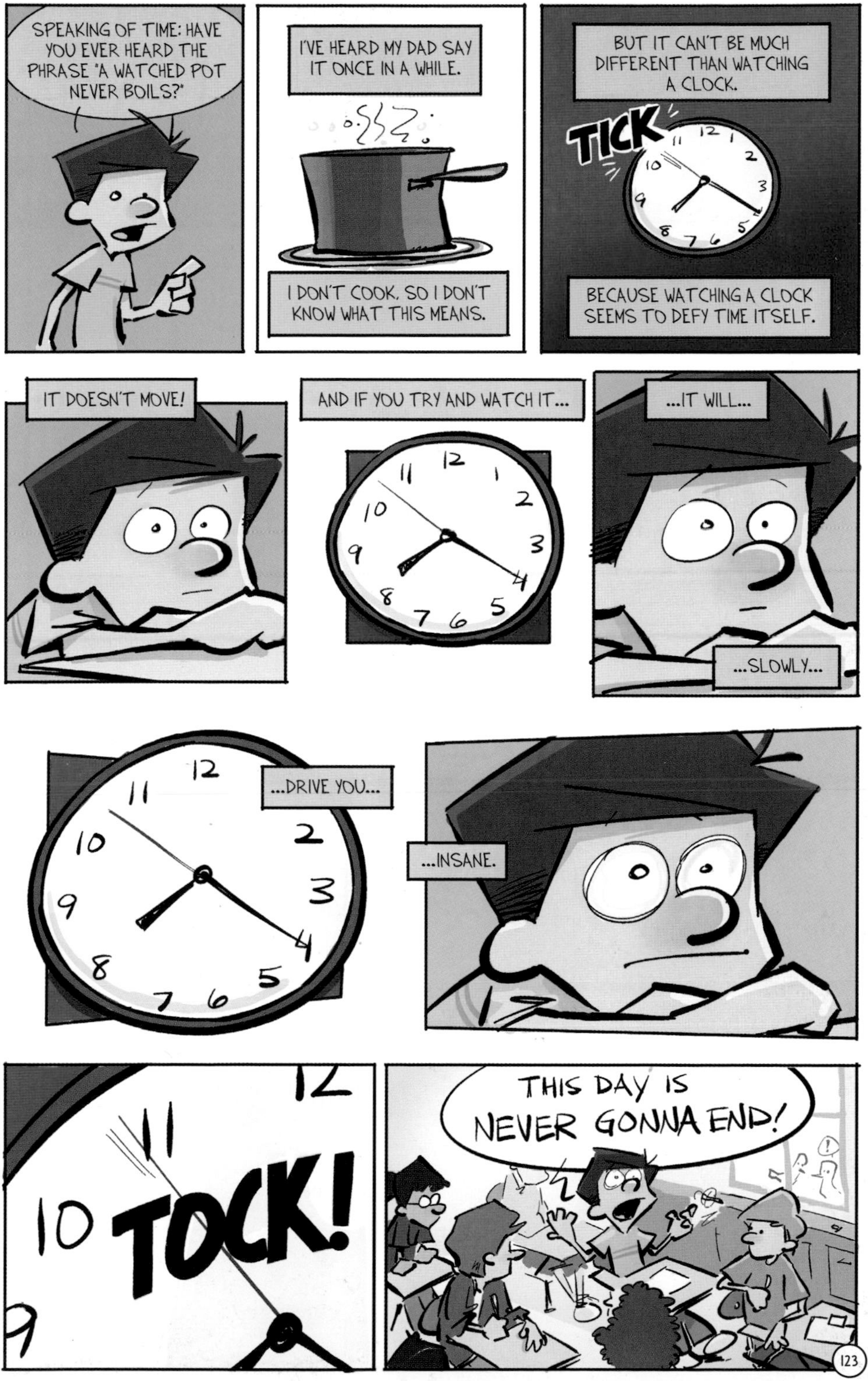

SPEAKING OF TIME: HAVE YOU EVER HEARD THE PHRASE "A WATCHED POT NEVER BOILS?"
I'VE HEARD MY DAD SAY IT ONCE IN A WHILE.
I DON'T COOK, SO I DON'T KNOW WHAT THIS MEANS.
BUT IT CAN'T BE MUCH DIFFERENT THAN WATCHING A CLOCK.
TICK
BECAUSE WATCHING A CLOCK SEEMS TO DEFY TIME ITSELF.
IT DOESN'T MOVE!
AND IF YOU TRY AND WATCH IT...
...IT WILL...
...SLOWLY...
...DRIVE YOU...
...INSANE.
TOCK!
THIS DAY IS NEVER GONNA END!

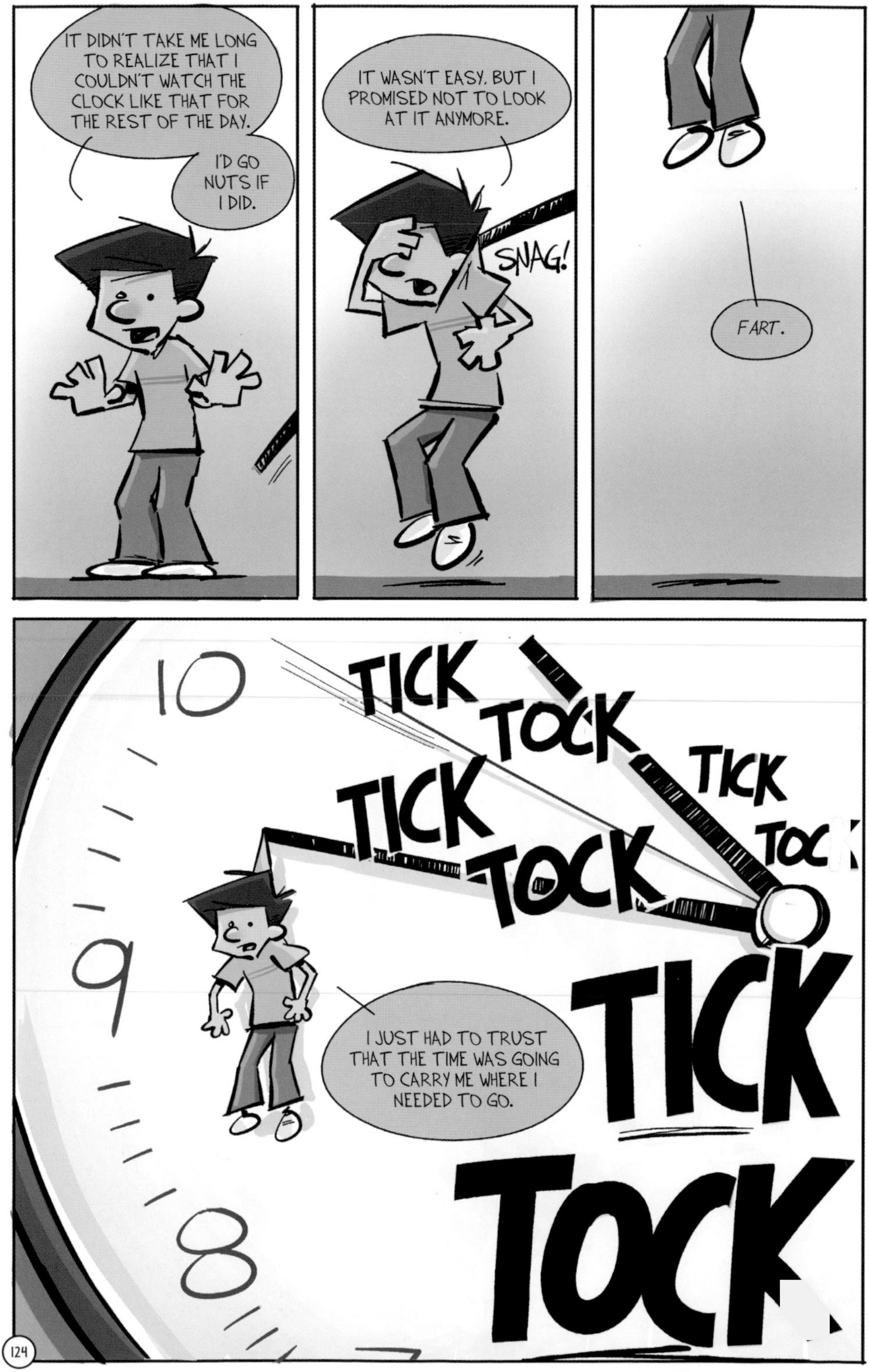
IT DIDN'T TAKE ME LONG TO REALIZE THAT I COULDN'T WATCH THE CLOCK LIKE THAT FOR THE REST OF THE DAY.
I'D GO NUTS IF I DID.
IT WASN'T EASY, BUT I PROMISED NOT TO LOOK AT IT ANYMORE.
SNAG!
FART.
TICK
TOCK
TICK
TICK
TOCK
TOCK
I JUST HAD TO TRUST THAT THE TIME WAS GOING TO CARRY ME WHERE I NEEDED TO GO.
TICK
TOCK

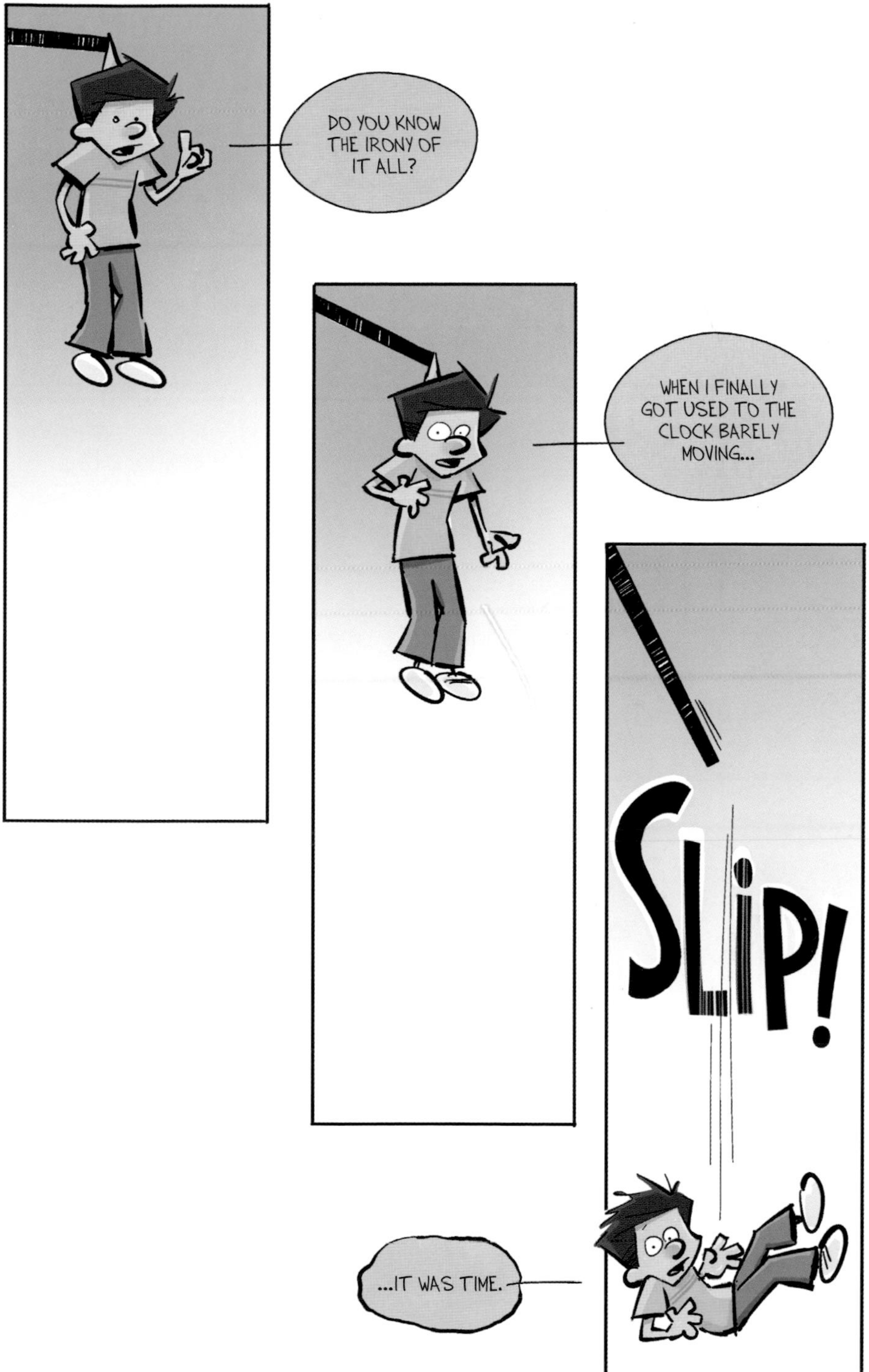
DO YOU KNOW THE IRONY OF IT ALL?
WHEN I FINALLY GOT USED TO THE CLOCK BARELY MOVING...
SLIP!
...IT WAS TIME.

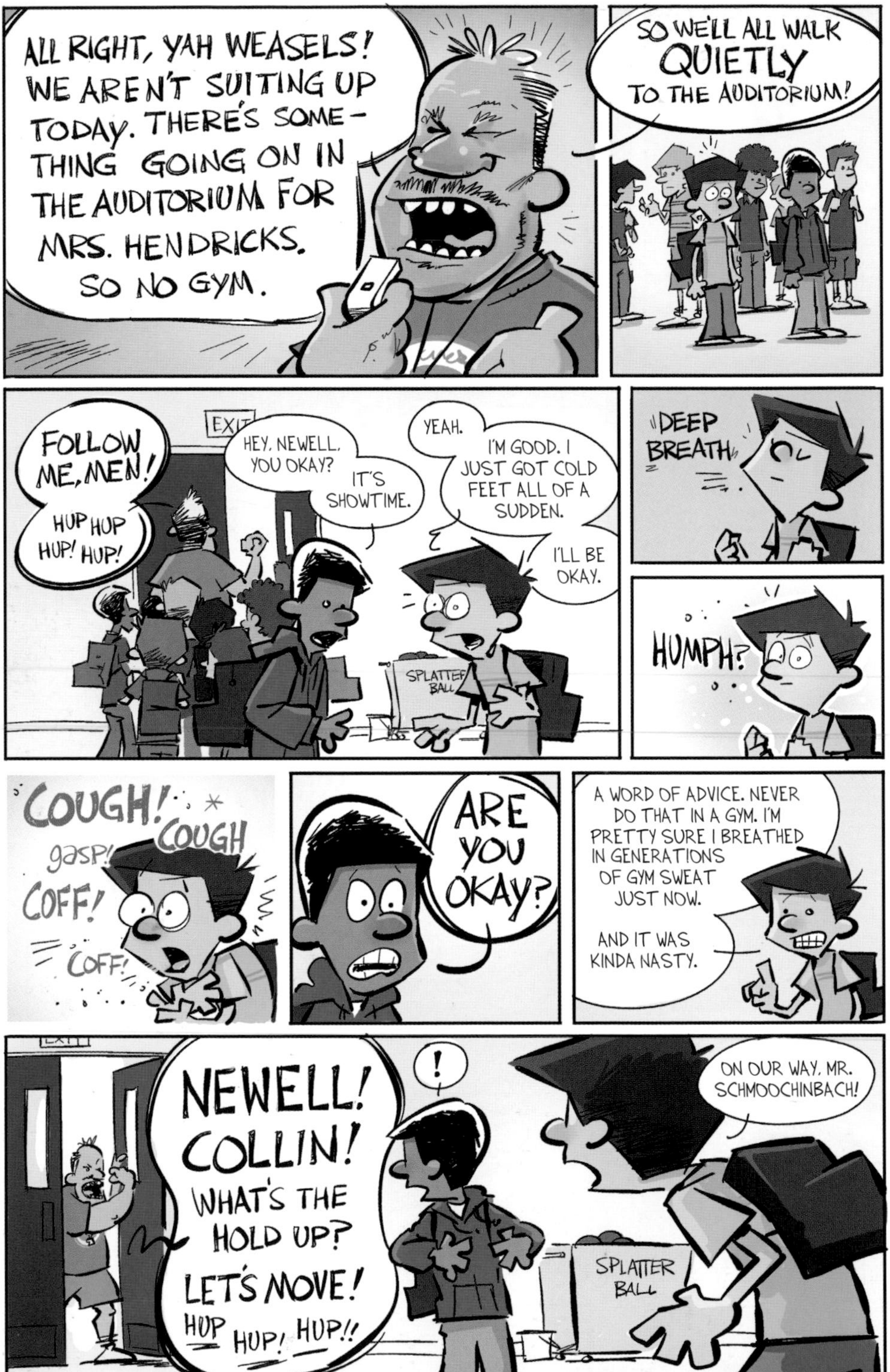
ALL RIGHT, YAH WEASELS! WE AREN'T SUITING UP TODAY. THERE'S SOME-THING GOING ON IN THE AUDITORIUM FOR MRS. HENDRICKS. SO NO GYM.
SO WE'LL ALL WALK QUIETLY TO THE AUDITORIUM!
EXIT
FOLLOW ME, MEN!
HUP HUP HUP! HUP!
HEY, NEWELL, YOU OKAY?
IT'S SHOWTIME.
YEAH.
I'M GOOD. I JUST GOT COLD FEET ALL OF A SUDDEN.
I'LL BE OKAY.
SPLATTER BALL
DEEP BREATH
HUMPH?
COUGH!
COUGH
gasp!
COFF!
COFF!
ARE YOU OKAY?
A WORD OF ADVICE. NEVER DO THAT IN A GYM. I'M PRETTY SURE I BREATHED IN GENERATIONS OF GYM SWEAT JUST NOW.
AND IT WAS KINDA NASTY.
NEWELL! COLLIN! WHAT'S THE HOLD UP? LET'S MOVE! HUP HUP! HUP!!
!
ON OUR WAY, MR. SCHMOOCHINBACH!
SPLATTER BALL

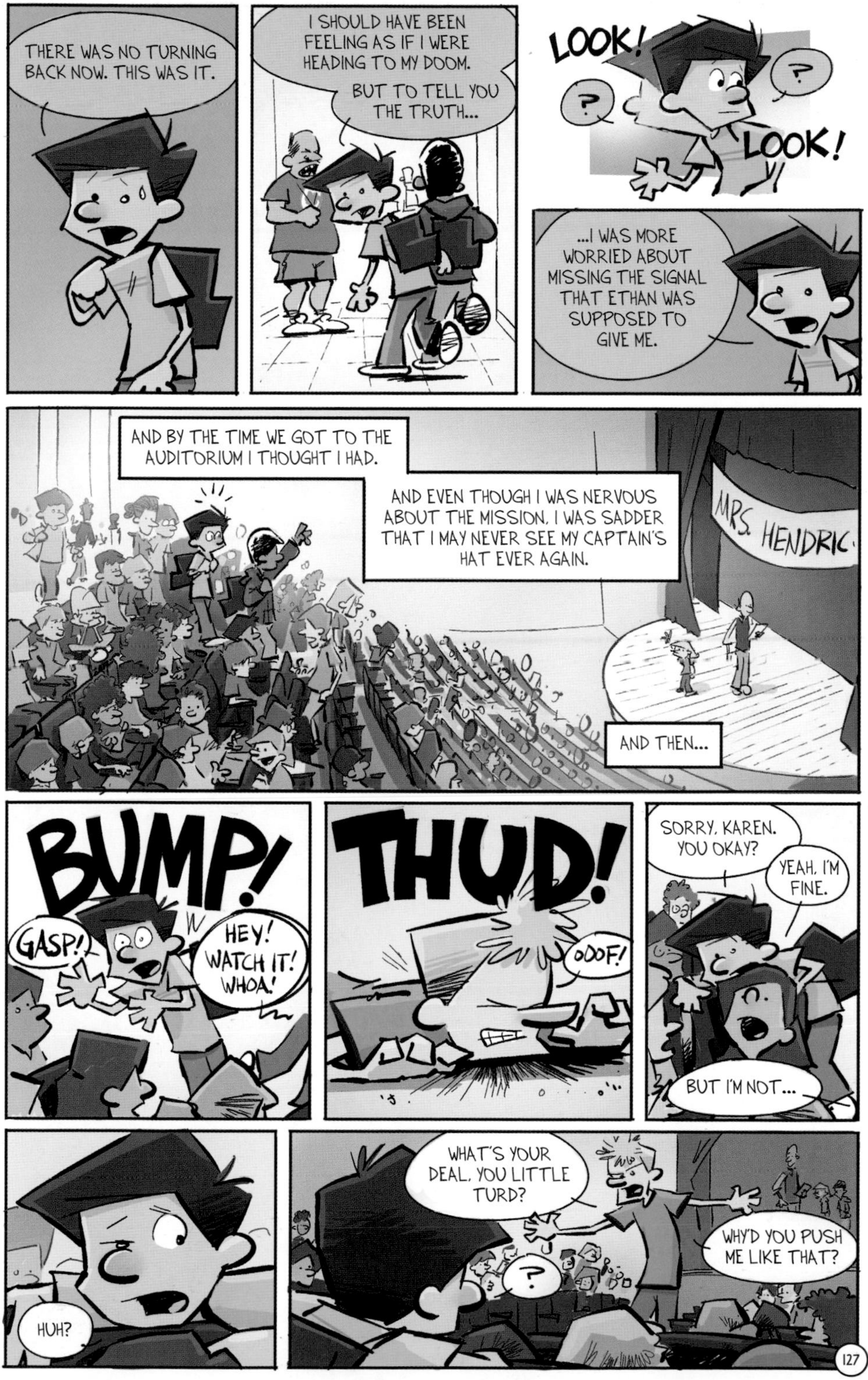

THERE WAS NO TURNING BACK NOW. THIS WAS IT.
I SHOULD HAVE BEEN FEELING AS IF I WERE HEADING TO MY DOOM.
BUT TO TELL YOU THE TRUTH...
LOOK!
?
?
LOOK!
...I WAS MORE WORRIED ABOUT MISSING THE SIGNAL THAT ETHAN WAS SUPPOSED TO GIVE ME.
AND BY THE TIME WE GOT TO THE AUDITORIUM I THOUGHT I HAD.
AND EVEN THOUGH I WAS NERVOUS ABOUT THE MISSION, I WAS SADDER THAT I MAY NEVER SEE MY CAPTAIN'S HAT EVER AGAIN.
MRS. HENDRIC
AND THEN...
BUMP!
GASP!
HEY! WATCH IT! WHOA!
THUD!
OOOF!
SORRY, KAREN. YOU OKAY?
YEAH, I'M FINE.
BUT I'M NOT...
HUH?
WHAT'S YOUR DEAL, YOU LITTLE TURD?
?
WHY'D YOU PUSH ME LIKE THAT?

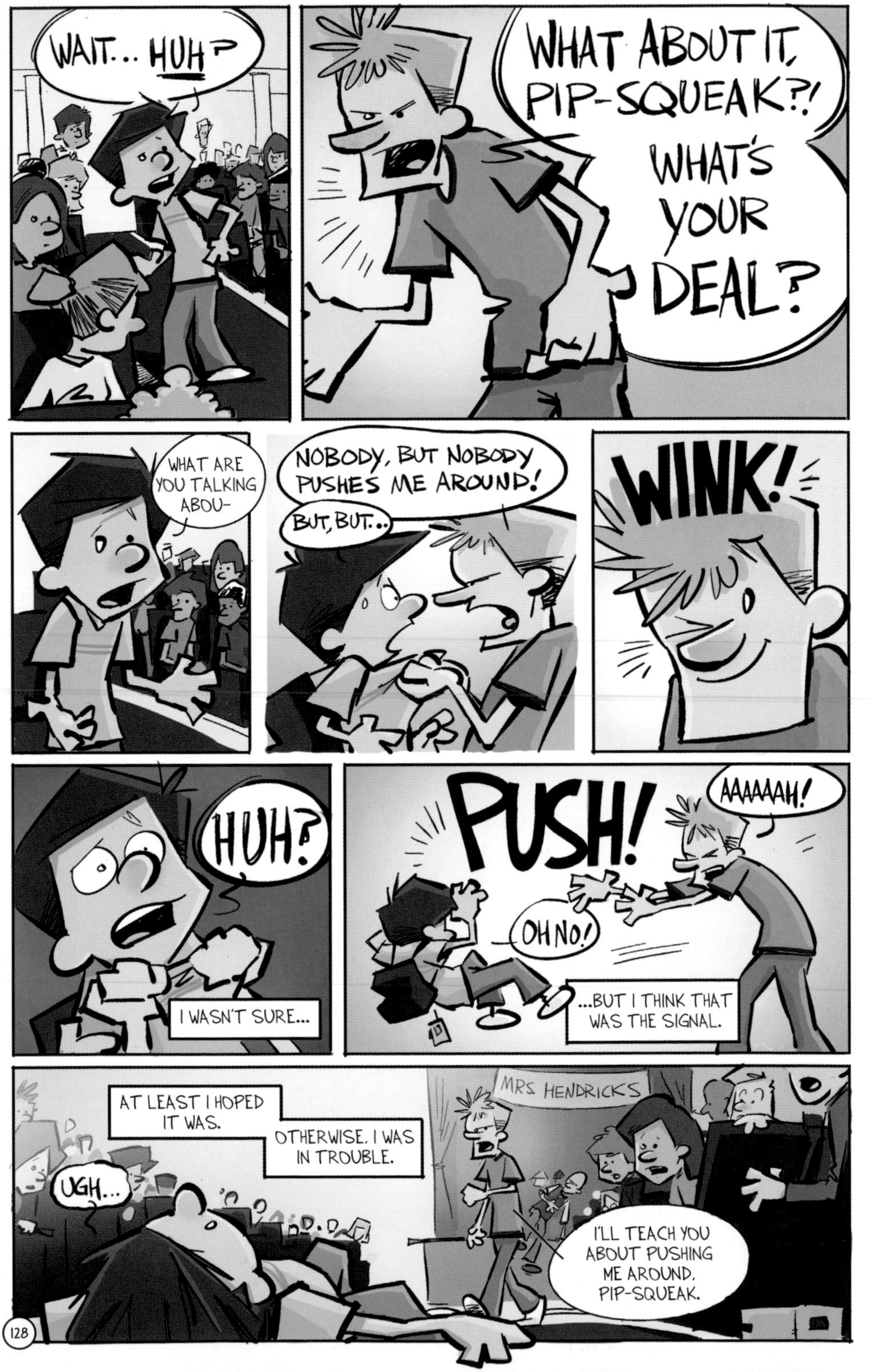

WAIT... HUH?
WHAT ABOUT IT, PIP-SQUEAK?!
WHAT'S YOUR DEAL?
WHAT ARE YOU TALKING ABOU-
NOBODY, BUT NOBODY PUSHES ME AROUND!
BUT, BUT...
WINK!
HUH?
I WASN'T SURE...
PUSH!
AAAAAAH!
OH NO!
...BUT I THINK THAT WAS THE SIGNAL.
AT LEAST I HOPED IT WAS.
OTHERWISE, I WAS IN TROUBLE.
UGH...
MRS. HENDRICKS
I'LL TEACH YOU ABOUT PUSHING ME AROUND, PIP-SQUEAK.

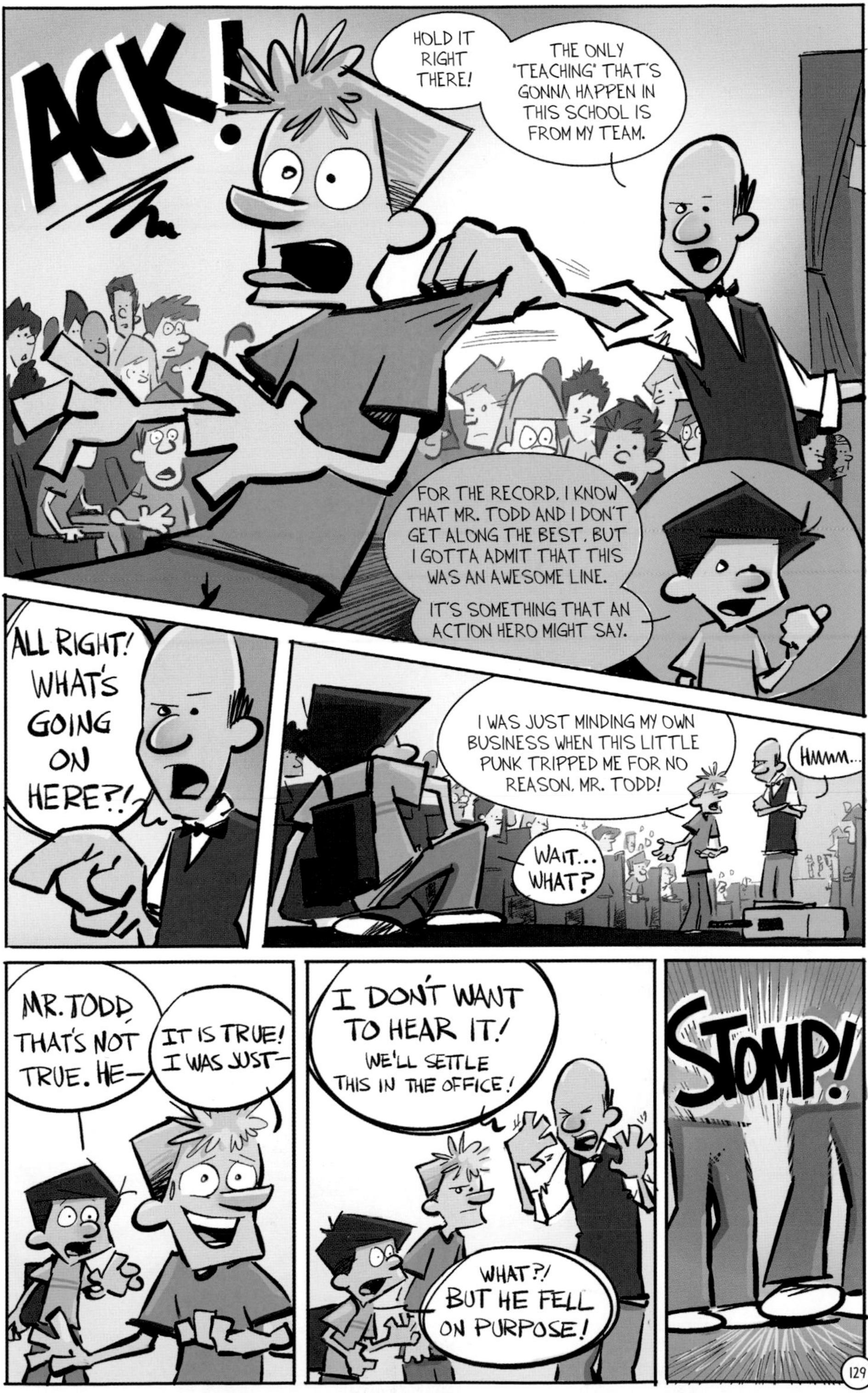
ACK!
HOLD IT RIGHT THERE!
THE ONLY "TEACHING" THAT'S GONNA HAPPEN IN THIS SCHOOL IS FROM MY TEAM.
FOR THE RECORD, I KNOW THAT MR. TODD AND I DON'T GET ALONG THE BEST, BUT I GOTTA ADMIT THAT THIS WAS AN AWESOME LINE.
IT'S SOMETHING THAT AN ACTION HERO MIGHT SAY.
ALL RIGHT! WHAT'S GOING ON HERE?!
I WAS JUST MINDING MY OWN BUSINESS WHEN THIS LITTLE PUNK TRIPPED ME FOR NO REASON, MR. TODD!
HMMM...
WAIT... WHAT?
MR. TODD, THAT'S NOT TRUE. HE—
IT IS TRUE! I WAS JUST—
I DON'T WANT TO HEAR IT! WE'LL SETTLE THIS IN THE OFFICE!
WHAT?! BUT HE FELL ON PURPOSE!
STOMP!

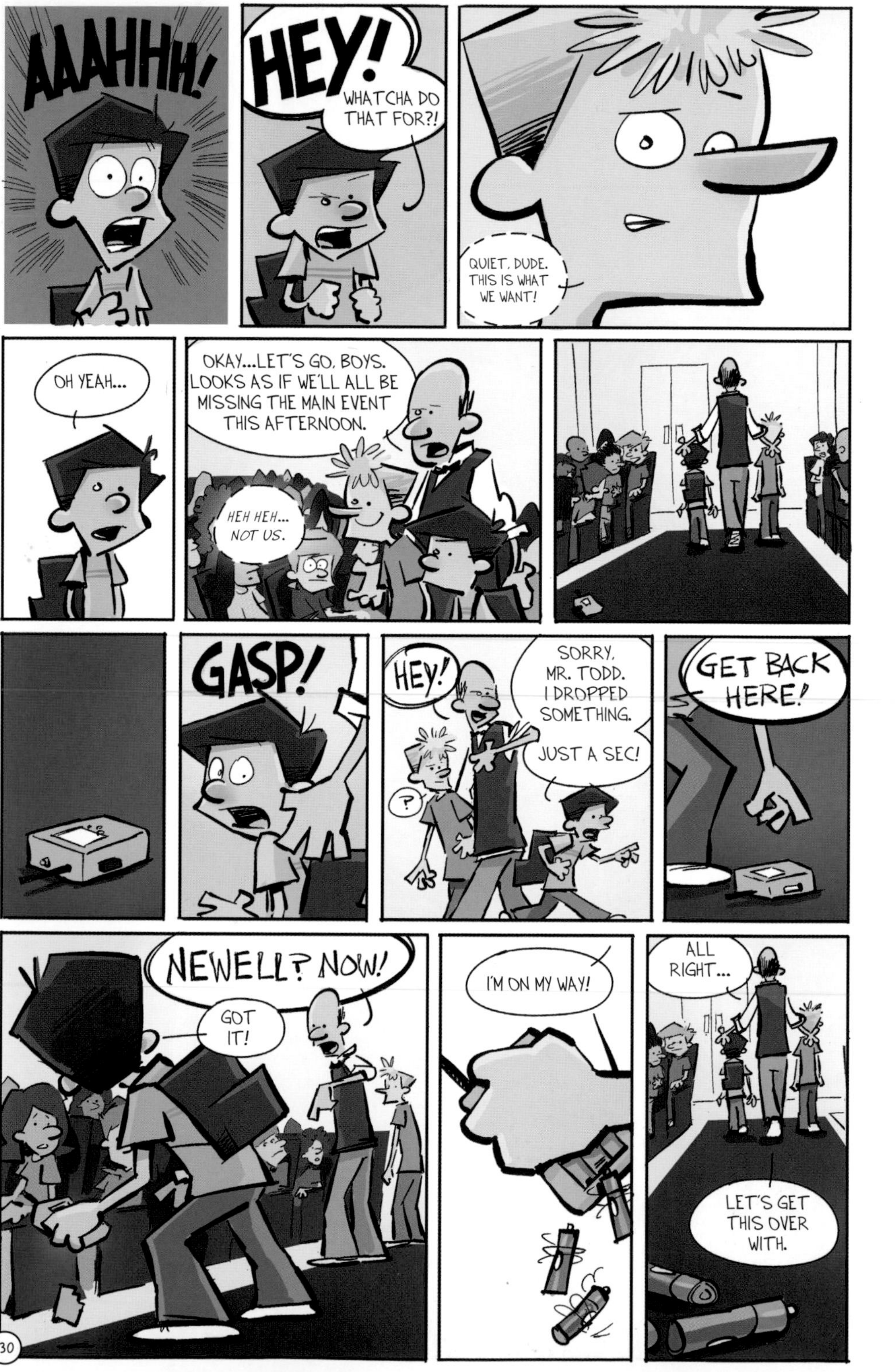
AAAHHH!
HEY!
WHATCHA DO THAT FOR?!
QUIET, DUDE. THIS IS WHAT WE WANT!
OH YEAH...
OKAY...LET'S GO, BOYS. LOOKS AS IF WE'LL ALL BE MISSING THE MAIN EVENT THIS AFTERNOON.
HEH HEH... NOT US.
GASP!
HEY!
SORRY, MR. TODD. I DROPPED SOMETHING.
JUST A SEC!
?
GET BACK HERE!
NEWELL? NOW!
GOT IT!
I'M ON MY WAY!
ALL RIGHT...
LET'S GET THIS OVER WITH.

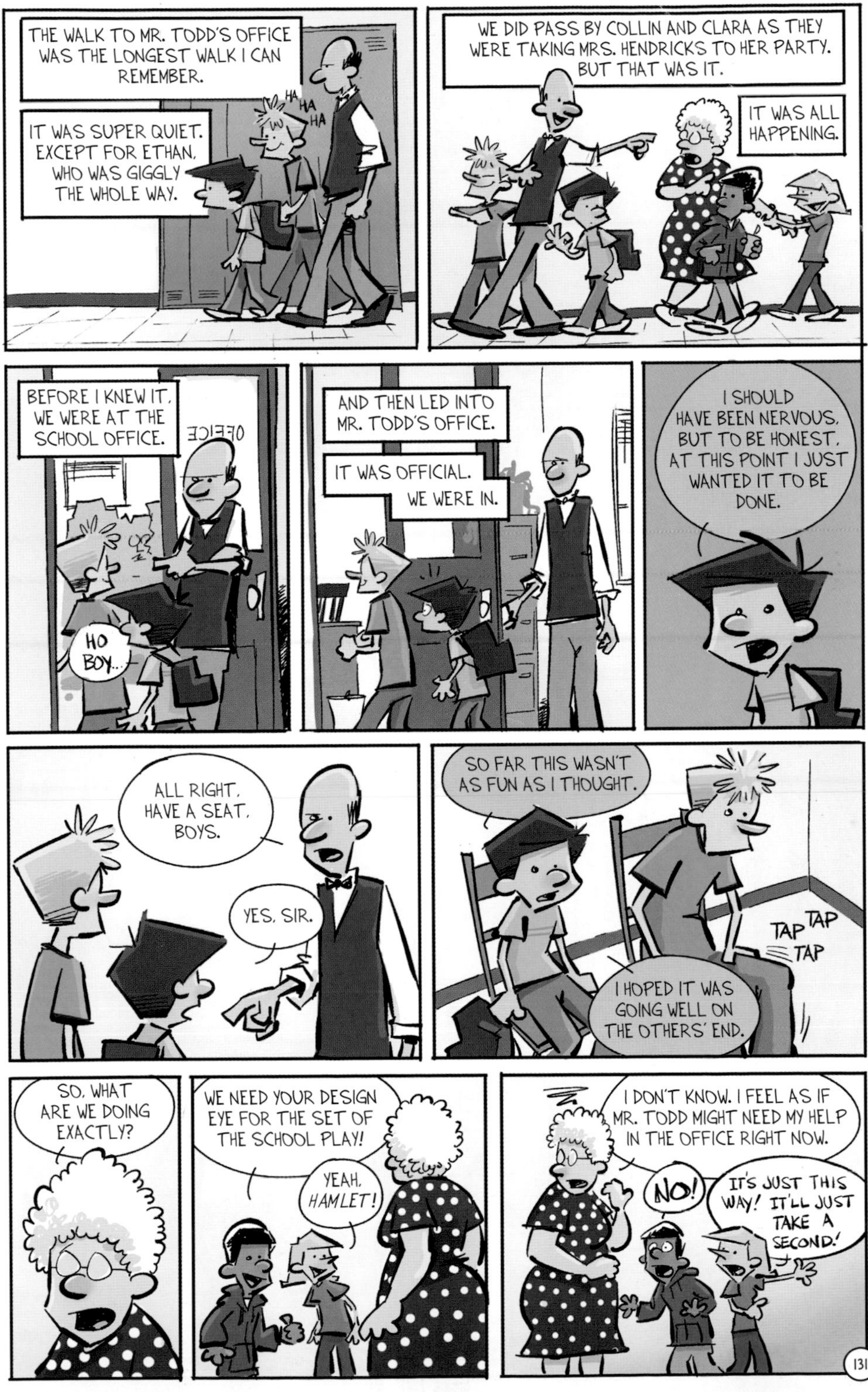

THE WALK TO MR. TODD'S OFFICE WAS THE LONGEST WALK I CAN REMEMBER.
IT WAS SUPER QUIET. EXCEPT FOR ETHAN, WHO WAS GIGGLY THE WHOLE WAY.
HA HA HA
WE DID PASS BY COLLIN AND CLARA AS THEY WERE TAKING MRS. HENDRICKS TO HER PARTY. BUT THAT WAS IT.
IT WAS ALL HAPPENING.
BEFORE I KNEW IT, WE WERE AT THE SCHOOL OFFICE.
OFFICE
HO BOY...
AND THEN LED INTO MR. TODD'S OFFICE.
IT WAS OFFICIAL.
WE WERE IN.
I SHOULD HAVE BEEN NERVOUS, BUT TO BE HONEST, AT THIS POINT I JUST WANTED IT TO BE DONE.
ALL RIGHT, HAVE A SEAT, BOYS.
YES, SIR.
SO FAR THIS WASN'T AS FUN AS I THOUGHT.
TAP TAP TAP
I HOPED IT WAS GOING WELL ON THE OTHERS' END.
SO, WHAT ARE WE DOING EXACTLY?
WE NEED YOUR DESIGN EYE FOR THE SET OF THE SCHOOL PLAY!
YEAH, *HAMLET*!
I DON'T KNOW. I FEEL AS IF MR. TODD MIGHT NEED MY HELP IN THE OFFICE RIGHT NOW.
NO!
IT'S JUST THIS WAY! IT'LL JUST TAKE A SECOND!

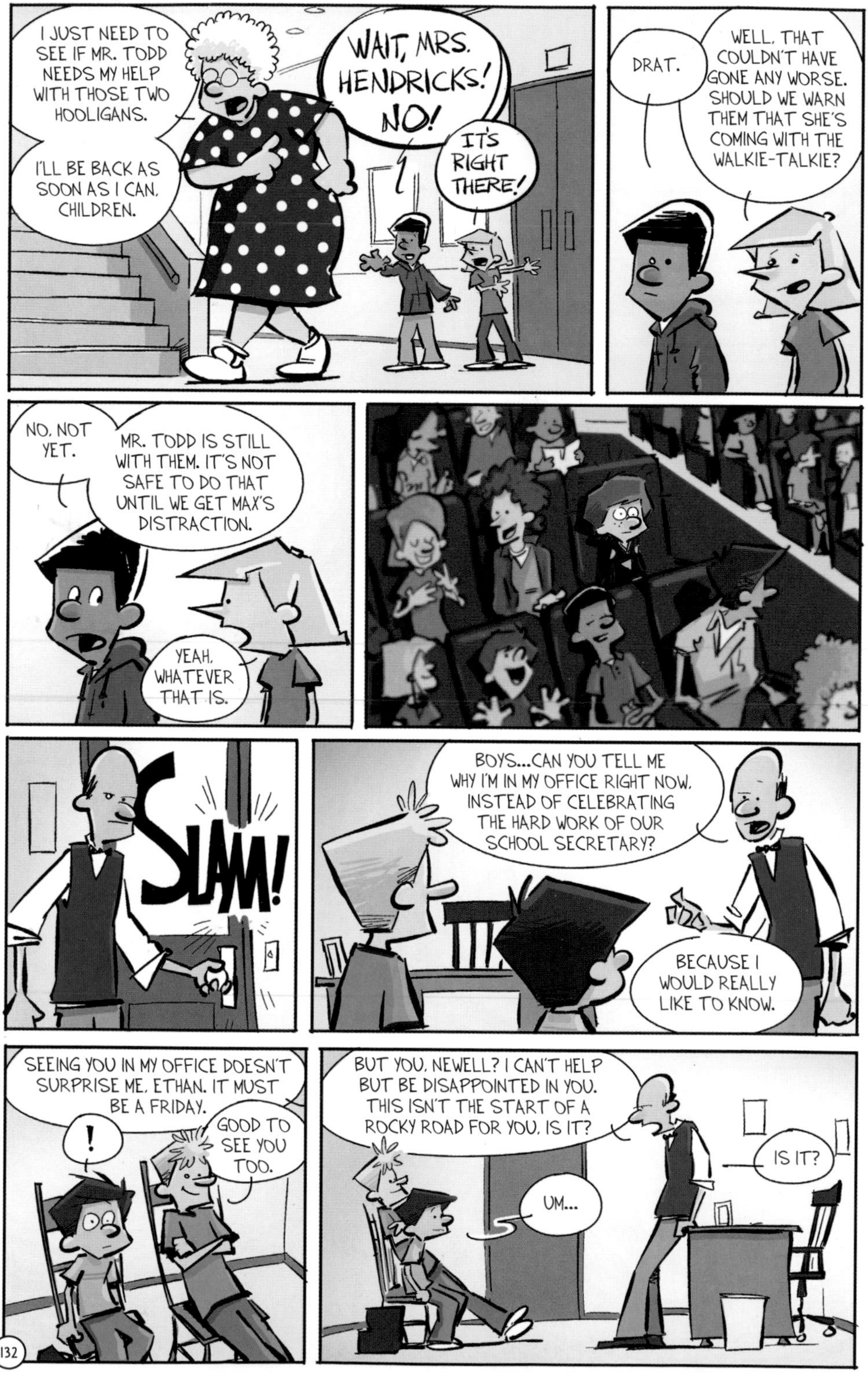
I JUST NEED TO SEE IF MR. TODD NEEDS MY HELP WITH THOSE TWO HOOLIGANS.
I'LL BE BACK AS SOON AS I CAN, CHILDREN.
WAIT, MRS. HENDRICKS! NO!
IT'S RIGHT THERE!
DRAT.
WELL, THAT COULDN'T HAVE GONE ANY WORSE. SHOULD WE WARN THEM THAT SHE'S COMING WITH THE WALKIE-TALKIE?
NO, NOT YET.
MR. TODD IS STILL WITH THEM. IT'S NOT SAFE TO DO THAT UNTIL WE GET MAX'S DISTRACTION.
YEAH, WHATEVER THAT IS.
SLAM!
BOYS...CAN YOU TELL ME WHY I'M IN MY OFFICE RIGHT NOW, INSTEAD OF CELEBRATING THE HARD WORK OF OUR SCHOOL SECRETARY?
BECAUSE I WOULD REALLY LIKE TO KNOW.
SEEING YOU IN MY OFFICE DOESN'T SURPRISE ME, ETHAN. IT MUST BE A FRIDAY.
!
GOOD TO SEE YOU TOO.
BUT YOU, NEWELL? I CAN'T HELP BUT BE DISAPPOINTED IN YOU. THIS ISN'T THE START OF A ROCKY ROAD FOR YOU, IS IT?
IS IT?
UM...

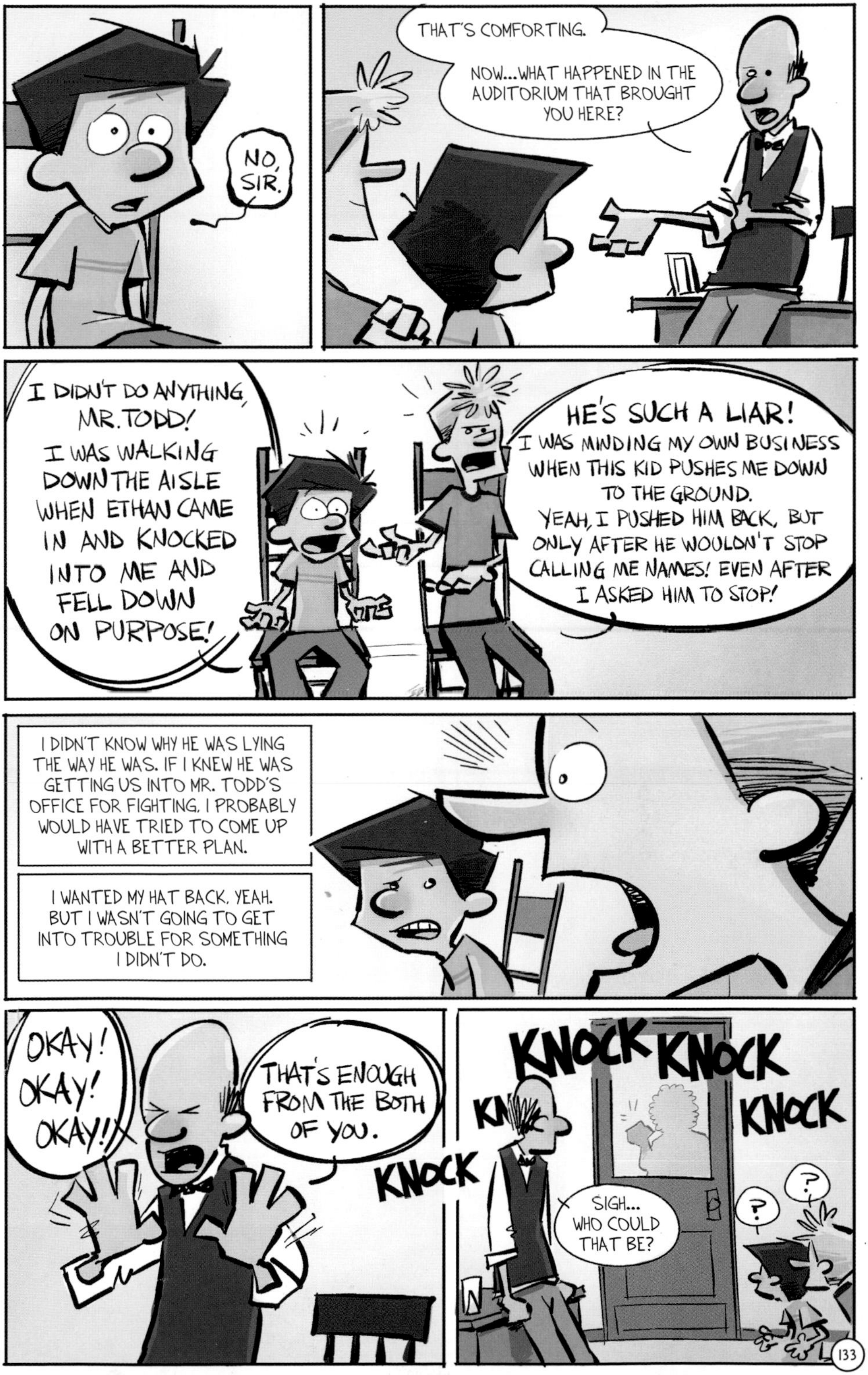
NO, SIR.
THAT'S COMFORTING.
NOW...WHAT HAPPENED IN THE AUDITORIUM THAT BROUGHT YOU HERE?
I DIDN'T DO ANYTHING, MR. TODD! I WAS WALKING DOWN THE AISLE WHEN ETHAN CAME IN AND KNOCKED INTO ME AND FELL DOWN ON PURPOSE!
HE'S SUCH A LIAR! I WAS MINDING MY OWN BUSINESS WHEN THIS KID PUSHES ME DOWN TO THE GROUND. YEAH, I PUSHED HIM BACK, BUT ONLY AFTER HE WOULDN'T STOP CALLING ME NAMES! EVEN AFTER I ASKED HIM TO STOP!
I DIDN'T KNOW WHY HE WAS LYING THE WAY HE WAS. IF I KNEW HE WAS GETTING US INTO MR. TODD'S OFFICE FOR FIGHTING, I PROBABLY WOULD HAVE TRIED TO COME UP WITH A BETTER PLAN.
I WANTED MY HAT BACK, YEAH. BUT I WASN'T GOING TO GET INTO TROUBLE FOR SOMETHING I DIDN'T DO.
OKAY! OKAY! OKAY!
THAT'S ENOUGH FROM THE BOTH OF YOU.
KNOCK KNOCK
KN
KNOCK
KNOCK
SIGH... WHO COULD THAT BE?
?
?

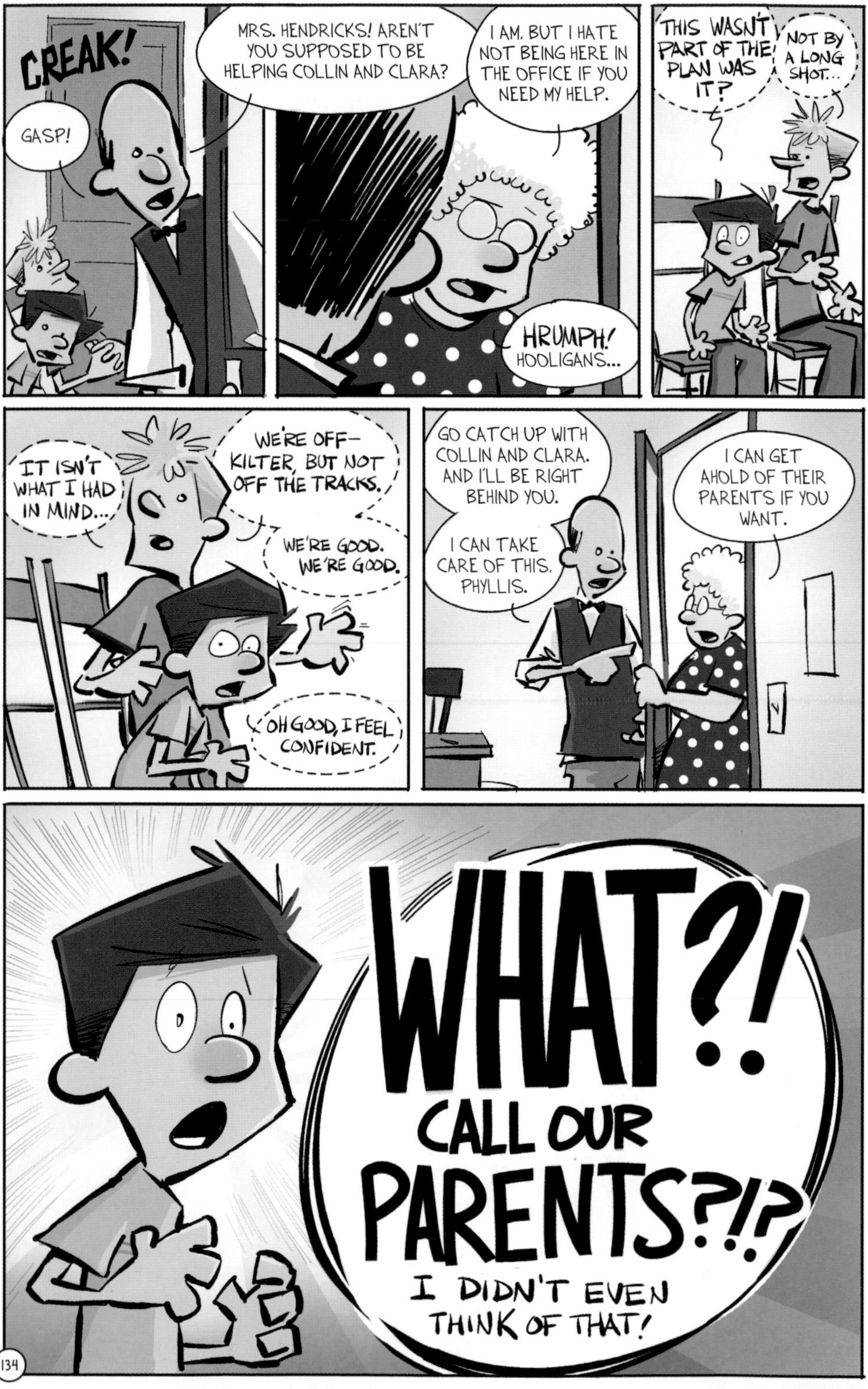
CREAK!
GASP!
MRS. HENDRICKS! AREN'T YOU SUPPOSED TO BE HELPING COLLIN AND CLARA?
I AM, BUT I HATE NOT BEING HERE IN THE OFFICE IF YOU NEED MY HELP.
HRUMPH! HOOLIGANS...
THIS WASN'T PART OF THE PLAN WAS IT?
NOT BY A LONG SHOT...
IT ISN'T WHAT I HAD IN MIND...
WE'RE OFF-KILTER, BUT NOT OFF THE TRACKS.
WE'RE GOOD. WE'RE GOOD.
OH GOOD, I FEEL CONFIDENT.
GO CATCH UP WITH COLLIN AND CLARA. AND I'LL BE RIGHT BEHIND YOU.
I CAN TAKE CARE OF THIS, PHYLLIS.
I CAN GET AHOLD OF THEIR PARENTS IF YOU WANT.
WHAT?! CALL OUR PARENTS?!?
I DIDN'T EVEN THINK OF THAT!

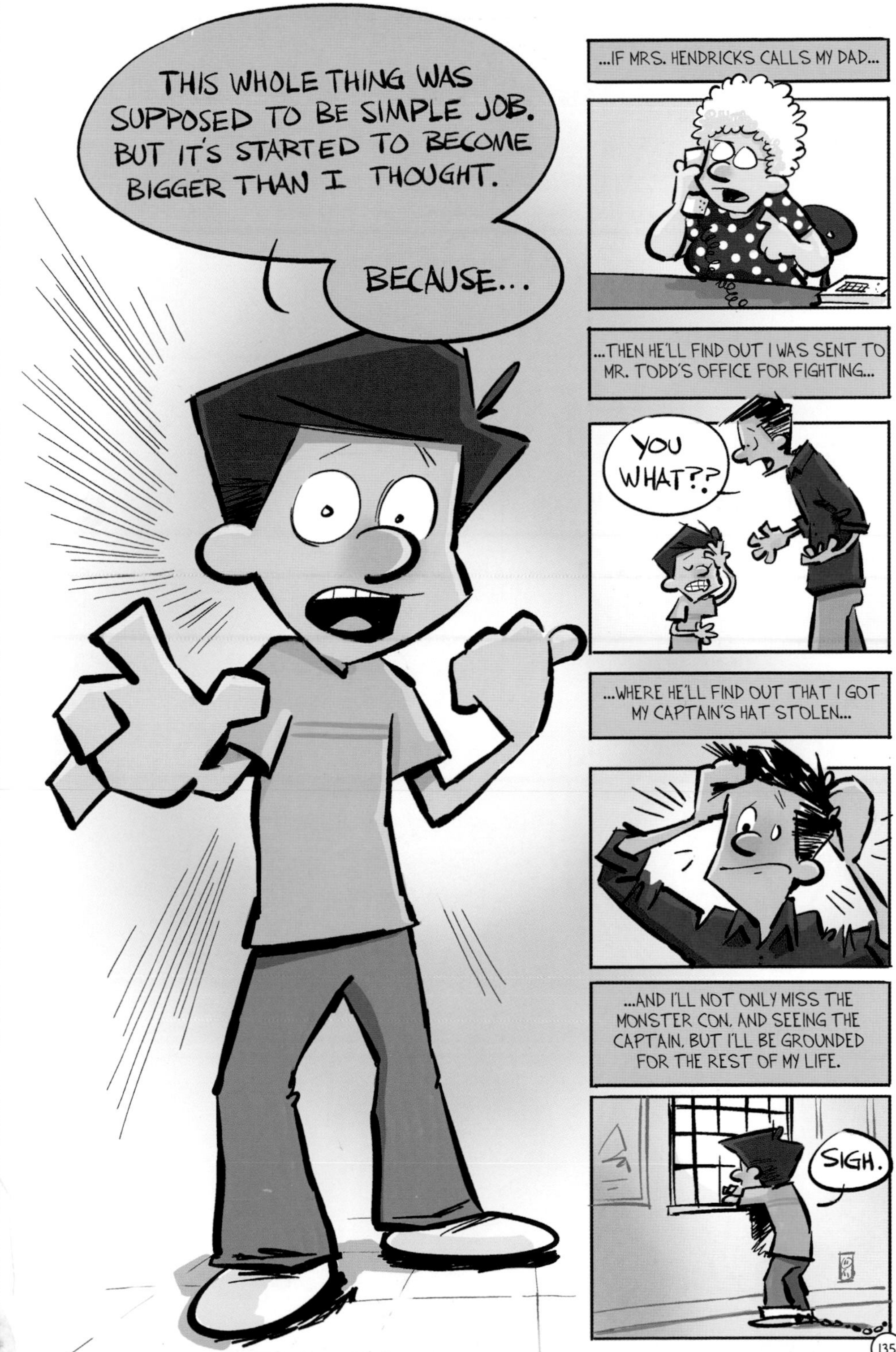
THIS WHOLE THING WAS SUPPOSED TO BE SIMPLE JOB. BUT IT'S STARTED TO BECOME BIGGER THAN I THOUGHT.
BECAUSE...
...IF MRS. HENDRICKS CALLS MY DAD...
...THEN HE'LL FIND OUT I WAS SENT TO MR. TODD'S OFFICE FOR FIGHTING...
YOU WHAT??
...WHERE HE'LL FIND OUT THAT I GOT MY CAPTAIN'S HAT STOLEN...
...AND I'LL NOT ONLY MISS THE MONSTER CON. AND SEEING THE CAPTAIN. BUT I'LL BE GROUNDED FOR THE REST OF MY LIFE.
SIGH.

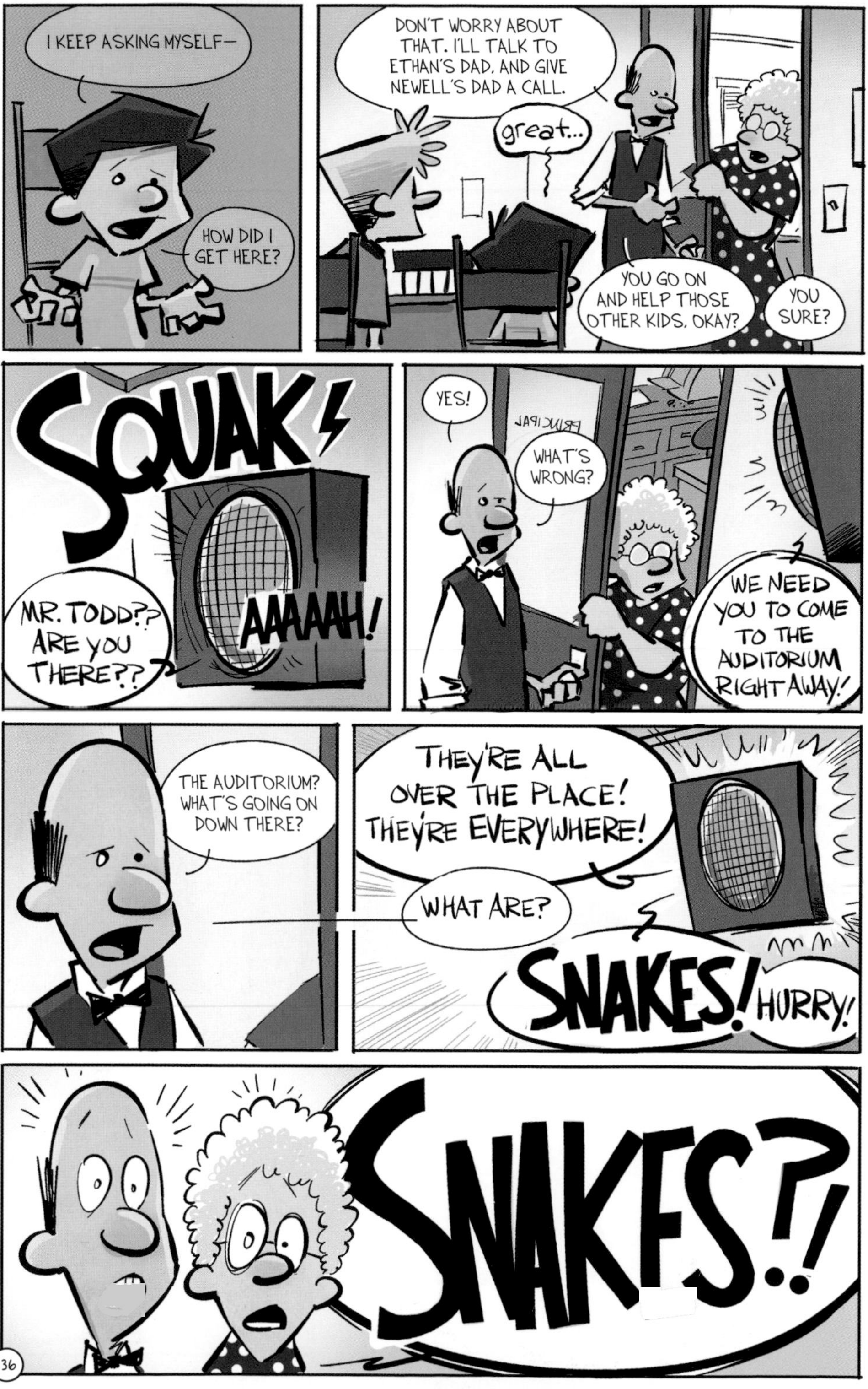
I KEEP ASKING MYSELF—
HOW DID I GET HERE?
DON'T WORRY ABOUT THAT. I'LL TALK TO ETHAN'S DAD, AND GIVE NEWELL'S DAD A CALL.
great...
YOU GO ON AND HELP THOSE OTHER KIDS, OKAY?
YOU SURE?
SQUAK
MR. TODD?? ARE YOU THERE??
AAAAAH!
YES!
PRINCIPAL
WHAT'S WRONG?
WE NEED YOU TO COME TO THE AUDITORIUM RIGHT AWAY!
THE AUDITORIUM? WHAT'S GOING ON DOWN THERE?
THEY'RE ALL OVER THE PLACE! THEY'RE EVERYWHERE!
WHAT ARE?
SNAKES! HURRY!
SNAKES?!

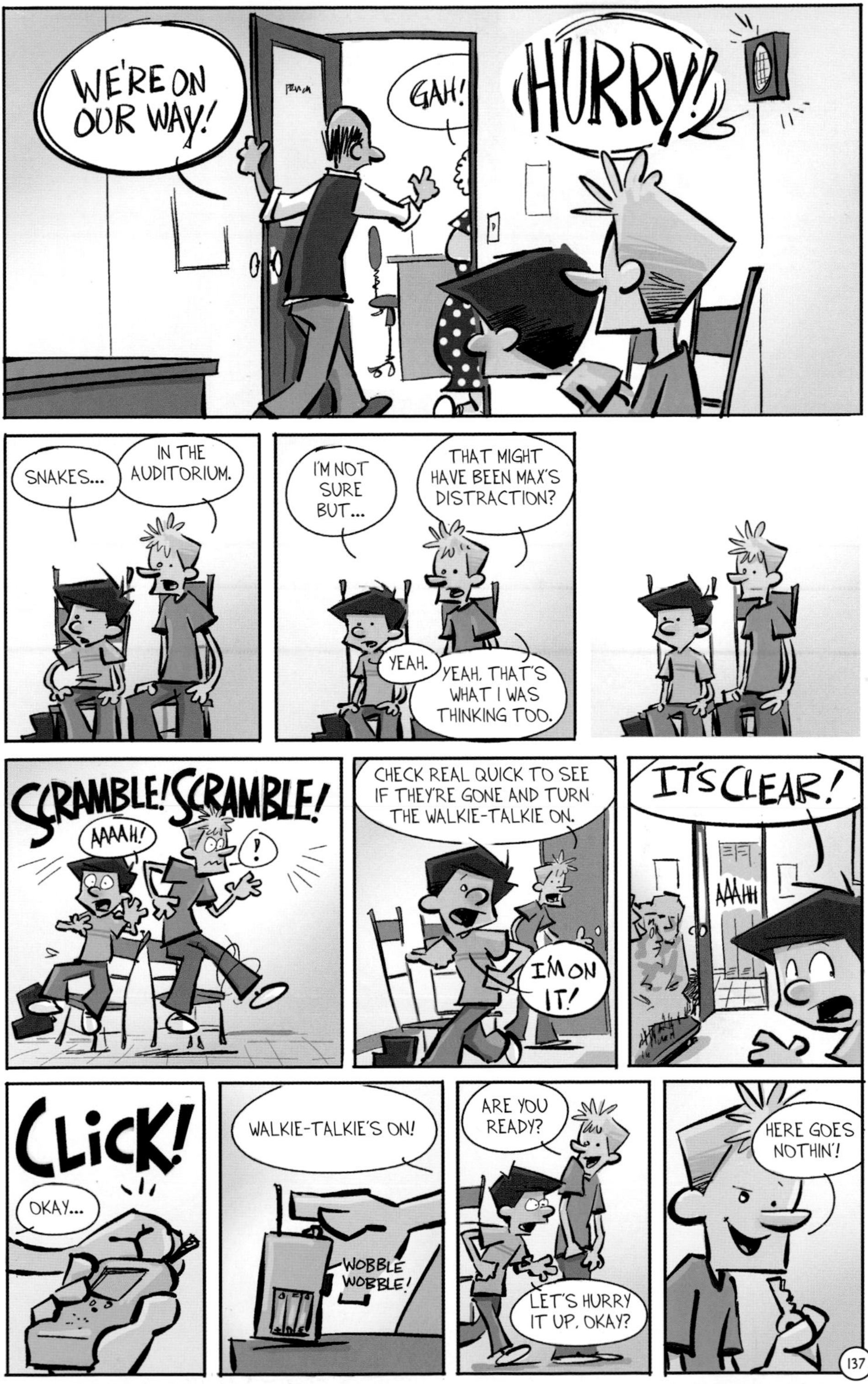
WE'RE ON OUR WAY!
GAH!
HURRY!
SNAKES...
IN THE AUDITORIUM.
I'M NOT SURE BUT...
THAT MIGHT HAVE BEEN MAX'S DISTRACTION?
YEAH.
YEAH, THAT'S WHAT I WAS THINKING TOO.
SCRAMBLE! SCRAMBLE!
AAAAH!
!
CHECK REAL QUICK TO SEE IF THEY'RE GONE AND TURN THE WALKIE-TALKIE ON.
I'M ON IT!
IT'S CLEAR!
AAAHH
CLICK!
OKAY...
WALKIE-TALKIE'S ON!
WOBBLE WOBBLE!
ARE YOU READY?
LET'S HURRY IT UP, OKAY?
HERE GOES NOTHIN'!

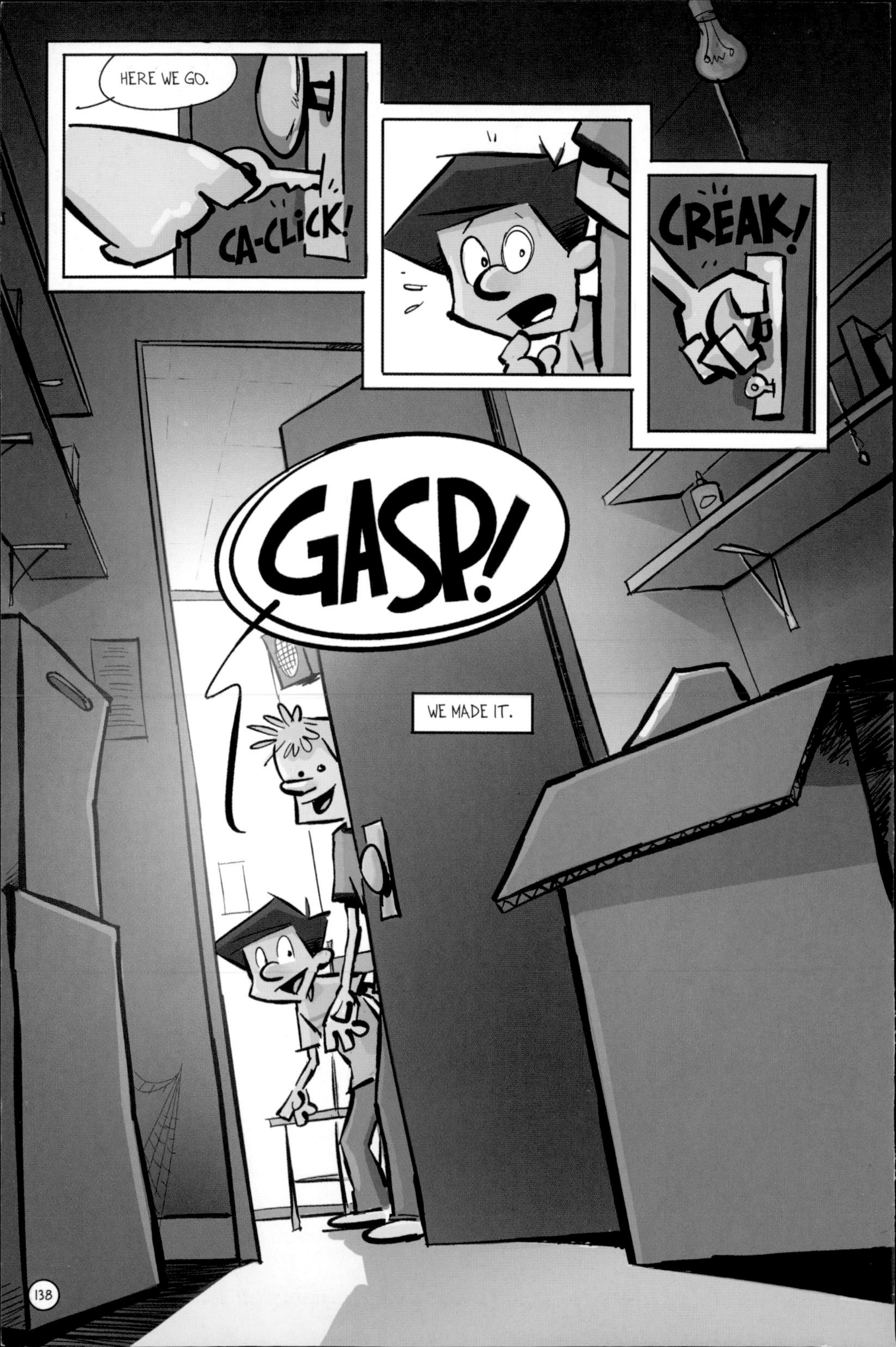
HERE WE GO.
CA-CLICK!
CREAK!
GASP!
WE MADE IT.

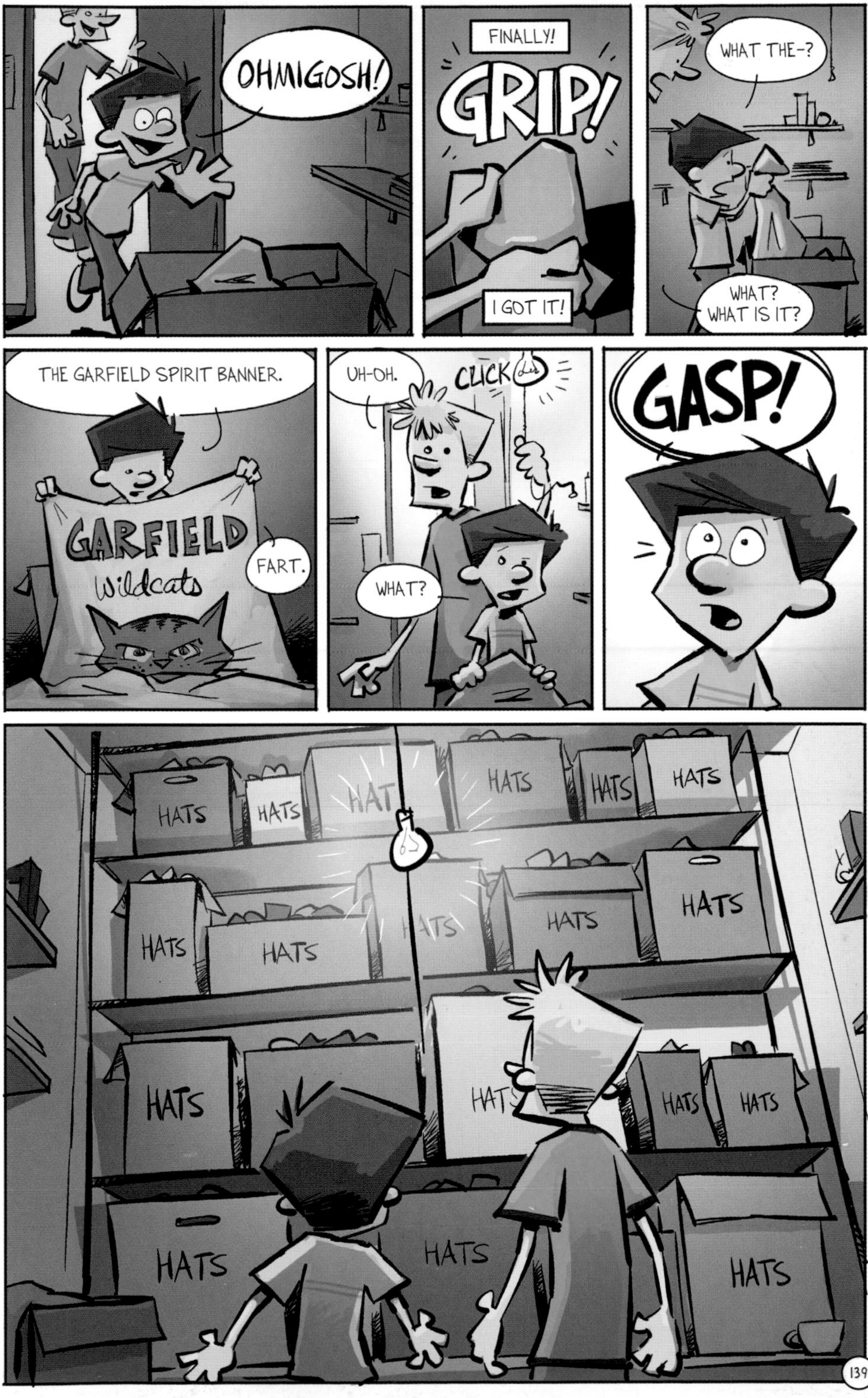
OHMIGOSH!
FINALLY!
GRIP!
I GOT IT!
WHAT THE-?
WHAT?
WHAT IS IT?
THE GARFIELD SPIRIT BANNER.
GARFIELD
Wildcats
FART.
UH-OH.
CLICK
WHAT?
GASP!
HATS
HATS
HATS
HATS
HATS
HATS
HATS
HATS
HATS
HATS
HATS
HATS
HATS
HATS
HATS
HATS
HATS
HATS

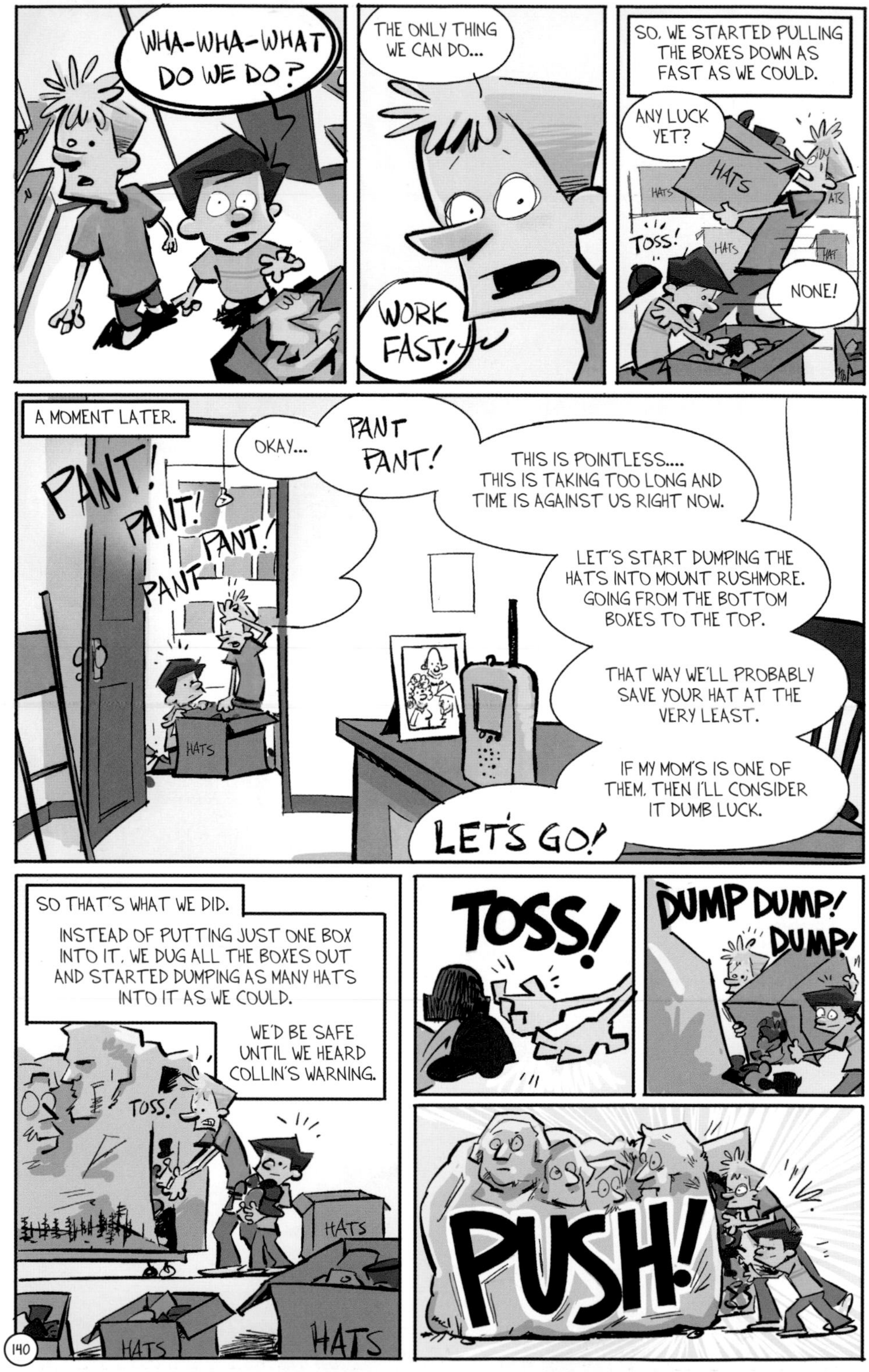

WHA-WHA-WHAT DO WE DO?
THE ONLY THING WE CAN DO...
WORK FAST!
SO, WE STARTED PULLING THE BOXES DOWN AS FAST AS WE COULD.
ANY LUCK YET?
HATS
TOSS!
NONE!
A MOMENT LATER.
PANT! PANT! PANT! PANT
OKAY...
PANT PANT!
THIS IS POINTLESS.... THIS IS TAKING TOO LONG AND TIME IS AGAINST US RIGHT NOW.
LET'S START DUMPING THE HATS INTO MOUNT RUSHMORE. GOING FROM THE BOTTOM BOXES TO THE TOP.
THAT WAY WE'LL PROBABLY SAVE YOUR HAT AT THE VERY LEAST.
IF MY MOM'S IS ONE OF THEM, THEN I'LL CONSIDER IT DUMB LUCK.
LET'S GO!
HATS
SO THAT'S WHAT WE DID.
INSTEAD OF PUTTING JUST ONE BOX INTO IT, WE DUG ALL THE BOXES OUT AND STARTED DUMPING AS MANY HATS INTO IT AS WE COULD.
WE'D BE SAFE UNTIL WE HEARD COLLIN'S WARNING.
TOSS!
HATS
HATS
HATS
TOSS!
DUMP DUMP! DUMP!
PUSH!

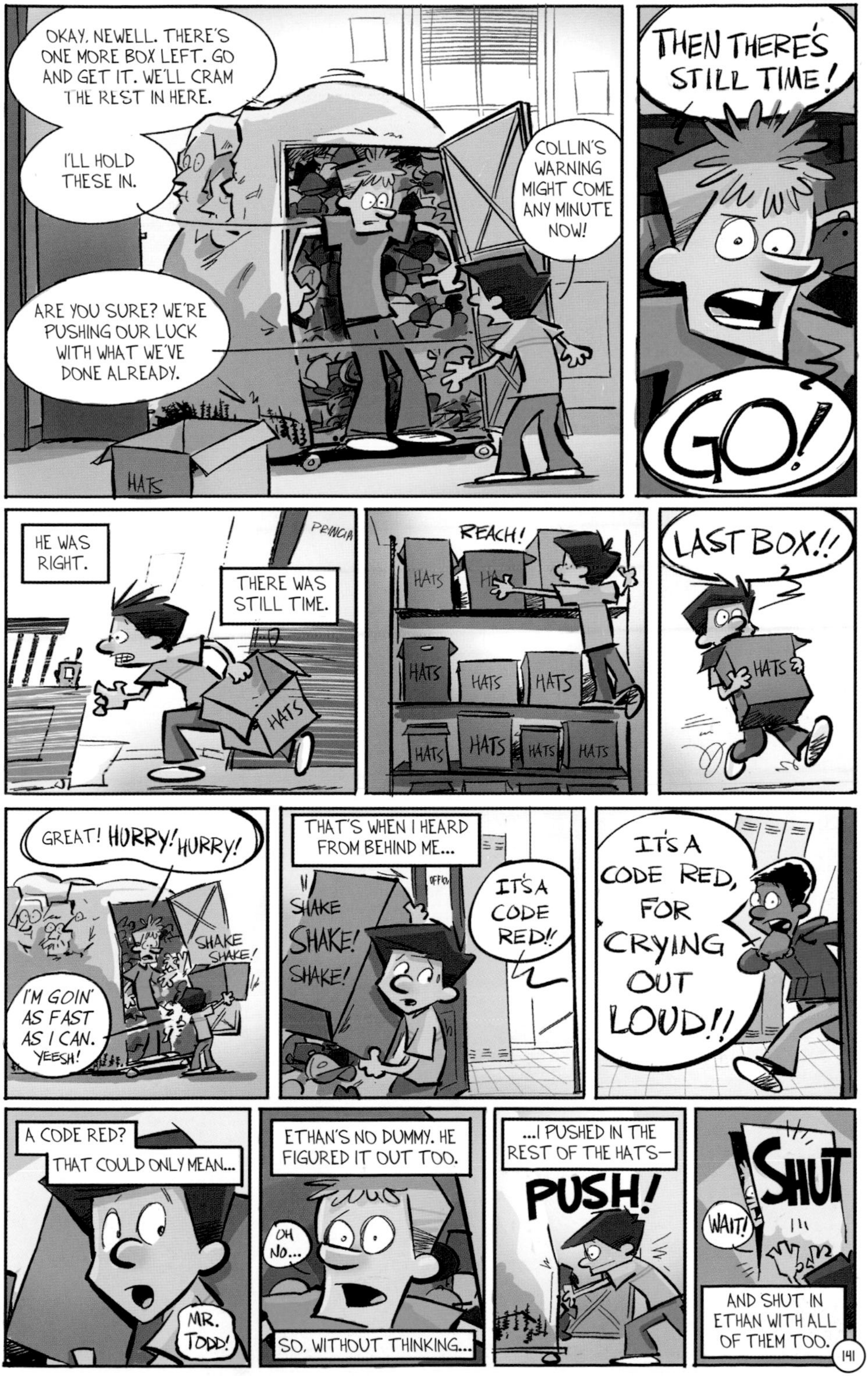

OKAY, NEWELL. THERE'S ONE MORE BOX LEFT. GO AND GET IT. WE'LL CRAM THE REST IN HERE.
I'LL HOLD THESE IN.
COLLIN'S WARNING MIGHT COME ANY MINUTE NOW!
ARE YOU SURE? WE'RE PUSHING OUR LUCK WITH WHAT WE'VE DONE ALREADY.
HATS
THEN THERE'S STILL TIME!
GO!
HE WAS RIGHT.
THERE WAS STILL TIME.
HATS
REACH!
HATS
HATS
HATS
HATS
HATS
HATS
HATS
HATS
LAST BOX!!
HATS
GREAT! HURRY! HURRY!
SHAKE SHAKE!
I'M GOIN' AS FAST AS I CAN. YEESH!
THAT'S WHEN I HEARD FROM BEHIND ME...
SHAKE
SHAKE!
SHAKE!
IT'S A CODE RED!!
IT'S A CODE RED, FOR CRYING OUT LOUD!!
A CODE RED?
THAT COULD ONLY MEAN...
MR. TODD!
ETHAN'S NO DUMMY. HE FIGURED IT OUT TOO.
OH NO...
SO, WITHOUT THINKING...
...I PUSHED IN THE REST OF THE HATS—
PUSH!
SHUT
WAIT!
AND SHUT IN ETHAN WITH ALL OF THEM TOO.

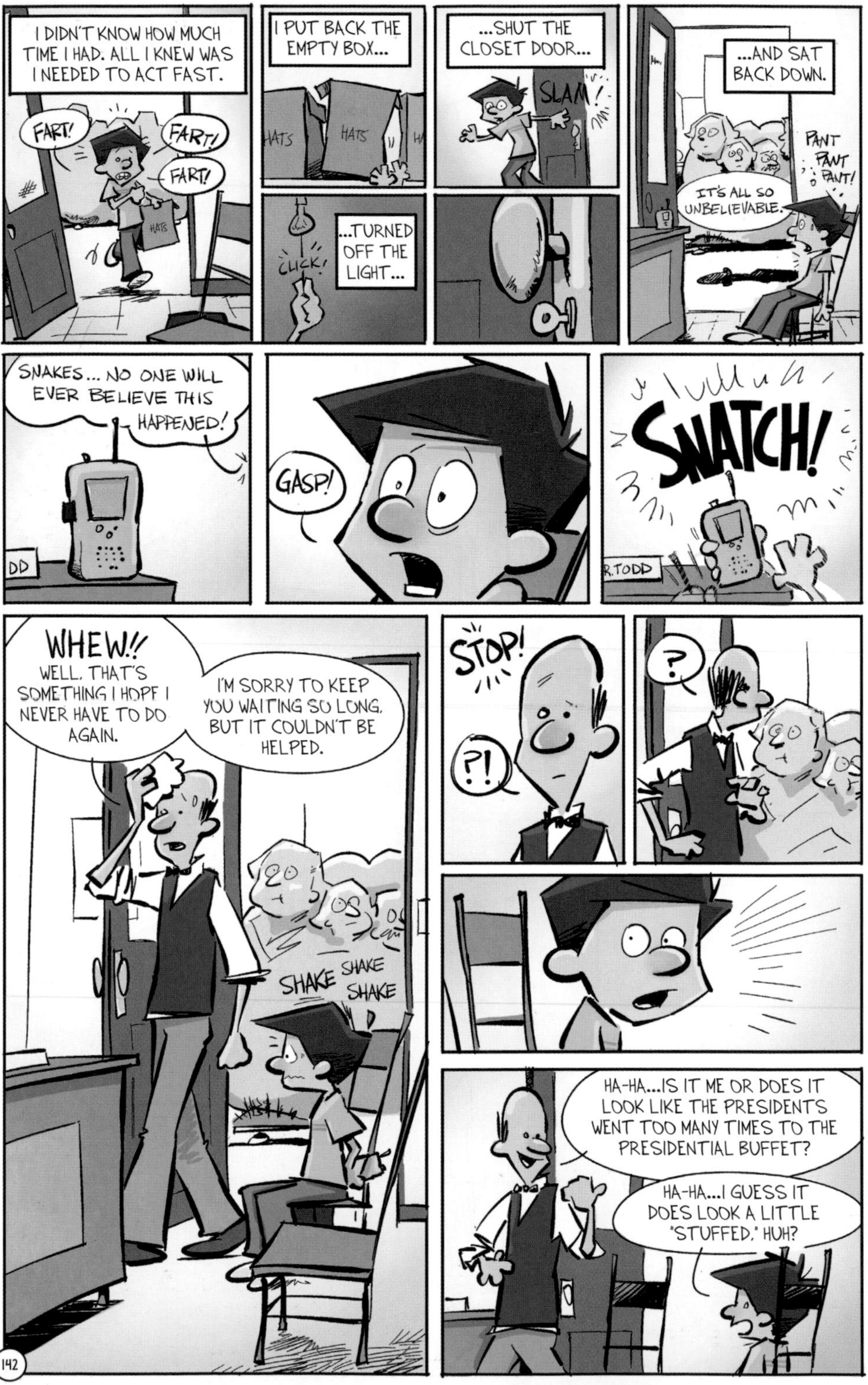
I DIDN'T KNOW HOW MUCH TIME I HAD. ALL I KNEW WAS I NEEDED TO ACT FAST.
FART!
FART!
FART!
HATS
I PUT BACK THE EMPTY BOX...
HATS
HATS
...SHUT THE CLOSET DOOR...
SLAM!
...TURNED OFF THE LIGHT...
CLICK!
...AND SAT BACK DOWN.
PANT PANT PANT!
IT'S ALL SO UNBELIEVABLE.
SNAKES... NO ONE WILL EVER BELIEVE THIS HAPPENED!
GASP!
SNATCH!
R.TODD
WHEW!! WELL, THAT'S SOMETHING I HOPE I NEVER HAVE TO DO AGAIN.
I'M SORRY TO KEEP YOU WAITING SO LONG, BUT IT COULDN'T BE HELPED.
SHAKE SHAKE SHAKE
STOP!
?!
?
HA-HA...IS IT ME OR DOES IT LOOK LIKE THE PRESIDENTS WENT TOO MANY TIMES TO THE PRESIDENTIAL BUFFET?
HA-HA...I GUESS IT DOES LOOK A LITTLE "STUFFED," HUH?

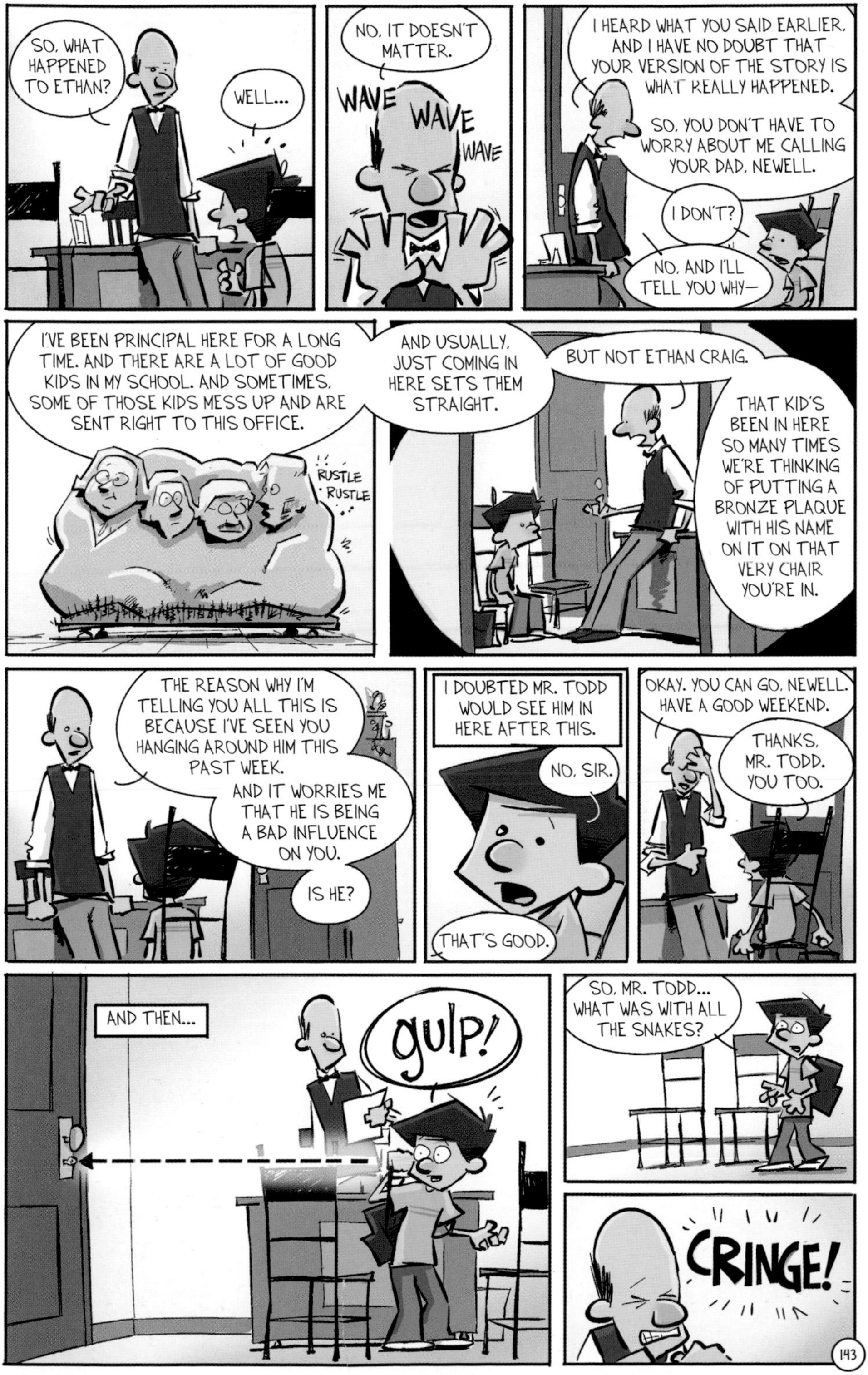

SO, WHAT HAPPENED TO ETHAN?
WELL...
NO, IT DOESN'T MATTER.
WAVE
WAVE
WAVE
I HEARD WHAT YOU SAID EARLIER, AND I HAVE NO DOUBT THAT YOUR VERSION OF THE STORY IS WHAT REALLY HAPPENED.
SO, YOU DON'T HAVE TO WORRY ABOUT ME CALLING YOUR DAD, NEWELL.
I DON'T?
NO, AND I'LL TELL YOU WHY—
I'VE BEEN PRINCIPAL HERE FOR A LONG TIME. AND THERE ARE A LOT OF GOOD KIDS IN MY SCHOOL. AND SOMETIMES, SOME OF THOSE KIDS MESS UP AND ARE SENT RIGHT TO THIS OFFICE.
RUSTLE RUSTLE
AND USUALLY, JUST COMING IN HERE SETS THEM STRAIGHT.
BUT NOT ETHAN CRAIG.
THAT KID'S BEEN IN HERE SO MANY TIMES WE'RE THINKING OF PUTTING A BRONZE PLAQUE WITH HIS NAME ON IT ON THAT VERY CHAIR YOU'RE IN.
THE REASON WHY I'M TELLING YOU ALL THIS IS BECAUSE I'VE SEEN YOU HANGING AROUND HIM THIS PAST WEEK.
AND IT WORRIES ME THAT HE IS BEING A BAD INFLUENCE ON YOU.
IS HE?
I DOUBTED MR. TODD WOULD SEE HIM IN HERE AFTER THIS.
NO, SIR.
THAT'S GOOD.
OKAY. YOU CAN GO, NEWELL. HAVE A GOOD WEEKEND.
THANKS, MR. TODD. YOU TOO.
AND THEN...
gulp!
SO, MR. TODD... WHAT WAS WITH ALL THE SNAKES?
CRINGE!

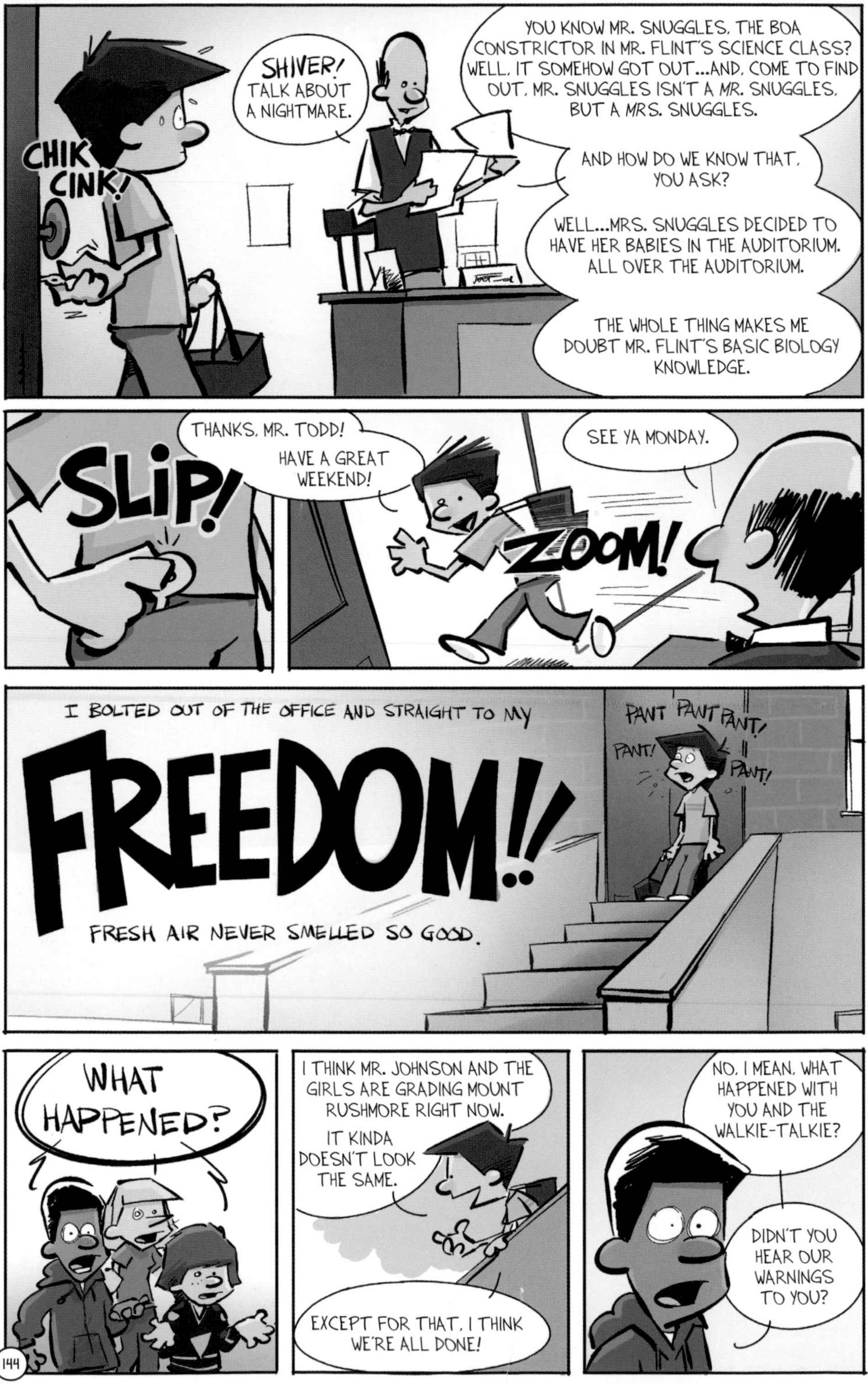
SHIVER! TALK ABOUT A NIGHTMARE.
CHIK CINK!
YOU KNOW MR. SNUGGLES, THE BOA CONSTRICTOR IN MR. FLINT'S SCIENCE CLASS? WELL, IT SOMEHOW GOT OUT...AND, COME TO FIND OUT, MR. SNUGGLES ISN'T A *MR.* SNUGGLES, BUT A *MRS.* SNUGGLES.
AND HOW DO WE KNOW THAT, YOU ASK?
WELL...MRS. SNUGGLES DECIDED TO HAVE HER BABIES IN THE AUDITORIUM. ALL OVER THE AUDITORIUM.
THE WHOLE THING MAKES ME DOUBT MR. FLINT'S BASIC BIOLOGY KNOWLEDGE.
SLIP!
THANKS, MR. TODD!
HAVE A GREAT WEEKEND!
SEE YA MONDAY.
ZOOM!
I BOLTED OUT OF THE OFFICE AND STRAIGHT TO MY
FREEDOM!!
FRESH AIR NEVER SMELLED SO GOOD.
PANT PANT PANT!
PANT!
PANT!
WHAT HAPPENED?
I THINK MR. JOHNSON AND THE GIRLS ARE GRADING MOUNT RUSHMORE RIGHT NOW.
IT KINDA DOESN'T LOOK THE SAME.
EXCEPT FOR THAT, I THINK WE'RE ALL DONE!
NO, I MEAN, WHAT HAPPENED WITH YOU AND THE WALKIE-TALKIE?
DIDN'T YOU HEAR OUR WARNINGS TO YOU?

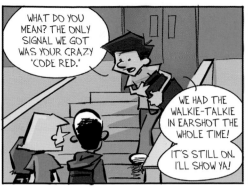

WHAT DO YOU MEAN? THE ONLY SIGNAL WE GOT WAS YOUR CRAZY "CODE RED."

WE HAD THE WALKIE-TALKIE IN EARSHOT THE WHOLE TIME!

IT'S STILL ON. I'LL SHOW YA!

BLINK BLINK

HUH... I GUESS I LOST THE BATTERIES.

WHOA...I GUESS WE GOT LUCKY THERE, DIDN'T WE?

AND WHAT ABOUT THE SNAKES? HOW'D YOU SWING THAT, MAX?

WELL...

TO TELL YOU THE TRUTH...IT WASN'T WHAT I WAS PLANNING.

MY ORIGINAL PLAN WAS A LITTLE LESS EFFECTIVE.

EARLIER.

OPE!

OKAY, KIDS. IT'S TIME. WE'RE ALL GONNA MAKE OUR WAY DOWN FOR MRS. HENDRICKS'S THING.

MAX? WANNA LEND ME A QUICK HAND?

SURE.

DO ME A FAVOR AND THROW THESE UP ON THE SHELF FOR ME? AND CATCH UP WITH ALL OF US, OKAY?

YEAH, SURE THING, MR. FLINT.

"IN MY DEFENSE, HE SHOULDN'T HAVE SAID THE WORD *THROW*."

TOSS

SO? THAT'S IT?

WELL, THE BOOKS MIGHT HAVE KNOCKED INTO THE OTHER BOOKS.

TOPPLE!

"AND THOSE OTHER BOOKS FELL."

"RIGHT ON MR. SNUGGLES'S CAGE."

BAM!

"WHERE..."

FLIP!

FLAP FLAP

FLAP

"SO, I BOLTED."

SLITHER!

HISS HISS

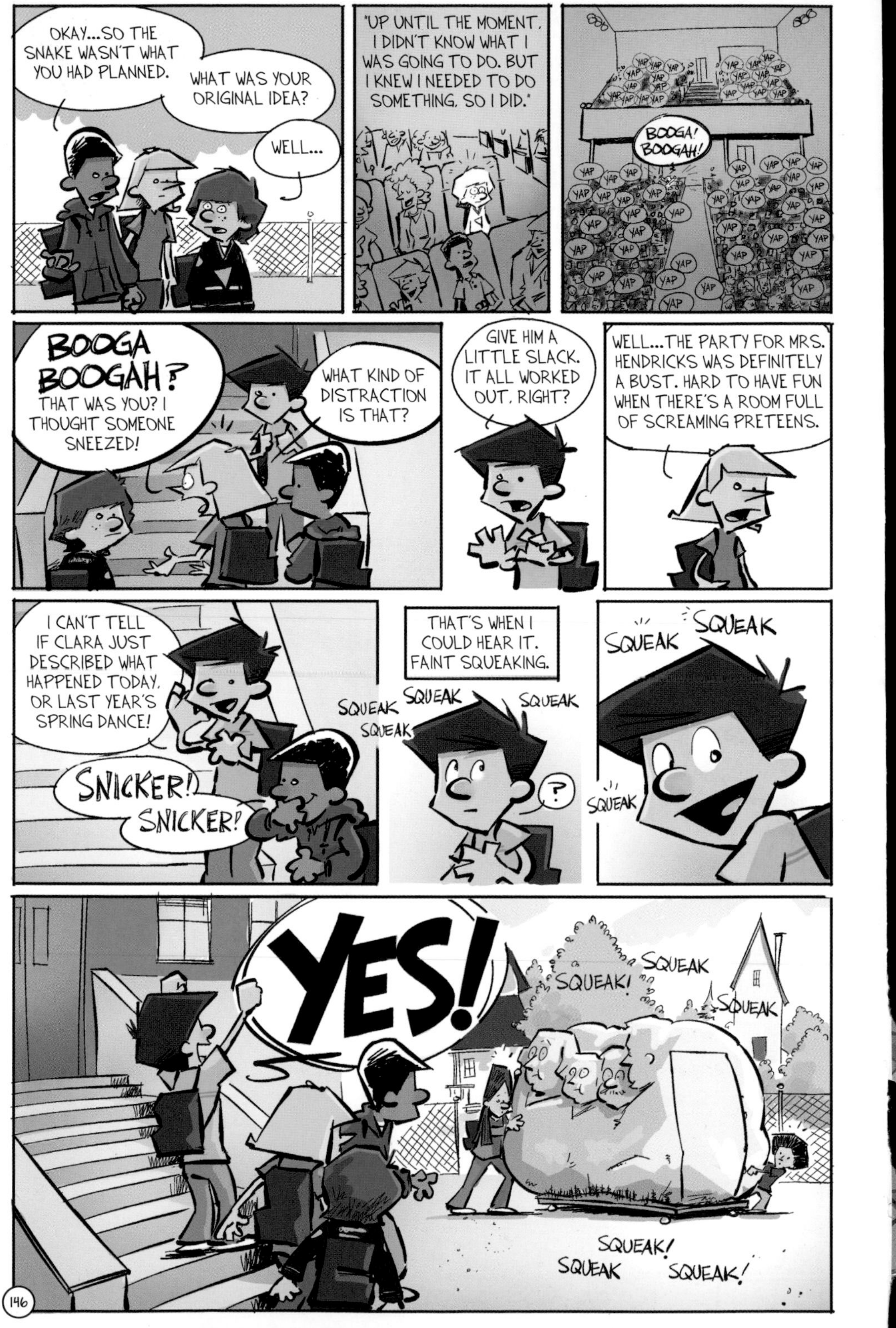
OKAY...SO THE SNAKE WASN'T WHAT YOU HAD PLANNED.
WHAT WAS YOUR ORIGINAL IDEA?
WELL...
"UP UNTIL THE MOMENT, I DIDN'T KNOW WHAT I WAS GOING TO DO. BUT I KNEW I NEEDED TO DO SOMETHING, SO I DID."
YAP YAP YAP YAP YAP YAP
BOOGA! BOOGAH!
BOOGA BOOGAH? THAT WAS YOU? I THOUGHT SOMEONE SNEEZED!
WHAT KIND OF DISTRACTION IS THAT?
GIVE HIM A LITTLE SLACK. IT ALL WORKED OUT, RIGHT?
WELL...THE PARTY FOR MRS. HENDRICKS WAS DEFINITELY A BUST. HARD TO HAVE FUN WHEN THERE'S A ROOM FULL OF SCREAMING PRETEENS.
I CAN'T TELL IF CLARA JUST DESCRIBED WHAT HAPPENED TODAY, OR LAST YEAR'S SPRING DANCE!
SNICKER!
SNICKER!
THAT'S WHEN I COULD HEAR IT. FAINT SQUEAKING.
SQUEAK
SQUEAK
SQUEAK
SQUEAK
?
SQUEAK
SQUEAK
SQUEAK
YES!
SQUEAK
SQUEAK!
SQUEAK
SQUEAK!
SQUEAK
SQUEAK!

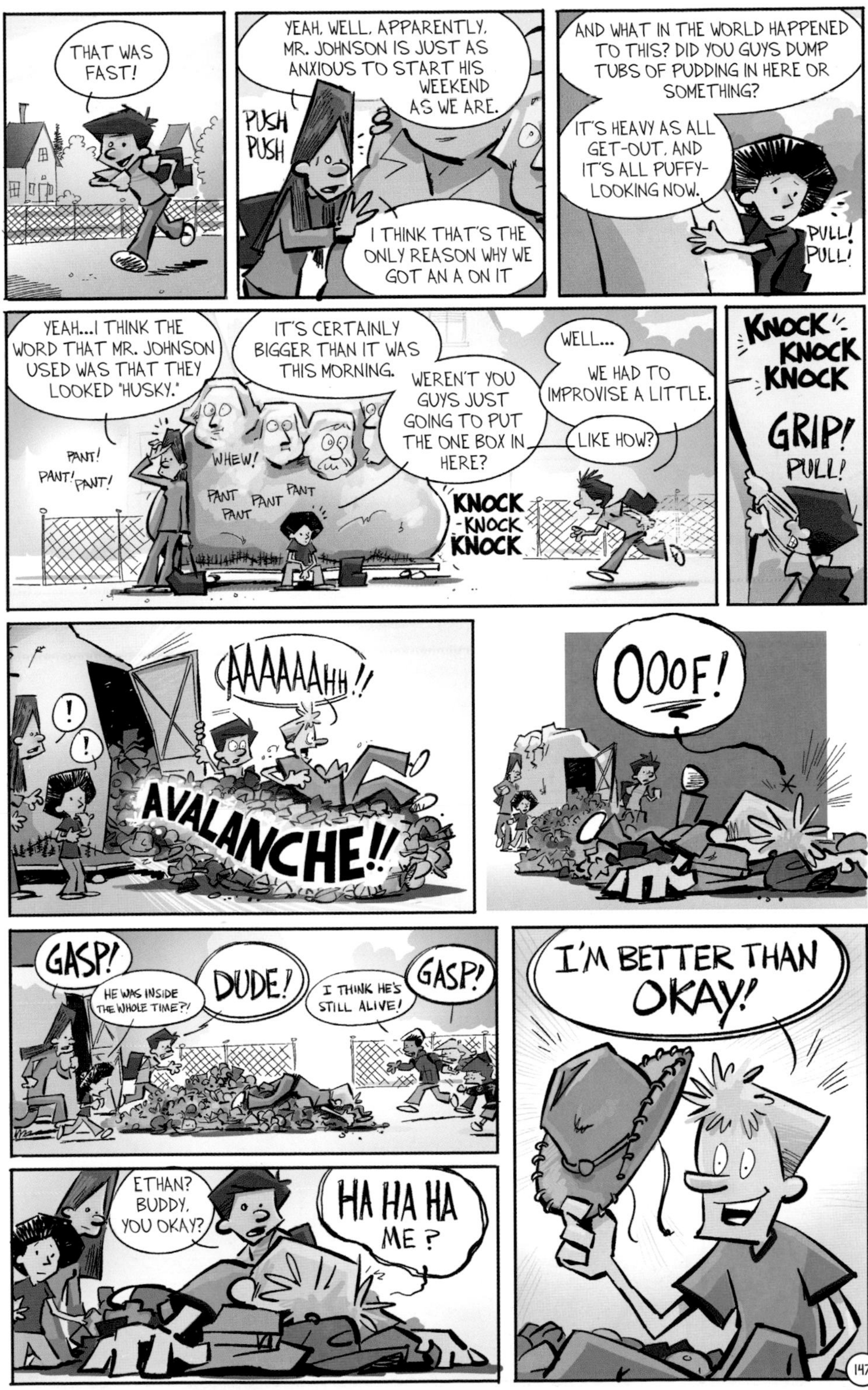
THAT WAS FAST!
YEAH, WELL, APPARENTLY, MR. JOHNSON IS JUST AS ANXIOUS TO START HIS WEEKEND AS WE ARE.
PUSH PUSH
I THINK THAT'S THE ONLY REASON WHY WE GOT AN A ON IT
AND WHAT IN THE WORLD HAPPENED TO THIS? DID YOU GUYS DUMP TUBS OF PUDDING IN HERE OR SOMETHING?
IT'S HEAVY AS ALL GET-OUT, AND IT'S ALL PUFFY-LOOKING NOW.
PULL! PULL!
YEAH...I THINK THE WORD THAT MR. JOHNSON USED WAS THAT THEY LOOKED "HUSKY."
IT'S CERTAINLY BIGGER THAN IT WAS THIS MORNING.
WEREN'T YOU GUYS JUST GOING TO PUT THE ONE BOX IN HERE?
WELL...
WE HAD TO IMPROVISE A LITTLE.
LIKE HOW?
PANT! PANT! PANT!
WHEW!
PANT PANT PANT PANT
KNOCK -KNOCK KNOCK
KNOCK KNOCK KNOCK
GRIP!
PULL!
!
!
AAAAAAHH!!
AVALANCHE!!
OOOF!
GASP!
HE WAS INSIDE THE WHOLE TIME?!
DUDE!
I THINK HE'S STILL ALIVE!
GASP!
ETHAN? BUDDY, YOU OKAY?
HA HA HA
ME ?
I'M BETTER THAN OKAY!

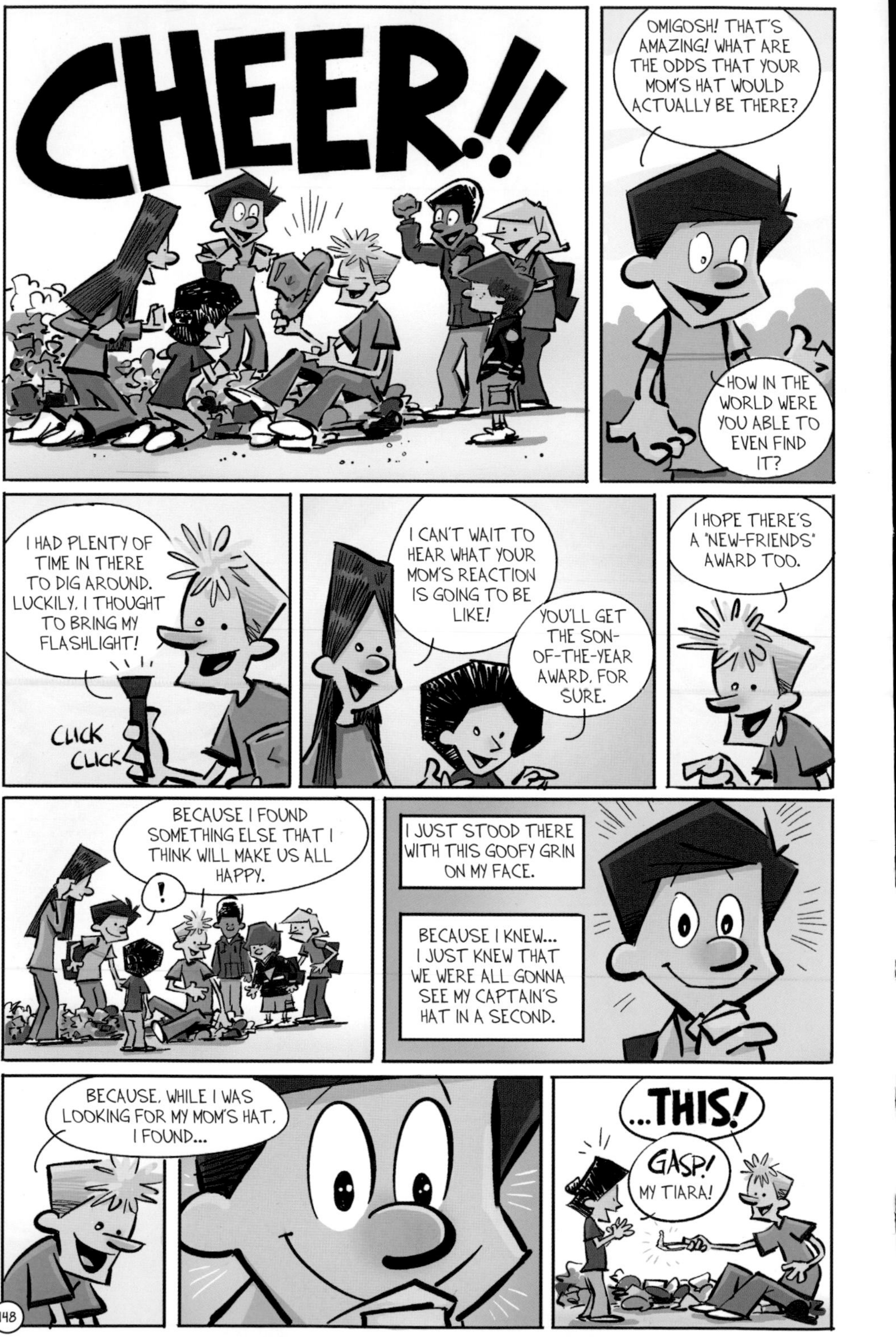
CHEER!!
OMIGOSH! THAT'S AMAZING! WHAT ARE THE ODDS THAT YOUR MOM'S HAT WOULD ACTUALLY BE THERE?
HOW IN THE WORLD WERE YOU ABLE TO EVEN FIND IT?
I HAD PLENTY OF TIME IN THERE TO DIG AROUND. LUCKILY, I THOUGHT TO BRING MY FLASHLIGHT!
CLICK CLICK
I CAN'T WAIT TO HEAR WHAT YOUR MOM'S REACTION IS GOING TO BE LIKE!
YOU'LL GET THE SON-OF-THE-YEAR AWARD, FOR SURE.
I HOPE THERE'S A "NEW-FRIENDS" AWARD TOO.
BECAUSE I FOUND SOMETHING ELSE THAT I THINK WILL MAKE US ALL HAPPY.
!
I JUST STOOD THERE WITH THIS GOOFY GRIN ON MY FACE.
BECAUSE I KNEW... I JUST KNEW THAT WE WERE ALL GONNA SEE MY CAPTAIN'S HAT IN A SECOND.
BECAUSE, WHILE I WAS LOOKING FOR MY MOM'S HAT, I FOUND...
...THIS!
GASP! MY TIARA!

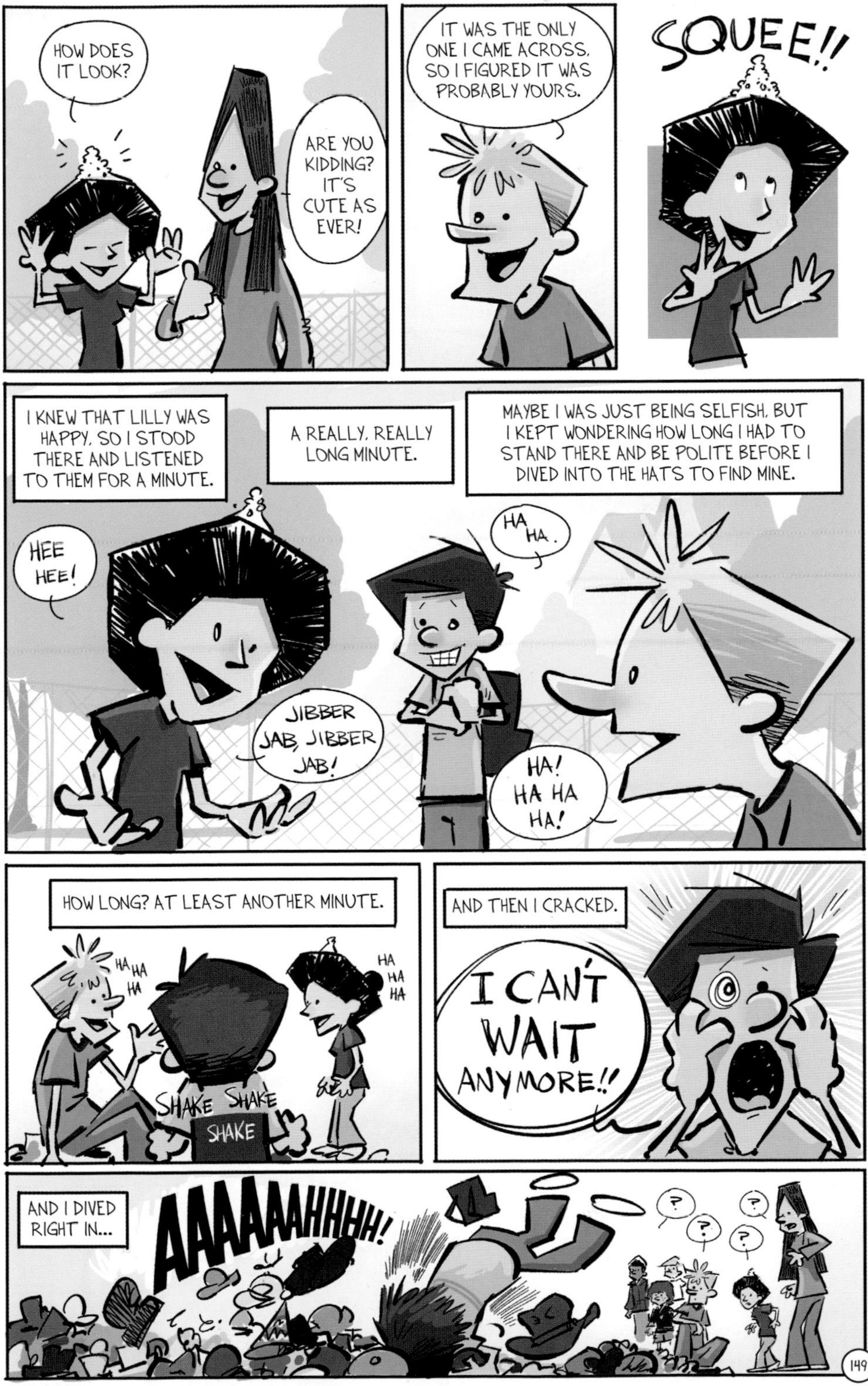
HOW DOES IT LOOK?
ARE YOU KIDDING? IT'S CUTE AS EVER!
IT WAS THE ONLY ONE I CAME ACROSS, SO I FIGURED IT WAS PROBABLY YOURS.
SQUEE!!
I KNEW THAT LILLY WAS HAPPY, SO I STOOD THERE AND LISTENED TO THEM FOR A MINUTE.
A REALLY, REALLY LONG MINUTE.
MAYBE I WAS JUST BEING SELFISH, BUT I KEPT WONDERING HOW LONG I HAD TO STAND THERE AND BE POLITE BEFORE I DIVED INTO THE HATS TO FIND MINE.
HEE HEE!
JIBBER JAB, JIBBER JAB!
HA HA.
HA! HA HA HA!
HOW LONG? AT LEAST ANOTHER MINUTE.
HA HA HA
SHAKE SHAKE
SHAKE
HA HA HA
AND THEN I CRACKED.
I CAN'T WAIT ANYMORE!!
AND I DIVED RIGHT IN...
AAAAAAHHHH!
?
?
?
?

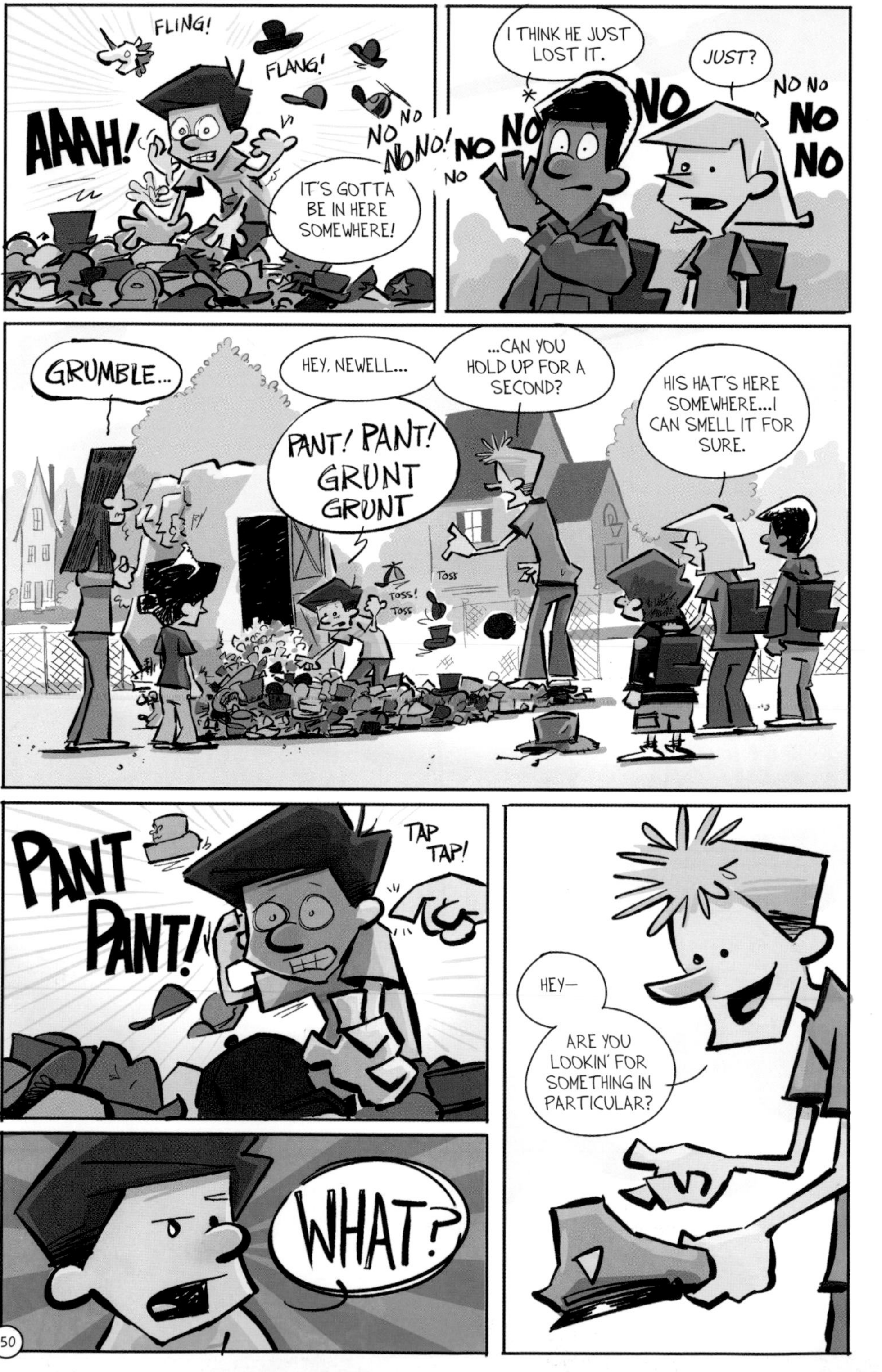

FLING!
FLANG!
AAAH!
NO NO NO NO NO!
IT'S GOTTA BE IN HERE SOMEWHERE!
I THINK HE JUST LOST IT.
JUST?
NO NO NO NO NO NO NO NO
GRUMBLE...
HEY, NEWELL...
...CAN YOU HOLD UP FOR A SECOND?
PANT! PANT! GRUNT GRUNT
TOSS
TOSS! TOSS
HIS HAT'S HERE SOMEWHERE...I CAN SMELL IT FOR SURE.
PANT PANT!
TAP TAP!
HEY—
ARE YOU LOOKIN' FOR SOMETHING IN PARTICULAR?
WHAT?

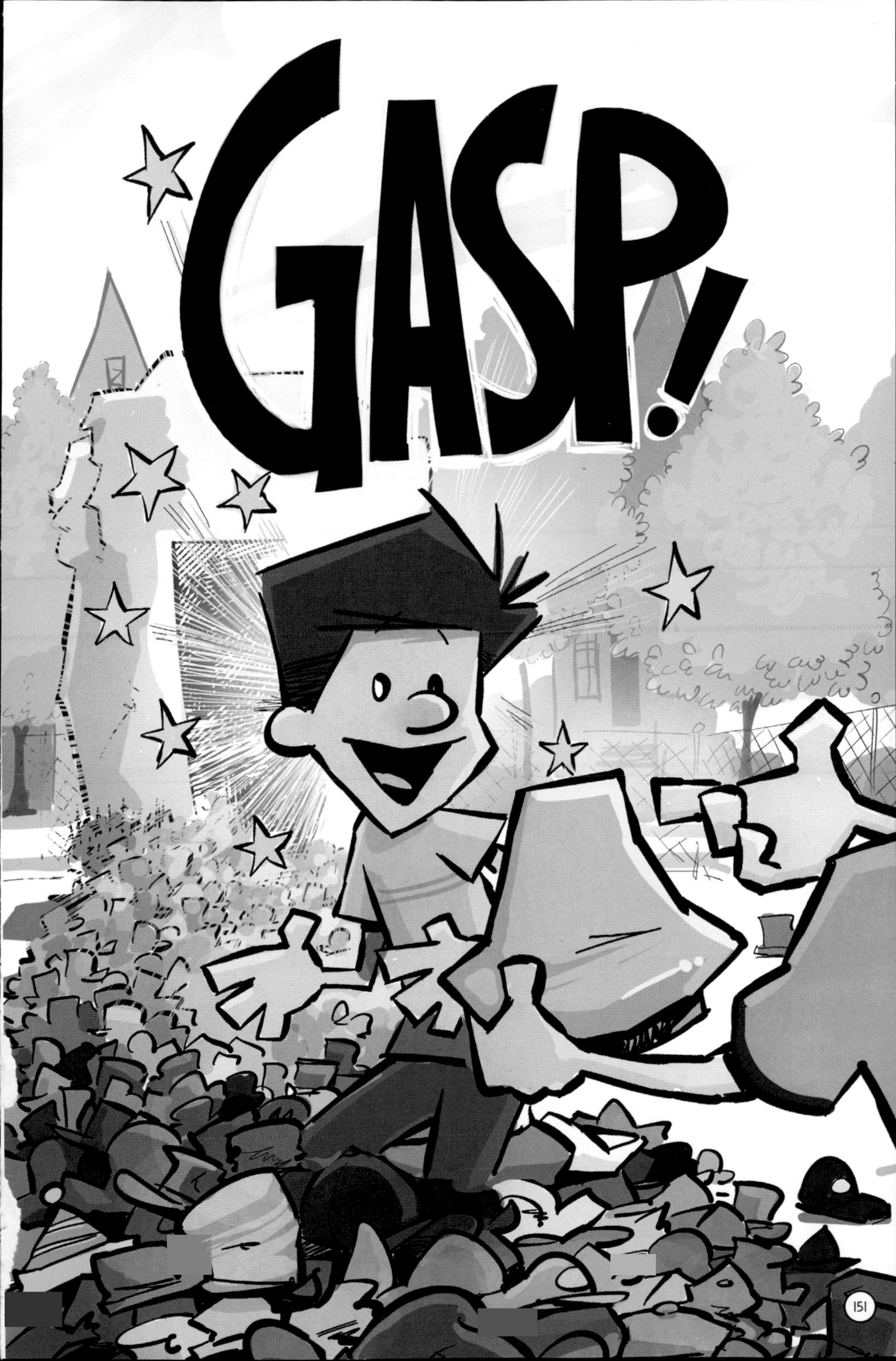
GASP!

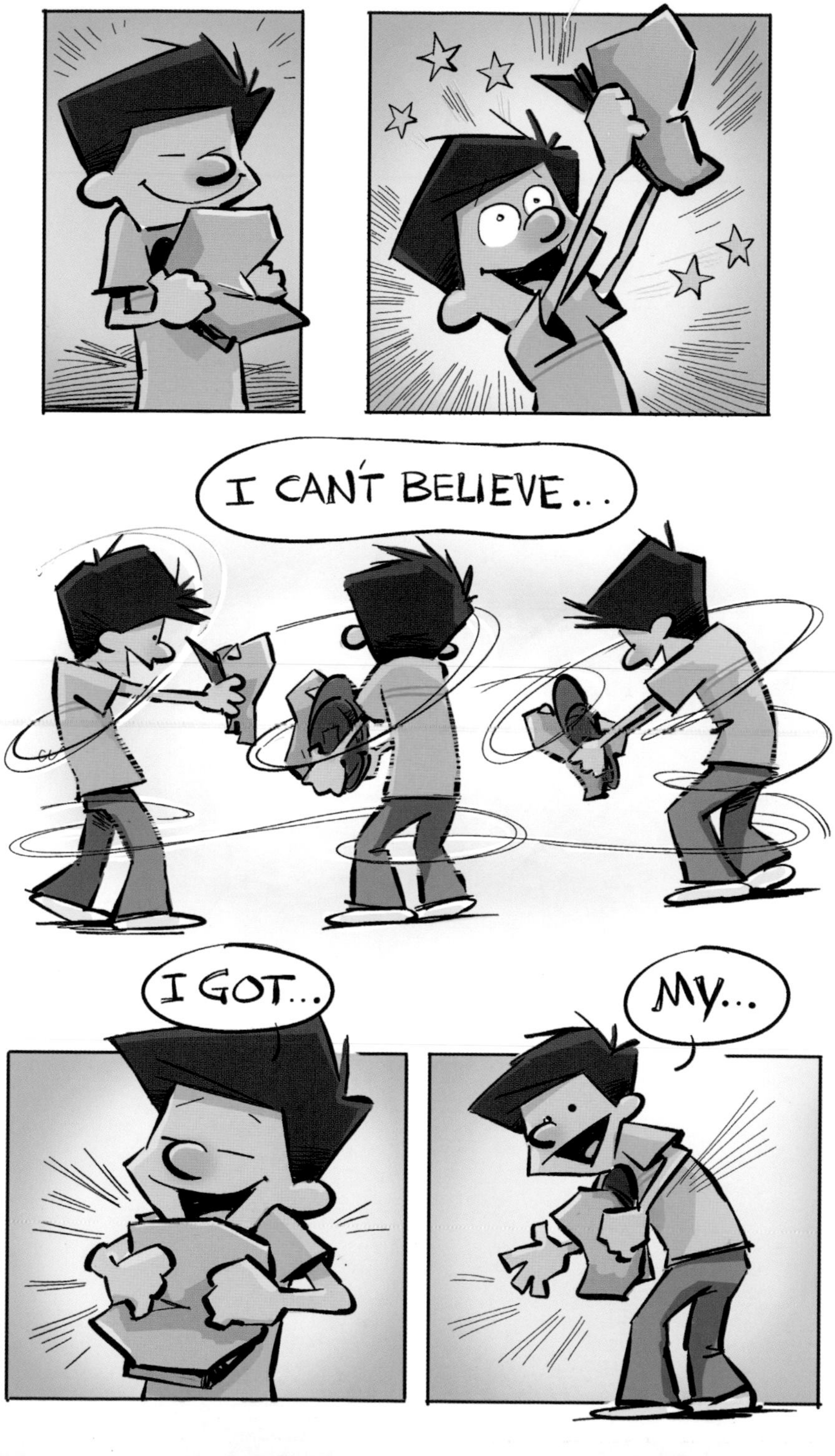
I CAN'T BELIEVE...
I GOT...
MY...

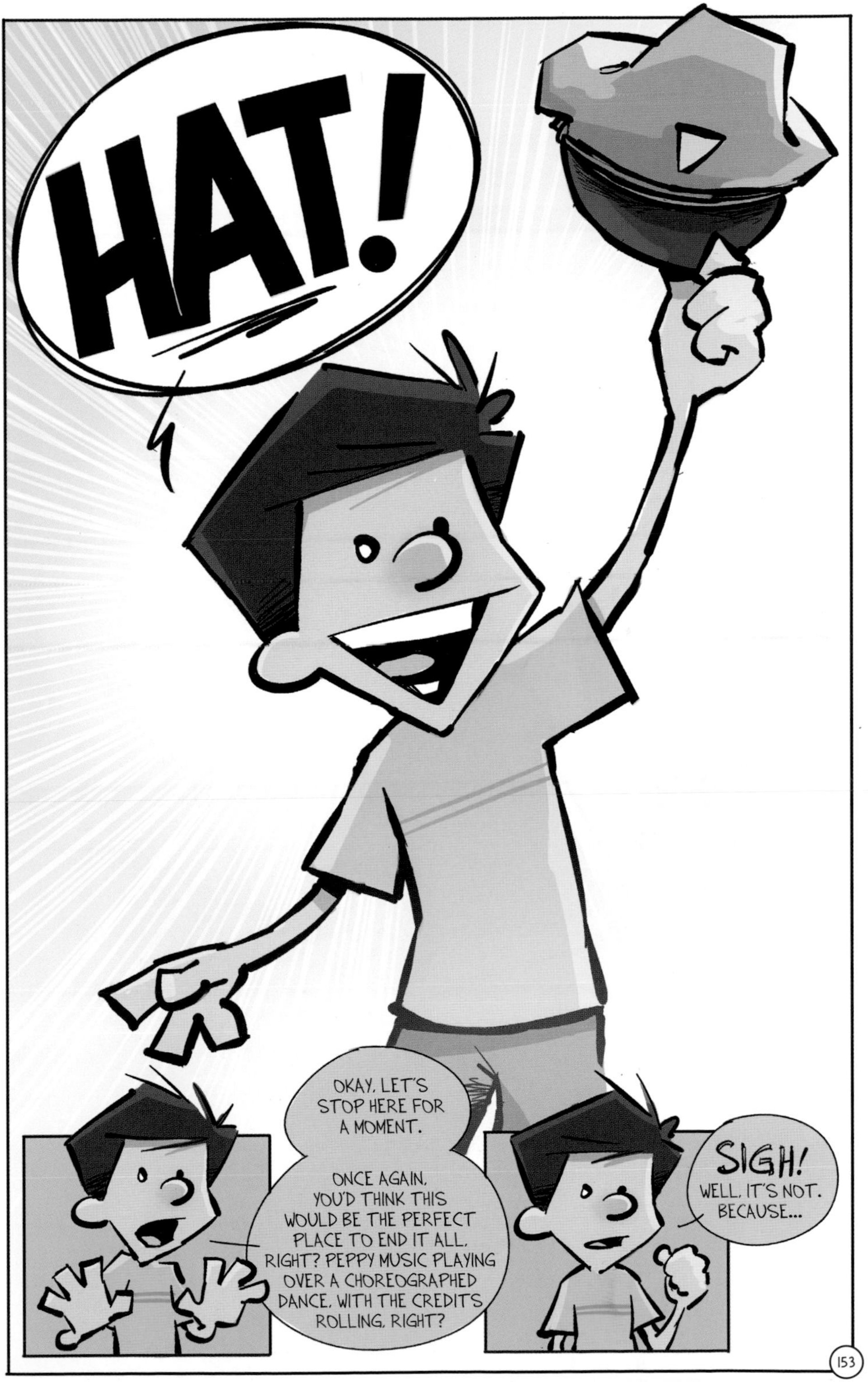
HAT!
OKAY, LET'S STOP HERE FOR A MOMENT.
ONCE AGAIN, YOU'D THINK THIS WOULD BE THE PERFECT PLACE TO END IT ALL, RIGHT? PEPPY MUSIC PLAYING OVER A CHOREOGRAPHED DANCE, WITH THE CREDITS ROLLING, RIGHT?
SIGH! WELL, IT'S NOT. BECAUSE...

CHAPTER EIGHT
IT'S ONLY THE BEGINNING...AGAIN

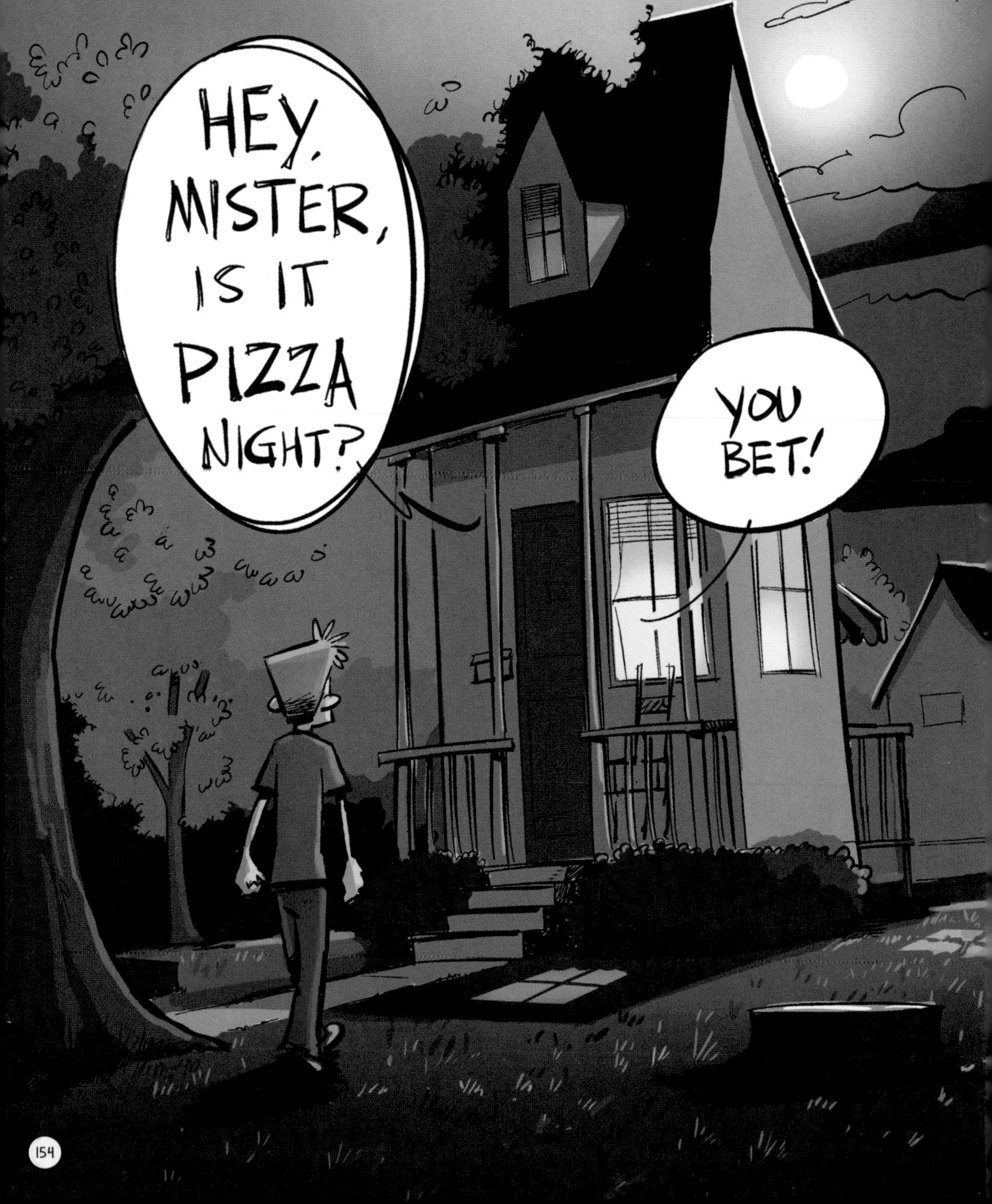

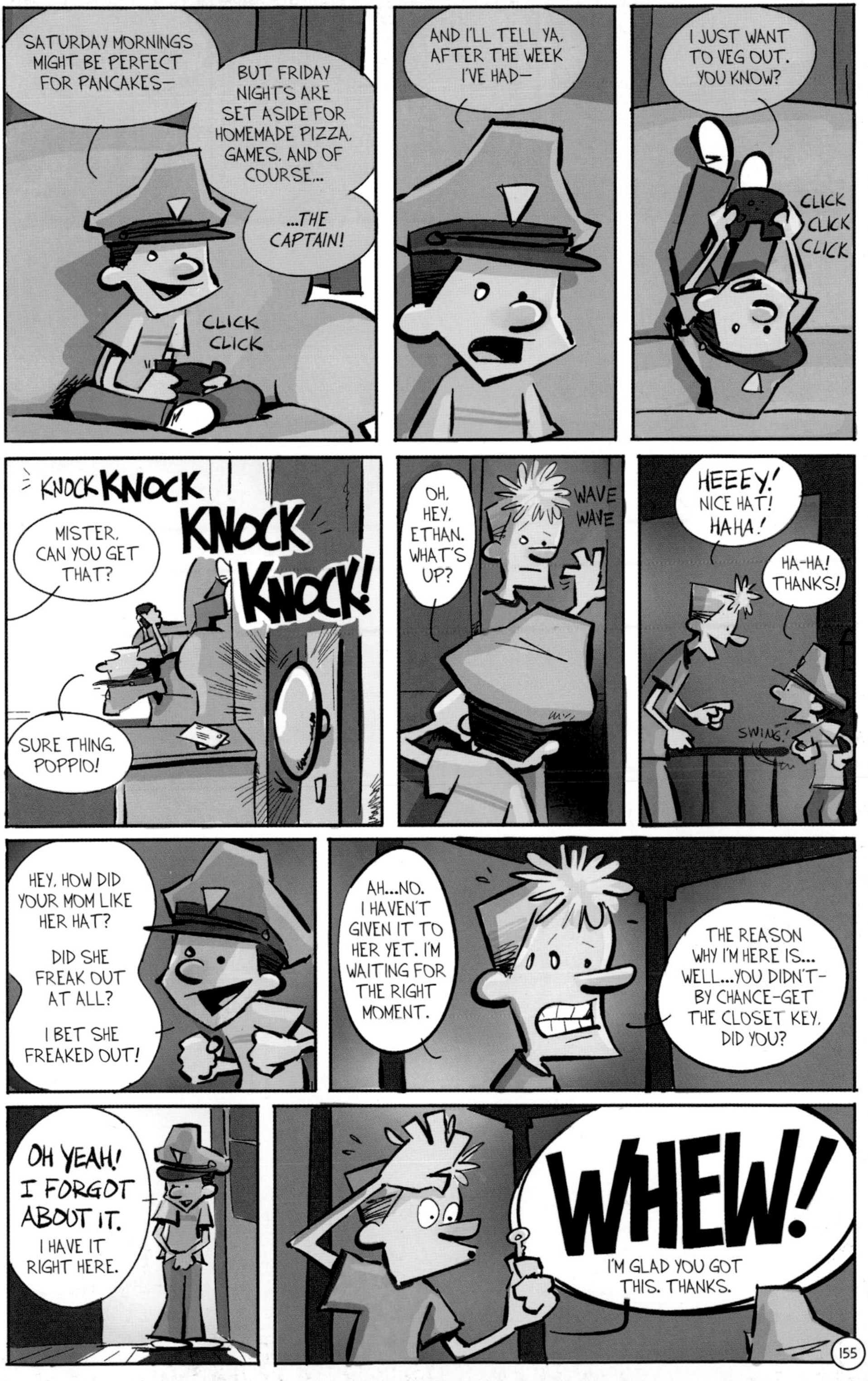
SATURDAY MORNINGS MIGHT BE PERFECT FOR PANCAKES—
BUT FRIDAY NIGHTS ARE SET ASIDE FOR HOMEMADE PIZZA, GAMES, AND OF COURSE...
...THE CAPTAIN!
CLICK CLICK
AND I'LL TELL YA, AFTER THE WEEK I'VE HAD—
I JUST WANT TO VEG OUT. YOU KNOW?
CLICK CLICK CLICK
KNOCK KNOCK
KNOCK
KNOCK!
MISTER, CAN YOU GET THAT?
SURE THING, POPPIO!
OH, HEY, ETHAN. WHAT'S UP?
WAVE WAVE
HEEEY! NICE HAT! HAHA!
HA-HA! THANKS!
SWING!
HEY, HOW DID YOUR MOM LIKE HER HAT?
DID SHE FREAK OUT AT ALL?
I BET SHE FREAKED OUT!
AH...NO. I HAVEN'T GIVEN IT TO HER YET. I'M WAITING FOR THE RIGHT MOMENT.
THE REASON WHY I'M HERE IS... WELL...YOU DIDN'T—BY CHANCE—GET THE CLOSET KEY, DID YOU?
OH YEAH! I FORGOT ABOUT IT. I HAVE IT RIGHT HERE.
WHEW!
I'M GLAD YOU GOT THIS. THANKS.

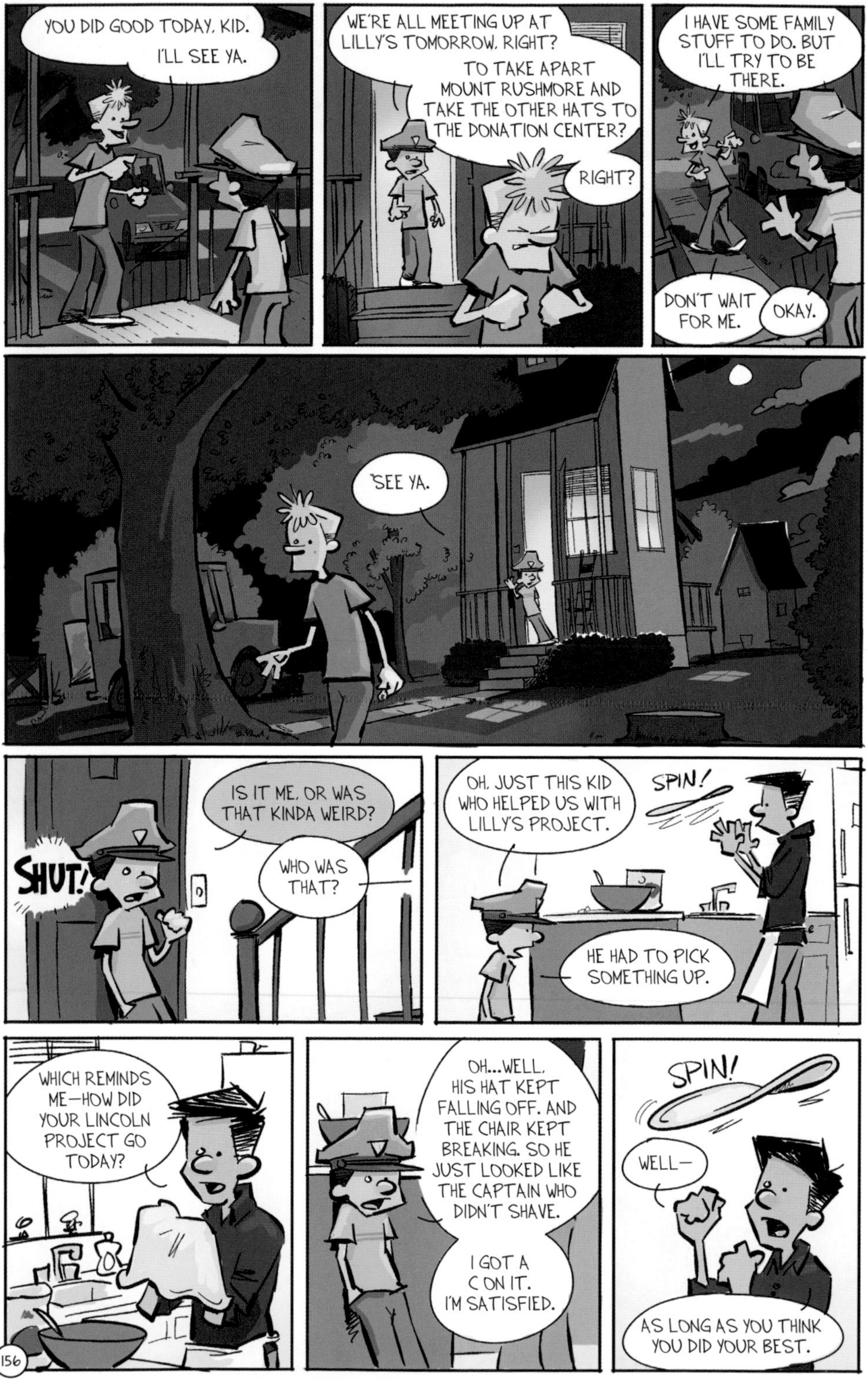

YOU DID GOOD TODAY, KID.
I'LL SEE YA.
WE'RE ALL MEETING UP AT LILLY'S TOMORROW, RIGHT?
TO TAKE APART MOUNT RUSHMORE AND TAKE THE OTHER HATS TO THE DONATION CENTER?
RIGHT?
I HAVE SOME FAMILY STUFF TO DO. BUT I'LL TRY TO BE THERE.
DON'T WAIT FOR ME.
OKAY.
SEE YA.
SHUT!
IS IT ME, OR WAS THAT KINDA WEIRD?
WHO WAS THAT?
OH, JUST THIS KID WHO HELPED US WITH LILLY'S PROJECT.
SPIN!
HE HAD TO PICK SOMETHING UP.
WHICH REMINDS ME—HOW DID YOUR LINCOLN PROJECT GO TODAY?
OH...WELL, HIS HAT KEPT FALLING OFF. AND THE CHAIR KEPT BREAKING. SO HE JUST LOOKED LIKE THE CAPTAIN WHO DIDN'T SHAVE.
I GOT A C ON IT. I'M SATISFIED.
SPIN!
WELL—
AS LONG AS YOU THINK YOU DID YOUR BEST.

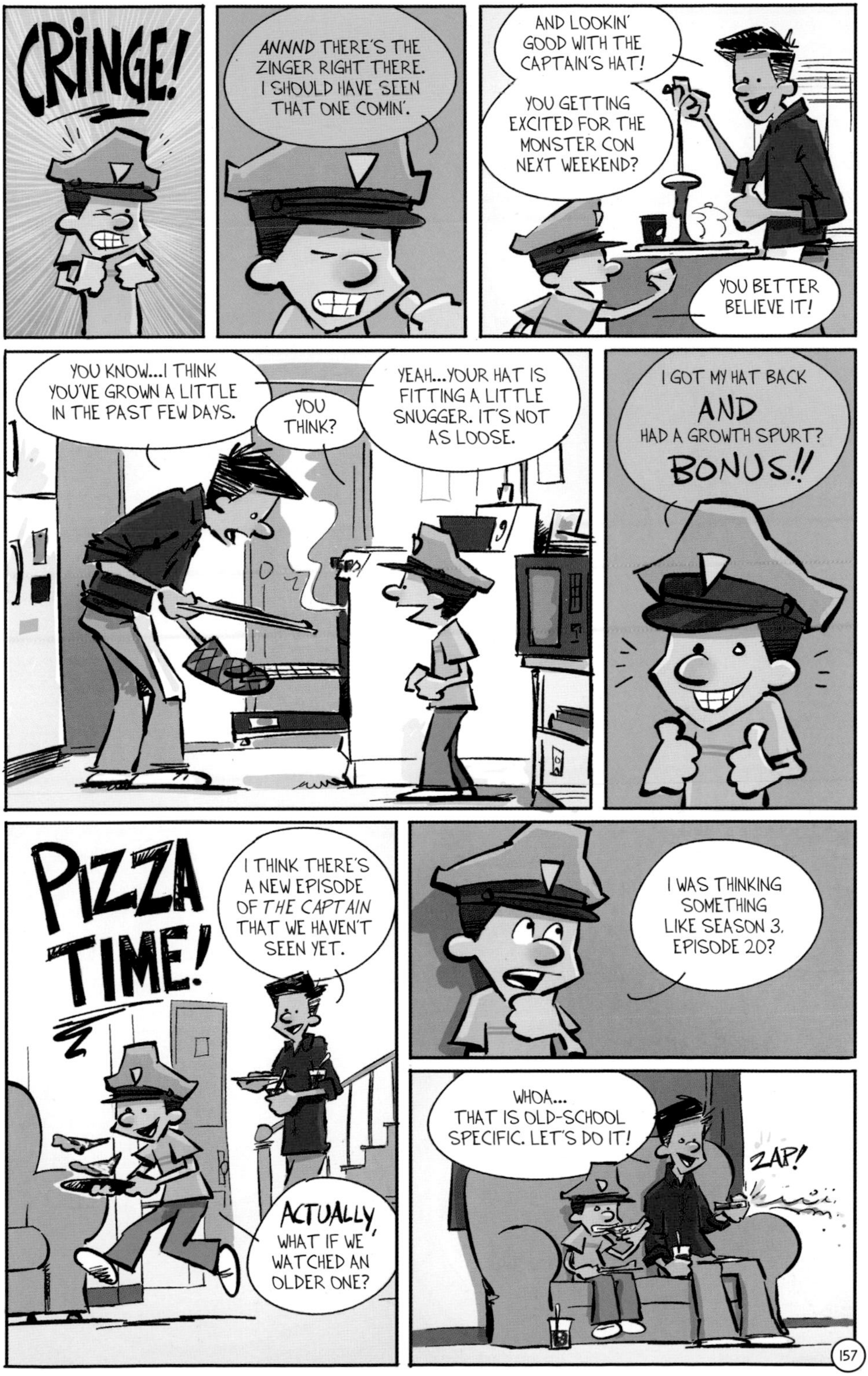
CRINGE!
ANNND THERE'S THE ZINGER RIGHT THERE. I SHOULD HAVE SEEN THAT ONE COMIN'.
AND LOOKIN' GOOD WITH THE CAPTAIN'S HAT!
YOU GETTING EXCITED FOR THE MONSTER CON NEXT WEEKEND?
YOU BETTER BELIEVE IT!
YOU KNOW...I THINK YOU'VE GROWN A LITTLE IN THE PAST FEW DAYS.
YOU THINK?
YEAH...YOUR HAT IS FITTING A LITTLE SNUGGER. IT'S NOT AS LOOSE.
I GOT MY HAT BACK AND HAD A GROWTH SPURT? BONUS!!
PIZZA TIME!
I THINK THERE'S A NEW EPISODE OF THE CAPTAIN THAT WE HAVEN'T SEEN YET.
ACTUALLY, WHAT IF WE WATCHED AN OLDER ONE?
I WAS THINKING SOMETHING LIKE SEASON 3, EPISODE 20?
WHOA... THAT IS OLD-SCHOOL SPECIFIC. LET'S DO IT!
ZAP!

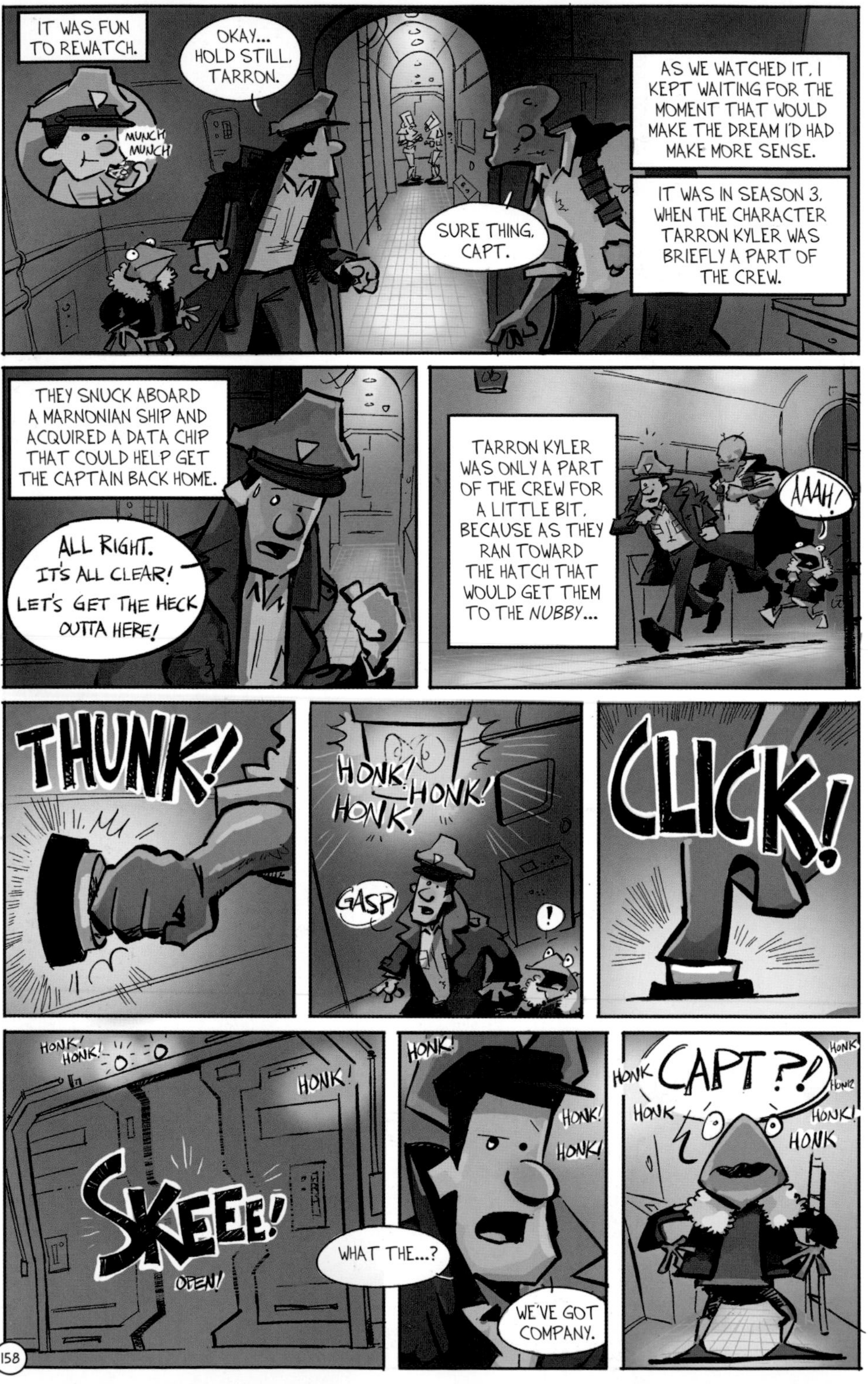
IT WAS FUN TO REWATCH.
MUNCH MUNCH
OKAY... HOLD STILL, TARRON.
SURE THING, CAPT.
AS WE WATCHED IT, I KEPT WAITING FOR THE MOMENT THAT WOULD MAKE THE DREAM I'D HAD MAKE MORE SENSE.
IT WAS IN SEASON 3, WHEN THE CHARACTER TARRON KYLER WAS BRIEFLY A PART OF THE CREW.
THEY SNUCK ABOARD A MARNONIAN SHIP AND ACQUIRED A DATA CHIP THAT COULD HELP GET THE CAPTAIN BACK HOME.
ALL RIGHT. IT'S ALL CLEAR! LET'S GET THE HECK OUTTA HERE!
TARRON KYLER WAS ONLY A PART OF THE CREW FOR A LITTLE BIT, BECAUSE AS THEY RAN TOWARD THE HATCH THAT WOULD GET THEM TO THE *NUBBY*...
AAAH!
THUNK!
HONK! HONK! HONK!
GASP!
!
CLICK!
HONK! HONK!
HONK!
SKEEE!
OPEN!
HONK!
HONK!
HONK!
WHAT THE...?
WE'VE GOT COMPANY.
CAPT?!
HONK
HONK
HONK
HONK
HONK!
HONK

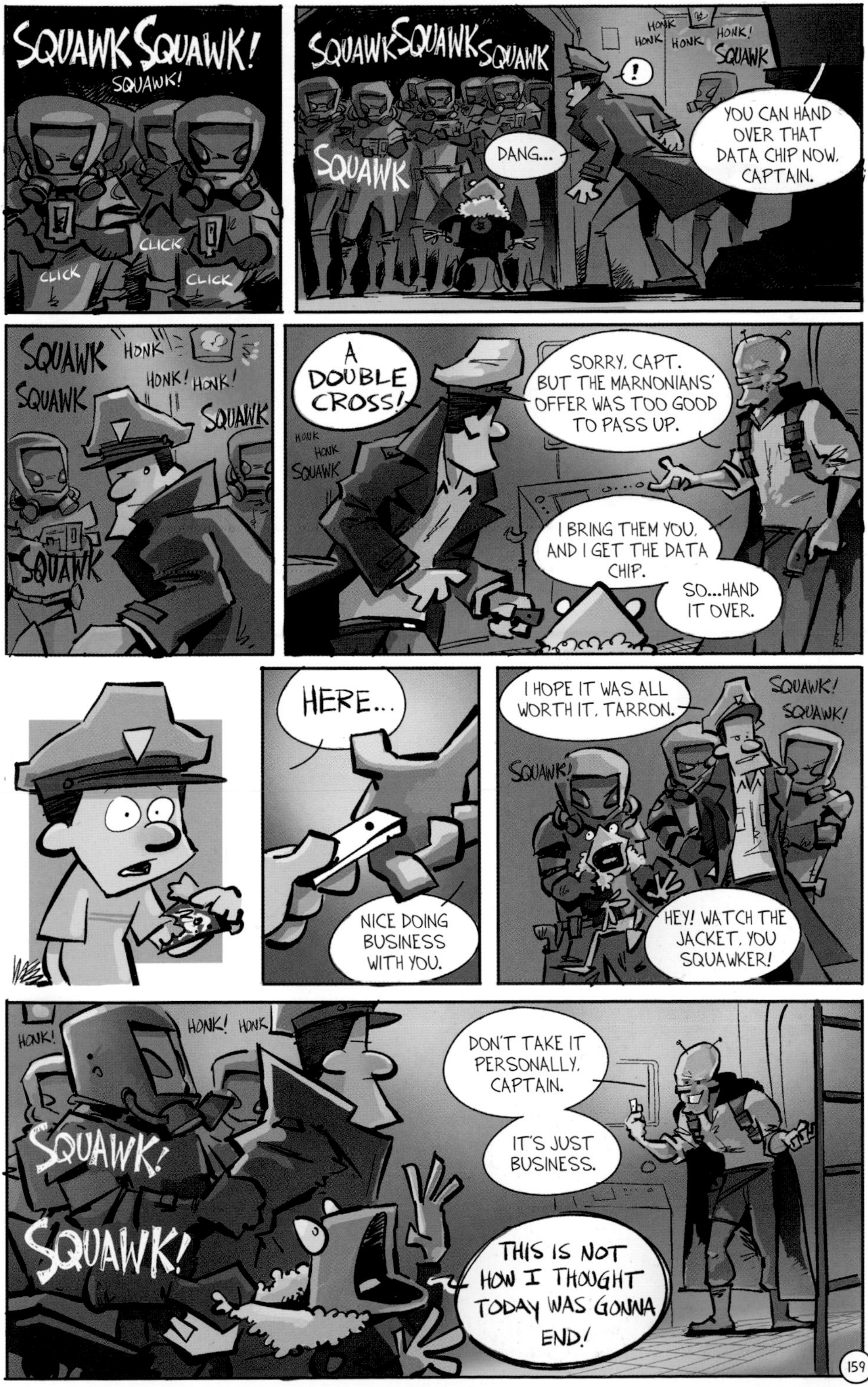
SQUAWK SQUAWK!
SQUAWK!
CLICK
CLICK
CLICK
SQUAWK SQUAWK SQUAWK
HONK HONK HONK HONK!
SQUAWK
!
SQUAWK
DANG...
YOU CAN HAND OVER THAT DATA CHIP NOW, CAPTAIN.
SQUAWK
HONK
HONK! HONK!
SQUAWK
SQUAWK
SQUAWK
A DOUBLE CROSS!
HONK
HONK
SQUAWK
SORRY, CAPT. BUT THE MARNONIANS' OFFER WAS TOO GOOD TO PASS UP.
I BRING THEM YOU, AND I GET THE DATA CHIP.
SO...HAND IT OVER.
HERE...
NICE DOING BUSINESS WITH YOU.
I HOPE IT WAS ALL WORTH IT, TARRON.
SQUAWK!
SQUAWK!
SQUAWK!
HEY! WATCH THE JACKET, YOU SQUAWKER!
HONK!
HONK! HONK
SQUAWK!
SQUAWK!
DON'T TAKE IT PERSONALLY, CAPTAIN.
IT'S JUST BUSINESS.
THIS IS NOT HOW I THOUGHT TODAY WAS GONNA END!

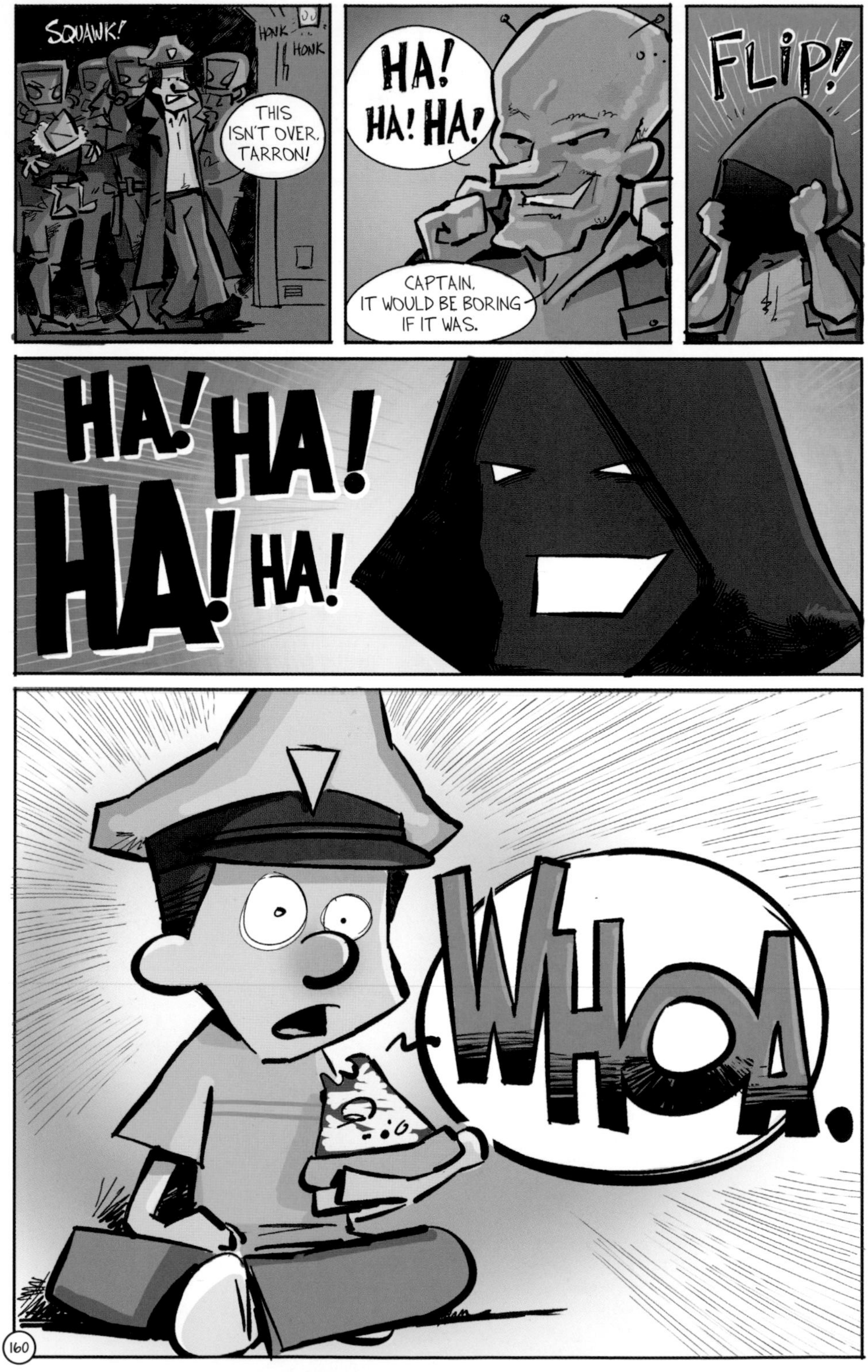
SQUAWK!
HONK
HONK
THIS ISN'T OVER, TARRON!
HA! HA! HA!
CAPTAIN, IT WOULD BE BORING IF IT WAS.
FLIP!
HA! HA! HA! HA!
WHOA.

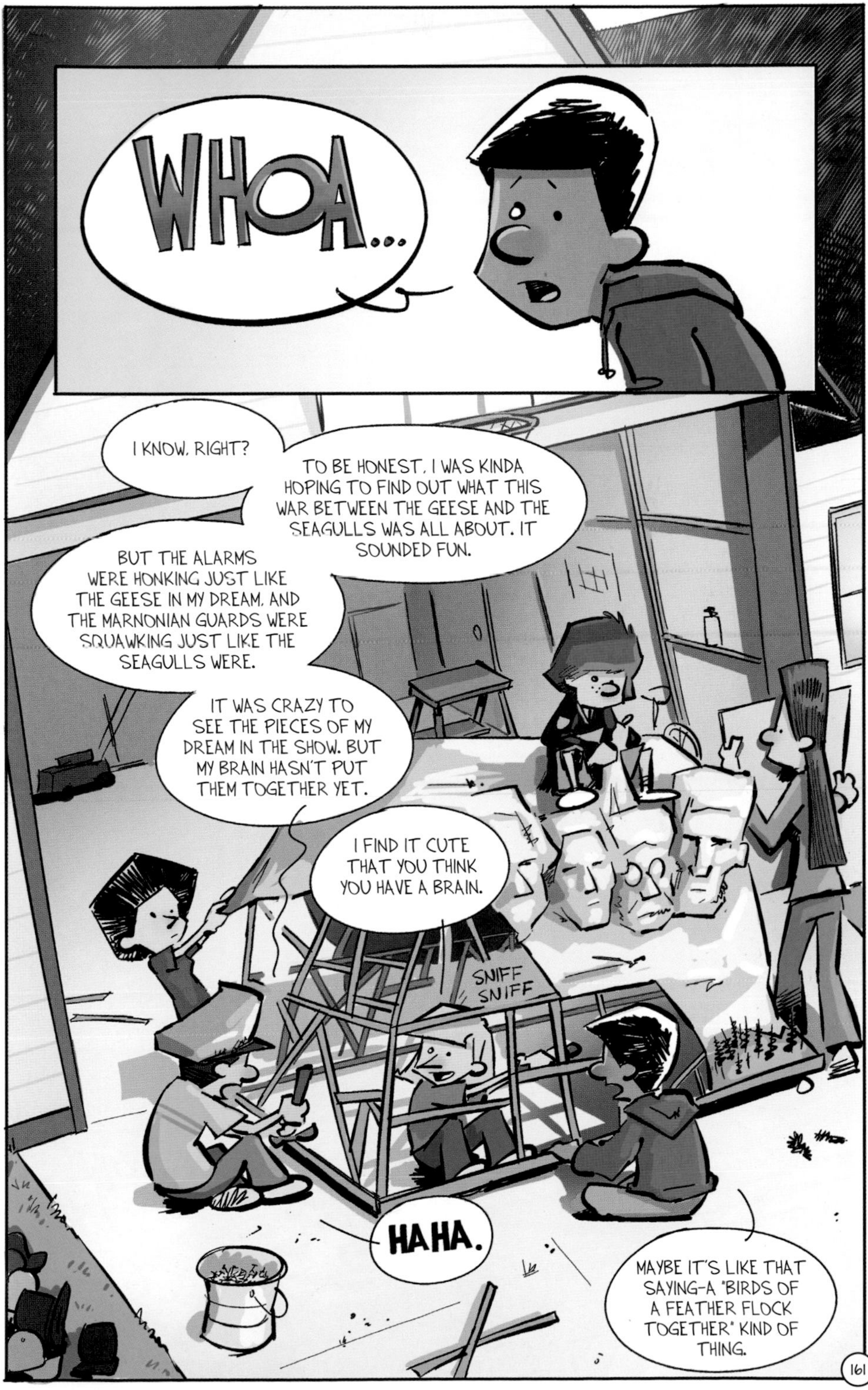
WHOA...
I KNOW, RIGHT?
TO BE HONEST, I WAS KINDA HOPING TO FIND OUT WHAT THIS WAR BETWEEN THE GEESE AND THE SEAGULLS WAS ALL ABOUT. IT SOUNDED FUN.
BUT THE ALARMS WERE HONKING JUST LIKE THE GEESE IN MY DREAM, AND THE MARNONIAN GUARDS WERE SQUAWKING JUST LIKE THE SEAGULLS WERE.
IT WAS CRAZY TO SEE THE PIECES OF MY DREAM IN THE SHOW. BUT MY BRAIN HASN'T PUT THEM TOGETHER YET.
I FIND IT CUTE THAT YOU THINK YOU HAVE A BRAIN.
SNIFF SNIFF
HAHA.
MAYBE IT'S LIKE THAT SAYING—A "BIRDS OF A FEATHER FLOCK TOGETHER" KIND OF THING.

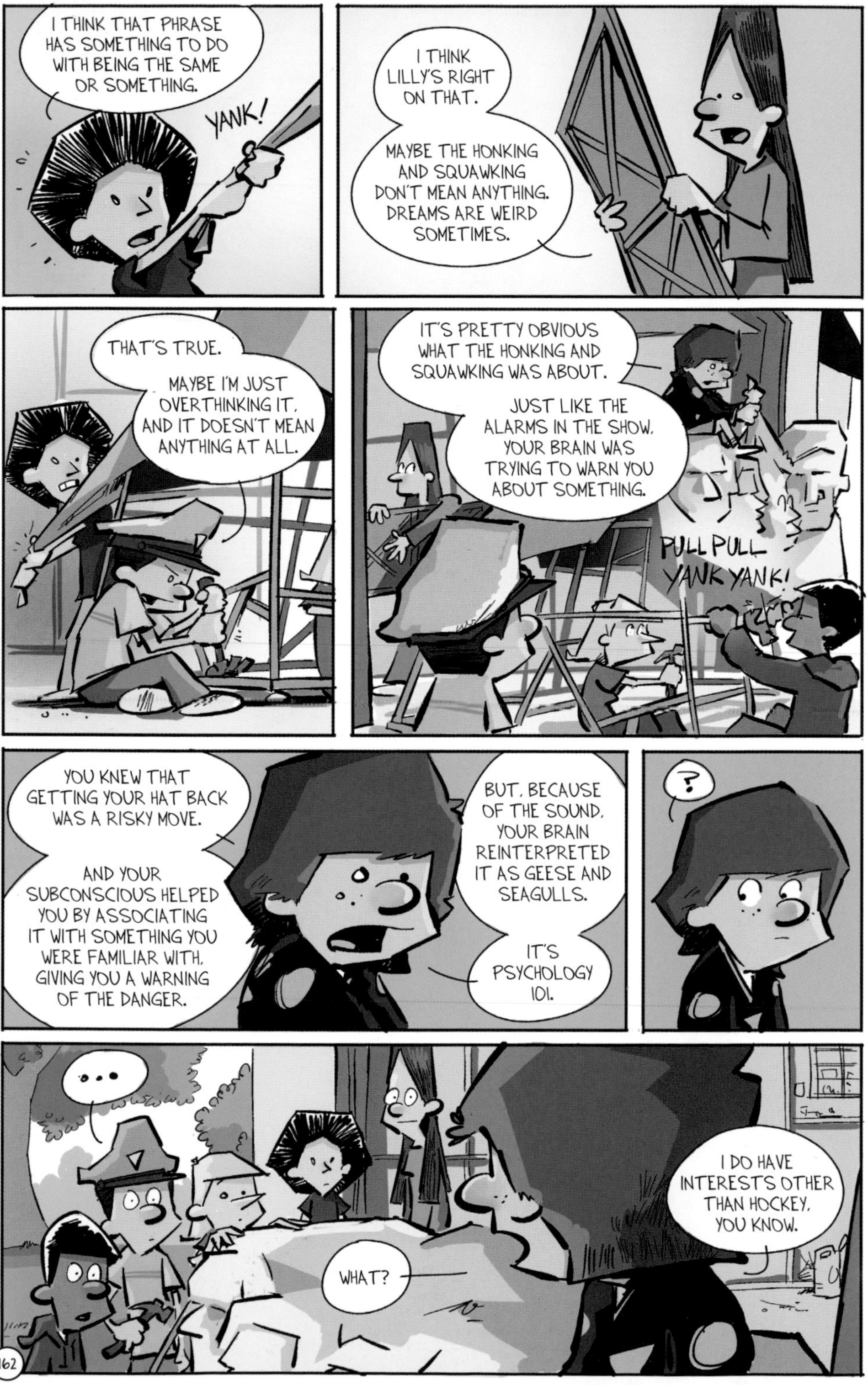
I THINK THAT PHRASE HAS SOMETHING TO DO WITH BEING THE SAME OR SOMETHING.
YANK!
I THINK LILLY'S RIGHT ON THAT.
MAYBE THE HONKING AND SQUAWKING DON'T MEAN ANYTHING. DREAMS ARE WEIRD SOMETIMES.
THAT'S TRUE.
MAYBE I'M JUST OVERTHINKING IT, AND IT DOESN'T MEAN ANYTHING AT ALL.
IT'S PRETTY OBVIOUS WHAT THE HONKING AND SQUAWKING WAS ABOUT.
JUST LIKE THE ALARMS IN THE SHOW, YOUR BRAIN WAS TRYING TO WARN YOU ABOUT SOMETHING.
PULL PULL
YANK YANK!
YOU KNEW THAT GETTING YOUR HAT BACK WAS A RISKY MOVE.
AND YOUR SUBCONSCIOUS HELPED YOU BY ASSOCIATING IT WITH SOMETHING YOU WERE FAMILIAR WITH, GIVING YOU A WARNING OF THE DANGER.
BUT, BECAUSE OF THE SOUND, YOUR BRAIN REINTERPRETED IT AS GEESE AND SEAGULLS.
IT'S PSYCHOLOGY 101.
?
...
WHAT?
I DO HAVE INTERESTS OTHER THAN HOCKEY, YOU KNOW.

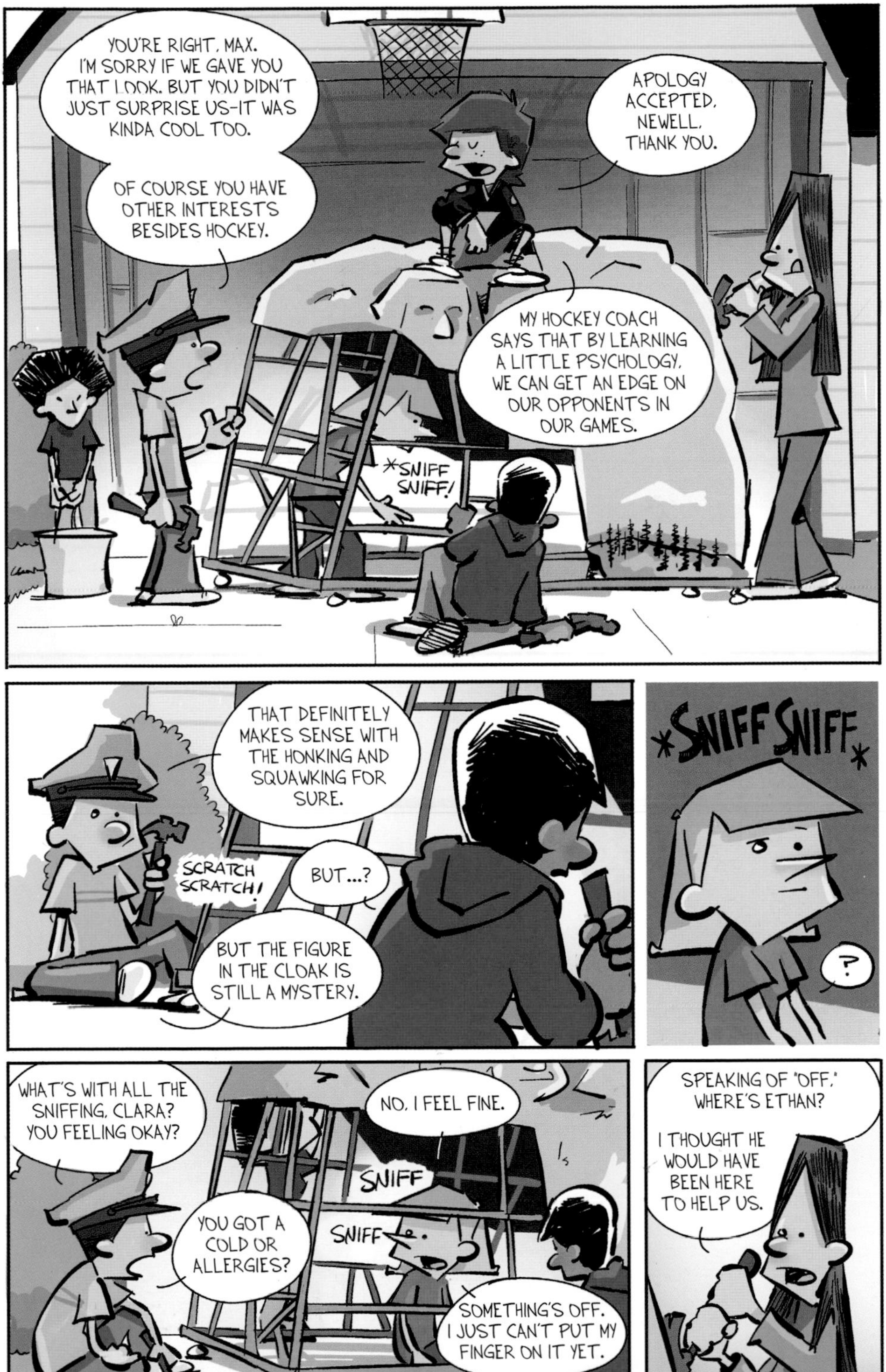
YOU'RE RIGHT, MAX. I'M SORRY IF WE GAVE YOU THAT LOOK. BUT YOU DIDN'T JUST SURPRISE US–IT WAS KINDA COOL TOO.
OF COURSE YOU HAVE OTHER INTERESTS BESIDES HOCKEY.
APOLOGY ACCEPTED, NEWELL. THANK YOU.
MY HOCKEY COACH SAYS THAT BY LEARNING A LITTLE PSYCHOLOGY, WE CAN GET AN EDGE ON OUR OPPONENTS IN OUR GAMES.
*SNIFF SNIFF!
THAT DEFINITELY MAKES SENSE WITH THE HONKING AND SQUAWKING FOR SURE.
SCRATCH SCRATCH!
BUT...?
BUT THE FIGURE IN THE CLOAK IS STILL A MYSTERY.
SNIFF SNIFF
?
WHAT'S WITH ALL THE SNIFFING, CLARA? YOU FEELING OKAY?
NO, I FEEL FINE.
SNIFF
SNIFF
YOU GOT A COLD OR ALLERGIES?
SOMETHING'S OFF. I JUST CAN'T PUT MY FINGER ON IT YET.
SPEAKING OF "OFF," WHERE'S ETHAN?
I THOUGHT HE WOULD HAVE BEEN HERE TO HELP US.

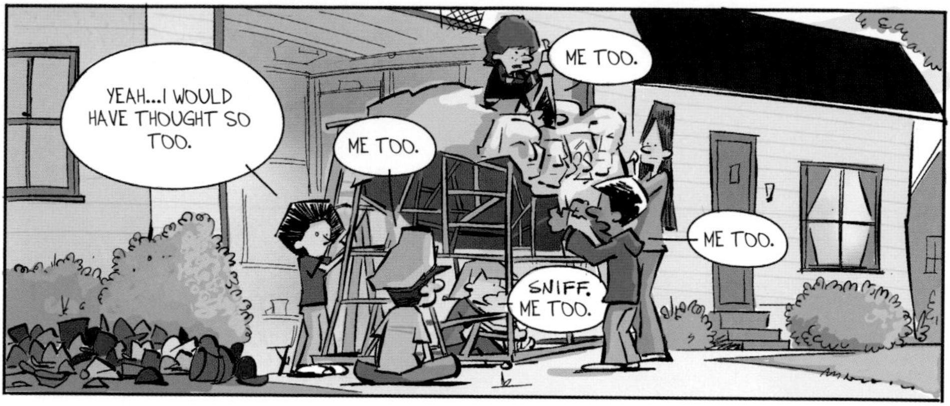
YEAH...I WOULD HAVE THOUGHT SO TOO.
ME TOO.
ME TOO.
ME TOO.
SNIFF. ME TOO.

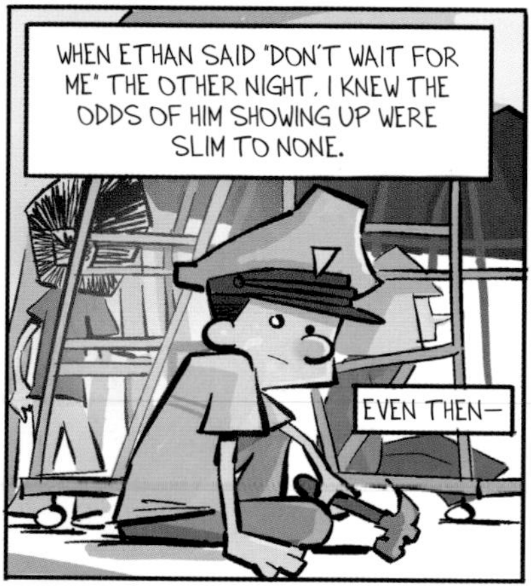
WHEN ETHAN SAID "DON'T WAIT FOR ME" THE OTHER NIGHT, I KNEW THE ODDS OF HIM SHOWING UP WERE SLIM TO NONE.
EVEN THEN—

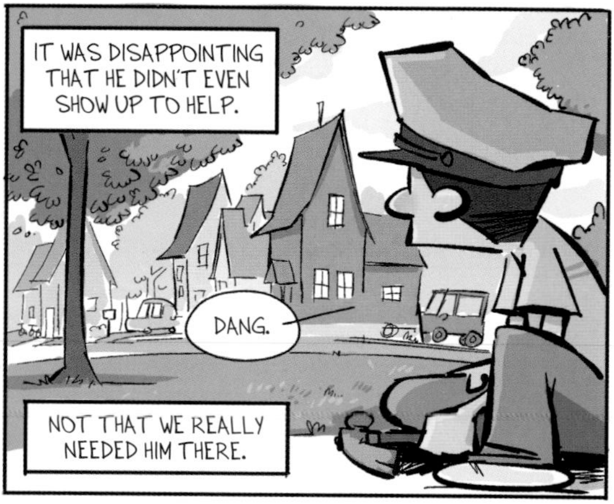
IT WAS DISAPPOINTING THAT HE DIDN'T EVEN SHOW UP TO HELP.
DANG.
NOT THAT WE REALLY NEEDED HIM THERE.

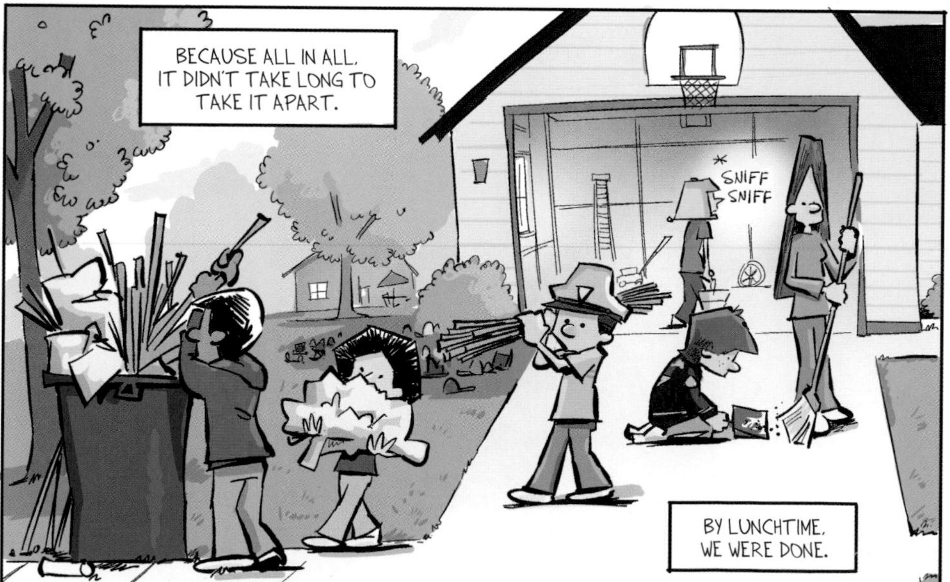
BECAUSE ALL IN ALL, IT DIDN'T TAKE LONG TO TAKE IT APART.
SNIFF SNIFF
BY LUNCHTIME, WE WERE DONE.

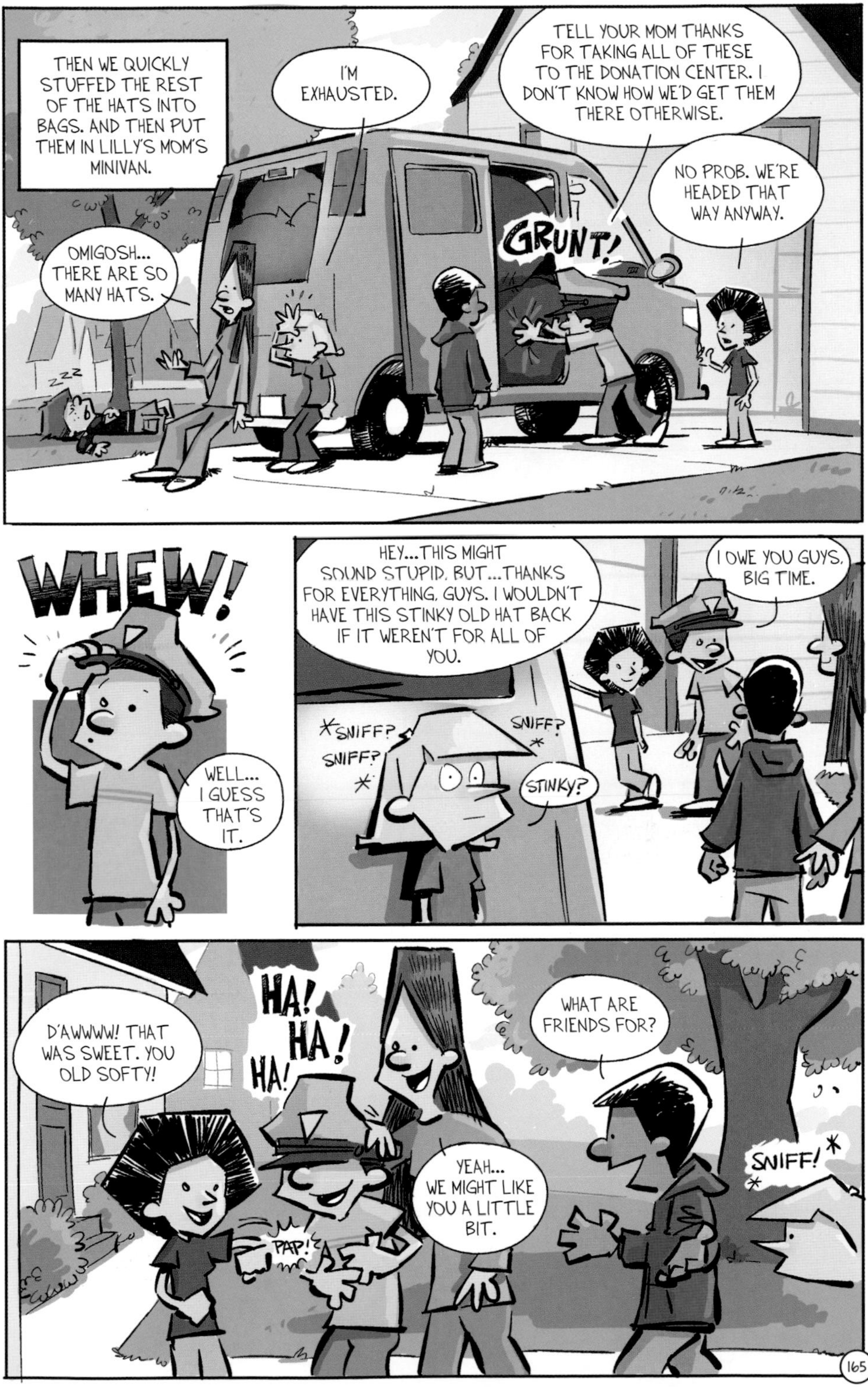

THEN WE QUICKLY STUFFED THE REST OF THE HATS INTO BAGS. AND THEN PUT THEM IN LILLY'S MOM'S MINIVAN.
OMIGOSH... THERE ARE SO MANY HATS.
I'M EXHAUSTED.
GRUNT!
TELL YOUR MOM THANKS FOR TAKING ALL OF THESE TO THE DONATION CENTER. I DON'T KNOW HOW WE'D GET THEM THERE OTHERWISE.
NO PROB. WE'RE HEADED THAT WAY ANYWAY.
WHEW!
WELL... I GUESS THAT'S IT.
HEY...THIS MIGHT SOUND STUPID, BUT...THANKS FOR EVERYTHING, GUYS. I WOULDN'T HAVE THIS STINKY OLD HAT BACK IF IT WEREN'T FOR ALL OF YOU.
I OWE YOU GUYS, BIG TIME.
SNIFF?
SNIFF?
SNIFF?
STINKY?
D'AWWWW! THAT WAS SWEET. YOU OLD SOFTY!
HA! HA! HA!
WHAT ARE FRIENDS FOR?
PAP!
YEAH... WE MIGHT LIKE YOU A LITTLE BIT.
SNIFF!

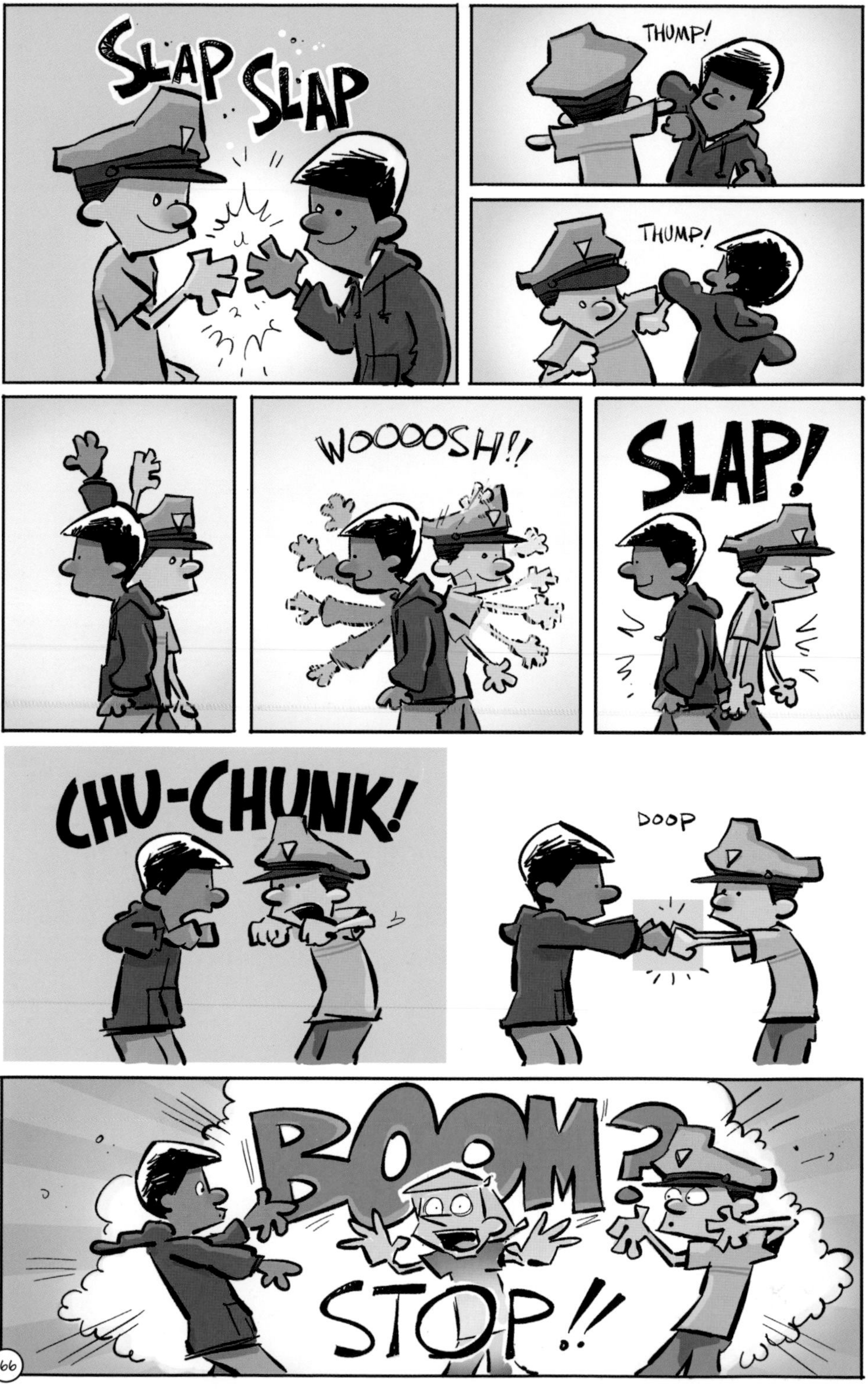
SLAP SLAP
THUMP!
THUMP!
WOOOOSH!!
SLAP!
CHU-CHUNK!
DOOP
BOOM?
STOP!!

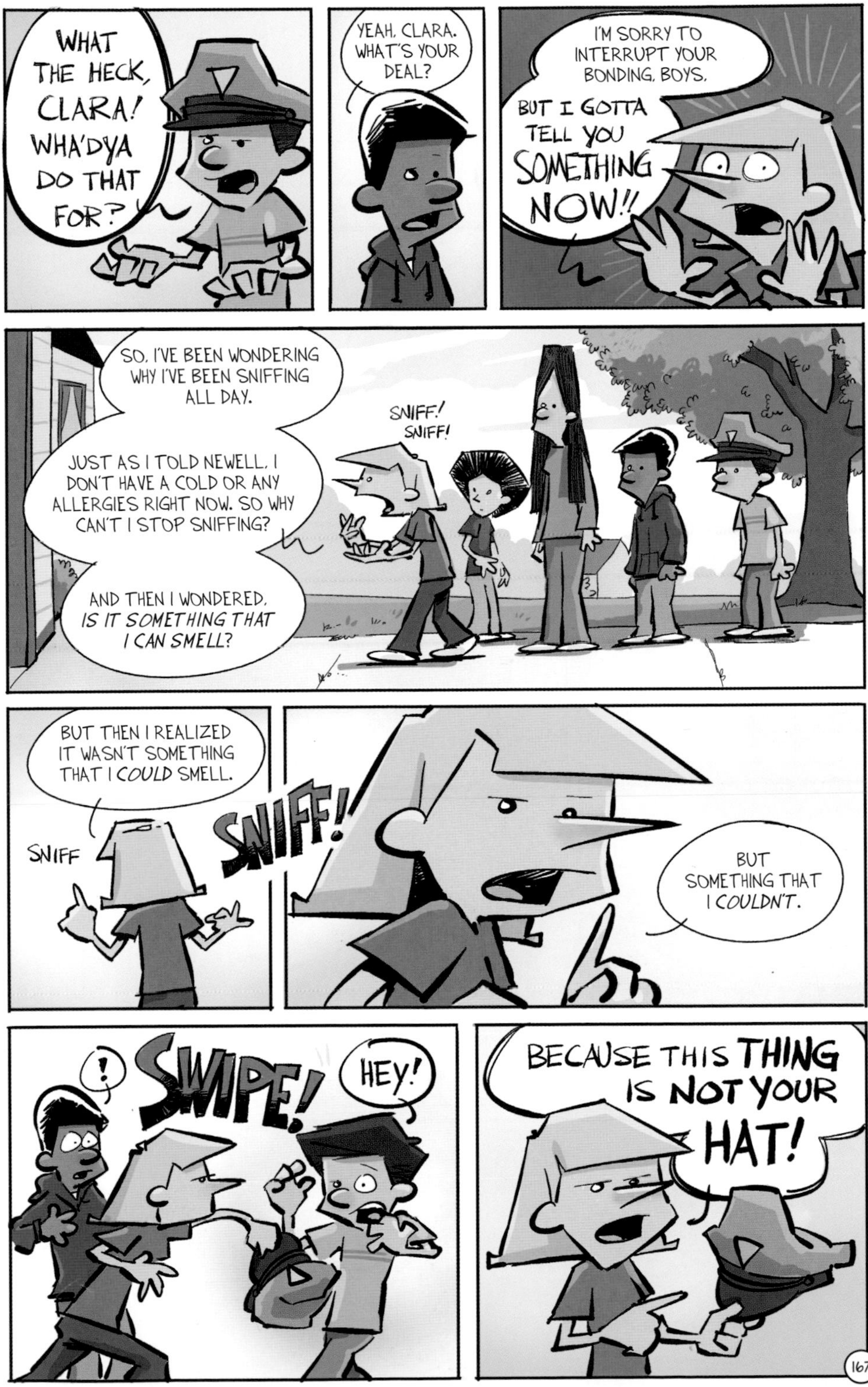

WHAT THE HECK, CLARA! WHA'DYA DO THAT FOR?
YEAH, CLARA. WHAT'S YOUR DEAL?
I'M SORRY TO INTERRUPT YOUR BONDING, BOYS,
BUT I GOTTA TELL YOU SOMETHING NOW!!
SO, I'VE BEEN WONDERING WHY I'VE BEEN SNIFFING ALL DAY.
SNIFF! SNIFF!
JUST AS I TOLD NEWELL, I DON'T HAVE A COLD OR ANY ALLERGIES RIGHT NOW. SO WHY CAN'T I STOP SNIFFING?
AND THEN I WONDERED, *IS IT SOMETHING THAT I CAN SMELL?*
BUT THEN I REALIZED IT WASN'T SOMETHING THAT I *COULD* SMELL.
SNIFF
SNIFF!
BUT SOMETHING THAT I *COULDN'T*.
!
SWIPE!
HEY!
BECAUSE THIS **THING** IS **NOT YOUR HAT!**

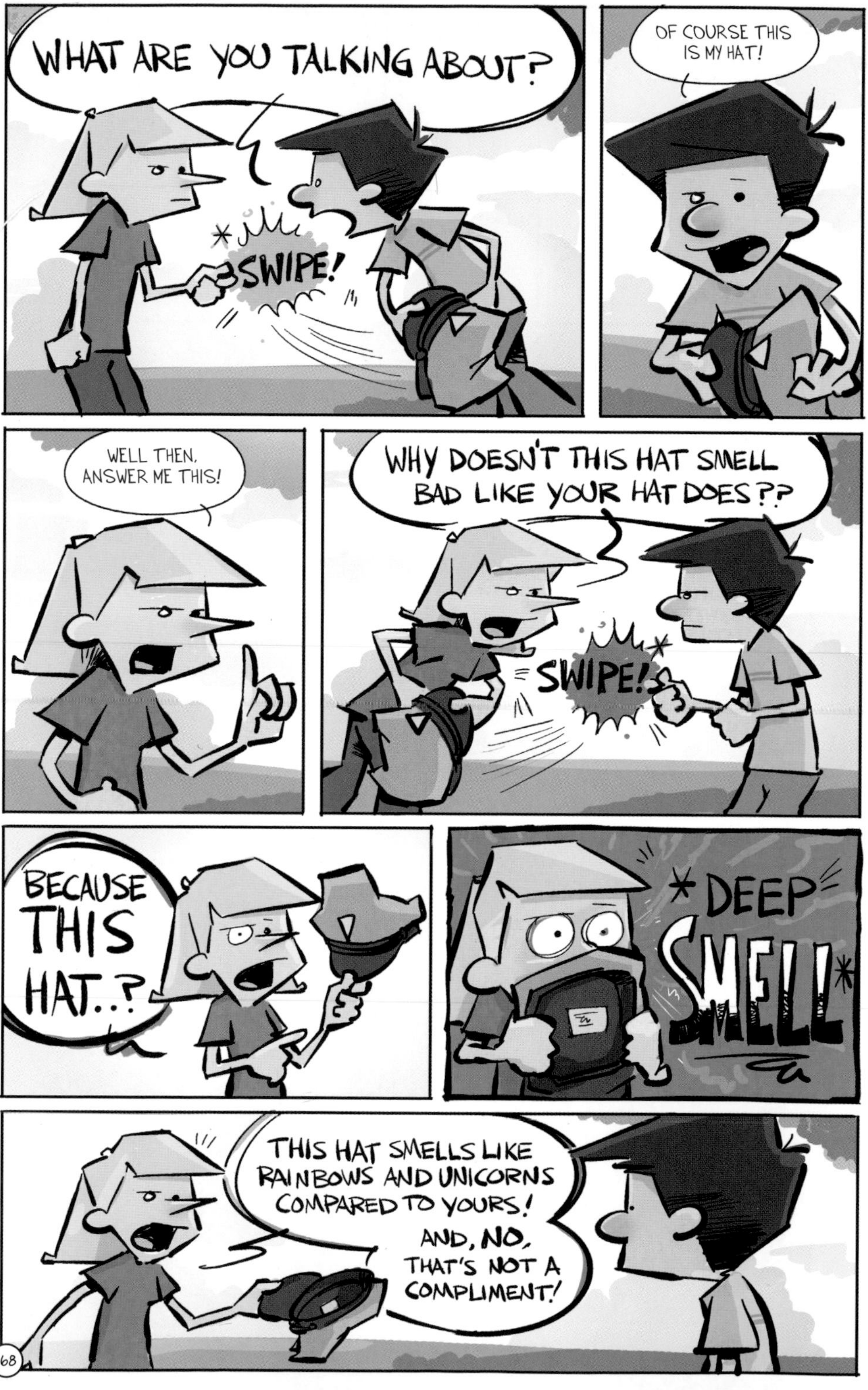
WHAT ARE YOU TALKING ABOUT?
*SWIPE!
OF COURSE THIS IS MY HAT!
WELL THEN, ANSWER ME THIS!
WHY DOESN'T THIS HAT SMELL BAD LIKE YOUR HAT DOES??
SWIPE!*
BECAUSE THIS HAT..?
DEEP SMELL
THIS HAT SMELLS LIKE RAINBOWS AND UNICORNS COMPARED TO YOURS!
AND, NO, THAT'S NOT A COMPLIMENT!

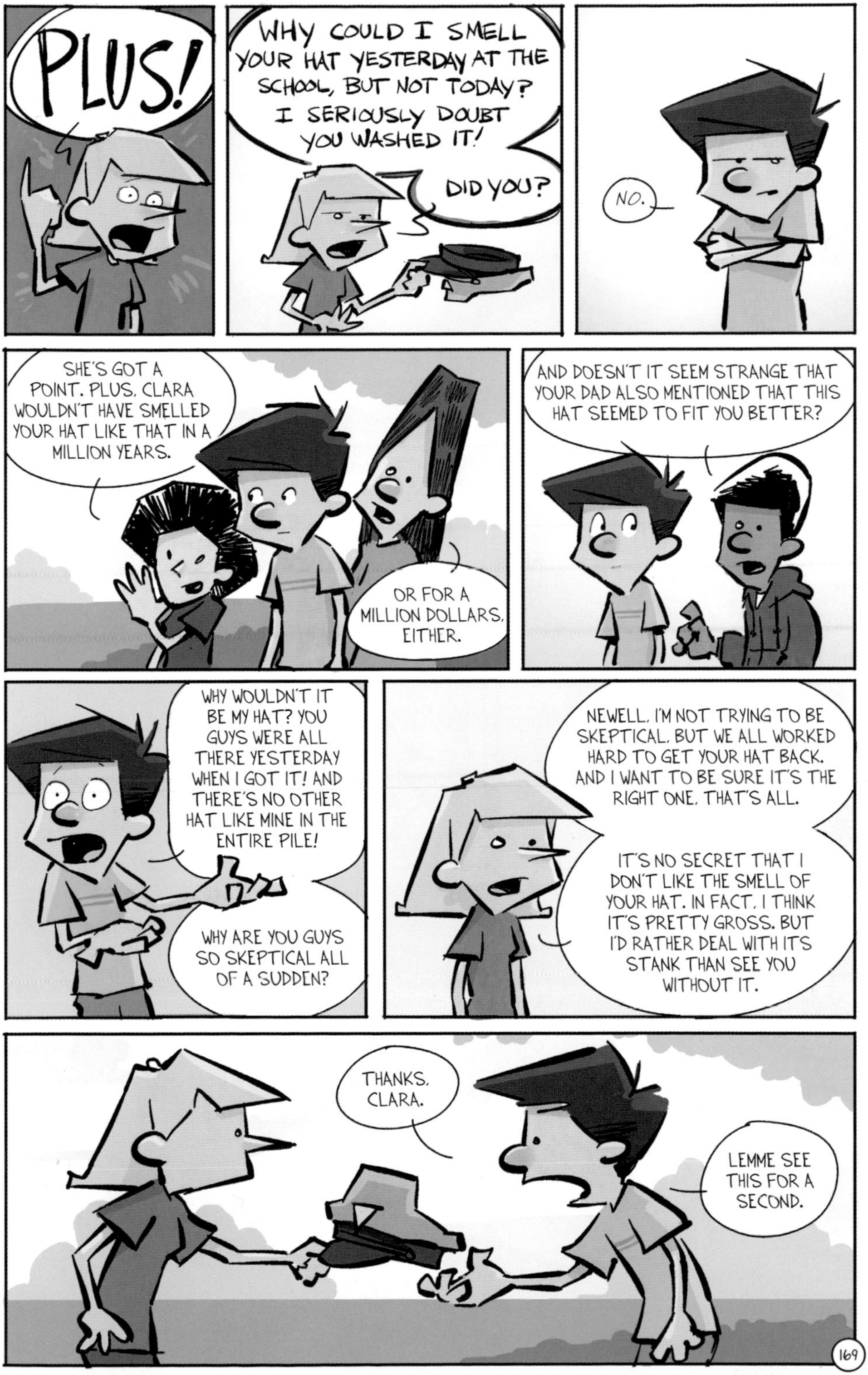
PLUS!
WHY COULD I SMELL YOUR HAT YESTERDAY AT THE SCHOOL, BUT NOT TODAY? I SERIOUSLY DOUBT YOU WASHED IT!
DID YOU?
NO.
SHE'S GOT A POINT. PLUS, CLARA WOULDN'T HAVE SMELLED YOUR HAT LIKE THAT IN A MILLION YEARS.
OR FOR A MILLION DOLLARS, EITHER.
AND DOESN'T IT SEEM STRANGE THAT YOUR DAD ALSO MENTIONED THAT THIS HAT SEEMED TO FIT YOU BETTER?
WHY WOULDN'T IT BE MY HAT? YOU GUYS WERE ALL THERE YESTERDAY WHEN I GOT IT! AND THERE'S NO OTHER HAT LIKE MINE IN THE ENTIRE PILE!
WHY ARE YOU GUYS SO SKEPTICAL ALL OF A SUDDEN?
NEWELL, I'M NOT TRYING TO BE SKEPTICAL, BUT WE ALL WORKED HARD TO GET YOUR HAT BACK. AND I WANT TO BE SURE IT'S THE RIGHT ONE, THAT'S ALL.
IT'S NO SECRET THAT I DON'T LIKE THE SMELL OF YOUR HAT. IN FACT, I THINK IT'S PRETTY GROSS. BUT I'D RATHER DEAL WITH ITS STANK THAN SEE YOU WITHOUT IT.
THANKS, CLARA.
LEMME SEE THIS FOR A SECOND.

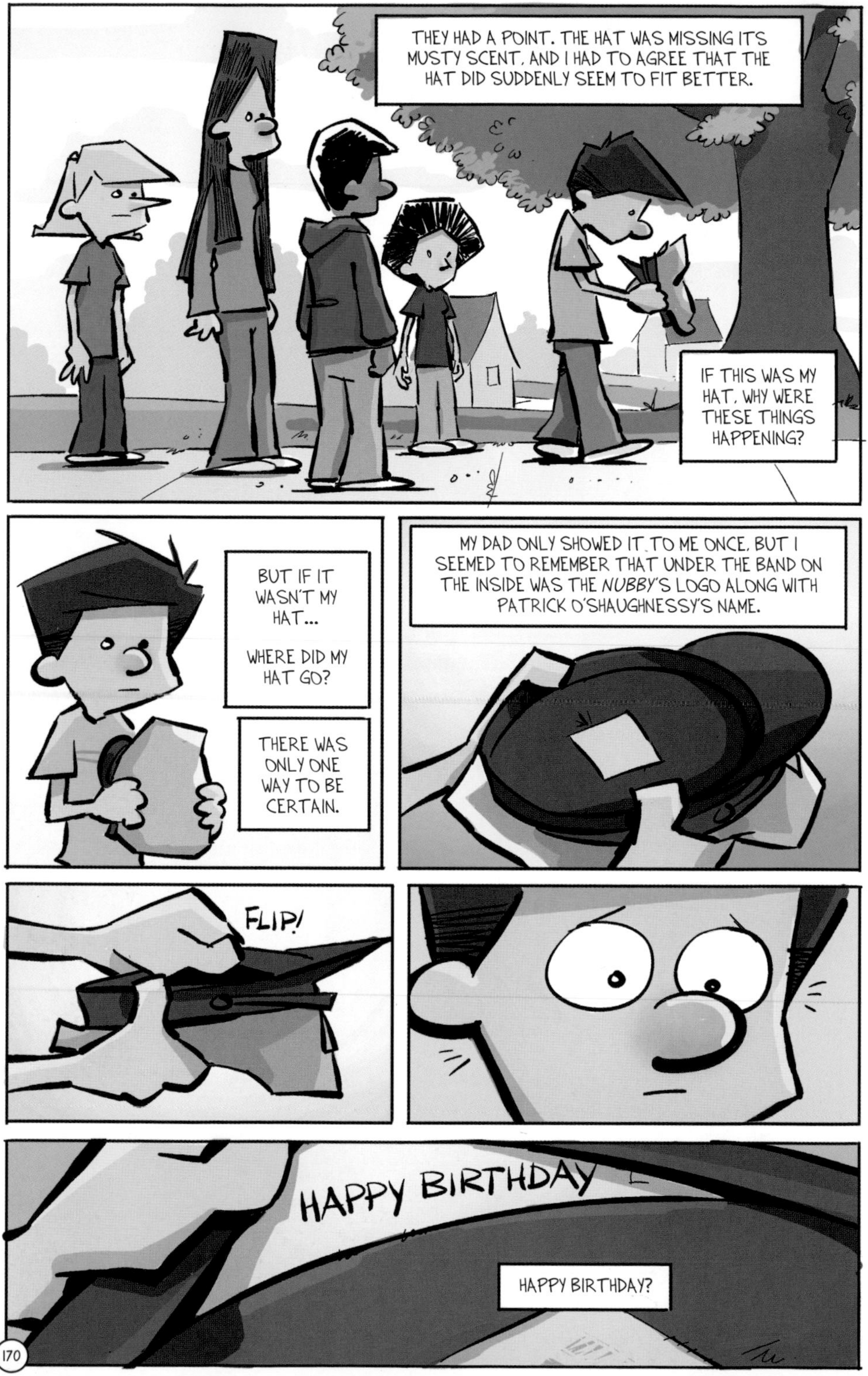
THEY HAD A POINT. THE HAT WAS MISSING ITS MUSTY SCENT, AND I HAD TO AGREE THAT THE HAT DID SUDDENLY SEEM TO FIT BETTER.
IF THIS WAS MY HAT, WHY WERE THESE THINGS HAPPENING?
BUT IF IT WASN'T MY HAT...
WHERE DID MY HAT GO?
THERE WAS ONLY ONE WAY TO BE CERTAIN.
MY DAD ONLY SHOWED IT TO ME ONCE, BUT I SEEMED TO REMEMBER THAT UNDER THE BAND ON THE INSIDE WAS THE *NUBBY'S* LOGO ALONG WITH PATRICK O'SHAUGHNESSY'S NAME.
FLIP!
HAPPY BIRTHDAY
HAPPY BIRTHDAY?

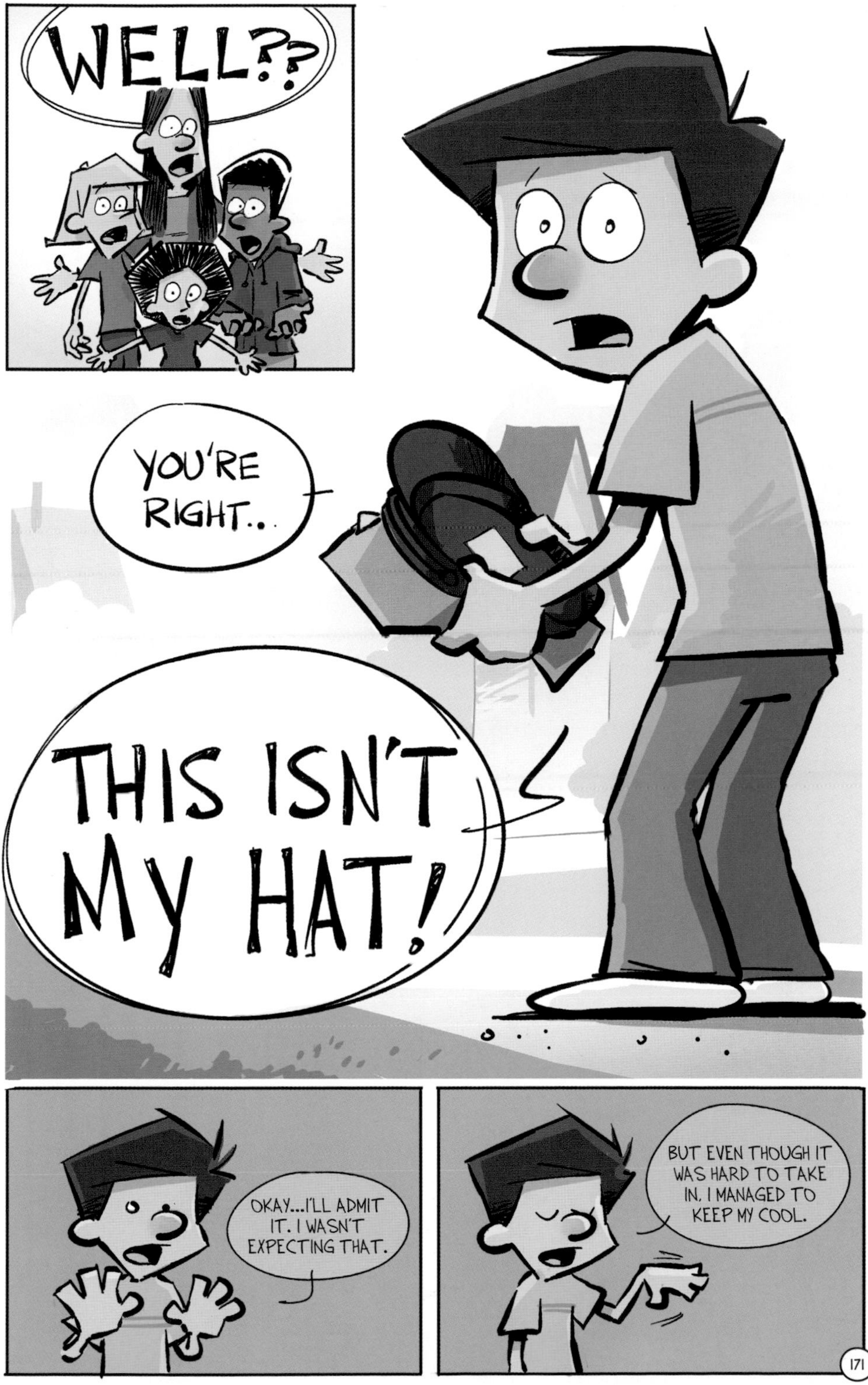
WELL??
YOU'RE RIGHT...
THIS ISN'T MY HAT!
OKAY...I'LL ADMIT IT. I WASN'T EXPECTING THAT.
BUT EVEN THOUGH IT WAS HARD TO TAKE IN, I MANAGED TO KEEP MY COOL.

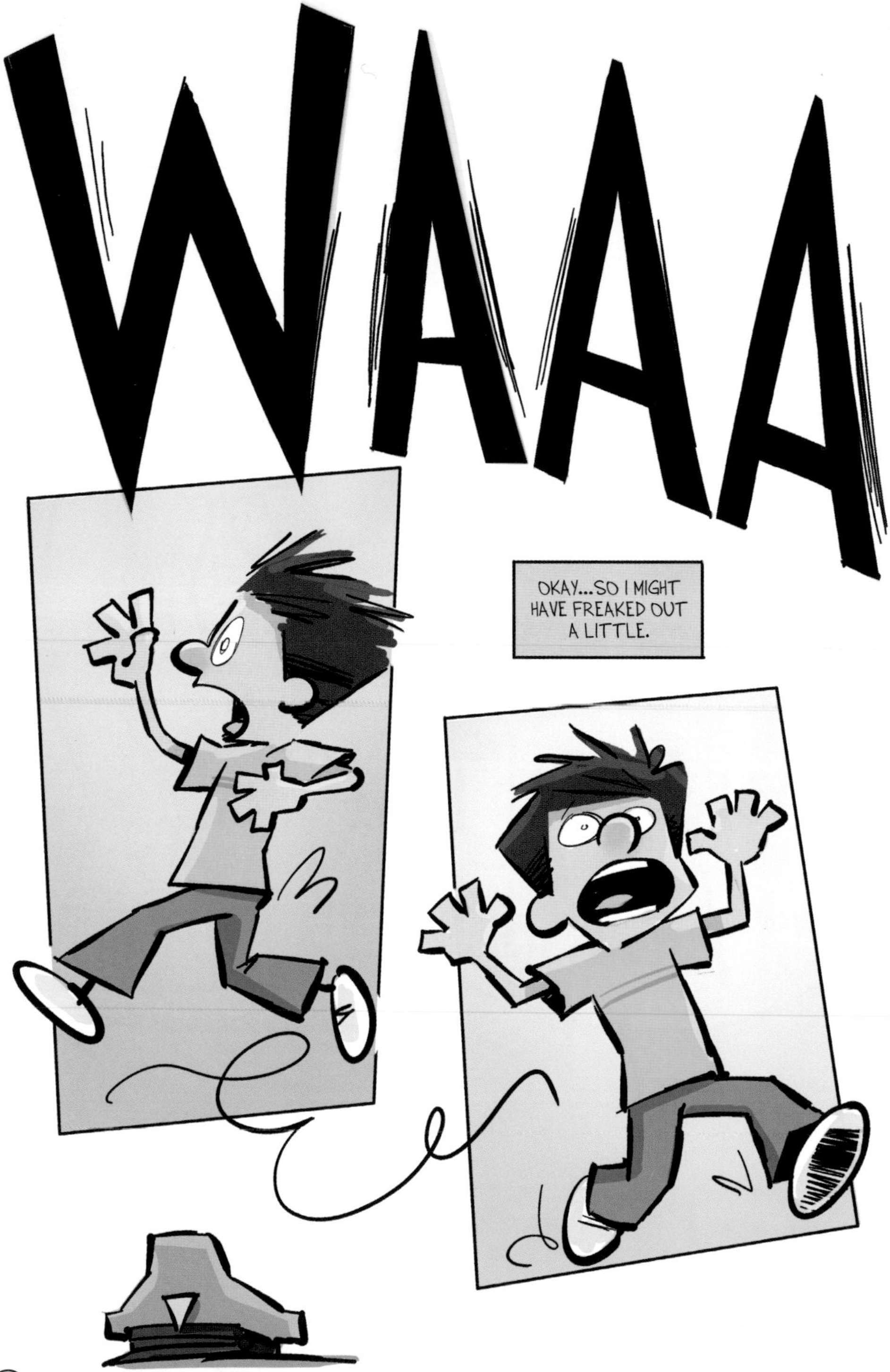
WAAA
OKAY...SO I MIGHT HAVE FREAKED OUT A LITTLE.

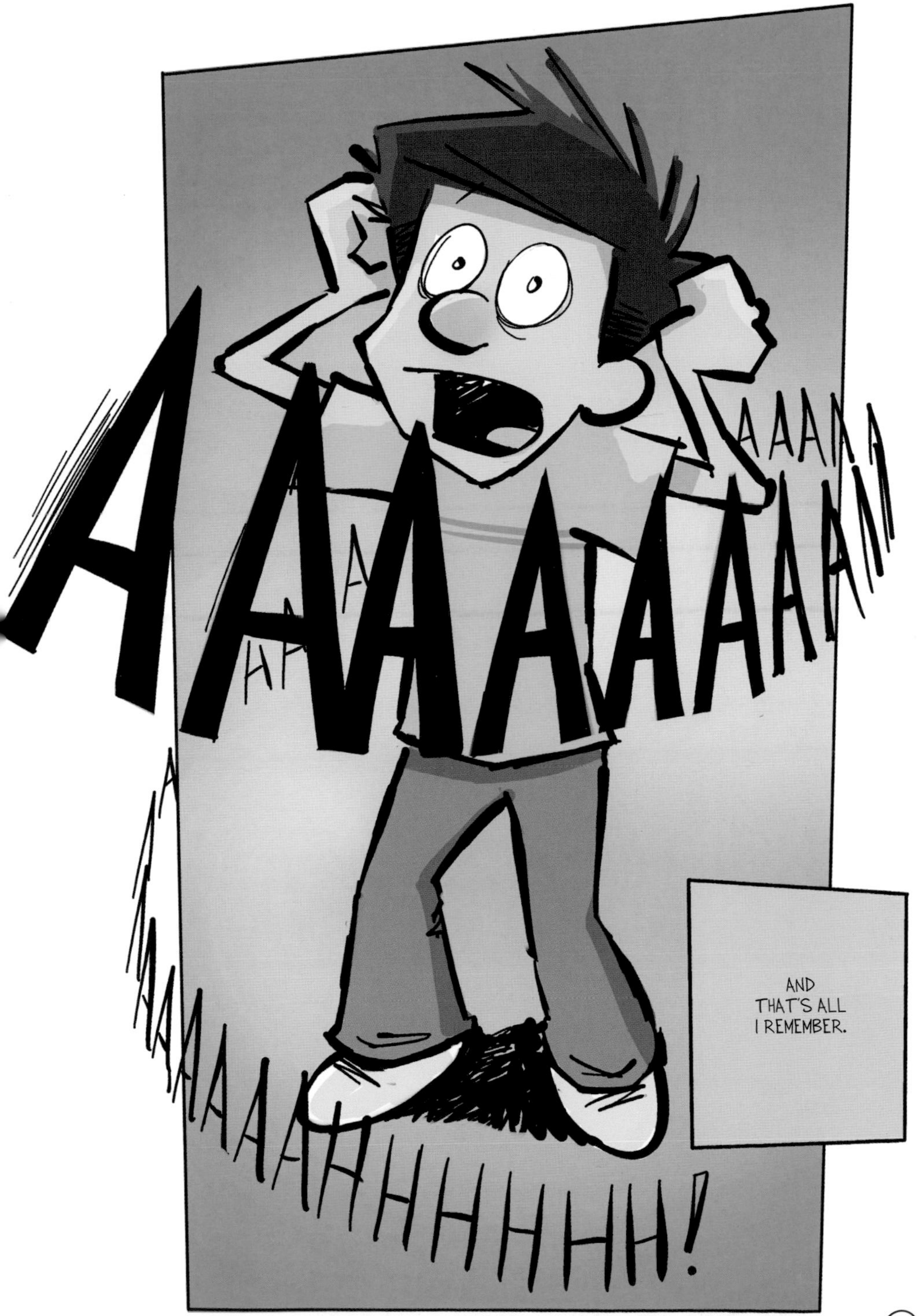
AAAAAAAAAAAAAAAAAAAAHHHHHHHHH!
AND THAT'S ALL I REMEMBER.

CHAPTER NINE
THE DOUBLE TAKE

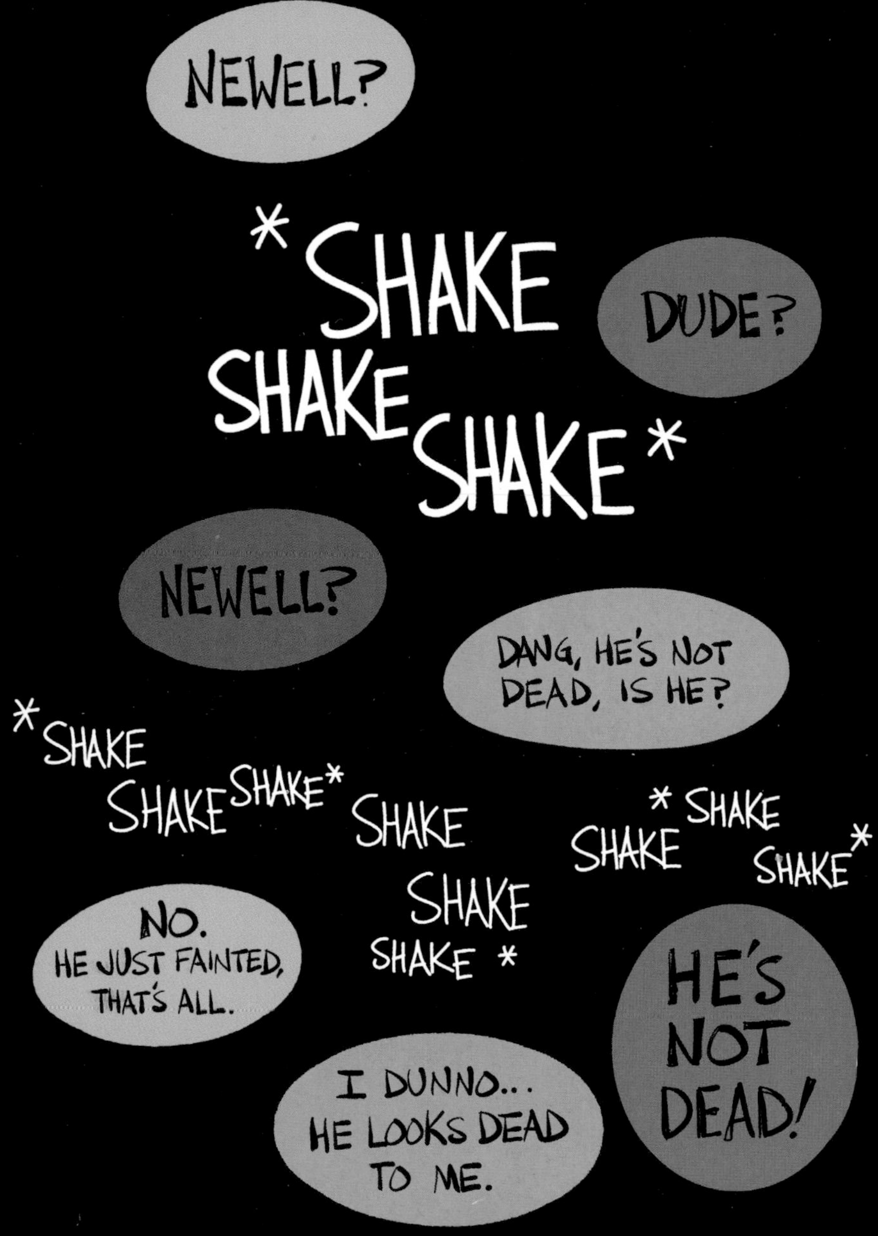
NEWELL?
SHAKE SHAKE SHAKE
DUDE?
NEWELL?
DANG, HE'S NOT DEAD, IS HE?
SHAKE SHAKE SHAKE
SHAKE SHAKE SHAKE *
* SHAKE SHAKE SHAKE*
NO. HE JUST FAINTED, THAT'S ALL.
HE'S NOT DEAD!
I DUNNO... HE LOOKS DEAD TO ME.

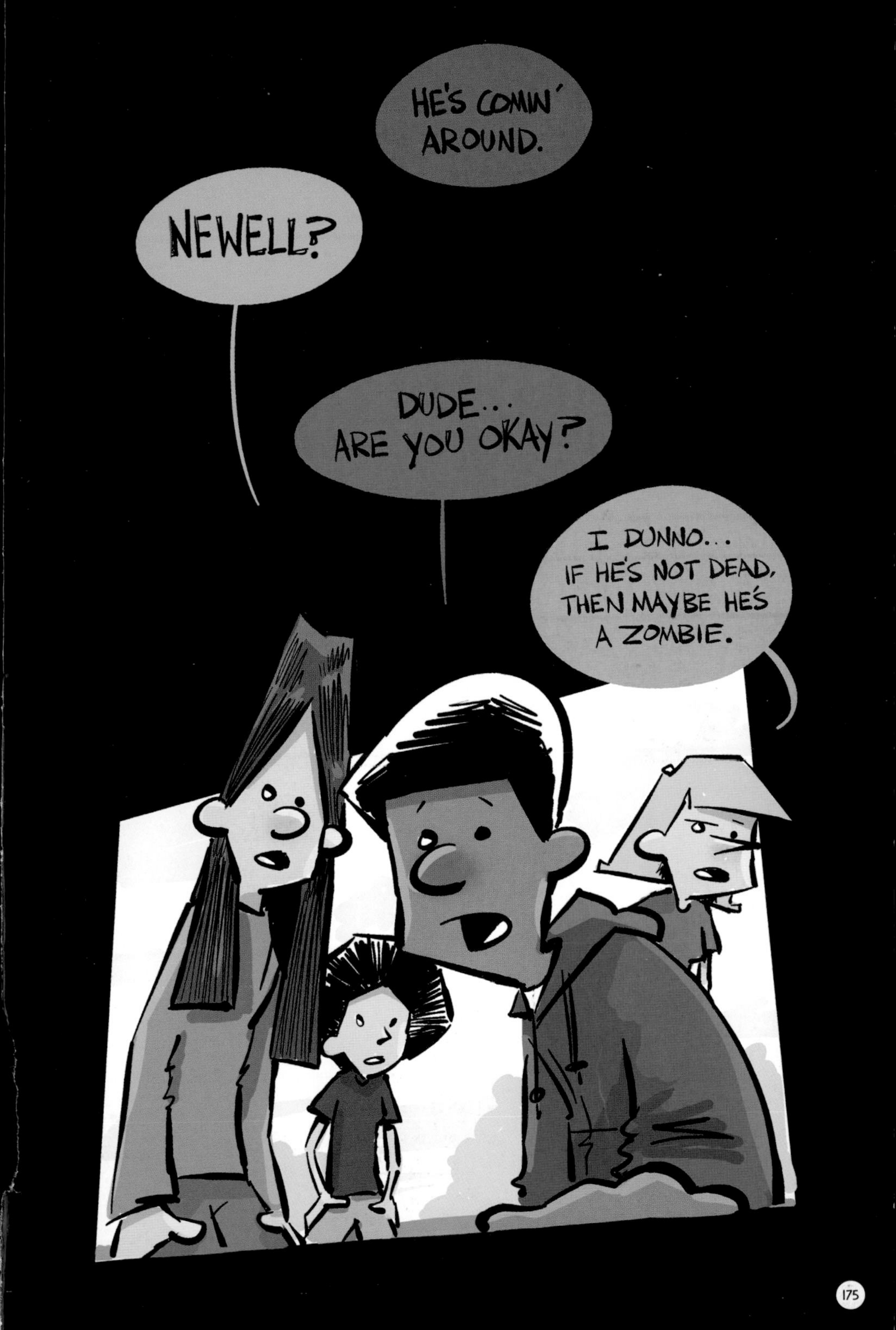
HE'S COMIN' AROUND.
NEWELL?
DUDE... ARE YOU OKAY?
I DUNNO... IF HE'S NOT DEAD, THEN MAYBE HE'S A ZOMBIE.

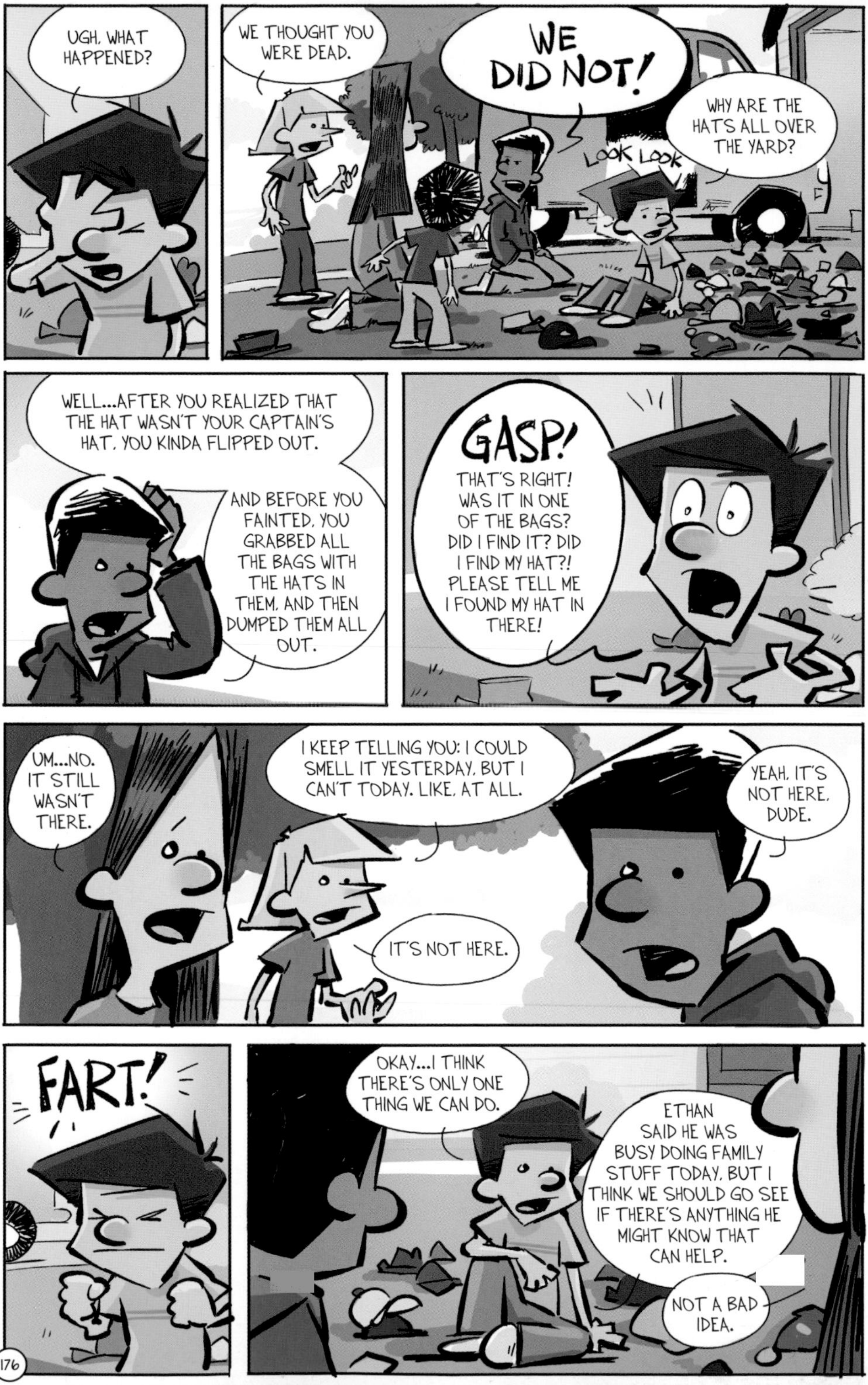
UGH, WHAT HAPPENED?
WE THOUGHT YOU WERE DEAD.
WE DID NOT!
LOOK LOOK
WHY ARE THE HATS ALL OVER THE YARD?
WELL...AFTER YOU REALIZED THAT THE HAT WASN'T YOUR CAPTAIN'S HAT, YOU KINDA FLIPPED OUT.
AND BEFORE YOU FAINTED, YOU GRABBED ALL THE BAGS WITH THE HATS IN THEM, AND THEN DUMPED THEM ALL OUT.
GASP!
THAT'S RIGHT! WAS IT IN ONE OF THE BAGS? DID I FIND IT? DID I FIND MY HAT?! PLEASE TELL ME I FOUND MY HAT IN THERE!
UM...NO. IT STILL WASN'T THERE.
I KEEP TELLING YOU: I COULD SMELL IT YESTERDAY, BUT I CAN'T TODAY. LIKE, AT ALL.
IT'S NOT HERE.
YEAH, IT'S NOT HERE, DUDE.
FART!
OKAY...I THINK THERE'S ONLY ONE THING WE CAN DO.
ETHAN SAID HE WAS BUSY DOING FAMILY STUFF TODAY, BUT I THINK WE SHOULD GO SEE IF THERE'S ANYTHING HE MIGHT KNOW THAT CAN HELP.
NOT A BAD IDEA.

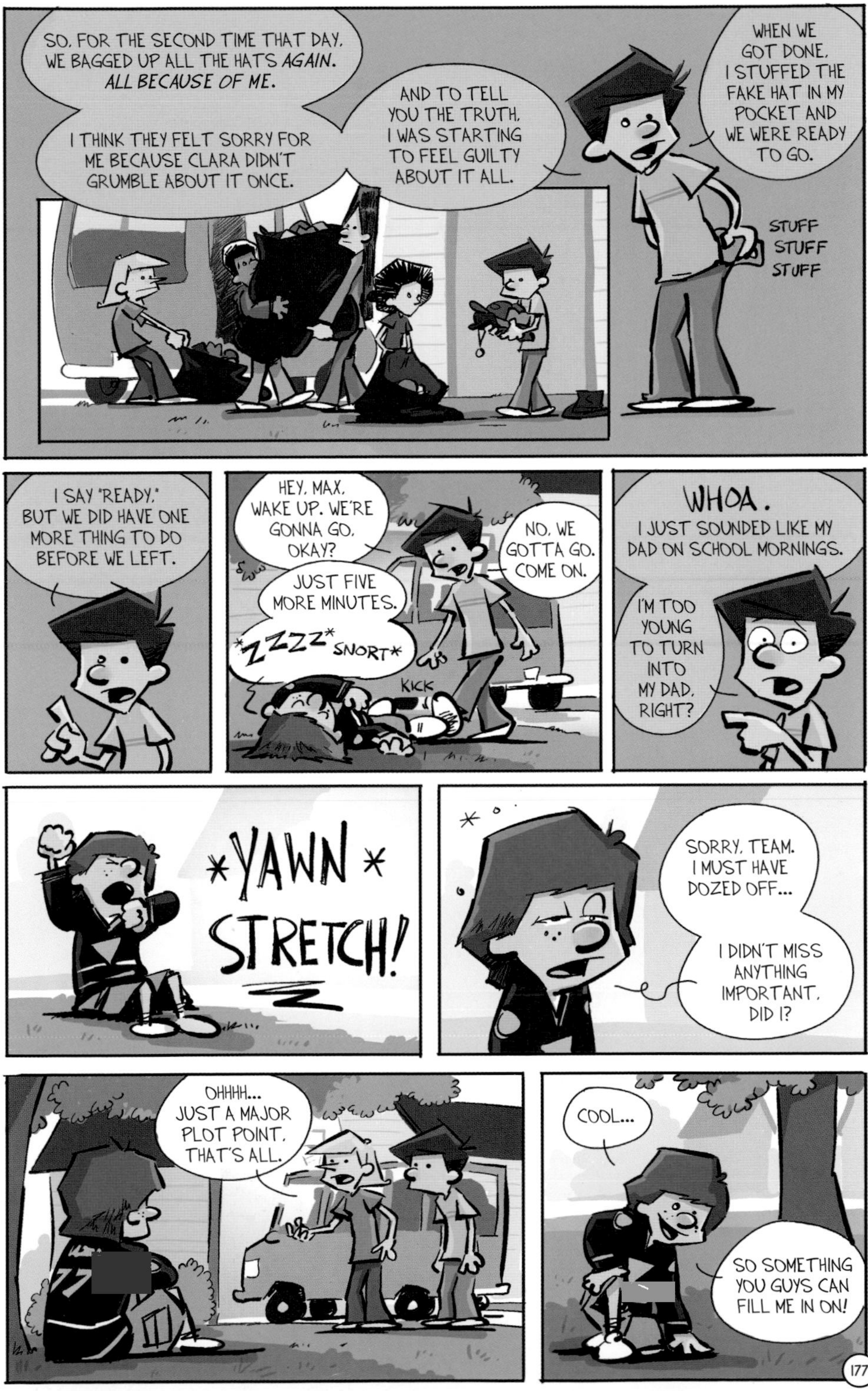
SO, FOR THE SECOND TIME THAT DAY, WE BAGGED UP ALL THE HATS *AGAIN*. *ALL BECAUSE OF ME*.
I THINK THEY FELT SORRY FOR ME BECAUSE CLARA DIDN'T GRUMBLE ABOUT IT ONCE.
AND TO TELL YOU THE TRUTH, I WAS STARTING TO FEEL GUILTY ABOUT IT ALL.
WHEN WE GOT DONE, I STUFFED THE FAKE HAT IN MY POCKET AND WE WERE READY TO GO.
STUFF STUFF STUFF
I SAY "READY," BUT WE DID HAVE ONE MORE THING TO DO BEFORE WE LEFT.
HEY, MAX, WAKE UP. WE'RE GONNA GO, OKAY?
JUST FIVE MORE MINUTES.
ZZZZ SNORT*
NO, WE GOTTA GO. COME ON.
KICK
WHOA.
I JUST SOUNDED LIKE MY DAD ON SCHOOL MORNINGS.
I'M TOO YOUNG TO TURN INTO MY DAD, RIGHT?
YAWN
STRETCH!
SORRY, TEAM. I MUST HAVE DOZED OFF...
I DIDN'T MISS ANYTHING IMPORTANT, DID I?
OHHHH... JUST A MAJOR PLOT POINT, THAT'S ALL.
COOL...
SO SOMETHING YOU GUYS CAN FILL ME IN ON!

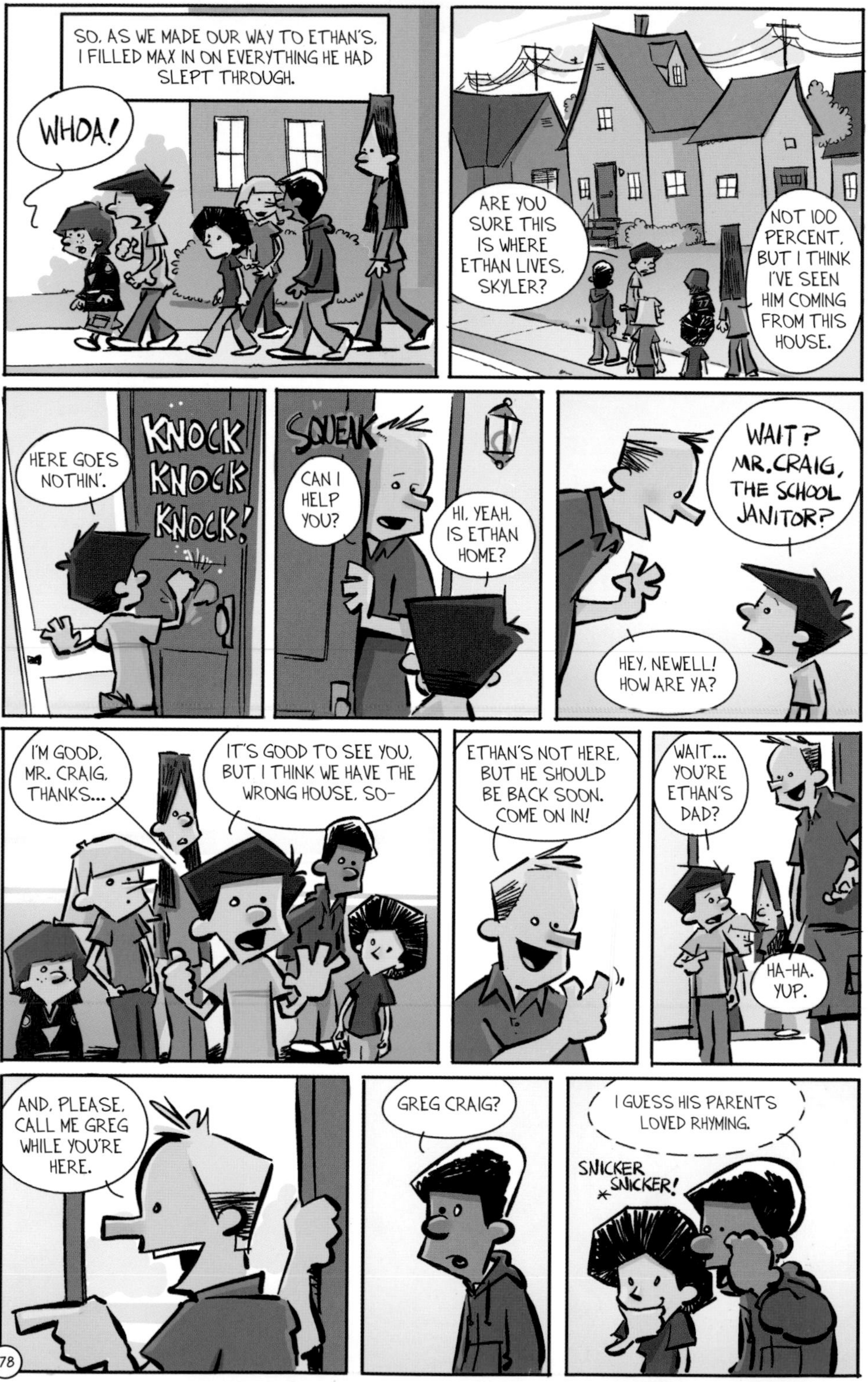
SO, AS WE MADE OUR WAY TO ETHAN'S, I FILLED MAX IN ON EVERYTHING HE HAD SLEPT THROUGH.
WHOA!
ARE YOU SURE THIS IS WHERE ETHAN LIVES, SKYLER?
NOT 100 PERCENT, BUT I THINK I'VE SEEN HIM COMING FROM THIS HOUSE.
HERE GOES NOTHIN'.
KNOCK KNOCK KNOCK!
SQUEAK
CAN I HELP YOU?
HI, YEAH, IS ETHAN HOME?
WAIT? MR. CRAIG, THE SCHOOL JANITOR?
HEY, NEWELL! HOW ARE YA?
I'M GOOD, MR. CRAIG, THANKS...
IT'S GOOD TO SEE YOU, BUT I THINK WE HAVE THE WRONG HOUSE, SO-
ETHAN'S NOT HERE, BUT HE SHOULD BE BACK SOON. COME ON IN!
WAIT... YOU'RE ETHAN'S DAD?
HA-HA. YUP.
AND, PLEASE, CALL ME GREG WHILE YOU'RE HERE.
GREG CRAIG?
I GUESS HIS PARENTS LOVED RHYMING.
SNICKER SNICKER!

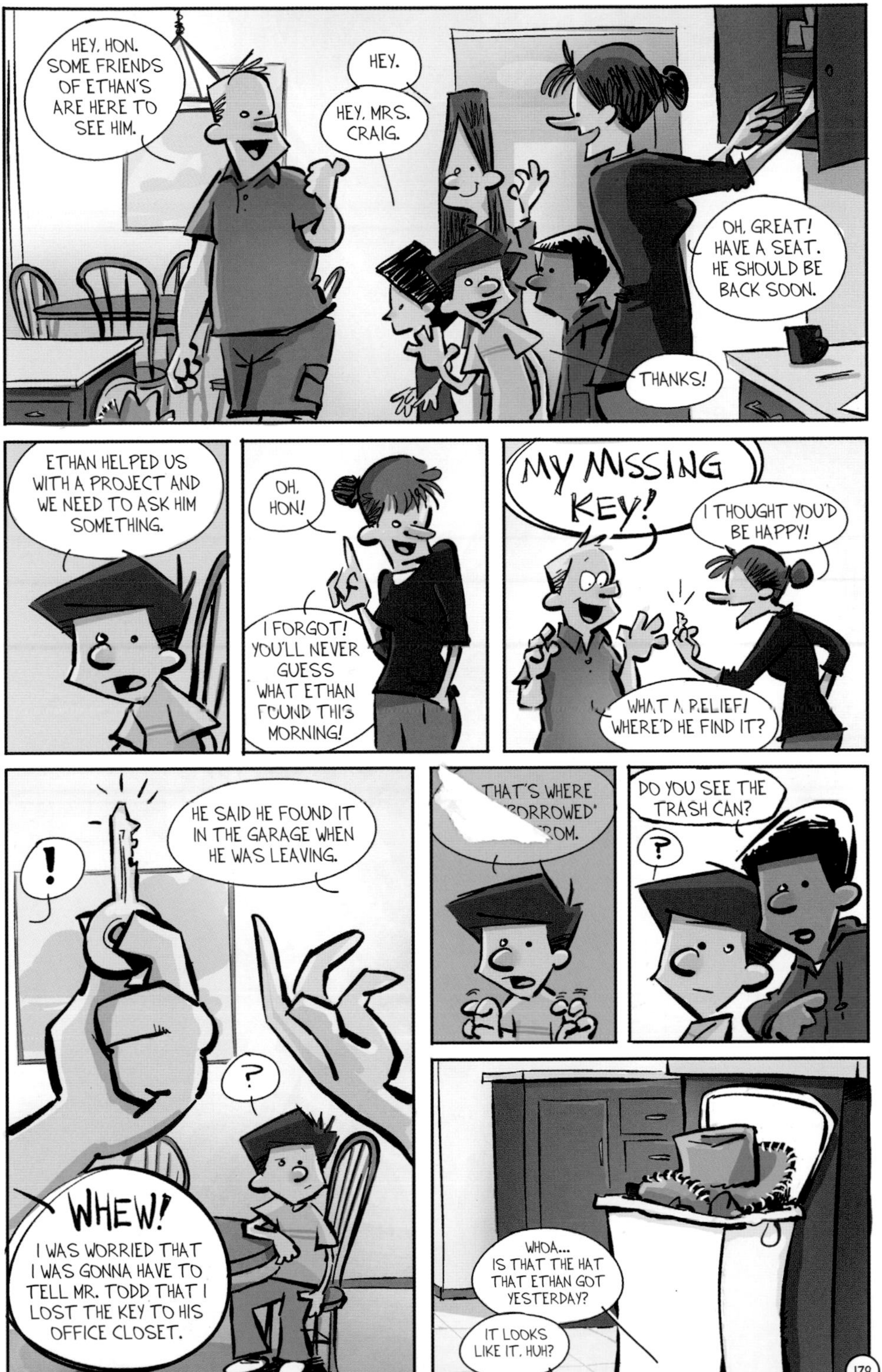
HEY, HON. SOME FRIENDS OF ETHAN'S ARE HERE TO SEE HIM.
HEY.
HEY, MRS. CRAIG.
OH, GREAT! HAVE A SEAT. HE SHOULD BE BACK SOON.
THANKS!
ETHAN HELPED US WITH A PROJECT AND WE NEED TO ASK HIM SOMETHING.
OH, HON!
I FORGOT! YOU'LL NEVER GUESS WHAT ETHAN FOUND THIS MORNING!
MY MISSING KEY!
I THOUGHT YOU'D BE HAPPY!
WHAT A RELIEF! WHERE'D HE FIND IT?
!
HE SAID HE FOUND IT IN THE GARAGE WHEN HE WAS LEAVING.
?
WHEW!
I WAS WORRIED THAT I WAS GONNA HAVE TO TELL MR. TODD THAT I LOST THE KEY TO HIS OFFICE CLOSET.
THAT'S WHERE
'BORROWED'
ROM.
DO YOU SEE THE TRASH CAN?
?
WHOA... IS THAT THE HAT THAT ETHAN GOT YESTERDAY?
IT LOOKS LIKE IT, HUH?

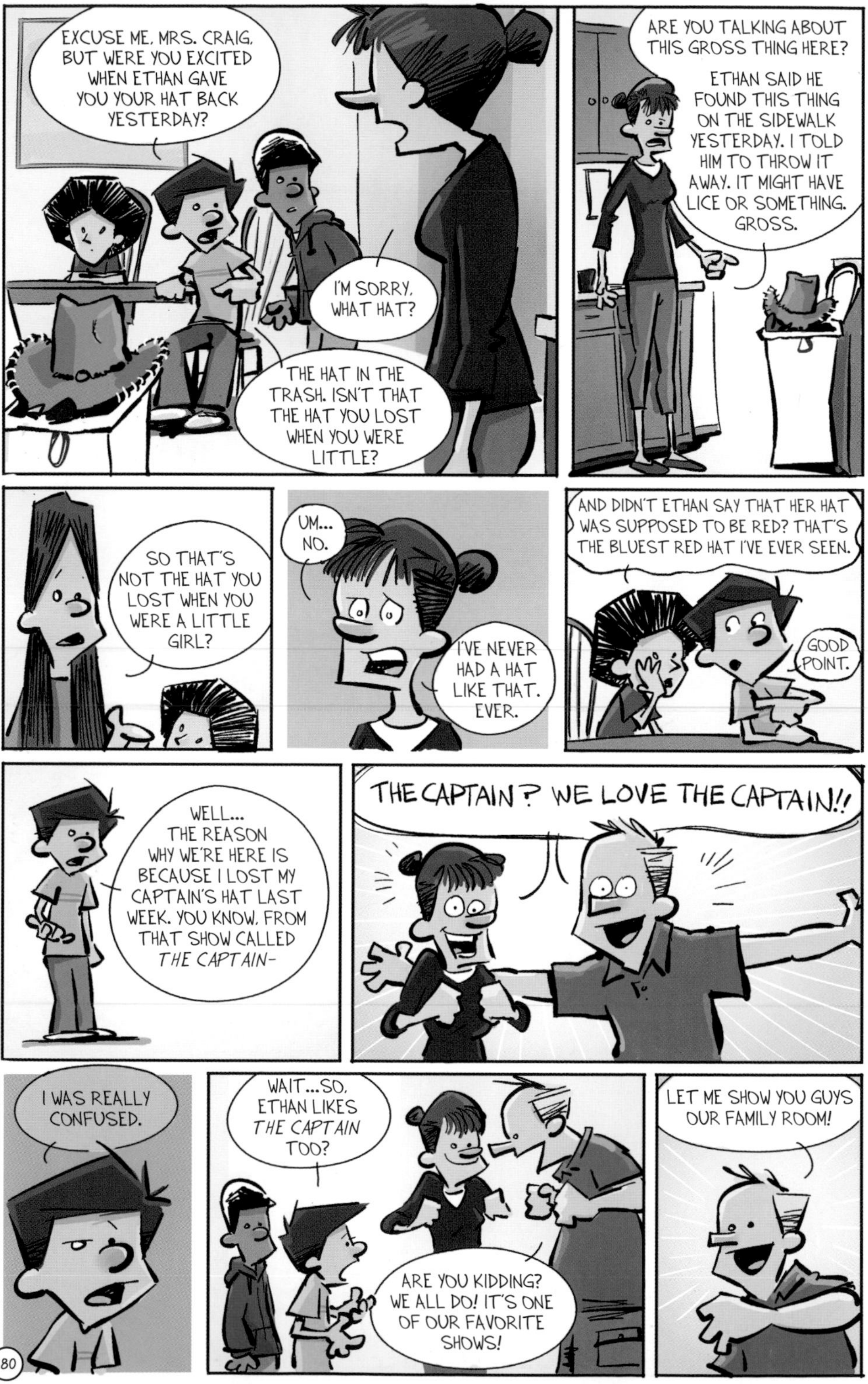
EXCUSE ME, MRS. CRAIG, BUT WERE YOU EXCITED WHEN ETHAN GAVE YOU YOUR HAT BACK YESTERDAY?
I'M SORRY, WHAT HAT?
THE HAT IN THE TRASH. ISN'T THAT THE HAT YOU LOST WHEN YOU WERE LITTLE?
ARE YOU TALKING ABOUT THIS GROSS THING HERE?
ETHAN SAID HE FOUND THIS THING ON THE SIDEWALK YESTERDAY. I TOLD HIM TO THROW IT AWAY. IT MIGHT HAVE LICE OR SOMETHING. GROSS.
SO THAT'S NOT THE HAT YOU LOST WHEN YOU WERE A LITTLE GIRL?
UM... NO.
I'VE NEVER HAD A HAT LIKE THAT. EVER.
AND DIDN'T ETHAN SAY THAT HER HAT WAS SUPPOSED TO BE RED? THAT'S THE BLUEST RED HAT I'VE EVER SEEN.
GOOD POINT.
WELL... THE REASON WHY WE'RE HERE IS BECAUSE I LOST MY CAPTAIN'S HAT LAST WEEK. YOU KNOW, FROM THAT SHOW CALLED *THE CAPTAIN*-
THE CAPTAIN? WE LOVE THE CAPTAIN!!
I WAS REALLY CONFUSED.
WAIT...SO, ETHAN LIKES *THE CAPTAIN* TOO?
ARE YOU KIDDING? WE ALL DO! IT'S ONE OF OUR FAVORITE SHOWS!
LET ME SHOW YOU GUYS OUR FAMILY ROOM!

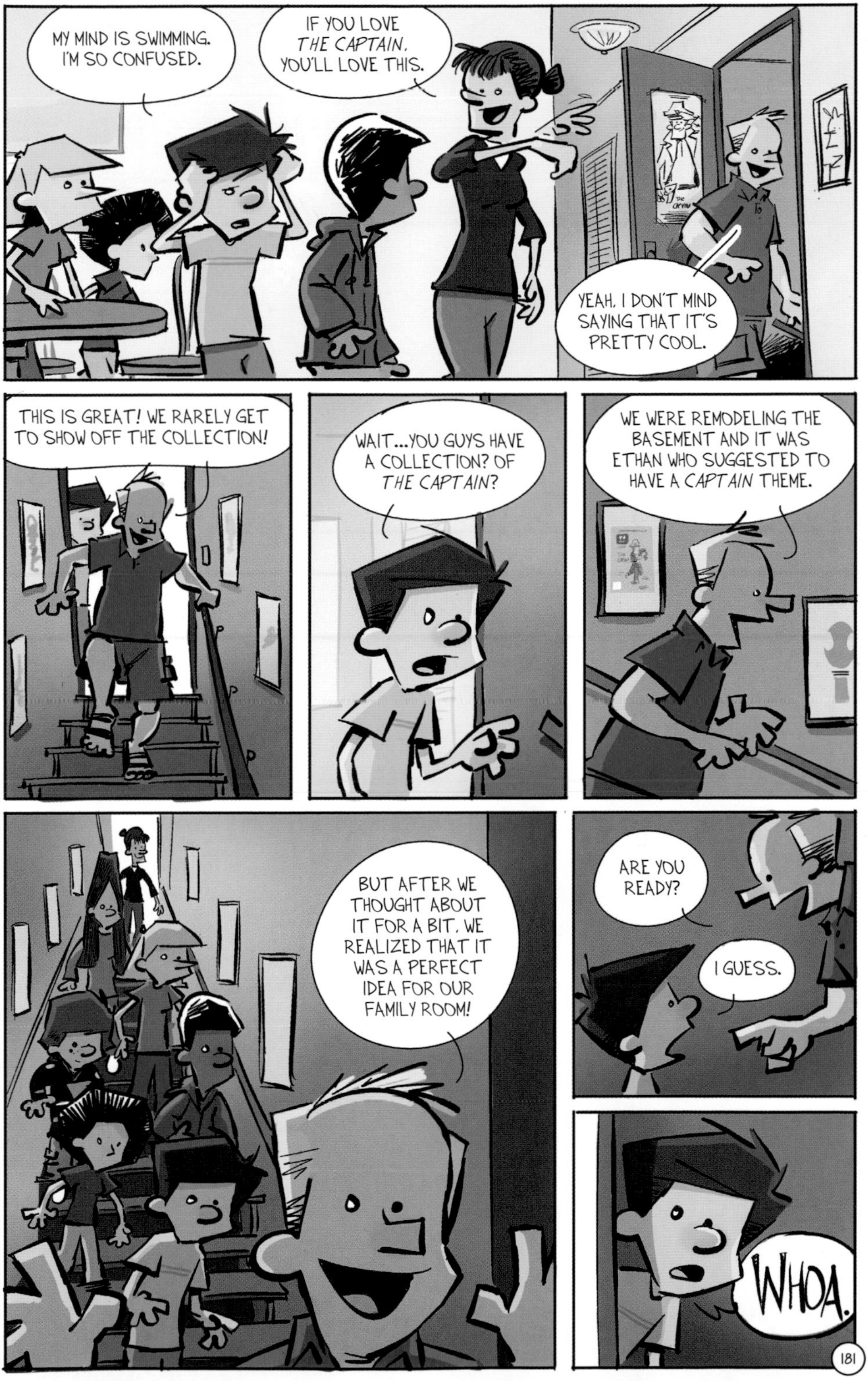

MY MIND IS SWIMMING. I'M SO CONFUSED.
IF YOU LOVE *THE CAPTAIN*, YOU'LL LOVE THIS.
YEAH, I DON'T MIND SAYING THAT IT'S PRETTY COOL.
THIS IS GREAT! WE RARELY GET TO SHOW OFF THE COLLECTION!
WAIT...YOU GUYS HAVE A COLLECTION? OF *THE CAPTAIN*?
WE WERE REMODELING THE BASEMENT AND IT WAS ETHAN WHO SUGGESTED TO HAVE A *CAPTAIN* THEME.
BUT AFTER WE THOUGHT ABOUT IT FOR A BIT, WE REALIZED THAT IT WAS A PERFECT IDEA FOR OUR FAMILY ROOM!
ARE YOU READY?
I GUESS.
WHOA.

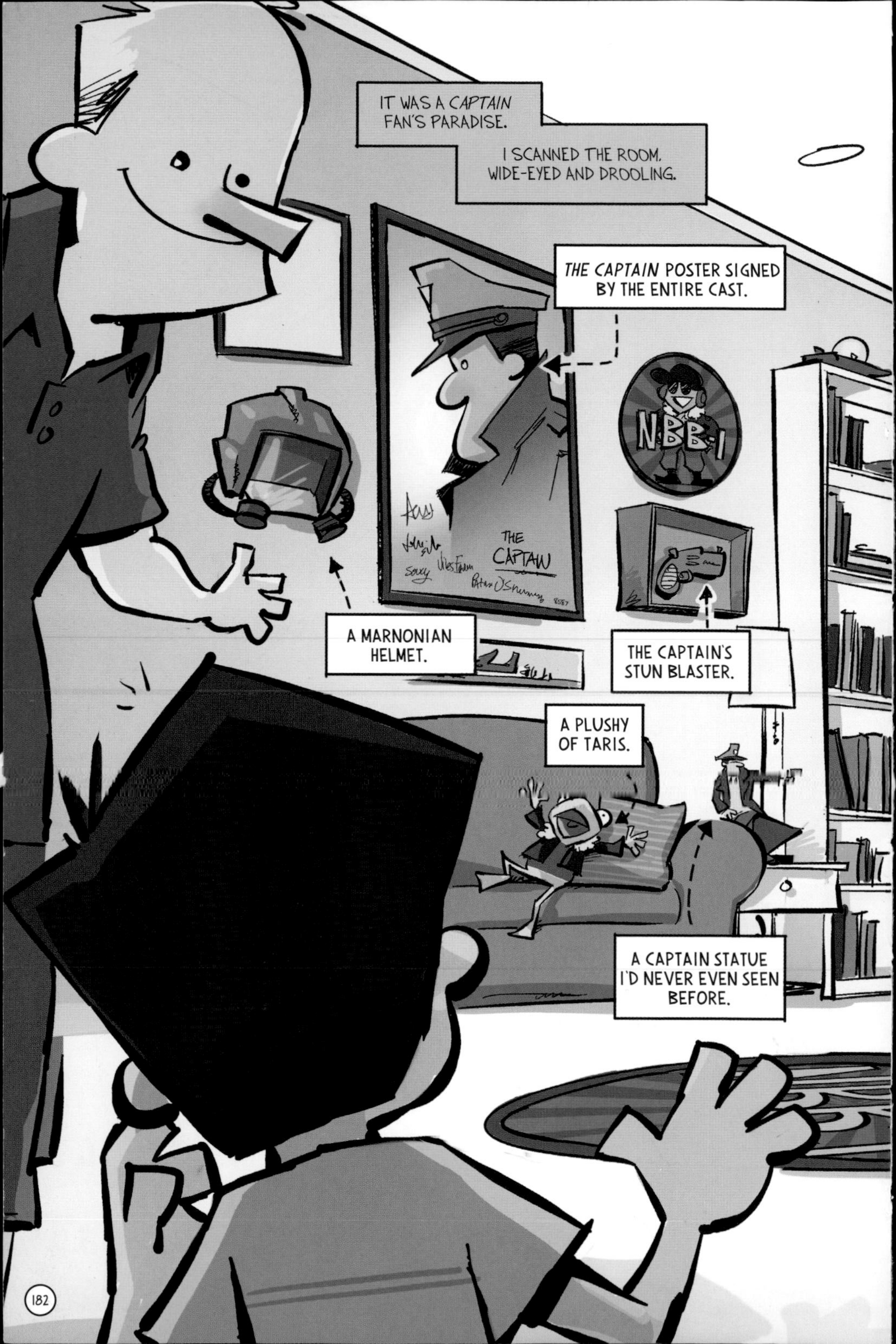
IT WAS A *CAPTAIN* FAN'S PARADISE.
I SCANNED THE ROOM, WIDE-EYED AND DROOLING.
THE CAPTAIN POSTER SIGNED BY THE ENTIRE CAST.
THE CAPTAIN
NBBI
A MARNONIAN HELMET.
THE CAPTAIN'S STUN BLASTER.
A PLUSHY OF TARIS.
A CAPTAIN STATUE I'D NEVER EVEN SEEN BEFORE.

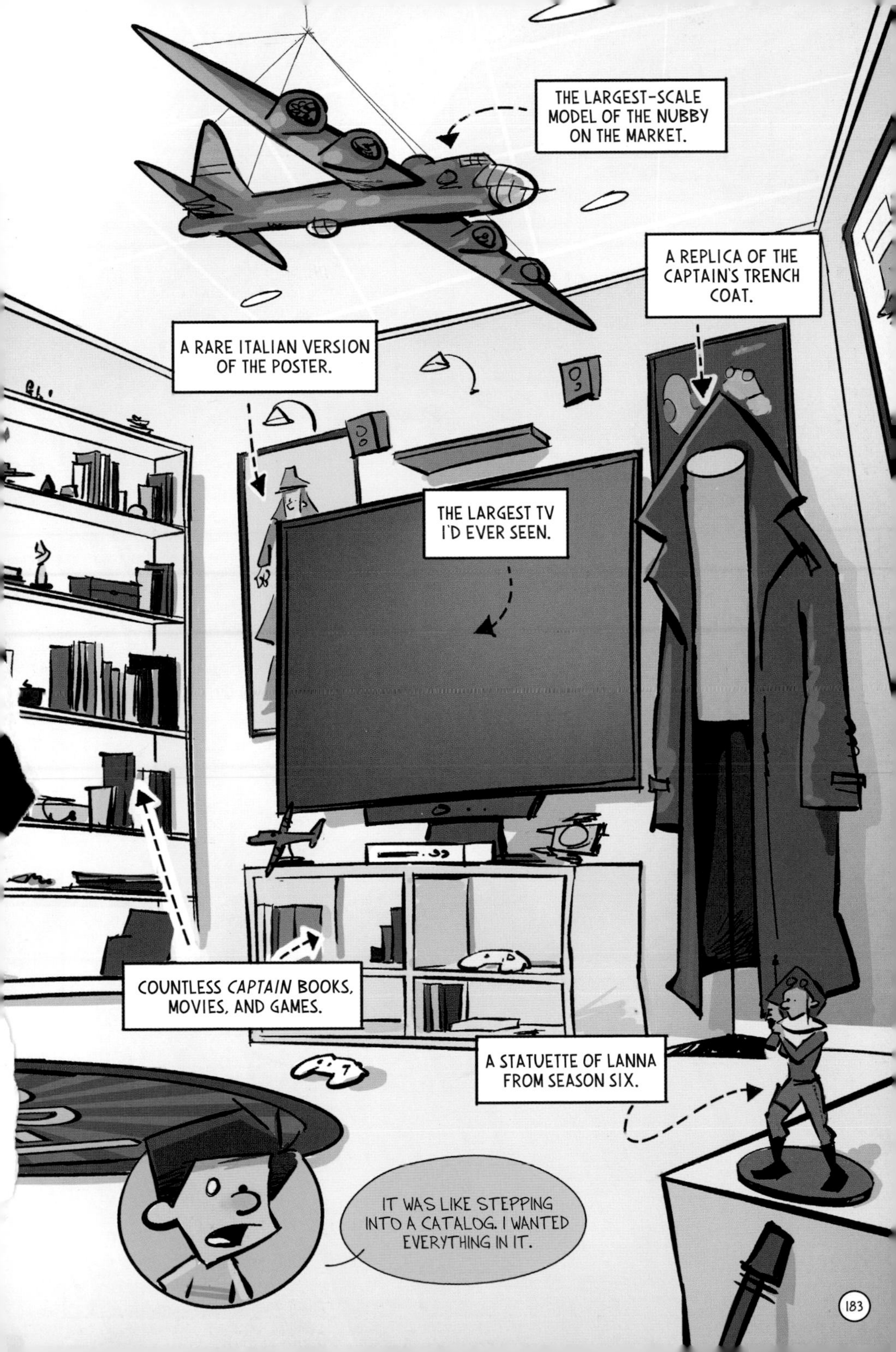
THE LARGEST-SCALE MODEL OF THE NUBBY ON THE MARKET.
A REPLICA OF THE CAPTAIN'S TRENCH COAT.
A RARE ITALIAN VERSION OF THE POSTER.
THE LARGEST TV I'D EVER SEEN.
COUNTLESS *CAPTAIN* BOOKS, MOVIES, AND GAMES.
A STATUETTE OF LANNA FROM SEASON SIX.
IT WAS LIKE STEPPING INTO A CATALOG. I WANTED EVERYTHING IN IT.

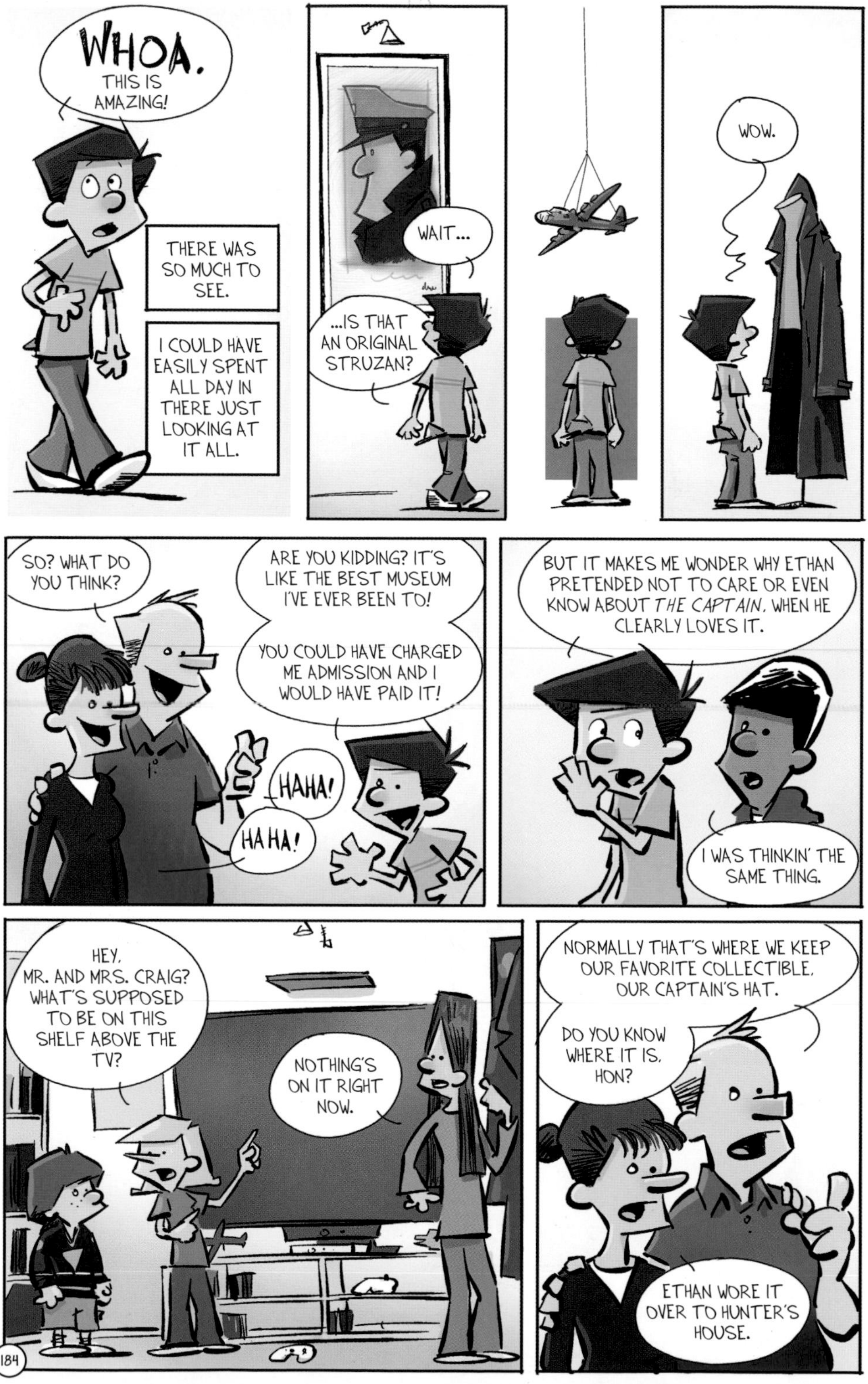
WHOA. THIS IS AMAZING!
THERE WAS SO MUCH TO SEE.
I COULD HAVE EASILY SPENT ALL DAY IN THERE JUST LOOKING AT IT ALL.
WAIT...
...IS THAT AN ORIGINAL STRUZAN?
WOW.
SO? WHAT DO YOU THINK?
ARE YOU KIDDING? IT'S LIKE THE BEST MUSEUM I'VE EVER BEEN TO!
YOU COULD HAVE CHARGED ME ADMISSION AND I WOULD HAVE PAID IT!
HAHA!
HA HA!
BUT IT MAKES ME WONDER WHY ETHAN PRETENDED NOT TO CARE OR EVEN KNOW ABOUT *THE CAPTAIN*, WHEN HE CLEARLY LOVES IT.
I WAS THINKIN' THE SAME THING.
HEY, MR. AND MRS. CRAIG? WHAT'S SUPPOSED TO BE ON THIS SHELF ABOVE THE TV?
NOTHING'S ON IT RIGHT NOW.
NORMALLY THAT'S WHERE WE KEEP OUR FAVORITE COLLECTIBLE, OUR CAPTAIN'S HAT.
DO YOU KNOW WHERE IT IS, HON?
ETHAN WORE IT OVER TO HUNTER'S HOUSE.

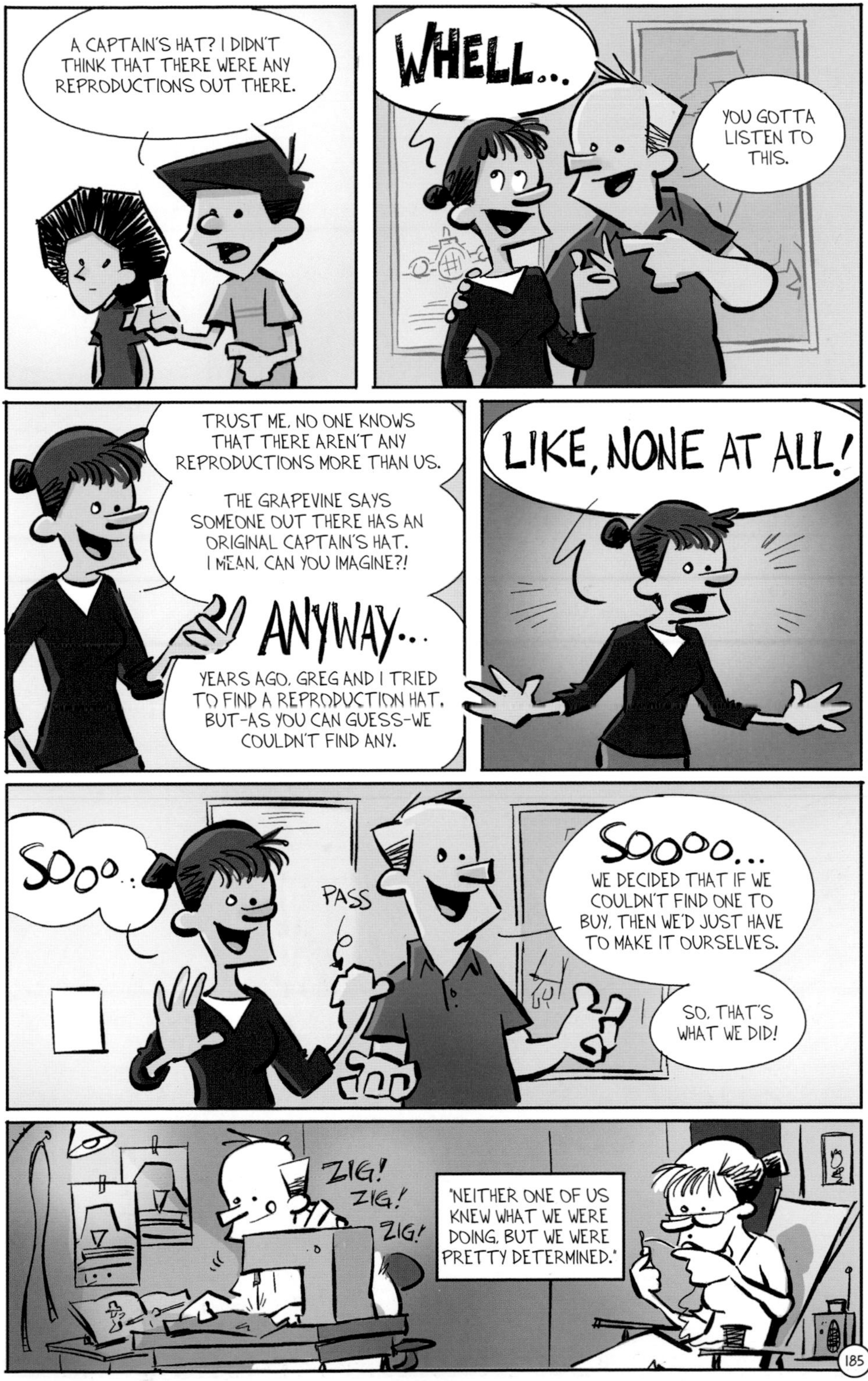
A CAPTAIN'S HAT? I DIDN'T THINK THAT THERE WERE ANY REPRODUCTIONS OUT THERE.
WHELL...
YOU GOTTA LISTEN TO THIS.
TRUST ME, NO ONE KNOWS THAT THERE AREN'T ANY REPRODUCTIONS MORE THAN US.
THE GRAPEVINE SAYS SOMEONE OUT THERE HAS AN ORIGINAL CAPTAIN'S HAT. I MEAN, CAN YOU IMAGINE?!
ANYWAY...
YEARS AGO, GREG AND I TRIED TO FIND A REPRODUCTION HAT, BUT–AS YOU CAN GUESS–WE COULDN'T FIND ANY.
LIKE, NONE AT ALL!
SOOO...
PASS
SOOOO...
WE DECIDED THAT IF WE COULDN'T FIND ONE TO BUY, THEN WE'D JUST HAVE TO MAKE IT OURSELVES.
SO, THAT'S WHAT WE DID!
ZIG! ZIG! ZIG!
"NEITHER ONE OF US KNEW WHAT WE WERE DOING, BUT WE WERE PRETTY DETERMINED."

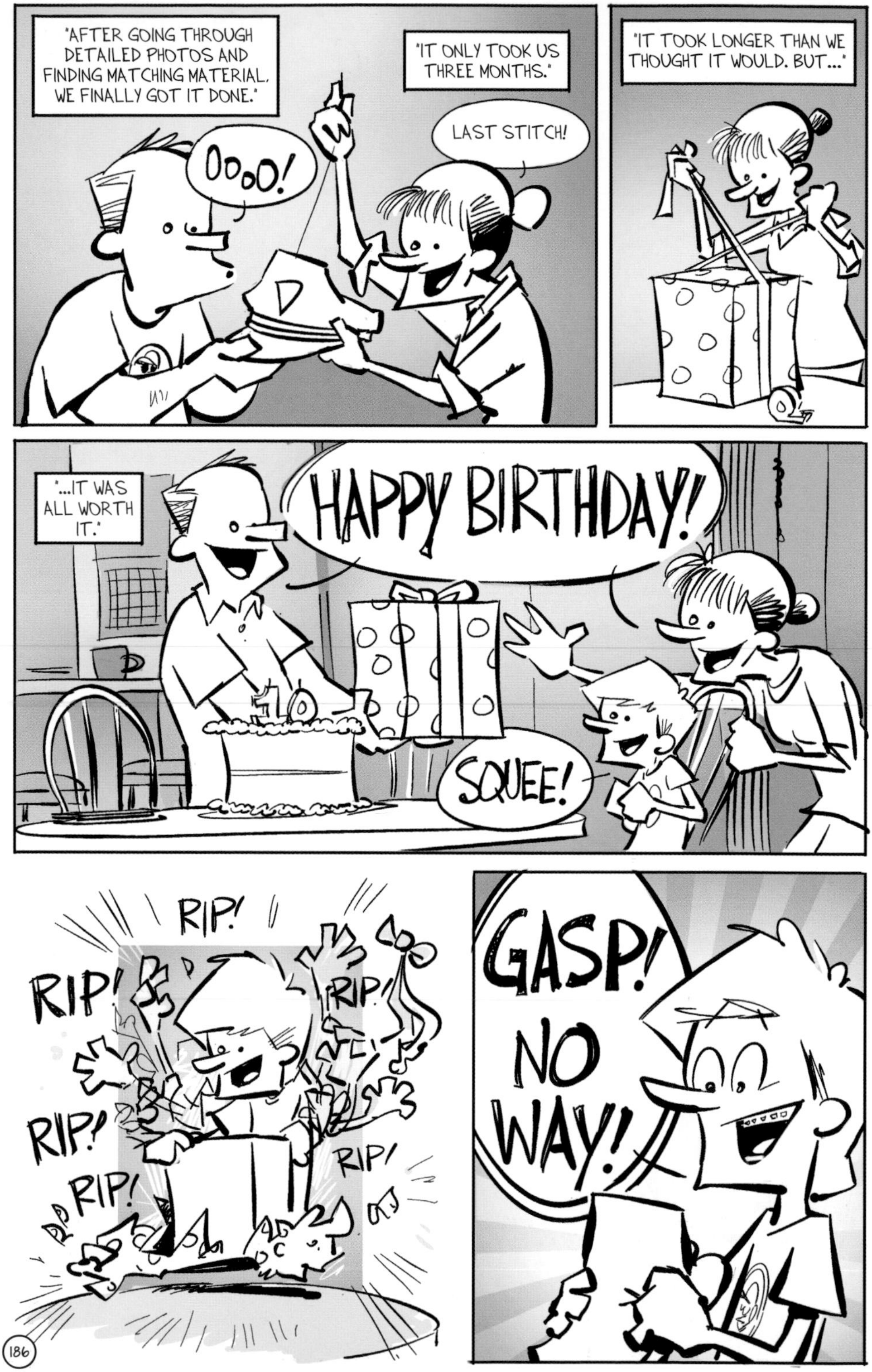
"AFTER GOING THROUGH DETAILED PHOTOS AND FINDING MATCHING MATERIAL, WE FINALLY GOT IT DONE."
OOoO!
"IT ONLY TOOK US THREE MONTHS."
LAST STITCH!
"IT TOOK LONGER THAN WE THOUGHT IT WOULD. BUT..."
"...IT WAS ALL WORTH IT."
HAPPY BIRTHDAY!
SQUEE!
RIP!
RIP!
RIP!
RIP!
RIP!
RIP!
GASP!
NO WAY!

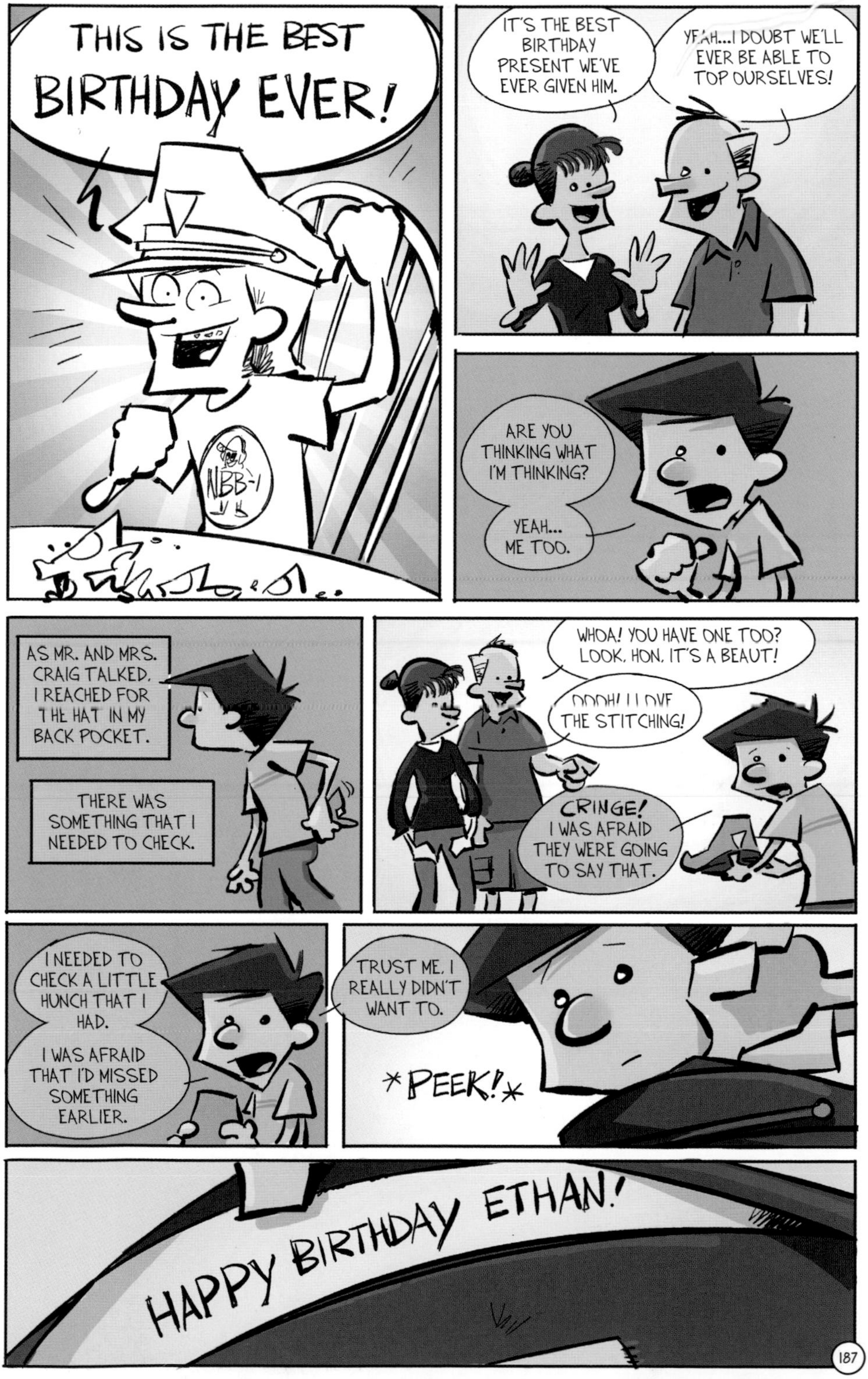

THIS IS THE BEST BIRTHDAY EVER!
NBB-1
IT'S THE BEST BIRTHDAY PRESENT WE'VE EVER GIVEN HIM.
YEAH...I DOUBT WE'LL EVER BE ABLE TO TOP OURSELVES!
ARE YOU THINKING WHAT I'M THINKING?
YEAH... ME TOO.
AS MR. AND MRS. CRAIG TALKED, I REACHED FOR THE HAT IN MY BACK POCKET.
THERE WAS SOMETHING THAT I NEEDED TO CHECK.
WHOA! YOU HAVE ONE TOO? LOOK, HON, IT'S A BEAUT!
OOOH! I LOVE THE STITCHING!
CRINGE! I WAS AFRAID THEY WERE GOING TO SAY THAT.
I NEEDED TO CHECK A LITTLE HUNCH THAT I HAD.
I WAS AFRAID THAT I'D MISSED SOMETHING EARLIER.
TRUST ME, I REALLY DIDN'T WANT TO.
PEEK!
HAPPY BIRTHDAY ETHAN!

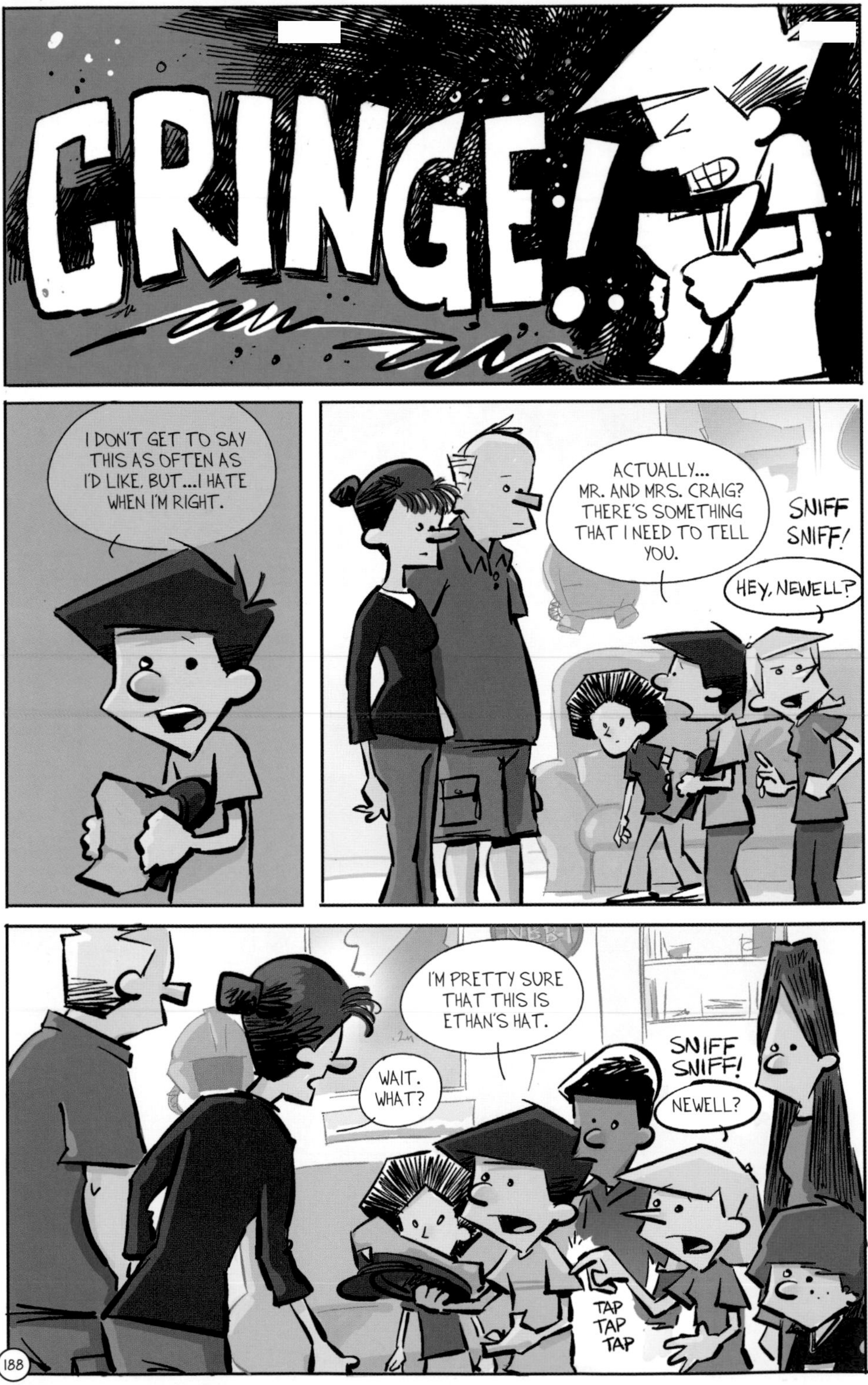
CRINGE!
I DON'T GET TO SAY THIS AS OFTEN AS I'D LIKE, BUT...I HATE WHEN I'M RIGHT.
ACTUALLY... MR. AND MRS. CRAIG? THERE'S SOMETHING THAT I NEED TO TELL YOU.
SNIFF SNIFF!
HEY, NEWELL?
I'M PRETTY SURE THAT THIS IS ETHAN'S HAT.
WAIT. WHAT?
SNIFF SNIFF!
NEWELL?
TAP TAP TAP

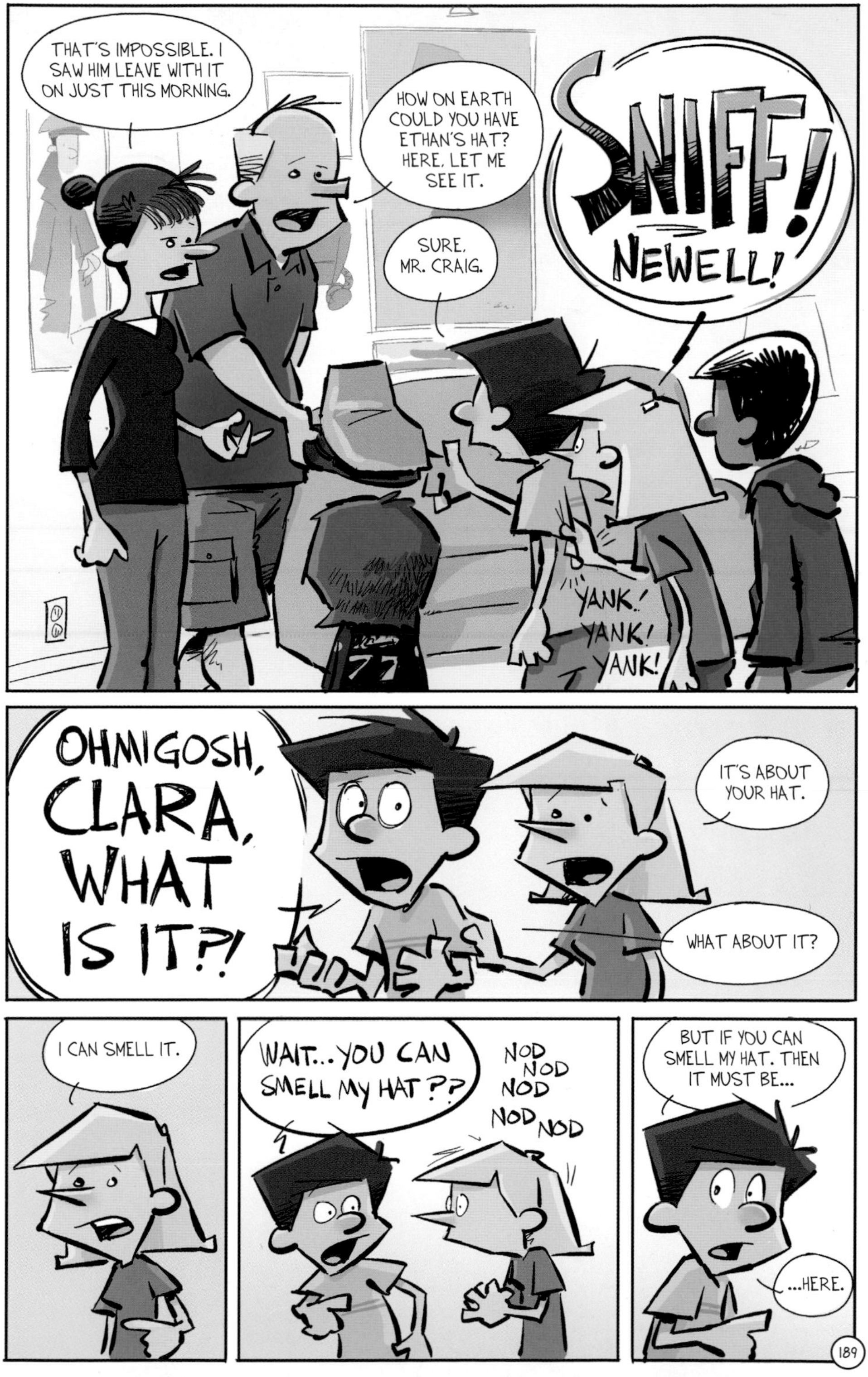

THAT'S IMPOSSIBLE. I SAW HIM LEAVE WITH IT ON JUST THIS MORNING.
HOW ON EARTH COULD YOU HAVE ETHAN'S HAT? HERE, LET ME SEE IT.
SURE, MR. CRAIG.
SNIFF! NEWELL!
YANK! YANK! YANK!
OHMIGOSH, CLARA, WHAT IS IT?!
IT'S ABOUT YOUR HAT.
WHAT ABOUT IT?
I CAN SMELL IT.
WAIT...YOU CAN SMELL MY HAT??
NOD NOD NOD NOD NOD
BUT IF YOU CAN SMELL MY HAT, THEN IT MUST BE...
...HERE.

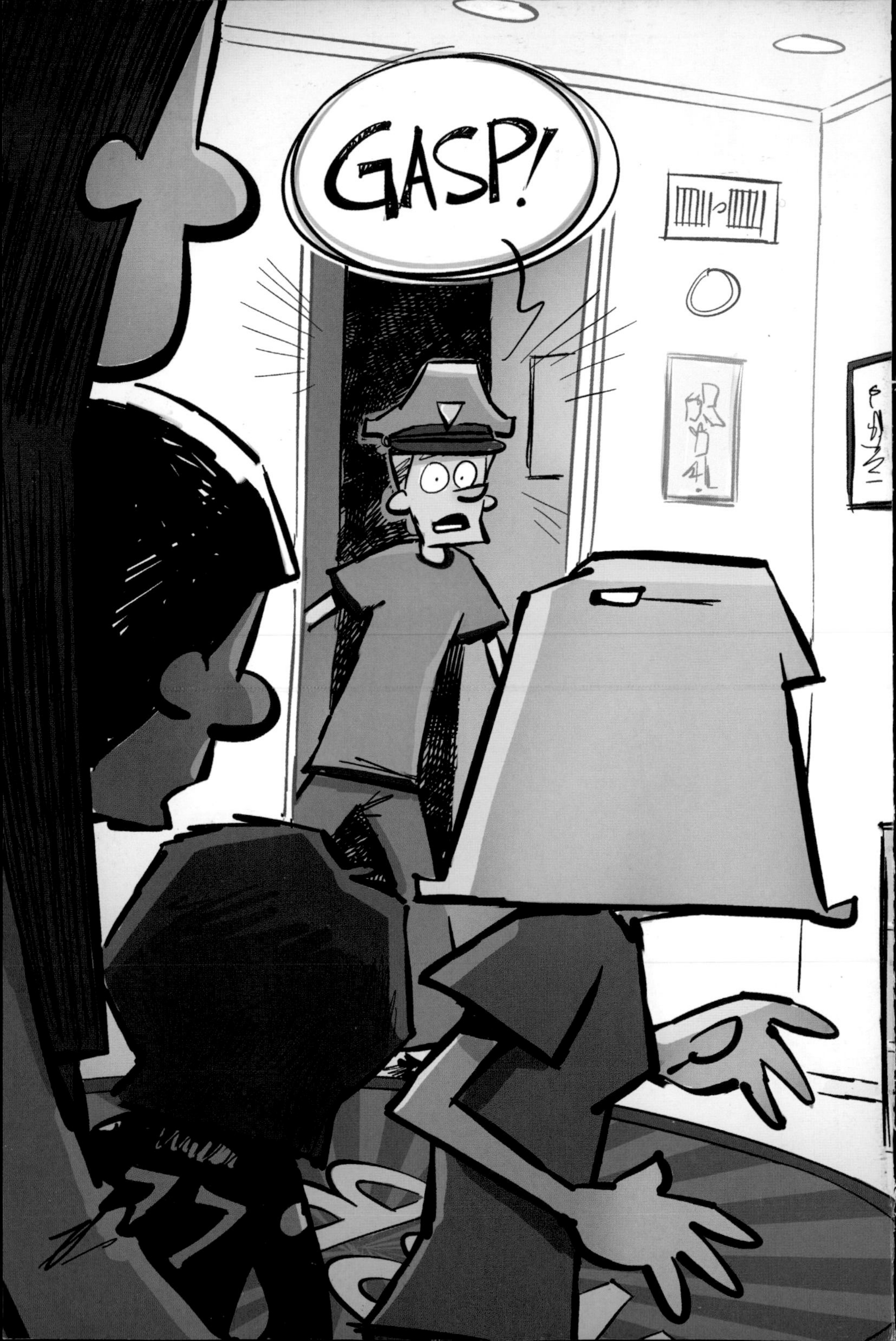
GASP!

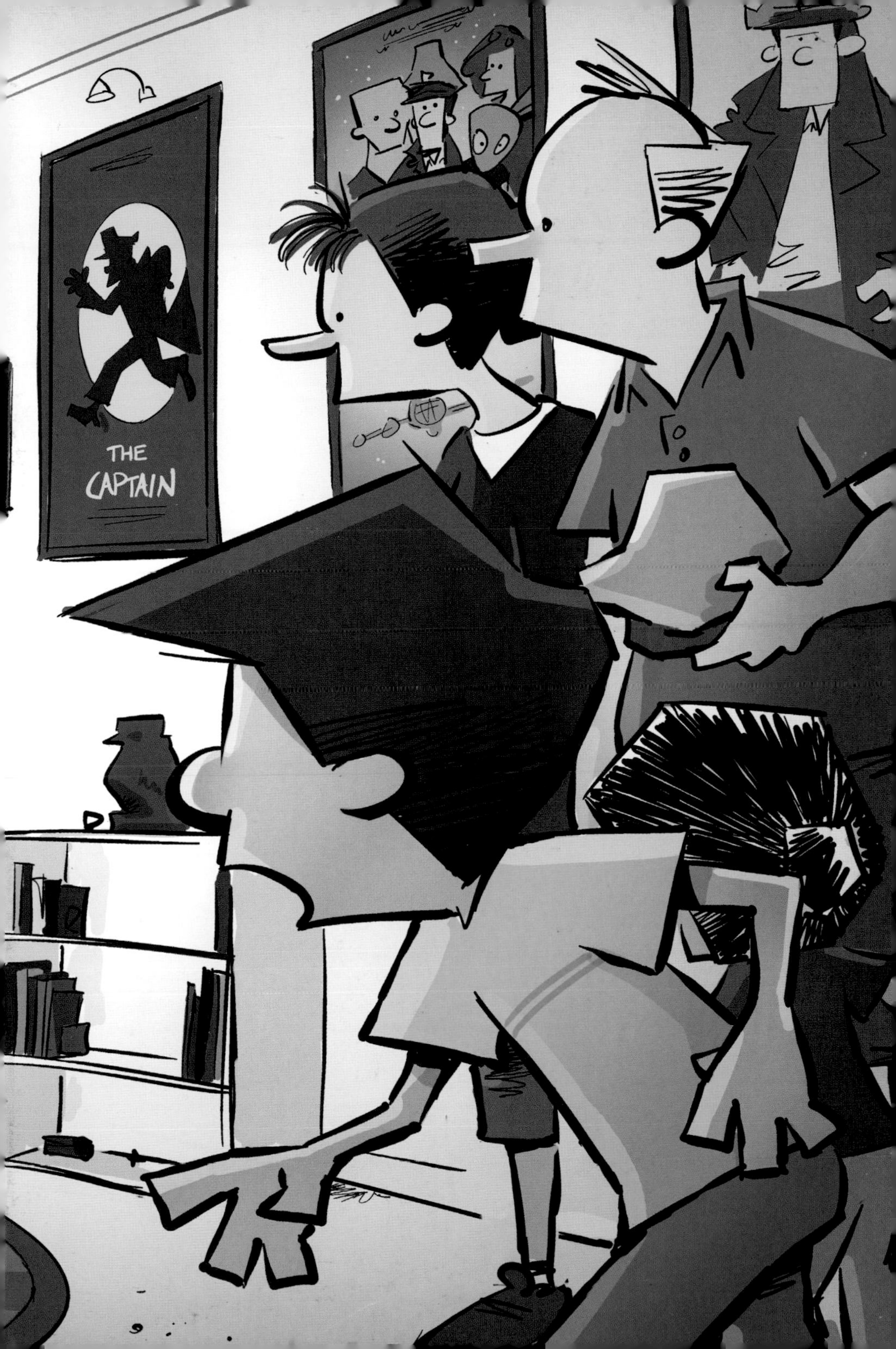
THE CAPTAIN

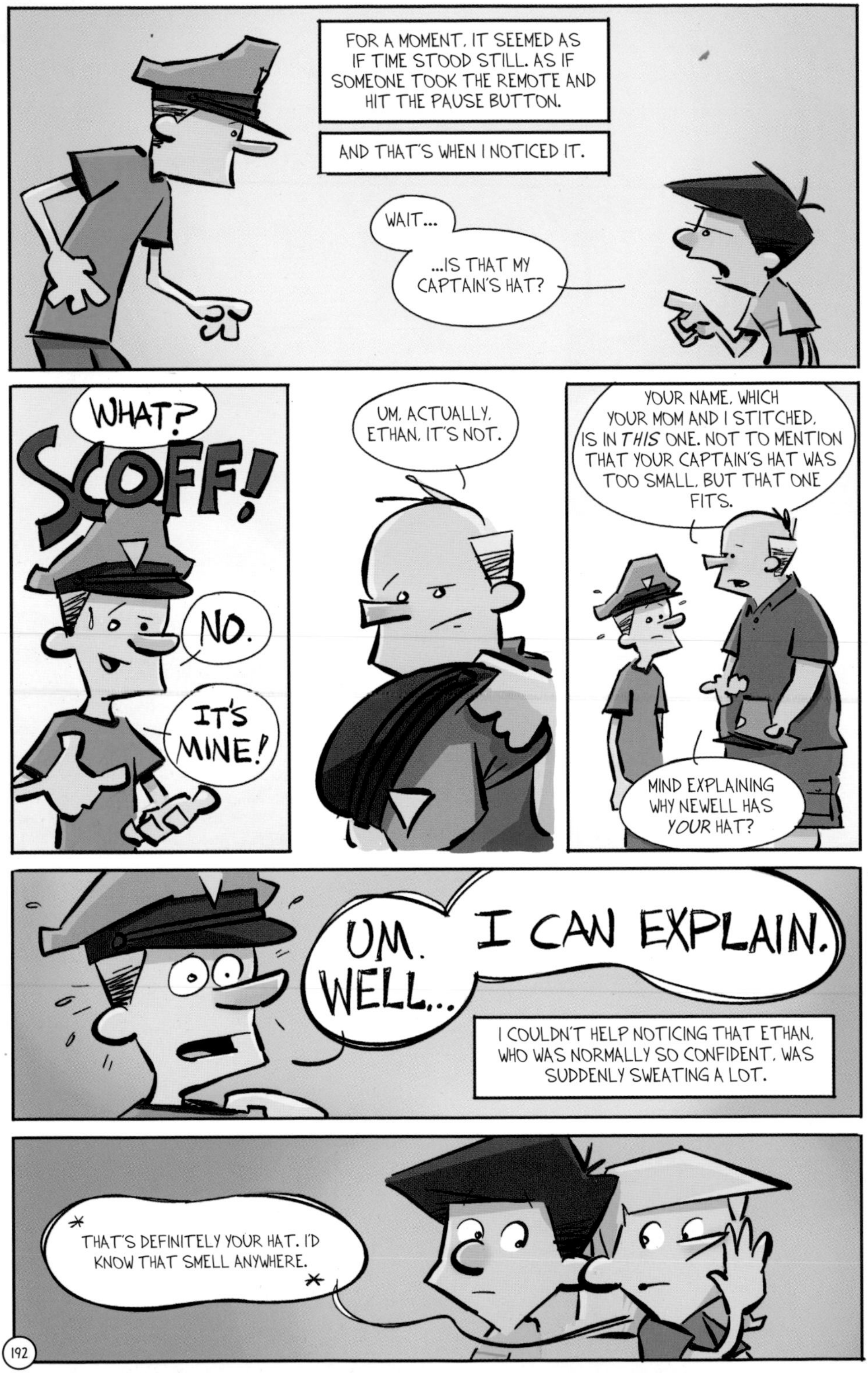
FOR A MOMENT, IT SEEMED AS IF TIME STOOD STILL. AS IF SOMEONE TOOK THE REMOTE AND HIT THE PAUSE BUTTON.
AND THAT'S WHEN I NOTICED IT.
WAIT...
...IS THAT MY CAPTAIN'S HAT?
WHAT?
SCOFF!
NO.
IT'S MINE!
UM, ACTUALLY, ETHAN, IT'S NOT.
YOUR NAME, WHICH YOUR MOM AND I STITCHED, IS IN *THIS* ONE. NOT TO MENTION THAT YOUR CAPTAIN'S HAT WAS TOO SMALL, BUT THAT ONE FITS.
MIND EXPLAINING WHY NEWELL HAS *YOUR* HAT?
UM. WELL...
I CAN EXPLAIN.
I COULDN'T HELP NOTICING THAT ETHAN, WHO WAS NORMALLY SO CONFIDENT, WAS SUDDENLY SWEATING A LOT.
* THAT'S DEFINITELY YOUR HAT. I'D KNOW THAT SMELL ANYWHERE. *

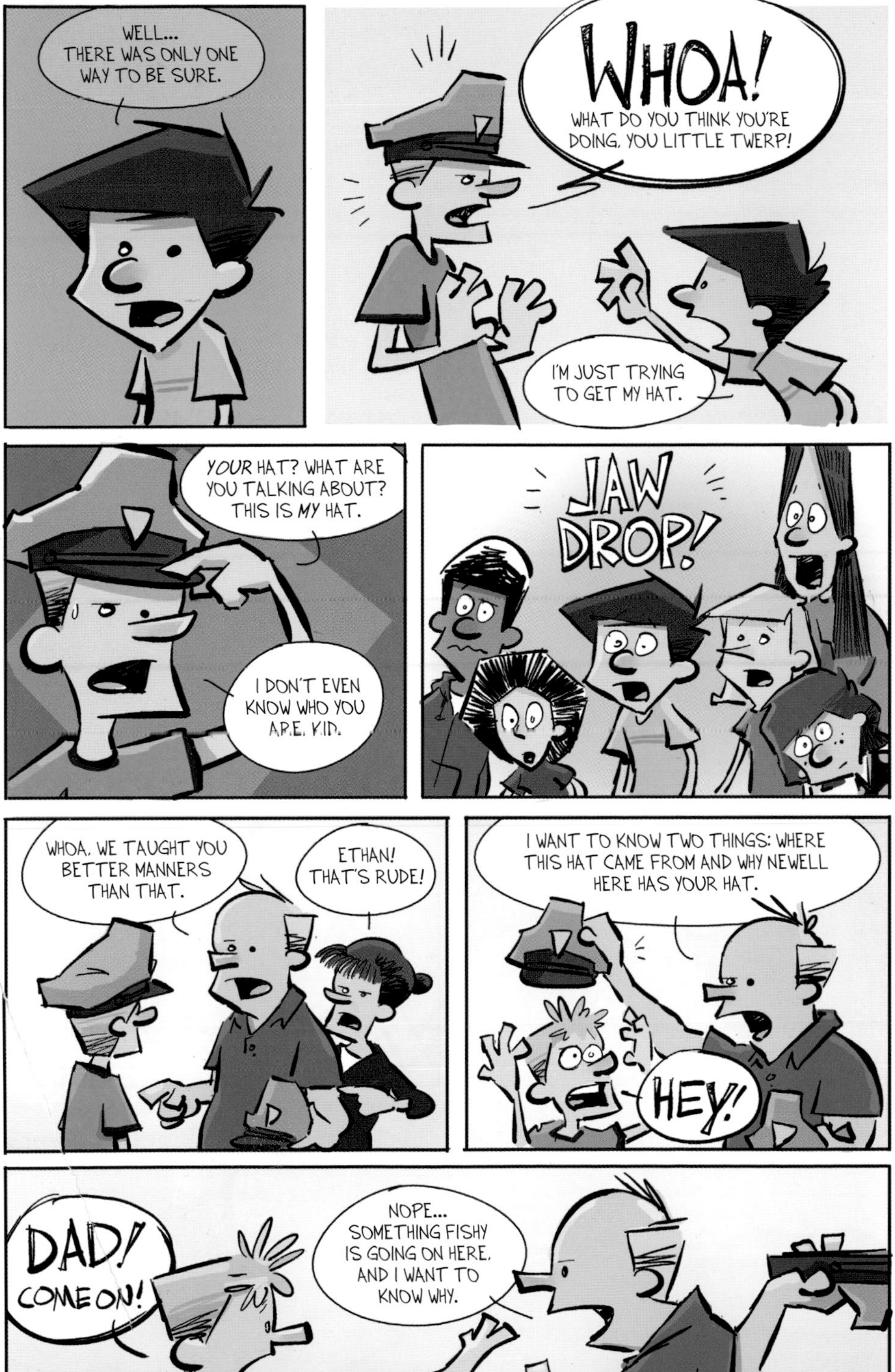
WELL... THERE WAS ONLY ONE WAY TO BE SURE.
WHOA! WHAT DO YOU THINK YOU'RE DOING, YOU LITTLE TWERP!
I'M JUST TRYING TO GET MY HAT.
YOUR HAT? WHAT ARE YOU TALKING ABOUT? THIS IS *MY* HAT.
I DON'T EVEN KNOW WHO YOU ARE, KID.
JAW DROP!
WHOA, WE TAUGHT YOU BETTER MANNERS THAN THAT.
ETHAN! THAT'S RUDE!
I WANT TO KNOW TWO THINGS: WHERE THIS HAT CAME FROM AND WHY NEWELL HERE HAS YOUR HAT.
HEY!
DAD! COME ON!
NOPE... SOMETHING FISHY IS GOING ON HERE, AND I WANT TO KNOW WHY.

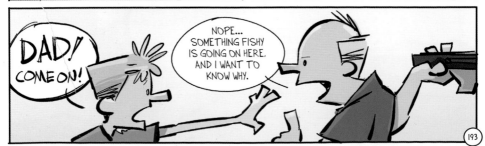

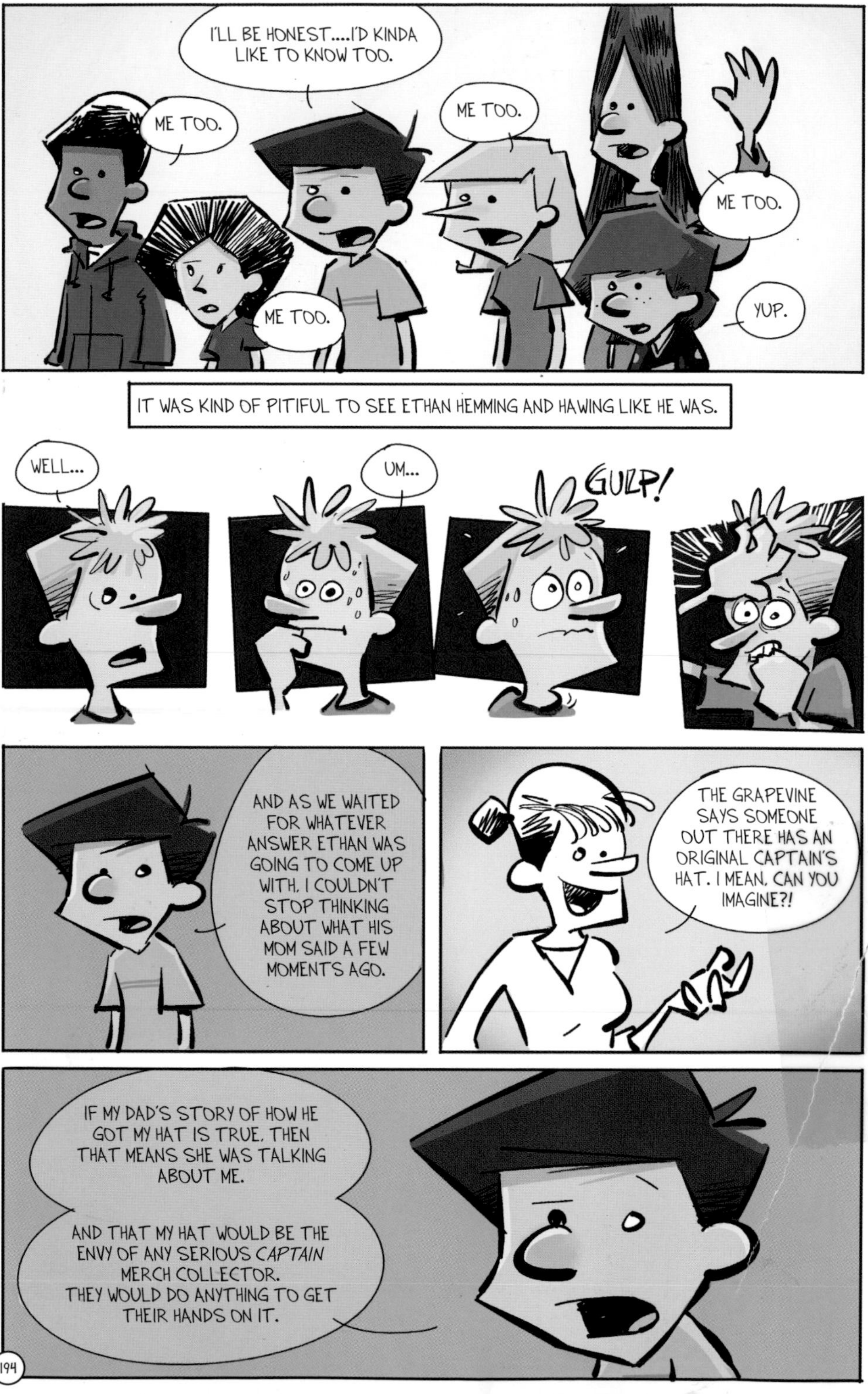
ME TOO.
I'LL BE HONEST....I'D KINDA LIKE TO KNOW TOO.
ME TOO.
ME TOO.
ME TOO.
YUP.
IT WAS KIND OF PITIFUL TO SEE ETHAN HEMMING AND HAWING LIKE HE WAS.
WELL...
UM...
GULP!
AND AS WE WAITED FOR WHATEVER ANSWER ETHAN WAS GOING TO COME UP WITH, I COULDN'T STOP THINKING ABOUT WHAT HIS MOM SAID A FEW MOMENTS AGO.
THE GRAPEVINE SAYS SOMEONE OUT THERE HAS AN ORIGINAL CAPTAIN'S HAT. I MEAN, CAN YOU IMAGINE?!
IF MY DAD'S STORY OF HOW HE GOT MY HAT IS TRUE, THEN THAT MEANS SHE WAS TALKING ABOUT ME.
AND THAT MY HAT WOULD BE THE ENVY OF ANY SERIOUS *CAPTAIN* MERCH COLLECTOR.
THEY WOULD DO ANYTHING TO GET THEIR HANDS ON IT.

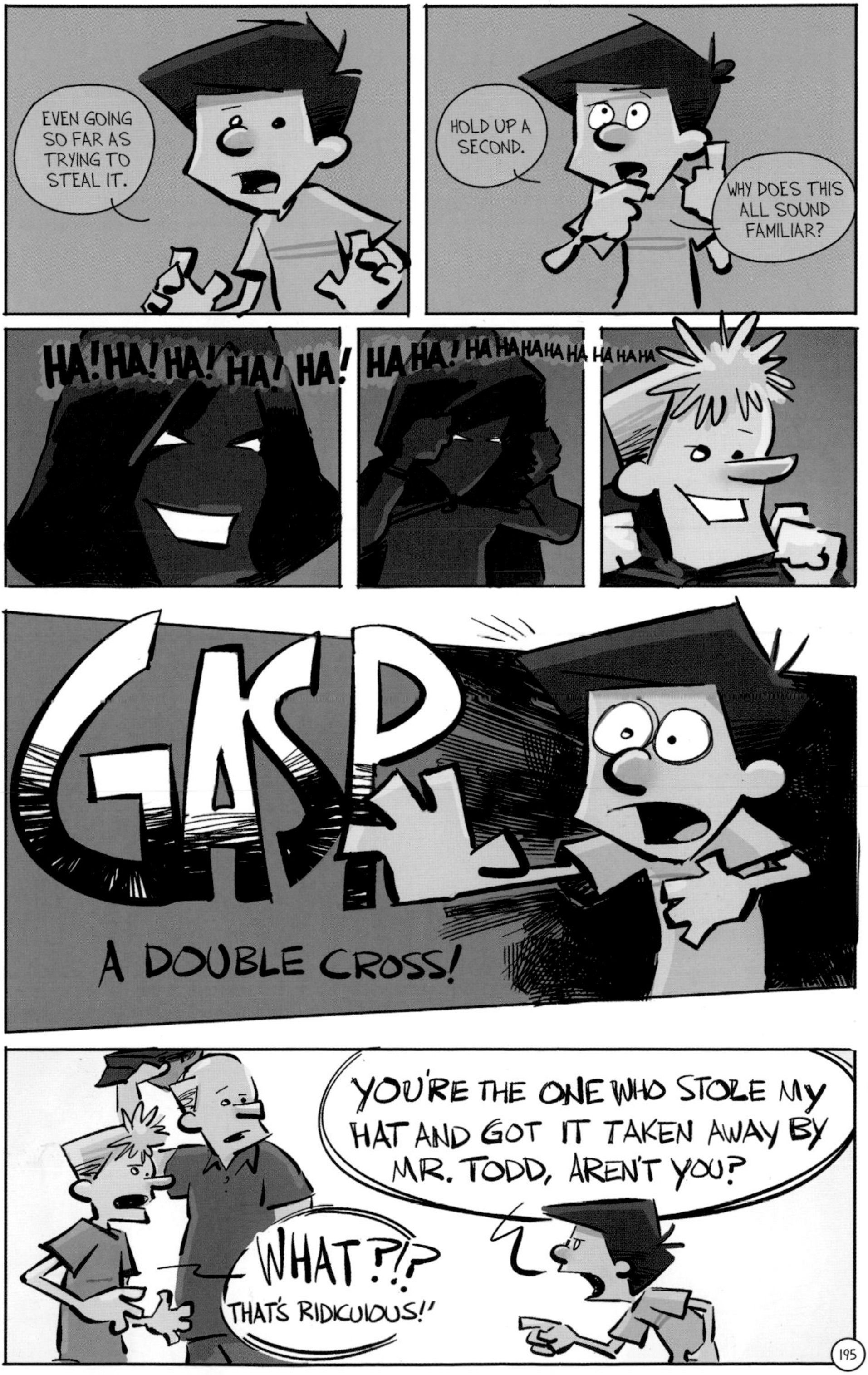

EVEN GOING SO FAR AS TRYING TO STEAL IT.
HOLD UP A SECOND.
WHY DOES THIS ALL SOUND FAMILIAR?
HA! HA! HA! HA! HA!
HA HA! HA HA HA HA HA HA HA HA HA
GASP!
A DOUBLE CROSS!
YOU'RE THE ONE WHO STOLE MY HAT AND GOT IT TAKEN AWAY BY MR. TODD, AREN'T YOU?
WHAT?!? THAT'S RIDICULOUS!

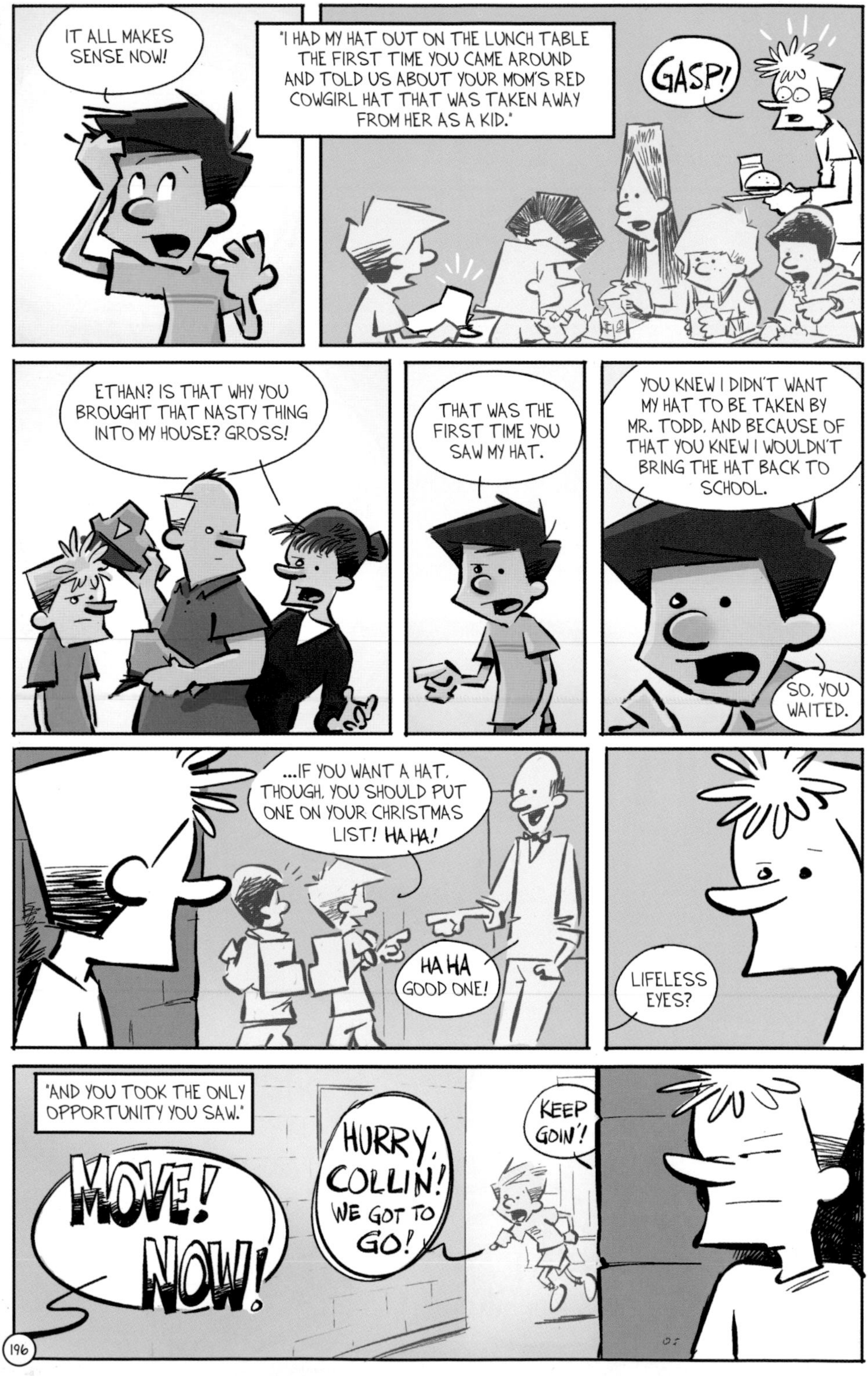

IT ALL MAKES SENSE NOW!
"I HAD MY HAT OUT ON THE LUNCH TABLE THE FIRST TIME YOU CAME AROUND AND TOLD US ABOUT YOUR MOM'S RED COWGIRL HAT THAT WAS TAKEN AWAY FROM HER AS A KID."
GASP!
ETHAN? IS THAT WHY YOU BROUGHT THAT NASTY THING INTO MY HOUSE? GROSS!
THAT WAS THE FIRST TIME YOU SAW MY HAT.
YOU KNEW I DIDN'T WANT MY HAT TO BE TAKEN BY MR. TODD, AND BECAUSE OF THAT YOU KNEW I WOULDN'T BRING THE HAT BACK TO SCHOOL.
SO, YOU WAITED.
...IF YOU WANT A HAT, THOUGH, YOU SHOULD PUT ONE ON YOUR CHRISTMAS LIST! HA HA!
HA HA GOOD ONE!
LIFELESS EYES?
"AND YOU TOOK THE ONLY OPPORTUNITY YOU SAW."
MOVE! NOW!
HURRY, COLLIN! WE GOT TO GO!
KEEP GOIN'!

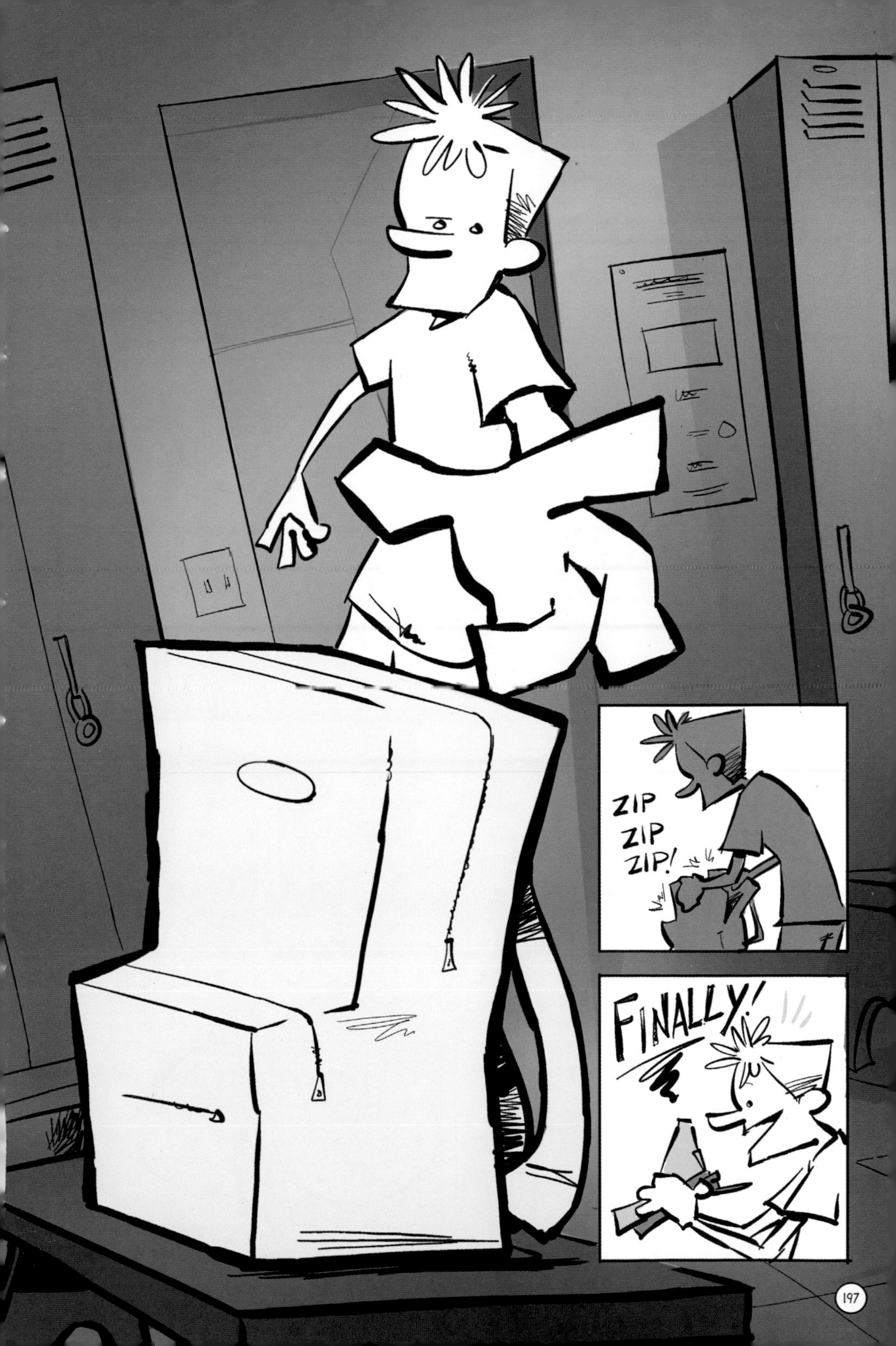
ZIP
ZIP
ZIP!
FINALLY!

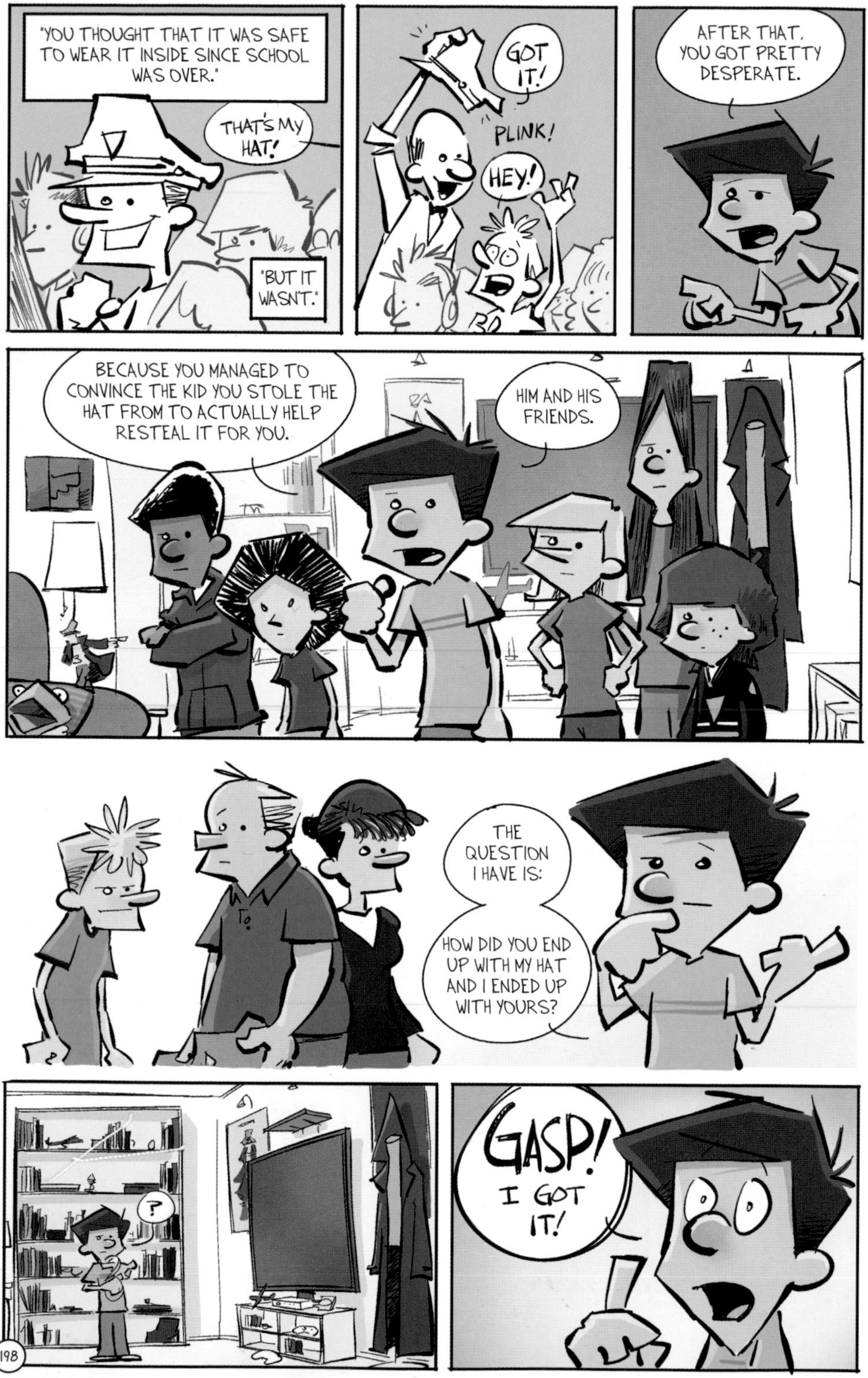

"YOU THOUGHT THAT IT WAS SAFE TO WEAR IT INSIDE SINCE SCHOOL WAS OVER."
THAT'S MY HAT!
"BUT IT WASN'T."
GOT IT!
PLINK!
HEY!
AFTER THAT, YOU GOT PRETTY DESPERATE.
BECAUSE YOU MANAGED TO CONVINCE THE KID YOU STOLE THE HAT FROM TO ACTUALLY HELP RESTEAL IT FOR YOU.
HIM AND HIS FRIENDS.
THE QUESTION I HAVE IS:
HOW DID YOU END UP WITH MY HAT AND I ENDED UP WITH YOURS?
?
GASP!
I GOT IT!

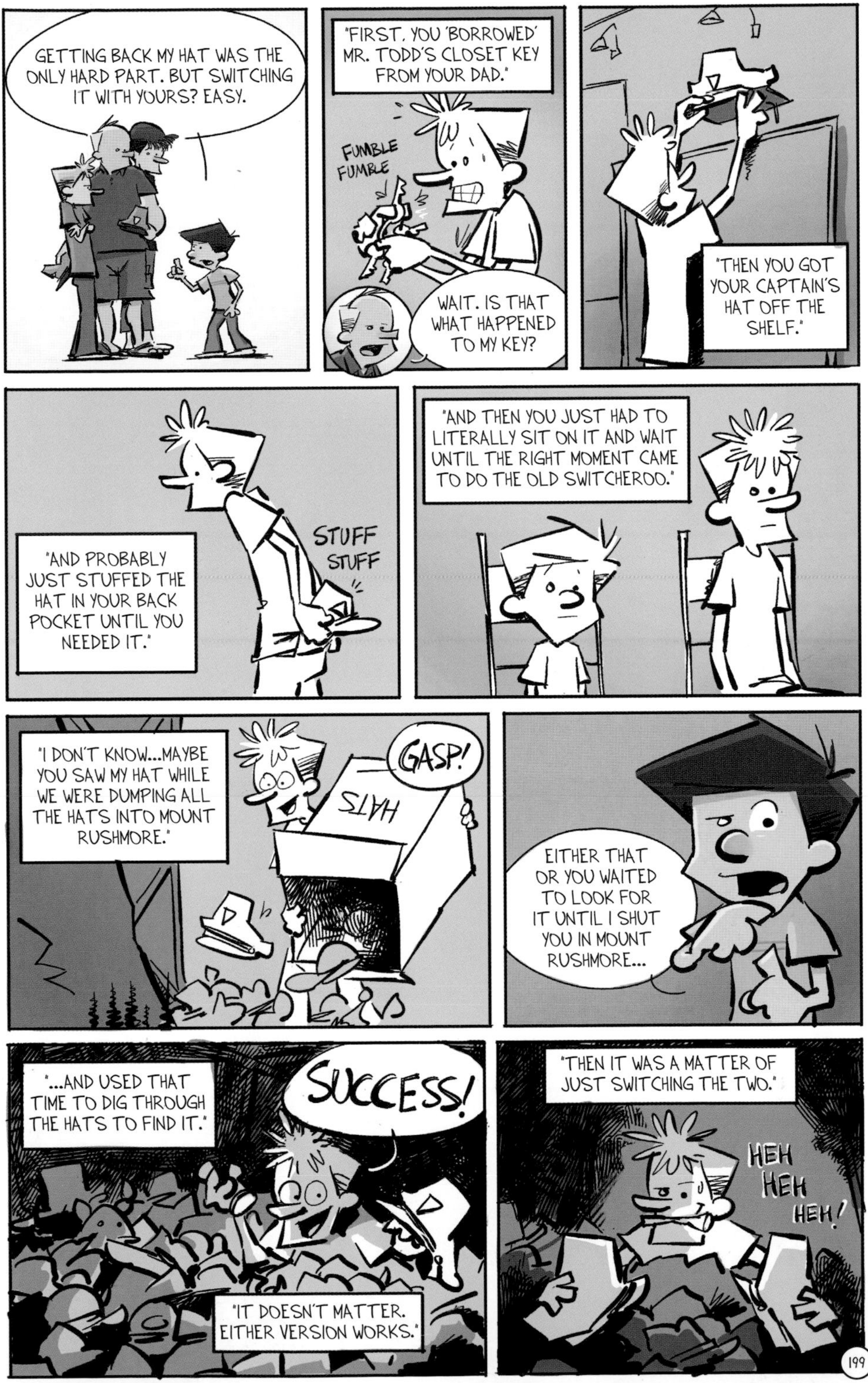
GETTING BACK MY HAT WAS THE ONLY HARD PART. BUT SWITCHING IT WITH YOURS? EASY.
"FIRST, YOU 'BORROWED' MR. TODD'S CLOSET KEY FROM YOUR DAD."
FUMBLE FUMBLE
WAIT. IS THAT WHAT HAPPENED TO MY KEY?
"THEN YOU GOT YOUR CAPTAIN'S HAT OFF THE SHELF."
"AND PROBABLY JUST STUFFED THE HAT IN YOUR BACK POCKET UNTIL YOU NEEDED IT."
STUFF STUFF
"AND THEN YOU JUST HAD TO LITERALLY SIT ON IT AND WAIT UNTIL THE RIGHT MOMENT CAME TO DO THE OLD SWITCHEROO."
"I DON'T KNOW...MAYBE YOU SAW MY HAT WHILE WE WERE DUMPING ALL THE HATS INTO MOUNT RUSHMORE."
GASP!
HATS
EITHER THAT OR YOU WAITED TO LOOK FOR IT UNTIL I SHUT YOU IN MOUNT RUSHMORE...
"...AND USED THAT TIME TO DIG THROUGH THE HATS TO FIND IT."
SUCCESS!
"IT DOESN'T MATTER. EITHER VERSION WORKS."
"THEN IT WAS A MATTER OF JUST SWITCHING THE TWO."
HEH HEH HEH!

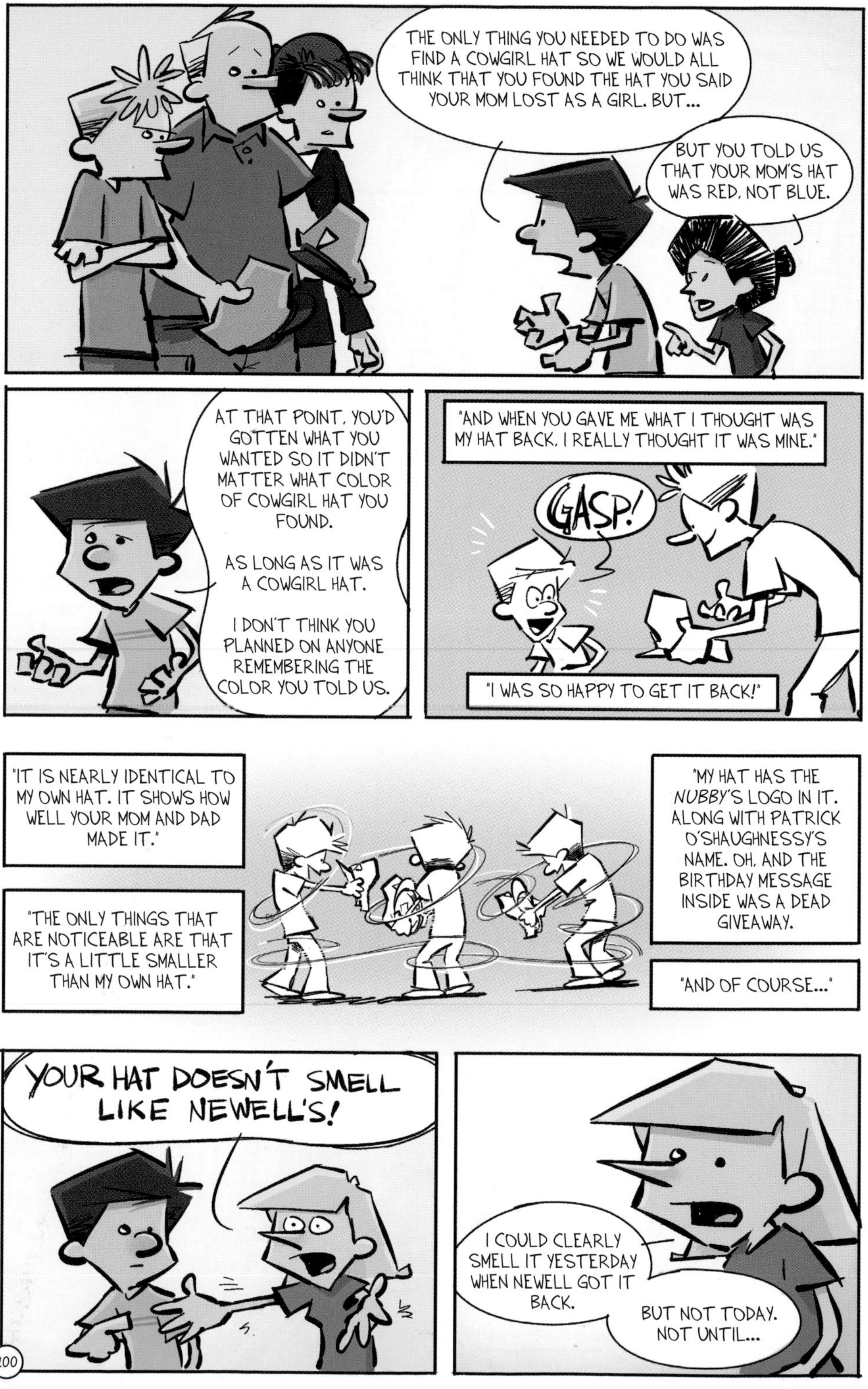
THE ONLY THING YOU NEEDED TO DO WAS FIND A COWGIRL HAT SO WE WOULD ALL THINK THAT YOU FOUND THE HAT YOU SAID YOUR MOM LOST AS A GIRL. BUT...
BUT YOU TOLD US THAT YOUR MOM'S HAT WAS RED, NOT BLUE.
AT THAT POINT, YOU'D GOTTEN WHAT YOU WANTED SO IT DIDN'T MATTER WHAT COLOR OF COWGIRL HAT YOU FOUND.
AS LONG AS IT WAS A COWGIRL HAT.
I DON'T THINK YOU PLANNED ON ANYONE REMEMBERING THE COLOR YOU TOLD US.
"AND WHEN YOU GAVE ME WHAT I THOUGHT WAS MY HAT BACK, I REALLY THOUGHT IT WAS MINE."
GASP!
"I WAS SO HAPPY TO GET IT BACK!"
"IT IS NEARLY IDENTICAL TO MY OWN HAT. IT SHOWS HOW WELL YOUR MOM AND DAD MADE IT."
"THE ONLY THINGS THAT ARE NOTICEABLE ARE THAT IT'S A LITTLE SMALLER THAN MY OWN HAT."
"MY HAT HAS THE *NUBBY*'S LOGO IN IT. ALONG WITH PATRICK O'SHAUGHNESSY'S NAME. OH, AND THE BIRTHDAY MESSAGE INSIDE WAS A DEAD GIVEAWAY.
"AND OF COURSE..."
YOUR HAT DOESN'T SMELL LIKE NEWELL'S!
I COULD CLEARLY SMELL IT YESTERDAY WHEN NEWELL GOT IT BACK.
BUT NOT TODAY. NOT UNTIL...

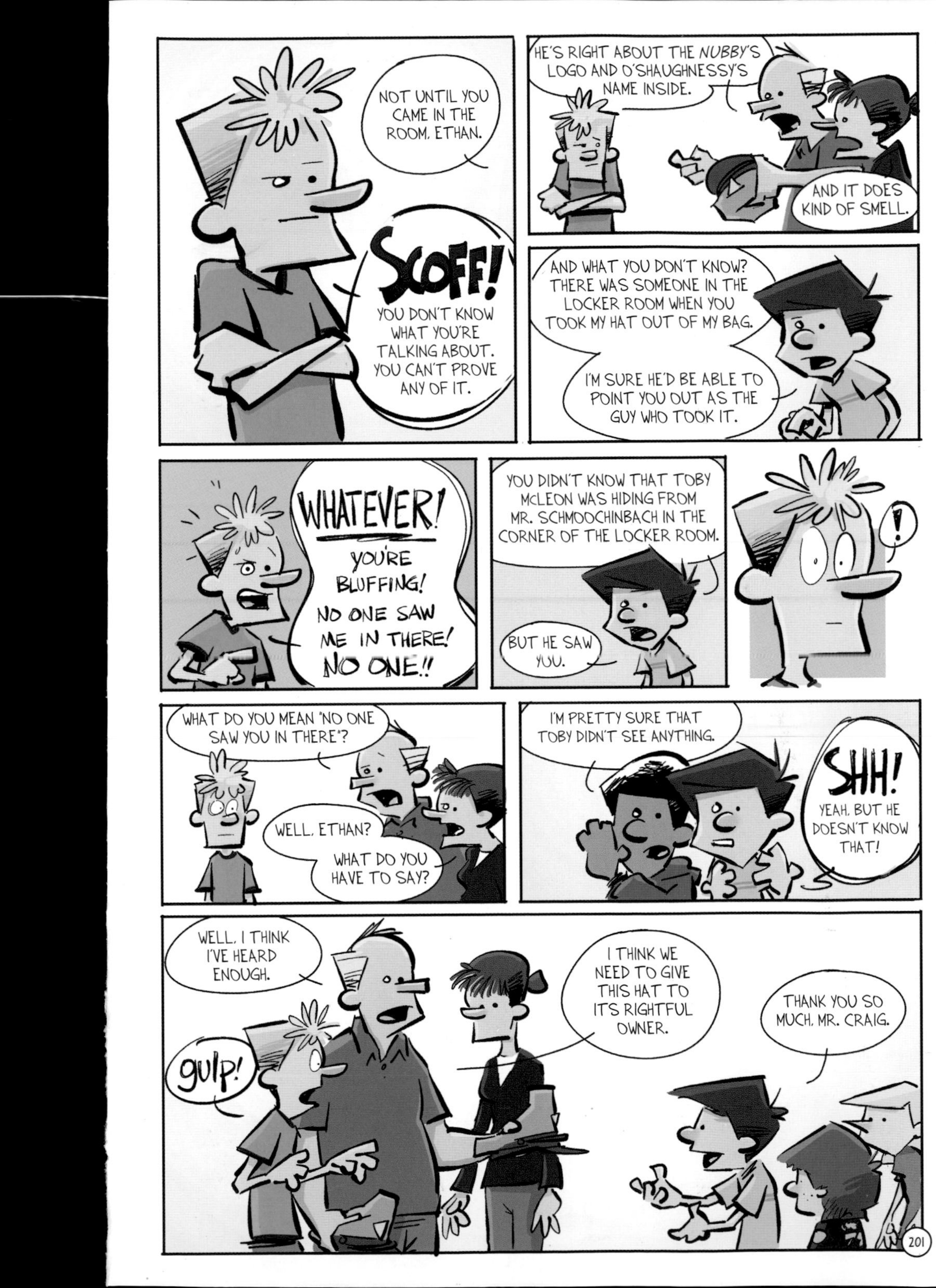
NOT UNTIL YOU CAME IN THE ROOM, ETHAN.
SCOFF!
YOU DON'T KNOW WHAT YOU'RE TALKING ABOUT. YOU CAN'T PROVE ANY OF IT.
HE'S RIGHT ABOUT THE *NUBBY'S* LOGO AND O'SHAUGHNESSY'S NAME INSIDE.
AND IT DOES KIND OF SMELL.
AND WHAT YOU DON'T KNOW? THERE WAS SOMEONE IN THE LOCKER ROOM WHEN YOU TOOK MY HAT OUT OF MY BAG.
I'M SURE HE'D BE ABLE TO POINT YOU OUT AS THE GUY WHO TOOK IT.
WHATEVER!
YOU'RE BLUFFING! NO ONE SAW ME IN THERE! NO ONE!!
YOU DIDN'T KNOW THAT TOBY McLEON WAS HIDING FROM MR. SCHMOOCHINBACH IN THE CORNER OF THE LOCKER ROOM.
BUT HE SAW YOU.
!
WHAT DO YOU MEAN "NO ONE SAW YOU IN THERE"?
WELL, ETHAN?
WHAT DO YOU HAVE TO SAY?
I'M PRETTY SURE THAT TOBY DIDN'T SEE ANYTHING.
SHH!
YEAH, BUT HE DOESN'T KNOW THAT!
WELL, I THINK I'VE HEARD ENOUGH.
gulp!
I THINK WE NEED TO GIVE THIS HAT TO ITS RIGHTFUL OWNER.
THANK YOU SO MUCH, MR. CRAIG.

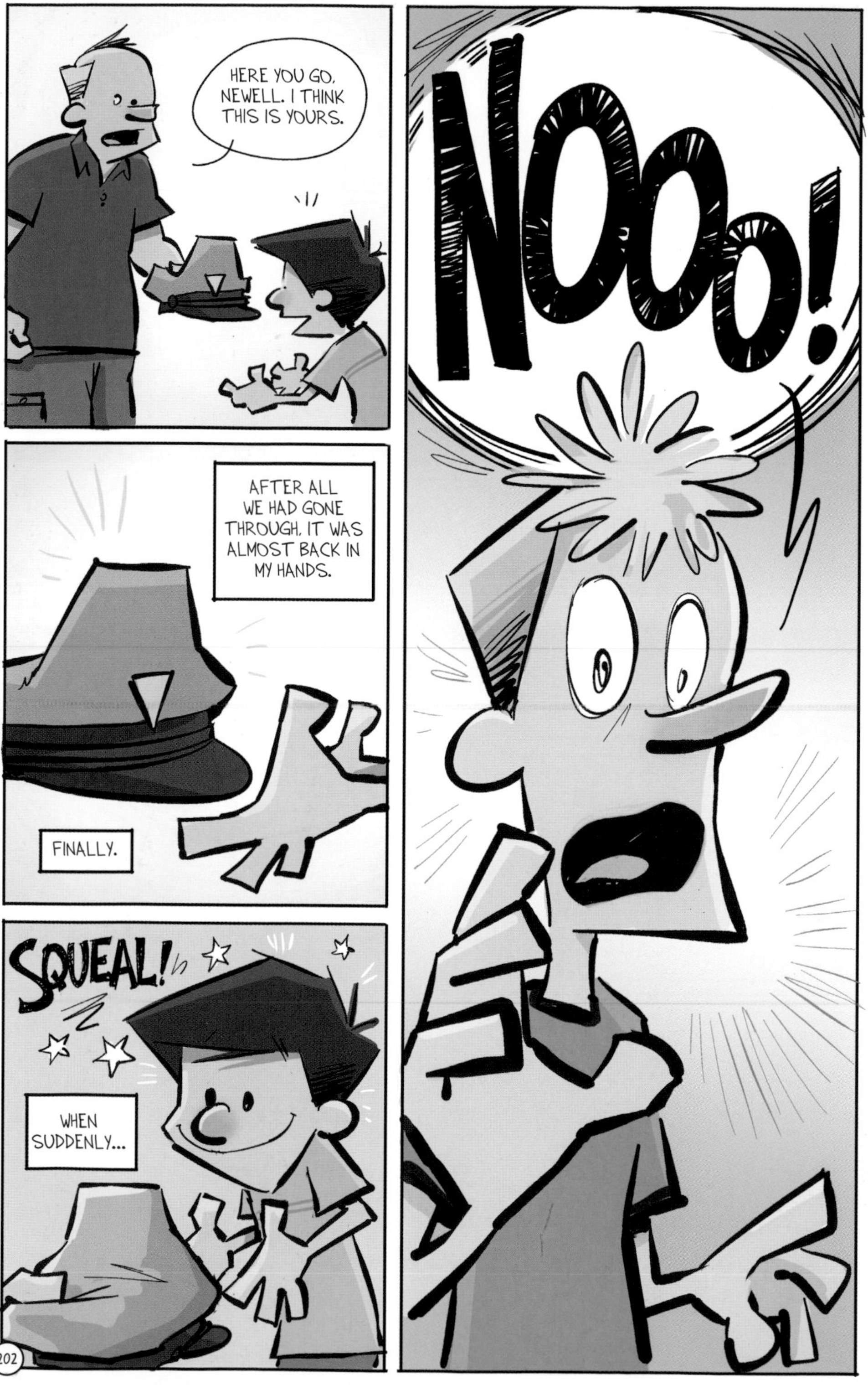
HERE YOU GO, NEWELL. I THINK THIS IS YOURS.
AFTER ALL WE HAD GONE THROUGH, IT WAS ALMOST BACK IN MY HANDS.
FINALLY.
SQUEAL!
WHEN SUDDENLY...
NOOOO!

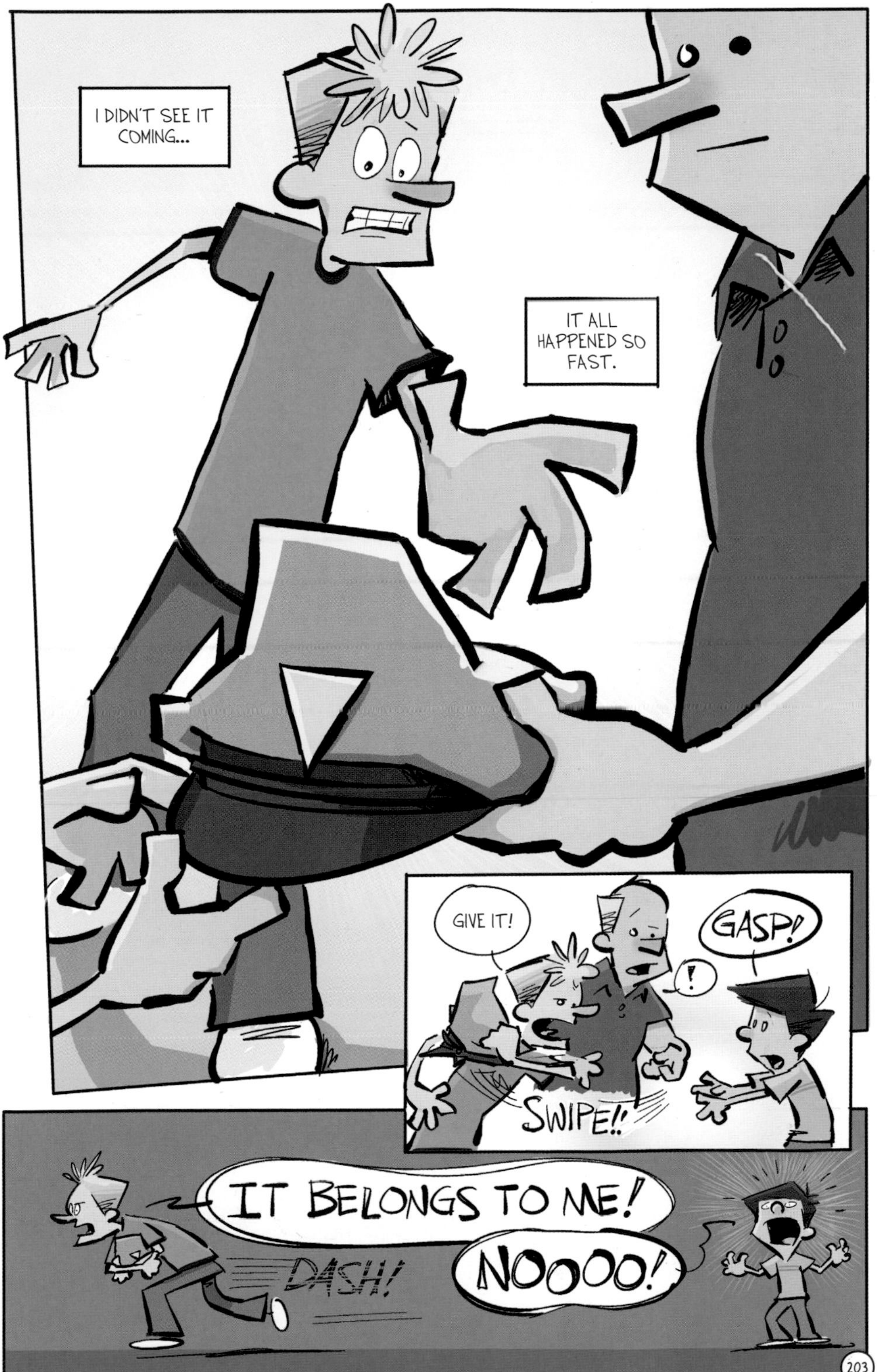
I DIDN'T SEE IT COMING...
IT ALL HAPPENED SO FAST.
GIVE IT!
!
GASP!
SWIPE!!
IT BELONGS TO ME!
DASH!
NOOOO!

CHAPTER TEN
THE SHOWDOWN

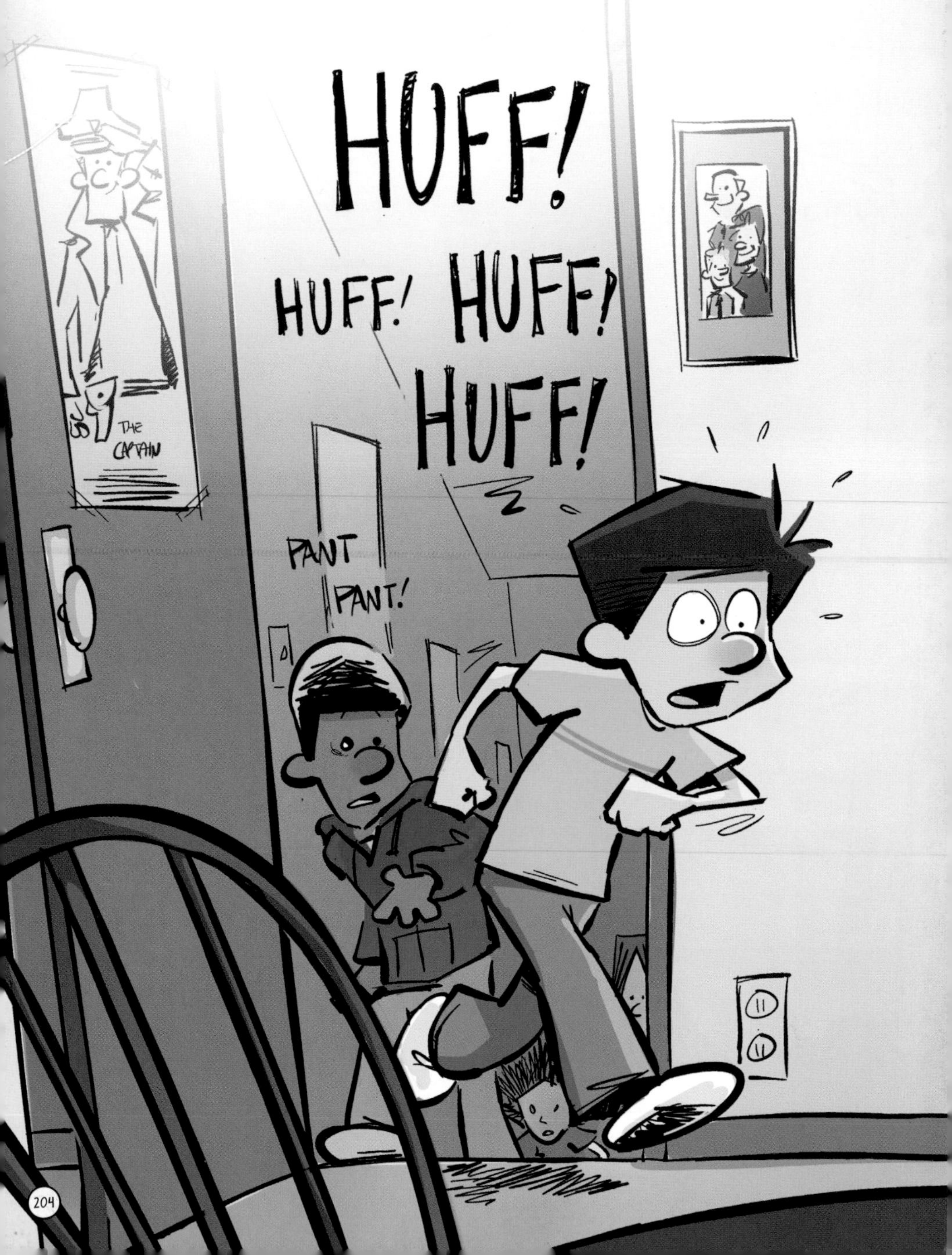
HUFF!
HUFF! HUFF!
HUFF!
PANT
PANT!
THE CAPTAIN

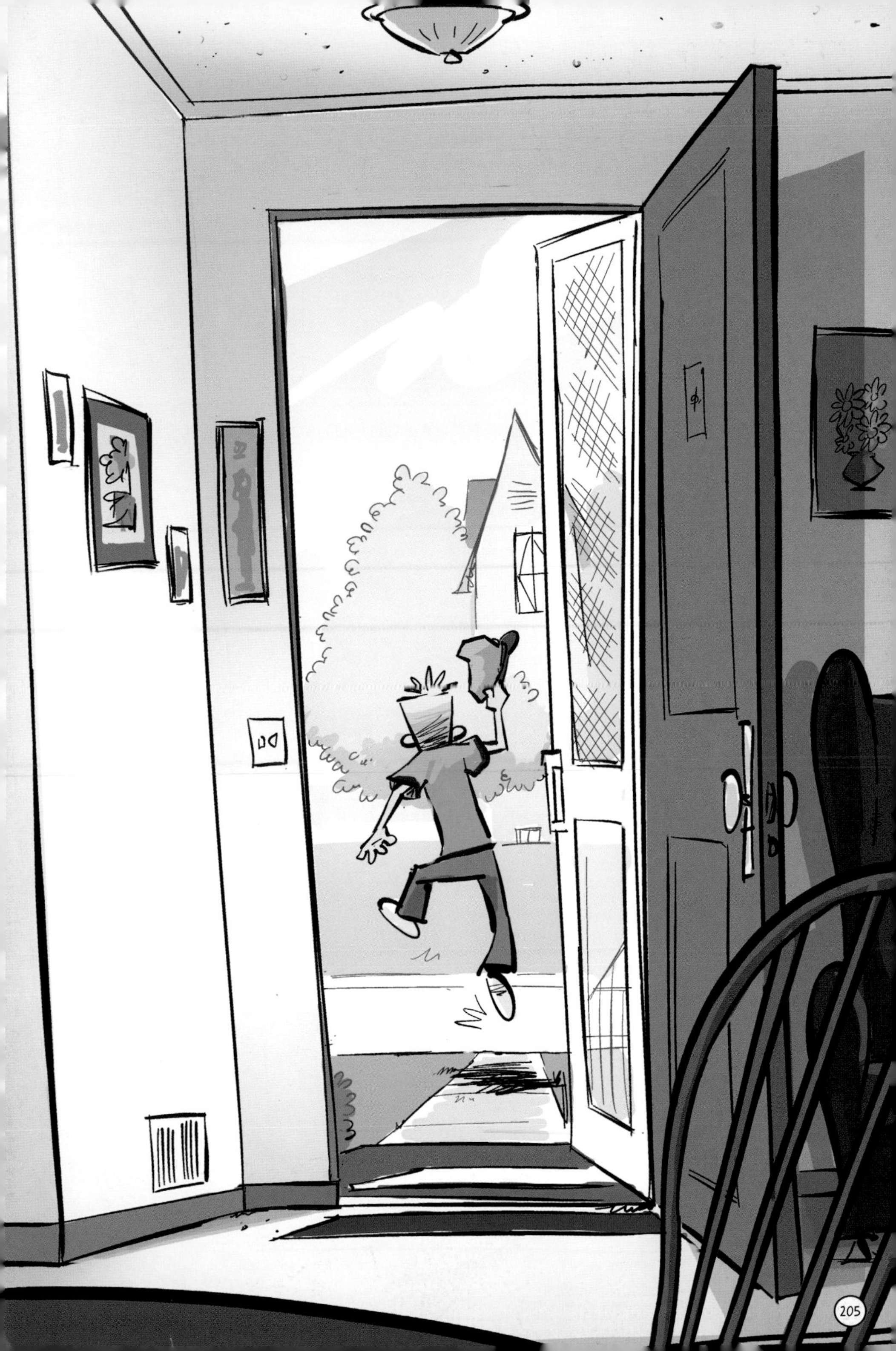

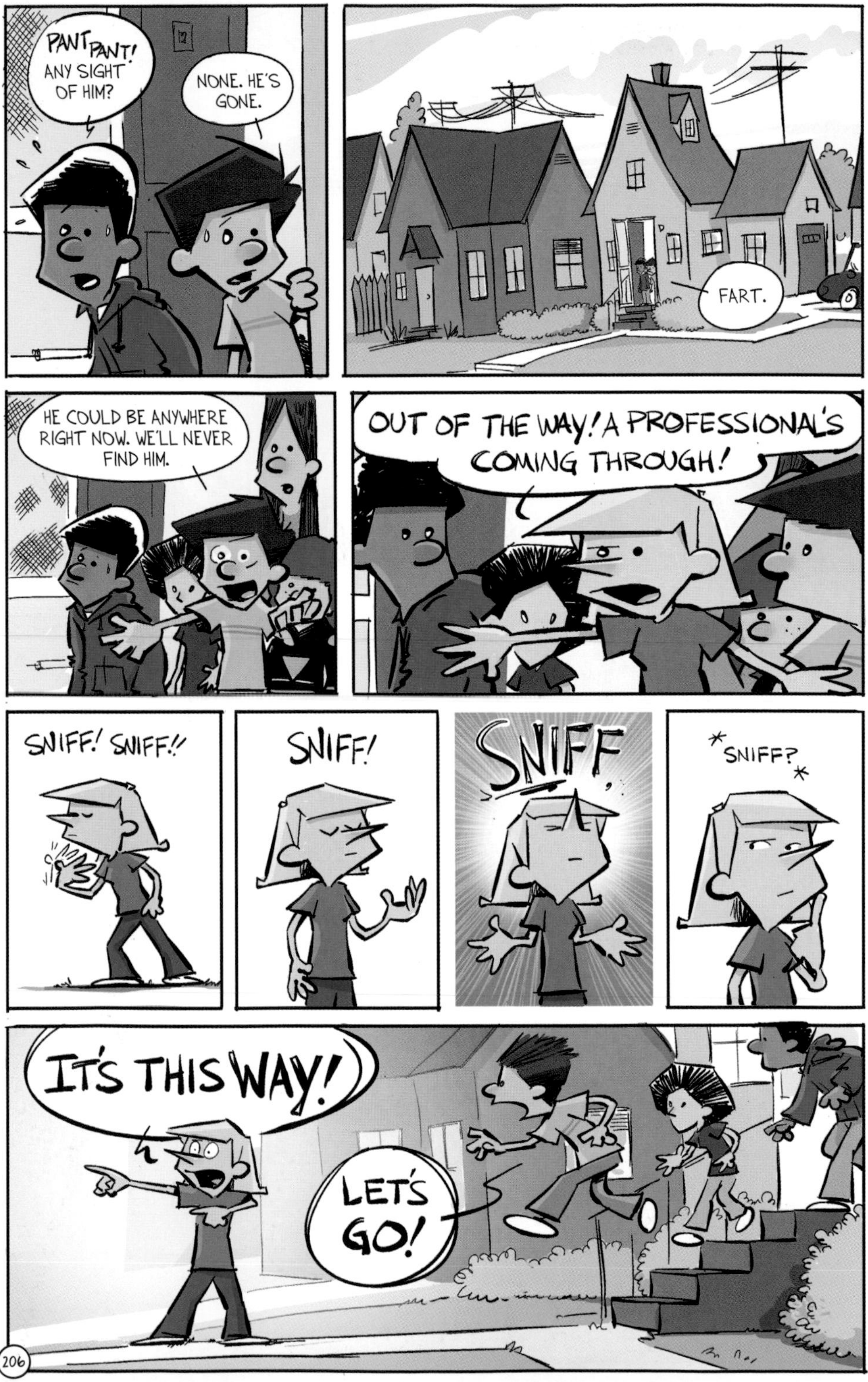
PANT PANT! ANY SIGHT OF HIM?
NONE. HE'S GONE.
FART.
HE COULD BE ANYWHERE RIGHT NOW. WE'LL NEVER FIND HIM.
OUT OF THE WAY! A PROFESSIONAL'S COMING THROUGH!
SNIFF! SNIFF!!
SNIFF!
SNIFF
SNIFF?
IT'S THIS WAY!
LET'S GO!

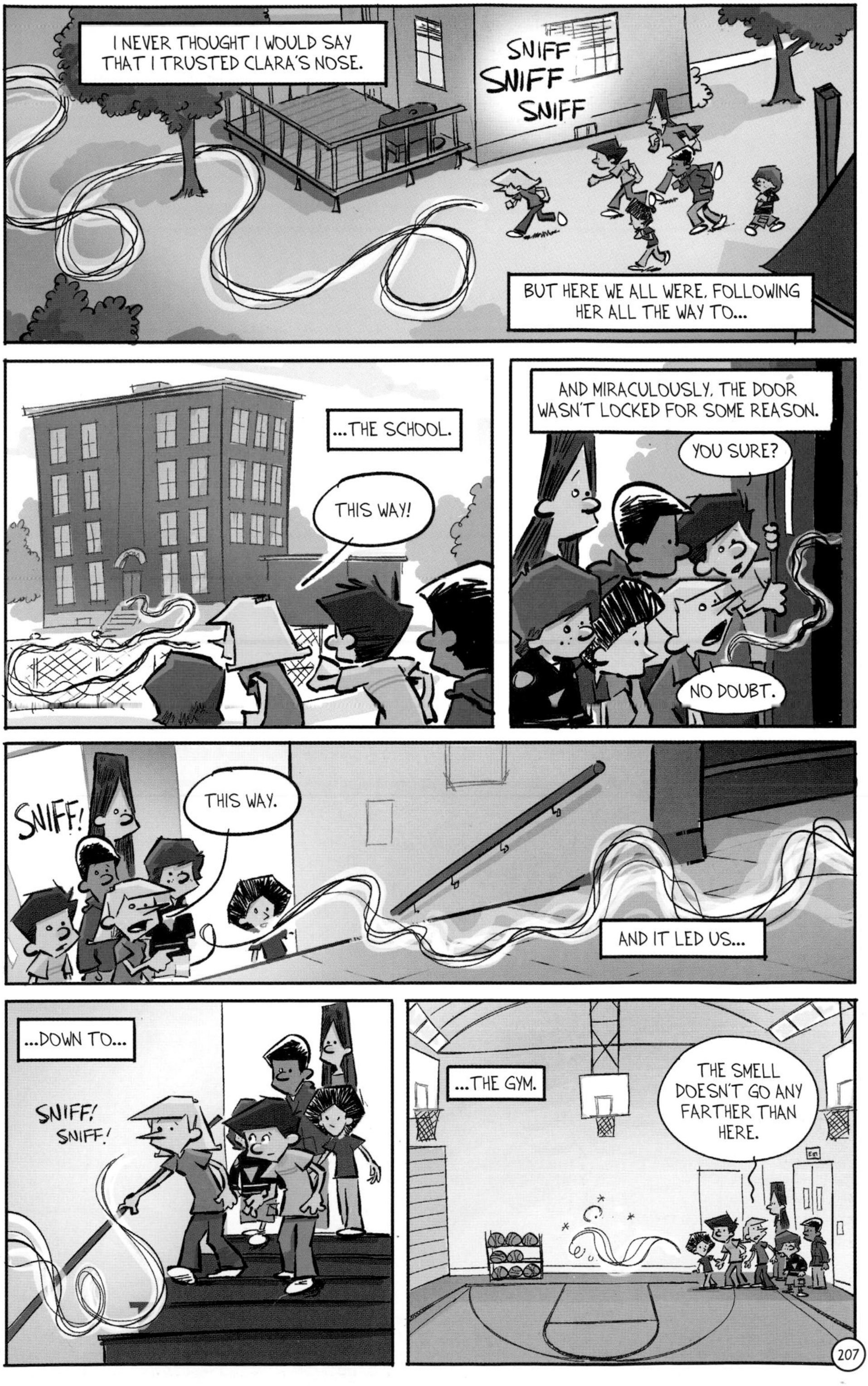
I NEVER THOUGHT I WOULD SAY THAT I TRUSTED CLARA'S NOSE.
SNIFF SNIFF SNIFF
BUT HERE WE ALL WERE, FOLLOWING HER ALL THE WAY TO...
...THE SCHOOL.
THIS WAY!
AND MIRACULOUSLY, THE DOOR WASN'T LOCKED FOR SOME REASON.
YOU SURE?
NO DOUBT.
SNIFF!
THIS WAY.
AND IT LED US...
...DOWN TO...
SNIFF! SNIFF!
...THE GYM.
THE SMELL DOESN'T GO ANY FARTHER THAN HERE.

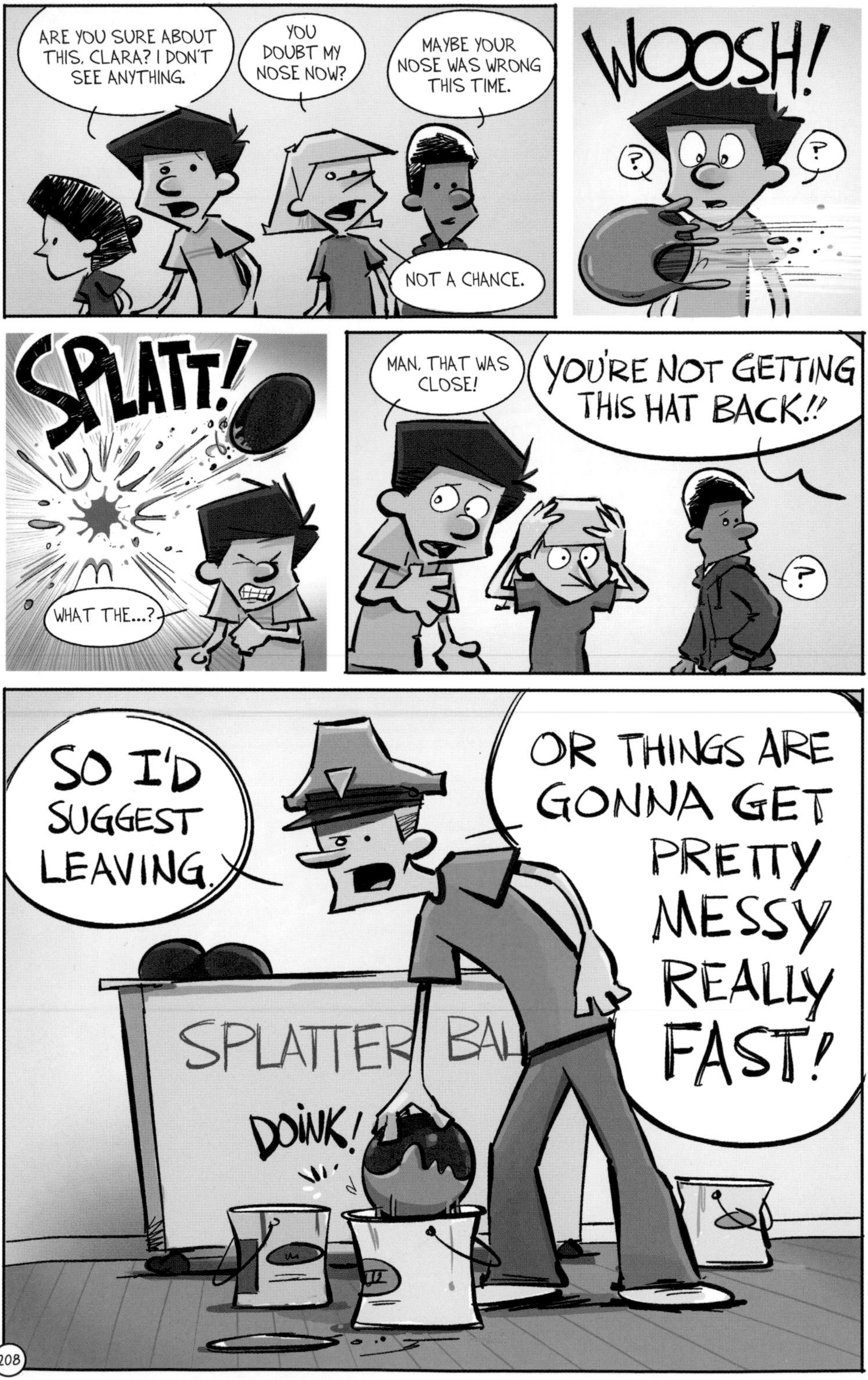
ARE YOU SURE ABOUT THIS, CLARA? I DON'T SEE ANYTHING.
YOU DOUBT MY NOSE NOW?
MAYBE YOUR NOSE WAS WRONG THIS TIME.
NOT A CHANCE.
WOOSH!
?
?
SPLATT!
WHAT THE...?
MAN, THAT WAS CLOSE!
YOU'RE NOT GETTING THIS HAT BACK!!
?
SO I'D SUGGEST LEAVING.
OR THINGS ARE GONNA GET PRETTY MESSY REALLY FAST!
SPLATTER BAL
DOINK!

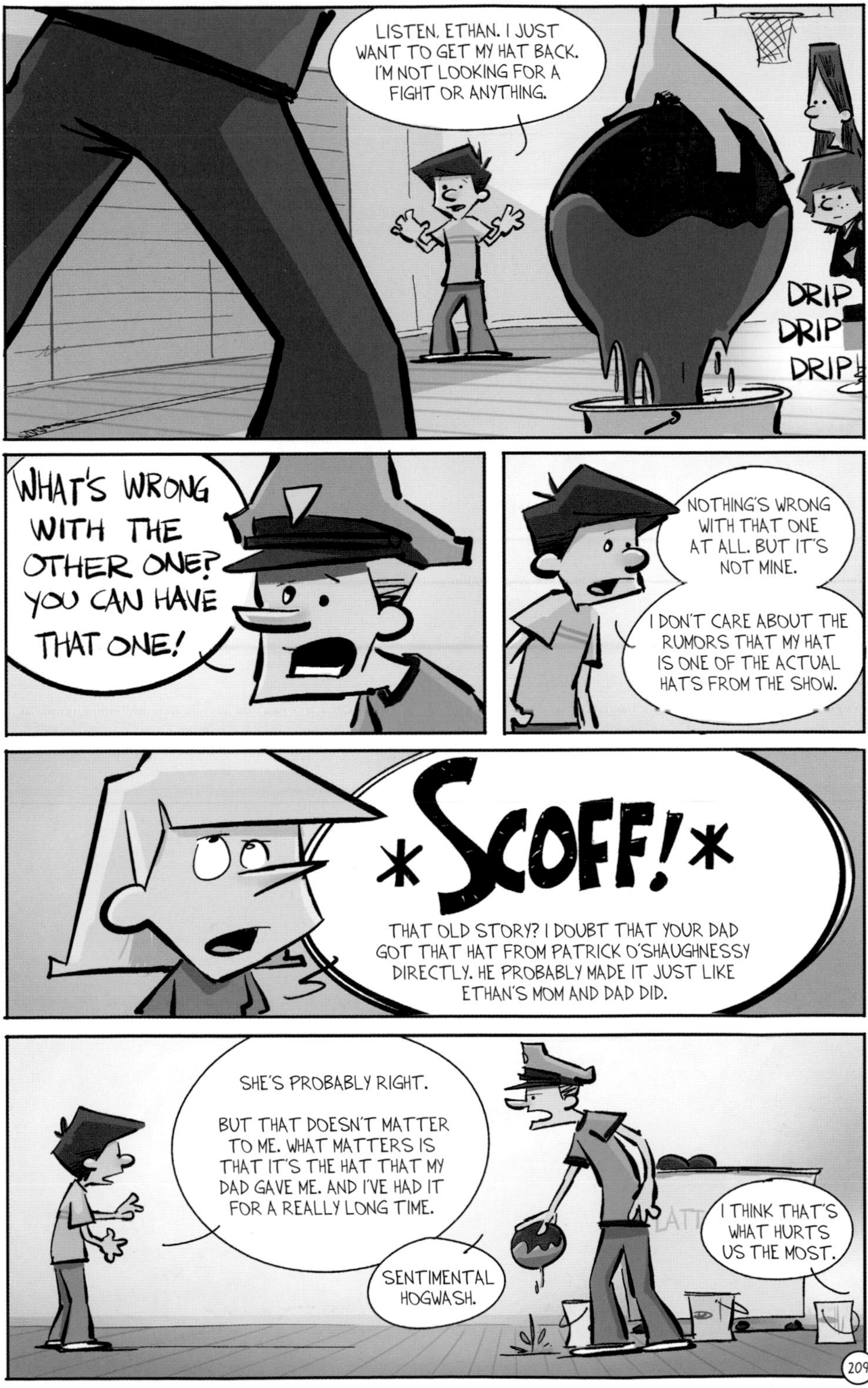
LISTEN, ETHAN. I JUST WANT TO GET MY HAT BACK. I'M NOT LOOKING FOR A FIGHT OR ANYTHING.
DRIP DRIP DRIP
WHAT'S WRONG WITH THE OTHER ONE? YOU CAN HAVE THAT ONE!
NOTHING'S WRONG WITH THAT ONE AT ALL. BUT IT'S NOT MINE.
I DON'T CARE ABOUT THE RUMORS THAT MY HAT IS ONE OF THE ACTUAL HATS FROM THE SHOW.
SCOFF!
THAT OLD STORY? I DOUBT THAT YOUR DAD GOT THAT HAT FROM PATRICK O'SHAUGHNESSY DIRECTLY. HE PROBABLY MADE IT JUST LIKE ETHAN'S MOM AND DAD DID.
SHE'S PROBABLY RIGHT.
BUT THAT DOESN'T MATTER TO ME. WHAT MATTERS IS THAT IT'S THE HAT THAT MY DAD GAVE ME. AND I'VE HAD IT FOR A REALLY LONG TIME.
SENTIMENTAL HOGWASH.
I THINK THAT'S WHAT HURTS US THE MOST.

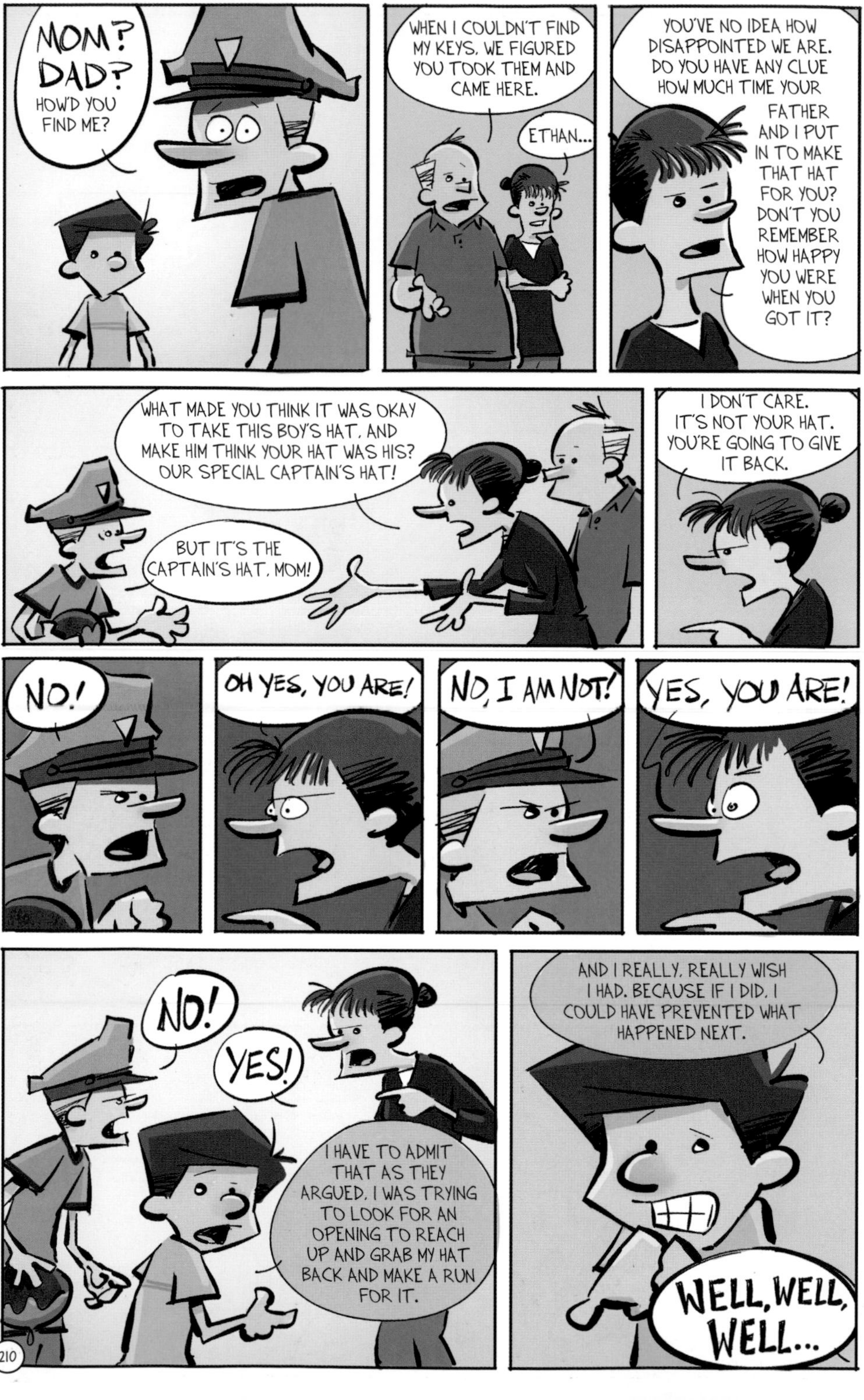
MOM? DAD? HOW'D YOU FIND ME?
WHEN I COULDN'T FIND MY KEYS, WE FIGURED YOU TOOK THEM AND CAME HERE.
ETHAN...
YOU'VE NO IDEA HOW DISAPPOINTED WE ARE. DO YOU HAVE ANY CLUE HOW MUCH TIME YOUR FATHER AND I PUT IN TO MAKE THAT HAT FOR YOU? DON'T YOU REMEMBER HOW HAPPY YOU WERE WHEN YOU GOT IT?
WHAT MADE YOU THINK IT WAS OKAY TO TAKE THIS BOY'S HAT, AND MAKE HIM THINK YOUR HAT WAS HIS? OUR SPECIAL CAPTAIN'S HAT!
BUT IT'S THE CAPTAIN'S HAT, MOM!
I DON'T CARE. IT'S NOT YOUR HAT. YOU'RE GOING TO GIVE IT BACK.
NO!
OH YES, YOU ARE!
NO, I AM NOT!
YES, YOU ARE!
NO!
YES!
I HAVE TO ADMIT THAT AS THEY ARGUED, I WAS TRYING TO LOOK FOR AN OPENING TO REACH UP AND GRAB MY HAT BACK AND MAKE A RUN FOR IT.
AND I REALLY, REALLY WISH I HAD. BECAUSE IF I DID, I COULD HAVE PREVENTED WHAT HAPPENED NEXT.
WELL, WELL, WELL...

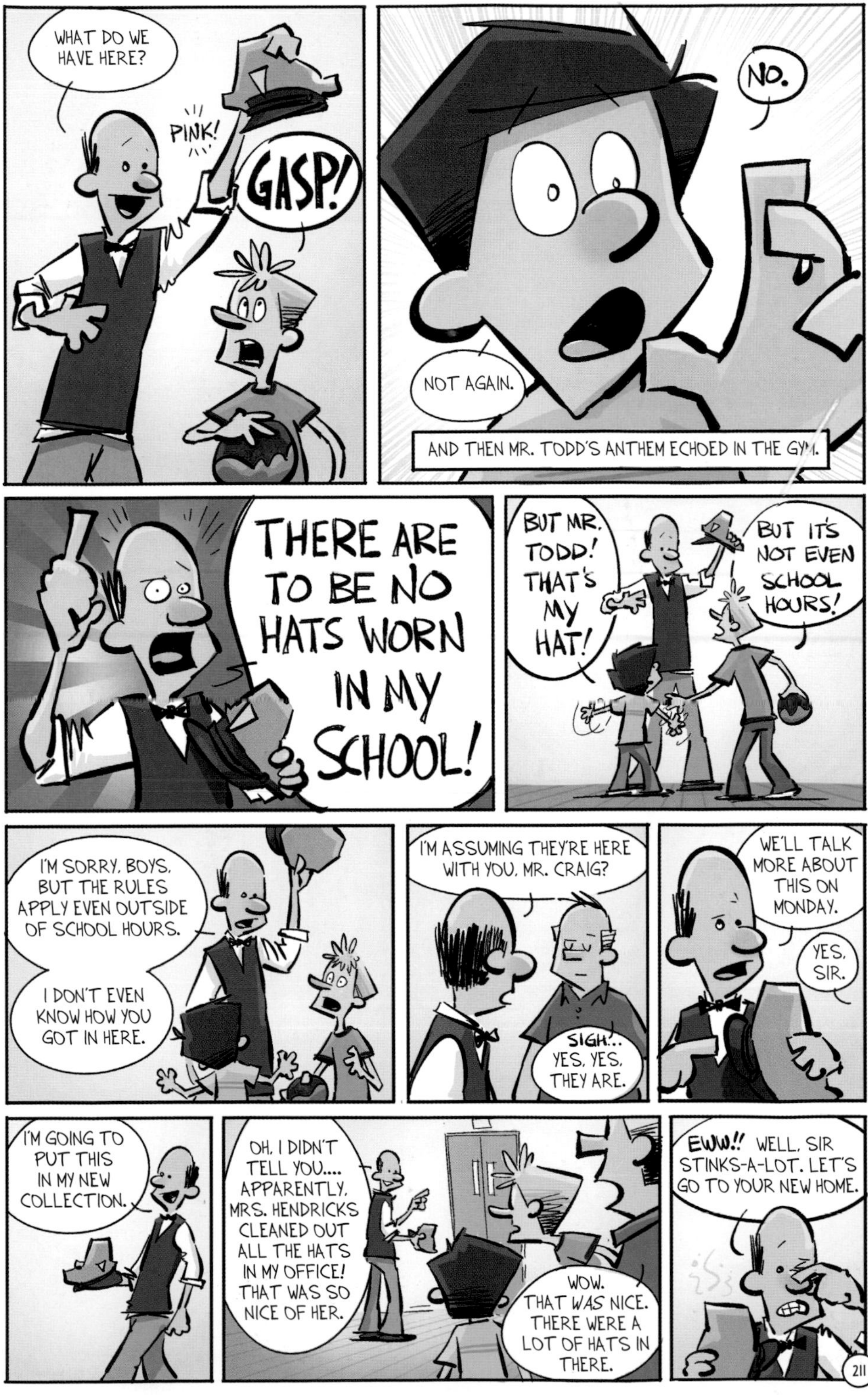
WHAT DO WE HAVE HERE?
PINK!
GASP!
NO.
NOT AGAIN.
AND THEN MR. TODD'S ANTHEM ECHOED IN THE GYM.
THERE ARE TO BE NO HATS WORN IN MY SCHOOL!
BUT MR. TODD! THAT'S MY HAT!
BUT IT'S NOT EVEN SCHOOL HOURS!
I'M SORRY, BOYS, BUT THE RULES APPLY EVEN OUTSIDE OF SCHOOL HOURS.
I DON'T EVEN KNOW HOW YOU GOT IN HERE.
I'M ASSUMING THEY'RE HERE WITH YOU, MR. CRAIG?
SIGH!... YES, YES, THEY ARE.
WE'LL TALK MORE ABOUT THIS ON MONDAY.
YES, SIR.
I'M GOING TO PUT THIS IN MY NEW COLLECTION.
OH, I DIDN'T TELL YOU.... APPARENTLY, MRS. HENDRICKS CLEANED OUT ALL THE HATS IN MY OFFICE! THAT WAS SO NICE OF HER.
WOW. THAT WAS NICE. THERE WERE A LOT OF HATS IN THERE.
EWW!! WELL, SIR STINKS-A-LOT. LET'S GO TO YOUR NEW HOME.

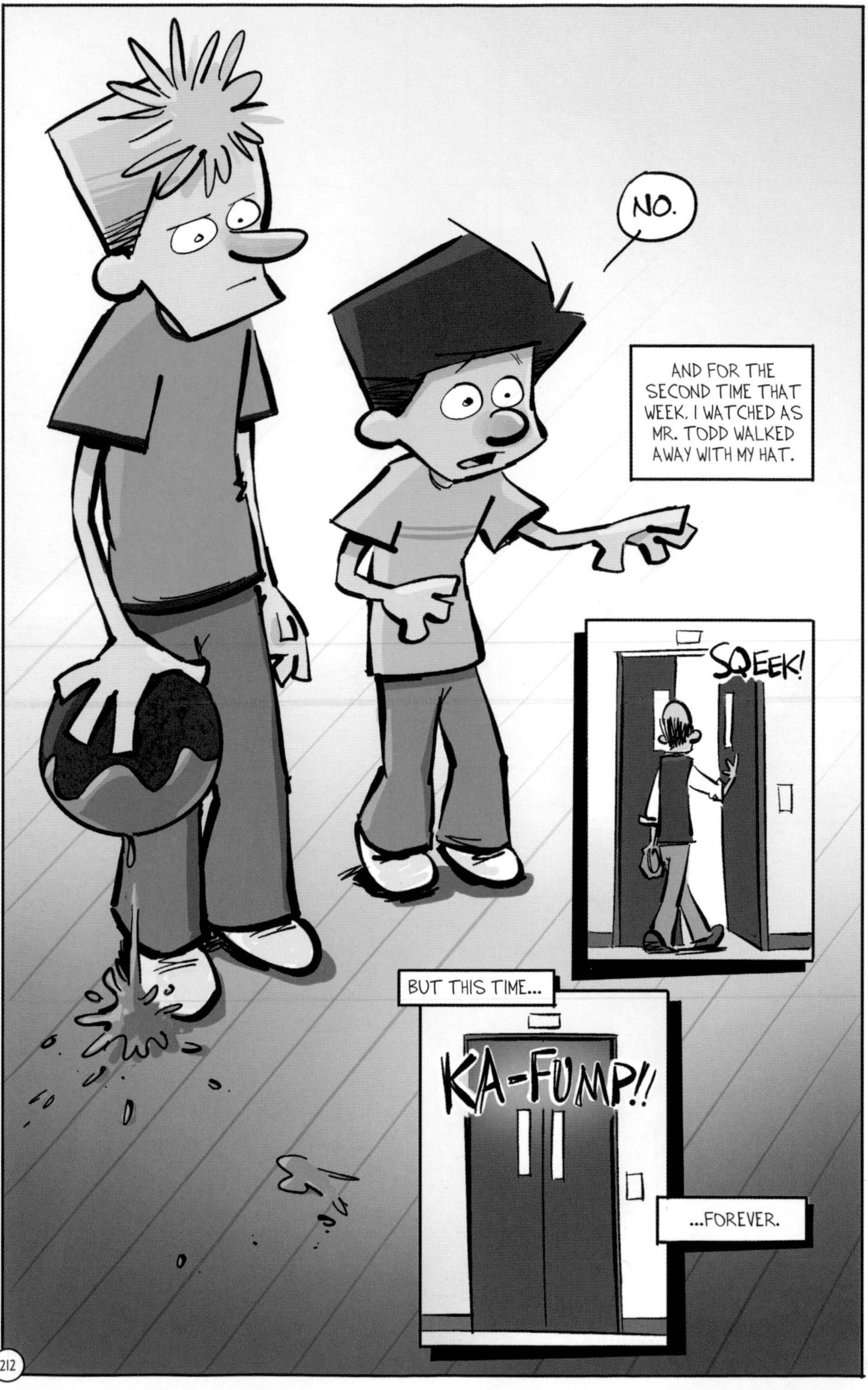
NO.
AND FOR THE SECOND TIME THAT WEEK, I WATCHED AS MR. TODD WALKED AWAY WITH MY HAT.
SQEEK!
BUT THIS TIME...
KA-FUMP!!
...FOREVER.

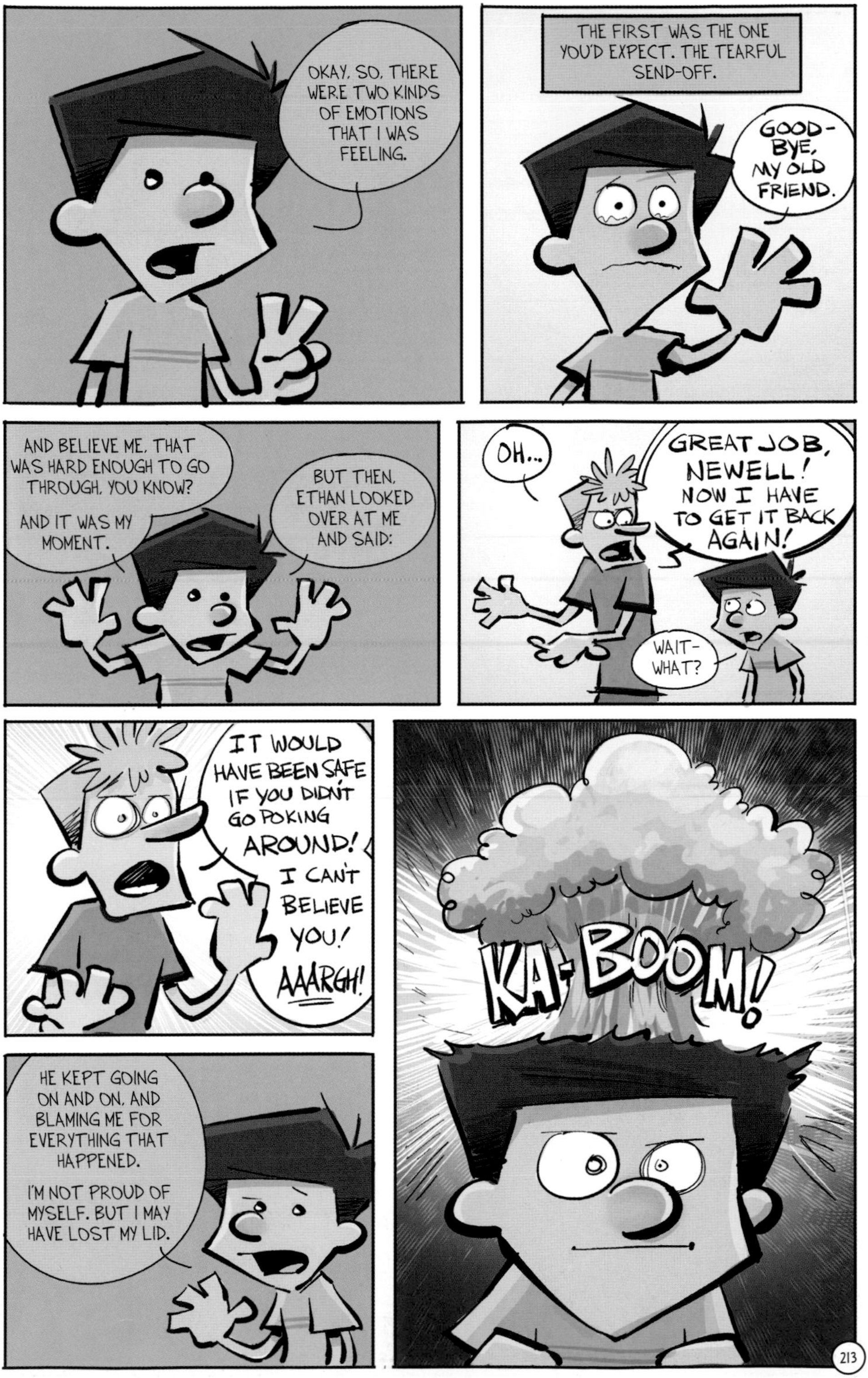

OKAY, SO, THERE WERE TWO KINDS OF EMOTIONS THAT I WAS FEELING.
THE FIRST WAS THE ONE YOU'D EXPECT. THE TEARFUL SEND-OFF.
GOOD-BYE, MY OLD FRIEND.
AND BELIEVE ME, THAT WAS HARD ENOUGH TO GO THROUGH, YOU KNOW?
AND IT WAS MY MOMENT.
BUT THEN, ETHAN LOOKED OVER AT ME AND SAID:
OH...
GREAT JOB, NEWELL! NOW I HAVE TO GET IT BACK AGAIN!
WAIT-WHAT?
IT WOULD HAVE BEEN SAFE IF YOU DIDN'T GO POKING AROUND!
I CAN'T BELIEVE YOU!
AAARGH!
HE KEPT GOING ON AND ON, AND BLAMING ME FOR EVERYTHING THAT HAPPENED.
I'M NOT PROUD OF MYSELF. BUT I MAY HAVE LOST MY LID.
KA-BOOM!

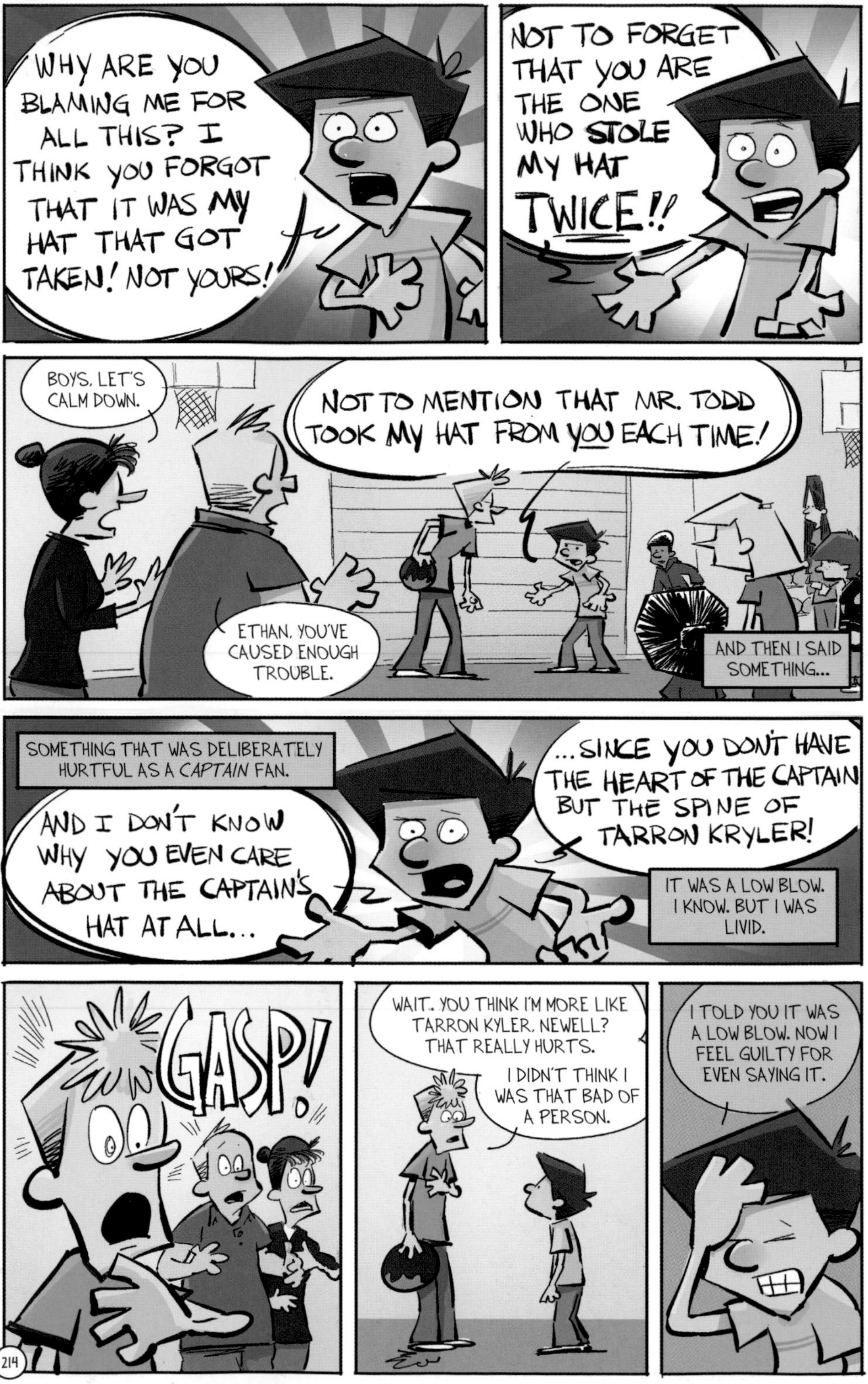
WHY ARE YOU BLAMING ME FOR ALL THIS? I THINK YOU FORGOT THAT IT WAS MY HAT THAT GOT TAKEN! NOT YOURS!
NOT TO FORGET THAT YOU ARE THE ONE WHO STOLE MY HAT TWICE!!
BOYS, LET'S CALM DOWN.
NOT TO MENTION THAT MR. TODD TOOK MY HAT FROM YOU EACH TIME!
ETHAN, YOU'VE CAUSED ENOUGH TROUBLE.
AND THEN I SAID SOMETHING...
SOMETHING THAT WAS DELIBERATELY HURTFUL AS A CAPTAIN FAN.
AND I DON'T KNOW WHY YOU EVEN CARE ABOUT THE CAPTAIN'S HAT AT ALL...
...SINCE YOU DON'T HAVE THE HEART OF THE CAPTAIN BUT THE SPINE OF TARRON KRYLER!
IT WAS A LOW BLOW. I KNOW. BUT I WAS LIVID.
GASP!
WAIT. YOU THINK I'M MORE LIKE TARRON KYLER, NEWELL? THAT REALLY HURTS.
I DIDN'T THINK I WAS THAT BAD OF A PERSON.
I TOLD YOU IT WAS A LOW BLOW. NOW I FEEL GUILTY FOR EVEN SAYING IT.

LISTEN, ETHAN, I'M SORRY FOR WHAT I SAID. I WAS ANGRY.

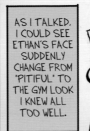

AS I TALKED, I COULD SEE ETHAN'S FACE SUDDENLY CHANGE FROM "PITIFUL" TO THE GYM LOOK I KNEW ALL TOO WELL.

WILD EYES

AND AS SOON AS I SAW ETHAN GRIP ON TO THE SPLATTER BALL TIGHTER, I KNEW IT WAS TIME.

TO RUN!

AAAAAAAAH

GASP!

ETHAN! STOP!

215

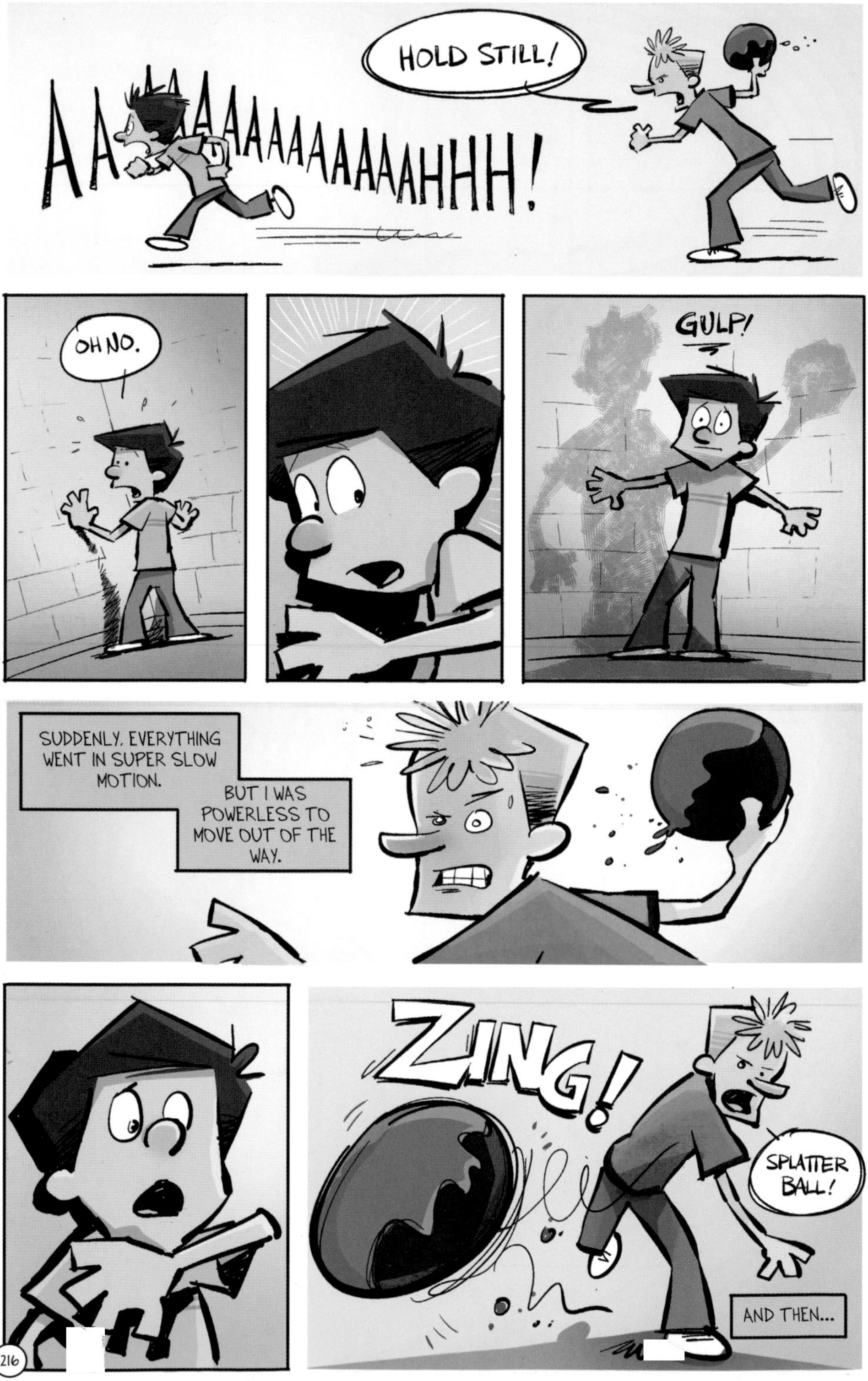

AAAAAAAAAAAAAAAHHH!
HOLD STILL!
OH NO.
GULP!
SUDDENLY, EVERYTHING WENT IN SUPER SLOW MOTION.
BUT I WAS POWERLESS TO MOVE OUT OF THE WAY.
ZING!
SPLATTER BALL!
AND THEN...

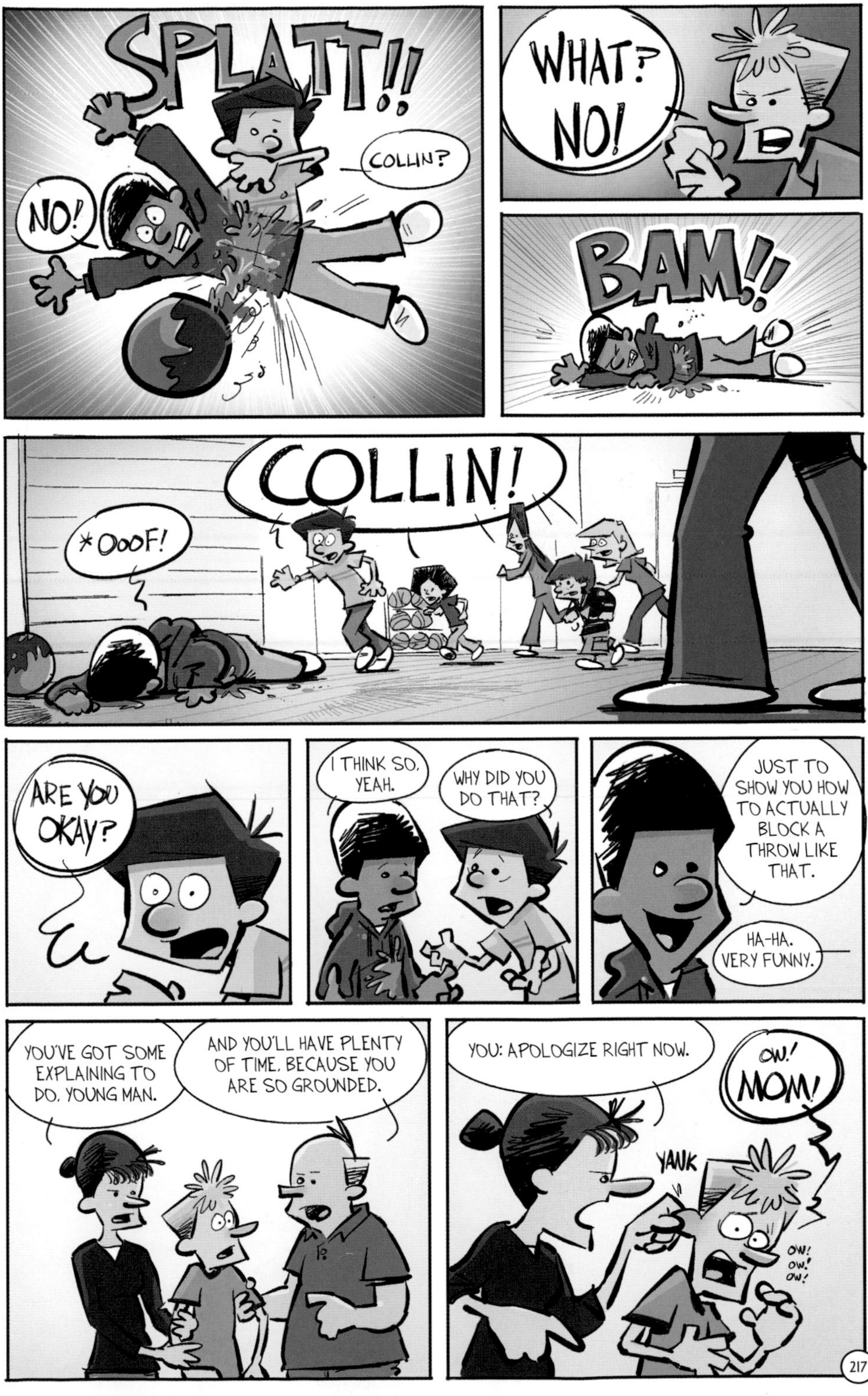
SPLATT!!
NO!
COLLIN?
WHAT? NO!
BAM!!
COLLIN!
*OOOF!
ARE YOU OKAY?
I THINK SO, YEAH.
WHY DID YOU DO THAT?
JUST TO SHOW YOU HOW TO ACTUALLY BLOCK A THROW LIKE THAT.
HA-HA. VERY FUNNY.
YOU'VE GOT SOME EXPLAINING TO DO, YOUNG MAN.
AND YOU'LL HAVE PLENTY OF TIME, BECAUSE YOU ARE SO GROUNDED.
YOU: APOLOGIZE RIGHT NOW.
OW! MOM!
YANK
OW! OW! OW!

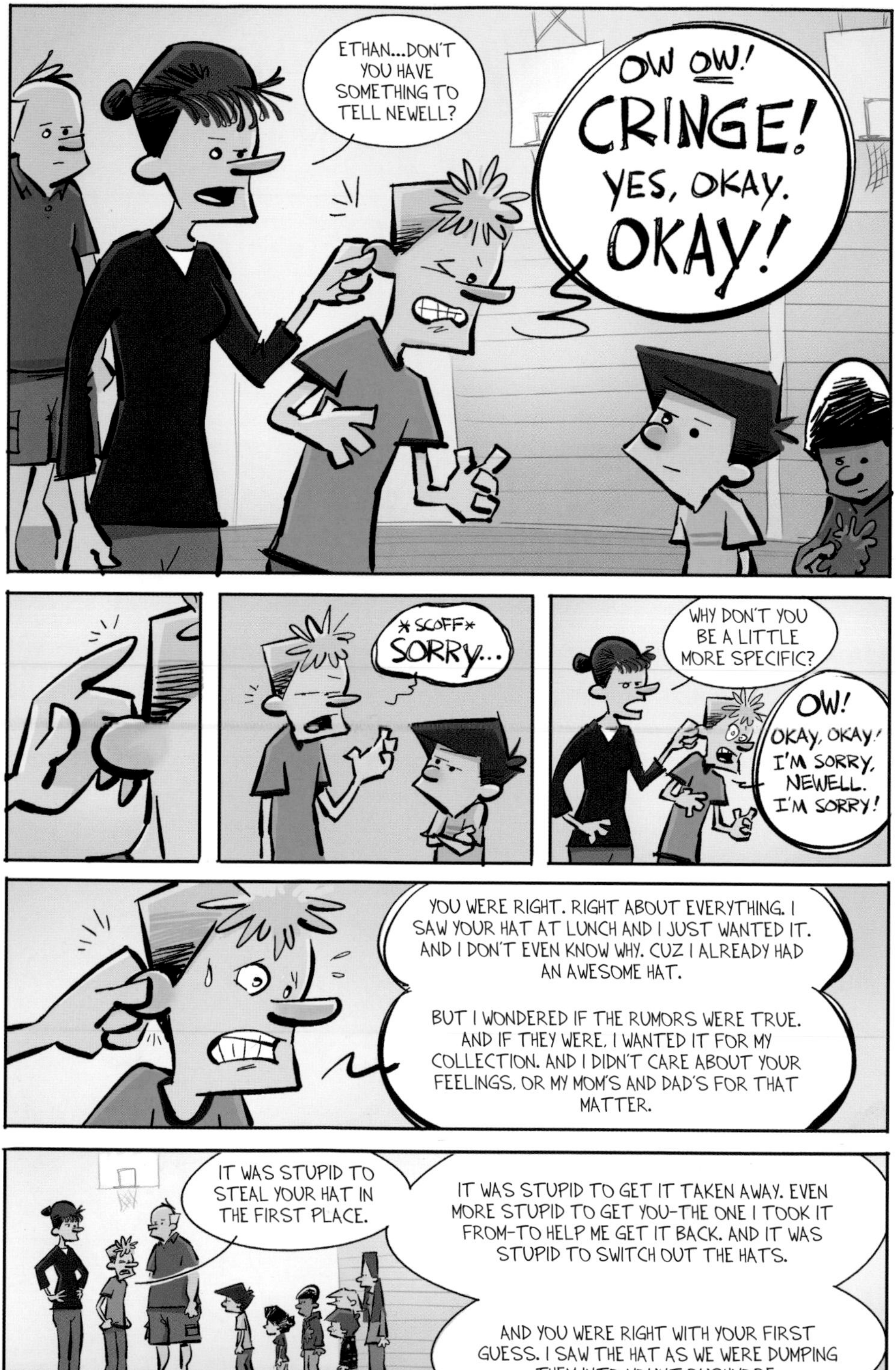
ETHAN...DON'T YOU HAVE SOMETHING TO TELL NEWELL?
OW OW! CRINGE! YES, OKAY. OKAY!
SCOFF SORRY...
WHY DON'T YOU BE A LITTLE MORE SPECIFIC?
OW! OKAY, OKAY! I'M SORRY, NEWELL. I'M SORRY!
YOU WERE RIGHT. RIGHT ABOUT EVERYTHING. I SAW YOUR HAT AT LUNCH AND I JUST WANTED IT. AND I DON'T EVEN KNOW WHY. CUZ I ALREADY HAD AN AWESOME HAT.
BUT I WONDERED IF THE RUMORS WERE TRUE. AND IF THEY WERE, I WANTED IT FOR MY COLLECTION. AND I DIDN'T CARE ABOUT YOUR FEELINGS, OR MY MOM'S AND DAD'S FOR THAT MATTER.
IT WAS STUPID TO STEAL YOUR HAT IN THE FIRST PLACE.
IT WAS STUPID TO GET IT TAKEN AWAY. EVEN MORE STUPID TO GET YOU—THE ONE I TOOK IT FROM—TO HELP ME GET IT BACK. AND IT WAS STUPID TO SWITCH OUT THE HATS.
AND YOU WERE RIGHT WITH YOUR FIRST GUESS. I SAW THE HAT AS WE WERE DUMPING THEM INTO MOUNT RUSHMORE.
TAP TAP TAP

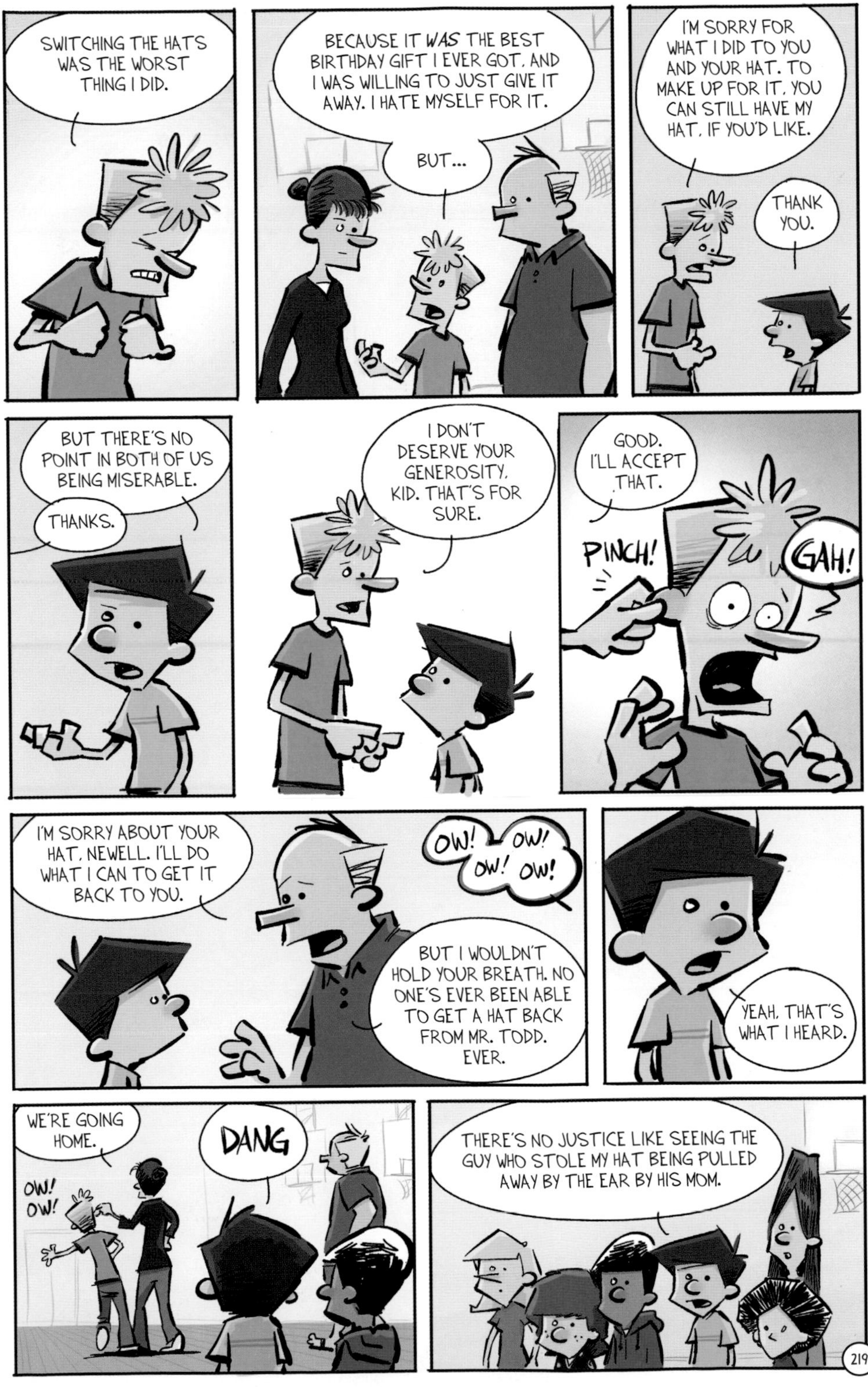
SWITCHING THE HATS WAS THE WORST THING I DID.
BECAUSE IT *WAS* THE BEST BIRTHDAY GIFT I EVER GOT. AND I WAS WILLING TO JUST GIVE IT AWAY. I HATE MYSELF FOR IT.
BUT...
I'M SORRY FOR WHAT I DID TO YOU AND YOUR HAT. TO MAKE UP FOR IT, YOU CAN STILL HAVE MY HAT, IF YOU'D LIKE.
THANK YOU.
BUT THERE'S NO POINT IN BOTH OF US BEING MISERABLE.
THANKS.
I DON'T DESERVE YOUR GENEROSITY, KID. THAT'S FOR SURE.
GOOD. I'LL ACCEPT THAT.
PINCH!
GAH!
I'M SORRY ABOUT YOUR HAT, NEWELL. I'LL DO WHAT I CAN TO GET IT BACK TO YOU.
OW! OW! OW! OW!
BUT I WOULDN'T HOLD YOUR BREATH. NO ONE'S EVER BEEN ABLE TO GET A HAT BACK FROM MR. TODD. EVER.
YEAH, THAT'S WHAT I HEARD.
WE'RE GOING HOME.
OW! OW!
DANG
THERE'S NO JUSTICE LIKE SEEING THE GUY WHO STOLE MY HAT BEING PULLED AWAY BY THE EAR BY HIS MOM.

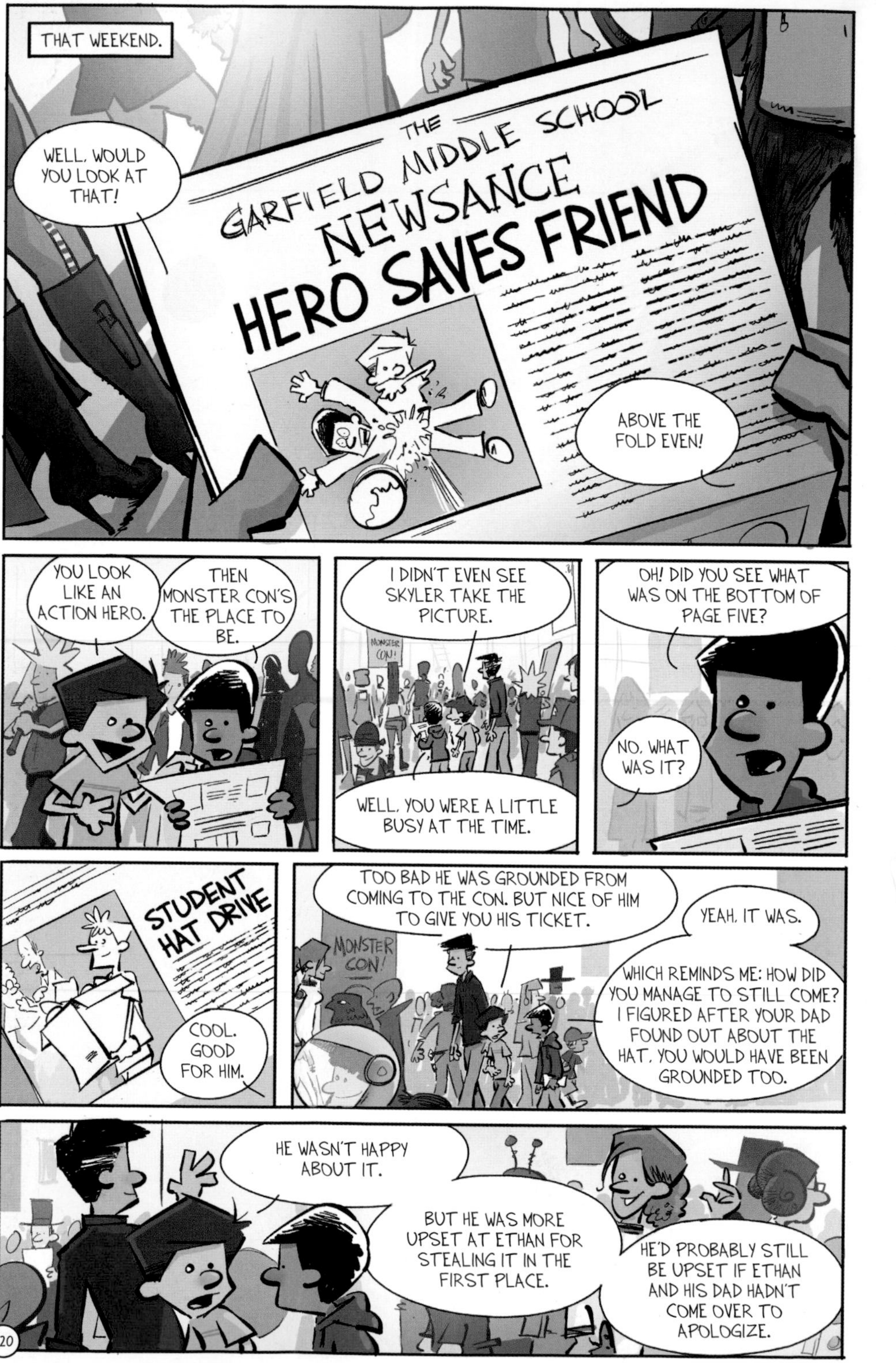
THAT WEEKEND.
WELL, WOULD YOU LOOK AT THAT!
THE GARFIELD MIDDLE SCHOOL NEWSANCE
HERO SAVES FRIEND
ABOVE THE FOLD EVEN!
YOU LOOK LIKE AN ACTION HERO.
THEN MONSTER CON'S THE PLACE TO BE.
I DIDN'T EVEN SEE SKYLER TAKE THE PICTURE.
MONSTER CON!
WELL, YOU WERE A LITTLE BUSY AT THE TIME.
OH! DID YOU SEE WHAT WAS ON THE BOTTOM OF PAGE FIVE?
NO, WHAT WAS IT?
STUDENT HAT DRIVE
COOL. GOOD FOR HIM.
TOO BAD HE WAS GROUNDED FROM COMING TO THE CON. BUT NICE OF HIM TO GIVE YOU HIS TICKET.
MONSTER CON!
YEAH, IT WAS.
WHICH REMINDS ME: HOW DID YOU MANAGE TO STILL COME? I FIGURED AFTER YOUR DAD FOUND OUT ABOUT THE HAT, YOU WOULD HAVE BEEN GROUNDED TOO.
HE WASN'T HAPPY ABOUT IT.
BUT HE WAS MORE UPSET AT ETHAN FOR STEALING IT IN THE FIRST PLACE.
HE'D PROBABLY STILL BE UPSET IF ETHAN AND HIS DAD HADN'T COME OVER TO APOLOGIZE.

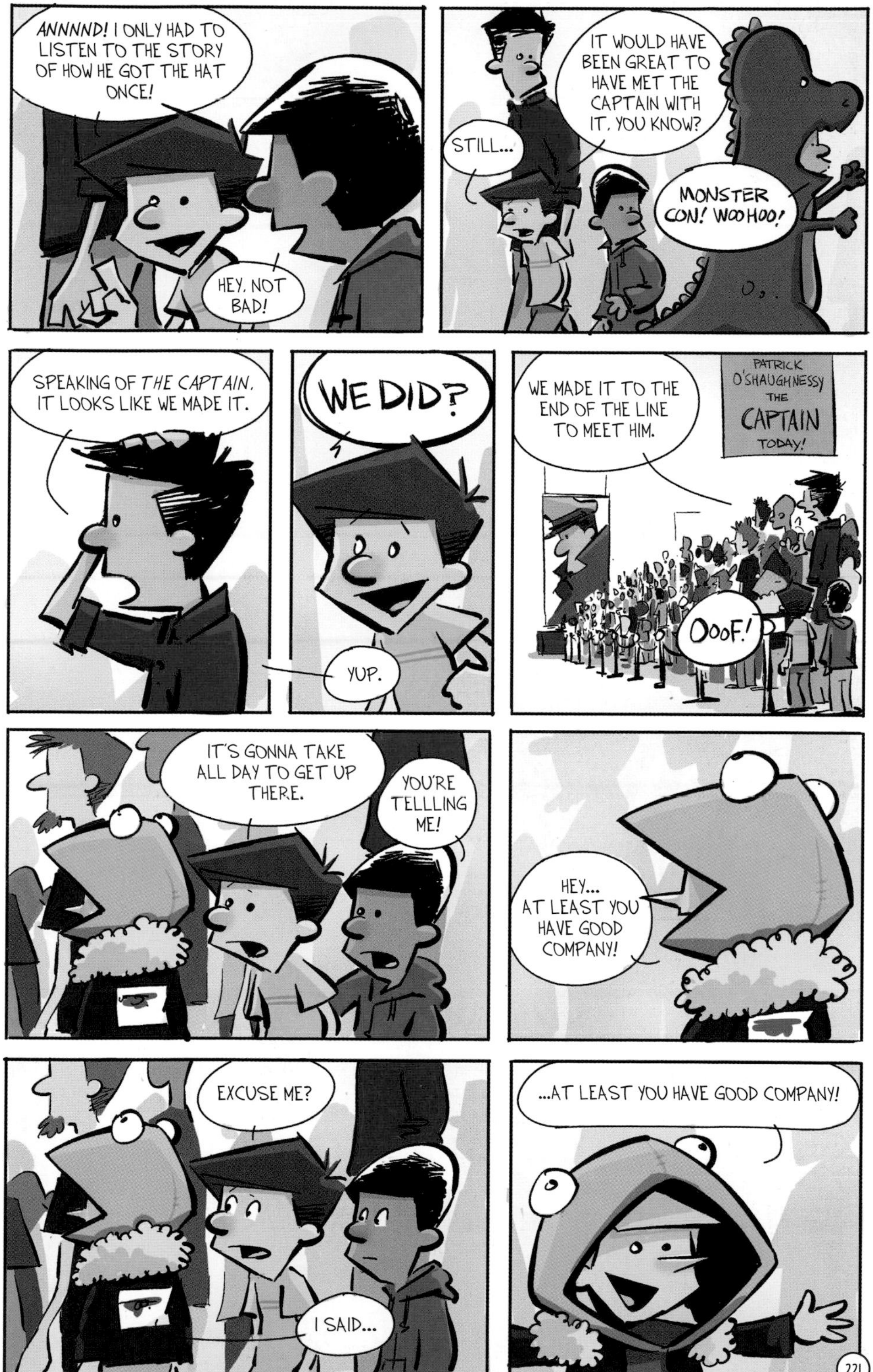
ANNNND! I ONLY HAD TO LISTEN TO THE STORY OF HOW HE GOT THE HAT ONCE!
HEY, NOT BAD!
STILL...
IT WOULD HAVE BEEN GREAT TO HAVE MET THE CAPTAIN WITH IT, YOU KNOW?
MONSTER CON! WOO HOO!
SPEAKING OF THE CAPTAIN, IT LOOKS LIKE WE MADE IT.
WE DID?
YUP.
PATRICK O'SHAUGHNESSY THE CAPTAIN TODAY!
WE MADE IT TO THE END OF THE LINE TO MEET HIM.
OOOF!
IT'S GONNA TAKE ALL DAY TO GET UP THERE.
YOU'RE TELLLING ME!
HEY... AT LEAST YOU HAVE GOOD COMPANY!
EXCUSE ME?
I SAID...
...AT LEAST YOU HAVE GOOD COMPANY!

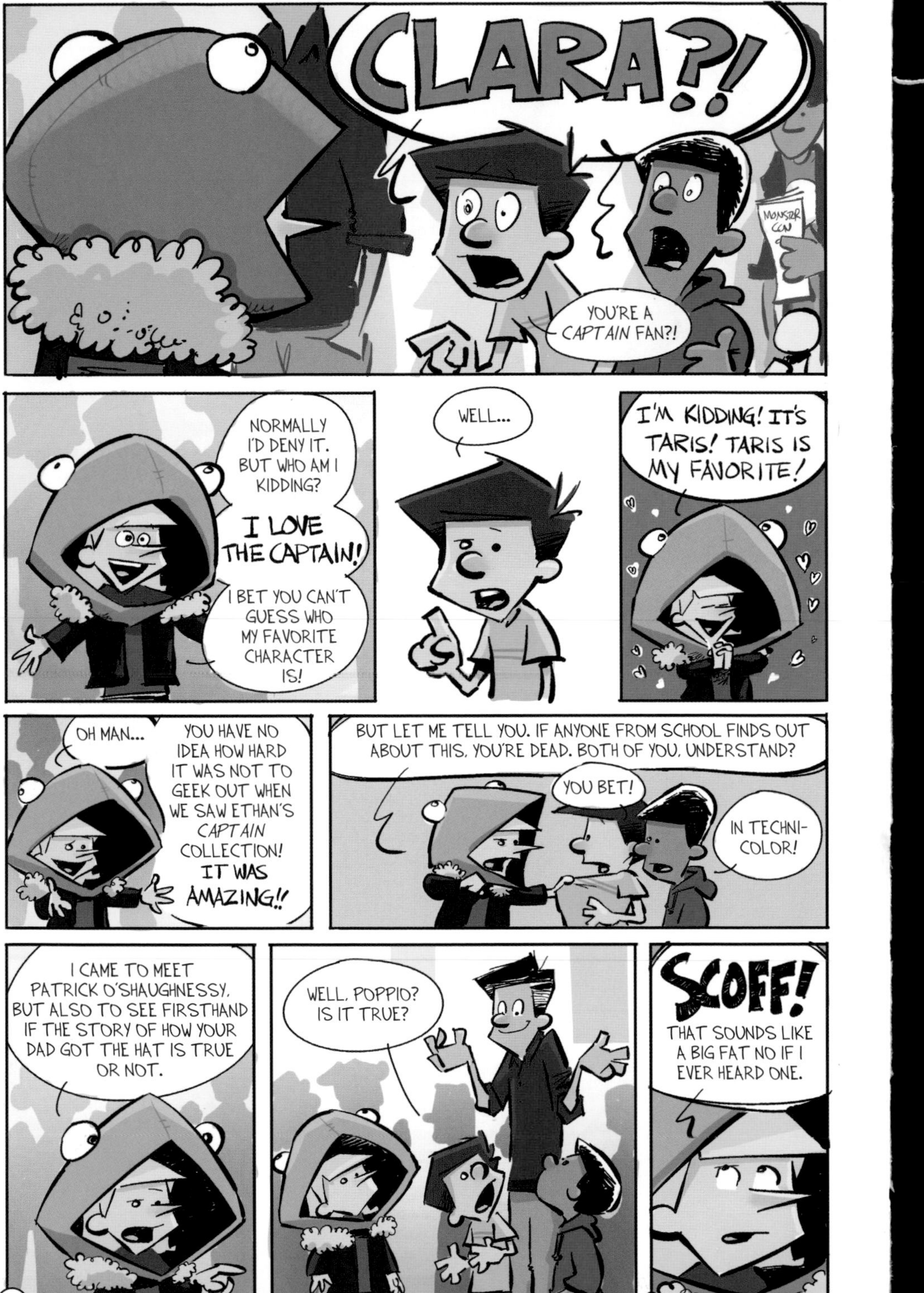
CLARA?!
YOU'RE A CAPTAIN FAN?!
MONSTER CON
NORMALLY I'D DENY IT. BUT WHO AM I KIDDING?
I LOVE THE CAPTAIN!
I BET YOU CAN'T GUESS WHO MY FAVORITE CHARACTER IS!
WELL...
I'M KIDDING! IT'S TARIS! TARIS IS MY FAVORITE!
OH MAN...
YOU HAVE NO IDEA HOW HARD IT WAS NOT TO GEEK OUT WHEN WE SAW ETHAN'S CAPTAIN COLLECTION! IT WAS AMAZING!!
BUT LET ME TELL YOU. IF ANYONE FROM SCHOOL FINDS OUT ABOUT THIS, YOU'RE DEAD. BOTH OF YOU, UNDERSTAND?
YOU BET!
IN TECHNI-COLOR!
I CAME TO MEET PATRICK O'SHAUGHNESSY, BUT ALSO TO SEE FIRSTHAND IF THE STORY OF HOW YOUR DAD GOT THE HAT IS TRUE OR NOT.
WELL, POPPIO? IS IT TRUE?
SCOFF!
THAT SOUNDS LIKE A BIG FAT NO IF I EVER HEARD ONE.

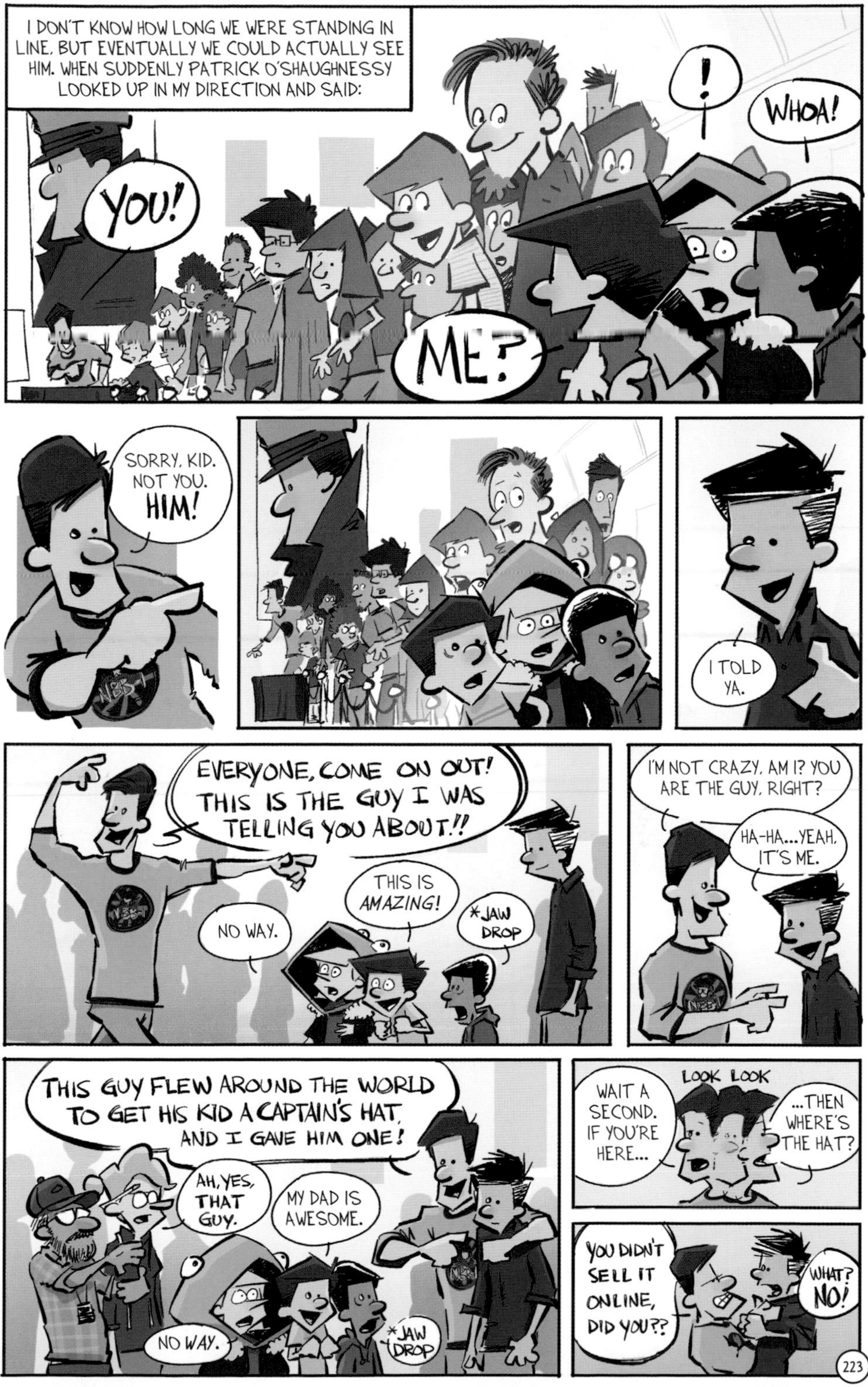
I DON'T KNOW HOW LONG WE WERE STANDING IN LINE, BUT EVENTUALLY WE COULD ACTUALLY SEE HIM. WHEN SUDDENLY PATRICK O'SHAUGHNESSY LOOKED UP IN MY DIRECTION AND SAID:
YOU!
!
WHOA!
ME?
SORRY, KID. NOT YOU. HIM!
I TOLD YA.
EVERYONE, COME ON OUT! THIS IS THE GUY I WAS TELLING YOU ABOUT!!
THIS IS AMAZING!
NO WAY.
*JAW DROP
I'M NOT CRAZY, AM I? YOU ARE THE GUY, RIGHT?
HA-HA...YEAH, IT'S ME.
THIS GUY FLEW AROUND THE WORLD TO GET HIS KID A CAPTAIN'S HAT, AND I GAVE HIM ONE!
AH, YES, THAT GUY.
MY DAD IS AWESOME.
NO WAY.
*JAW DROP
LOOK LOOK
WAIT A SECOND. IF YOU'RE HERE...
...THEN WHERE'S THE HAT?
YOU DIDN'T SELL IT ONLINE, DID YOU??
WHAT? NO!

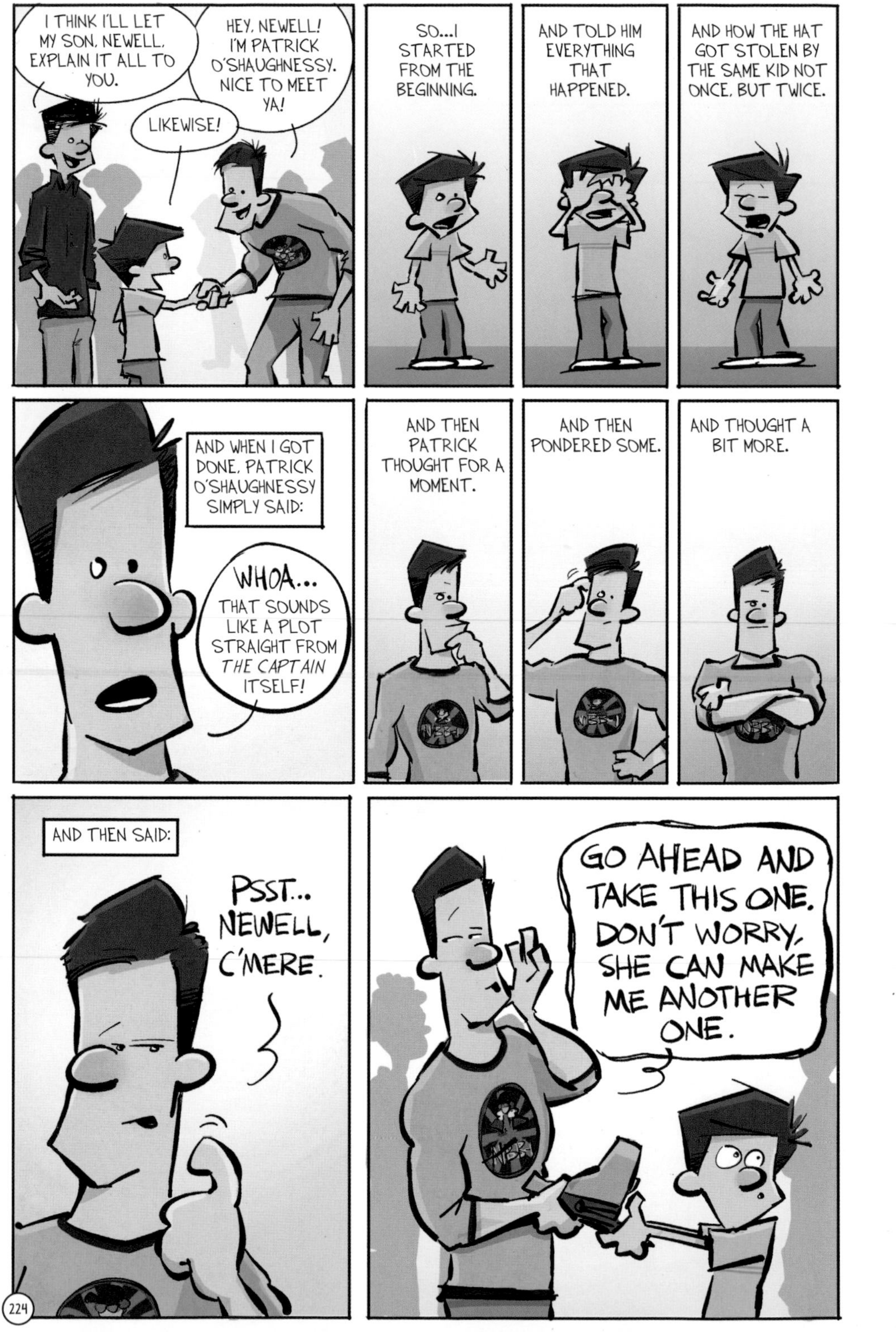
I THINK I'LL LET MY SON, NEWELL, EXPLAIN IT ALL TO YOU.
HEY, NEWELL! I'M PATRICK O'SHAUGHNESSY. NICE TO MEET YA!
LIKEWISE!
SO...I STARTED FROM THE BEGINNING.
AND TOLD HIM EVERYTHING THAT HAPPENED.
AND HOW THE HAT GOT STOLEN BY THE SAME KID NOT ONCE, BUT TWICE.
AND WHEN I GOT DONE, PATRICK O'SHAUGHNESSY SIMPLY SAID:
WHOA... THAT SOUNDS LIKE A PLOT STRAIGHT FROM *THE CAPTAIN* ITSELF!
AND THEN PATRICK THOUGHT FOR A MOMENT.
AND THEN PONDERED SOME.
AND THOUGHT A BIT MORE.
AND THEN SAID:
PSST... NEWELL, C'MERE.
GO AHEAD AND TAKE THIS ONE. DON'T WORRY, SHE CAN MAKE ME ANOTHER ONE.

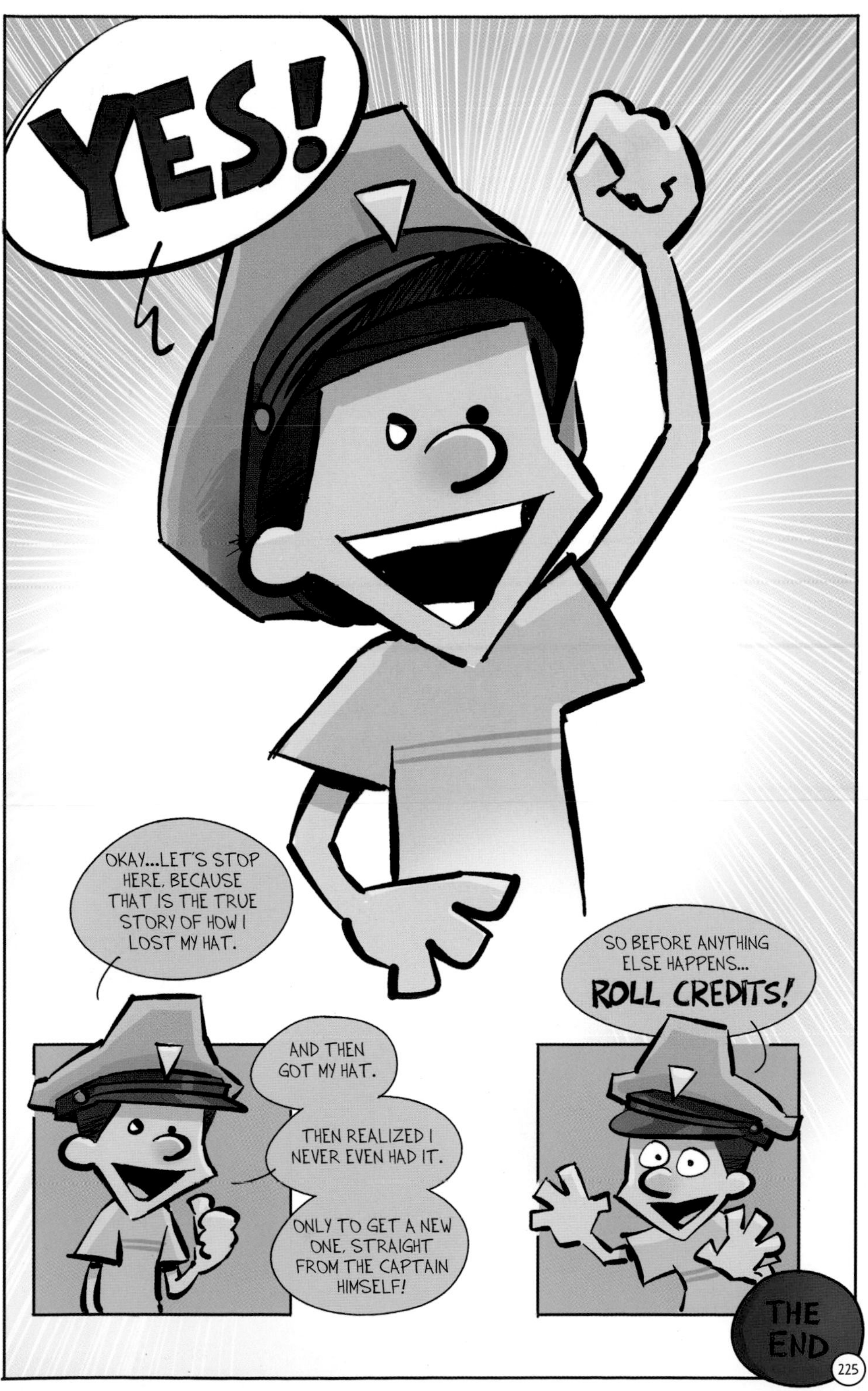
YES!
OKAY...LET'S STOP HERE, BECAUSE THAT IS THE TRUE STORY OF HOW I LOST MY HAT.
AND THEN GOT MY HAT.
THEN REALIZED I NEVER EVEN HAD IT.
ONLY TO GET A NEW ONE, STRAIGHT FROM THE CAPTAIN HIMSELF!
SO BEFORE ANYTHING ELSE HAPPENS... ROLL CREDITS!
THE END

JASON PLATT IS A PROFESSIONAL CARTOONIST
AND MEMBER OF THE NATIONAL CARTOONISTS SOCIETY.
WHILE BORN IN THE MIDWEST, HE GREW UP IN DURHAM,
NORTH CAROLINA, AND LATER GRADUATED WITH
HONORS FROM THE SAVANNAH COLLEGE OF ART AND
DESIGN, IN SAVANNAH, GEORGIA. IN HIS FREE TIME,
JASON CAN BE FOUND PERFORMING OR WRITING FOR
THE THEATER. JASON LIVES IN DAVENPORT, IOWA,
WITH HIS WIFE, SON, AND CAT.

ACKNOWLEDGMENTS

* * *

THANK YOU TO EVERYONE AT LITTLE, BROWN BOOKS FOR
YOUNG READERS WHO HELPED BRING THIS BOOK TO LIFE.
SPECIAL SHOUT-OUTS TO MY WONDERFUL EDITOR,
RACHEL POLOSKI; DESIGNER CHRISTINA QUINTERO (WHO
PATIENTLY WORKED WITH ALL THE PAGES I SENT ALONG);
AND DEIRDRE JONES. I COULDN'T HAVE DONE IT
WITHOUT YOU. YOU GUYS ROCK.

TO BOTH TIM TRAVAGLINI AND SAMANTHA HAYWOOD:
THANK YOU FOR ALL THE GUIDANCE YOU GAVE ME AT THE
BEGINNING OF THIS ADVENTURE.

AND TO BOTH J&J AND RUSS BUSSE, WHO ORIGINALLY
HELPED BRING MY FUNNY MISADVENTURES TO LIFE,
THANK YOU.

AND, OF COURSE, TO THE MAIN THREE. NO MISADVENTURE
IS WORTH HAVING IF YOU DON'T HAVE ANYONE TO SHARE IT
WITH. AND I GET TO SHARE MINE WITH THE BEST.
TO MY SON, WYETH; MY WIFE, ERIN; AND MY MOM, KATHY.
YOUR ENCOURAGEMENT HAS MEANT THE WORLD TO ME, AND
YOU HAVE MADE MY OWN MISADVENTURES ALL THE BETTER.
HOW ABOUT WE GO AND HAVE SOME MORE?!

JASON

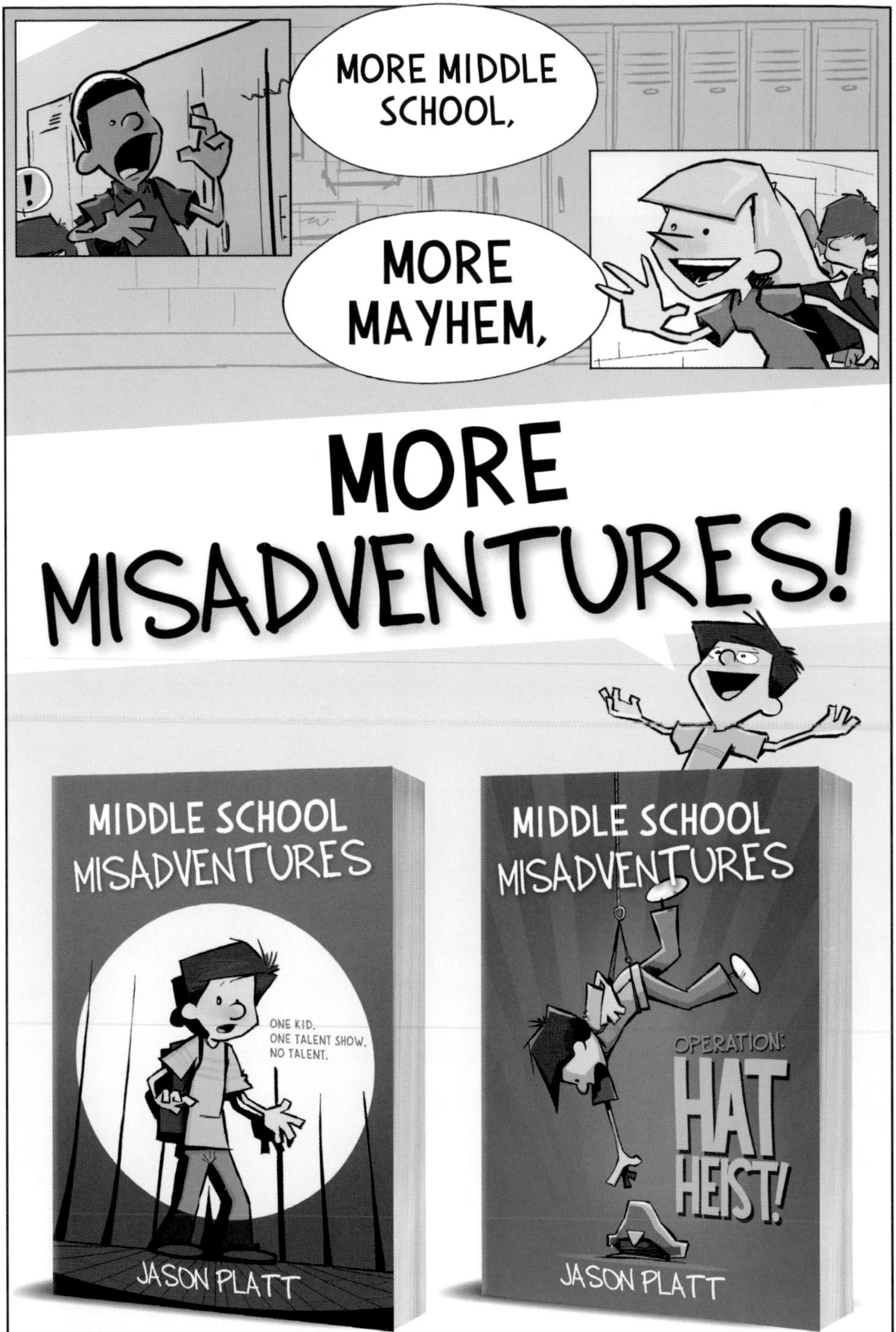
MORE MIDDLE SCHOOL,
MORE MAYHEM,
MORE MISADVENTURES!
MIDDLE SCHOOL MISADVENTURES
ONE KID. ONE TALENT SHOW. NO TALENT.
JASON PLATT
MIDDLE SCHOOL MISADVENTURES
OPERATION: HAT HEIST!
JASON PLATT
LITTLE, BROWN AND COMPANY
BOOKS FOR YOUNG READERS
LBYR.COM

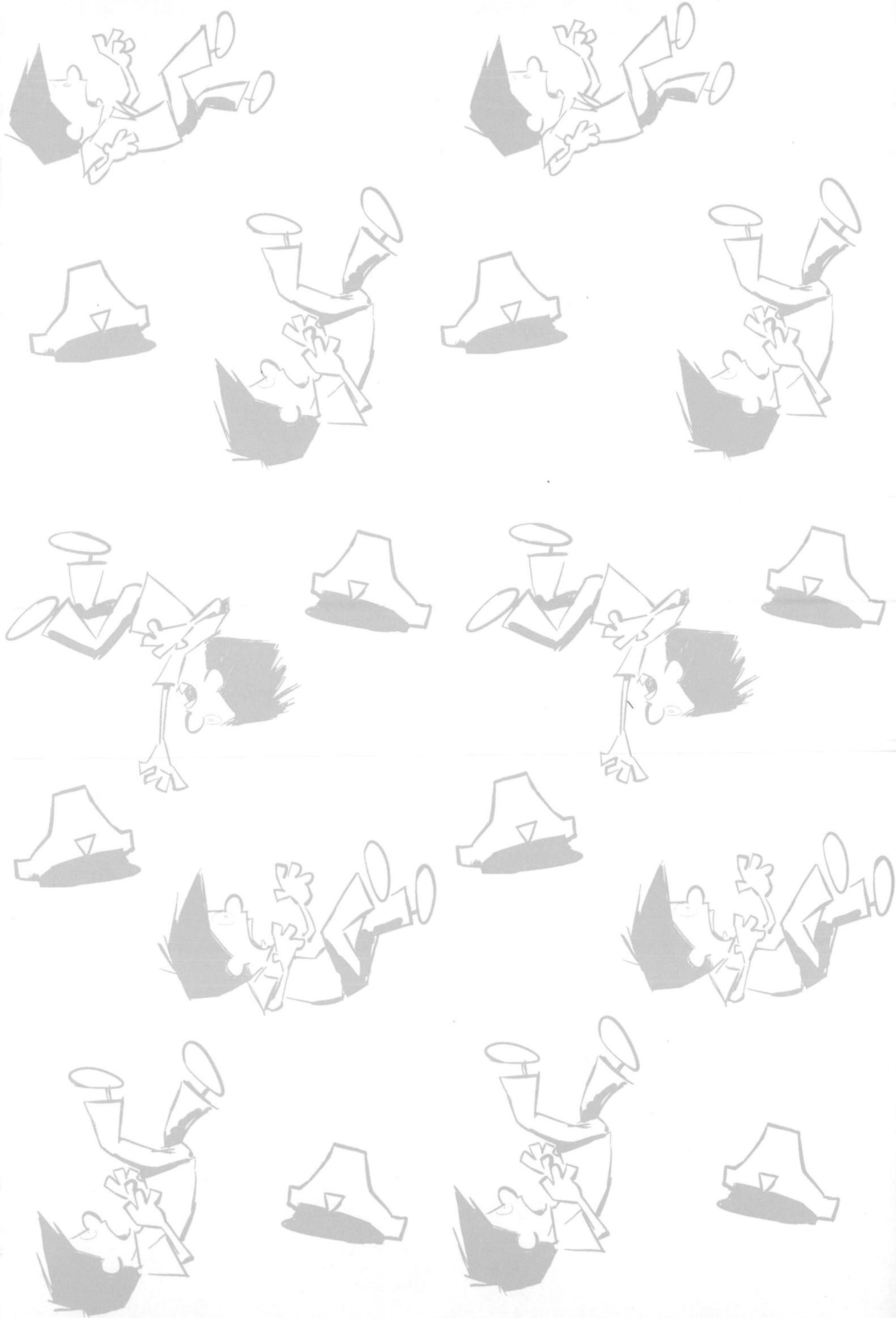

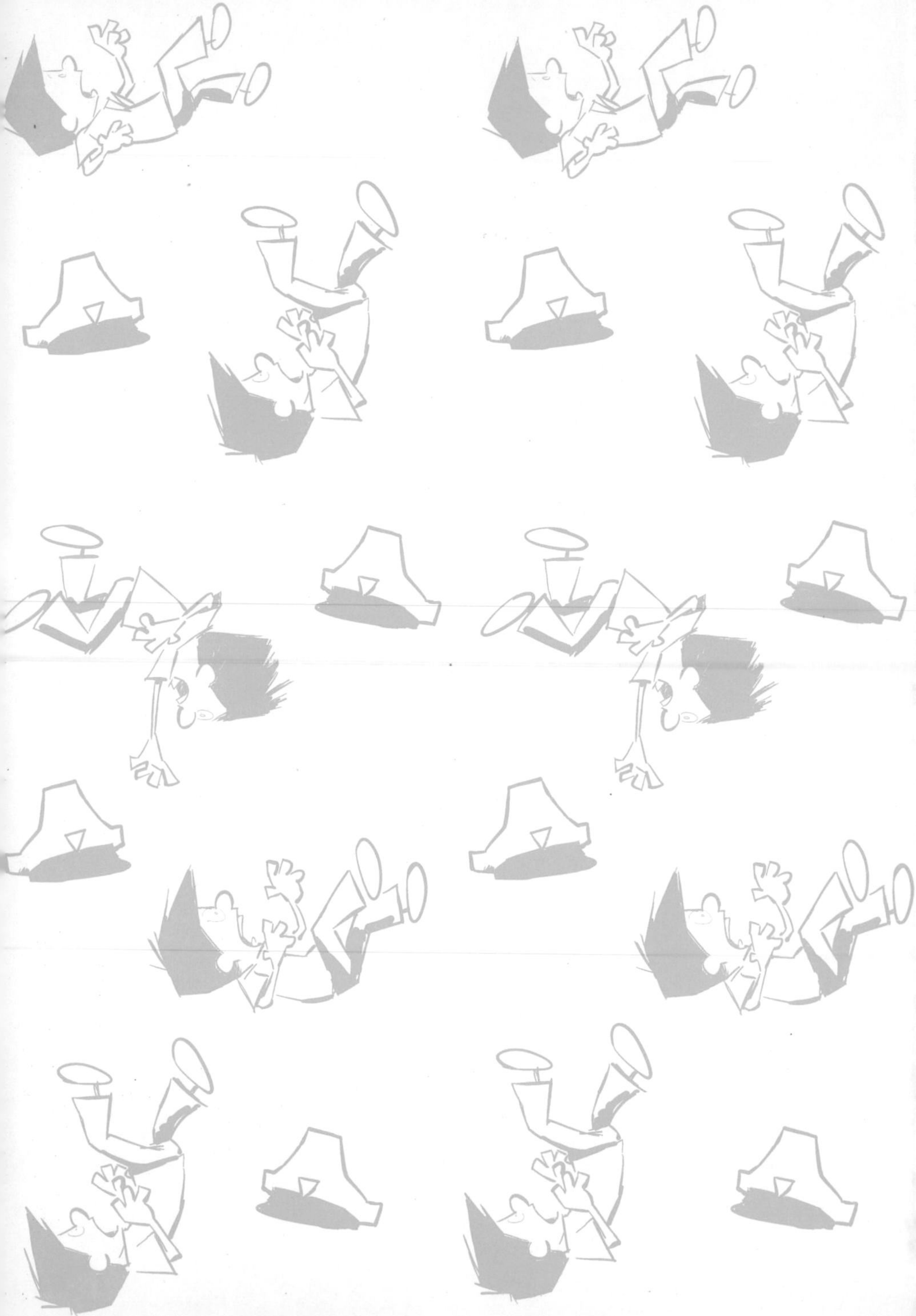